By Sam Barone

DAWN OF EMPIRE

Forthcoming in hardcover
EMPIRE RISING

DAWN
OF
EMPIRE

SAM BARONE

HARPER

An Imprint of HarperCollinsPublishers

This book is a work of fiction. The characters, incidents, and dialogue are drawn from the author's imagination and are not to be construed as real. Any resemblance to actual events or persons, living or dead, is entirely coincidental.

HARPER

An Imprint of HarperCollins*Publishers*
10 East 53rd Street
New York, New York 10022-5299

Copyright © 2006 by Saverio N. Barone
Excerpt from *Empire Rising* copyright © 2007 by Saverio N. Barone
ISBN: 978-0-06-089245-6
ISBN-10: 0-06-089245-5

First Harper paperback printing: September 2007
First William Morrow special printing: September 2006
First William Morrow hardcover printing: September 2006

Printed in the United States of America

Visit Harper paperbacks on the World Wide Web at
www.harpercollins.com

10 9 8 7 6 5 4 3 2 1

. . . when the storm of arrows, speeded by the strings,
Shot above the shield wall, swift on feathered wings.
Every shaft fulfilled its duty, and drove the barb to goal.

—BEOWULF

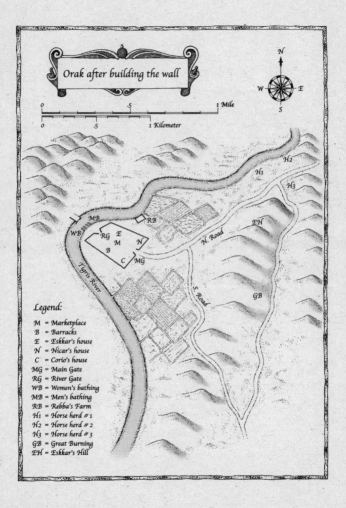

Orak after building the wall

Legend:

M = Marketplace
B = Barracks
E = Eskkar's house
N = Nicar's house
C = Corio's house
MG = Main Gate
RG = River Gate
WB = Women's bathing
MB = Men's bathing
RB = Rebba's Farm
H1 = Horse herd #1
H2 = Horse herd #2
H3 = Horse herd #3
GB = Great Burning
EH = Eskkar's Hill

DAWN
OF
EMPIRE

Prologue

The eastern bank of the river Tigris, 3158 B.C.E. . . . .

The village lay before him like a lamb trapped by a pack of wolves. Thutmose-sin halted his sweat-soaked horse on the crest of the hill, while his men formed up on each side. He surveyed the plain beneath him, taking in the crops in the fields and the irrigation canals that watered them. His eyes soon fixed on the village barely two miles away. There the Tigris curled sharply around the cluster of mud huts and tents that nestled against it. Today the river that brought the very sustenance of life to the dirt-eaters would be the obstacle that prevented their escape.

Those who hadn't fled already, Thutmose-sin corrected himself. He had planned to catch the village by surprise, but word had preceded his band, as it so often did. The warriors had ridden hard for five days with little sleep. Despite that effort, the dirt-eaters had received a few hours' warning. News of his approach must have traveled down the river, faster than a man on a horse. Even now, Thutmose-sin could see a few small boats paddling frantically to the far side of the Tigris. Those lucky ones would use the river to elude the fate he had planned for them.

His men had settled into place. Nearly three hundred warriors formed a single line across the hilltop, with Thutmose-sin at their center. Each man strung his bow, unslung his lance, and loosened the sword in his scabbard. They had done this so many times that now they spoke little and needed few commands, as they prepared themselves not for battle but for conquest. Only after the weapons were ready did they look to themselves. Every rider drank deeply from his water skin, then emptied what remained over the head and neck of his horse. There would be plenty of water for both man and beast in the village.

His second in command, Rethnar, pulled up just behind him. "The men are ready, Thutmose-sin."

The leader turned his head, saw the eagerness in Rethnar's face, and smiled at the man's excitement. Thutmose-sin looked left and right along the line, and saw that every tenth man had raised bow or lance into the air. The warriors were more than ready. Their reward for the days of hard riding awaited them. "Then let us begin."

With a touch of his heel to the horse's ribs, Thutmose-sin started the descent, the men following his lead. They took their time negotiating the downslope. With fresh horses, they would have raced down the incline and covered the last two miles in an exuberant rush. But after five days of riding, no man wanted to risk a valuable but weary horse— not with the end of their journey so near.

When they reached the plain, the line of horsemen became more ragged as the land flattened out. Small bands of riders detached themselves from the wings and began sweeping the countryside. They would search the outlying fields and scattered farmhouses, driving any inhabitants toward the village.

The main body of warriors cantered through fields of golden wheat and barley, Thutmose-sin at their head. They soon reached the broad, well-trodden path that led up to the village. Two minutes at a smooth gallop and they had passed the outermost dwellings.

Now the youngest warriors on the freshest horses took the lead, their war cries ringing over the thudding of the horses' hooves. They rode past a few scattered dirt-eaters, ignoring the screaming women, frightened men, and crying children. A rough wooden fence as tall as a man might have slowed them for a moment, but the crude gate stood open and undefended. The warriors swept through unopposed.

Thutmose-sin saw the first dirt-eater die. An old man, stumbling in fear, tried to reach the safety of a hut. A warrior struck downward with his sword, then raised the now-bloodied blade high into the air and shouted his war cry. Arrows snapped from bows, striking down men and women caught in the open. The riders fanned out, some dismounting to search the huts, sword or lance in hand, looking for victims. Anyone who resisted would die, of course, but many would be killed just for the sport or to satisfy a thirst for blood. The rest would be spared. The Alur Meriki needed slaves, not bodies.

Thutmose-sin ignored the clamor as he rode slowly through the village, the ten members of his personal guard now surrounding him in the narrow lane. He saw that a few of the dwellings stood two stories tall, a display of their owner's wealth and prestige. Some houses hid behind high mud walls, while others had small gardens setting them back from the lane.

He reached the gathering place at the heart of the village, a large open space with a wide stone well in its center. More than a dozen carts, their dirty linen awnings flapping in the light breeze, crowded the marketplace. A few still had their wares upon them, though all stood deserted. A rich village, as his scouts had promised.

After a pause to let the horses drink some water from the well, Thutmose-sin picked out a wider lane that led toward the rear of the village. They followed its path until they reached the river. Here he halted, then slid easily to the ground, handing the halter to one of his men. A wooden dock extended a dozen paces into the Tigris. Walking to the jetty's end, he tightened the wide strip of blue cloth embroidered with red thread that held his hair away from his eyes. Then he stopped and stared at the opposite bank.

Even at this fording place in midsummer, the Tigris reached nearly to the tops of its wide banks and flowed deeper than a man's height in places. A ferry provided passage to the other side, but the abandoned craft sat on the opposite bank, along with three smaller vessels, all empty. He noticed that the flat-sided ferry rested at an odd angle. Some dirt-eaters must have opened its bottom.

On the opposite shore, the land rose steeply into a hillside dotted with date palms and poplars. Thutmose-sin could see hundreds of people moving frantically up those slopes, some leading animals, others carrying their meager belongings, men helping their women and children. Most followed a crooked road that climbed toward a gap between the nearest hills. Almost all stole quick glances back toward the river, terrified that the grim riders would pursue them. The cowardly dirt-eaters would run as far as they could, for as long as they could, then hide in the rocks and caves, shaking with fear and praying to their feeble gods for deliverance from the Alur Meriki.

They'd slipped beyond his reach, and the knowledge enraged Thutmose-sin, though he kept his face emotionless. The tired horses didn't have the strength to fight the current, let alone chase fleeing villagers, nor did they have the means to bring any captives or goods back to this side of the river.

He hated the Tigris, hated all rivers almost as much as he hated the dirt-eaters who dwelt beside them. The rivers with their boats that could travel farther and faster than a galloping horse while carrying men and their burdens. More important, the flowing waters gave life to villages—abominations—such as this, and let them grow large and prosperous.

Thutmose-sin took a deep breath, then walked back up the jetty. Nothing showed of his disappointment. Thutmose-sin swung back onto his horse and led his bodyguards back into the village, where the captives' laments rose to greet him. When he reached the well, Rethnar was waiting.

"Hail, Thutmose-sin. A fine village, isn't it?"

"Hail, Rethnar." Thutmose-sin answered formally, to affirm

his authority. The two men were of much the same age, a few months under twenty-five, but Thutmose-sin commanded most of the men, and the clan's sarrum, or king, had given him responsibility for the raid. The fact that the sarrum happened to be Thutmose-sin's father made no difference in his authority.

"Yes, but too many escaped across the river."

Rethnar shrugged. "One of the slaves said they learned of our coming a few hours ago. Word came down the river."

"Just enough time for most of them to escape." Thutmose-sin had driven the men without respite the last three days, trying to avoid this situation. "Did the slave say how many were in the village?"

"No, Thutmose-sin. I will find out."

"Then I leave you to your task, Rethnar." The remaining villagers would be hiding under their beds or in holes dug beneath their huts. It would take a few hours to find them all.

Thutmose-sin dismounted and stepped over to the well. One of his men brought up a bucket of fresh water and Thutmose-sin drank his fill, then washed the dust from his face and hands. He dismissed most of his guards, so they could join in the looting. They wouldn't be needed here.

With only three men, he began to explore. Thutmose-sin entered several of the larger houses, curious to see what they contained and how the people lived. He did the same at a half dozen shops. Signs of their owners' hasty departures abounded, from half-eaten meals to the goods still displayed for sale on carts or pushed indoors before the owners fled. Taking his time, he examined the leather belts, linens, sandals, and pottery scattered about. He even ducked into an alehouse, but the sour stench made him move on.

Choosing another lane, Thutmose-sin wondered how the dirt-eaters could live behind walls of mud that blocked out the wind and sky, while surrounded by the stench and filth of hundreds of others as dirty as one's self. A true warrior lived free and proud, unfettered to any particular place, and took what he needed or wanted with his sword.

A larger house, nearly hidden behind a wall, caught his

eye. He pushed open the wooden gate. Instead of the usual garden, he found a smith's shop, with two forges, a bellows, and three different-sized cooling pots. Half-mended farm implements lay on the ground or on the empty benches. But nearly half the workspace held tools for making weapons. Clay molds for swords and daggers leaned against the garden wall. Sharpening and finishing stones filled a shelf, and a large block of wood, nicked and hacked, showed where the swordsmith tested his new blades. The craftsman had taken his tools with him, of course, or hidden them someplace. Weapons and tools could be as valuable as horses. The blacksmith would have made a useful slave, but so important a laborer would have crossed the river at the first warning.

The smith must be a master craftsman to have such a large house. The thought gave him no pleasure. The best bronze weapons the Alur Meriki carried came from large villages like this one. He hated the fact that village smiths could create such fine weapons with apparent ease. Swords, daggers, lance and arrow points, all could be made here, and better than his own people could make.

Not that his clansmen didn't know the mysteries of bronze and copper. But their smaller, portable forges couldn't match the quality or resources of a large village. Forging a strong bronze sword required care and time, two luxuries his people didn't have, living in permanent migration.

Few warriors among his people cared about the dirt-eaters' ways, but Thutmose-sin had a wise father, who taught him the mysteries of life. Of all the many sons of Maskim-Xul, only Thutmose-sin had been born at the fullness of the moon, the birthing time for those to whom the gods gave extraordinary perception and cunning. By the time Thutmose-sin came of age, his father had appended the rare *sin* to his name, to signify his wisdom and judgment.

Thutmose-sin understood the importance of learning about his enemies. The dirt-eaters harbored a threat even to the Alur Meriki, something his father understood well. Everyone else in the clan would have scoffed at the thought of the soft villagers competing with them. To the warriors, an enemy was some other rival steppes tribe they might encounter in their wanderings. The pathetic dirt-eaters possessed few fighters and even fewer skilled horsemen. Any of his fighters, stronger, taller, and trained in fighting and horsemanship at an early age, could kill three or more dirt-eaters in battle without difficulty.

No, the dirt-eaters didn't know the arts of war, nor could they ever become strong fighters. But they possessed another weapon deadlier than any bow or lance: the food they coaxed out of the ground. The food that allowed them to multiply like ants, without having to hunt or fight for their nourishment. The more food they took from the earth, the more they multiplied. And some day, there might be so many of them that even the Alur Meriki could not kill them all.

That day must never come, Thutmose-sin vowed. His father grew old and soon would have to pass on the authority he had wielded for so long. On that day, Thutmose-sin, already the favorite of the clan's elder council, would rule the Alur Meriki. It would be his responsibility to make sure the clan grew and prospered as it always had, by conquest and pillage. He would not fail in his duty.

Hours passed before he returned to the marketplace. Warriors and their captives filled the area. Most of the crying had ceased. The new slaves knelt in the dirt, crowded together, shoulder to shoulder. The stink of their fear overpowered even the five-day-old horse smell of the warriors. He found Rethnar sitting on the ground, his back against the well, awaiting his leader's return.

"Greetings, Rethnar. How many are there?"

"Two hundred and eighty-six taken alive, after we dug the last of them out of their burrows. Another seventy or eighty dead. More than enough for our needs. All the huts and fields have been searched. Not one tried to resist."

"How many lived here?"

"Nearly a thousand dirt-eaters, living in this filth," Rethnar answered, a look of disgust on his face. "A few hours earlier and we could have captured another four or five hundred."

"We'll need horses with wings, then." They'd ridden as hard as they could. "Did you get any horses?"

"No, not one. No doubt anyone with a horse rode south. There are some oxen still in the fields."

Oxen had no value, not this far from the Alur Meriki's encampment. Thutmose-sin had hoped for at least a few horses. Extra horses could carry more booty back. He put the thought away. "Are you ready to begin?"

"Yes, Thutmose-sin. After we select our slaves, do we let the rest live?" Rethnar fingered his sword.

Thutmose-sin smiled at the man's anticipation. His second in command enjoyed killing. "No, not this time. Too many escaped us. Begin."

Rethnar stood as he gave the orders. The warriors moved among the prisoners, selecting those unfit for work. At swordpoint, they separated the old, the young, the sick, and the infirm, driving them away from the original group. They pulled babies from their mothers' hands, knocking the women down with their fists if they tried to resist. Two men struggled against the warriors and were cut down swiftly. Rethnar's men wanted only those strong enough to endure what awaited them. The others, of no use, would die. Thutmose-sin had decreed it.

The culling went rapidly. Thutmose-sin watched as the warriors divided the dirt-eaters into two groups, his lips moving as he did his own count. Scarcely more than a hundred and forty would live.

When his men completed the division, Rethnar shouted the order and the killing began. Warriors moved methodically through those selected to die. Swords rose and fell. The smell of blood quickly saturated the air. Shouts and screams again echoed from the walls, as loved ones cried out to each other. The killing, efficient and swift, took little time. Warriors found no glory in such slaughter. Few resisted. Three children tried to run, urged on by their helpless mothers, but the line of warriors held the victims in. Some called out to their gods, imploring Marduk or Ishtar to help them, but the false gods of the dirt-eaters had no power over the Alur Meriki.

When the carnage ended, Thutmose-sin mounted his horse and moved in front of those left alive, his guards standing before him, weapons in hand, as much to intimidate as to protect. Fresh tears streaked the terrified faces of both men and women. Silence quickly fell over the survivors as they looked up at this new warrior.

"I am Thutmose-sin of the Alur Meriki. My father, Maskim-Xul, rules all the clans of the Alur Meriki." He spoke in his own language, even though he could speak the villagers' dialect well enough. If the village had resisted, if some of them had fought bravely, he might have spoken to them directly. But to do so now would dishonor him. One of his men interpreted, speaking in a loud voice, so that everyone could hear their fate.

"In Maskim-Xul's name, you are to be slaves of the Alur Meriki clan for the rest of your lives. You'll work hard and you'll obey every order. You will now learn what awaits those who disobey or try to run."

He turned back to Rethnar. "Teach them."

Rethnar called out to his men, and they began the next phase of the slaves' training. One of his subcommanders quickly selected two men and two women. The warriors stripped the men naked, then staked them, legs spread wide apart, on the ground. The ropes stretched their limbs as much as possible to prevent the slightest movement. At the same time, other warriors herded the remaining slaves even closer together, still on their knees, so they could see the torture. All must watch and none could turn away or close their eyes.

Warriors knelt next to each bound victim. Rethnar nodded and his men began, using their knives to slice into their captives, or fist-sized stones to break or crush their flesh. The helpless men cried out in terror even before the first cut or blow. When the actual torture began, shrieks of pain rebounded off the mud walls. The torture must be drawn out, so that the victims suffered as much as possible for as long as they could endure. Their fate would serve as an example to those forced to watch. A few spectators trembled uncontrollably in their fear, others cried in grief, but most just stared in shock. Anyone who turned away or closed his eyes received a blow from the flat of a sword.

At the same time other warriors attended to the women. A cart, one used by the villagers to display fruits or vegetables, now served another purpose. Their simple shifts ripped from their bodies, they found themselves side by side, bent backward across the cart and held down by laughing warriors, while the first group of grinning Alur Meriki lined up to take their pleasure. Both women would be raped into near insensibility, then cut to pieces, a practice that always instilled the proper amount of terror in newly captured women.

The process wouldn't take long. Afterward there would be no resistance. The new slaves would learn the lesson their new masters intended: obey every command instantly, suffer any abuse, or face even worse punishment. The Alur Meriki had few problems with their slaves, male or female. Death by slow torture for the slightest offense, real or imagined, made for an effective deterrent that kept slaves docile while their masters worked them to death.

Thutmose-sin turned back to Rethnar and saw his subcommander pushing aside his undergarment. He'd be the first to take one, or both of the women. "Don't let them die too soon, Rethnar."

The rising screams of the victims drowned out Rethnar's reply.

Thutmose-sin turned his horse and rode out of the village, three guards still accompanying him. This time he inspected the neighboring farms, studying the farmhouses, fields, and even the endless irrigation that carried water to the crops. No warrior would ever stoop to farming, but Thutmose-sin wanted to know how this village had grown so large, how so many could be fed from these fields. The answer eluded him, however, and by the time he returned, Rethnar's lesson had ended. The four bodies, now covered with flies, lay sprawled where they had died. Silence filled the marketplace. Obeying their new masters, the slaves kept silent. They'd learned the first lesson.

He dismounted, then stepped past the bodies to where the

villagers knelt, their gaze fixed on the victims as they'd been ordered. A few had glanced at the Alur Meriki leader as he approached, but one brief look at his unsmiling face, and they turned their eyes back to the grisly tableau in front of them. Ignoring the men and children, he examined the women's faces. Three or four looked comely enough.

"Bring them out for me," he ordered his bodyguards. They grabbed those he indicated, pulling them to their feet, out of the crowd of kneeling bodies. It took only moments to rip off their garments and force them to their knees in the dirt.

These looked to be the prettiest of the lot, though Thutmose-sin knew that tears and terror could change a woman's face. Two women, their bodies shaking, cried softly, bitter tears that would soon pass. Eyes could only hold so much water, after all. The other two just looked at him, fear and shock already fading into hopelessness.

Thutmose-sin examined each in turn, grasping their hair and pulling their faces upward. The two he chose looked older, about sixteen or seventeen seasons. He liked them at that age, when they'd learned enough about how to satisfy a man. They would please him, he knew. After what they'd seen today, they'd be frantic in their efforts to give him pleasure.

Rethnar walked over. "The lesson is ended, Thutmose-sin. Should we begin dividing the spoils? The men are eager to take the rest of the women."

Thutmose-sin glanced at the sun, still high in the afternoon sky. "No, not until darkness. Put the slaves to work. Anything we don't want is to be destroyed. If it can burn, I want it carried here and set afire. Everything, including the fence, the wagons, tools, clothing, everything. Smash whatever can't be burned. Then tomorrow, have the slaves knock down every house. When the dirt-eaters return, they must find nothing of value. And before you begin the march back to camp, burn all the fields as well. Everything, every animal, is to be destroyed."

Thutmose-sin looked around at the houses surrounding him. "This village grew too large and prosperous. These dirt-eaters must be taught not to build such places again. And when you begin the journey home, load the slaves with as much as they can carry. Let only the strongest survive to reach our camp."

Rethnar smiled. "I'll teach them. Then you go back to the council?"

"Yes. Tomorrow I'll take fifty men and return to my father. I'll bring the choicest wine and women for him. If you like, send ten of your own men with gifts for your grandfather." Rethnar's grandfather sat on the council as well.

"Grandfather will be pleased."

"You've done well, Rethnar. I'll speak of you to my father and the council."

It would take Rethnar close to three weeks to rejoin the clan, burdened with so many slaves and goods. And the number of slaves would increase, as Rethnar's men visited the farmhouses they'd bypassed in their rush to the village.

Thutmose-sin mounted his horse, then turned to his guards. "Bring my women to the river." He guided the animal through the lane, until he again reached the water's edge. First he would see to his horse, then wash himself in the Tigris. The two women would also bathe, so that they wouldn't bring the village stink to his bed tonight.

As he dove into the cool and cleansing water, he thought about what he'd accomplished. They'd taken much booty and slaves, and a large village would be destroyed as a lesson to the dirt-eaters. The health and power of the Alur Meriki would be greatly increased. The capture of a few hundred more slaves would have made the raid more successful, but nothing could be done about that. All in all, everything had gone well. His father and the council would be pleased.

Eleven years later, near the headwaters of the Tigris . . .

Thutmose-sin rode slowly through the scattered huts until he reached the edge of the bluff. From this height he observed the chilled waters of the Tigris, sparkling in the sunlight and fresh from their birth-mountains, stretching all the way to the distant northern horizon. Directly beneath the hilltop, a caravan of men and animals had begun the difficult crossing to the eastern bank.

This caravan would prove far mightier than the watery obstacle nature had placed in its path. The people of the steppes, the Alur Meriki, traveled wherever they chose and nothing stood in their path. They dominated all the peoples of the world, just as Thutmose-sin dominated them. He was their king, and he ruled the world.

In his thirty-fifth season, the leader of the Alur Meriki stood as strong and powerful as in his youth, with not a trace of fat on his tall, muscular frame. Around his neck hung a copper-linked chain with a three-inch gold medallion identifying the Alur Meriki leader. Unlike his followers, he wore no other jewelry or rings to show his importance or his conquests. The medallion proclaimed his power—only the strongest and most capable ever earned the right to wear it.

Thutmose-sin regarded the scene beneath him with satisfaction. The clan extended in a wide and crooked line for nearly four miles, a snakelike procession that sent a long plume of reddish dust into the still air. Four hundred warriors shepherded them along, helping the wagons get through places where the earth turned to soft sand, keeping the flocks of sheep, goats, and cattle moving, and occasionally dismounting to add their own muscles to those of the weary animals that struggled over the rough ground. The caravan traveled slowly, but it never stopped.

The column consisted of horses, oxen, wagons, stock animals, women, children, old men, and slaves, in roughly that order of importance. The real strength of his people, its great force of warriors, traversed the land many days' ride ahead and to each side of the line of march. Some searched out the best and easiest route for the clan's travel. But most plundered the countryside, taking whatever of value they found, to enrich themselves and to keep the clan alive and growing.

The Alur Meriki had become the largest gathering of those

who'd come forth from the northern steppes many generations ago. They now numbered more than five thousand people, not counting slaves. That meant that Thutmose-sin had nearly two thousand fighting men at his command. No other steppes clan had produced so many warriors. More important, the Alur Meriki warriors had never suffered defeat in battle. It had been more than twenty years, in the days when Maskim-Xul led the Alur Meriki, since another clan had even dared to challenge them.

Satisfied with his peoples' progress, Thutmose-sin turned his horse away from the edge of the promontory. As he did so, a small band of riders approached, a clan leader at their head.

"Greetings, Sarrum." Urgo, clan leader and kinsman to Thutmose-sin, used the formal title to refer to his lord. The first to swear allegiance to Thutmose-sin after the death of Maskim-Xul six seasons ago, Urgo stood a hand's width shorter but a little broader than his cousin. Though seven seasons older, Urgo looked just as fit. Eight or ten hours a day on the back of a spirited horse kept any man in fighting shape.

"Greetings, Urgo."

"I bring news, Thutmose-sin."

Of the twenty clan leaders who ruled the Alur Meriki, Urgo's clan had grown into one of the most powerful, with two hundred warriors under his standard.

Not that Urgo or any of the clan leaders made life easier for Thutmose-sin, even though half of them shared kinship to one degree or another. At times the entire Alur Meriki horde, with their endless disputes over women, horses, or some warrior's honor, took less effort to manage than the fractious disputes of the twenty council members.

Thutmose-sin led Urgo back toward the crest of the hill. They left their bodyguards behind, out of earshot, and sat near the promontory's edge where they could watch the procession below. It would take three or four days before the clan could ford the Tigris. They'd camp here for at least a week, resting while repairing the wagons, and letting the sheep and goats graze on the plentiful grass, fattening themselves before moving on.

"A river trader told me something of interest," Urgo began without ceremony. "He said there's a great village far to the south. It's called Orak. The trader claims there are two thousand dirt-people living there."

"Two thousand?" Thutmose-sin's voice rose in disbelief. That was easily twice as large as anything the Alur Meriki had ever encountered before. A village that size, if it could feed itself, would have great resources that would provide much plunder. "Can that many dirt-eaters live in one place? Are you sure your trader speaks the truth?"

"Yes, Sarrum, I believe him," Urgo answered. "Others have spoken of this place before. Let me show you." He began to trace out a map in the sand. With a few light strokes of his knife and the help of some pebbles to represent the mountains and other landmarks, Urgo made the rivers appear and the mountains to the east rise up. As always, he impressed his sarrum as much with his memory as with his skill at mapmaking. Urgo could re-create maps from all the places the clan had traveled as accurately as if he'd seen them yesterday, instead of five or even ten years ago.

"When we cross the Tigris," Urgo said, "we'll continue east. In a few weeks we'll have to choose a route to the south. If we turn here, or here," he indicated places on the map, "as we planned, we'll pass this Orak far to the northeast. It will be too distant to raid. So if we wish to capture this place, we must turn sooner. We could head more toward this village, perhaps even following the path of the Tigris. The lands along the river are fertile. There'd be much grain and goods to capture. It's not the line of march that we planned, but this great village would yield many spoils."

Urgo took a deep breath. "With whatever route we choose, when we're a few months closer, we can send raiding parties ahead to capture this Orak. Two thousand dirt-eaters will have plenty of valuables and no way of hiding them all."

Thutmose-sin looked down at the lines in the sand. "This place, it seems familiar."

"It should," Urgo said with a laugh. "You raided it a few years before you became sarrum. Orak was a fat village even then, and you brought back many slaves."

Thutmose-sin fingered the hilt of his sword, trying to re-call one raid out of so many. The name meant nothing to him, but he recognized the bend of the Tigris. "Yes, I re-member. A good raid. But the village wasn't so large then, and we killed everyone and destroyed it. Can it have grown back so quickly?"

Urgo shrugged. "It must have."

It seemed a simple decision, easy to make, no different from many other such choices the clan faced every day. Still, Thutmose-sin hesitated.

"A village that big defies our way of life, Urgo," he said, "and for that reason alone it should be destroyed. But we hadn't planned to go so far south. If we do, we'll add many more miles to our journey. We'd have to hurry to reach our winter camp. What we find when we reach this Orak may not be worth the extra weeks of travel."

"Yes, that may be so," Urgo answered. "It's the usual problem."

Thutmose-sin understood the man's prudence. Urgo did not make such decisions. Only Thutmose-sin or the entire council could change the route. But Urgo had the responsi-bility of collecting information about the land through which they passed and suggesting possible raids or routes to fol-low. While the Alur Meriki would eventually begin to move south, what route they chose and how fast they traveled would be critical to the prosperity and health of the clans. The sar-rum understood the problem Urgo referred to all too well. If they sent raiding parties, that meant delays and difficulties of carrying the loot back to the main camp. A mounted warrior, burdened by weapons, water, and whatever he needed for his horse, could carry little else. Loaded-down slaves traveled slowly and required large quantities of food and water, which must also be carried. If instead they took the entire clan closer to Orak, then they'd be nearly two hundred miles west of where they wanted to be. As always, not every need could be satisfied. No matter what decision he reached, some would be displeased.

"If we head toward this place," Thutmose-sin said, tapping the pebble that represented Orak, "they'll learn of our coming. These large villages empty themselves long before our warriors arrive. Even the farmers along the way will flee, after first burying their tools and seed crops deep in the ground. No matter what route we choose, word of our coming will soon spread."

Ideally, they would capture this Orak with all its people and goods inside, but such an occurrence almost never happened, even with raiding parties that could travel far and fast. Tools, grain, and valuables would disappear, while horses and herd animals would be scattered or hidden. The clan would be lucky to capture a third of what the village possessed.

Thutmose-sin turned away from the map and stared at the land below. But his thoughts stayed focused on this Orak. Such an abomination could not be allowed to exist. Villagers scratched in the dirt like pigs for their food, instead of hunting or fighting for it like true men. The dirt-eaters lived and bred like ants. You could kick over their anthill, but in a few years it grew back, with more of them than before. Just like this Orak. He had leveled it years ago and already it had risen again, with more dirt-eaters than before.

Now Thutmose-sin wanted to obliterate it and destroy everyone within it. The Alur Meriki might tolerate small villages. They'd be plundered but not destroyed, so that they could be raided again in the future. But a village of two thousand was more than an insult. He considered what might happen if they returned in another ten years to find the village had again doubled in size. No, this Orak must be destroyed to make sure such a thing could never happen.

It wouldn't be easy. Thutmose-sin needed to find a way to keep all the villagers inside, with their goods, until it was too late to get away.

"This village," Thutmose-sin said, "the ford there is a good one?"

Urgo nodded. "According to the trader, it's the only easy crossing for thirty or forty miles in either direction. Likely that is what helps the place grow so large."

"Then most of the important villagers will flee across the Tigris or down the river." Thutmose-sin took his dagger from his belt and moved closer to Urgo's map. "Perhaps there's a way to take it before too many escape."

His knife inscribed fresh lines in the sand as he spoke. The plan he sketched was simple, but unlike anything they had ever done. The lay of the land would help, as would the Tigris. By the time Thutmose-sin finished, their heads nearly touched as they leaned over the map.

"It's a cunning plan, Thutmose-sin. We'll gain many slaves."

"The tactics are simple enough, and we've twice as many warriors as we need. And the dirt-eaters will do what they always do, and so help destroy themselves."

Finally Urgo nodded. "Yes, Sarrum, I can't think of anything that can go wrong. We'll capture much of value to the clan. I'll begin the preparations. There are many months to work out the details, and we can always change our tactics if something unexpected happens."

"Then it's decided." Thutmose-sin rose to his feet, his subcommander doing the same. "We'll discuss it tonight with the council." They'd approve it, of course, especially if Urgo supported it.

He swung back up on his horse, his bodyguards again forming up around him, then rode back to the edge of the escarpment for one last look at the caravan. His people continued their inexorable march. Their traveling pace would be slow, but the rulers of the world had no need to hurry.

Thutmose-sin smiled in anticipation as he turned his horse around and put him to the gallop. He had set in motion the route and the objectives of the Alur Meriki for the next six months. Those plans meant that some villages would be spared, their foolish inhabitants thanking the gods for their deliverance, never realizing that they existed only at his sufferance.

This great village of Orak would be taken just as easily as

the smallest farmhouse in their path. Orak's inhabitants would die or become slaves. He, Thutmose-sin, had decided and so it would be. No clan, no village, no force of nature could stop the full might of his people. And this time when he finished with it, Orak would be sunk back to the mud from which it came. This time, the anthill would not recover.

PART 1

The Gathering

1

The eastern bank of the river Tigris, two hundred miles north of the great sea . . .

Awake, Eskkar, awake now! Nicar sent for you. You must come at once!" Eskkar realized the words had been spoken several times, accompanied by vigorous shaking. Now they ceased being mere sounds and became instead a message, one that slowly found its way through the haze that still clutched at his mind and body from last night's drinking.

"Enough," Eskkar grunted, swinging an arm clumsily at the messenger. But the nimble youth dodged easily. Eskkar pushed himself up to a sitting position on his hard pallet, while the room revolved around him and the blood pounded in his head from the sudden motion. His throat felt dry, like the gritty dirt floor beneath his naked feet, and his skull seemed ready to split apart at any moment as he paid the price for last night's vinegary wine.

"Water," he growled. After a few moments, the messenger placed a wooden cup in Eskkar's shaking hands. He swallowed a few mouthfuls, though much of the liquid dribbled down his chin onto his bare chest. His eyes refused to focus, and the bright sunlight that streamed through the open doorway into the shadowy soldiers' quarters added to his misery.

As soon as Eskkar lowered the cup, the boy started again. "Hurry, Eskkar. Nicar awaits you now! You must come at once."

What in the name of the gods could Nicar want from him? But Nicar's name and position as the ruler of the village of Orak started him moving, stumbling first to the rank chamber pot inside the soldiers' common room, then back to his pallet to don his tunic.

Leaving the barracks, his eyes half-shut against the sun, Eskkar managed to find his way to the well. He leaned against the rough stones for a moment, then upended the bucket to splash water on his face before drinking.

Somewhat refreshed, Eskkar looked up, surprised to see the sun so high. Demons below, he must have drunk a whole skinful of that bitter date wine. He cursed himself for being a fool.

When Eskkar turned away he saw a handful of guards, men who should have been busy at their daily tasks, standing uneasily near him. "Where is Ariamus?" he asked no one in particular, his voice sounding hoarse in his ears. Ariamus, captain of the guard, maintained the few laws of Orak and defended the village from bandits and marauders.

"Ariamus is gone," a gray-bearded veteran answered, spitting in the dirt to show his disgust. "He's run off, taken a dozen men with him, as well as extra horses and arms. The talk in the market says that barbarians are heading south, coming toward Orak."

Eskkar let the words penetrate as he studied their faces. He saw fear and uncertainty, mixed in with the shock of losing their master. No wonder they looked toward him. If Ariamus had run off, then Eskkar would be in charge, at least until a new captain could be chosen. That would explain the summons from Nicar.

The grinning messenger plucked at Eskkar's tunic. He refused to hurry, taking his time to draw another bucket

from the well. He washed his hands and face before returning to the barracks to lace on his patched and worn sandals.
Only then did he follow the boy through the winding streets
to the imposing mud-brick and stone house of Nicar, Orak's
leading merchant and foremost among the Five ruling Families that dictated the daily comings and goings of the village.

The youth pulled Eskkar past the gatekeeper and into the
house, then guided him up the narrow steps to the upper
rooms. The house seemed quiet, with none of the usual visitors waiting their turn to see the busy merchant.

Nicar stood on the tiny balcony that looked out over the
village. Quite a bit shorter than Eskkar, the gray-haired
merchant carried the extra weight around his middle that
marked him as a man of wealth.

Eskkar grunted something he hoped sounded like a greeting and stood still as the most important and richest man
in the village looked him over. Eskkar realized Nicar was
studying him with the same care used when selecting the
best slave from a bad lot.

Nearly three years ago, Eskkar had limped into Orak,
with nothing but a sword on his back and an infected leg
wound. Since then he'd seen Nicar many times, but Orak's
most important person had never paid any particular attention to the tall, dark-haired subcommander who rarely spoke
and never smiled.

When Nicar finished his scrutiny, he turned away and
looked out over the village. Suddenly Eskkar felt uncomfortable in his shabby tunic and worn sandals.

"Well, Nicar, what do you want?" The words came out
harsher than intended.

"I'm not sure what I want, Eskkar," the merchant answered.
"You know Ariamus is gone?"

Eskkar nodded.

"You may not know that the barbarians have recently
crossed the Tigris, far to the north. The killing and burning
have already begun there."

It took a moment before Nicar's words struggled through

the vapors clouding Eskkar's mind. Finally he understood their meaning. So rumor spoke the truth for once. He leaned heavily against the balcony wall, aware of his aching head. His belly cramped painfully, and for a moment he thought he would vomit. Eskkar struggled to keep control of his thoughts and his stomach.

Nicar continued. "From the far north, through the foothills, then down the plain toward the river." He hesitated, to give Eskkar time to comprehend his words. "They're moving steadily south. It's likely they'll turn in this direction, though it will be months before they arrive."

Nicar spoke calmly, but Eskkar heard a faint hint of fear and resignation in his voice.

Eskkar ran his fingers through his unruly hair, then fingered the thin beard that outlined his chin. "Do you know which clan?" Even after all these years, the word *barbarian* grated on his ears.

"I believe they're called the Alur Meriki. They may be the same clan that raided here last time."

Eskkar grimaced. His own birth clan. Not his people anymore, not for many years, not since they'd cast him out. "The Alur Meriki are a fierce clan with many men and horses."

"What clan are you from, Eskkar? Or is that a question I shouldn't ask?"

"Ask what you like. But I never raided this place, if that's what you wish to know. I had barely started riding with the warriors when they killed my family."

"Is that what happened? Is that why you left?"

Eskkar bit his lip, cursing at himself for even mentioning his past. Even the ignorant villagers knew warriors never left their clans willingly, only in disgrace.

Nicar let the silence lengthen, until Eskkar felt compelled to answer.

"I didn't leave, Nicar. I ran for my life. I was lucky to get away."

"I see. You're right, it makes no difference."

Eskkar's thoughts returned to the Alur Meriki. So his family's clan marched toward Orak. No, *marched* didn't properly convey the slow and steady movement of the steppes people. Migration came closest to a real description of the steady movement that might take months to advance but a few miles. "How long have you known of their coming, Nicar?"

Nicar stroked his gray-speckled beard. "Word came to me three days ago. I told only Ariamus. He cautioned me to tell no one for a few days while he considered how to defend the village."

Eskkar jerked his head in derision, the sudden movement sending a wave of sharp pain through his head that made him regret the gesture. Ariamus, as leader of the village's small garrison, had certainly planned well. But his plans hadn't been for the defense of the village, nor had they included Eskkar, his lowly third in command. The second in command, one of Ariamus's fawning friends, had died a week before from the pox. Eskkar already knew he would not be promoted. He'd never bothered to toady up to Ariamus.

Instead, two days ago Ariamus ordered Eskkar off on a chase after an inconsequential runaway slave, a task that might have taken a week except for the fortunate accident of the foolish slave breaking his leg in some rocks. Eskkar remembered the brief look of surprise on Ariamus's face when he'd returned yesterday afternoon.

Then last night a comradely Ariamus had invited the soldiers to the tavern for wine and song, paying for the powerful spirits that kept flowing long into the night. Eskkar should have been suspicious after the first drink, since the tight-fisted Ariamus never bought more than one mug of barley ale for any of his men. But tired, thirsty, and smug with satisfaction at recovering the slave so quickly, Eskkar hadn't noticed. Again he cursed himself for being so easily tricked.

Eskkar's head began to throb again, and his throat felt dry.

"Well, Nicar, what do you expect me to do? Go after Ariamus and the others? I'm sure he took the youngest and wildest men. He's probably stolen the best horses as well. He'll be long gone by the time we're ready to give chase, and with a dozen fighting men he can match any force we send after him."

The hoarseness returned to Eskkar's voice, and he could scarcely get the last few words out.

Nicar recognized the rasp in his visitor's throat, and called out for a servant. The same boy who'd escorted Eskkar, no doubt waiting on the steps outside, appeared at once. Nicar turned to his visitor. "Water or wine?"

Eskkar wanted wine, wanted it badly, and wanted it right now, but he'd shown enough stupidity for a while.

"Water, for a start. Perhaps wine later, eh, Nicar?" Eskkar didn't try to conceal the sarcasm. He had lived in Orak for almost three years but had entered the fine house of Nicar only once before, and then only to deliver a message. Now Nicar offered him wine, almost with his own hand. He wondered what would come next.

While the boy poured a cup of water, Eskkar thought about the captain of the guard, who might easily have looted the village before he vanished. Eskkar briefly wondered why his own throat hadn't been cut. The gods knew he'd argued with Ariamus numerous times. The thought of himself lying in bed helpless, a drunken pig ready to be butchered, sent a shiver through him. Evidently Ariamus hadn't considered him worth killing.

Eskkar drank some water, then turned back toward the balcony. Despite the grim news, the cool drink made him feel better. He remembered his manners. "Thank you, Nicar. But I ask you again. Do you want me to chase after Ariamus?"

"No, I don't want him back. I was fool enough to trust him to defend Orak. Now I'd kill him if I could. What I want is to make the village ready for defense. We must be ready to fight off the barbarians."

The thought of the soft merchant fighting the hard-bitten Ariamus almost made Eskkar smile. He started to speak, then hesitated, trying to think as he rubbed his hand over the rough surface of the balcony wall. Nicar hadn't summoned Eskkar to his home for casual conversation. No, Nicar wanted to know what could be done for Orak. More to the point, what Eskkar could do for Orak.

The thirty-odd fighting men who remained would likely follow Eskkar, at least for a while, either out of loyalty or necessity. Most had women and children in the village or had grown too old to go looting across the countryside.

Eskkar thought of his thirty-one seasons. He'd been fighting since he turned fourteen, when he'd killed his first man with a knife thrust in the back. His father, a leader of twenty, had somehow offended Maskim-Xul, the ruler of the Alur Meriki, and the punishment had been death for the whole family. Eskkar had seen his mother and younger brother die, and his sister carried off. But the man who killed his brother would never kill again. He never learned what sent Maskim-Xul's enraged guards to his father's tent. Eskkar managed to slip away in the darkness, never to return to the campfires of his kindred.

He would have to leave Orak. He couldn't chance being captured. His former clansmen would kill him merely for leaving the clan. And if they remembered Eskkar's family, his fate would be even worse.

Eskkar brought his thoughts back to the present and realized that Nicar had continued to study him.

"We'll have to run, Nicar. Even with Ariamus and his men still here, the village would fall. Thirty, even a hundred soldiers will make no difference. If the clans are truly in migration, there will be many hundreds of warriors, maybe even a thousand."

Eskkar shook his head at the idea. A thousand barbarians, an incredible number of fighting men, mounted and well armed, could sweep any force of mere villagers aside without pausing.

Nicar said nothing, drumming his fingers on the same stones that Eskkar still gripped. "No. We must stay. Stay and fight. Orak must be held. If we run, there will be nothing left when we return, and we'll have to rebuild all over again."

He heard determination in Nicar's words. They turned

toward each other at the same moment, standing eye to eye.

"This village is mine, Eskkar. When I arrived here, Orak was hardly more than a collection of mud huts. I built it myself, along with the other Families. Twenty-seven years I've been here, and all of us have prospered nearly every day. Everything I have is here. Never have so many men lived before in one place, in safety, with food and drink and tools to share. Look around you, Eskkar. Do you want to return to the ways of your fathers, living in tents, fighting each day for food, killing others to take what is theirs? Or do you want to dig your food out of the earth, at the mercy of any band of murderers?"

Eskkar, like everyone else, knew what Nicar had accomplished. He also knew that the village had existed here for uncounted years before Nicar arrived. Nor had Nicar done it alone. Other powerful traders and farmers had worked closely with him to rule Orak, and together their fortunes and power had grown, until they reserved the title of "Noble" for themselves and their sons. For years, the Five Families had settled disputes and reconciled customs, as their Houses and influence increased.

"Nicar, I know what Orak means to you. But even if we managed to drive off a small band, they'd only return with more warriors. If the main force of the Alur Meriki comes against us . . ."

"No, Eskkar. I will not hear it." Nicar's hand smacked down on the balcony stones. "Ten years have passed since they last came. That time there was no warning. I remember how men fought to get into the boats, to get across the river. Many were trapped in the village. They became slaves or died. Those who got to the other bank, we ran until our hearts were ready to burst. When we returned, nothing remained. The huts had all been destroyed, the crops burned, the animals slaughtered and dumped in the wells. It took two years to rebuild then. Two wasted years. Do you know how long it would take us to rebuild now?"

Eskkar shook his head. Two years seemed like plenty of time to replace mud huts and plant a few more crops.

"Orak is more than twice as big as it was then. Now I think it would take five years to rebuild, assuming our trade doesn't go to another village up or down the river. Orak might never grow so great again. I cannot waste five years, Eskkar. I will not."

Eskkar had lived among villagers long enough to understand their fears, but to complain about raiders merely wasted breath. "Nicar, bandits from the north and east have been raiding this land for generations. Nothing can be done about it. At least this time you'll have plenty of time to prepare your . . . departure."

Nicar looked out over the village again. "You're like all the others. They all say nothing can be done. You surprise me, Eskkar. You're supposed to be a fighting man, and yet you're afraid to fight."

"Watch your words, Nicar. I have fought the Alur Meriki before. But I'm not a fool. Much as I'd enjoy killing more of them, I won't fight where there's no hope of winning. If there were some way to hold them off, if something could be done . . . but they're just too strong. You'd be better off taking your gold and leaving."

"No. I will not run, and I will not give my hard-earned gold to the barbarians! Better to use it to try and defend Orak. I'm too old to start over again. This village is mine, and I will stay. That is, if you can defend Orak."

"Nothing can stop the Alur Meriki."

"Perhaps you're right. Perhaps nothing can be done. But before we run away again, I want to know why we cannot defend ourselves against them. I want to understand why Orak, with so many people, is so helpless. Tell me that, Eskkar."

Nicar was right about the village. In all his travels, Eskkar had never seen a village as big. A day seldom went by without someone moving into Orak. A few even used a new word to describe it, calling it a city, the City, the biggest gathering of people ever built. A place with a real stockade made from rough-cut logs and two solid gates to deny entrance. But Eskkar knew that the palisade and gates served only to deter petty thieves or small bands of marauders, not a migration of the steppes.

Of all the raiders who plagued the land, the steppes barbarians aroused the most terror. Ruthless warriors and superb horsemen, no force could stand against them. No force ever had, at least not in Eskkar's memory, or even in the legends of others.

"Nicar, where were the barbarians found? How far away are they?"

"Many miles across the steppes to the far north," Nicar answered. "It will be midsummer before they reach this place. The great curve of the Tigris will force them far to the east before they can head south. But this time their path seems to point toward us. It may be more than a raiding party that comes to Orak next summer. Word of our prosperity has reached even them, so the traders tell me."

"So we have nearly six months to prepare. Of course, raiding parties could be here sooner, Nicar, much sooner."

The steppes people always had two or three groups of raiders operating around the tribe's center, looking for opportunities to take horses, tools, weapons, or women, and not necessarily in that order, although none would pass up a good horse to waste time on a woman. A village this size would attract them as it attracted everyone. There might even be almost as many people here as in the migrating tribe. Strange he hadn't thought of that before.

Eskkar drained his water cup. The sharp pain behind his eyes had lessened, replaced by a dull throb. Nicar's earlier words came back to him, and now they seemed to contain a challenge. "You want to understand why we must run, Nicar, is that it? It's because we don't have warriors. We have farmers, tradesmen, and a few dozen men trained to fight. The Alur Meriki can send hundreds of warriors against us. Even soldiers won't fight against those odds."

"If we fight them from behind our palisade. . . ."

"The palisade will not stand. A few ropes over the top and they'll pull it down."

"Then we need a stronger barrier," Nicar said, a little more forcefully. "Could such a barrier be constructed in time?"

Eskkar glanced out over the balcony. The fence that surrounded Orak stood almost directly below him, only a dozen paces away, and he studied it as if seeing it for the first time. Not high enough, not strong enough, he knew. Orak needed a solid wall. A mud wall, if it could be built high enough and strong enough, might give the barbarians pause. But even a wall wouldn't stop fighting men. Well, one thing at a time. They just needed something with enough resistance to make the attackers move on to easier pickings.

"I need to think about this, Nicar. What you ask may not be possible. Give me some time. I'll come back to you by sundown and tell you what I think."

Nicar nodded, almost as if expecting the delay. "Come for dinner, then, after sundown. We'll talk again."

Eskkar bowed and left the house. He walked through the twisted lanes back to the soldiers' compound, thinking about Nicar's words. At the barracks he ignored the idle men standing around and went instead to the stables. He called for a horse and while the stable boys readied it, Eskkar crossed back into the lane. He approached the nearest street vendor and spent the last of his copper coins to buy some bread and cheese.

Shoving the food into his pouch, Eskkar filled a bag with water, then mounted up and rode slowly through the village. He passed through the main gate and nodded to the guard who looked at him nervously, no doubt wondering whether he'd be returning. Rumors must be spreading, fanned by the news of Ariamus's sudden departure.

The fresh air cleared the last effects of the wine from his mind, and Eskkar gave his full attention to the spirited horse, which seemed equally glad to escape the village's confines. He put the beast to an easy canter until he reached the top of a small hill about two miles east of the village. From this vantage, he had an excellent view of both Orak and the river Tigris that looped behind it.

He reined in the horse and began eating the good bread and poor cheese he'd purchased, letting many different thoughts drift through his head. To his surprise, he had several ideas of what could and could not be done. Licking the last of the cheese from his fingers, he studied the village, almost as if seeing it for the first time.

Orak sat on a broad slab of hard earth and stone that forced the river to bend around it, so that the fast-flowing currents protected almost half the village from direct approach. The bedrock supporting the village had once been surrounded by marshland. As the settlement had grown, farmers had drained the marshes, growing crops and building huts on the recovered land. Dozens of canals, large and small, crisscrossed the countryside around the village, bringing water from the river to the farms.

Perhaps the land could be flooded again, leaving only one main approach to the village's gates. In his mind's eye, Eskkar pictured a line of archers atop a wall, standing shoulder to shoulder, launching flights of arrows into a swarm of mounted attackers beneath them. The bow, he decided. Only that weapon could make the soft dirt-eaters equal to Alur Meriki warriors, and then only if the bowmen had a wall to hide behind.

Faced with a strong wall, most of the mounted warrior's advantages disappeared. No storm of arrows to devastate the defenders, who could then be overwhelmed and cut apart by the charging riders. Against such a wall, the Alur Meriki's greater physical strength and skill with sword and lance would be lessened. Yes, it might work. If Orak could build the wall, the village might have a chance. Whether Orak could transform itself remained to be seen.

Orak resembled every other village Eskkar had seen. Small huts built from river mud and straw accounted for most of the dwellings, though the homes of the rich merchants and nobles tended to be much larger or two-story affairs. A fence surrounded the village, but numerous huts and tents had sprung up outside the stockade, including some that, against Nicar's orders, butted up against the structure.

As for the villagers, they, too, were much the same as people everywhere. Most had few possessions: a cotton tunic, a wooden food bowl, perhaps a few crude tools. But the farms around Orak yielded plenty of grain, which the bakers turned into a hearty bread, the one clean smell that constantly scented the village air.

The farmers produced enough not only to feed themselves and their families, but enough extra to trade or sell in the village. That surplus filled Orak with people who didn't need to farm to survive, merchants, traders, carpenters, shopkeepers, innkeepers, smiths, and dozens of other tradesmen. These skilled laborers provided any craft required to support the village, the river traffic, and the surrounding farms, taking payment in grain as well as the coins hammered out by the wealthy traders and nobles.

Only its size made Orak different from any other place Eskkar had visited. The village had been large when he arrived, and since then it had nearly doubled. In his travels Eskkar had learned that the larger the village, the easier he would be accepted. A big village always needed men to defend it, so a skilled fighting man who knew horses could usually find employment and a safe place to sleep at night, even if the villagers might laugh behind his back at his barbarian heritage. They seldom laughed to his face; the battle scars on his body intimidated most villagers. At least they didn't drive him away in their fear, something that had occurred more than once in his wanderings.

Those wanderings had taken him as far as the great sea to the south. Three years ago, Eskkar decided to return to the land of his youth. He'd thrown in with a trader's caravan destined for Orak, one of half a dozen guards hired to safeguard the merchant's goods. When twenty bandits attacked the caravan at night, the outnumbered guards, caught by surprise, had been overwhelmed. Wounded, Eskkar and a few servants had escaped, reaching Orak a week later. The servants he'd rescued had not only vouchsafed him, but they stood by him until he recovered. Deciding to stay for a few months, Eskkar joined the force that guarded the village as a common soldier, and never got around to leaving. Since then he managed to work his way up to third in command, riding most of the patrols and chasing after runaway slaves or petty thieves.

Putting thoughts of the past aside, he decided to look at Orak as the Alur Meriki would. Taking a gulp from the water bag, Eskkar rode down the hill and headed toward the river.

The breeze refreshed him, the air cool and invigorating. Eskkar often longed for the feel of the wind in his face. The feel of a horse on the open lands always called to him, sometimes making each day spent in the village's confines seem a day of torment. You'll always be a barbarian, even though your own people cast you out. For years he had drifted aimlessly across the lands, scorned by the villagers and farmers he encountered, even beaten and abused.

Three years he had lived in Orak, longer than he had ever spent anywhere, and lately he'd thought about moving on, frustrated by Ariamus and his petty orders. Perhaps now was the time to forget Orak, move east and visit lands still new to him.

No matter what Nicar wanted, trying to fight off the Alur Meriki would fail, and simply get him killed for his trouble. Eskkar owed the villagers nothing. To them, he was just another barbarian, just as capable of murdering them in their sleep. He'd seen the distrust and fear in their faces often enough.

The idea of leaving tempted him, but only for a moment. A new place would be no better than Orak and probably a good deal worse. He'd have to start again from the bottom, a mere soldier, treated scarcely better than a callow recruit. No, he felt the same way as Nicar. Eskkar wouldn't run away to start that life all over again. Not if he could find another option, especially one that didn't end with him dead.

The Alur Meriki had murdered his family, driven him from the clan, hounded him across the plains, and nearly killed him more than once. Eskkar hated the thought of running from them again. Assuming something could be done that didn't leave him with his throat cut, he wanted the chance to strike an avenging blow against them for a change, to repay them for his father's death.

If he could accomplish it, Orak and Nicar would owe him much. As captain of the guard, he'd have more than enough gold to settle down for the rest of his days. Perhaps he'd join the ranks of the nobles and become one of Orak's rulers. That would be almost as satisfying as crushing a part of the Alur Meriki.

Eskkar put the fanciful thoughts aside. He studied the landscape, riding slowly to the southwest, stopping from time to time to examine the approaches to Orak, picturing what the steppes people would see when they turned their eyes here.

He rode for nearly three hours, until he completed a circle around Orak and found himself back at the hilltop where he'd begun his observations. Eskkar dismounted and sat down with his back to a rock. He let his mind turn over the ideas he had this day.

No one had ever called him quick in his wits, but Eskkar could build a simple plan as well as the next. That ability, plus his size, strength, and quickness with sword and knife, had won him promotion until he stood at Ariamus's side. Now Eskkar stood alone, and Nicar had asked him to do something no man had ever done before—prevent the steppes people from looting and destroying the village.

The sheer scope of what needed to be done threatened to overwhelm him. He forced himself to remember that a plan had many parts and that each part could be considered separately.

Carefully, he reviewed the many tasks needed to defend the village, repeating them out loud several times to make sure he'd remember all of them. When he finished, Eskkar saw that the sun had moved far into the western sky. Grunting a little, he stood and stretched, then he mounted his horse and retraced his path back to the village and his appointment with Nicar. At least he knew what he would say tonight, though he doubted Orak's leading merchant would like his words.

2

Riding back into Orak, Eskkar found two soldiers guarding the gate instead of the usual sentry. Both called out to him, looks of relief on their faces. Nicar must have ordered the extra guard to reassure the villagers. By now everyone must know about the barbarians sighted in the north.

As his horse picked its way through the narrow lanes, people stopped their activities and stared. A few tried to stop him, to ask him what he knew about the barbarians. Eskkar paid no attention to them. Everyone seemed to know that Nicar had summoned him, so now they looked at him for some sign of hope and protection. That thought deepened his frown. Eskkar had no idea what to tell them.

At the barracks, the soldiers waited outside, squatting on the dirt or leaning against the wall, regular duties ignored, anxiety on their faces. The soldiers knew about tonight's meeting with Nicar. Nearly thirty men, and some of their women, awaited him, eager to learn anything new. He dismounted and handed the horse to a stable boy.

Eskkar considered ignoring them, then thought better of it. "You know the barbarians are coming?" Heads nodded. "They won't be here for at least five months, so you can sleep easy tonight." He hesitated, not sure what to tell them. "I'm meeting with Nicar, to talk about the defense of the village. When I return, I'll tell you what I know."

He strode past them into the barracks and dumped his gear on his pallet. Eskkar thought about moving into Ariamus's private room, but decided that could wait until after tonight's meal. Reminded of his meeting, he stripped to his undergarment and wrapped his rough blanket around himself. Leaving the barracks, he went down the winding street and through the village's rear gate, heading straight to the river. Eskkar ignored anyone who tried to speak to him and pushed past those few brave enough to try to block his path.

At the water's edge, Eskkar tossed the blanket on a low bush, stripped, then dove in. At first he stayed in the calm of the eddy pool that hugged the river's east bank, then moved away from the shore and took strong, overhand strokes against the current. That demanded hard work, and after a few strokes he had to use all his strength to avoid being swept downriver. When Eskkar returned to the eddy pool, he rested in the chilled water. Finally he pulled himself out of the river, reclaimed his blanket, and used it to dry off before returning to the barracks.

At least tonight he wouldn't meet Nicar in a ragged garment with the smell of horses and wine on him. Putting on his one clean tunic, he considered wearing his short sword, then decided he wouldn't need it. The men who might want him dead had left with Ariamus, and he doubted he had one enemy left in the village.

He returned to Nicar's house. A few paces before Eskkar reached the gate, five men came out of Nicar's courtyard and headed toward him.

Noble Drigo and his son, with three bodyguards, filled the narrow lane, and Eskkar had to stand aside to let them by. Noble Drigo glanced at him and smiled as he passed, the knowing smile of a man who already had all the answers.

When Eskkar stepped through Nicar's gate, he found the boy who'd fetched him that morning again waiting for him. Once inside, the boy closed and bolted the door, then knelt with a damp cloth to clean Esskar's feet and sandals, removing the dirt of the street.

Nicar's wife, Creta, had nearly as many years as her husband, and her hair had long since turned to silver. Everyone knew that Nicar preferred young slave girls as bed companions, but he treated his wife honorably and she managed his household efficiently.

Creta greeted Esskar warmly enough, after a quick inspection to see if he were reasonably clean and presentable. She'd walked past him in the street many a time without ever noticing him. She escorted him to the dining chamber at the rear of the house, where he found a large table spread for only two. Creta gave him the briefest of bows and left him alone. A matronly servant brought wine, but Esskar asked for water. In a few moments she returned, handing him a cup of chilled water as Nicar entered the room.

"Please sit down, Esskar." Nicar wore a different tunic tonight, one with red and blue stitching around the collar. "You had a long ride today, and we should eat first so that we have time to talk afterward. You'll have something to drink, I trust?"

The servants began bringing food, one course at a time, and Esskar found that somewhat strange. When the soldiers ate, everything got dumped on the plank table at once, to be wolfed down as quickly as possible before it disappeared.

Esskar copied his host's pace and ate slowly, taking small bites of the warm vegetables after dipping them in spiced oil imported from some distant land to the west. While they ate, Nicar did most of the talking, asking Esskar about his early life and the many places he'd seen in his travels. He even asked about the steppes clans, what kind of people they were, why they lived the way they did. He talked of everything except the coming of the steppes people.

Esskar realized that Nicar continued to study him, wanting to know what kind of man Esskar was. More important, Nicar wanted to learn whether Esskar had the wits to make any plan succeed.

The food was easily the best Esskar had ever eaten. But the wine, like the portions, was served in small quantities.

He decided that Nicar wanted him to have a clear head. When the servants finally cleared the table and refilled the wine cups, Nicar dismissed them, then closed the door.

Eskkar caught a glimpse of Creta sitting outside the door, sewing a garment by the light of a lamp, to make sure the servants didn't eavesdrop on their master's conversation. Not that it would do any good. Household slaves always knew everything that went on.

"So, tell me about your ride, Eskkar. What did you see?" Nicar returned to the table, eyes fixed on his guest.

"You want to know if Orak can be defended against the barbarians? It can be done, but the cost will be great, and you may not want to pay it." He looked hard at Nicar, but his host said nothing.

"We cannot defeat them in battle. But we can make it too difficult to capture the village. If we can hold out for a month or two, they'll have to move on, driven by a lack of food. So that's what we must do—make it too costly for them to take the village, too expensive in terms of warriors and horses killed, too much time for a place that will be barren of food and horses even if they do capture it. That means we'll have to kill many warriors, kill enough of them to make their leaders worry."

Eskkar saw the questioning look on Nicar's face. "The barbarians always have too many warriors, and not enough horses, women, or food. That's why they're always fighting, even among themselves. The clan would actually welcome a chance to thin out the ranks, kill off the foolish, the young, or the weak. If they lose fifty or sixty warriors in return for the capture of a rich village, they'd be happy with the trade."

Nicar nodded thoughtfully. "I understand. So they will welcome the fight, at least at first. So what must we do to make it too painful for them?"

"First, you must build a wall around the village. A real stone wall, something that cannot be pulled down or burned, at least four times the height of a man. And it will have to enclose a much larger area than the palisade does now."

"The nobles have talked about building such a wall before,

Esskar, but nothing ever came of it. There was no need, and the cost and effort were too great. Now the barbarians come. Now, there is a need."

"Remember, Nicar, we have to consult the masons to see if such a wall can even be built."

"Yes, of course. What else is needed?"

"Second, all the huts and farmhouses outside this new wall must be torn down, removed completely, the ground leveled and stripped bare, and the farms and fields flooded again. The marshland mud will slow the horses down, and force them to approach the village from the land in front of the main gate.

"Third, every man must be trained to fight. That means training and arming as many archers as possible. Only the bow can drive off the Alur Meriki. We'll need thousands of arrows and hundreds of bows, and men will have to train every day until they can hit their targets with confidence, while standing atop the wall. Also, there must be training with axes, spears, and swords, and finally with rocks to hurl at the attackers and forked staves to push their ladders away from the wall. Even the women and children must work and fight. We'll have to train every day, build every day, and prepare for every possible attack. Everyone must work as they've never done before, so that when the barbarians arrive, all will be ready."

Esskar took a deep breath and sipped from his wine cup, grateful that he'd gotten the words out with scarcely a stumble.

"Orak must be stocked with food and water, enough for everyone for two or three months. The rest of the herds must be sent far away, across the river, where they'll be safe. That will take men away from the village, as well as soldiers to guard them from bandits. The animals will be a tempting target. When the barbarians arrive, they must learn that we have no horses for plunder, no cattle, goats, or sheep."

Nicar looked closely at him, sensing something more was coming. "And what else must we do?"

Esskar was ready. "The slaves. We'll need the slaves to labor as they've never done before, and we won't have the time or men to guard them. They must work on their own, and use all their skill. You'll have to promise to free the slaves, Nicar, at least some of them, so they'll have an incentive to work and fight."

Nicar's wine cup stopped halfway to his lips. "Free the slaves! You can't be serious. After what we've paid for them? And if we free the slaves, how will we keep the village running?"

"Not all the slaves. Only those we need to work on the defenses, probably no more than half of them. You ran the village before you had so many slaves, didn't you? Besides, if the barbarians come, you'll lose your slaves along with your lives or be enslaved yourself. Either way, your slaves will be gone.

"If we succeed, instead of slaves you'll have servants that you can pay until you find new slaves to replace them. Without the promise of freedom, Nicar, they won't work very hard or they'll slip away into the night, thinking that even the barbarians might treat them better. Don't forget, many will die, both villagers and slaves, and you'll need to replace them anyway.

"And one last thing, Nicar. You must speak for the entire village and the Five Families. I can organize the defense and determine what needs to be done, but there must be no quarrelling or arguing amongst the nobles or from any of the leading tradesmen. We must speak in one voice to everyone, so that all can see we're determined to resist and to win. And whatever I ask for in the defense of the village, you'll have to supply. I will not argue with you or anyone else. My orders must be obeyed by all, and without question. Even by you, Nicar. So I ask you. Do you speak for the Five Families?"

For a moment, Nicar looked a little taken aback by Eskkar's demands. "You ask for much. But there is truth in your words. The many quarrels among the Five Families are public gossip. They must be put aside to defend Orak."

"And you will speak for all the Families?"

"Yes, I think they can all be persuaded, all except House Drigo. He will likely choose to go his own way."

Eskkar didn't think Noble Drigo could be dismissed so

lightly. For the last few months, in Orak's day-to-day affairs, Drigo's men often acted as if their master alone ruled the village. Even Eskkar, who rarely had any interest in gossip, knew that Drigo contested with Nicar for authority, that Drigo constantly tried to sway the other Families to his side. So far, most preferred Nicar, who was certainly a more just and even-handed administrator.

"And if you cannot control Noble Drigo, what then?" Eskkar asked. "He's powerful, and many will follow whatever path he chooses."

Nicar stared at him again, openly sizing him up. "It seems you are not quite as simple a soldier as I've been told." He drank from his cup. "If you can develop a good plan to defend Orak, we may not need Drigo and his gold. Let me worry about Drigo." Nicar waved his hand as if dismissing the matter. "But afterward, if we succeed in fending off the barbarians, what will we owe you, Eskkar?"

"Not that much, Nicar," he laughed. "I have no grand ambitions. The Five Families will become six, and I'll be your equal in the running of the village. Each of you will give me two ingots of gold, enough for me to set up my own house. For that, I will remain in Orak and we can start the planning for the barbarians' next visit, because they'll be back in another five or ten years. If we're lucky enough to drive the Alur Meriki off, they will never forget the insult. They have long memories. They'll be back someday, and we'll have to fight them again. So I think you'll need me again, and the sooner we start preparing, the better."

Nicar shook his head. "So much waste and destruction. It would be better for all of us if they'd leave us alone."

"They can never do that, Nicar. They live by taking what they need from others. It's the only way they know. So, they will be back. This struggle may never be truly over until one or the other of us is destroyed."

Nicar obviously hadn't considered that the barbarians might return. He said nothing for a moment, spinning the wine cup in his hands.

"One more thing, Eskkar. Some may wonder why you'd fight against your own kind. What would I say to them?"

"Tell them the truth, that they're not my kind anymore. When you leave the clans, your life, your memory . . . all gone." For the first time Eskkar's voice took on a hard edge, an intensity of raw emotion. "I want . . . even your gold isn't enough to make me fight them. I want the chance to avenge my family's murder, to kill enough of them to satisfy their spirits. This is the only chance I'll ever have."

Nicar nodded in understanding. "Enough talk about the past and the future. Do you think we can defeat the barbarians, if we do all that you ask?"

Eskkar met his gaze. "No village has ever surrounded itself with a wall such as the one we will need. I don't even know if such a wall can be built before they arrive. But if it can, then we may have a chance. Whether it's a good chance or not, we'll find out in the coming months. If we put our hearts and bodies into the preparation, we may have a fair chance, perhaps an even chance. If we don't prepare well, then we know what will happen.

"That is the best hope I can offer you, Nicar. As I said, the price you will pay to defend the village may be more than it's worth or more than you can afford. And even then, we may fail. You'll be risking more than just your gold. All who have tried to resist the Alur Meriki have been destroyed."

Nicar drained the wine cup, then set it down. "So we must build a wall around Orak if we wish to resist." He sat there, drumming his fingers on the table for several moments, before he lifted his eyes. "I can see, Eskkar, that you're honest. You don't promise success. If you had, I wouldn't have believed you." He looked at his guest for a few more moments, as if making up his mind. "You don't have a woman, do you?"

The odd question surprised Eskkar, though he gathered that Nicar already knew the answer. Women, good ones at any rate, were both scarce and expensive in Orak, and fathers did not approve marriages for eligible daughters to soldiers with no futures, let alone to those who didn't have two coins to rub together.

"No, I haven't been able to afford one yet," Eskkar replied, unable to keep a hint of embarrassment from his voice. Once a week or so, Eskkar spent a copper coin for one of the girls at the alehouse, or visited the prostitutes who sold themselves at night along the river's edge. Nearly a month had passed since his last visit.

"I received some new slaves a few weeks ago," Nicar continued. "One is a girl, still a virgin, I'm assured. I think she's about fourteen, not pretty, but attractive enough. I was going to bed her myself when I found the time . . . and the will," he added, with a smile.

"Unlike most women, she can count, as well as read and write the symbols, and she seems levelheaded enough. I will give her to you, and I think you'll find her useful for many things in the coming months. She'll be much more than a simple bed companion. You'll need someone to help you with the planning and to keep you out of the alehouse at night."

Even through his surprise, Eskkar knew it to be an exceptional and costly gift, given graciously and with subtle advice. "I thank you, Nicar." Eskkar suddenly realized what else it meant—that Nicar had agreed to his demands.

"All of us will need your advice and guidance, Nicar. If we are to do this, we'll need many men working together. So, again, I thank you."

"You may not have the wit of Ariamus, but you can think and I know you can fight," Nicar replied. "The rest you can learn, and I and the others will help you. Not many men can know and do everything. Most of us need to learn to accept all the help we can be given. Don't let your pride stand in the way of what you can accomplish with the help of others."

Nicar remained silent for a moment. "Know one other thing, Eskkar. If we succeed, then I will owe you much, more than I and my family can repay. And if we fail, then let us fail together.

"I meet with the nobles the day after tomorrow, when Noble Nestor returns from the south. Until then, you are captain of the guard. When we meet, we'll confirm our decision to resist the barbarians. Take the girl tonight and move into Ariamus's quarters. I'll send you some gold tomorrow so you can buy whatever else you need. In the next few weeks, I'm sure there will be a house available for you. The other Families will provide servants as well, to help free you from everything except the defense of the village."

Eskkar understood his meaning about the house. Despite what Nicar said, many would flee Orak in the coming months. Eskkar suddenly understood that a bond had formed between them. They shared at least one trait—neither gave up easily. They would live or die in this together.

No matter how it ended, Eskkar knew that his life had changed—that he would never again be the simple warrior who lived by his sword for so many years. Now he'd have to learn to think, plan, prepare defenses, and train people. Not for the first time that day, he wondered whether he was up to the task.

But he'd taken the first step—persuading Nicar that he could save Orak. To accomplish that, he would have to change even more, become someone different, someone better than the drunken fool who passed out last night in the tavern. That would never happen again, he swore.

Nicar stood, signaling the end of the dinner. "Then it's settled. We'll do what's never been done! We will save the village."

Eskkar smiled, already thinking of the girl who'd accompany him to the barracks. "No, Nicar, if we succeed, we'll use the new word and call it the City of Orak."

"Let us pray for that day," Nicar said. He reached out his hand and clasped Eskkar's arm, sealing the agreement. Then the merchant strode to the door, calling to his wife, speaking quietly to her before they disappeared into the living quarters.

After a few moments Eskkar heard women's voices raised in heated debate, followed by an anguished cry, cut short by the sharp sound of a slap. Then Nicar's wife reappeared, dragging a girl by the shoulder. Creta pushed the girl in front of Eskkar.

"Here's the slave, Eskkar. Her name is Trella." Creta's voice now cut like a rasp. "Of course, you can change it to anything you like. I suggest you give her a good beating to make sure she understands her place. She's willful and proud."

The girl flashed a look of hatred at her former mistress, and Eskkar guessed Nicar might have more than one reason for getting rid of the girl. Life in the rich homes of the Five Families might be more complicated than he'd thought.

Eskkar took a step and lifted up the girl's chin. She had large, dark brown eyes that refused to meet his gaze. Her slightly darker skin, clear except for a few faint scars from the pox on both cheeks, told him she came from the lands to the south. Her narrow face held a thin nose and small even teeth, hiding behind a trembling lip that still held a drop of blood in the corner, where Creta had slapped her. She looked rather thin and plain, but she had one treasure. Her hair, dark and heavy, fell in a wave around her shoulders.

He saw the fear in her eyes, the fear that came to any slave handed from one man to another. Eskkar had seen that look many times before. She moved her head away from his hand and returned her gaze to the floor. Suddenly the image of another girl, about the same age and just as frightened, came to mind. A few years after leaving the clan, he'd befriended Iltani, saving her life and protecting her from rape and worse. She'd repaid that debt by giving herself to him, his first time with a woman. And twice afterward, she risked her life to save his, an obligation he'd never managed to repay. Perhaps the gods had sent Iltani's image, to remind him of that debt.

"Listen to me, girl," he said, again lifting her chin, and keeping his tone gentle. "Don't be afraid. You're to help me, and I will need your help. Do you understand?"

Her eyes turned up to him and Eskkar held her gaze, seeing this time the strength that lay behind the dark, wide-set eyes. Her lips stopped trembling and she gave him a quick nod, the movement making her hair swirl gently around her face.

"Good. Come with me, then." A thought struck him and he turned to Creta. "Does she have anything of her own that she should bring?"

"She has some things," Creta admitted grudgingly. "She can return for them in the morning."

Whatever trinkets or possessions she might have would

be long gone by morning, taken either by Nicar's wife or the other servants. He started to turn away, hesitated, then faced Creta once again. "A cloak. She'll need her cloak against the night's chill. She does have one, doesn't she?" He made his tone reasonable. "Or perhaps you could find one for her?"

Nicar's wife must have remembered her husband's words. She pursed her lips, then gave in. "She has no cloak of her own," Creta admitted. "But I'll give her one of mine."

She clapped her hands and another girl appeared almost instantly, no doubt standing just out of sight beyond the doorway. Creta told the servant to fetch a particular cloak. In moments the girl returned, carrying a faded and patched cloak that looked serviceable enough.

Esskar took the garment and draped it around the girl's shoulders. "Thank your mistress for her gift, Trella." He watched her closely. Now he'd start to learn what kind of girl he had acquired.

Trella looked first at Esskar as if trying to read his face. He said nothing, just stared at her. The silence began to lengthen. Then Trella turned to Creta and bowed her head. "Thank you, mistress." She spoke softly, her words properly servile.

When she straightened up, she looked at Esskar as if to say, "Is that what you wanted?" and he found himself hiding a smile. He turned to Creta and bowed low. "And I thank you, Mistress Creta. The food you prepared was delicious and well served." He'd rehearsed the unaccustomed words earlier and was happy to get them out without stumbling.

Out of the house and into the lane, Esskar laughed aloud as he took Trella's hand, finding it soft and warm in his own as he guided her toward the barracks. "Did you have a cloak of your own?"

A shake of her head answered him, as she kept her eyes on the rough ground underfoot.

"Good, then. At least you got something from her."

The girl stole a glance at him, then looked down again.

Esskar's thoughts raced ahead to the big bed in Ariamus's chamber and he quickened his pace, glancing up at the stars.

Only a few hours before midnight. He'd have to be up before dawn.

Turning the corner at the alehouse, he nearly stopped in surprise. Two torches lit the common area outside the barracks, illuminating a crowd of soldiers, their women, and villagers. Apparently they all had nothing better to do at this late hour than wait for his return. Automatically Eskkar took a quick count and guessed there might be as many as sixty villagers mixing with the soldiers, probably a hundred people all told.

All thoughts of enjoying Trella in his warm bed now vanished, as he remembered his promise. He would have to say something, a prospect that dried his mouth and put an uneasy feeling in his stomach.

Everyone started speaking as soon as they spotted him. A rush of men surrounded him, hands picking at his tunic, eager questions tossed at him like stones. Eskkar knew he must speak to silence the crowd, but his mind remained as empty as last night's wine cup as he reached the barracks, stopping only because the soldiers waiting there blocked the doorway. He had to face the crowd.

Eskkar felt his hand squeezed hard and realized the boisterous crowd had frightened Trella. He looked down at her and saw the question in her eyes.

"What do they want?" she asked, her voice uncertain.

He tightened his lips before answering. "Nothing, girl. They're only afraid of what is coming. They think the barbarians are already camped outside the gate." Somehow her worry gave him strength, and he faced the crowd. "Stay here," he commanded Trella, letting go of her hand and moving a few steps toward one of the mounting stones, then standing on it to rise a little above the crowd.

"Silence," Eskkar said loudly. He repeated the word, this time using his command voice. "You'll wake the whole village with your chattering, and no one will get any sleep tonight." He jerked his head at the soldiers, and they began to move in front of the crowd, ordering the excited crowd to be silent. When the voices finally died down, Eskkar began to speak.

"Yes, it's true. The barbarians are coming." Eskkar let the words run through the crowd, let them jabber for a moment, watching their faces as he confirmed their worst fears. "But they won't be here for months, so go back to your beds—before your wives cut your throats for being out so late."

That brought nervous laughter from some, but others shouted at him, asking from what direction the barbarians would come, whether they should leave the village, or whether Orak would try to fight them off. Eskkar raised his hand and eventually they fell silent.

"In two days, Nicar and the other Families will meet. Then we can begin preparing to resist the barbarians. We will fortify Orak so that it can turn back any attack."

Shouts of disbelief rose up, as well as questions, and the clamor grew louder. Eskkar glanced down at the soldiers. "Quiet them down," he commanded. His men moved through the crowd, silencing the loudest, pushing back the most aggressive.

Strange, now these soldiers watch my every gesture and obey my smallest command. Yesterday only his fists, backed if necessary by his sword, had provided the slimmest shred of authority. This must be what real power is like, Eskkar realized, more than a little amazed at the sensation. The people are afraid. Even the soldiers are worried. They want to be told they'll be safe, told by someone in charge, someone in whom they can believe, even if only for a little while.

"I know you have many questions," he went on when the murmurs abated, "but they'll have to wait until Nicar speaks. But hear this, my friends. We have the means and the men to make Orak strong enough to stop the barbarians—if we stand together. I will guide you all in this, and I tell you it can be done, and it will be done. Now, return to your homes and to your beds. Let Nicar speak in two days. By then you'll know what you must do."

They shouted at him, but Eskkar ignored them as he jumped down and grabbed Gatus, a grizzled veteran approaching fifty seasons. A subcommander when Eskkar joined Orak's guards, Ariamus had demoted Gatus back to the ranks for questioning his orders. Esskar had no real friends among the soldiers, but he respected the old fighter, who knew his trade better than most.

"Gatus, you're second in command now." Esskar raised his voice so as many soldiers as possible could hear him. "Clear out this crowd. Make sure the gates are fastened for the night and guards stationed there. Have a few men patrol the streets until dawn as well. They don't have to do anything, but have them armed and looking impressive. Then come see me."

The man nodded, accepting without question his new authority as well as Esskar's.

"And Gatus, I'm moving into Ariamus's quarters. Put a guard at my door. Otherwise some of these fools will be pounding on it until dawn."

Esskar turned to Trella and found her staring at him, her fright gone, her wide eyes now locked firmly on his as he returned to her side. Taking her hand, he led her away from the crowd, toward the rear of the barracks where his new quarters were located.

Guiding her inside, Esskar noted in surprise that somebody had cleaned and packed down the dirt floor, thrown out most of the refuse, and moved his few belongings in there as well. Some of the men had anticipated his promotion.

The thought of his possessions made him smile. It wouldn't have taken long to move a thin blanket, a tunic, an old horse sword, and a common short sword.

A fire burned in the tiny hearth and someone had piled a stack of wood nearby. A soldier entered, bringing a precious candle that he set in a pool of wax on the rough table in the center of the room. The soldier glanced admiringly at Trella, then grinned at Esskar before he left them.

Esskar closed the door and leaned against it, the crowd noises already fading as his men started herding the villagers away. The candle flared up, adding its light to that of the fire.

Trella walked slowly around the room. Esskar's eyes followed her as she took in her new home. She removed her cloak, then hung it on a peg near the door. From a pocket of her dress she removed a small pouch that no doubt contained the rest of her possessions, and hung it over the same peg. She crossed over to the fireplace, then turned and stood facing him, her head held high.

Eskkar saw the swell of her breasts against the thin dress as she took a deep breath and let her eyes meet his.

"I was told your name is 'Eskkar,' that you're a barbarian, and that I'm given to you as your slave." She couldn't keep the hint of bitterness out of her voice when she uttered the word *slave*. "Creta didn't say that you are now captain of the guard."

"The steppes people don't consider themselves barbarians, Trella. They're the same as any other clan, except they move from place to place. But I left them long ago, when I was fourteen, and I've lived among the farms and villages ever since, selling my sword. I'm just a soldier, and only the cowardice of Ariamus has made me captain of the guard."

Eskkar still had his back to the door, and faintly he heard a guard take up position outside. The crowd noise had disappeared, save for an occasional distant shout as his men went about their assignments.

His men. The words sounded good. The day had started badly, but by day's end, he'd become captain of the guard with his own room, his own woman slave, and a bag of gold arriving in the morning. Perhaps the gods smiled on him after all. His future prospects seemed good, at least for the next few months, when the Alur Meriki would likely cut off his head and impale it on a lance. No sense worrying about that tonight, though.

"My father was advisor to the ruler of the village of Carnax," Trella went on. "They were both killed by treachery, and my brother and I sold into slavery. Now I belong to you."

Eskkar wondered whether she told the truth. Everyone knew that all slaves lied about their past. Her parents could be peasants in the field who sold their daughter for a few coins because the rains came late or the sow died. He'd never heard of Carnax and in truth, it mattered little what she said or claimed. Trella was a slave and would be so for the rest of her life. He saw the tension in her body and guessed that she would resist him when he took her.

To his surprise, the thought of taking her brought no excitement, and suddenly his legs felt as weary as his head. He pushed himself away from the door. The movement brought fear to Trella's eyes. She took a step backward, her hands coming up to cross over her breasts.

He sat down at the table and stared at the burning candle for a moment. "Trella, today has been long, and filled with many surprises for both of us."

Until now he hadn't realized how much effort it had taken him to talk to Nicar, forcing himself to think and to present his plans and ideas clearly. Swinging a sword or cracking skulls took less effort, and he knew he'd spoken more words today than in the last month. His head wasn't used to this much activity, and now he felt too tired even to force himself on the girl. He was getting old. Thirty seasons gone, and he knew he was lucky to be alive.

"And tomorrow will probably be worse. I'm weary. I've eaten too much food and drunk too much wine, and there are too many thoughts in my head. Tell me if there's anything you need, and we'll go to sleep."

Her head came up, and he thought he saw color come into her cheeks, though the flickering light made it hard to be sure.

"I have never been with a man."

He smiled at her, though at this particular moment he didn't know whether that was good news or bad. "I think you'll be safe tonight, girl. I need my sleep more than I need to wrestle with you."

He stood up, looking around the room. "There's the chamber pot. I don't think you should use the latrine outside, not tonight, anyway." He turned away from the table and went outside, nodding to the guard as he headed down to the barracks' privy.

Finishing at the latrine, he found Gatus waiting for him. The old soldier wasted no words. "Did Nicar make you captain of the guard?" Gatus looked him straight in the eye, standing directly in front of his new commander.

"For now. But I told him I would be in charge of all the village and its defenses or nothing at all. He'll confirm that when he meets with the nobles. Or perhaps not."

"And if not?" Gatus asked.

"If not, then I and my slave will be leaving the village. But Nicar will confirm it, I'm sure."

Gatus shrugged, then shook his head. The motion swirled his long gray hair around his shoulders. "Do you really think the village can withstand the barbarians?"

"Gatus, I won't lie to you. I know it's never been done. But this is no small village. There may be as many people here as there are barbarians on the move. I think we can make its defenses strong enough to resist until they are forced to move on."

The thought that he might slip out of the village at any time in the next few months had also occurred to him, and the promise of Nicar's gold kept the thought in the back of his head.

The man looked dubious, and rightly so. Still, Gatus had to be persuaded, or Eskkar's tenuous authority with the men would vanish. They respected Gatus and his words would matter.

"Follow me for a few weeks, and let's see what we can do. I've spent the day thinking about this, and it can be done. I'm certain of it. Meanwhile, your pay is doubled, and you're second in command."

Gatus moved a step closer. "You are changed from what you were yesterday. Have you been touched by the gods?"

Eskkar's laugh rang out into the night. The gods and he were not exactly on good terms. "No, I'm not out of my head, though my skull does spin with all these new ideas." He started to walk past the man, but Gatus gripped his arm hard and now their faces were inches apart.

"You are changed, Eskkar. A fool can see that, even the rest of the men. I'll follow your orders for a while, at least. But if you lie to me, I'll put a sword in your back. I swear by the gods, I will! I've a wife and two boys, and I'll not have them taken by the barbarians."

"Tend to your duties, then. Tomorrow will be a long day, and you'll have much to do." He moved away, and Gatus's hand slipped from his arm.

Eskkar thought about how quickly things had changed. Yesterday he would have struck anyone who laid hands on him. Now it meant nothing.

When Eskkar returned to Ariamus's room, the candle had been extinguished and the fire had burned itself down to glowing embers. Dropping the wooden bar across the door, he untied his sandals and stripped off his tunic and undergarment, ignoring the growing chill in the room.

He took his short sword from the wall where it had been hung, drew the blade from its scabbard, and placed it next to the bed. Since he'd run from the Alur Meriki, there had never been a night when he didn't keep a weapon close at hand. Briefly, he wondered whether the girl would use it on him in the middle of the night, but decided he was too tired to worry about it.

The bed had more than enough room for two, as Ariamus had liked his women large. For a moment, Eskkar thought it was empty until he realized the girl had wedged herself against the wall, as far from him as possible. Fine, let her stay there. Tomorrow, maybe even in the morning, he'd take her, and there'd be no more nonsense.

Eskkar rolled onto his side, putting his back to her while facing the door. He pulled the single blanket up over his shoulder and let his body relax as he prepared for sleep.

But his mind refused to obey. Thoughts of Nicar, the Alur Meriki, the command of the guard, the village itself, all kept running through his head. A week ago, Eskkar couldn't have imagined this could happen. Now he could have power, gold, slaves, anything he wanted—if he could save Orak from the barbarians.

A big *if*, despite what he had told Nicar and Gatus. There was so much to do, it was difficult to know where to start. Tomorrow there would be many tasks to set in motion. He would have to talk with Gatus, choose new subcommanders, prepare to meet with Nicar, and speak to the soldiers. Eskkar knew he faced long odds, but there might be a chance, and if he could win, if he succeeded, if the gods gave him luck, if . . . if . . . if.

His thoughts kept traveling in circles, going from Nicar's dinner to the meeting of the nobles, thinking of all the things he should have said to his men and the crowd tonight, what else he should have discussed with Nicar, all the tasks he would have to do tomorrow, how he must address the men, what he must say to the Families. Each time he tried to follow one particular thought, another popped into his mind and started the cycle all over again.

The blanket shifted a little, and abruptly he felt Trella's body against his back, her legs barely brushing against his, something softer touching his shoulder.

"You're still awake," she whispered, almost as if it were an accusation. "It's cold against the wall," she explained further, to justify moving closer to him. "What are you thinking about?"

Whatever he'd been thinking about vanished with the first contact of her flesh. "You. I was thinking about you." Thoughts of Orak, along with his tiredness, disappeared, and he felt himself beginning to harden.

"Don't lie. You were thinking about Nicar and his gold."

He laughed a little. She was certainly quick about her wits and bold enough to challenge her new master. "Well, I was thinking about Nicar, but not about his gold. But now I can't remember my thoughts, only the touch of your body. You are very beautiful, Trella."

She didn't answer for a long moment. Then her arm crept over his shoulder, and somehow it seemed both cool to his skin and warm to his touch. Eskkar took her hand in his and held it firmly, the way he'd held it in the street earlier that night. She drew a little closer to him, and now he could almost feel the length of her body against his, warm and soft.

"And what do you think about now?"

He felt her breath against his ear.

"I think about holding you in my arms, holding you and

kissing your lips." His manhood raged now, almost painfully, with an intensity he hadn't felt in a long time, but he didn't want to move or do anything to break the spell cast by her words and touch.

"I am your slave, Eskkar," she said, her voice low in his ear, moving more of her body against his back.

Her words surprised him, but he rolled to face her, putting his arms around her, feeling the muscles in her back as he pulled her against him. Eskkar could feel her whole body against his, her skin almost hot to his touch. Something strange had come over him. Perhaps the events of the day aroused him, or the fact that she belonged to him. Suddenly he wanted her more than any woman he could remember. Most of all, he wanted her to be willing, wanted her to want him as well.

"A slave is taken. If you were just that, I would take you whether you wished it or not. But you're more than a common slave girl. Even Nicar knew that, and I'm only a simple barbarian, not someone good with words." But he couldn't stop his hands from reaching out for her, and he heard Trella catch her breath as he cupped the softness of her breast.

"I saw the fear in your eyes when you first beheld the crowd outside. But you said the right words, and I think now that you believe them."

He said nothing, surprised at her words and a little shamed that his nervousness had been visible, at least to the girl. But he thought he'd managed it well enough, and perhaps no one else had noticed.

Her mouth brushed his cheek, banishing all such thoughts once again.

"I'm afraid, too, Eskkar. Afraid of the barbarians, afraid of the future. But it is past time for me to become a woman, and I think you will not hurt me too much." She let her body relax under his touch, burying her head against his shoulder. After a few moments, her hand slipped down between his legs and she gasped.

He kissed her cheek, then her mouth, gently at first, then harder and deeper as she clung to him. Caressing her body, touching her, stroking her stomach, he held off as long as he could, until he thought he would burst with desire, held off until she moaned for him and he could feel the wetness between her legs, before he mounted her, moving as slowly as he could, knowing he would hurt her, but trying to be as gentle as possible. Then she cried out, a sharp exclamation of pain and intake of breath as her nails dug into his back, then smoothness and a gasp of delight as he entered her.

Eskkar lay still for a moment until she relaxed and her arms encircled him tightly once again. He began to rock against her, and now her small sounds of pain and pleasure mixed as her desire grew. When it was over, all too soon, he held her close, stroking her hair, enjoying her presence, until he fell asleep in her arms, sleeping the deep sleep of the emotionally spent as well as physically exhausted, feeling a sense of comfort in her clasp he hadn't known since childhood.

Trella waited until she was sure she wouldn't wake him. Then she gently disengaged her arm from around Eskkar's neck, though she stayed close to him and could feel his breath against her breast. He stayed on his side, breathing heavily, with his arm thrown across her stomach. She stared up at the darkness, thinking about their lovemaking as silence surrounded them while the village slept. Now her troubled thoughts kept her awake.

It had been lovemaking, something she had wanted, though not for all the same reasons as the man beside her. Her virginity had become a problem. Nicar, his son, the other servants in Nicar's home, even the slave traders who had delivered her to Orak, all of them had desired her, and her maidenhead offered an added attraction. This Eskkar, he'd wanted her as well, and he would have taken her willing or unwilling this night, except for the events of the day.

But tomorrow would have been different, and as captain of the guard he would have lost respect with his men if he hadn't taken her. If she'd resisted, he would have beaten her, and she didn't want such a beginning with him. No, better to get it over with, while she still had the gift to give to him.

Much would be happening in the coming months and she'd need all her wits to stay alive, especially if the barbarians did come.

Still, he had wanted her, and the thought pleased her. Back at Nicar's house, she'd seen it in his eyes, despite her cast-off garments and the tears sprinkling her cheeks. Trella recalled the despair that had washed over her when she first saw the tall barbarian with the grim face who now owned her.

Thus she reasoned, though occasionally the memory of her own desires questioned her logic. How strange, she admitted to herself, that when he chose not to take her, when he left the room, that was when she decided that, despite her apprehension, she wanted him to be the one. And by offering herself, rather than just letting herself be taken, she'd kept some dignity. A man must be more than an animal, and this Eskkar, barbarian or not, had shown that he possessed something more than what appeared on the surface. She might be a slave, but even a slave could share in her master's life. His life was now hers, and Trella meant for both of them to rise in the future.

She hadn't heard anything of what Eskkar and Nicar discussed during dinner, but she had overheard much of Nicar's earlier talk with his wife, Creta, and later with Noble Drigo, including how Nicar's worries about the coming barbarians had forced him to send for Eskkar. Somehow this barbarian had convinced Nicar that he could handle the village's defense, and that accomplishment had surprised even Nicar, who had sharp wits of his own—as keen as those of her father.

The thought of her father sent a pang of sorrow through her, but she forced her mind away from the image of his body lying on the floor, blood pouring from his wounds, eyes staring sightlessly at the ceiling. He'd taught her well, too well, her mother used to say, recognizing in his daughter a mind as keen as his. Someday she hoped to avenge his death. But for now, she had no more tears to shed over her parents or her own misfortune.

This barbarian, she needed to learn all about him, as quickly as possible. He might be a strong fighter and experienced in battle, but she needed to know whether he had the wits to survive long enough even to meet the barbarians, let alone defeat them. That concerned her the most. Tomorrow she would learn much more about her new master. Everything in her future now depended on him.

Starting tonight, she belonged to a soldier, and a barbarian at that, so her status was little more than that of a camp follower or prostitute. However, if Eskkar succeeded as captain of the guard and took the lead in Orak's defense, then his status, and hers, would be immeasurable. Though she knew even that feat might not be enough to overcome the stigma of his being both an outsider and a barbarian.

Nonetheless, if Nicar had seen something worthwhile in this man, then she must look for it also. And any place or any owner would prove better than remaining in Nicar's house, with his disgusting son fondling her at every opportunity. A servant by day, she soon would have passed from father to son to the servants. Even life as this barbarian's slave would be preferable to that existence.

This one's lovemaking had surprised her. Her mother had warned her of the first night's pain, but that had passed in one brief moment, her fear turning to surprise and pleasure. He'd treated her gently, more so than she had expected, and her own reactions to him made her twitch with embarrassment. Trella knew she'd been shameless, and she could still feel the wetness between her legs that brought back the sensations that had spun through her body faster than she could control them.

At last her thoughts slowed and she began to drift off to sleep, thinking about the man in her arms and knowing that tomorrow she would begin a new life as slave to this upstart captain of the guard. It wouldn't be the life she had foreseen, the one she and her father had discussed often as he trained her. Instead of guiding and helping some wealthy and powerful trader, she now had to help this rough soldier turn back a barbarian invasion, a task that daunted her the more she thought about it.

She was too young for this, halfway into her fourteenth season, but she had to attempt it and hope her father's teachings would be enough to overcome her inexperience.

Still, even Eskkar admitted that no one had ever driven off barbarians before, so perhaps her new master would listen to her advice. Trella decided she must use all she'd learned and her body as well, to keep him close. He would need her, need her more than he could know, just as Nicar had said.

And if Eskkar succeeded, then only the gods knew what the future could bring for them. There would be much work in the days ahead. Her final thought before she drifted off to sleep was that tomorrow night she would once again be in his bed and his arms, and this time there would be no fear, only pleasure.

3

The pounding on the door woke Eskkar with a start. His hand reached for the sword even as he bolted upright, confused momentarily by the unfamiliar bed and surroundings until he remembered the events of last night. The pounding increased until the door shook on its already loose hinges.

"Gods, cease that noise!" he shouted. "Who is it?"

"Gatus, Captain. Get yourself up. Nicar's messenger is here."

"Curse you and all the gods," he muttered, then raised his voice. "I'm coming." Eskkar glanced at the tiny window covered with its scrap of leather for a shade. A bright wedge of sunlight slanted onto the dirt floor. Almost an hour after sunrise. He should've been up and about long ago. Last night's good food and better lovemaking had let him sleep deeply, and he felt wonderfully refreshed. In fact, he couldn't remember when he'd last slept so soundly.

Eskkar arose and looked at the empty bed. Trella had vanished, her cloak missing from the peg. Run off, no doubt, after playing me for the fool. But the recollection of the night's intimacy brought a smile to his face, and a closer look at the bed showed the small stain of blood from her virginity. Well, he had no time for the girl now.

Dressing rapidly, he opened the door, buckling on his

short sword as he stepped outside, squinting against the sunlight. Gatus had gone, but two men stood waiting. Eskkar recognized the older one as one of the merchant's trusted servants. The other, much younger, wore a short sword and must be a guard in Nicar's pay. The older man's face plainly showed his impatience.

"What is it?" Eskkar growled. Had Nicar decided to call the whole thing off? Or perhaps demand that his slave be returned?

The servant stepped forward, nodding in the shortest bow possible. "Nicar sends his greetings and asks that you come to his house tomorrow at midmorning."

The man waited a moment, then continued when Eskkar said nothing. "I am to give you this." He handed over a small leather pouch that jingled pleasantly as Eskkar took it.

"Tell your master that I'll attend him at that hour." Deciding he might as well be gracious, he added, "and I'm sorry I kept you waiting. I was up late thinking about the barbarians."

Mollified, Nicar's messenger bowed also, more respectfully this time. He wished Eskkar a good morning, then headed back toward his master's residence, his escort scrambling behind him.

Eskkar turned toward the guard, leaning on his spear. "Wipe that smile off your face or I'll rip out your insides." The man's smile broadened further before it disappeared.

"And where's the girl? Did you let her run off in the night while you slept at your post?"

The man's smile returned. "No, Captain, she went out a little while ago to get food. She told me to let you sleep. She'll be back shortly."

Yes, if she wasn't halfway across the fields. Trella had probably charmed the guard as easily as she'd beguiled him. Curse the gods, he should have told the man to watch her. He'd be the butt of every joke in Orak, the great captain of the guard who couldn't keep his girl slave even for one day. He kept his grim thoughts to himself as he went first to the latrine, then to the well to wash.

Walking back to his room, he saw smoke coming from the tiny opening that served as a chimney. Inside, he found Trella heating water at the fire that seemed to smoke as much as it burned. An oval of fresh bread lay on the table, scenting the air, with a solitary dark sausage on the room's single cracked plate.

He gaped like an idiot at the sight of her and couldn't stop himself from smiling when she turned toward him. She watched him as he sat down at the table before turning her attention back to the blackened and dented copper bowl resting amid the flames. Grasping it with a bit of rag, Trella carried it to the table and poured the warm water into the wooden cup before him.

"Good morning, master," she said tonelessly as she set the pot on the table.

"I thought you'd run off. When I awoke and saw you gone, I thought you'd slipped away in the night."

"And what would you do if I had run off?" she asked, her voice still empty of emotion.

"I'd have gone after you, Trella." He reached across the table and touched her arm, enjoying the feel of her flesh as his thoughts returned to last night.

"You talk with Nicar tomorrow, as everyone knows. How could you chase after me if you were meeting with him?"

"There are more important things to me than Nicar and Orak. If you ever run from me, I'll come after you."

A smile appeared briefly on her face, turning her instantly back into a young girl. She touched his hand.

"I'll not run away, at least not today," she said, her voice more pleasant now. "Eat your breakfast, master. You have much to do today, to prepare for your meeting tomorrow."

"Join me then." He broke the bread in half, then ripped the sausage in two equal pieces. She carried the pot back to the fire and returned to the table. Picking up the sausage, she took a bite, but returned most of her portion to the plate.

"You'll have a long day and you'll need your strength," Trella said, indicating the meat. "Besides, it's not fit for the slave to eat as much as the master."

Eskkar washed down the bread with a mouthful of warm water, then pushed the meat back to her. "Eat, woman. You'll need your own strength tonight."

She turned red with embarrassment and looked away.

Women were a great mystery, Eskkar decided. Tearing the skin off your back in the night, then refusing to meet your gaze in the morning. He changed the subject. "How did you pay for this? Did Creta give you some coins before you left?"

"That old cow? She gave me nothing, only took the few things I owned. No, I just asked the guard where to find food, then went to the street vendor with the best-looking wares. I told him I was Eskkar's woman and I needed food for your breakfast. He gave me the bread and meat. I told him you would pay him later."

"And he gave you the food?" Eskkar asked, amazement in his voice. No one in the village had ever given him credit before.

"He was eager to help." She chewed on a piece of bread for a moment. "Master, may I speak?"

He rapped his water cup sharply against the table. "Say what you like, Trella. I told you last night you were to be more than a servant and that I'd need your help. So speak your mind."

"Men say things at night they forget in the morning." She toyed with the scraps of bread in front of her.

"As women say things to get what they desire. What is it you want, girl? Do you want to leave? Or go back to Nicar? I'll not stop you if that's what you wish. So speak your mind and be done with it."

She touched his hand again, then met his eyes for the first time. "Eskkar, I'm just a girl. No, not even that, a slave. But last night, after you fell asleep, I thought long about what I want."

She took her hand away. "My father is dead, my family is gone, either dead or sold, and I'll never see any of them again. So, last night I decided that I want to stay and help you. Help you succeed against the barbarians. Because if you do, then you can have the wealth and power to establish your own House. That's what I want now, to be part of your family. And so I'll help you in any way I can."

For a few moments, he just looked at her. "Last night, in the darkness, I began to doubt if I could truly defend the village from the barbarians. This morning it seems even more impossible."

"I can help you, Eskkar." She leaned across the table. "I'm sure I can help. That's why Nicar gave me to you. But you must tell me everything, all your thoughts, all your plans, everything."

He stared at his plate while he considered her request. He'd never made any friends in Orak, certainly no man he trusted enough to confide his doubts. As for Gatus and the rest, they had little to offer. Eskkar had no doubt that he knew more about what needed to be done than they did.

He could talk to Nicar, but Eskkar didn't want to approach Orak's ruler so soon with his own misgivings. No, Eskkar had no one he could confide in. Nicar said she would be useful, so he might as well talk to her as anyone else, though he doubted how much she could help. Still, he had little to lose by talking to her.

Nevertheless, he hesitated. She'd come from Nicar's house. Perhaps what Eskkar told her would find its way back to her former master. Even if Nicar trusted his new captain of the guard, the noble might still wish to know Eskkar's private thoughts. But she'd been given to him, not loaned, and the hatred between the girl and Creta seemed real enough.

"Master, whatever you tell me, I'll repeat to no one."

Her words made him wonder if she could read his mind. He more than half-believed she'd cast a spell upon him last night. In the end, the look in her eyes convinced him, a gaze so intent that it seemed to pierce his thoughts, as she leaned forward across the table, waiting for him to make up his mind.

"I'll tell you what I know, Trella," he began, "though I don't see how you can help."

"It may be I can do more than you know. Since I was a child, I've been trained in many things. My father was a noble and taught me to understand their ways. I sat at his feet as he worked and I listened to him advise the leader of our village. And I learned many things in Nicar's house. Because I could read the symbols and count, I worked with Nicar and his stewards nearly every day. I heard them speak about Orak, about Noble Drigo, and the other nobles."

He wanted to believe her. More than that, he wanted to trust her. Even if she repeated his words to Nicar, what did it matter? Eskkar had the gold and the slave, and enough of the soldiers would follow him if he decided to leave. No one would try to stop him. What did he have to lose?

"Very well. Where should I start?"

They spoke for nearly two hours. Eskkar described building a wall, explained about using the bow to keep the attackers at arm's length, about flooding the lands around the village. He told her how he would train the men, what arms he would need, what forces he hoped to muster, and what the coming months would bring.

She asked about the barbarians, and he described them, why they fought, and their tactics. He pointed out every detail of the coming struggle as best he could, answering her questions and endless requests for details.

When he'd finished, she leaned across the table and took his hand in both of hers. "Thank you, master. But you talk only of the fighting, of the men and the wall. You don't tell me what you fear, what you worry about, what concerns you the most. Please, master, tell me about those things."

Eskkar stroked her hands. They felt as warm and exciting as they had last night. The girl had surely cast a spell on him, but it didn't matter anymore. "All right, Trella. I worry about the nobles. I don't know how to deal with them. They're quicker in their wits and easy with their words. Nicar is a good man, but I don't fully trust him. He only sent for me because he had no one else. The rest of the nobles are worse. And Drigo—last night Drigo looked at me in the street, and I saw the laughter in his eyes. He mocked me without speaking a word, and I could do nothing."

The memory stirred him to anger, and he tightened his grip on her hand just for a moment. "I'm not afraid of Drigo, but he has power and men who obey his will. I could kill any one of them easily enough, but even a small pack of wolves can bring down one man." He took a deep breath. "But most of all, I fear looking foolish in their eyes and in front of others."

Never in his life had Eskkar admitted fear to anyone, let alone a slave girl. Now that the words had been spoken, they couldn't be called back. He decided to go on. "And it's the same with the merchants. I don't know how to ask for bows, or swords, or any of the other things I'll need, let alone how many, or when I'll want them. Even with Nicar's help, I wonder if I'll be able to get what I need."

He'd voiced his doubts and fears. But instead of shame at admitting his weakness, Eskkar felt a feeling of relief.

Trella's hand gripped his with surprising strength. "Master, you worry about these things because you don't know these men. I've lived with such people all my life. They're nothing to be afraid of. As you've spent your life fighting, they've spent their lives talking and counting and bargaining. But with the barbarians coming, the time for talk is past. Now they will both fear and need you, because they know only fighting men can save them and their gold. May I tell you what I think will happen?"

That the nobles might fear him seemed odd at first. "Go on, Trella."

She told him how she thought the Five Families would react, what the men of power would likely do and say, and how their arrogant need to dominate everyone and everything might overcome even their fear of the barbarians. She told him of Nicar's doubts and concerns, especially his worries about the other noble families, particularly Noble Drigo.

"Remember, no matter what happens with the barbarians, the nobles will never fully trust you or accept you. You're not their kind."

Eskkar thought back to last night, when he'd casually assumed that Nicar and the other nobles would welcome him into their circle. How childish that must have sounded to Nicar.

"I thought that they'd be grateful if I saved their village. But you're right. They will always think of me as a barbarian."

"They are what they are, master. And none of them likes to share power, especially with a stranger, not even Nicar. He may be good to you now when he needs you, but later he will take his authority back."

"And what about you, Trella? You don't mind belonging to a barbarian?"

"You are not a barbarian, master. You treat even a slave girl with respect. I saw that and more last night. And I'm a stranger here, too. Perhaps the gods sent us to each other." Her last words came with a brief smile that disappeared quickly. "Now, can we talk about your meeting with the nobles tomorrow? You should prepare yourself to meet with the Families."

With growing confidence, she talked about what questions might arise at Nicar's meeting and how he should respond. Her ideas surprised him, though once she explained, he saw how likely they were to come up. Eskkar realized his offer to defend Orak was even more complicated than he'd thought.

"Last night, you said that you came from . . . ?"

"Carnax. It's a large village, close to the Great Sea, in Sumeria."

"You said your father was advisor to the village's ruler. I doubted you then, but now I see that you spoke the truth. You think like a noble. You understand power and how it can be used."

"Yes, master. My father trained me differently than the other girls. He taught me the nobles' ways, and instructed me in the mysteries of gold, the farm, and many other subjects."

"You must teach me all these secrets." He smiled. "If it is not too late to learn them."

"In time, you will learn them all. Now we should go over your preparations once more."

She led him through several situations that might arise, what he should say, and how he should deal with each. The more they spoke, the more his trust increased. And of all the things they discussed, they talked longest about Noble Drigo.

Trella's thoughts about Drigo startled Eskkar. She believed Drigo presented the biggest problem and the greatest danger. She'd learned much in Nicar's house about Drigo and his plans, and her words sent a chill through him. He hadn't realized the immediate threat Drigo represented.

Slowly his resolve hardened. Nothing, he decided, nothing and no one would push him aside again, not in the street, not in Nicar's house. He would be captain of the guard and even Drigo would acknowledge him.

When they finished speaking, their hands joined again across the table. He looked at her differently now, seeing someone with fire in her heart and bronze in her thoughts. Eskkar knew he'd found a woman worth more than a fistful of gold coins. With her beside him, he felt he could accomplish anything, dare the Five Families, and even defeat the horde of barbarians. "You give me strength, Trella," he said simply. "Stay at my side."

Her grip tightened on his hand, and again her strength surprised him.

"You have the power now, Eskkar, but you must learn to use it, and quickly, or it will slip away. You must act as if you have always had it. When you speak, speak with authority and certainty. If you're not sure what to say, say nothing, just look confident. The crowd will follow if you lead them. I saw that last night, and again in the streets this morning. Even the soldiers looked to you for direction.

"And don't be in awe of any man from now on, Eskkar, not even any of the Five Families. They're just merchants, and they're all frightened. Only you seem not to be afraid, and that is your power. Don't hesitate to show that power. Starting today everyone will look to you, searching for

weakness or doubt. If you have any, conceal it. If any oppose you, push them aside—kill them if you have to. No one
will question you. In times of trouble, people look to strong
leaders, not merchants and tradesmen, no matter how much
wealth they have. Tomorrow you must take the power, or not
at all."

The hard words no longer surprised him, not even her
casual reference to killing. The nobles thought that way,
careless of lives other than their own. He'd stopped thinking of her as an inexperienced young girl, a slave, or even
a woman whose ideas didn't matter. She'd become a window into the lives of the nobles, perceiving their plots and
plans, and offering herself as a partner to his own ven-
tures.

But Trella's strength of will did surprise him. Some
women could be stronger than their men, though the idea
made him a little uncomfortable. Such women often eclipsed
a man in reading people's thoughts and faces. Trella had all
those qualities, the toughness of a man in the body of a
young woman.

A thought crossed his mind. He reached into his tunic
and brought out Nicar's leather pouch. He hadn't even looked
inside, but he opened it now and dumped the contents on the
table. Counting slowly, he found twenty gold coins. He knew
Ariamus had gotten only ten each month. For a moment Eskkar played with the small golden squares, touching them,
enjoying the feel of the cool metal and the power it represented. Many men worshipped gold, he knew, schemed and
plotted to obtain it, then caressed it at night behind locked
doors before burying it deep in the ground.

Looking up, he found Trella observing him, not the gold.
Abruptly, Eskkar pushed two coins across the table. "Take
these and change them for copper, then pay the street vendor
for the food. I'll not owe any man for my bread. Make sure
you're not cheated in the exchange. Use the rest to buy a
decent dress for yourself and anything else you need. And
buy new sandals for me, the sturdiest you can find, the kind
a man can fight in."

Eskkar pushed the rest of the coins toward her, trying not

to think he was trusting her with what until today he would have considered a small fortune. "Keep the rest of the gold safe for me. There will be more things to buy in the coming weeks."

He put his finger on one coin, the brightest and shiniest of the lot, then picked it up and held it to the light. "This one is a gift for you. One gold coin is enough to buy a good female slave. If you ever desire to leave me, give me this coin, and you can have your freedom."

A look of confusion covered her face, and Eskkar sat back and laughed. "It will save me the time and trouble of chasing after you. Otherwise, for now and between us, let there be no more talk of master and slave." He put the coin in the palm of her hand and closed her fingers lightly over it.

Trella opened her hand and looked at the gold glittering brightly on her palm. "May I have your sword?" she said quietly.

Surprised, he hesitated, then drew the sword from its scabbard, reversed it and handed it to her.

She stood up, put the coin near the edge of the table, and placed the middle of the blade, where the edge was sharpest, against the coin. Using both hands, she leaned on it with all her strength, the muscles straining in her tanned arms.

When she lifted the blade, the coin was nocked down its middle by a thin crease. She handed him back the sword, then gathered the rest of the coins and put them in the pouch. "Now it is marked, and I'll keep it safe." She put the pouch around her neck, then tucked it inside her dress. "You should get ready for your meeting with the men. It's nearly noon."

Eskkar stood, glancing at the window and seeing the sun race ever higher into the sky. "I have time for this, Trella." He pulled her to him, kissing her hungrily, feeling an unaccustomed thrill of pleasure when she stood on her toes and wrapped her arms around his neck, her body pressing against him. He would have thrown her across the bed and taken her right then, Orak and Nicar be damned, if she hadn't pushed herself away, face averted, and gone outside.

Esskar picked up the last scrap of bread and followed her out the door. The guard still held his post, watching Trella as she walked away. "Watch your eyes, dog," Esskar snapped, "if you know what's good for you."

He grabbed the startled man's spear and pulled it from his hand. "Follow after her and stay at her side. At her side, you hear me? Make sure she comes to no harm and that everyone knows she's Esskar's woman. If any man bothers her, slit his throat. Now, go!"

He shoved the man on his way, making him stumble as he hurried to catch up. Esskar twirled the heavy spear easily in his hand a few times, then turned and hurled it with all his strength at the side of the house. Fragments sprang from the mud wall as the heavy spear buried itself in the structure. Esskar grunted in satisfaction, before he went off in the other direction, looking for Gatus. Time to prepare for tomorrow's meeting with Nicar.

This time Trella paid more attention to her surroundings. The soldiers hanging around the barracks stopped whatever occupied them and turned to stare at her as she walked by. Some called her by name, while others made rude remarks about her first night with Esskar. At first the words and bold looks made her uneasy, but then she realized they all knew who she was, that their words were spoken in rough jest, and that there was little chance of any of them hurting her.

When she passed into the street, she realized one of the soldiers had followed, walking a few steps behind. Turning, she recognized the sentry who'd guarded Esskar's room this morning.

"Captain Esskar told me to escort you around the village, Trella, to protect you, in case anyone should not know who you are."

She didn't know what to say, and briefly wondered if Esskar

had ordered him to ensure that she didn't run off. But the man's simple expression couldn't conceal any guile. And she remembered the touch of Eskkar's hands only moments ago. "Thank you, soldier. What is your name?"

"I'm called Adad, Trella."

"Well, Adad, can you tell me where I can find a merchant who sells good clothing? I need to buy some things for my master."

He directed her as they walked, slipping through the stream of people who walked Orak's narrow dirt lanes, a noisy mixture of men, women, children, and animals. She saw that most of the mud-brick houses had a single story. But the homes and shops of the better-off merchants usually had a stall or table in front to display some wares. Images painted on the wall identified the type of establishment or what goods could be had.

Though she had lived in Orak for almost two months, she'd rarely been allowed outside Nicar's courtyard, and then only to accompany Creta or one of the senior servants. Now she looked closely at the people and stalls that lined the streets. At each stall a merchant, his wife, or an older child tended the merchandise, both to deter petty thieves and to encourage those looking to buy. Orak seemed much like her former village, only much bigger and with more fine houses.

She would have liked to take her time and explore, but she wanted to get back to Eskkar. So she hurried until she reached the shop Adad had suggested.

Entering the low doorway of the merchant Rimush, she found two other women ahead of her. The older dressed like the wife of a well-off tradesman. Her younger companion looked to be a servant or slave, in more humble clothing. The large room, illuminated only by the sunlight coming through the door and a small hole cut in the ceiling, held several rough-cut tables and shelves, all covered with clothing or lengths of wool and linen. The intense smell of the fresh linen tingled her nose. Goods were stacked on the floor as well, covering nearly every open space, and Trella had to be careful where she stepped. A colorful blanket curtained off another room at the rear.

The women and shop owner gave her a quick glance, then ignored the poorly dressed slave. Ignored her, until Adad followed her inside, looked around, then leaned in the doorway. The sight of the armed soldier accompanying Trella stopped all conversation, and now Rimush turned to her, taking only a moment to guess who she was.

"You're the new slave of the soldier Eskkar?" Rimush spoke rapidly, his curiosity plain. Eskkar and his new status were the main topic of conversation everywhere in Orak since sunrise.

Although not particularly tall, Trella knew how to stand properly and how to deal with merchants, so she drew herself up before answering. "My master is Eskkar, captain of the guard. He wishes me to purchase sandals and a tunic for him. Do you have such items, or should I seek elsewhere?" She kept her head high, her voice low but firm. The merchant would recognize the tone of one accustomed to dealing with shopkeepers and servants.

The older woman seemed annoyed at the interruption. "When I'm finished, slave, you may buy whatever it is you can afford."

"I'll look elsewhere, then," Trella said calmly and turned to go.

"No, wait, girl," Rimush called hastily after her. "I have what you need here." He turned to his other customer. "I will return to you when I have finished with . . . what is your name, girl?"

"Trella." She watched in amusement as Rimush ignored the tradesman's wife to go to the darkest corner of the shop, returning in a moment with a pair of sandals. While he went to fetch some tunics, Trella inspected the sandals, then called to him. "These sandals are not strong enough, Rimush. I want the finest, strongest pair you have, sturdy enough to fight in."

Muttering under his breath, he returned in an instant, handing her another pair of sandals he'd picked up without stopping, then went again to the back room. His other customer, angered at Rimush's treatment, banged down the cloth she'd been inspecting and left the shop. Her companion gave Trella a broad smile as she passed, trailing behind her mistress.

Trella inspected the sandals, then rapped one sharply on the counter. Next she twisted it with both hands, to make sure nothing shifted. "These are of fair quality," she commented as Rimush returned, carrying half a dozen tunics. "I'll take them, upon my master's approval, of course."

"There are no better sandals in Orak. Your master will be pleased." He pushed a bolt of cloth out of the way with his elbow, then put the tunics down on a narrow table, fanning them out. "Your master is tall and has broad shoulders. Not many carry tunics of his size."

"You know my master, then?"

"No, he has never come here. But I know who he is."

Trella ignored the first four garments, soft, decorated tunics for rich merchants or nobles. The one she selected looked more fitting to a captain of the guard, well made but unadorned except for a red stripe around the simple square collar. She wet her finger and rubbed the stripe to make sure the dye stayed true, then reversed the garment to check the stitching and the seams, tugging on the half sleeve to make sure it held fast.

"This one will do," she announced. "Also, I need a dress for myself, something simple. Have you anything for me?"

This required the assistance of Rimush's wife, who had come out from the back of the house to stare at the captain of the guard's new slave. She helped Trella make her selection, then escorted her into the back of the house where she could try it on. "You look very pretty in it, Trella, like a fine lady," she added, admiring the way the dress fit. "Are you sure you don't want a newer one, or something of finer quality?"

Trella smiled at the compliment. "This is good enough. Now I must be on my way." She took the new garment off and put her old one back on.

The haggling over prices went faster than Trella had expected. Five silver coins for the expensive sandals, four for the tunic, and two for the dress. The price seemed reasonable enough, but she countered with an offer of eight coins for everything. Rimush complained about being robbed, but eventually accepted a price of ten silver coins when Trella tossed everything on the counter and prepared to leave.

Rimush looked surprised when she handed him a gold coin. Gold was scarce and slaves not often trusted with such coins. He took the coin, pinching it hard with his fingernail to make sure it was real and noting Nicar's mark on it before he gave her ten silver coins in change.

Trella smiled as she watched him. Rimush would spread the word that Eskkar had access to Nicar's gold. Gathering up her goods, she thanked him and his wife.

"No, Trella, our thanks to your master. The gods protect him, and may he save us from the barbarians. And from Noble Drigo as well. I'm too old to start over in another place."

"Noble Drigo?"

"Yes, Noble Drigo." Rimush spat the words out. "His bullies take what they like and pay as little as they can, if they pay at all. They say Drigo will take charge of Orak soon."

"Nicar won't allow that," Trella answered. "Nor will my master. He will protect you, Rimush," she told him confidently. "He'll protect all of us."

Outside in the street, Adad waited patiently for his charge. They walked back toward the barracks, the soldier two steps behind her, stopping once for Trella to purchase a good quality comb to manage her hair, her own having more broken teeth than good ones, then again to buy a small oil lamp.

As she walked and shopped, however, Trella noticed that everyone was staring at her. No one had ever seen a soldier assigned to protect a slave before. She'd have received quite a bit of attention for that reason alone. But they all knew her status as Eskkar's slave, the man who claimed he could defend Orak against the barbarians. That made her someone of importance.

A few people asked what she knew about the barbarians or about Eskkar's plans. She smiled at anyone who spoke to her but said nothing. Fear of the barbarians showed in their faces, so worried that they looked even to her for some sign of hope.

The walk through Orak's streets gave her much to think about. She'd seen the villagers' apprehension, the anxiety she had warned Eskkar about, and that meant anything could happen in the next few days, for good or evil. Trella pushed the thought from her mind. She had more than enough to worry about in the next few hours.

4

~~~~~~~~~~

Eskkar found Gatus sitting against the barracks wall, dozing in the early afternoon sun while waiting for his captain. Climbing to his feet, Gatus yawned loudly, then led the way to the stable. Fewer than a dozen horses remained. Ariamus had taken the best, leaving behind animals past their prime. Not that Eskkar would have trusted any of them in a hard fight, including those taken by Ariamus. It took gold to buy, maintain, and train good horses, and the miserly nobles spent as few of their coins as possible on the soldiers' mounts.

They picked two horses that needed work, and Eskkar led the way to the hilltop where he'd done his thinking yesterday. The two men sat facing each other, and Eskkar repeated everything he'd told Nicar, this time in much more detail. Gatus made suggestions about the food and supplies needed, the quantity and quality of weapons, and how the men would be paid. They discussed the soldiers, talking about individual abilities and how best they could be used. Gatus agreed with the three Eskkar had in mind for subcommanders.

They tried to come up with everything needed to raise, train, and support a large number of fighting men. Then they attempted to put tasks in order, what must be done first, what could wait a few weeks longer. Last, they discussed the barbarians, guessing what they might do when they saw the wall, how they'd use their weapons and horses, and the most likely points of attack.

Eskkar had never had such a discussion before. All his life, fighting was something you just did, not something you planned for. You might try to ambush your enemy, or catch them asleep, but for horsemen, there was little else in the way of tactics. In true steppes tradition, Eskkar believed the best plan of all was to have more men and better horses than your enemy. If outnumbered, barbarians tended to avoid battle, preferring to fight another day. Neither Eskkar nor the Alur Meriki felt any loss of honor in turning away from such unfavorable conflicts. Now Eskkar had to devise ways to resist not only a numerically superior foe, but one whose individual warriors were stronger and more capable. Just as important, he had to convince villagers that his tactics would be effective.

For someone village-bred, Gatus had plenty to contribute. He had survived years of fighting and had ideas of his own and no hesitations about putting them forth, especially those concerning weapons and training. He kept challenging Eskkar, looking for weaknesses or flaws that would doom Orak's defense. When Gatus did find a weakness, they worked out how to resolve it.

Nearly three hours later, Eskkar nodded in satisfaction. They had reached agreement on every item. Gatus had helped him specify his plans. For the first time Eskkar felt confident he could answer any question at Nicar's meeting, that no one could brush off either his ideas or his facts. They might not share his beliefs, but that would be a matter for debate.

The two men rode down the hill to repeat Eskkar's survey of the land. This time they paid particular attention to the farmlands north and south of the village. Flooding these would change the usual approach to Orak's main gate. When they finally finished their circuit, Gatus admitted Orak might have a chance, with luck, of surviving the invasion.

Eskkar wanted more than just Gatus's approval. He wanted the old soldier waiting outside Nicar's house, in case the nobles wanted a second opinion. Gatus had lived in Orak for more than five years, and most of them would respect his words.

"But we'll need to train bowmen, three or four hundred of them at least," Gatus said. "And assuming you can provide weapons for all of them, it's still going to take at least two months to train a good archer."

Eskkar didn't understand why it took so long to teach someone how to use such a simple weapon, but he had to defer to Gatus's experience with villagers. "Then we'd better get started at once, Gatus. You know how to train men better than anyone. They'll do as you say."

And they would do it faster for Gatus than for a barbarian. Eskkar might be captain of the guard, but he hadn't proven himself to the men. They'd follow him for now, but for a real battle, where men had to trust their commander completely and be willing to risk their lives . . . that needed a leader with a different kind of authority.

"And what of everything else that must be done? Are you sure you know what's needed from Nicar and the nobles?"

"Yes. I went over all that with Trella. She thought of a dozen things I'd missed. She knows how to ask for what we'll need. We just have to tell her. Then she can deal with the craftsmen. She knows the symbols, she can count, and she remembers what she hears. She comes from a noble family. Her father taught her the ruling ways."

"Ah, she's one of those."

"Those what?" He looked toward Gatus.

"One of the special ones. You've spent time in other villages, haven't you?"

"Yes. Now stop talking in riddles. What about her?"

Gatus took his time before answering. "How many women in Orak know the symbols, or can count higher than ten?"

"I don't know," he shrugged. "None, I suppose. All the clerks and scribes are men."

"You don't know the symbols; I don't know them. But Nicar's wife knows them." Gatus saw the surprise on Eskkar's face. "There are a few others, wives of the big traders and merchants. Who do you think runs their trading business when they're away or sick? There are some women, you ignorant barbarian, who are trained for more than just bedding. If she's one of those . . . tell me what else Trella said."

Eskkar grimaced at the slur, but told him everything he'd learned.

"Then she was raised to be a wife to someone like Nicar or Drigo," Gatus mused, "a ruling noble."

"What does that . . ."

"Listen to me. You were raised to fight, trained from childhood, taught how to use weapons, how to be strong."

"Yes, that's the barbarian way. You spend your whole life learning how to fight, how to . . ."

"Trella was raised to help rule. She probably spent her whole life at her father's feet, watching the rulers of her village, learning how to read men's faces, listening to what they say, judging when they lie. Trella's what, fourteen seasons? She may have spent every day for the last five years watching her village's nobles, learning the mysteries of gold and bronze, the secret symbols, studying the ways of farmer and villager. If her wits are as sharp as you say . . ."

"They are," Eskkar said, trying to grasp this new concept. It had never occurred to him that the nobles in Orak might have trained to learn their ruling ways. As he'd been trained to fight, Trella learned to use her wits, to study men and their ways. Their talk this morning . . . he realized that Trella had guided him through the preparations for tomorrow's meeting with more than just her knowledge of Nicar's house. If she knew the secret ways of the nobles, could read men's thoughts, then she might be worth even more than he'd thought.

"Not used to dealing with women who have their wits about them, are you?"

Eskkar closed his mouth and frowned at Gatus. "No. I didn't know such women existed."

"Well, think about what that means, Eskkar, before you have her fetching water from the well and washing your feet. Nicar may have given you a bigger prize than you know."

"At first I thought she was just for remembering things . . . helping out. After last night's bedding and our talk this morning . . ."

"She's bewitched you already. I saw the way you look at her." Gatus laughed at the memory. "But will the nobles listen to a slave girl?"

"When the time comes, I'll make sure they do, Gatus. And she'll speak in my name. If the nobles refuse or give us trouble, we'll leave Orak. I won't argue with Drigo or any of them. That's what I told Nicar yesterday, and that's what I'll say at tomorrow's meeting. That's why you'll be there, in case they want to hear your thoughts."

"My thoughts are that you're going to get us both killed, Eskkar."

Eskkar laughed. "Perhaps. But don't tell them that. Besides, we've time to get out, if things start going badly. And enough men to follow us, if it comes to that. So we'll just have to see what happens."

"Time will tell, then," Gatus said, putting his heels to the horse.

They cantered through the gate before slowing to a walk. Gatus was right. The next few days would decide all. But Eskkar had persuaded the old soldier, a difficult enough task, and now Gatus would stay as long as he believed they could endure. Winning over Gatus would help persuade the soldiers, too. A good day's work, Eskkar decided. He just needed to do the same at Nicar's meeting tomorrow.

Carrying her purchases, Trella returned to Eskkar's room. She sat at the table, enjoying a rare moment of privacy. The events of last night and this morning threatened to overwhelm her.

Sunlight streamed in through the open door, illuminating her new home. Only a few months ago, the stark surroundings would have seemed bleak and wretched, even worse than the tiny, unventilated nook she'd shared with two other girls at Nicar's house. Now everything within these walls was her responsibility. She had become mistress of Eskkar's house, if you could call a single room attached to the soldiers' barracks a house.

Her new duties might be limited, but at least she didn't have Creta or more senior servants ordering her around. And she'd avoided the distasteful fate of having to pleasure first Nicar and then his son and the other servants. She could have accepted being Nicar's occasional bedmate. He was, after all, the kind of man her father planned for his daughter, though she'd hoped for one closer to her own age. No, Nicar wouldn't have been a problem. She knew she could have pleased him enough to earn further responsibilities. The troubles in Nicar's household came from Creta and Nicar's youngest son, Caldor.

The servants had described their degrading experiences with Caldor, and even now Trella couldn't repress a shudder. She'd seen him enjoying one of the other slaves, a girl even younger than Trella and barely into the secrets of womanhood. He'd taken her from behind, positioning her on her knees with her head and shoulders on the floor. The poor girl couldn't stop crying and her sobs echoed throughout the house. But a slave's tears meant nothing, not even to the other servants. Caldor had prolonged the act, no doubt reveling in the girl's humiliation as much as her body, while ignoring all those who walked by his room.

Trella wondered what she would have done when Caldor had finally sent for her, told her to remove her dress, and display herself. She shook her head in anger. Like the other girl, Trella would have obeyed, and later cried herself to sleep, comforted by the older women. Slaves did not resist their masters, no matter what they commanded, and pleasuring a master sexually was expected, as routine a task as washing his clothes or serving his food.

She pushed the dark thoughts away. Instead she recalled last night's lovemaking, and that memory sent a wave of pleasure through her, a pleasant anticipation of tonight's intimacy. No, whatever this new life brought would be a definite improvement, and she wouldn't waste any time complaining about her surroundings. Not with so much to do.

A slave's duty was to please her master, she reminded herself. She'd accomplished more than that last night and today. Eskkar had unburdened himself, confided in her. He'd also offered her a compliment without realizing it. He'd treated her differently, almost as an equal, something she hadn't enjoyed since her enslavement. More than that, Eskkar respected her ideas. Uneducated he might be, but he knew the truth when he heard it, no matter who spoke it. So that would be her role from now on. Advisor by day, lover by night.

Last night she'd been a frightened virgin and unsure of herself. Tonight would be different, and she'd start learning how to satisfy Eskkar's desires, how to keep him aroused and hungry for her body. Her mother had warned her about men and their needs, about how they could lose interest in a woman after a few bouts in bed. Fortunately, her mother had instructed her in the mysteries of the love act. With what she had learned, and what she would soon discover, Trella would keep Eskkar close to her.

Nevertheless, she felt her secret places grow warm at the thought of having him inside her tonight. She might be a slave, but she'd become a woman. She determined to make him desire her, to make herself the most important thing in his life.

But right now Trella needed to pay attention to her other duties. She stood and looked around the room, wondering where to start. Eskkar hadn't given her any commands. He likely wouldn't have minded if she sat around all day combing her hair and waiting for his return. The chamber was dirty and unkempt, though she doubted Eskkar or the previous owner noticed such things. That meant work to be done. Trella didn't plan to live in filth.

She went to the door. Adad glanced up, then smiled. For a moment he reminded her of her brother.

"Adad, I'd like you to get me some things." She found herself speaking in what her father called her "serious voice," the tone she used when she wanted something.

"What do you need?"

"A broom, a bucket, and some rags. Then I want you to go and buy some mats, plain ones, three, no, four of them, at least this big." She held her arms wide apart. "Tell the merchant who they're for, and that I'll pay him later. Can you do that for me?"

"I'm not supposed to leave you alone. Eskkar told me . . ."

"I know what he told you. I promise I'll stay inside until you return."

He hesitated, then gave in, aware that Eskkar wouldn't return for some time. "I'll be right back. Don't go anywhere." He leaned his spear against the doorway and walked off.

Trella smiled. The soldier obeyed her almost as quickly as if Eskkar had given the command. She went back inside, looked at the bed, and decided she might as well start there.

She dragged the heavy frame away from the wall, revealing a mix of trash and debris accumulated beneath it. A fat brown spider scuttled through the pile, unaccustomed to the light. She frowned at the sight of it. It looked large enough to give a nasty bite. A layer of clean sand might once have covered the dirt floor, but over time the topping had vanished. What remained looked more like soil from the fields.

Adad returned, carrying a broom in one hand and an empty bucket in the other. "I'll go get the mats." He moved off at a trot, anxious about leaving her alone.

Trella took the broom and started sweeping the debris toward the door. As soon as she finished sweeping and smoothing under the bed, she shoved the heavy pallet back into the corner, grunting with the effort. Then she started on the rest of the floor.

She worked steadily, most of the time on her knees, using her hands to scoop and move whatever objects she encountered, tossing all the pebbles and refuse into the bucket. She used her fingers to strain the mix of sand and dirt, and squashed the occasional insect with the heel of her hand.

By the time Adad returned, she'd cleaned the room. Together they moved the table, then set the mats down, one near the bed, one just inside the entrance, and the other two under the table and its rickety benches. Smoothing the dirt, she made sure the mats lay flat, with no lumps underneath.

Finished at last, Trella examined the room. It looked as clean as she could make it on such short notice, and at least tonight there would be no scraps of food or bits of bone to attract bugs or mice. On her next visit to the market, a copper coin would purchase a cartload of clean sand, enough to re-cover the dirt.

If this were to be their home, she'd have the inner walls recoated with fresh mud, then smoothed and whitewashed. That might get rid of the stale odors that lingered within. That reminded her of the mattress. Only the gods knew when it had last been changed. She'd have that refilled with fresh straw, too.

She looked down at herself and laughed. Covered with dust and grime, she thought half the dirt from the floor now covered her body. She needed a bath. Taking her cloak, she tossed it over her arm, then gathered up the garments purchased earlier and the greasy rag she'd used at the fire. Bundling them together, she set out toward the river. Adad fell in behind her and had to stretch his legs to keep up with her rapid pace.

Trella enjoyed her newfound freedom. The guard actually made things easier, since she could now go wherever she chose and feel perfectly safe.

She knew the way to the river, and it didn't take long to reach Orak's rear gate. They passed through and headed to the left, moving quickly through the crowd. Trella kept a step ahead of Adad, and this time no one noticed her. They passed the jetties where men worked the boats, and soon reached the start of the women's area, fringed by a few willow trees that lined the riverbank.

"Wait here, Adad. I need to wash Eskkar's clothes and bathe myself. Please hold my cloak."

Adad looked uncomfortable, but complied. By custom, men did not venture too close to the women's bathing place, though often enough boys or men took their time passing by, laughing and staring at the women.

Trella went to the riverbank, then climbed down to the rocky bank. This late in the day only three people labored there, washing clothes. An elderly matron and her granddaughter seemed to spend more time splashing than cleaning. The remaining woman looked only a few years older than Trella.

A glance back toward Adad showed him standing where she'd left him, about fifty paces away. She took a few steps into the river and ducked beneath the cool water, letting it flow over her entire body. When she came up for air, she turned her back to the bank and pulled her dress up over her head, then held it under the water and rubbed it vigorously.

She cleaned herself, rubbing the cold water all over her body. She finished up by ducking her hair several times, then retrieved her dress, pulling the wet garment over her head and wriggling it down around her body.

Gathering the other garments, she washed them as well. As she finished, the other girl came over to her, moving slowly through the water, her dress bunched up around her waist.

"You are Trella, the new slave of Eskkar?"

Trella examined the young woman. A large bruise covered her left eye and her lower lip was split and swollen. "Yes, I'm Trella. And you are . . ."

"Shubure. I'm a slave in Noble Drigo's house. I must finish cleaning my master's clothing, then return home. His son may summon me to pleasure him again before supper." She lifted her hand to her face.

Trella had heard stories about Drigo's son, and felt pity at Shubure's plight. Trella thanked the gods Nicar, not Drigo, had purchased her. At least in Nicar's home the master and his sons did not beat their women, not even their slaves. "Why did your master hit you, Shubure?"

Shubure ignored the question as she moved closer. "Tell your master to be wary. Noble Drigo is not happy with Nicar's choice for captain of the guard."

A chill went through Trella, not entirely caused by the cold water swirling around her thighs. "What did you hear?"

Shubure moved back to the rocks, picked up a garment from her basket, and dipped it into the water. The girl looked around, to see if anyone was watching. The matron still chattered with the little girl, and only Trella's guard glanced in their direction.

"Not much. Just Noble Drigo speaking to his son. He said this Eskkar took too much upon himself and needed to be taught a lesson. One he and the other soldiers wouldn't forget. That's all." She shrugged and turned slightly away, concentrating on washing the already clean garment in her hands.

Trella moved her own hands through the water. "Why did he beat you, Shubure?"

The girl turned back to face her, and a shudder passed through Shubure's body.

"My mother is too ill to work. She doesn't have any copper to buy food for my brothers and sisters. They're all hungry. Soon my mother will have to sell them as slaves, as I was, just to keep them fed. So last night, after young Drigo bedded me, I asked if I could have a copper coin or two for my family, to keep them from starving. I promised to work extra hard to please him, to do anything he asked." Her eyes closed, as if reliving the memory. "He hit me once to shut me up, then again for bothering him with such things."

A slave could be well treated or badly treated. A hard master, Drigo had put one of his slaves to death a few weeks ago. The whispers said the son was even worse than the father.

Trella had never been beaten at Nicar's house, not even slapped until the night Eskkar took her away. Yet young Drigo used his fist on Shubure merely for trying to feed her family.

Whatever Shubure's misfortune, Trella needed to know more about Drigo's plans. "Stay a moment, Shubure." Trella turned away from the shore and opened the pouch that still hung around her neck. Copper and silver coins now mixed with Eskkar's gold. She removed two copper coins from the pouch and reclosed it tightly before turning back. Keeping her hand in the water, she waded closer to Shubure.

"Take these for your mother. If anyone finds them, say you picked them up in the street." Shubure's hand met hers underwater. "If you hear anything else about my master, return here tomorrow. I'll have more coins for you. What hour can you come?"

"An hour after sunrise, Trella . . . Mistress Trella. I'll thank the gods for your gift."

Mistress Trella. For the first time in her life, someone had acknowledged Trella as the head of a household. "It's little enough, Shubure. You'd better go, before they wonder why you dally so long and give you another beating."

Shubure nodded and moved off, slipping the coins inside her dress.

Trella waited, splashing water around her as if she still worked, until Shubure disappeared behind the jetties. Then Trella gathered her garments and climbed up the riverbank.

Walking back toward Adad, she saw his eyes staring at her body, her wet dress outlining her breasts and hips. What would be a disgrace in her father's house meant nothing now. No one cared about a slave's clothing or lack of it. Adad finally remembered his manners and looked away as he handed her the cloak. She rubbed her hair vigorously with it for a few moments, then wrapped it gratefully around her body. Carrying the wet clothes in her arms, she started back home, thinking hard about what she'd just heard.

Nicar knew of Drigo's ambition to become the first man in Orak, to lead the nobles and decide the future of the village. Drigo had pressed that goal more and more in the last few months. But with the barbarians coming, Nicar believed Drigo would leave, removing himself and his ambitions, and solving at least one problem for Nicar.

He wanted the council of nobles to vote to stay and fight. If Drigo abandoned Orak and the barbarians were driven off, he'd find it difficult to reestablish his authority. But if Drigo persuaded the other nobles to leave Orak, Nicar's authority would be weakened. When they returned to pick up the pieces and rebuild, it would be Drigo wielding the power and influence. He'd take Nicar's place as the first man in Orak.

But Nicar wielded great influence. If Eskkar proved he had a workable plan, and if Nicar chose to stay and resist, the nobles would likely side with him.

Trella stopped short, so suddenly that Adad bumped into her. They'd passed back through the gate. She stepped away from the center of the lane and leaned up against the closest wall, hugging the wet bundle to her chest and ignoring the looks from those who passed by.

Until now, Trella hadn't really worried about the consequences of tomorrow's meeting. If they all stayed and fought, Eskkar would win great honor and be able to establish his own House in Orak. That made it worth the risk, though Eskkar had repeated that he wouldn't remain unless he thought they could prevail.

If Drigo left and Orak survived, the noble would have lost face and honor, but would've saved all his gold, and would soon reestablish his trading routes. Then why would Drigo want to discredit Eskkar's plan? Surely the arrogant noble would benefit if the village held out, even without his presence.

What Trella had just worked out, Nicar must have reasoned as well. That's why he told Eskkar not to worry about Drigo. Even Eskkar, though not politically astute, knew that Drigo's choice mattered, that it would influence many in Orak.

Perhaps Drigo had a different plan, something Nicar hadn't thought of. Trella considered Drigo's alternatives. They seemed simple enough: go or stay. Leave, taking everything of value with him, or remain, and risk his life and his fortune under Nicar's orders. The choices seemed straightforward, so clear. Unless Drigo had discovered a third course of action.

She recalled everything she'd heard about Drigo. Ambitious, arrogant and cruel to his servants, miserly with his goods and gold, always seeking more and more gold. But gold, she reminded herself, could be obtained in more ways than just buying and selling. For Drigo, the barbarian invasion might be seen as a blessing from the gods, not the disaster that Nicar foresaw.

And then Trella knew the answer. Knew that she'd guessed Drigo's plan, something even Nicar had failed to do. She looked at Adad, but then her eyes focused on the sword belted to his waist. She needed to learn something else, just to be sure.

"Come, Adad, we must get back. I must speak with Esk-kar."

Eskkar handed off his horse, then went to the well to wash the dust and horse smell from his body. He looked forward to an hour in bed with Trella. Afterward they'd go to one of Orak's better inns, one where they could get decent wine and food, a previously unheard-of luxury, before returning to bed.

Entering his room, Eskkar looked about in surprise. Even in the afternoon shadows, the room seemed brighter. He noticed the new flaxen mats that covered half the floor, then saw that the rest of the dirt had been cleaned and brushed evenly. The place looked almost as clean as one of Nicar's rooms, though the poor furnishings and begrimed walls left much to be desired. The fact that Trella had managed all this in a few short hours whetted his desire. His previous women had cared little for cleanliness.

He'd just hung his sword up when Trella entered, a bundle of damp clothes in her arms. His satisfied mood vanished as soon as he saw her face.

"Master, we need to talk." She looked toward the open doorway. Adad had gone, his duties done for the day. Another soldier already stood guard outside. She lowered her voice. "Can you send the guard farther away, so we can talk privately?"

The last of Eskkar's feelings of warmth disappeared. He stepped outside and told the guard to watch the door from beneath the tree, out of earshot. Eskkar returned, shutting the door behind him.

Trella had finished spreading the clean clothes to dry. She came into his arms, putting her face against his chest and squeezing him tight, surprising him with this show of emotion. He felt her body outlined by the damp dress and inhaled the clean river smell from her hair.

Before he could react, she stepped back, took his hand, and led him to the table. They sat facing each other, but she kept hold of his hand.

"Master, I met a girl at the river this afternoon, a slave from Noble Drigo's house. She had bruises on her face.

Drigo's son had beaten her. She told me that Drigo wants to 'put you in your place' before the meeting tomorrow. I fear Nicar has underestimated Drigo's intentions."

A wave of anger went through him at the idea Drigo might interfere with his newfound happiness and prosperity. Then he shrugged. Probably just talk, women's gossip at the river.

"What can Drigo do, Trella? He can refuse to fight and leave. Or he can stay, and ask that someone else be named captain of the guard. It doesn't matter to me. I told Nicar I'd deal only with him. If the nobles don't want to fight, or want someone else for captain of the guard, then you and I will take Gatus and some men and leave."

"Who else could Drigo put forward as captain?"

Eskkar thought about that. Among the soldiers, only Gatus had enough experience, and he didn't want the job. Gatus hated Drigo and his gang, and wanted nothing to do with them. He'd been ready to leave before Eskkar talked him out of it last night.

Drigo had plenty of men, all of them carrying swords as they strutted through the village. Their leader, Naxos, Drigo's personal bodyguard, was dirty and crude. Neither Nicar nor any of the others would entrust their lives and fortunes to Naxos, even if Drigo suggested him.

"I don't know of anyone else in Orak. Unless there's someone here I don't know about, someone who's fought the barbarians and led men in battle."

"How many soldiers does Noble Drigo have, master?"

"They're not soldiers," he corrected, annoyed at the usual villager confusion between hired guards and trained fighting men. "They're big and carry swords, but mostly they bully the farmers and tradesmen, men weaker than themselves or unarmed. They're brave when there's enough of them, but not one of them could kill the youngest Alur Meriki warrior."

She said nothing, and it took a moment before he realized he hadn't answered her question. "Drigo has plenty of guards, more than the other nobles. Maybe nine or ten."

The determined expression on her face made him consider his words. Each of the nobles hired his own guards.

Paid better than the soldiers, they tended to drink and congregate among themselves. They looked down on the soldiers, and the soldiers had always given way to them. "I think Drigo may have hired a few more in the last few weeks."

"And the other nobles, how many men do they have?"

Eskkar had already started down that path. Each of the nobles had at least seven or eight armed men. Even without Nicar's guards, that meant the others outnumbered the thirty remaining soldiers. The last of his feelings of contentment vanished.

"Would those other guards follow Drigo's man, this Naxos?"

Eskkar took a deep breath. "I don't know, Trella. They'd do as their masters told them, but without orders . . . they'd probably listen to Drigo's man."

"Tomorrow morning I'll go back to the river. Drigo's slave said she might return an hour after sunup. You won't meet with Nicar until midmorning, and perhaps she'll be able to tell us something more."

"If she doesn't get her throat slit for telling tales on her master," Eskkar said. He'd heard the same stories about Drigo's household.

"I gave her two copper coins for what she told me and promised her more tomorrow, master. If you approve."

The polite request made him smile. "Give her a handful, if she learns anything useful." Eskkar certainly had changed his ideas about gold overnight. "I'll need to think about what Drigo and Naxos might do in the next few days."

She shook her head. "Tomorrow, master. You don't have two or three days. Whatever Drigo plans, it will be tomorrow." She squeezed his hand across the table. "What do you think he might try?"

He looked at her, wondering how she had gotten him so worried over a few chance words. If he'd heard the same words himself, he might have laughed them off or ignored them. Trella's perception gave them weight.

"I was surprised when Nicar sent for me. There must not have been anyone else he could turn to. If I'd said last night that Orak couldn't be defended, Nicar would have given up the idea of resisting." That much seemed true enough, he decided. "If I were gone, then . . ."

"Or if you were dead," Trella said. "Then Drigo could take charge of the soldiers, get rid of the ones he didn't need or couldn't control, and Orak would be his."

"What would that gain him? The barbarians would still come, and he still wouldn't fight them."

"The barbarians won't be here for months. If Drigo controls the sixty or so soldiers and guards, plus any more that he might hire, then who could stop him from doing whatever he wants? Taking whatever he wants? He could plunder the entire village, take the loot across the river, then return when the barbarians left. With enough men and gold he could rebuild Orak as his own. He wouldn't need Nicar or any of the other nobles. He'd rule Orak alone."

She waited a moment, but he didn't say anything. "Drigo didn't count on you, didn't expect you to convince Nicar. Now even the villagers think of you as the one man not afraid of the barbarians. I don't think Noble Drigo likes that."

Eskkar's anger rose up. He wanted Trella to be wrong. Curse these nobles and their schemes. Now he was threatened by them. He struck the table with his fist, saw Trella's eyes go wide. He got up and went to the door. Opening it, he called out to the guard. "Find someone to fetch Gatus right away. Then get back here to your post."

Trella's hand touched his arm. She'd followed him to the door. "Send for Adad also. You should keep him close by tonight. He was with me today and saw me talk to the girl. He might mention to someone that I spoke to one of Drigo's women."

Her suggestion annoyed him. Eskkar knew Trella had gone to the river and a guard had accompanied her. But he would never have thought of what that guard might do or say in his off-duty hours. He raised his voice and called after the already moving guard. "Bring Adad back with you! I want him guarding my quarters tonight."

He closed the door so hard it shook, then stepped over to the hook where his sword hung. He belted it around his

waist. The gesture might look foolish, but he felt better with
the sword at his hip. The room seemed to close in around
him, the air close and stale. He had to get out. "It's almost
dark, Trella. Stay inside for the rest of the night."

"Where are you going?"

"Nowhere. I need to think by myself for a moment." In
truth he felt himself coming under her influence, doing what
she wished instead of making his own decisions. He jerked
the door open and went outside.

He walked over to the tree, then leaned against it. The
scent of roasting chickens hung in the air, floating in from
the street.

Eskkar had lost his appetite. He'd wanted to walk with
Trella into the village tonight, showing her off to everyone,
then stopping at one of the inns for wine and dinner. His
hand clenched the sword hilt in frustration.

Now he'd stay here, afraid to leave his room, worried
about a knife in his back. He didn't fear any of Drigo's hired
bullies. Not alone. But three or four together could bring
down any man. The urge to leave Orak swept over him. Take
Trella and go. There was plenty of Nicar's gold left. In moments he could be on a horse. The guards at the gate would
open it for him, one way or another.

Eskkar swore a string of oaths at Nicar, the nobles, Ariamus, and especially the villagers who'd distrusted and hated
him behind his back for years, and who now wanted him to
save their cowardly lives and miserable property. He de-
spised them as much as they feared him. To them he was
just an outcast, a tame barbarian, but one who would still
turn on them if given a chance.

He should go, leave Orak. Nothing good would come of
staying, trying to fight the Alur Meriki, gambling his life on
the will of these dirt-eaters. He'd take Trella and . . . she
didn't want to go. She hadn't answered when he'd spoken
about leaving. There'd be nothing for her, a noble-born girl,
accompanying a soldier selling his sword. He didn't even
know if she could ride. Few enough women knew how to
handle a horse. He swore again. And he couldn't leave her,
not after last night.

The guard returned, accompanied by an annoyed Adad, interrupted at his supper. The two men slowed when they saw their captain under the tree. He stepped toward them, his hand on the sword hilt.

"Stay together and stay alert. Don't leave your post for any reason. Call out if you see anything suspicious. There may be trouble tonight. I'll have more men join you later."

He brushed past, ignoring their questioning looks, and went inside. In the darkening room, he could just make out Trella sitting at the table. Without food, she had nothing to do.

Eskkar closed the door, went over to the fireplace, and began building a fire. The task gave him something to occupy his hands while he kept thinking. Finally he got the fire going and added more wood than necessary. He carried a burning stick back to the table and lit the new lamp she'd purchased.

Trella hadn't said anything. When the lamp added its light to the firelight, he turned toward her. "Can you ride a horse?"

"No, master. But I'm sure I can learn."

She kept her voice even, but he heard the disappointment. She knew what the question implied. Eskkar felt disappointed, too, but for a different reason. He'd taught enough dirt-eaters how to ride. Even for an apt pupil with strong hands, it took at least a week to stiffen thigh and leg muscles properly, maybe longer. Assuming that Trella didn't fall off and break something. Still, she could always walk while she learned.

A knock sounded on the door as Gatus pushed it open and stepped inside. "What's going on? Why . . ." he saw the sword on Eskkar's hip.

"Shut the door," Eskkar said. "We need to talk."

Gatus sat down, his eyes moved from Eskkar to Trella and back. He'd seen the extra sentry standing guard outside. "What's happened?"

"Nothing yet. Trella overheard something at the river. Drigo's men may try something, maybe to beat or kill me. It seems Noble Drigo is unhappy with Nicar's choice for captain of the guard, and doesn't want to wait for tomorrow's meeting." Eskkar turned to Trella. "Tell him everything."

She related what she'd learned at the river and added her ideas of what Drigo meant to do.

Gatus sat there, chewing on his lip, taking his time while he thought. He turned toward Eskkar. "What will you do? I don't plan on taking orders from that fool Naxos or even Drigo, not that they'd want me around. Maybe it's time to forget all this silly talk and leave Orak."

Moments ago, that would have been what Eskkar wanted to hear. But he'd watched Trella as she related the story. He knew she wanted to stay, wanted him to stay, though she hadn't said it. Suddenly he didn't want to disappoint her, didn't want to admit that he couldn't meet Drigo's challenge.

"No, Gatus. I'm going to stay and fight." The words came out almost without thinking. "I won't let Drigo's bullies chase me off, not as long as Nicar wants me for captain of the guard. That is, if you'll stay with me."

Eskkar hated to ask any man for help, but he had no choice. "I'm not sure which of the men we can trust. You've lived here for years and know them better than anyone, certainly better than me."

"Most of 'em hate those guards," Gatus said, scratching his beard, "but there might be a few fools eager to earn Drigo's silver." He took a breath. "But there won't be more than three or four. If they try something, when will it be?"

"It has to be tonight, Gatus, or tomorrow at Nicar's house. Either before the meeting or after it, I'd guess." He turned to Trella. "What do you think?" Those words surprised him, too. He was treating her as an equal partner in the planning.

"Master, if anyone attacks you after Nicar has confirmed you captain of the guard, it will be taken as a challenge to Nicar. The other nobles won't like such a thing. But if Drigo can humiliate you before the meeting, then the nobles will not be eager to give you their trust, no matter who's at fault, not with their lives and property at stake."

"Well, that seems simple enough," Gatus said. "We just take all the men to Nicar's, and if anyone gets in our way . . ."

"The nobles might take that as a threat, Gatus, showing up at Nicar's house with thirty armed men."

Trella had voiced her opinion unasked, but by now neither Eskkar nor Gatus cared that a slave girl was giving them advice. She went on before they could say anything. "And there must not be bloodshed, nothing to make the nobles think they'll be risking their lives at your hands."

Eskkar tightened his fist on the table, but restrained the impulse to smash it down again. He'd faced death in battle often enough, but Drigo had more than enough gold to hire a dozen men willing to take their chances. The thought that a pack of curs would be at his throat sent a wave of anger through him, though he kept his voice calm. "Blood will flow, Trella. Unless we leave."

"Blood in the streets will not give the nobles confidence in you, master. Can't you find another way?"

"Damn the gods." This time it was Gatus who pounded the table with his fist. "My wife was happy to hear we were staying, even if it meant a fight with the barbarians. If I leave now . . . if we leave with you, Eskkar, there'll be women, children, carts, animals, a regular little caravan. I'd hoped we could stay."

So he had three choices, Eskkar thought. Leave alone with Trella, lead a group of soldiers with their wives and children, or stay and fight both the nobles and the barbarians. Well, the time for prudence had passed. He couldn't admit to being worried in front of Trella and Gatus, and he wouldn't take back his words. "We're staying, Gatus, if you will."

Gatus snorted. "Put it on my shoulders, will you? I'm too old to go wandering about the countryside, not while there's a chance to stay here."

"Then we'll fight," Eskkar said. "We just need to have Nicar confirm me as captain of the guard. After that, we can take care of Drigo."

Eskkar felt better now that he'd decided. "Gatus, make sure no one leaves the barracks tonight, and keep a dozen men awake and ready."

"Yes, Captain." Gatus stood and gave Trella a grin. "You've earned your keep already, girl. You may have saved my head as well as your master's from being broken. Try to keep him out of trouble for the rest of the night." He turned to Eskkar. "Will you still meet with the men tomorrow?"

"Yes, right before Nicar's meeting, as we planned."

"And what are you going to do tomorrow?"

"I'll think of something before then," Eskkar said.

He walked Gatus outside, watching the old soldier disappear into the darkness. Eskkar leaned against the house, thinking about what the last few hours had brought. For the last fifteen years, he'd been on his own, making his own decisions and living with the consequences. He'd survived, thanks to his fighting skills, but there wasn't much more that he could add to that accomplishment.

Now he was listening to a girl, someone trained to look beyond the obvious, to see what he would likely have missed. More than listening, he and Gatus were starting to rely on her. Eskkar had never given heed to any woman's advice before, and now he was seeking it out. Part of him wanted to ignore her words, to make his own decisions, even mistakes, if it came to that.

That would be foolish, he knew. More than that, it might get him killed. He hadn't survived this long by ignoring the truth. Realistically, if Trella hadn't put the pieces together, he would probably have walked unaware into whatever Drigo's men had planned for tomorrow.

So he might even owe her his life. Eskkar didn't like admitting such a debt, but no warrior could ignore such an obligation. Between her and Nicar, his life had changed. Nicar's summons had offered him a future. Now Trella's advice might offer even more. At the very least he owed her the chance to help. He still wanted her, wanted her even more every hour, and if keeping her with him meant having to swallow his pride and accept her advice, then he would do it. She'd saved his life once. Maybe she could do it again. After all, things couldn't get much worse. Perhaps the time had come to try a different way.

Eskkar took one last look at the guards, then went back inside, closing and securing the door behind him. She still sat there, outlined by the remnants of the fire, waiting. Waiting for him to decide not only his fate, but hers.

Nothing mattered, he realized. He needed to be with her, keep her for his own. Everything else meant nothing, including his foolish pride.

"We will think of something, won't we?"

Trella awoke before dawn, slipped out of bed and dressed. The night had passed uneventfully. Eskkar sent out for a roasted chicken, bread, nuts, and wine, and they'd eaten the dinner with the door closed. The fresh chicken had been well cooked, though neither noticed it. She'd filled his wine cup but refused any herself. When he drank half the cup, she watched as he refilled it with water, leaving the rest of the wine untouched. She hadn't said anything, but felt grateful her master knew better than to drink too much on such a night.

Gatus came back twice, once to report everything in order and men in place, and the second time to grab a hunk of chicken and tell Eskkar to get some sleep. Before retiring, Eskkar blocked the entrance with the table and benches, and he'd placed his sword and knife next to the bed.

In the darkness he held her in his arms, but didn't speak, and she knew he was thinking about tomorrow. To her surprise, Eskkar soon came up with a plan for handling the guards. Dangerous to be sure, but perhaps a way to avoid bloodshed.

When nothing more remained to discuss, Trella moved astride him, feeling a thrill at her boldness. She kissed him again and again, then leaned down and rubbed herself against him, moving her breasts slowly over his chest and stomach, then to his lips and back again. Suddenly she felt him inside her, heard herself moaning at the wave of pleasure. She kept her movements slow, enjoying the new sensations that passed through her, holding him back until he cried out, both of them forgetting all about the world outside.

When the lovemaking ended, he'd fallen asleep almost at once, a deep sleep that permitted no worries to interrupt it. She slept lightly, waking often, waiting for the dawn. Today she wanted to be at the river early.

At the first sign of daylight, she woke Eskkar and they opened the door. Nothing greeted them except two tired guards standing at their post. Moments later Gatus arrived, yawning and carrying a long wooden trencher filled with bread and cheese, breakfast for all of them, including the men who'd watched Eskkar's door all night. Afterward, Trella went with Gatus into the barracks and offered to clean some of the soldiers' garments.

They filled a basket with as much as she could carry. She'd hoped Adad would accompany her back to the river, but he'd already gone to get some sleep, tired after his all-night vigil, so Gatus chose another man to accompany her.

At that early hour, only a few women had come to wash their household's clothes, but more would arrive soon. The women recognized her immediately. They gathered around while she worked, introducing themselves, eager to hear the latest gossip from someone who might actually know something.

Trella reassured them, but kept busy with her washing. Eventually they took the hint and moved away. Trella found herself washing the same tunic over and over before she saw Shubure approaching.

Unnoticed now, Trella moved farther downriver, wading out into deeper water that reached nearly to her waist. Even so, Shubure did not come near until her own washing was well begun. This time Trella's eyes studied the shore and the other women, but no one was paying any attention to them, only the bored guard whose gaze wandered up and down the river.

As Shubure drew near, Trella let the tunic slip from her hands. The current took it straight to Shubure, who caught it up, then handed it back to Trella. As their hands touched, Trella let three copper coins slip into the girl's hand. Shubure's eyes looked down for a moment. Then she turned slightly away, searching those along the river bank.

"Your master meets with Nicar at midmorn. Drigo has ordered Naxos to keep Eskkar from Nicar's house. They want to embarrass him and Nicar before the meeting, in front of the other nobles. If he resists, Naxos will kill him. Naxos will be the new captain of the guard."

So it would happen this morning. Trella turned away, so no one could see them talking. "Did you learn anything else?"

"No, nothing. Except Drigo said he will rule in Orak within a few days. He and his son are already making plans. They expect to gather much gold before the barbarians arrive."

"I thank you for your news, Shubure."

"My mother and I thank you for your coins, Mistress Trella. She'll be able to feed our family for a few days."

"If your mother can be trusted to keep her tongue, I'll send more coins to her. If you learn anything more, you tell her and she can tell me." It would certainly be easier and safer for Shubure to meet with her mother.

Shubure nodded. She moved away as new arrivals splashed closer to them, eager to speak with Trella. But Trella gathered up the wet clothes and waded carefully back to the shore. She lifted the heavy bundle in her arms, the wet dress clinging to her legs, as she walked back toward the gate. The guard followed, no doubt watching her figure.

She found Eskkar waiting for her outside the barracks. He followed her inside and closed the door.

"Did she come?"

"Yes." She repeated what Shubure had said. Surprisingly, the news seemed to calm him. He went to the table and sat down, his brow furrowed. She spread the wet garments across the bed, then sat down across from him. "Will you keep to your plan, master?"

He looked up, his face grim. "Oh, yes. I'll take care of Naxos."

She knew what he meant. "If you kill Drigo's servant, he'll hire someone else to murder you. He won't tolerate the insult. And the nobles . . ."

"If Naxos's death is too bloody for them, Trella, then we'll move on. I won't spend my days wondering when Drigo's assassin will find me."

Trella studied him carefully. Not a hint of worry in the man. He seemed relaxed and assured, no trace of last night's doubts. She realized how different he was from the merchants and traders she'd grown up with. A warrior, he needed only to know what to do. He would work out the how, and once begun, he would be like an arrow launched from a bowstring—no hesitation and no turning back.

"Is there anything I can do to help?"

He smiled at her, a real smile full of warmth and caring. "Perhaps. I've been thinking about the meeting. I still need to talk to the men. But I think I will need your help."

She smiled back and reached her hand out to his across the table. "Tell me what to do."

5

In two hours, I meet with Nicar and the Five Families," Eskkar began, speaking to Gatus and the three men he'd selected as subcommanders. They sat shoulder to shoulder at the small table in Eskkar's quarters. Gatus sat next to Eskkar. Bantor, Jalen, and Sisuthros faced their new captain across the table. A water jar and cups rested between them.

Bantor, a reliable man who could follow orders, was a little older than Eskkar. Jalen, about five years younger, had come to Orak from the west. An excellent fighter and one of the few good horsemen in Orak, Jalen had quarreled with Ariamus and his toadies even more than Eskkar. Sisuthros had just reached his twentieth season, but had sharp wits to match his skill with a sword.

Except for Gatus, none had commanded any significant number of men before. Ariamus had kept them in the ranks, promoting his favorites who followed his orders without thinking. Eskkar had marked these three as men of courage and ability who could be relied on. Most of all, they'd dared to disagree with Ariamus.

"There'll be much arguing at Nicar's meeting, but most of the nobles will decide to stay and fight. Afterward, Nicar will go to the marketplace and speak to the people, as will I. You and the men will be there, to keep order. Follow my lead, and help sway the villagers. If any in the crowd get out of control, don't be afraid to break a few heads. There will be plenty of blood shed before this is over, so we might as well start today."

Esskar studied them. They seemed steady enough. "Bantor, you'll take charge of the gates. Assign three men to each. No one leaves the village without permission from Nicar or me. No one—and that includes any of the Five Families."

Their faces showed disbelief, their doubts clearly visible. Breaking a few heads—that they could understand. But standing up to the Five Families and their armed guards clearly involved more danger.

Esskar saw the question on the man's face. "We cannot have men leave the village and take with them anything or any slave we'll need to defend it," he explained. "So if a man wants to leave and take, say, a craftsman or builder slave with him, we must not allow that. Our lives may depend on such men."

"What about those going out to the fields?" Bantor cocked his head.

Better to question than not, Esskar knew. "I don't mean those just going for the day, Bantor, only those planning to leave the village permanently and taking their goods with them. If any want to leave on their own, fine. But no men of property, taking either slaves or tools or baggage, leaves without our approval."

"Noble Drigo's men are in the streets and in the market, talking to everyone," Bantor offered. "They're acting as if they already rule the village. Some are saying Drigo will take command of Orak and the soldiers."

"Well, I have a surprise for Noble Drigo," Esskar said, thanking the gods for Trella's warning, "but we'll talk of that later."

"Men won't want to give up their slaves, Esskar," Gatus remarked. "They'll make trouble if you try to stop them."

Esskar nodded. "If they have something we want, we'll pay them for it, be it slave or tool or weapon. Nicar and the Families will pay them, that is."

The men exchanged glances but said nothing. He ignored

the looks. He needed them to believe in him, at least until after today, when they'd see for themselves how events played out.

"Starting tomorrow, we begin recruiting and training. In the next few months, hundreds of people will be pouring into the village, fleeing the barbarians. We must be ready to arm and train them."

"You can't train men to fight barbarians, not in a few months," Jalen objected, his voice rising in protest.

"We're not going to go out and fight them man-to-man. Instead, we'll battle them from the wall we build around the village. We will fight them with archers. Any man can bend a bow. Gatus and I have discussed this and it can be done." Eskkar turned toward Gatus, who nodded agreement.

"I've always wanted to train a large group of men to fight as one," Gatus said. "Now I'll have my chance."

The old soldier had many strange ideas about how to train men, and nothing gave him more pleasure than sweating recruits into shape.

"They'll surround us and rush the village from all sides," Jalen insisted. "Even bowmen cannot stop that kind of attack."

"Not so fast, Jalen." Eskkar gave a short laugh. "We'll make sure they can come at us in force from only one direction, against our strongest point. We'll wait behind our wall, wait until they run out of food, wait until they must move on. We don't have to defeat them or drive them off. We just have to make them grow tired of attacking us. I know we can do that."

Eskkar rapped his cup on the table. "And every time they attack our wall, we'll slaughter them. We'll force them from their horses and kill them with arrows." He saw the skepticism in their faces. They'd seen action against barbarians at one time or another. They knew how tough they were.

"You know once a man is off his horse," Eskkar went on, "he's easy to kill, and barbarians are even easier. From childhood, they fight from their horses. Their swords and lances are meant to strike from the horse, their bows to fire while racing at the enemy. Once dismounted, they'll be poor fighters and easy targets for archers standing behind a wall."

"The barbarians are archers, too, Eskkar." Sisuthros had encountered the barbarians before and still carried the scar. "They can shoot our men off the walls just as easily."

"Perhaps not as easily as you think, Sisuthros, but I'm glad all of you are thinking of these things. Barbarians use short, curved bows. We'll use hunting bows, longer and more powerful, with a heavier arrow. We'll start killing them before they can get into range, and the wall will protect our men from their arrows."

"You really think a wall can stop them, Captain?" Sisuthros asked.

"Yes. They've never faced one before, a wall full of well-armed and well-trained men."

Gatus pulled at his beard. "Can a wall strong enough and high enough be built in time? I mean, how high must it be?"

Eskkar shrugged. "Now you're ahead of me. That's one of the things I need to find out, and it will take several days of working with the artisans and builders. That's why none of them can be allowed to leave."

He looked at each of them in turn. "The hardest part of this battle against the barbarians is going to happen in the next few hours," he said, glancing at the window. He didn't have much time.

"If the Five Families accept our plan, the village can be held. That's why it's important that you all be in the market and that you follow my lead. Nicar and I will sway the Five Families. You must help us convince the crowd."

"You're asking us to risk our lives, Eskkar, as well as our families," Sisuthros said. "If we stay and fight . . . if we fail . . ."

"Nicar and I will risk as much. Or would you rather take your families and start roaming the countryside, looking for a safe place to live? When we drive the barbarians off, your places here will be secure. Besides, I've doubled your pay. That should stiffen your backbones. When the barbarians are driven off, you'll each receive twenty gold coins, plus a double share of any loot taken from the barbarians."

The mention of gold had the desired effect.

"But that's not enough to keep men fighting. I've fought them many times, and even when I've killed them, I've always had to give ground. I'm tired of giving way to them, and I'm tired of being told what great fighters they are. It's time to make them afraid of us."

Eskkar's words hung in the air for a long moment before Jalen spoke up. "I have not spoken to anyone of this, but seven years ago, barbarians overran my village, murdered my father, and took my mother and sister as slaves. I've killed many of them since, and I want only the opportunity to kill more. I'll follow your orders, Eskkar, as long as you stand and fight them. I'm not afraid of them, even on their horses."

Eskkar nodded, understanding the man's pain. The village held many more like him. And now he knew why Jalen had often looked at him with anger in his eyes, seeing only a man from a barbarian clan, not the soldier Eskkar had become.

"We're all fighting men, and our fight against the barbarians begins today. The first step will be to stop Drigo from taking control of Orak. Even with Nicar's backing, I expect we'll see some blood spilled before dark. What I'm asking won't be easy. It will likely be the most danger you've ever faced. But if we win, the rewards will be great. So I ask you: will you follow me down this road, to win gold for ourselves and to save Orak? Or must I look to other men to join me?"

One by one, they looked at each other, and slowly nodded assent.

Eskkar smiled in satisfaction. He'd gotten them this far. Now he'd find out just how much they were willing to risk. He glanced up at the sun. "Good. Now there's one more thing we have to plan, and cursed little time to do it."

The crowds thronged the narrow lanes. Eskkar had never seen so many in the marketplace. Every man wanted to stop and question him as he pushed through on the way to Nicar's house. Gatus, Sisuthros, Adad, and two others accompanied Eskkar. Dressed in his new tunic and sandals, Eskkar moved confidently, taking long, purposeful strides that parted the crowd ahead of him. His short sword hung from his belt, freshly oiled to stay loose in its scabbard.

Behind him walked Trella, head properly downcast, wearing her new dress. The garment hadn't been woven from the fancy cloth worn by rich merchants or wealthy farmers, but it fitted her new station and looked much better than the cast-off garment she'd worn as Nicar's slave. Eskkar hadn't thought to tell her what to buy or how much to spend, but it didn't surprise him that she had sense enough to buy something practical.

Turning into the lane where Nicar lived, Eskkar found what he'd been told to expect. Almost twenty men lounged about, the hired bodyguards of the Families. Using the authority of their masters, they lorded it over both the villagers and the soldiers for at least as long as Eskkar had lived in Orak. When they saw him approach, most of them straightened up and a rough line formed across the lane, a dozen paces from Nicar's gate. Most of those blocking the way wore Drigo's emblem on their tunics.

Naxos, Noble Drigo's chief bodyguard, had broad shoulders and a coarse red beard that failed to cover a poxed face and a missing tooth. He stood in the center of the lane, directly in Eskkar's path.

"The meeting of the Five Families is closed to soldiers," Naxos said in a loud voice, as Eskkar's party approached, making sure everyone heard his authority. Naxos hooked his thumbs on the thick leather of his sword belt.

"I've been summoned by Nicar," Eskkar answered reasonably, stopping about five paces from the line. "Am I forbidden to enter as well?"

Naxos, one of the few men in the village as tall as Eskkar, stared him in the eyes and took his time before replying. "You may enter," he answered, still speaking in a forceful tone that carried the length of the lane, as if deciding the matter himself, "but the rest of your men must return to their shit-hole of a barracks. There's no need for play soldiers here."

So they wanted him alone. No doubt Drigo didn't want too much bloodshed either. Then they'd jump him as he passed through their line. Eskkar mentally thanked the man for his offensive words. Nothing could have provoked his men or stiffened their resolve more. They'd all been bullied and ridiculed by Naxos and the other guards. Eskkar looked at the men standing boldly beside Naxos, hands on their swords, smiles on their faces, confident in their authority. Eskkar could hear the crowd behind him begin to melt away.

"My men go where I tell them, Naxos," Eskkar said firmly. "Stand aside and let us pass."

Naxos's laugh boomed across the alleyway. "You're a pig of a barbarian, Eskkar, and should have been taught a lesson long ago. I'll have your head on a plate if your men aren't on their way."

The man standing next to Naxos, burly and young, drew his sword, eyes wide with excitement. "Let me kill him for you, Naxos," he said eagerly.

Eskkar didn't reply. Instead, he slowly raised his left hand above his shoulder, palm outward, as if to appease the man. But instead of saying anything, Eskkar simply pointed his finger at the troublemaker. There was a hiss in the air and a soft thud, and the man looked down to see a long arrow buried in the center of his chest.

No one moved as the dying man first gasped a long breath, then looked up, the sword slipping from his hand and falling to the ground. Then he was on his knees, pitching facedown into the dust. Nobody moved. All of Naxos's men looked up, open-mouthed, at the rooftops along the alleyway where ten archers rose up, five on each side of the street. Jalen commanded them and they stood ready, bows drawn to the nock, targets selected, waiting for Eskkar's next signal.

The rest of the bodyguards made no movement, their eyes locked on the archers, as Gatus shouted an order. Bantor and a half-dozen men, raced up to stand on either side of Eskkar and Gatus. They carried shields and drawn swords as they quickly fanned out in a line, facing Naxos and his men.

The bodyguards' bravado had changed to fear in an instant, and now they were paralyzed with indecision. No one attempted to draw a weapon, and most took their hands off their hilts. A few, especially those serving the other nobles, stepped back a little, as if to distance themselves from Naxos and Drigo's men.

Eskkar calmly drew his sword, but kept the tip pointing toward the ground as he crossed the five paces that separated him from Naxos. The man's eyes stared up at the roof, looking at the three men aiming arrows at his chest. He didn't even react when Eskkar raised the blade and held it against his stomach. Instead, Naxos looked down at the sword as if he'd never seen such a weapon before.

"All of you men," Eskkar called out, "don't move. Throw down your weapons. Anyone who draws a sword dies here in the dirt." Nothing happened. The guards seemed rooted to the ground. Most of them still stared at the archers above them.

"Now!" Eskkar barked the command savagely. His voice broke the spell, and in a moment the dull sound of weapons striking the dirt was heard.

Eskkar looked into Naxos's eyes and saw fear replace the shock of seeing the line of bowmen. Eskkar gave him no more time, either to speak or to act, thrusting the sword deep into the man's belly. A grunt of pain and astonishment escaped from Naxos's lips even as he tried to grasp the blade that pierced him. Viciously, Eskkar turned the blade, wrenching another groan from Naxos's open mouth, then jerked it from his body.

Blood spurted everywhere, escaping through the man's hands as he tried to cover the fatal wound, sagging to his knees as his legs gave way, then falling hard on his back, one leg under him, the other twitching in the dust. Naxos tried to speak, but couldn't get the words out. Even before he died, Eskkar's men had moved, closing to within striking distance of the guards.

Stooping down, Eskkar wiped his sword on the dying man's tunic, ignoring his death sounds and twitches. Eskkar even changed hands and cleaned his right hand and arm, both spattered with the blood gushing from the man's stomach. None of Naxos's men moved or said a word.

Eskkar returned his blade to its scabbard. Turning his

back on the cowed guards, Eskkar faced the frightened villagers who'd hung back behind him, hoping to see some excitement. They, too, stood rooted in place and stunned into silence.

"I do not like to be called a barbarian," Eskkar said, his voice carrying down the lane. "Nor do my men like to hear their commander so addressed."

He turned to Gatus. "Gather their weapons and keep them quiet." Trella had stopped a few paces behind Gatus and his men. Eskkar called her name, and she followed him as he pushed past the still-shocked bodyguards. They walked through the open gate and entered the spacious garden that separated Nicar's house from the street.

The door stood slightly ajar and unattended, and they entered without knocking. Once inside, Eskkar realized that no one was aware of what had happened in the lane outside. The house servants, busy waiting on Nicar's guests, had no time for events in the always noisy lane.

Trella held his arm for a moment, took a scrap of cloth from her pocket, moistened it in her mouth, and wiped a drop of blood from his cheek and another from his arm. She examined him carefully for any other blood traces. Her face looked pale and her hands shook a little, but her eyes showed no panic. He guessed she had never seen men die like that.

"Killing people is never pretty," he kept his words low, so only she could hear. "If I hadn't killed him, he'd have challenged my authority every day." He touched her arm for a moment. "Can you still face what may come inside?"

She nodded.

They turned at the sound of footsteps to find Creta coming toward them.

"Good day, Eskkar," she glanced at Trella, then stared more closely, noting her new dress. "Come this way, they're waiting for you. You're already late."

"Good day, Creta," Eskkar answered, nodding his head. "We'll follow you."

Creta stopped abruptly, and Eskkar spoke before she could protest. "Nicar said I should use Trella to assist me, and I need her with me." He kept his voice firm and hard.

Without a word, Creta turned and led them to the same room where he'd dined with Nicar. She knocked once, then opened the door. Eskkar and Trella moved past her, and she shut the door behind them.

Today the room looked different, set up for business rather than dinner. Gone were the soft chairs and cushions used for dining. Another table had been brought from somewhere and joined to the one Nicar and Eskkar had eaten from last evening, forming a large expanse of wood that nearly filled the room. The scent of wine hung in the air, noticeable even over the thick spray of jasmine in the far corner of the room, set there to mask the odors of so many men in such a confined space.

Ten men sat around the table: the leaders of the Five Families, each accompanied by an eldest son or a trusted advisor. Nicar sat at the head of the table, with Nobles Rebba and Decca to his right. The two cousins owned several shops and many of the boats that plied the river. Drigo and Nestor took the other side. Nestor owned most of the large farms surrounding the village.

One empty stool at the foot of the table remained and Eskkar crossed to it, and bowed low to the assembly. His doubts had vanished. The killings in the lane committed him fully, and he could not turn aside. He had to leave this room as captain of the guard. Otherwise he'd be lucky to get out of Orak with his skin intact. Drigo would certainly put a price on his head for killing Naxos. Eskkar realized he had one, although temporary, advantage—no one in the room knew what had happened outside, that their guards had been disarmed and now sat in the dirt under the soldiers' control.

"Noble Nicar, I come at your request." He looked at the other men, and noted the brief look of surprise on Drigo's face. "Greetings to you all."

Trella had stressed that he be polite at all times and keep his temper in check, no matter what provocation or disagreement might arise.

"Your slave does not belong here," Drigo said, though the meeting was supposedly under Nicar's control. "This is the meeting of the Five Families, and we follow our customs. Women and slaves are not permitted."

Drigo had recovered quickly from his surprise. Strange, Eskkar thought, yesterday he would have been in awe of the noble's authority. Now he was merely an obstacle to be overcome.

"Nobles, I'm a simple soldier. I have no training or memory to speak with you. My slave is here to remember what we discuss, so that I don't forget anything of importance."

"My father told you to send the slave away." These words came from Drigo the Younger. A few years ago, as a young bully, he had terrorized the weaker children with his fists. Now he'd reached manhood and considered himself a leader of men. Taller and broader than his father, he had nineteen seasons. Three men who had offended him died mysteriously, murdered in the night. At least two others had died by young Drigo's own hand.

His words brought stern glances from the other leaders, and Eskkar guessed only the elders could speak freely.

"She stays with me," Eskkar answered firmly. "Or I can go if you wish."

The first test of wills, even as Trella had foretold. One of the leaders looked to Drigo, the other two glanced at Nicar. Eskkar stood there at ease, his hands relaxed at his sides. Trella remained two paces behind him, eyes down.

"And where would you go, Eskkar," countered Drigo, ignoring his son's comments. "Back to the barbarians from whence you came? Perhaps we should send you to them."

"Today the wind blows in many directions, Noble Drigo," Eskkar answered. "But I thought the Families wished to defend Orak. If that's not true, merely say so, and I'll leave you to your business. Fighting men can always find work in these troubled times."

"You're an impudent dog," snarled Drigo the Younger. "I've a mind to have you thrown out into the street."

This time the reaction came from Nicar. "Drigo, your son speaks out of turn. If he cannot restrain his tongue, perhaps it would be best if he left the room." Nicar glanced around the table, and the others nodded their agreement.

"My son will keep silent," Drigo responded, "but I will not. We don't need this 'soldier.' We cannot resist the barbarians in any case."

Several members of the Families began speaking, but Eskkar's voice sounded clearly over theirs. "Nobles, if you don't wish to fight, then your village will be destroyed. The barbarians will tear your houses down to the ground and burn everything they don't toss into the river. Or you can resist them, drive them off, and save your village. The choice is yours, and you must make it today."

His words silenced them momentarily. Eskkar looked around the table and saw doubt in their eyes, mixed with confusion at the boldness of a man they'd thought of only as a common soldier. He went on before they could say anything.

"Whatever you choose, the people are waiting to hear your words. I told them you would speak to them today. So you'll have to decide now. If you tell them the nobles are not going to resist, many will begin to leave. Once gone, they won't come back. And so you'll all have to leave, taking what you can carry, crossing the river, and hoping to avoid the barbarians."

"You had no right to speak to the people," Noble Rebba said, speaking for the first time. "Only the Families can speak for Orak." Noble Decca nodded in agreement.

"The villagers know the barbarians are coming," Eskkar answered, keeping temper and voice under control. "They know Ariamus took men and horses as well as all he could carry before he fled. They know that I'm meeting with you now. If you don't say something today, many more will go, including myself and the rest of the soldiers. No one will stay here guarding your wealth until it's too late to escape. So Orak will fall in a few weeks, months before the barbarians arrive. When you leave here, I think you'll find that many things have changed."

He looked at Nicar for a moment. "As I said, if you don't want me to defend the village, say so, and I'll be gone. I don't need to risk my life defending Orak."

"Nothing can stop the barbarians, Eskkar," answered

Nestor, the oldest member of the Families. Nestor had lived in and around Orak even longer than Nicar. Nestor resided in one of the large farms that ringed the village. "You should know that, more than any of us."

"Noble Nestor, I believe they can be stopped, and that I know how to stop them. As I discussed with Nicar, it can be done. But it's only possible if we start now, and only if everyone puts their hearts and backs into it. The villagers must believe Orak can resist, or they'll leave."

"We don't need the villagers," Drigo answered easily. "We rule here, and we decide what is to become of Orak."

"You may rule here, but the people of the village give you power," Eskkar countered. "Without the craftsman, the baker, the winemaker, the tavern keeper, even the farmers in the fields, what will you do? Make your own bread, plant crops yourself, rule over your own family?"

"There are other villages," Drigo said, sure of himself, still speaking down to Eskkar.

"Yes, and they have their own rulers," Eskkar said, recalling Trella's words. "You'd have to buy your way into them. Perhaps you would not find yourself a noble in your new village."

"We can start our own village," said Drigo the Younger, ignoring the admonishment to keep silent. "We don't need the villagers here for that."

Eskkar laughed. "Yes, ruler of a dung heap of fifty or a hundred people. Here is the river, fertile soil, trade with the other villages, hundreds of tradesmen, and crafts of many kinds. Where else can you find all that?"

"Keep silent, my son," the elder Drigo said, glancing at his heir. "But my son's words have truth in them. We can return here after the barbarians have gone."

"True, you can start over again," Eskkar replied, mentally thanking Trella for her foresight. So far they had said nothing she hadn't anticipated.

"Of course, the barbarians will return again in another five or ten years. Or perhaps other strangers may come, and maybe they will be interested in being rulers of a new Orak." Eskkar looked at Nicar and saw him leaning back in his chair, at ease, clearly enjoying the debate as he gauged the faces of the other leaders.

"But I don't want to waste your time, Nobles," Eskkar went on. "And I don't think it is my place to explain to you the value of a village the size of Orak." He stumbled a little with the words, trying to get the sense that Trella had voiced. But they didn't seem to notice his lapse.

"Perhaps we should ask Eskkar to tell us how he plans to stop the barbarians," Nicar said quietly. He waited a moment, but no one spoke. "Please sit, Eskkar. Would you care for some wine?"

Eskkar sat down, mindful of the sword at his waist that no one seemed to have noticed. "Water, Noble Nicar. My slave will fetch it." He nodded to Trella. She went to the water jug standing on a side table and filled a cup, then placed it in front of him.

"Wine for me, slave," sneered Drigo the Younger, sliding his cup hard across the table toward Trella. She caught it deftly before it could fall over the edge.

She looked at Eskkar, her face expressionless, and he nodded. "Wine for Master Drigo," Eskkar repeated, even as he decided he would kill the young fool for the insult. Some hint of his thoughts must have crept into his voice, because all eyes turned toward him, including those of the elder Drigo, as if they sensed something beneath his words.

"No, no more wine for my son," Drigo said, his tone somewhat more cautious. "We're finished here. The rest of you can waste your time talking about stopping the barbarians, but in the end, you'll all be leaving the village." He stood up, his son joining him. "I have more important things to attend to."

Eskkar smiled tolerantly at Drigo's son, even as he saw the dagger under the young man's tunic when he stood.

No one else left their seats. Father and son started for the door, but the youngest couldn't resist the urge to speak one more time. He stopped a few steps from Eskkar. "And barbarian, you'd better watch your tongue, or you'll find it gone from your head."

Trella's musical laugh surprised everyone, including Eskkar, and stopped all talk. Everyone's eyes turned toward her.

All except Eskkar, who kept his eyes on young Drigo's hands.

"My apologies, Nobles, my tongue betrayed me," Trella said contritely, but the laughter remained in her voice and her eyes.

"What's so funny, slave?" A crease appeared in the elder Drigo's brow, as if he'd missed something important.

"Nothing, Noble Drigo," she answered humbly enough, "except that the last man to call my master a barbarian is dead."

"We care not if he slits some pig farmer's throat," spoke young Drigo, his temper matching the flush rising on his face.

The girl's laugh had pushed the boy past his senses. Young Drigo wasn't used to being laughed at in public, and by a slave at that.

"No, young Master Drigo, it was not some peasant," Trella responded, her voice steady and with just the tiniest hint of insolence needed to further fan the flame of anger. "It was Naxos, and one of his men, who lie dead in the street outside." The smile stayed on her face as she looked at the boy.

Every eye turned to Eskkar, who picked at a fingernail, still keeping an eye on young Drigo. The youth's hand moved toward his tunic, inches from the dagger.

"Is this true?" Nicar asked, unable to keep the indignation and anger out of his voice.

"Yes, it's true," Eskkar replied, leaning against the table with his left arm as he turned sideways on the stool to face Nicar. "Drigo's man tried to keep me from your house. Naxos also said my slave wasn't permitted to enter. He called me a barbarian, then he and another tried to attack me."

Not quite true, but close enough. Eskkar waited a moment before he went on, shifting his body even further so that his sword was pinned against the table as he turned to face the elder Drigo, his right side now turned toward the younger man.

"But don't worry, Noble Drigo. I spared the rest of your guards. You'll find them outside, and they'll be much more polite to my men in the future." From his new position, Eskkar glanced back at Drigo the Younger, saw his face had flushed an even deeper red, and smiled at him, the way a man smiles at a small child.

With a cry of rage, the youth snatched the dagger from his tunic and lunged toward Eskkar, certain he could strike before Eskkar could stand or free his sword. But instead of trying to rise up and meet the thrust, Eskkar shifted more of his weight to the heavy table and lashed out with his leg. His sandal caught the boy squarely in the chest, the knife point stopping inches from Eskkar's body before the kick sent the boy reeling back into the wall, staggering him for a moment, but long enough, as Eskkar sprang from the stool, the sword flashing from its scabbard and crossing over his body before thrusting home in the boy's throat.

Eskkar's move had been so quick, so unexpected, that the rulers of Orak sat rooted in their chairs, stunned by the death blow, the usual reaction of men who gave orders, not sword strokes.

Only Drigo the Elder found his voice. "No, stop!" he screamed, too late, as he watched his son take the death cut. He threw himself at Eskkar.

He had no weapon, and a stiff arm in the chest would have sent him staggering back. But not today, Eskkar thought, as he twisted his body to meet the man's rush, stepped back and extended his sword arm, letting Drigo run himself against the blade, his weight and momentum carrying him forward until the hilt nearly touched his chest. His right hand twitched in front of Eskkar's face, and Drigo's eyes widened with amazement for a moment before they turned up in their sockets. Death had taken him even before his son, who gurgled and twitched for a few more moments before the loss of blood killed him.

Everyone was on their feet, but nobody said anything. They stood there, in shock, eyes wide as they watched the Drigos die. Eskkar tried to jerk his sword free as the father's body slumped to the floor, but the flesh had closed tight around the blade. Eskkar had to put his foot on the body and pull hard.

Still no one said anything. Blood continued to ooze from

the two bodies. Esskar handed the sword to Trella. "Take this and clean it."

Stooping, he recovered the dagger the foolish boy had dropped and sat back down at the table, dropping the knife in his lap. Esskar picked up his water cup and drained it, though much of its contents had spilled when he pushed against the table. "I think you should all sit down," he said, his voice calm. "We still have many things to discuss."

He noticed a sharp knocking on the door that grew louder. "See to the door, Trella, then find Gatus."

The door opened before Trella reached it, and Creta stood in the doorway, two of Nicar's guards behind her. She started to speak, then glanced in horror at the bloody scene at her feet, her hand flying up to cover her mouth. The guards behind her looked as frightened as their mistress.

"Noble Nicar," Esskar began, "perhaps you should tell your men that there's no danger."

To Esskar's relief, Nicar quickly recovered.

"Yes, of course. Creta! Wine for everyone. And have slaves remove these bodies immediately." He looked at the crowd of servants gathering in the antechamber and raised his voice so all could hear him. "An unfortunate incident has occurred. Drigo and his son tried to kill Esskar, the new captain of the guard," he paused, "and were themselves slain."

For the next ten minutes, chaos ensued as frightened servants dragged the bodies out, wiped the floor clean, and straightened the furniture. Trella returned with Gatus in tow. She handed Esskar his sword, wiped clean of blood, resting her hand on his arm for the briefest of moments. The still-nervous nobles gulped their wine, even as more was poured, before a still-trembling Creta closed the chamber door.

During this time, Esskar studied the men around the table. The Five Families—no, now it was the Four Families—had been given a fright, and were no doubt all thinking it could have been any of them. They needed to be reassured, and quickly.

"Noble leaders," Esskar began humbly, "I offer sorrow for

what happened here. But I didn't provoke anyone, not outside in the street nor here in this room."

Mostly true, he thought, but he'd certainly been prepared to kill anyone who tried to stop him. Looking around the table, he saw his words sinking in. Now these men would start thinking again, trying to discover what in Orak's power structure had changed and who would benefit. Eskkar took another breath.

"But Noble Drigo wasn't interested in defending Orak, only in taking control. He planned to seize your village and your property."

Watching them, he decided that Trella had been right. Better to pour a bucket of oil than a cupful. "You're Orak's leaders. My men and I will stay and fight to defend the village, *if you wish it.*"

He looked at each man in turn. "Nicar said that he wants to fight. I told him Orak could be defended and that I would lead the battle, if the Families agreed to my conditions. Now it's time to decide. We hold this place to the death, or we all move on. Which do you choose?"

6

For the next two hours the nobles argued, as much among themselves as with Eskkar. Nicar sent out for more wine, and voices rose as Eskkar explained what happened outside, and what Drigo and his men had planned for Orak. Finally satisfied with Drigo's demise, the talk shifted back to the wall and the coming invasion. Eskkar explained his plans again and again, repeating how the barbarians could be beaten from behind a wall. The tide turned when Rebba posed a key question.

"Suppose, Eskkar, the wall cannot be built high and strong enough in the time we have. After all, it can take months to build even a house. What then?"

"Noble Rebba, that's the most important question, and the one I can't answer. We must meet with the builders and masons and learn whether a wall can be built. If it cannot, then we're all free to stay or go."

Rebba wasn't finished yet. "Suppose they say it can be done and we start work, but the barbarians come before the wall is finished. We'd be trapped here, defenseless."

Eskkar and Trella had spoken of that possibility. "We can only try, Rebba. But the first moment we learn we can't finish in time, then we can leave. I don't want to fight them in the open."

Eskkar recalled more of Trella's thoughts. "But if we run

now, we abandon everything you've built here, and Orak will never be so great again. The trade up and down the river will dry up. Remember, too, we face danger in leaving a place and starting over. Every man becomes a looter, and every clan becomes a robber tribe. But if we drive them away, we break the old cycle of death and destruction. Orak will become the greatest village in the world. And you will own it."

Rebba stared down at his wine cup. Eskkar wondered if all of them had drunk too much to think clearly. He'd wanted some wine himself, but one look at Trella standing behind him and he'd stayed with water. Now Rebba shifted his gaze toward Nicar and nodded.

"Eskkar," began Nicar, "leave us for a moment. We need to discuss some things privately."

"I understand." He stood up, and it felt good to stretch his legs. "Come, Trella, we'll wait in the garden. Take this," he said, handing her Drigo's blade. Small and well made, it would be a fitting gift. She might need it in the coming days.

When Eskkar opened the door, he found Creta there, and this time he knew she overheard every word. Her attitude had changed, and she bowed nervously toward him, this time with genuine respect. At the front entrance a manservant, his mouth agape, rushed to open the door for them.

Eskkar found Gatus and his men bunched inside the front garden. They'd moved the nobles' bodyguards into the courtyard. They sat weaponless on the ground, their backs to the wall that hid Nicar's sanctuary from the street. Through the open gate, Eskkar saw villagers filling the lane, jammed together as tightly as possible in the narrow confines. Soldiers using spears kept them away from the entrance.

A shout went up from the crowd when they saw Eskkar emerge. The rising clamor was a mixture of people cheering and calling his name. Gatus strode over, a broad smile on his face.

"Greetings, Captain," he said formally, bowing properly so that everyone could see Eskkar's authority. "When they brought out Drigo's body, word spread like a steppes fire.

We had to bring the guards inside. It's a good thing Drigo and his whelp were so unpopular."

He moved closer so that only Eskkar could hear him. "I sent for the rest of the men when I saw the crowd growing. Maybe you should say something to them."

Eskkar could barely hear him over the noise from the street. At least five hundred people packed the lane, more villagers than he'd ever seen gathered together before. He turned to Trella. "What shall I say?" Just as he'd gotten accustomed to speaking freely with the Families, he now had to speak to a rabble and had no idea what to tell them.

She pulled his arm down so she could speak in his ear. "It doesn't matter. You're a hero to them now. Tell them that all will be well, that Nicar and the others will speak to them soon."

"But the nobles haven't finished talking yet. Suppose they decide to run?"

"Never! They decided to stay and fight an hour ago. They just needed to talk themselves into it."

He forced a smile to his face and strode toward the gate. Propping his foot on the gate's crossbar, he pulled himself up so he rose above the throng and held up his hand for silence. It took time for the noise to cease, helped along by stern words from the soldiers in front, which gave him time to think.

"People of Orak," he began, raising his voice. "The Four Families will speak to you soon. You'll hear from them what we plan to do."

An angry roar answered him, some people shouting that the Families would run, others that he must save them, some merely crying his name over and over. They began to press against his men. Soon they'd push their way into the garden.

"Silence," he roared in his battle voice, loud enough to be heard the length of the street. "Silence, or I'll leave you to the barbarians!" That stopped both the noise and the push of the crowd toward the house. He took another deep breath. "Go to the marketplace and await Nicar and the other Families. Go now!"

He swung down from the gate but his sandal caught in the crosspiece and he lost his balance. Only Gatus's strong arm kept him upright. Gods, if he'd fallen on his ass, the villagers would have laughed themselves senseless. He and Trella went back into the house, the door already opened wide by the waiting servant. When it closed safely behind them, he breathed a sigh of relief, then looked up to find Nicar walking toward him.

"Well, Eskkar, what other surprises do you have for us? Perhaps you should tell us what you've decided to do. I begin to wonder what I have unleashed."

Despite the irony in Nicar's words, Eskkar heard respect in them as well.

"Nothing you need worry about, Nicar. I only want to hear your decision. Do we stay and fight, or do we run?"

"The Families have decided to stay and lead the defense of Orak," Nicar answered, raising his voice and knowing his words would be heard and repeated. "You'll be in command of Orak until the barbarians have been driven off." He lowered his voice so only Eskkar and Trella could hear. "Though I wonder what will happen then." Nicar shrugged resignedly. "It doesn't matter. What must we do now?"

"Take the nobles to the marketplace. Let everyone see that all are united in this. You know better than I what to say. After all of you speak, then I'll tell them how hard it's going to be."

Nicar nodded, pulling at his beard. "Is there anything else?"

"No, nothing. I'm sure there will be . . ." Trella grasped his arm and whispered in his ear. "Oh, yes . . . I think you should send men to take possession of Drigo's house and goods. We can begin paying for the defense of Orak with his gold."

"Yes, an excellent suggestion, Eskkar." Nicar glanced at Trella. "That may soften the blow to the Families as well." Nicar hesitated for a moment. "And what do you want from Drigo's goods for yourself?"

"I want nothing to do with his gold." Murdering men for their goods might bring down the anger of the gods, or so the priests said, and he'd tried to avoid their wrath as much as possible since he ceased his raiding days. "But his house is large and will make an excellent headquarters for my men, as well as a place to begin storing our weapons. When you have emptied it, perhaps you'll approve our using it."

"And after this is over, you'll keep it, I suppose," Nicar answered. "Well, why not? I did promise you a house, though I wasn't expecting it to be larger than my own."

"Nicar, if I live long enough to keep his house, I'll pay you and the other Families fairly for it. You can tell that to the nobles, if any ask."

Nicar studied him for a moment. "You continue to surprise me, Eskkar. Take the house at sundown tomorrow. That will give us time to search it and discover Drigo's hiding places."

Nicar faced Trella once again. "I wonder if I made a mistake in giving you away. Your laughter started the killing as surely as a blow. For a moment I thought you both planned it in advance." He shook his head. "No, that can't be true. Young Drigo, the fool, brought it on himself."

Nicar turned back to Eskkar. "Though you didn't need to kill his father. You could have . . ."

"If I hadn't, he would have killed me. If not today, then soon enough." Eskkar had acted instinctively, but he knew he'd done the right thing. Father and son both had to die.

"Yes, I suppose so," Nicar agreed reluctantly. "Anyway, it's too late to think about such matters. Let's go to the marketplace and reassure the people. We've much to tell them, if we're going to convince them to stay and fight."

It was five hours after sundown before Eskkar blew out the flame from the lamp. Since the morning, they'd not had a moment alone in the long day that changed Eskkar's fortune more than any day since his birth. He crawled under the blanket, where her waiting arms folded around him. For a long time they held each other, the events of the day still a whirlwind in their minds.

"We made it through the day, thanks to you, Trella."

That was true enough. She had probably saved his life by warning him about Naxos. And by provoking Drigo at the right time, she'd guided the outcome as surely as his own actions.

In the market, Nicar had spoken to the crowd. He promised grain, silver coins, and new or better houses for those who stayed and fought. He guaranteed the craftsmen protection in their trade. Food and grain would be stockpiled in the village, enough to feed everyone until after the danger had passed. And finally, slaves and bound servants who worked on the wall would earn their freedom in return, and their owners would receive compensation.

Shouts of anger from some and cheers from the slaves greeted that announcement, but Nicar stood his ground. Orak had to survive, and the village's defense needed skilled men. He repeated the warning that those trying to leave with critical tools or slaves would be stopped.

The other nobles and even Orak's two priests spoke to the crowd. They all answered questions and stressed the need to stay and defend their homes and families.

Only Nicar's pronouncement that Eskkar would be in charge of the village's defense put the crowd at ease.

"Your words pleased the villagers, Eskkar. I could see they trusted you."

In the market Trella had sat at his feet, her back to the crowd, to make sure that he didn't forget anything of importance. He'd warned the people about the dangers of leaving Orak, the risk of traveling on the roads, and the bandits that would follow the barbarians. Again and again he assured them the barbarians could be driven away and that a wall would protect them. He promised he would defend all of them.

And it had worked. In the end, most of the crowd roared approval of both Nicar and Eskkar as men who would save their families and their lives. They ignored Eskkar's origins; he was one of them now, their protector. The shouting and talking continued long after Eskkar and the nobles left the marketplace.

"I hope we persuaded enough of them to stay. Many will need to work on the wall."

Trella stayed silent for a moment, then clasped him tightly again before she spoke.

"I've never seen men killed like that before . . . I mean . . . so suddenly. In Carnax I watched an execution, but I never saw men . . . killing like that . . . it was more bloody than I expected." She pushed closer to him, moving her leg over his, rubbing herself against him. "And you could have been killed. When Drigo rushed at you with the dagger, I thought you would die. And I provoked him, wanted him to attack you, laughed at him until he lost control."

"Men die all the time. And men like Drigo and his foolish child, they die more easily because they know nothing of real fighting. I've fought many battles, and I've learned something from all of them."

"What of Naxos? He was no pampered brat, and he was standing close enough to you."

Her concern was real. She'd been truly frightened for him.

"Naxos was different, but he was already beaten when the archers rose up behind me. If his men had been trained fighters, they would have rushed us when the first arrow struck, and the bowmen would have had no targets. Instead they just stood there, and their will to fight vanished. Killing him only made it easier to provoke Drigo and control his men."

"And what would you have done if they had attacked you?"

He laughed softly in her ear as his hand found her breast. The touch excited him.

"Naxos and his guards were bullies, used to swaggering through the streets and breaking villagers' heads. Guards don't expect to fight archers. That's why they frightened so easily."

But that arrow had passed closer than he liked to admit, flying just above his head. The archer and Jalen had split one of Eskkar's new gold coins as a reward, an act of generosity he already regretted. A few silver coins would have sufficed. And that was in addition to the three silver coins he'd promised each of the archers.

She shivered under his touch, and her hand moved from around his neck to begin stroking his chest. "Now the people will follow you. Even the Families will do what you say, now that Drigo is gone." She moved her hand down to his hip, letting her fingers explore.

"Drigo would have made himself ruler of Orak. It was better that he died quickly, rather than stand in our way."

Her touch made him even more eager, and his worries faded as his desire hardened. The picture of Drigo running onto his sword flashed into his mind, and that image made him even more excited. Killing often did that, he knew, made a man lust for a woman, any woman, simply to prove that you still lived after the fighting stopped, that you'd survived and someone else was dead.

And what a woman was in his bed tonight, he thought, as his hands began to roam her body—one more precious than any in the village. Perhaps the killings had excited her as well. Women often became aroused after seeing a kill. She had, after all, helped bring them about.

The warmth in the bed grew, and not all of it from the thick blanket. Trella's mouth found his for a long kiss that left them both breathless.

"And what plans does my master have for me in the morning?" she whispered seductively, as her hand reached down to touch his manhood.

"Tomorrow will take care of itself." He rolled onto her stomach, unable to restrain himself any longer and feeling her legs part easily beneath him. "Tonight you have much more important duties."

The next morning Eskkar's regular habits asserted themselves and he rose before daybreak. He dressed quietly and left Trella asleep in the warm bed. At the well he washed his hands and face in the cold water as the first rays of the sun reached over the eastern hills and covered Orak with its soft light. A long drink from a second bucket satisfied his thirst. Then he strode toward the barracks room to wake the men. But the door stood open, and Gatus, dressed and wearing a short sword, emerged as Eskkar approached.

"I just woke them up, Captain. The lazy brutes will be surly all day. Not many went to bed early last night."

"Thank you, Gatus." His second in command must have arisen even before Eskkar. They went over the orders for the day as men still half-asleep stumbled forth into the sunlight. Nicar had stressed to Orak's inhabitants that they must remain under control and go about their daily affairs, and the soldiers needed to keep order. Eskkar and Gatus had discussed these plans briefly last night, but Eskkar wanted to make sure the men kept busy for the rest of the day.

By the time Eskkar returned to his room, the sun had cleared the horizon. He found the door open to freshen the air. Trella had laid out their breakfast. Today the bread came from a baker who specialized in a different, more expensive type of grain. A glass bottle, scarcely taller than his thumb and with its own wooden stopper, held a handful of brown salt. Water from the well now rested inside a graceful pitcher, next to another that contained weak beer. A new clay plate had also joined Eskkar's increasing supply of worldly goods. Two dark-brown sausages, both larger than yesterday's, mixed their aroma with that of the still-warm bread.

"Good morning, Trella." He took her by the shoulders and kissed her, enjoying the taste of her lips. After a moment, she put her arms around his neck and returned the kiss. The sight of the bed only a step away began to tempt him. She must have sensed what he was thinking, because she pushed herself away.

"Good morning, master. You must eat. Corio will be here soon."

They sat down at the table and began to eat. Trella explained her new arrangement with one of the street vendors. A boy would deliver their breakfast each morning. Eskkar knew he could look forward to more good meals from now on.

When they finished, Eskkar and Trella went over ideas about the wall. They'd discussed this last night, but Eskkar wanted to be sure he didn't forget anything.

Trella's ability to anticipate problems continued to impress him. She was teaching him to think like a ruling noble, something his years in and around Orak and other villages had never succeeded in doing.

Not that her wits or ideas mattered to him any longer. If she were deaf and dumb, he'd keep her for her lovemaking. Already he looked forward to the coming night.

A tall shadow appeared in the doorway, darkening the room, and a voice called out. "Greetings, Eskkar. Nicar asked that I speak with you."

"Enter, Honored Corio." Eskkar put thoughts of Trella in his bed aside, rose from the table and extended his hand to the master artisan. "Join us at table. Would you care for some wine?"

"Not at present, thank you," Corio spoke in a deep bass voice. He sat down at the table. The builder's eyes examined his host closely, no doubt sizing up the new Eskkar, who yesterday had magically been transformed from a common soldier into a leader of men.

"Trella, this is Master Corio, the most important builder in Orak." Eskkar looked at Corio. "Trella will join us. I find her most useful to keep track of things."

If Corio found anything strange in that, he said nothing. Eskkar noticed that he did give Trella a thorough look.

"Well, then, Eskkar, what's all this about a wall? I wasn't at the marketplace yesterday, but I heard you and Nicar promised a wall would be built around the village, a wall big enough to stop the barbarians." He tightened his lips. "I meant no disrespect with the word."

Eskkar laughed. He guessed the thoughts in Corio's head. Yesterday Eskkar would have bowed to him in the street. Today Corio would worry that he might be killed as easily as young Drigo—and with as little consequence. Eskkar smiled to put the man at ease.

"I'm well civilized, Corio, so use the word as you wish. As you say, I promised a wall to the villagers yesterday, and now I must ask you to help me keep my promise. I need a wall around Orak, high enough and strong enough to keep the barbarians at bay, a wall that I can fill with bowmen to pour arrows into their ranks. Can you build such a wall?"

"Any wall can be built, Captain. How high a wall would be needed?"

"At least twenty-five feet high. That height gives my archers a clear field of fire even as it increases their range. Of course, the wall would have to be strong enough so that it could not be easily pulled down."

When Corio didn't respond, Eskkar went on. "The wall need not surround all of Orak. We'd have the outlying houses torn down and the fields on both sides flooded. I rode around the village two days ago. The wall would have to be bigger than the palisade is today, but not too much more."

Corio shifted a little on the bench, as if he found it uncomfortable. "A wall such as you describe would take at least a year, perhaps as many as two, to build. You expect the barbarians to arrive in five months?"

"Your pardon, Master Corio." Trella's voice was properly subservient. "My master does not mean to tell you what to construct. You are the master builder. He only asks what can be built that will stop the barbarians. Is that not correct, master?"

Eskkar kept his face impassive. "Yes, of course, that's what I meant. I would not tell the blacksmith how to cast me a sword. I can only ask for what I need." Eskkar leaned back in his chair. He'd asked Corio, politely and respectfully, for his services. Honor required that the artisan give an honest answer.

Corio drummed his fingers on the table. "Assuming that I remain in Orak to work on such a project, how many men would be available to work on this wall? Also, materials would need to be purchased from other places along the river. And we might need craftsmen from other villages as well. How much coin is Nicar willing to pay?"

"You'll have every man in the village, Corio. Everyone, including myself and my soldiers if necessary, plus the hundreds of new men who'll begin arriving, driven south by the oncoming barbarians. Seven days a week and long into the night. No man will be spared. Even Nicar has promised to labor on it. And all the gold of the Families will be made available to buy whatever is needed."

As the master artisan sat contemplating this information, Eskkar did some sizing up of his own. About the same age, Corio stood a few inches shorter, with thinning hair already tinted with gray. His face had almost no trace of a beard, and his eyes gleamed with intelligence. Eskkar knew him to be a skilled craftsman, used to naming his own prices, working at his own pace, and following his own rules. Nothing could compel him to build the wall. They needed a key to get him involved, something that would make him want to stay. Eskkar remembered what Trella had suggested.

"Listen, Corio," Eskkar leaned across the table, "if we can hold off the barbarians, Orak will be the biggest and most important village for a hundred, no, two hundred miles in every direction. The man who builds the wall that saves Orak will be the most famous and skilled artisan in the land. It will be the wall that defeats the barbarians, not the soldiers, not the villagers. Your fame would spread up and down the river, and you'd be remembered forever. And you'd be well paid for your efforts."

And if you can't, Eskkar thought to himself as he settled back, then we'll all begin planning our departure.

"Master, I recall that Noble Nicar spoke about establishing another House to replace Drigo's," Trella added. "If Corio agreed to build such a wall, surely Nicar and the Families would accept him as their equal."

Nicar had said no such thing, but Eskkar liked the idea anyway. Even he knew of Corio's reputation as an honest man who treated everyone fairly. Nicar and the Families could do worse. "It's a chance to join the nobles, Corio. Think of the honor. You'd become one of Orak's rulers."

The artisan sat there, glancing from one to the other. "And Nicar has agreed to that?" he asked pointedly.

"If he's forgotten, my master will remind him."

Eskkar nodded. "Yes, I'm sure nothing will be denied the man who raises the wall that saves Orak." We have him now, Eskkar decided—even Corio couldn't resist the thought of establishing his own noble house.

Eskkar had run out of words, so he waited in silence,

watching as Corio thought some more, the artisan's fingers again drumming on the tabletop.

The drumming stopped abruptly as Corio stood up. "Excuse me a moment, Captain." He stepped to the doorway and called out to someone. Immediately a young man carrying a large cloth pouch rushed to his master. Taking the pouch, Corio returned to the table, extracted a cylinder of leather about the size of a quiver of arrows and removed its cap. Carefully, he withdrew a roll of papyrus and set it out on the table, holding down the corners with four small weights that also came from the pouch.

The papyrus proved to be a map, one that showed the bend of the river and the village. Eskkar had heard of such a thing before but had never seen one. Even the papyrus sheet itself was rare, not something found in the lands nearby, but an expensive item traded on the river.

As for the map, it was as if Eskkar were a bird flying high in the sky, looking down at the Tigris and the village from above. The river flowed in a pale blue stream, but everything else had been stroked in black or brown. The village showed clearly, with a line around it that indicated the palisade. Eskkar caught the excitement in Trella's eyes and knew that she had never seen such a treasure either.

"This is a map prepared by my slave several weeks ago. After yesterday's . . . events, I sent him round the village and palisade again, and then we worked on other details most of the night. So . . . what's shown here is correct in most respects."

Eskkar's eyes stayed on the map, but he thought about Corio's words. Working through the night meant burning lamps or candles, expensive items even for Corio. Even more interesting was that Corio had heard all the talk about the barbarians and the wall, and prepared himself for this meeting. That meant that Corio had the wit to see what would be asked of him even before he'd received the summons. It also meant that Corio had his answers ready—and that Eskkar had better ask the right questions.

Trella kept telling me to anticipate everything. Under the table and out of Corio's sight, his hands tightened into fists.

"Can you understand the map, Eskkar? Many men have trouble understanding the lines and representations."

The question had been repeated, and Eskkar focused his thoughts on the map again, looking carefully to see the location of the village, river, docks, palisade, farms, and the two roads that met a mile from the village before joining to carry the traffic into and out of Orak.

"Yes, it's clear enough."

He'd scratched out enough maps in the dirt while campaigning, and the papyrus made everything easier to follow. Reaching out with his finger, he started to trace the river.

"Please, Captain, don't touch the sheet with your hands. The inks may smear from the wetness of your fingers, and papyrus is delicate. Use this pointer." He handed Eskkar a small piece of soft wood with a bluntly rounded tip.

Taking the pointer, Eskkar identified aloud the key points on the map, even noting the directions for north and south, indicated by an arrow point in one corner. Corio explained the few details he didn't understand. A glance at Trella showed she, too, grasped what the map represented.

"You do well, Eskkar," remarked Corio. "Some men have trouble with the scale of the drawing. Now, show me where you'd have your wall and what you would exclude."

Eskkar didn't know what Corio meant by the word *scale*, but he decided not to ask, especially since he was supposed to understand it. He repeated the word to himself, to remind himself to ask Trella later.

"The wall should go to here, Corio, here, and then back to the river's edge." Eskkar touched the map lightly with the pointer. "And these places will be flooded, turned into a swamp. I want to force the barbarians to send their main force at the front of Orak, where my men can kill them from the top of the wall.

"Also, the wall on the river side should be extended as close to the bank as possible so that the barbarians cannot gather enough men to rush the wall from the rear or sides. At the front of the village, I will kill them by pouring arrows down on them."

Corio sat silent for a long moment before he looked up.

"The barbarians have seen wooden fences before and learned to use ladders and ropes against them. They'll use the same tactics against a wall. If your men are busy using their bows, how will they stop men on ladders?"

"I've used such ladders myself, against stockades such as our own. A length of wood with a fork on the end can be used to throw the ladder down. Two women, pushing together, can shove back a ladder, even with a warrior on it."

Eskkar didn't bother to add he had firsthand experience with that practice, having been thrown down himself and nearly skewered on his sword in the process. "That's why we need a true wall, a strong structure that cannot be pulled down or burned, and that gives us enough room to position two or three rows of archers to defend it."

Corio went into another of his long trances, seeming to stare at the map. Eskkar used the moment to glance at Trella. She appeared confident and gave him a quick smile of encouragement.

The master builder took a deep breath and looked up. "When I came here this morning, I expected to tell you truthfully that it was impossible to build a wall around Orak in the time we have. It is not possible to construct a wall of that length and twenty-five feet high, not in the time available. Such a height would require too much strengthening and support work. Also, the base would require preparation and settling. How about a height of about fifteen feet?"

Eskkar had to stop and think, trying to visualize the height in his mind. He knew fifteen feet to be a little less than the height of three village men. Barbarians tended to be taller, though most of them stood less than six feet tall. But a fit rider could stand on the back of his horse and jump high enough to pull himself over fifteen feet of wall. Even dead horses and men could be used as stepping stones, and ladders that high could be easily constructed and carried.

"No, that's not high enough," Eskkar replied, explaining his reasons, sensing even as he did so that Corio already had an answer.

"I suggest, Eskkar, that we make the wall fourteen or fifteen feet high, but that in the front of the wall, we dig a ditch at least ten feet deep and at least thirty feet wide. That would effectively make the height of the wall the twenty-five feet you want."

When Eskkar didn't reply, Corio hastened to add, "It's much easier to dig a ditch than build a wall. And any villager can dig. The dirt from the ditch can be used to make the mud bricks that will form the wall, and the earth and stones can be used for fill."

Corio had thought all this through. The idea of a ditch was new, something Eskkar had never seen or heard of. He pictured himself standing at the bottom of such a ditch, looking up. The wall would indeed appear to be twenty-five feet high. "Wouldn't the ditch weaken the wall at the base?" Eskkar knew solid earth was needed to support a walled structure.

A smile crossed Corio's face. "You're quicker than most men, Eskkar, to think of that. But no, the ditch wouldn't come all the way to the wall's base. It would stop about one long pace away, and we would taper the slope to make it difficult to stand on. The bottom of the wall would be reinforced with stones to make it difficult to dig through. That way, the base of the wall retains its support, and the attackers cannot easily dig the foundation away."

Corio's own words seemed to give him some discomfort. "You realize, Captain, that if the barbarians begin digging at the base of the wall, then eventually it will weaken and begin to crumble."

"If we allow them time to dig at the base of the wall, then we are lost. Stones, arrows, spears, everything will be used to stop them. No, they'll not have time to dig."

"Master Corio," Trella asked politely, "could the ditch be flooded with water from the river?"

Corio started to say something, then paused, perhaps remembering again what happened to young Drigo. "No, if we flood the ditch, then the water itself might weaken the earth at the wall's base. If we had more time, we could line the ditch with stones and logs to reinforce it." Corio finished with a condescending smile.

Trella hadn't finished. "Still, Master Corio, if we flooded

the ditch just a little, for a day or two, might it not turn the ditch into a river of mud which would rob the attackers of their footing?"

"Yes, but the mud would dry after a few days, and the ditch would be as it was before," he explained a little less patiently, again drumming his fingers on the table.

Eskkar decided Corio wasn't used to listening to suggestions from slaves, and young female ones at that.

"Master Corio, what if we were to flood the ditch every few days, or whenever it began to dry out?"

"If we are locked inside the walls, Trella, we won't have access to the river to open trenches at our will." The fingers drummed even faster on the tabletop, and Corio's reply sounded final.

Trella went on, ignoring the little signs of impatience. "We could use water from the wells inside the village. The wells in Orak are steadily refilled from the river. Could not a water wheel be built to lift the water over the walls?"

The fingers stopped their drumming and the confident smile vanished from Corio's face. What in the name of the gods was a water wheel? But Eskkar saw that the master builder understood the words. The man went into another of his long moments of thought. Abruptly, Corio arose from the table, strode to the doorway, and passed outside into the sunlight.

Eskkar got up also, curious about whatever was outside, winked at Trella and went to stand in the doorway. To his surprise, he found five of Corio's apprentices and helpers squatting in the dirt, each carrying a different bundle. One boy had only a large drawing slate hanging from his neck. Corio spoke quietly with his senior apprentice, a man about his own age. The talk went on for some time. Eskkar felt Trella's arm on his back, slipping up under his tunic and rubbing at the hard muscles on his shoulders.

"What's a water wheel?" he asked absently, watching Corio. Another apprentice had been summoned into the conversation. This one handed his bag to another and dashed off down the lane. Corio resumed his discussion with his assistant, both of them becoming more animated.

"It's a tool we used in our village to draw water from the

river. With it, a few slaves could easily lift many barrels of water from the river."

Corio turned from the assistant and walked back toward them.

When they were all seated again, Corio turned to Trella. "My apologies, Trella, I see both you and your master are wiser than you appear. Sometimes it's better to keep one's wits hidden and so conceal your abilities.

"Your idea is a good one," Corio went on, "and one I should have thought of myself. I've sent a boy off to find the well maker. We need to know about the force of the water inside the wells and how long it takes to dig new ones and where they could be placed. The water wheel would be an excellent way to lift and move the water. But I don't think we would need to lift the water over the walls. Holes can be constructed in the wall just above the ground to pass the water through to the ditch. Yes, I think that would work."

Corio paused for a moment. "We could use clay pipes inside the holes, and build some lengths of wooden troughs to carry the water from the wells to the pipes. The dirt in the ditch would remain a pool of mud, forcing the attackers to move slowly in it, but not so wet as to threaten the base of the wall, or rob it of its strength."

Eskkar thought about Corio's comment about hiding one's wits and realized the master builder included himself in that group. Eskkar had always believed that people like young Drigo who spoke sharply and arrogantly all the time were smarter than he was, smarter than most others. Perhaps it wasn't true. Perhaps there were many like Corio and Trella who kept their wits and their mouths to themselves and so avoided the difficulties of appearing to know too much. He would talk about it with Trella later.

"Captain, for the first time, I begin to believe what you propose is barely possible. Whether it can be built in time, I'm not sure, but I will study the matter, and give you an answer tomorrow. It will be close, I warrant that much. But it may be that we can do what you ask."

"Master Corio," Trella said, "what of the gates to the

village? Can they be made strong enough, if that is where the barbarians will attack?"

"The gates can be strengthened until they're stronger than the wall, and the ditch can be twice as wide and even deeper there. We'll need great logs from the forests of the north for that. As long as we keep them wet enough, they won't burn. The barbarians will try to use a ram against them, but that will take time, and your soldiers will have to kill them."

He looked at Eskkar. "I hope you've thought about barbarians shooting arrows at whatever sticks out over the wall?"

"Yes, Corio, I have." He didn't explain further, since he didn't know yet whether the bows could be crafted in time or men trained.

Eskkar tightened his lips and remained silent, until Corio realized nothing further would be forthcoming. Corio wasn't the type to ask again.

At that moment, the apprentice returned, accompanied by the village's well maker. Solus had been appointed by the Families and was the only one in Orak allowed to construct wells. One of the oldest men in the village, short and stooped, he claimed nearly sixty seasons. The man had lived in and around the river all of his life.

"Yes, Master Corio, I come at your summons. What is it you wish to know?" Solus had trouble speaking, mostly because he had so few teeth left in his bald head.

"How difficult is it to construct new wells inside Orak, Solus?" Corio asked, getting right to the point.

"We already have four large wells for public use as well as many private ones that provide more water than we can use. Why would we want more wells?"

Another man with pride in his station and his trade, Eskkar thought with amusement. The old man had ignored him completely. Obviously Corio had worked with Solus before because he took the question in stride.

"We plan for the defense of Orak, and I need water supplies closer to the palisade. I need to know how much pressure is in each well, in case I need to draw large quantities of water each day. So tell me, Master Digger, how long does it take?"

Solus scratched his bald pate and took his time answering, plainly not used to rushing at the beck and call even of Corio, let alone some upstart captain of the guard. "To do it properly, cutting through the rock and walling the sides, about two months." Solus looked around the table, as if waiting for someone to challenge his estimate.

Corio said nothing, just drummed his fingers on the table.

Solus went on. "As for the water pressure, the force of the river is powerful and the wells in Orak cannot be emptied. As fast as you take water, it will be replenished."

"Even with a water wheel?" Corio asked.

"Why would you need a water wheel?" When he saw Corio's expression darken, Solus hastened to amplify his answers. "Yes, even with a water wheel. Further inland, the ground is dry and even a good well can be emptied in three or four days of heavy use."

Corio stood up and bowed to the digger of wells. "Thank you for your time and your wisdom, Solus. You've been of great assistance. I've taken you away from your work for long enough."

When the man left, Corio turned to Eskkar. "He's an old fool, but a good stone mason. As for the wells, I'm sure a working well could be dug in about a week or two. Solus is very good about taking his time and lengthening out the work. But I believe he's correct about the pressure of the water." Corio glanced out the door at the sun, then carefully rolled up his map, replacing it in the case, which he sealed tightly.

"I'll go and review my estimates. By noon tomorrow, I'll return and tell you what you need to know."

"My thanks to you, Master Corio," Eskkar replied. He stood and clasped Corio's arm. "I've learned much this morning."

"As have I." Corio's smile this time was more relaxed. He started for the door but then stopped and turned back. "Honorable Captain," he began formally, "I don't wish to offend, but I would ask something." He looked at Trella, then continued. "If you should ever wish to sell your servant, then I would be prepared to pay almost any price. In my trade, I must search constantly for people with certain skills and talents. Your servant seems to have many such skills." His eyes flickered from Eskkar to Trella and back to Eskkar.

"Master Builder, I thank you for your generous offer, but Trella is not for sale." Eskkar smiled to show that he hadn't taken any offense. "And we look forward to meeting you tomorrow." He bowed to Corio, as did Trella.

Corio hesitated as if wanting to add something, but instead merely smiled. He bowed and left the room, calling out to his apprentices as he did so. Eskkar went to the doorway and watched him depart with his entourage. The master artisan had given him much food for thought, but now Eskkar's thoughts were elsewhere.

He stepped out into the bright sun and called out to the guard, standing patiently at his post. "I don't want to be disturbed by anyone for the next hour. If someone asks, tell them I'm busy planning the defense of Orak."

The guard looked at him and nodded his understanding, keeping his face under control. Returning inside, Eskkar closed the door and dropped the wooden bar across the entrance. Trella was clearing the table of the water cups, but looked up at the sound, put down the cups, and walked into his arms.

"You should be meeting with Nicar and with the tradesmen," she put her arms around him and her head against his chest. "Master Corio seems to be the most important person in Orak right now, and we should . . ."

"Be quiet, girl," his voice already hoarse with passion, "or I'll sell you to Corio. I'm sure he could keep you busy building things." His hands slid under her dress. Feeling her softness, he marveled once again at how she roused him.

"Maybe I would like him better. He might not keep me up all night." Her hands were under his tunic now, making him even more excited.

He lifted the dress up over her head and tossed it toward the table, then picked her up, carried her to the bed, and deposited her gently on the blankets. He stood over her looking down at her naked body as he removed his tunic. She moved sinuously in the bed, looking up at him and arching her back a little in anticipated pleasure. Remembering his promise from last night, he vowed to keep better control of his desire.

"Trella, my woman, you belong to me, and with me you will stay." He sat down on the bed and began kissing her breasts, and then he had no more words in his head for anyone or anything.

7

An hour later, Eskkar unbarred the door and stepped out into the courtyard. The guard still attended. Gatus had joined him, both men sitting under the tree. From the grim look on Gatus's face, Eskkar guessed that his own contentment was about to vanish. "Yes, Gatus, what is it?"

"Can we speak privately, Captain?" he glanced toward the house.

Trella was up and dressed, but the room still reeked of sex.

"Yes. Let's go to the tavern for some food and beer." Eskkar had worked up an appetite, and what had formerly been an unheard of luxury was nothing now. He started walking and Gatus followed. Bypassing the cheaper alehouse near the barracks, Eskkar strode two streets over to a smaller tavern, one not usually frequented by soldiers. This tavern's wine and ale didn't wrench your stomach, and if you wanted something other than bread, they'd fetch it from the street vendors.

The innkeeper tried to seat his guests near the doorway so anyone passing by could see them. But Eskkar chose a dark corner and told the owner they wanted privacy along with some bread and beer. Eskkar might have gold now, but he didn't plan to waste it on drink.

"Well, Gatus," he began after taking a deep draught of the ale. "What's the problem now?"

"The men. While you're taking your pleasure, they're standing about, worried about the barbarians and all this talk about fighting them off." Gatus stopped to take a sip of his ale. "They know there aren't enough of them to resist the barbarians, even with a wall. You need to talk to them. Some are getting ready to run, like Ariamus. I see it in their eyes. They turn away when I look at them. Say something to them, and soon, or they'll be gone."

Eskkar's hand had tightened on the ale cup when Gatus mentioned his time with Trella, but he relaxed it immediately. He couldn't get angry at Gatus over that. When Ariamus had wasted away hours or even the whole day, his dalliances annoyed all those who needed him, including Eskkar. Besides, Gatus kept close to the men. If he said they had a problem, then there was one. Otherwise Gatus would have handled it himself.

A week ago Eskkar would have stormed out of the tavern, returned to the barracks, and started knocking some heads. That response wouldn't work, not with the threat of the barbarians moving toward them. Now he needed the soldiers more than they needed him.

Without them, any wall would be useless. Worse, the wall would never be built without the threat of force from Orak's guards. Eskkar sat there, thinking, listing in his mind what he could say and do. Some ideas occurred and he examined them, slowly and in more detail than was his wont. Perhaps Trella was right. He should think everything through before he spoke or acted.

They sat there in silence. "What did Corio have to say?" Gatus finally asked as he finished his beer. "Can the wall be built in time?"

Eskkar told him what Corio said. "Now that you know as much as I do, let's get back to the men. Here's what I want you to do."

Ticking them off on his fingers, he listed the items he wished Gatus to assemble. When he finished, Gatus smiled as he leaned back against the rough stone wall, and called for more beer.

Two hours of preparation later, including some time telling Trella what he would do and say, Eskkar walked around the barracks to the training area. Gatus had brought in all the men, leaving only a single man at each gate. Eskkar wore only a short linen skirt, leaving his chest bare. He carried his long horse sword in his hand.

Gatus, Jalen, Bantor, and Sisuthros waited together in the open space in front of the men. Two blankets at their feet concealed what lay beneath. A high wagon with four large, solid wheels stood behind them.

"Sit down, in two ranks," Eskkar growled at the men. He counted twenty-seven seated before him. At least none had run yet, though the day and week were far from over. He looked at each of them as he strode up and down in front of their ranks.

"You men, scum that you are, are going to help me defeat the barbarians. You're going to do that by training all the hundreds of new men and villagers that will be pouring into Orak in the next few months. Before you can do that, however, you'll have to be trained properly yourselves, and that's what we," he waved the sword toward Gatus and the others, "are going to do, starting today."

He watched their eyes shift and a few squirmed in their positions. But they said nothing, proving they'd learned the two basic lessons of soldiering—never volunteer and never be the first to ask a question.

"I see you have your doubts," Eskkar said with a smile. "Well, good. Maybe we'll have a little wagering. You all like to wager, don't you? Let's pretend that I am a fierce barbarian warrior. Gatus, come here."

Gatus stepped forward at the command, drawing his short sword as he did so, and faced Eskkar ten feet away.

"Now, men, let's make a little wager. The barbarian against Gatus." Eskkar hummed his horse sword through the air. It was nearly twice the length of the short swords carried by the soldiers. "Who would win?"

No one said anything, so he shouted at them. "Answer me, dogs! Who would win?"

Grudging replies of "you" or "the barbarian" answered him this time.

He waited a moment. "So, nobody thinks the soldier can win. And why not?" He prodded them until he heard the reply he wanted. "Because of the long sword, I can cut him down before he even reaches me." He glared at them. "Or can I? Jalen!"

Gatus stepped back. Jalen reached under the blanket, put on a thick leather vest, and lifted up a stout wooden shield reinforced with two thick strips of weathered copper. Sliding his arm into the straps, he drew his sword, and walked aggressively toward Eskkar, raising the shield to his eyes as he did so. The short sword that had looked so puny a moment before now seemed much more menacing.

Eskkar instinctively gave back a pace as he raised his sword before Jalen halted, the same ten feet away.

"Well, men, let's get back to our wager. The barbarian or Jalen? Who'd win now?"

After a moment, most of them began muttering Jalen's name.

"What happened to change your minds? The shield makes the difference, doesn't it? Now the barbarian's long sword is of little value. Instead the protected short sword becomes deadly. Jalen can move in to close quarters with the barbarian, take the sword stroke on his shield, and kill him easily."

One of the men called out, "The barbarians don't fight on foot. They use their horses as shields."

"Ah, we have a leader of men here, I see," Eskkar remarked and nodded at Gatus again.

Lifting his fingers to his lips, Eskkar gave a shrill whistle, and in a moment a stable boy ran up, leading a horse. Eskkar leaped on the animal and raised the sword on high. The horse reared up, showing high spirits, and forcing Eskkar to grip him tightly with his knees and pull back hard with the halter rope.

Gatus, meanwhile, had dragged out a training post, a four-foot-tall post he set into a block of wood buried in the ground. The block held the post upright, and on its top, he set a melon from the market.

Eskkar wheeled the horse and rode a short distance away, then turned and raced the animal back toward the post, giving voice to a barbarian war cry that acted like a whip to the excited animal. As he flashed by the post, Eskkar leaned outward and struck down hard with his sword, exploding the melon as a man might crush a grape and splitting the post as he thundered past in a spray of flying dirt and splattering fruit.

He rode back slowly, talking to the horse soothingly and smiling to himself because he'd nearly missed the melon. Eskkar stopped in front of the men. "Who wants to stand against the barbarian and his horse?"

No one answered. "Come now, men, I'll even give you a horse of your own, though I'll warrant you'll have a better chance on the ground. What, still no takers?"

He looked down at them and laughed. Turning toward Gatus, he nodded again. This time Gatus and Bantor jumped into the wagon and gathered bows and arrows which they notched but did not draw. The two of them stood shoulder to shoulder, standing over the side of the wagon.

"Now who will you wager on, the barbarian on his horse, or the men standing with drawn bows on their wall? Because that's what the barbarians are going to see when they reach Orak. Only the wall will be twenty-five feet high. Show them, Jalen."

Jalen and Sisuthros jogged to the rear of the barracks and returned with two saplings bound together end-to-end with rope to make a crude joint. Jalen set his end on the ground and braced it with his foot while Sisuthros, at the other end, lifted it with a grunt and walked it upright, hand over hand, until he joined Jalen. The two men now held the beam vertical.

"That pole is twenty-five feet high. When the barbarians are beneath it, their swords and horses will be useless." He walked the horse closer to the pole so that they could see the height difference, clucking to the animal to overcome its nervousness at the strange object looming over its head.

"Picture yourselves on top of the wall, pouring arrows down on the barbarians and their horses. Now, who would you wager on?"

He looked at their open mouths, hoping his message was getting through. One of the men called out to him. "Captain, the barbarians have bows as well. They can shoot back at men on the wall."

It was Alexar, the same man who had asked the first question.

"Ah, I see our leader of men has his wits about him," Eskkar replied, getting down from his horse. Walking to the wagon, he reached up and Bantor handed him his bow and arrow. Walking back to the men, he held up the bow in one hand, the arrow in the other.

"This is the bow used by the barbarians," he explained, talking as if they'd never seen one before. "It's short because it must be fired from the back of a horse while at a dead run. It's curved because it must be bent to provide enough force. This bow is made of three different kinds of wood glued together, and tipped with horn for strength. A craftsman takes about six months to make a bow like this."

Eskkar knew most of the men had no idea how much effort it took to make a bow, or how many were discarded or shattered in the process.

He held out the arrow. "The arrow is short because it must fit the bow and be carried on the horse. The tip may be of hardened bone or bronze. It weighs almost nothing." Eskkar tossed the arrow in the air a few times, so they could see how light it was, then put the arrow to the bow. He turned toward the wagon, bent the bow, and launched the shaft. The arrow quivered into the thick wheel.

"With a bow such as this, even the slowest barbarian on his horse can launch ten to fifteen arrows per minute."

Whether these men knew it or not, that was a frightening number of missiles for any massed group of men, since a mere fifty horsemen could shoot at least five hundred arrows per minute, and each rider might carry thirty or forty arrows in his quiver.

Warriors could empty their quivers and completely break

a mass of men five times their size. They could inflict huge casualties on their hapless opponents, shattering their ranks and making them easy prey for the final attack with lance and sword.

"But the killing range of this arrow is less than one hundred paces with any accuracy. A few shafts might kill at one hundred and fifty paces." Eskkar let that sink in. "At close range, the arrow is deadly. After a hundred paces, it will not pierce armor or shield. At two hundred paces or more, the arrow is nearly spent and won't penetrate even a leather vest.

"Most of you men know how to use a bow. Even Forno," Eskkar pointed with the bow at the marksman who'd killed Naxos's henchman, "at least when he's sober, can put a shaft in a man at fifty paces. Our own bows will be longer and heavier and they'll cast a heavier weight of arrow, enough to kill a man at two hundred paces unless he's wearing bronze. And since they don't have to be small and compact, we can make our bows in less than three months."

Eskkar gave them a grim smile. "So, men, you will have to train others, many others, in how to fight with bow, spear, and short sword. Master Builder Corio will construct our wall, and it will enclose most of Orak. We'll tear down the rest of the village and then flood the surrounding land. We'll force the barbarians to come up against us at the main gate, and we'll kill them with arrows from the wall. Starting tomorrow, all of us will put in three hours a day with the bow. Gatus and Forno will lead the training."

He glanced over at Gatus, who nodded agreement.

"In three months, I want every one of you to be able to shoot the eyes out of a man at two hundred paces. When the wall is ready, we'll mark out the distances on the ground so you'll know the range."

He had their attention now, and could almost read their thoughts from the looks on their faces. They were thinking that maybe, just maybe, it might work. Give them something to believe in, something to keep them here a few more months. As long as they thought they had a chance, they'd stay.

"When you can shoot at least ten arrows per minute,

standing behind the wall, wearing leather armor and picking your targets, you'll do to the barbarians what they usually do to others. You will smash their ranks and kill hundreds of them. Remember, a horse is a big target. If you kill or wound the horse, the man goes down. As he falls, he may lose his bow and quiver, his sword, or his wits, even if he doesn't break his neck.

"In five months, I expect we'll have between three hundred and four hundred men, well trained in the use of the bow, to defend the wall, with all the remaining men and women of Orak to back us up. We will have food and water, while the barbarians will find nothing to eat outside the village. When they get hungry enough, they'll move on.

"We'll have other tricks for the barbarians as well, but I don't want to burden your heads with too many things at once. But remember this—when the arrows start flying, I'll be standing beside you on the wall.

"So, tomorrow starts our training. And I'll be training with you. As more men arrive, you'll begin training them, as Gatus and Forno have trained you."

He saw more doubt on their faces.

"Oh, don't worry, men will come—driven from their homes by the barbarians, men whose families have been killed by them, men who are tired of running from them every few years. Even now, dozens of men in the village are looking for a chance to pay off old scores. When they hear we intend to fight, more will join us."

Eskkar stopped, as if to consider his words, glancing at every man.

"We can beat the barbarians as long as we fight them our way and on our terms. I know how they fight and I know they can be beaten. You men will be the ones who do it. Unless you would rather run than fight." He let that thought take root for a moment.

"Starting today, your pay for each month is doubled and you'll get better food. You get your first payment tomorrow. And there will be an extra month's pay when the barbarians are beaten off." No doubt Nicar could handle that small sum easily enough, especially with Drigo's gold.

That brought the expected cheer, and he waited until it stopped.

"But starting tomorrow, you work, you train, and you guard the village. If you train well, many of you will become leaders-of-ten, and there'll be more pay for that."

He let his voice go hard, to make sure they understood his meaning. "But if you slack off, I may not even kill you." They went silent again. "I might just have you thrown out of Orak and let you fend for yourself."

He glanced up at the waning sun. "Gatus, take these poor excuses for soldiers to the alehouse and feed them some beer. But not too much. They start training at sunrise."

Eskkar walked off, thinking he'd have to be there himself, at least for the next few days. He could use some practice with sword and bow. Sitting around the barracks had weakened his muscles, and he didn't feel ready yet to meet the barbarians one on one. Killing fools like Naxos and Drigo was easy enough, but hardened Alur Meriki warriors would be a different matter.

Turning the corner, he found Trella waiting for him. Behind her stood more than a dozen women as well as an assortment of children and dogs.

"I kept them away, master, as you ordered," she said, raising her voice so all could hear. "They were sure to be a distraction."

His eyes widened in surprise. The barracks women barely obeyed their men, let alone the female slave of another man. She'd managed it somehow, imposing her will on others twice her size or age. Some of the women began making rude comments about Eskkar's body parts, and he felt glad that Trella had kept them away, though he'd told her no such thing. "Good, Trella. Come with me." He nodded politely to the women, who already pushed past him, eager to learn what new fate had befallen their men.

"We must get ready for the evening meal, and you must wash and dress," Trella told him, then wrinkled her nose. "You smell like a horse."

Nicar had invited Eskkar to his home for dinner. Whether or not the invitation included Trella didn't matter, as he had decided to take her anyway. "Yes, I'm sure I do. But before dinner, I want to see to the village bowyer and the fletcher. I've just made some more promises about bows and arrows, and I need to make sure they're kept."

Back at his quarters, he told the guard to have the bow-maker and the arrowsmith brought there in an hour. Then Eskkar and Trella walked down to the river to bathe, separating into the two areas customarily reserved for men and women. After a quick wash and even quicker swim, he dried himself, then waited a few moments before Trella appeared, her hair wet and stringy, but glistening in the fading sun. His eyes lingered over her dress, which clung tightly to her still-wet body, and he regretted his summons to the craftsmen. He took her by the hand, ignoring the smiles of the villagers at the gesture, and they walked back to the barracks.

The knock on the open door came as Eskkar finished belting on his sword. Two men stood there, men who differed in aspect as much as any two men could. The bowyer, Rufus, was a hunched-over old man with long stringy gray hair and yellowed teeth. He wore a dirty tunic marked with multicolored stains, and carried with him the scents of the glues and resins of his profession.

The fletcher stood much taller, and his clean tunic marked him as a well-to-do craftsman. He carried a goodly amount of weight on his frame that proved arrowmaking to be a more lucrative occupation than soldiering, though that could be said of almost any trade, even farming. Basically a carpenter who specialized in making tools and small implements, Tevana created many different items for the local tradesmen. As a profitable sideline, Tevana had been making arrows for the soldiers for years. Eskkar knew him by sight but had never spoken to him.

The fletcher spoke first, in a deep and pleasant voice, bowing to Eskkar and giving Trella a quick glance. "Good afternoon, Captain."

Rufus, the bowyer didn't bow. "Your summons interrupted me in my work and I lose time while we speak. What is so important it couldn't wait until morning?" His tone was irritating.

Eskkar had met twice with Rufus, once to accept delivery of some bows and again to complain when one of the weapons had broken after a few days. Eskkar had been ignored on the first occasion and laughed at on the second, for Rufus gave no guarantees. "After all, how do I know what some fool will use it for when it leaves my shop—to hammer a nail or dig a hole? It bent properly here, you paid for it, and that's the end of it." Eskkar had to report to Ariamus that he failed to get a replacement.

"Please sit down, Rufus, Tevana. Bring wine for our guests, Trella." Eskkar kept his voice calm and resisted the urge to draw his sword and sweep Rufus's head from his shoulders. The old man made the best bows not only in Orak but in the surrounding regions. Now his sons and apprentices did most of the work, but their reputation matched their master's.

The three men sat down and Trella poured wine, then took her place on her stool behind Eskkar's bench. Rufus practically snatched the cup from her hand and gulped down half the cup, then gave Eskkar a look that seemed to say he didn't think much about the taste. Once again Eskkar's sword hand twitched at the insult.

"Thank you, Captain," Tevana said after taking a sip. "How may we help you?"

"I won't keep you long from your work, Rufus," Eskkar began. "I meet with Nicar tonight. But I wanted to make my needs known to you both as soon as possible. The barbarians are moving toward us, and I'll need bows and arrows to resist them."

"I think you'll need more than that to stop barbarians," Rufus said with a dry cackle that tempted Eskkar's sword hand yet again. "But I can sell you all the bows you need, if you can afford to pay for them."

"Good, Rufus, I'm glad to hear that." If the old fool was going to take that attitude, so be it. "Trella, tell Rufus and Tevana what we need."

Trella scraped her stool closer to the table. "My master desires four hundred bows, all of them five feet in length and capable of penetrating leather armor at two hundred paces. As for arrows, we will need one hundred thousand war arrows, plus at least ten thousand target arrows, all properly feathered and tipped with bronze."

Arrows could be tipped with almost anything, though hardened bone or bronze was preferred. While the bone tip could actually penetrate deeper, the bronze point left a more vicious wound and was more difficult to remove.

"And, of course, my master will need all the other materials—bowstrings, thumb rings, and wrist pads."

Tevana's wine cup stopped an inch before his lips while Rufus laughed outright, slapping his hand on the table, his cackle rising in volume until even Tevana turned toward him in annoyance.

The fletcher regained his voice first. "Captain, that's impossible. No one has ever asked for such a quantity of arrows before—and bronze tipped! Why, that's at least three, maybe four tons of bronze by itself. And then there's the wood, the feathers, the glues. I couldn't possibly make that many . . ."

Rufus leaned forward, interrupting, and pushing his face toward Eskkar. "If you'd asked for fifty bows, perhaps I would have made them for you. But four hundred? I'll not even try." He picked up his cup and drained it, then held it out to Trella for more, staring at her, his business with Eskkar apparently finished.

Eskkar raised his hand as she rose to fetch the wine jug. "No more wine for Master Rufus. We still have much business to discuss."

"Not with me, you don't," Rufus answered, standing and starting for the open doorway. "I'm returning to my shop before the last light is gone."

Eskkar raised his voice. "Guard!" Outside, the guard straightened up and gathered his spear into a ready position as he moved quickly toward the doorway. "Guard, if Master Rufus tries to leave, kill him."

They could hear the spear as it hummed through the air, spun down to a level position. The slim bronze tip hovered a foot from Rufus's skinny chest as he stood in the doorway. He stared at the weapon. Then he turned back into the room. "You can't threaten me, Eskkar."

"I'm not trying to threaten you, Rufus, I'm only telling you what's going to happen. If you cross the doorway, you die on the spear. Now get back here and sit down. We have things to discuss and not much time."

Rufus returned to the table and sat. "You don't scare me, Eskkar. I'll appeal to Nicar and the Five Families."

Eskkar shook his head. The man must be senile not to understand the events of yesterday. "Rufus, in case you haven't heard, things have changed in Orak. Do you really think that you can tell the Families you're too busy to make bows right now? That you're too important to work to save Orak?"

"I plan to leave the village anyway, Eskkar. I'll not risk my life trying to stop barbarians. Nothing can stop them. Find someone else to make your bows."

"If you wish to leave, Rufus, you may. I'll escort you to the gate myself, right now if you like. But your family stays in Orak and lives and dies with the rest of us. Maybe you didn't hear Nicar's words yesterday. He said no one was to leave without his permission. But I'll make an exception for you. I'm sure all your sons and apprentices will be glad to see you gone. You're obviously too old to be the master bowyer any longer." He watched Rufus's face blanch as the harsh words hit home.

"You can't keep me here. I'm a free man and a master craftsman. I have a right to leave if I choose. Besides, there's no way to make that number of bows in five months."

"I didn't say you had to make them all yourself, Rufus. Find others to make them. This is why I've asked you and Tevana here today. Both of you must figure out a way to meet my needs. Wood, copper, bronze, cordage, feathers, glue, bindings, skilled craftsmen, whatever you require. If you cannot do the work yourself, find others to share in the labor. Send word to other villages up and down the river."

Eskkar turned to Tevana. "The same for you, Tevana. If you can't make that many arrows yourself, then hire others, or buy them. Nicar will arrange payment. So I suggest that each of you return to your homes and begin planning to meet my needs." The two men looked at each other but said nothing.

Trella's voice broke in. "Master, you asked me to remind you about the quality of the goods."

"Oh, yes, of course. Don't think that you can throw some sticks together and call them bows. They must be perfect. Our lives will depend on them, and I want not more than one broken bow for every fifty delivered. Tevana, the same goes for the arrows. The shafts must all be straight and true, nocked, feathered, and tipped properly, and all of the same length and weight. I want no differences in the shafts to make my archers miss their targets."

"Master, do you wish to discuss payment now?" Trella added.

Damn, he'd forgotten the gold, always the most important factor when dealing with a tradesman. He leaned back from the table. "Payment. Yes, we should discuss that. Rufus, whatever your price is for a top quality bow, that's what we'll pay. But for every twenty bows you deliver, we'll pay you for twenty-five. And there will be a bonus of twenty gold coins when the barbarians are driven off."

He turned to Tevana. "The same for you, Master Fletcher. For every twenty arrows, you'll receive payment for twenty-five. But you will be personally responsible for the quality of the shafts, no matter who shapes them. My men's lives will depend on how true they fly and how hard they strike. If the quality of your weapons isn't perfect, I'll not hesitate to take your heads off."

"And the same bonus," Tevana asked slowly, a hint of a smile on his face, "if the barbarians are defeated?"

Esskar understood the smile. Tevana had the better deal, since it was a lot easier to craft an arrow than a bow. "The same arrangement for you, Master Fletcher. I just want the weapons, and you'll both get rich in the process. And when this is over, you'll be the heroes of Orak, the men who made the weapons that saved the village."

"Master, it's time to go, or we'll be late."

"Yes," Esskar said, "and now we can tell Nicar the good news—that work on our weapons has already begun." He smiled at the men. "And what time should these fine crafts-men return tomorrow to discuss their plans for making or obtaining the bows and arrows?"

"At one hour past noon, master," she answered. "If the plans are not complete, we can work on them together."

"Ah, yes, I had forgotten that. Trella will be working with you both to make sure your plans and schedules for delivery are sound and that you get all the supplies and materials you need. You'll work with her as you would work with me or Nicar. You'll find she has a keen mind for details. So bring what help you need and don't waste time trying to fool her. It would not be good for your health." He stood up, noting that dusk had arrived. They really would be late soon.

"Good evening, Rufus, Tevana. I look forward to hearing your plans." He saw the guard standing ready at the door-way. The man had heard everything and would spread the word about Eskkar's treatment of Rufus. "Guard, the master bowyer may depart."

When they were gone, Eskkar draped his arm around Trella's shoulder. "I think you'll have no trouble with them now. But if you do, let me know." He felt her head lean against his shoulder.

"There should be no problems, master. But I did think of someone else we need to speak to. The dockmaster."

"The dockmaster? Why him?" The dockmaster managed the six wooden jetties that allowed the river boats to land and the slaves to load and unload cargoes. He also arranged for the transportation of goods into and out of Orak, or onto other boats or carts for portage into the countryside.

"You told Rufus not to leave, but you think only of the roads. It would be easy for either of them to arrange passage on a ship. They and their families could be well away before we even knew it."

Frowning, he realized she was right. A horseman, he'd only been on a boat once, and he had no desire to repeat the experience.

"That means guards at the docks as well, I suppose. And we'll have to talk to all the boat captains, too." Everything he needed required more men, more attention to details, more time that he didn't have. He sighed. "Arrange a meeting tomorrow with the dockmaster and Bantor."

Eskkar looked down at her and felt wonderfully happy. "Now let's go and join Nicar. Think how glad Creta will be to see you and to feed you at her table. I'm sure you'll both have much to talk about."

8

Nicar's dinner unexpectedly turned into a family affair. His two sons, Lesu and Caldor, had returned that afternoon from a two-week trading trip.

Nicar's eldest, Lesu, had overseen the small caravan. Leading a pack train of animals loaded with trade goods, he'd escorted seven new slaves his father would resell, no doubt for a fat profit. Trella knew Lesu to be bright and courteous. Only nineteen, he planned to take a wife in a few weeks and would soon be fully capable of carrying on his father's trading business.

Caldor, a year or so younger than Lesu, sat directly across from Trella. He fidgeted in his chair for most of the meal, reminding Trella that Nicar's youngest boy lacked the patience and self-control of his elders. Not that she needed any such reminder. At least tonight he avoided staring at her breasts. She remembered the rough touch of his hands on her body and resisted the urge to shiver.

Nicar must have warned both boys not to provoke Eskkar or to speak disrespectfully to her. Dining in the very room where Eskkar killed two people, Nicar must have wanted to make very sure there wouldn't be any more *accidents*. Nobody made the mistake of calling Eskkar a barbarian.

The meal ended at last, Trella and Eskkar left Nicar's

house and passed through the courtyard. As soon as they reached the street, Trella took Eskkar's hand and held it tight, thankful the evening's activity had ended. She took several deep breaths, trying to cleanse the memories of that house from her lungs. Nevertheless, she resolved never to return there if she could avoid it.

They walked briskly and Trella had no problem keeping up with Eskkar's longer stride. She felt Eskkar squeeze her hand in anticipation of the warm bed that awaited them.

"You were very quiet tonight. I thought you'd have more to say to Nicar."

"It's not my place to give advice to Nicar, master. Nor should women speak about such things to their men in front of others. At the tables of the nobles, women keep silent when the affairs of men are discussed." She paused for a moment. "And I didn't like returning to that house, even to eat. Nothing good happened to me there. I'd prefer never to go back there again."

They followed the lane as it twisted around a sharp corner. A torch burned at the entrance to the barracks.

"Was it so bad there, Trella? I mean . . . tell me about it."

"Please, master, not tonight. It's just that I'm grateful to be away from that place."

"Then we won't speak of it." He placed his arm around her shoulder as they passed through the rickety fence that marked the entrance to the soldiers' area. "Perhaps we can speak of other things in our bed."

She leaned briefly against him in a silent promise. The cool night air had finally driven away the smells and memories of Nicar's household. She felt a wave of anticipation rush through her loins, her body already eager for the coming lovemaking.

Once inside their room, Eskkar hung up his sword, then took her into his arms. Her arms went around him, and she held him tightly. They stood that way for a few moments, and she began to relax, enjoying the sensation of being safe once again. The warmth built up between them, and she felt him harden against her.

Eskkar pushed himself away and removed his tunic. "Get under the blanket, Trella."

She heard the hoarseness in his voice, the first sign of his passion. "Don't you want me to build a fire?"

"No. You're fire enough for me. I'll keep you warm, I promise."

He kept his promise, and their body heat soon spread under the blanket. When their lovemaking ended, she relaxed in his arms while he stroked her hair. The excitement of lovemaking, still so new to her, kept her passion high, and she enjoyed the feel of his body against hers.

"Master, I saw . . ."

"Eskkar . . . call me that when we're alone, and especially in bed."

She snuggled against him. "Eskkar, I saw tonight that you did not drink much wine, or even eat much. Didn't the wine and the food please you?"

"I've never tasted better wine in all my wanderings. But now I have to train with the men, and too much spirits make a man weak. If I have to make love to you each night, girl, I'll need all my strength."

"Nicar worried you drank too much, that you couldn't be depended on. I heard him say that the day he gave me to you."

He sighed. "Nicar was right. In the last few months, I spent too much time in the alehouse. If I'd had more coins, I'd have drunk even more." He laughed, then his voice took a serious tone. "The night Ariamus ran off, I passed out in the tavern and the men carried me to my bed. I could have been killed in my sleep. That must never happen again."

"You are wise to keep your head clear, master . . . Eskkar. You will need all your wits, especially when you work with Corio."

"I'm glad the Families will accept Corio into their ranks. He's a good man, I think."

During dinner Nicar had agreed to elevating Corio to the rank of Noble, mentioning that the nobles had considered his name before.

"Young Caldor didn't think much of your suggestion that Corio join the noble families."

"Caldor's just a boy, Trella, fresh off his first caravan, if you can call it that. Scarcely more than sixty miles to the east and back. Two days' ride for a man with a good horse." He kissed the top of her head. "How much gold do you think they took from Drigo's house?"

Nicar refused to reveal how much had been found, though he did say one-quarter of it had been given to Drigo's wife. She and her daughter, along with their most trusted servants and guards, had boarded a boat and been sent downriver to return to her father's village.

"At Nicar's house, I worked with his clerks, and they said that Nicar had more than twelve hundred gold coins," Trella mused. She remembered her first day in Orak. Nicar had questioned her for almost an hour, tested her, to ensure she could count and write the symbols before he assigned her to work with his senior clerk. She needed only a single day to learn the differences between the symbols used in Orak from those in her native village. Nicar's clerk soon found her more useful than the other two slaves who served as Nicar's record keepers. She'd quickly learned the full extent of Nicar's holdings.

"The clerks gossiped that Drigo was nearly as rich as Nicar. I'd guess at least a thousand gold coins were found, more than enough to start paying for the defense of Orak."

"No wonder Drigo walked the streets as if he owned them. So much gold and he sought even more. And he wanted to be the First Family in Orak."

"My father said greed can do such things to a man. Drigo would have torn Orak apart. Do you regret killing him?"

"If he were a beggar in the street, I'd have killed him for insulting you. No one will ever do that again, I promise."

His words pleased her, and she turned to him. They shared a long kiss, enjoying the taste of each other. That kiss led to other caresses, and Trella sighed contentedly as she felt Eskkar becoming aroused once again.

"Trella, tomorrow will be a special day for you. After I

finish the morning training, we'll stand before Nicar and the other Families."

Startled, she raised herself on an elbow to face him. "What? Why do we need to see them?"

"Tomorrow I'll give you your freedom. I spoke with Nicar when we were alone and asked him how the thing could be done. Nicar will enter it as a contract, with another of the nobles as a witness."

His words caught Trella by surprise. She pushed herself upright in the bed.

"Why are you doing this, Eskkar? This isn't the time for such a thing. Later, perhaps, or when the barbarians are gone. Now, as your slave, I have your status, and I can speak for you. As a free woman, I'll be just another camp follower, a soldier's woman."

"I thought you'd be pleased." Eskkar sounded stunned. "Besides, I don't want brats like Caldor looking down at you. As a free woman, you can choose to be my servant, and you can still speak for me."

"Is that why you're doing this? So you won't be embarrassed by a slave who thinks and talks too much?"

"By the gods, no! I do this because I want you with me." He grasped her roughly by her arms. "And I want you to choose me freely. All my life I've never cared for a woman as I do for you. If you say the word, we will leave Orak tomorrow and let the village fend for itself. Orak means nothing to me. Only you mean anything."

Trella stayed silent for a long time. When she spoke, her voice was firm. "No, we must stay here, and you must defeat the barbarians. Only then can we have power and be secure. And . . ." She hesitated now, unsure of what to say. "You say that you want me . . . that . . . do you wish to take me for your wife?"

When he didn't answer immediately, Trella poked him sharply in the ribs. "Well, what are you thinking about? Can't you make up your mind?"

He laughed and rubbed the spot where she had hit him before lying back on the bed. "Well, I hadn't thought about taking a wife. I was thinking about that new slave that Lesu had brought back. She looked pretty enough, and well rounded as well. She might do . . ."

Trella pushed him away and tried to leave the bed, but Eskkar caught her and pulled her back. She struggled hard to break free, but he pinned her with his weight and held her by her wrists as he rolled on top of her.

"You're very strong for a girl, Trella. I suppose we could be married at Ishtar's temple after Nicar seals your freedom. Though I'm sure you'll make a terrible wife, and I will have to beat you regularly."

He bent down to kiss her but she turned her head away, still struggling. When she wouldn't meet his lips, he kissed her neck and her hair, then forced her legs apart, letting her feel his desire against her. Finally she turned her lips to his.

"Trella, I'm not sure what people mean by love, but I'm sure I love you, and want you to be my wife. I swear it before all the gods in the sky and under the earth."

His body had aroused her. She stopped struggling and moved her legs farther apart, and he slid easily inside her. Her body remained moist from their earlier lovemaking. Trella gave a long sigh of pleasure and her legs slowly wrapped around him.

"I suppose I could marry you. You need someone to look after you." Her arms went around him, and she suddenly tightened all of the muscles in her body, gripping him as hard as possible. After a moment, she slowly relaxed, letting Eskkar move against her once again. "And our children will need their father's name."

"Children? I hadn't thought about children." His hand slid down to her hip.

"Yes, master," she answered, reverting to her role as his slave. "If we make love like this every night, the gods are sure to send a child soon. Or hadn't you thought of that?"

The thought of getting her with child excited him. He thrust himself against her even harder, moving faster and faster until she cried out at the pleasure he gave her.

Eskkar made no answer, just forced himself against her with all his strength. Trella felt her body begin to spin out of control and she heard herself moaning. He held back, waiting for her, until her moans of pleasure increased, until she tightened herself around his manhood and cried out his name. She felt his seed flow as he cried out, and a wave of pleasure rippled through her, through both of them, that went on and on until they were exhausted.

He stayed inside of her, not moving, for a long time, until she could barely breathe and she had to ask him to move off her. They held each other for a long time, until her pleasure subsided and she could think again.

Trella felt him drifting off to sleep, so she raised her voice to keep him awake. "You need me to manage your household, to make sure everything is done properly. And there will be many tasks to make sure the village is safe. Drigo's house is ready for us. We can move in there tomorrow."

She stayed silent for a few moments. "But you will not free me or marry me yet, though your offer pleases me greatly. I can better help you in the coming months as your slave than as a wife. I will wait. When the barbarians are driven off, then you can set me free if you still wish to."

"I never heard of any slave refusing their freedom. Suppose I change my mind?"

She touched his lips with her finger. "Then I still have my coin, master. Or have you forgotten your words already?"

"Keep your golden coin, Trella, or return it to me on our wedding night. And I would never take back my words. No warrior would ever do such a thing." He kissed her tiredly. "Now can I get some sleep?"

"I'm not the one keeping you awake. Instead of working to defend the village, you spend much of your day and night taking your pleasure. Who else did you tell about setting me free?"

"Only Nicar, and he will tell no one. I made sure of that."

"Good. Then tell Nicar tomorrow that you've decided to wait for a while. Now sleep."

He turned on his side and fell asleep in seconds. Trella

stared up at the darkness, relaxed but wakeful, her body pleasantly reminding her of their passion, her mind turning over Eskkar's startling offer.

For a soldier recently too poor to afford a decent tunic, he'd been ready to give away a valuable gift. Not that she needed the offer of her freedom to know he cared for her. She could see that in his eyes, and she'd known it from their first morning together when he gave her the gold coin.

Somehow that gift changed her, made her look at him differently, and now she saw in him many admirable qualities that counterbalanced his rough edges and soldier's habits. His unexpected offer had surprised her. She had already decided that at some point she'd ask for her freedom, certain that he would give it.

For a moment her thoughts returned to Drigo and his son. Eskkar had killed the son not only to provoke the father but because the boy had insulted her. When the boy demanded his wine, Eskkar's eyes went cold, and for a brief instant she saw the pitiless warrior that still dwelt within him. Blood flowed quickly among the barbarians, where an insult could lead to drawn swords and death in moments.

Young Drigo and his father should have left quietly. If they had, they'd still be alive, and the nobles in Orak split in two factions, fighting with each other and creating havoc. Now Drigo's gold would pay for the village's defenses, and the nobles stood united behind Nicar.

No man would insult her again, she thought. Tonight, even Caldor had been polite, keeping his eyes off her, no doubt well lectured by his father. Nicar showed caution as well, seeing Eskkar as a new man, one who now dealt easily with the likes of Corio and Rufus. Nicar would have his own concerns about the future should the barbarians be defeated. But first the village must survive. Like Nicar, she would bend all her efforts to make that happen.

Taking her freedom now would be a mistake. Better to work in the background, both for Eskkar and for herself. A slave's mistakes could be easily ignored or brushed aside, and they both might need that excuse at any time. Trella had been a slave for over three months, more than enough time to learn the bitter realities.

Unlike someone who sold himself into bondage for a season or two and consequently was treated more like a servant, a bound slave became the property of her master for the rest of her life, with no rights and no expectations. The slave traders had beaten her twice the first week until she learned to obey. A shudder passed through her at what they might have done if they hadn't wanted the extra price for her virginity. Even so, they'd stripped her naked for their amusement or for any prospective buyers, who examined her much the way they would look at any breeding animal.

Even Nicar had looked at her with lust in his eyes, running his hands over his property. He'd seen only a young girl to be used to give him pleasure. No, the life of a slave was too bitter for her to bear. Trella had lived too well in her father's house and learned too much to accept such a fate. With the barbarians coming toward them, her status, or even Nicar's, meant little. Eskkar had told her how even the meanest-treated slave in the village had a better life than any captive in the barbarians' tents.

Trella shook off the dark thoughts. Much work remained ahead, and the future was uncertain, with no clear path before her. She'd wait for her freedom.

The words of her father came to her: "A good leader thinks six months ahead for his people; a great leader thinks six years ahead." She pondered the words for a long time. Her master did not seem accustomed to planning more than a few days ahead. He'd need her to guide him and chart out the coming years. Still, he continued to surprise her, coming up with ideas and plans in response to her questions. But only in response to her prodding. She could see he had the wits but had never learned to use them.

All that would have to change. Yes, she must begin now if she and Eskkar were to survive. Orak would stand or fall by what she and Eskkar did in the next few months, not by what happened when the barbarians arrived on the plain before the village. Her fate and Eskkar's depended on Orak's survival. Such thoughts surprised her now, so different from a few days ago. Now she not only wanted Eskkar to survive, but to take his place as a powerful noble in the years ahead.

Her father had planned for her to join some noble family through marriage, and he'd trained her hard for such a role. She'd learned the mysteries of trade and barter, gold and silver, of the farm, and even of the bronzemaker. And each night her father had spoken to her of the events of the day, explaining the choices the rulers faced and the decisions they made. In her time with Nicar, she saw nothing that she did not understand.

Her father's dream ended with his own death. Now the barbarian threat loomed over her, providing both great danger and a rare opportunity. If the village survived, Trella would be the wife of the soldier who saved Orak. Eskkar's family, her children that would come, must survive and grow powerful. Eskkar was a strong man. There would be many babies from his seed.

She felt the first wave of sleep approaching and her thoughts began to slow. Their House must be rich and powerful to protect her and their children. The thought of her children gave her pause and she breathed a prayer to Ishtar. *Goddess, give me a son, but not yet. Please, goddess, not yet.* Repeating the prayer, she fell asleep, nestled within Eskkar's clasp.

Next morning, Corio sent word postponing their scheduled meeting to midafternoon and asking that Eskkar come to the master builder's home. Eskkar didn't mind. He felt good, having spent the morning training, then watching Gatus put the men through their paces. His second in command loved nothing better than sweating men into soldiers.

None of the men had run off during the night, though of course they had many months and opportunities to do so. In high spirits, they seemed to take pride in the fact that Eskkar would stand and fight beside them. The news that, starting today, Eskkar and Nicar would begin taking in new men to swell the ranks, added to the soldiers' good dispositions. Most of the new recruits would be farmers, or villagers driven from their homes, or even just men searching for a new life. Nevertheless, there would be some fighting men among them as well.

Two guards accompanied Eskkar, Trella, and Sisuthros as they walked to Corio's house. The show of force might not be necessary, but a few of Drigo's followers still remained within the palisade. And many of Orak's villagers felt displeasure at Eskkar's rules forbidding them to leave.

The builder's home stood on the northeast side of Orak, about as far as one could get from the barracks and the river's edge and yet be within the palisade. The house had two stories and stood behind a high wall that protected it from the busy street. A stout wooden door led into a small courtyard adorned with well-tended beds of tulips, roses, geraniums, and other greenery that gave a pleasant scent to the air. Parts of the garden were paved with flat stones from the river, set in a mix of hardened mud and straw that would resist all but the strongest rains.

Bringing Sisuthros along had been Trella's idea. When she'd asked Eskkar which of his subcommanders had the quickest wits, he'd named Sisuthros.

"Choose a man of quick wits to work with Corio while he builds the wall. You'll have many other things to occupy your time."

The young subcommander hadn't looked pleased with the assignment. Sisuthros wanted to fight, not help build a wall.

Telling the guards to wait in the garden, Eskkar, Trella, and Sisuthros entered Corio's workroom. Inside, a large plank table awaited them, its surface covered by a thin cotton cloth. Corio, his two sons, and assistants surrounded the table. This time Trella stood at Eskkar's left, an equal participant in the proceedings.

Corio seemed in a fine mood, no doubt because of his earlier meeting with Nicar and his elevation to noble family status. Corio extended greetings to all, then introduced his sons and apprentices. Eskkar noticed Corio pointed to each of them with great care, even the youngest, giving honor to all of them. Their chests swelled with pride as he announced their names.

That's how one builds loyalty, Eskkar realized, by showing respect for one's people in front of others. Perhaps he could learn from men like Corio and Nicar. Eskkar resolved to remember this practice in dealing with his men.

"Captain of the Guard," Corio began in a formal manner, "I told you I would answer your question about building a wall to defend Orak. My sons and I have worked long into the night and this morning to answer that question." He nodded to his assistants and they removed the cloth from the table.

Trella gasped while Sisuthros slapped his sword hilt in amazement. Eskkar just stared. The map of yesterday had come to life as a model of Orak, only larger, and now it revealed the village and its surroundings. Little blocks of wood represented rows of buildings; the palisade was made of twigs; the river of pale green pebbles. The whole structure stretched about four feet long by three feet wide. Thin, flat strips of wood painted green indicated the farmlands. Corio pointed with his measuring stick, explaining what each miniature item represented.

"This is Orak today," Corio went on. "Now we'll change it." Like magicians, his sons began moving things around, removing some features, adding others. In moments, they'd transformed the model. The tiny blocks that represented houses and farms outside the palisade disappeared, a green cloth covering them. A taller wall represented by thin strips of wood set on edge replaced the original palisade, now surrounded on all sides by a narrow cloth ribbon, dyed the brown of the earth to represent the ditch Corio had proposed. The docks vanished, the gates changed to bigger and thicker sticks.

"A wall can be built, Eskkar." Corio touched the model's wall with his pointer for emphasis. "The wall will be fourteen feet high around three sides of the village and sixteen feet high on either side of the main gate. We'll flood the marshlands and, using water from Trella's wells, keep the ditch in front of the wall wet and muddy at our need. The distance from the bottom of the ditch to the top of the wall will measure at least twenty-five feet."

A rare compliment from any master, to give credit to a slave, especially the slave of another. "All this can be built in five months time?"

"It will be a close thing, Captain, but, yes, I believe so, providing everyone works on it as you promised. We must start at once, tomorrow, gathering the things we'll need, such as wood from across the river and from the forests up north. Only willow and poplar trees grow around Orak, and they're too soft and too small for our needs. We'll need hundreds of logs of all sizes, including large ones for the main gate my son will build for you. Most of these will have to come down the river by boat. Messengers and traders must be dispatched at once to buy them. Then stones must be taken up from the riverbed. Fortunately those are close at hand and in good quantity. Next we must set up a site to make the sun-dried bricks in huge numbers. They take weeks to harden properly, so we must start soon with them. We'll need every shovel and digging tool we can find as well as sand from the hills to the south, wagonloads of sand. And slaves, of course, to do the digging and the other heavy work."

"Then we start tomorrow," Eskkar said, staring at the miniature Orak, studying where the wall ended and the marshland began. It looked remarkably like what he'd envisioned from the hillside only a few days ago. "You must show this to Nicar and the Families. He will be pleased, I'm sure."

Eskkar turned to Sisuthros and gripped his subcommander's arm. "Sisuthros, you see what must be done. A strong hand will be needed to make sure the lumber arrives, the stones moved, the bricks made. Both slaves and villagers must be pressed into work as soon as Corio is ready and kept at it until they drop from exhaustion. Everyone must do his share, even the women and children. There must be no villagers hiding in their huts while others labor. I'll give you ten soldiers to start. It will be a difficult task, but I'm sure you can accomplish it."

Sisuthros nodded, fascinated by the model and now eager to undertake the assignment he'd questioned only this morning. "I'll do it, Captain. It will be worth it to see the faces of the barbarians when they see Corio's wall blocking their path."

"Come, there is more. Follow me." Corio went outdoors, then along the side of the courtyard. Two apprentices waited there.

"These boys built a model of the wall, so that you can get an idea of the scale you'll be using."

Using common river mud, the boys had built a wall, about three feet high and four feet in length. At the front side, dirt had been scooped out to represent the ditch. On the back of the wall a platform made of wood rose almost as high as the wall itself.

Corio squatted down and pointed to a doll. The figure held a tiny wooden sword on high and had been positioned in the ditch before the wall. "That's how high a man will be, standing before the wall. They'll need long ladders to reach the top."

He shifted his position to the other side of the wall. "Inside, the wall will be braced every twenty feet by a support wall, which will also carry the weight of the fighting platform. That platform, which we call a parapet, will be built of rough planks and will be four feet lower than the wall and ten feet across. That should be wide enough to allow men to pull a bow or swing a sword or even for some to move along the wall as others fight."

Eskkar joined Corio, squatting down beside him. "How high will the parapet be inside the village?" Eskkar wondered how he was going to get men up and down so that they could fight. Another detail he hadn't thought about before.

One of the apprentices giggled, apparently at Eskkar's ignorance, and received a sharp smack across his arm from the measuring ruler Corio still carried. "Keep your mouth still, boy."

Corio looked annoyed, clearly embarrassed by this flaw in his presentation. All of Corio's staff must have been warned not to laugh or say anything should any of the ignorant soldiers, particularly their barbarian captain, fail to understand what they saw or be unable to do a simple sum in their heads.

But Sisuthros had the same question. "Yes, Master Corio, how high will it be? We'll need to move men up and down very rapidly, and they'll be carrying heavy loads. And we'll need clear space at the base so men can move quickly from one point to another."

"The parapet will be ten feet high. We will put wooden ramps or steps inside so your men may mount the wall. We can use lifting poles to haul heavy stones to the top so that you can hurl them down at the attackers."

"Not wooden ramps, Corio," Eskkar commented. "At least, not anything that will burn easily. We'll be getting fire arrows shot over the wall. I want nothing nearby that can burn or even make smoke."

Fire was always a major hazard in the village, even in the best of times. The walls of the huts might be made of river mud, but their roofs could be any combination of cloth, wood, or straw, and most burned easily. Cooking fires set roofs ablaze often enough. During the siege, if the villagers detected smoke, many would panic. The defenders would have to be prepared for fire and smoke, Eskkar decided. Yet one more detail to think about.

"A good point," Corio conceded. "We'll build everything using as little wood as possible."

"Master Corio, if I may," Trella began, "perhaps we can coat anything inside the walls that might burn with a layer of mud. And we can have women and old men standing by with water buckets to fight any fires that break out. But besides fire arrows, won't there be many arrows shot over the wall into the village itself?"

"Trella's right," Sisuthros agreed. "Arrows will be landing everywhere. We may need to shelter some of the ground just inside the wall. It may be safest right under the wall."

Corio nodded thoughtfully. "There will be many such

things to consider in the next few weeks." He stood up and
turned to Eskkar. Eskkar rose with him.

"I'll work with Sisuthros starting tomorrow." Corio's eyes
looked directly into Eskkar's. "We'll give you your wall,
Captain. Now you must make sure you have the men to defend it."

9

Five days later, much had changed. Eskkar and Trella had moved into Drigo's house. The lower story of the spacious home contained five good-sized chambers, in addition to a large central space that could be used for meeting or dining, and a separate area for cooking. The upper floor, which Eskkar took for himself and Trella, held only two large rooms, one for sleeping and one for working.

With all that extra space, Eskkar provided quarters for Bantor and Jalen. Bantor had a wife and a daughter of eight seasons. After meeting Bantor's wife, Trella hired mother and daughter to help run the house. Bantor's family was more than grateful to get out of their wretched hut, all Bantor could afford.

A clerk, provided by the Noble Nestor and skilled in writing the symbols, arrived the morning after Eskkar and Trella moved in. The clerk kept track of expenses, but returned to Nestor's house each night, where he no doubt reported everything of interest.

Gatus's two boys and their friends began spending their days at the new headquarters and right away became runners, relaying messages at Eskkar's or the subcommanders' need. Nicar contributed an older woman slave as a cook. He'd planned to put her on the auction block, but she would have fetched little. Instead, he made her a gift to Eskkar. The grateful slave took over the cooking, and soon Eskkar and Trella began to enjoy bread and vegetables fresh from the market, to go with the occasional chicken.

To men used to communal living in the filthy and crowded barracks, the house seemed vast and luxurious, but Eskkar knew that soon more commanders would be eating and sleeping there. Meanwhile he ordered each commander to sleep three nights in a row in Ariamus's quarters. This would keep them close to the men, not only to keep an eye on the soldiers but also to stay aware of what they thought and felt.

The main house had a smaller, single-story building adjoining it, where Drigo housed his guards and slaves. It had five separate rooms, each large enough for four or five men. Eskkar decided to keep a force of ten soldiers near him at all times, should the villagers or even the Families grow troublesome. He had to put men there anyway, since the old barracks could at best provide beds for fifty men. Gatus helped pick the ten soldiers, making sure only the steadiest and most reliable men moved into Eskkar's quarters.

Eskkar and Trella began to settle into a routine. Each day he trained until midmorning with his men. After a brief break to wash up, he met with his four subcommanders and Trella to plan the rest of the day. They gathered in what had been Drigo's workroom, the large room outside Eskkar's bedroom and sanctuary. While Nicar had stripped the house of most of its furnishings, no one had wanted the workroom's two tables. Eskkar purchased them at a good price. He used the smaller one as his private work table, while the other easily accommodated Eskkar's meetings with his four subcommanders.

At the initial session, Eskkar had spoken first, according to the custom. Afterward, Trella suggested he allow the others to speak first. By doing so, he would not be contradicted by facts or new information he didn't have when he spoke. She added he didn't need to impress his men with his authority. Eskkar saw the wisdom in her suggestion so the next morning he let Gatus begin.

"The target range has been completed," Gatus announced. "Since Sisuthros wanted some building materials and we needed the space, we tore down almost all the huts on the northeast side of the palisade. We set up a range of up to three hundred paces, right up to the river's edge."

"And the training?" Most of the soldiers could bend a decent bow, but these men needed to train others. That required better than average archery skills, plus the knowledge of how to teach others.

"They're doing well, but slower than I'd like. I won't trust the best of them on their own for another week at least."

Gatus went on to the next topic. "In the last few days, we've taken in forty recruits. When I reached that number, I stopped accepting new men, at least until we've got these other men trained."

"Gatus, we need men as soon as possible, so move them along as quickly as you can," Eskkar said. "But I don't want half-trained men strutting around Orak carrying weapons, or fools killing themselves or some villager. How long before you can take more men?"

"At least two weeks, maybe longer." Gatus's words brooked no argument. "After that, we'll be able to take in another forty or fifty. Tevana already supplies us with target arrows, though he has requested four tons of bronze, plus a new forge and a dozen other wood and metal-working tools. I think Master Tevana wants to make sure he never has to buy anything again."

Eskkar grimaced at that, but nothing could stop Tevana or other craftsmen from taking advantage of the situation. If Orak survived, many tradesmen would profit handsomely by their dealings with Eskkar and Nicar.

"And thanks to Trella," Gatus continued with a smile, "we now have plenty of bows to work with, good ones, too. Tell them, Trella."

All eyes turned to Trella. She sat to Eskkar's left and always a little away from the table. "When I went to work with

Rufus at his home, I said I was ignorant of the bowmaking process and asked him to show me everything. At first he resisted, but finally he took me to the room where the bows were shaped and assembled, and the glues were prepared. I saw the tubs where they soaked the wood and the presses where the wet shafts were bent. But I never saw any finished bows.

"After I finished, I went to Gatus. He brought some men, and we searched the house. In a tiny attic above the bowmaster's sleeping chamber we found the drying and storage room. Inside were twenty-two finished bows, ready for use. I told Gatus to take them. Since Rufus had denied having any inventory, I told him there would be no payment. He wasn't happy."

Gatus laughed at that. "No, not a bit. He started to scream at Trella. His sons were quick to restrain him. Good thing, too, or I would've knocked the old fool down."

"Make sure the tale is told throughout the village," Eskkar said, laughing as well, though he'd already heard the story. "It may persuade others to be more honest. And keep training the men, Gatus. Archery first, then sword and spear. Practice everything from behind a wall if you can. Sisuthros, how goes our wall?"

"Captain, I'm worried," Sisuthros answered gloomily. "For the last five days, Corio and his helpers have been digging small holes in the ground, driving stakes here and there, and mixing batches of mud and straw. There are many meetings with his apprentices where they talk and talk. The masons are working from dawn to dusk making bricks, but Corio has yet to lay one brick on another, though he seems busy enough. I asked when he'd begin, but 'soon' was all he said."

Eskkar frowned. "What have you done for him?"

"We've confiscated lumber and tools and set up three different work crews. I also cleared some land near where the new gate will be, but that's all that has happened so far."

"Master, do not be concerned yet," Trella offered. "I've watched houses built, and there's much talking and preparation before the actual construction begins. It's always this way at the beginning, much confusion and seemingly little progress. Better to have them certain of what they must do, than to begin wrong and have to start over."

"Well, let's hope so, for our sakes." Eskkar shook his head. "Though I'd like the wall finished at least a day or two before the barbarians arrive." He turned to Bantor. "And the guards at the gates?"

Bantor's duty had turned into the busiest of all. Larger numbers of people came into and out of the village, and traffic on the road had increased to match. Already he'd stopped two fights at the gate involving people trying to leave. The second struggle had nearly overwhelmed the gatekeepers. Eskkar had to assign additional men, and now four men guarded both gates at all times.

"We search every cart and wagon that leaves Orak," Bantor answered. "No slaves or tools of value have left, and we make sure that no villager on Nicar's list leaves without his approval." He looked around the table. "Captain, the men are growing tired of guarding the gate. They complain they train for ten or twelve hours a day, then stand a four-hour watch at the gate or patrolling the streets."

"Bantor, I know the duty is hard right now. Tell the men it's only for a few more weeks until the recruits are trained." Not that Eskkar believed it. Any slack time created by the new recruits would likely be used up somewhere else. "You can lead them in this, Bantor. Treat yourself no better than they, and your men will endure it because you do."

Bantor nodded, then sat back, relieved to know his commander understood his problems.

Trella leaned forward again. "Bantor, has anyone tried to bribe your men to get out of Orak? If not, they will soon. Some rich tradesman or merchant will offer your men gold, and the temptation will be great."

"Like Rufus, you mean," Gatus said with a laugh. "I'm sure he's planning it as we speak."

Eskkar hadn't considered that possibility, though, of course, he should have thought of something so obvious. He sat thinking about what he would do if he were a rich merchant who wanted a few underpaid guardsmen to look the other way.

"Bantor, tell your men that anyone offered a bribe is to accept it. Once he has it in his hand then he's to report it, and you will double it. No matter how much the bribe, we'll double it."

"Where will this additional gold come from?" Sisuthros asked.

"Why, from the person who offered the bribe," Eskkar answered. "If a man can offer five silver coins, then he must have at least another five somewhere. This way, any man offering a bribe will pay twice and still be kept in Orak. Bantor, tell your men. If they can keep it to themselves, it may give them some incentive for their labors. A few may get some extra pay before the word gets out."

They all smiled at that. Everyone could picture the look of consternation on some merchant's face when he found out he'd been swindled. Eskkar turned to Jalen and listened to him report about the condition of the docks for a few moments, then held up his hand to interrupt. "Jalen, you haven't been given any tasks of importance this week because I've got something special for you. I want you to take four men, good riders, and the five best horses in the village. Then I want you to ride north and find the barbarians. I want to know where they are and when we can expect them to reach Orak."

"You're the best horseman in Orak," Eskkar went on, "and you've seen the barbarians in action. We need to know as much as we can about their movements, how many Alur Meriki there are. Anything you learn would be useful, but most of all, we need to know how much time we have."

All eyes turned to Jalen. The young man looked calm.

"I know this is risky. This will be dangerous, because if you get too close, you'll likely end up dead or captured."

"I'll do it, Captain," Jalen answered, "though it might be better if I took more men."

"No more men. I don't want you fighting. I want you scouting and reporting."

Jalen exhaled a long breath, but didn't argue. "How soon do you want me to go?"

"Leave in the morning," Eskkar replied. "Spend today picking your men and getting ready. Each of them will receive ten gold coins when they return, in addition to their regular pay. And double that for yourself, Jalen." For that much gold, most men would risk their lives gladly.

"You'll travel light and travel fast. And you can only take two experienced soldiers. Choose the others from the new recruits. Pick only good horsemen who are steady and will do as you tell them and not get their blood rushing if they see the barbarians." Eskkar intended that advice as much for Jalen as for any men he might pick.

"And the horses, take any in the village, even from the Families. Didn't Drigo have some good horseflesh?" Eskkar slapped the table in irritation for forgetting Drigo's horses, no doubt already appropriated by the Families. Breeding and maintaining a riding horse took plenty of silver coins, and only the richest could afford the luxury. The soldiers' mounts, provided grudgingly by the nobles, were mostly inferior animals, used for local patrols or as pack animals.

"Those horses must be around somewhere. We'll find them. But remember, Jalen, your task is to get information, not fight. I want you back here alive, not with your head on some warrior's lance. If you think fit, send two men back early to report. Take a boy as a servant and to ride an extra horse." A boy could always be abandoned, should the horse be needed.

Trella stood and went to the other table, returning with a small leather pouch. She removed a light brown cloth and spread it out on the table.

Everyone leaned forward to look, then gasped. The cloth was a map with details sewn into the material using green, blue, and red threads. The river and Orak were clearly marked, as were most of the villages in the northern countryside.

She set a slim wooden needle and two small spools of thread, one red and one white, on the table. "You can sew these threads on to indicate what you find and where you find it. My master obtained this for you yesterday."

Eskkar didn't mind explaining. "When I saw Corio's map, it stayed in my thoughts, so I went to him and asked if he could make one for me. Corio told me he got his from Noble Rebba who had a slave skilled in making such things. So I went to Rebba's house and convinced him that I needed the slave to work on this."

It had taken more than polite conversation. Eskkar had threatened to take the slave by force if the map wasn't completed by this morning. "I spent an hour with the slave. He said a cloth map is easier to carry and use than a papyrus one. He'll explain certain things to you about the map, and show you how to judge the distance between landmarks. Stay with him, Jalen, until everything is clear in your head."

"Now, men, let's get back to work," Eskkar said. "Jalen, join us for dinner at sunset, and we can discuss things. I'm going to visit Corio and see how things are progressing." He stood up to indicate that the meeting had ended, and that another day in the transformation of Orak had begun.

Eskkar's following was already so routine as to be scarcely noticed by the villagers. He traveled with Trella and two guards, one a seasoned veteran and the other a recruit, expected to watch his elder and follow his example. With Sisuthros leading the way, they found Corio working outside the main gate, leaning over a small table and talking with one of his sons. A half-dozen slaves and craftsmen surrounded them.

No one seemed to be doing any building. Most of the men just stood around. Tools lay on the ground. A few shallow holes had been dug and piles of wood were scattered about. Not one brick sat atop another.

"Good morning," Corio greeted each of them by name, an expansive smile on his face. "I expected a visit from you, Captain. I fear Sisuthros is dissatisfied with our progress."

"We know work such as this takes time, Corio," Eskkar

replied, determined to show the master artisan he understood something about the nature of his craft. "But I wanted to see what's been done and get some idea of when the wall is likely to be finished."

"Actually, Eskkar, we are almost ready to begin. Come, I'll show you." He walked toward the north, stopping in front of a shallow trench.

Eskkar estimated the hole to be four feet wide, six feet long, and three feet deep.

"This is the start of the wall. We'll dig it down a little deeper to make sure the base is solid, and we will layer the base with stones. Then sun-dried bricks of mud and straw will form two walls, and we'll fill in the center with dirt, stones, and upright bricks to add strength. We'll add the dirt slowly and tamp it down tightly as we go. Some bricks will be placed inside at angles to the face of the wall to give it additional strength. That way, the wall will be solid enough even though it will only have bricks on the front and back. Naturally, if we had more time, we would make the wall deeper, taller, and thicker."

Corio spoke to his son, who ran off and returned in a moment carrying a heavy mud brick with a few strands of straw sticking out of it. "This is the brick we will use."

About eighteen inches long, six inches wide, and four inches deep, it looked quite heavy. Eskkar started to take it from the boy, but Corio spoke first. "Captain, if you hold the brick, do not grasp it by the ends. It might break in half. Hold it from underneath and support its weight."

Eskkar took the brick as instructed, surprised at its weight. He handed it to Sisuthros, who hefted the brick before giving it back to the boy, who took it and carefully laid it flat in the bottom of the hole, then ran off to fetch a second brick. When he returned, he placed the second brick in a straight line with the first one, leaving a finger-sized gap between the two. He raced off to fetch another while Corio explained further.

"The bricks are placed thus in the hole, then covered with a thin layer of wet mud and sand, then a third brick is placed atop the middle of the first two. Then we add more mud and repeat the process. The wall grows out of the earth and becomes stronger as the mud and sand dry around the bricks. Then we smooth the outer face of the wall with a different mixture of sand and mud, which will also harden quite well."

"Master Corio," began Sisuthros, poking at the bricks with his foot, "it doesn't seem very strong. Isn't it just mud? I mean, won't the barbarians just be able to push it down?"

Eskkar thought much the same thing, but he'd learned not to ask the obvious questions. Nevertheless, he felt relieved Sisuthros had voiced his doubts.

"Sisuthros, the wall will be strong enough to protect your men and give them a fighting platform. It won't be easily climbed or torn down. But if they bring tools to dig at the wall, or a ram, to try and punch through it, then the wall won't stand for very long. To make the wall strong enough to resist tools or a determined assault of that kind would take more time than we have."

"Master Builder," Eskkar said, "your task is to build the wall; ours, to defend it." He turned to Sisuthros. "If we allow the barbarians time to stand before the wall and dig at it with shovels and axes, then we'll be lost. If we give them that much time . . . no, we must kill any of them that make it to the ditch or to the base of the wall."

Corio thought about Eskkar's words for a moment. "The wall will not yield easily, and the packed dirt will be difficult to dislodge. But if enough men with the right tools attack the base of the wall, then in twenty or thirty minutes' hard work, they could make a small breach."

Less time than that, Eskkar thought, knowing Corio had never witnessed the ferocious energy of the steppes people at war. "We'll not give them even ten minutes, Corio. Just make sure the wall doesn't fall down." He looked at Trella to see if she had anything to add.

"Master Builder," she began, "if you think it a good idea, perhaps you could build a small section, one that Eskkar and his men could pretend to attack to see how long it would take them to break it apart. What they learn might help you in your designs."

Corio rubbed his chin as he considered her words. "An excellent suggestion, Trella. I've never tried to tear down anything I've built. We're almost ready to begin anyway, so we will construct for you a ten or twenty-foot section of wall wherever you desire."

"And how long before we see an actual wall standing before us?" Eskkar asked. They still needed to know if it could be done in time. But that question didn't seem to worry Corio very much.

"Return in ten days, and you'll see the first section of the wall completed," he answered. "Right now, it's more important for you to make sure that all the supplies and men that I require are delivered."

"Then I go to attend to my task." Eskkar gave a formal bow to Corio. "And I leave you and Sisuthros to yours."

Eskkar walked away with Trella at his side, ignoring the custom of having the slave walk behind the master. "Well, what did you think?"

"Corio is sure he can complete the wall in time unless something unexpected occurs. But I don't think he gave much thought to how strong the wall would actually be. He'll think about it now, and I'm sure he will make the base of the wall stronger than he'd planned, at least at the places you say the barbarians will attack." She gave him a smile. "So, master, you have done well this day. Corio will build you a fighting wall, not a house wall."

Eskkar laughed, then put his arm around her, giving her a hearty squeeze and a slap on her backside, ignoring the looks and smiles from the people in the lane. "Well, then, tonight you will have to work extra hard to make sure your master is rewarded for his quick thinking."

When their lovemaking ended and Eskkar slept, Trella lay in the crook of his arm. She had to force her thoughts away from the warm glow of their passion, but she finally cleared her mind and thought about her future. The coming months would require long hours of hard work. She knew she'd be busy enough helping Eskkar manage the details of the defense, to make sure no key item was forgotten.

But all the coordination and planning for the attack would be only background to the real struggle that lay ahead. Her few days with Eskkar had convinced her, somewhat to her surprise, that her master possessed many good qualities and more wits than many gave him credit. He had proven capable and resourceful. Uneducated and rough he might be, but he had a personal code of honor that had won her respect and then her heart.

Eskkar had convinced Nicar, then the soldiers, and finally the rest of the villagers he could defend Orak, and now even she believed in him. Give him the men and supplies, make sure that nothing is overlooked and every detail well planned, and he would have an even chance against the barbarians. And so she promised herself that she would do everything she could to give him that chance.

Nevertheless, Trella knew that even a successful defense of Orak would not guarantee Eskkar would survive. The moment the threat disappeared, the nobles and the leading merchants would remember Drigo's destruction and how much gold Eskkar had cost them. They'd want to eliminate or remove the upstart captain of the guard. The nobles considered themselves too clever, too wealthy, and too powerful to submit to the rule of an outsider like Eskkar. Even less would they want someone like him to share in their rule, a constant reminder of what they owed to him. So while his dream of joining the nobles might be possible, it seemed doubtful that he, a barbarian himself, could long survive in that group.

No, they'd find a way to get rid of him, and that now included her as well. They'd remember she had provoked Drigo, that she had given Eskkar the help he needed to win over the merchants, and most of all that she'd been a slave. Her fate was bound up with her master's and just as sealed. Even if she survived, even if she were not kept as a slave, she'd be given in marriage to some minor son who would keep her in his household, a mere plaything or a source of children, locked away from everything and everyone, and soon forgotten.

Thus Eskkar might win the battle but lose the victory. So that must be where her true efforts should go, all her wits and resources committed to making sure that Eskkar and she retained the fruits of their victory. Not only would it prove difficult, she must do it quietly, so quietly that nobody knew what she was about. Even Eskkar, for now, was better off knowing nothing of her activities.

Knowledge would be the key. To know everything that went on in Orak would be her goal, and already she had several ideas about how to begin that task. Today, as they walked hand-in-hand through the village streets, she'd seen how the people looked at her, the slave girl who walked side-by-side with her master, the slave who'd surely cast a spell on the tall soldier, the slave who had brought down the House of Drigo, the slave who attended the councils of the Nobles. Those looks had reinforced her own assessment.

Tomorrow she'd begin winning over the common people, starting with the women. Once she'd swayed them to her side, she would use them to gather information. She would win allies and friends from among the villagers, especially the new ones that would flock to Orak in the next few months, the landless and friendless ones who would have little loyalty to the nobles or the wealthy merchants.

That started a new train of thought, and she shifted her body slightly, the small movement causing Eskkar to turn on his side but not to wake from his slumber. She smiled as she thought about herself and Eskkar—the barbarian soldier and the educated slave. Everyone in the village thought she'd bewitched him, used magic or potions to turn him into a leader of men. Even Nicar half-believed it. Perhaps that could be another ally. Let all of them think she had the gift of power over men.

Her wits were sharp, she knew, sharp enough to see quickly and easily many things that others saw only slowly or not at all. The common people would be one of the keys to power in the new Orak, she decided, a strong balance against the might and money of the nobles. Well, she would find a way to win the hearts of the crowd. She already had piqued their interest, a good first step. Yes, that was the way to power and security for herself and her lover. She smiled in the darkness and turned on her side, her arm crossing his body as she pulled herself close to him and fell asleep almost at once, feeling safe in his arms.

10

~~~~~~

The next four weeks passed quickly for Eskkar, who started every morning before the sun rose and climbed exhausted into bed at night. Each day brought some new crisis or an unexpected setback. But the first group of recruits had joined the ranks, and another group of forty had started.

At last Bantor and Gatus had enough soldiers to man the gates, the docks, and the lanes, allowing Eskkar the luxury of sending out local patrols. Their reports confirmed men were converging on Orak. Some looked for a chance to fight the barbarians, others simply sought refuge or a place of safety to bring their families. More arrived each day, and as many came to stay as had left. Bantor's men stopped everyone at the gate, where the arriving refugees learned they could either fight, dig, or move on. Only traders with their caravans and goods passed freely into Orak.

Patrols walked the village each day to make sure every man performed his assigned work task. Slackers received only one warning. At the second offense, Eskkar simply ordered them out of the village, forcing them to leave behind anything of value to the defense.

One foolish craftsman had resisted the order and drawn a knife. Bantor killed the man. His death was less than a pebble thrown into the great river, but the villagers, rich and poor, understood the warning. Since then, no one tried to leave the village by force. All those who remained worked on the wall, adding their sweat and blood to the sand, stones, and mud that comprised it.

The Wall. It became the focal point of everyone's lives and the main theme of conversation. The first topic of discussion centered around the backbreaking labor as men toiled under heavy loads of earth, bricks, or stones. Nicar, Corio, and the village elders walked the construction area each day, encouraging slaves and freemen to keep up their efforts. Sisuthros's soldiers made sure everyone did their fair share of the work, adding their own muscles to the toil, and using the whip only to deal with slackers. Men labored and sweated, and the wall began to grow out of the earth. But it grew slowly, as if resisting the efforts of impatient men to lift it from the dust.

The soldiers' training was the next subject of discussion. As hard as the villagers labored to build the wall, so did Eskkar's men sweat in their brutal training, cursing their drillmasters as they first hardened their bodies, then learned how to use their weapons. They trained in the shadow of the new wall as they tested their archery from makeshift platforms.

Use of the bow took first place in the training. For at least three hours every day, each group of soldiers devoted their time to archery. They fired hundreds of arrows daily until their fingers ran red with blood and muscles trembled from the strain. When they finished with the bow, they learned to fight with sword, spear, and axe, practicing from the makeshift walls. Day's end brought them no respite, for Eskkar still needed soldiers to guard the gates and the docks, patrol the village, and enforce discipline on the work crews. Everyone complained, but to no effect, as their commanders labored as hard as their men.

The third topic, which was usually the most interesting, was the captain of the guard and his female slave. Few villagers had known or noticed Eskkar before Nicar appointed him captain. Those who recalled him from those days admitted he'd changed. Still aloof and rarely smiling, he now stood out from other men as he strode about the village.

Everyone deferred to him. Everyone looked to him to defend Orak and save them from the barbarians. All watched him carefully each day, searching for the slightest sign of fear or doubt. But he gave no such sign. And each day the wall grew a few feet longer, the soldiers trained a little harder, and gradually the villagers began to believe they might survive.

If Eskkar made for poor conversation, Trella was another matter. As she went about her duties or accompanied her master, everyone found something to say about the slave girl who'd cast a spell on the soldier. Defying custom she walked at Eskkar's side, and he often put his arm around her, letting everyone see how much she meant to him.

The village women began to respect her, and their men soon grew as awed as their wives. Trella showed wisdom beyond her seasons, and her voice commanded attention in the councils. She seemed to radiate a power over men and women, and now many sought her advice as she passed through the streets.

Nevertheless, at each day's end, the tired villagers wondered whether there would be enough soldiers to defend Orak, and the soldiers worried if the laborers could complete the wall in time.

Eskkar threw himself into the effort, as if by hard work he could single-handedly guarantee success. His daily training soon made him the most proficient swordsman in the village, but many a time Eskkar found himself knocked to the dirt by some especially skillful or lucky opponent.

The men always cheered at that, and Eskkar learned to nod approval to his challenger, though it seldom happened twice. Several times each week Eskkar took a horse and rode the countryside around Orak, studying the land while he practiced his horsemanship. Each day brought some new bruise or scrape, and each night Trella would massage her master's stiff muscles.

Trella worked just as tirelessly. She took charge of all the weaponry and supplies needed by the soldiers. She met daily with Rufus and Tevana, coordinating their needs, and doing the same for those making the spears, shields, and axes.

She spent an entire day with Eskkar and Gatus, learning everything about the men's weaponry and clothing. They showed her the leather vests, caps, and wrist guards they wanted for the archers. Since bowmen standing atop the wall would be exposed from the waist up, leather armor would provide a great deal of protection. While the vest would not stop an Alur Meriki arrow at close range, it would certainly save some lives.

Trella did the same with the other weapons. Gatus showed her the kind of short sword, spear, and axe that he wanted, demonstrated how each would be used, and taught her how to judge their quality. She noticed Eskkar listened intently to Gatus. The old soldier knew his weapons, and knew what he wanted.

Soon Trella knew all she needed to know in order to deal with merchants and traders. Gatus would inspect and accept each new weapon, but the haggling over prices and delivery schedules were off his shoulders.

Trella made sure all the weapons and supplies arrived on time, even as she kept track of the gold needed. By taking care of the logistics, she allowed Eskkar to concentrate on the recruiting, training, and organizing of the men. It also gave him more time to meet with Nicar, Corio, and the rest of the noble families. At the end of each week, she spent a day with Nicar's clerks, going over the accounts and making sure no merchant received payment for something not delivered.

It took Trella only a few days to discover how much silver the previous Captain had stolen by purchasing poor quality food, and as little of that as possible. Honest bargaining with the farmers, as Eskkar's representative, made sure that sufficient and wholesome fare arrived regularly and at a reasonable price.

For the first time the soldiers had decent food to eat, and enough of it to maintain them through their strenuous training. Fresh bread and vegetables complemented the lamb and chicken the soldiers normally ate. Trella dealt directly with the farmers who supplied the food, and added a staff of cooks to prepare the meals. For that alone the soldiers would have loved her, but she did even more. Using Eskkar's gold, she paid a few copper coins to those willing to clean out the barracks and the grounds around them. After a few days even the malodorous barracks smelled and looked cleaner.

Not satisfied with her accomplishments, Trella looked for other opportunities to expand her influence. The first such she found involved working with Nicar and Nestor on the housing problem.

By Nicar's order, anyone leaving Orak forfeited their house and any belongings left behind. This policy forced any villagers who thought of leaving to make a hard choice. If the village survived and they returned, their homes would be gone, given to someone else. Or they could stay and fight.

Nevertheless, many left Orak, and those who remained clamored for even the humblest of the abandoned houses and huts. Working with the clerks, Trella inventoried each hut and home and recommended new owners, favoring those who could best help Orak. She argued skillfully, forcing the clerks to abandon their plans of helping friends or those willing to pay. Trella focused on those who had the skills needed for the village's defense. If they possessed those skills and were willing to stay and work, Trella would present their case.

Only once did she have to involve Eskkar. The clerks wanted to give an empty home to a wine merchant, while Trella insisted that the dwelling be given to a family of five that included a father and two grown sons willing to fight. Eskkar lost his temper and threatened to have every clerk run out of the village. Trella had to plead with him not to go to Nicar. After that, she had no more problems with the clerks.

With each day that passed, Eskkar and Trella's lives became more entwined with the fate of Orak—and the fate of Orak depended on the wall.

Everyone who could worked on the wall. Fight, dig, or move on. No other choice existed for anyone hoping to remain in Orak. Eskkar made that decision, backed by Nicar. The soldiers' swords enforced it. Everyone labored in Orak's defense, including the members of the Families.

No work on anything else was permitted unless approved by Nicar and Eskkar. Those caught away from their tasks received some punishment, and Eskkar would make no exceptions for the sons of the Families, though he did allow them to be assigned lighter duties than digging or rock carrying as long as they performed their duties well.

Gatus sent more men out to patrol the roads and to keep bandits and robbers from attacking those bringing goods to Orak. Sisuthros now had twenty men to make sure those working on the wall put their backs into it, while Corio directed a workforce of over four hundred men and boys, and even women and old men. The master builder walked back and forth among the workers, driving himself and his apprentices as hard as any laborer.

Slaves and free villagers alike worked, all covered with dust and mud, except those who gathered rocks from the river and could occasionally wash themselves clean. Each evening, their work completed, villagers came to stare at the wall, which grew longer and longer each day.

The wall now extended one hundred feet on both sides of where the new gate would be. Each side grew at least twenty feet every day, arms spreading themselves wide to encompass all of Orak.

Corio's oldest son, Alcinor, directed the construction of the main gate. It would be made of heavy beams carefully shaped and closely joined by the carpenters, all firehardened to resist flame arrows, and reinforced with wide bronze strips. Inside the gate, holes were lined with stones for the bracing logs that would reinforce the structure when closed.

Underneath the gate, a trench six feet wide and ten feet deep had already been dug. This pit would be completely filled with heavy stones and packed with the usual mud and straw mix, creating a solid foundation that would frustrate any attempts to dig under the structure. Soon the gate would be functional, though not fully completed, and would enclose the new, extended boundaries of the village.

Each day more than a dozen boats arrived carrying timber of all types and sizes. Finished tools, weapons, and leather goods came by land and by river. Food and wine disembarked as well, to help swell Orak's storehouses for the siege. Word had gone out throughout the countryside as well as up and down the great river, and other villages proved eager either to assist in resisting the barbarians or simply to make a profit.

Boats filled with costly copper and tin arrived regularly. Desperately needed by the bronze workers for dozens of items, the ores were in short supply and difficult to obtain. The mines lay many miles distant, and produced only a small output from their pits each day, since only slaves could be forced to labor in them. For some mysterious reason, slaves died quickly in the mines, few of them lasting more than six months. Eskkar learned this was why it took so much gold and silver to buy copper and tin.

But Eskkar demanded bronze weapons, and only these ores could be turned into the lustrous metal, and so Nicar's gold kept flowing. Orak's smiths labored from dawn to dusk, transmuting the raw ores into gleaming bronze weapons and tools.

Timber from the north ranked as the second most important cargo, as wood was needed not only for the gate, but to reinforce the walls and parapets, to make shields for the soldiers, and even as firewood for the forges. Other ships brought the first deliveries of weapons—finished swords, spears, and even bows and arrows, in addition to those made in Orak. The boats used by the river's sailors were small, propelled by a few oars and perhaps a tiny sail, and they couldn't carry much cargo, but more arrived daily as word about Orak's needs continued to spread throughout the land. Each boat captain rushed to unload his vessel, take on his trade goods or payment, and return whence he came for another consignment.

The dockmaster permitted no other cargoes to land,

except for food and wine, though Eskkar had no doubt other goods somehow managed to smuggle their way inside.

A large market had sprouted at the docks where traders bought and sold the ships' contents each day. The Families of Decca and Rebba took responsibility for that function, buying and selling, and making sure the prices stayed reasonable.

Eskkar didn't trust any of the Families, certain that if they had the opportunity, they would steal from the village. To guard against that, Nicar and his clerks assisted as well, checking the accounts and watching the cargo manifests. It seemed to be working, since every merchant and shipmaster complained of being robbed, while the Families shouted that they were being reduced to poverty. But the trading never stopped, and each day the boats continued to arrive and depart.

Gatus trained the men hard each day. He and Eskkar argued for a full day before Eskkar gave his approval to Gatus's novel ideas. The old soldier wanted to train the men to fight in units of ten. Eskkar had never heard of such a thing before, nor had any of the men. But Gatus fought hard for his ideas, declaring the archers would be more effective if they fought this way, and that foot soldiers could support each other in battle. Eskkar eventually agreed, since there would soon be so many men under arms that some organization would be needed just to control them.

As soon as Gatus began his new regimen, Eskkar saw the benefits—the men's morale improved along with their effectiveness.

Veterans had four hours of training, either at sunup or an hour past noon. When they finished training, they worked for Sisuthros or Bantor, or taught the new recruits, who trained all day long. The training for the new men was even harder because they needed to be physically fit in order to fight well. In exchanging sword strokes, the weaker man or the one who tired first usually died, and Eskkar wanted men who could fight and kill for hours if need be.

So Gatus made them run holding heavy logs over their heads until they staggered and fell, then put swords in their trembling hands and made them hack at the posts until their hands blistered and bled before hardening into calluses. Sometimes the men formed ranks and marched with their shields and spears, holding the heavy weapon aloft to strengthen arm muscles.

Then, thirsty, shaken, and exhausted, they stood at the archery range and shot arrows until each man hit his target fifty times, no matter how many arrows it took. Gatus and his men watched to make sure each man drew the shaft fully and aimed it properly. Wooden rods awaited any that shirked. And each day the targets moved a few feet farther back, until after three weeks of training, even the newest recruits could hit the mark at sixty paces five times out of six.

When the men finished their session, they rested by retrieving the target arrows from the butts and preparing them for the next group. Bowstrings had to be checked and replaced as needed. A well-made bowstring would launch between two and three hundred arrows before breaking or stretching, and it took the effort of a dozen women working all day to weave and braid the coarse flax into suitable bowstrings.

Eskkar did his part as well, first training with regular men, then working with the recruits. The new men felt proud, knowing their captain didn't think himself too haughty to sweat with them for a few hours each day. It made the training more bearable for them, as did his encouragements. "You miserable dogs," he shouted at them, "I want you to be more afraid of Gatus and me than any barbarian."

And each day a few villagers, mostly old women and children, came to watch the training and cheer the men on. Eskkar permitted this so everyone would know the soldiers worked as hard as those straining at their loads of dirt and rock.

Trella constantly reminded Eskkar that he must befriend the villagers, make them aware of what he did for them, and change them into his supporters. "Your strength," she reminded him, "lies in making sure the people believe you are defending them, not just the rich merchants."

So he forced himself to say a few words of encouragement or a simple hello to the villagers each day. Eskkar
felt strange doing it, but he soon grew used to it. He now
trusted Trella completely. If she believed something was
important, then Eskkar would do it even if he didn't understand why.

Amazingly, all of it was working. The mood of the soldiers and recruits stayed positive, reinforced by the steady
progress of the wall as it slowly crept across the face of
Orak. It grew at least twenty feet each day, and Corio promised more as the workers' skills improved.

Eskkar's body had hardened once again, and he made
sure that he grunted under the logs with the weakest men to
build his own strength. If they could keep up this pace and
the barbarians didn't arrive before the wall's completion, the
whole plan might work.

Eskkar had never thought villagers could be trained well
enough to beat barbarians one on one, but now, seeing their
progress, he began to think differently. Men had been trained
as soldiers before, but never under the threat of a barbarian
migration. Gatus and the other commanders became more
experienced and efficient in their training methods. If the
villagers could fight the barbarians on their terms, if the barbarians did what Eskkar expected, if they didn't come too
early, if . . . if . . . if.

Each night in bed, Eskkar whispered his doubts and worries to Trella. He, who'd never shared his thoughts with anyone in his life, talked openly to Trella, who reassured him if
she could or held him tight when she couldn't. Their lovemaking became less frequent but more intense, as if they
shared a burden that threatened to overwhelm them.

Each day Eskkar learned something new, looked at someone or something differently, gained a new insight or made
some mistake. Each day brought a dozen different decisions, a dozen situations for which he had no experience. He
had no sympathy for his commanders when they erred, and
he was harder on himself.

The worst of his errors were those he was unaware of.
Those Trella or somebody else pointed out to him were

bitter in his mouth. He forced himself to listen to Trella's explanations, silently vowing never to repeat the same mistake again.

Nothing in Eskkar's life had prepared him for this situation, and more than once he considered leaving it all behind, taking a horse and just riding off. But always the thought of Trella kept him to his task.

He now wanted the future she foresaw. He also knew that slowly, subtly, he was changing, learning to think before he spoke, to consider before he acted, and, most of all, to listen to and take the advice of others. Somehow he knew the gods had linked his fate to hers, and that both of them would face whatever future the barbarians brought to Orak. And each day, the wall continued to grow.

Those same weeks passed even faster for Trella, who set for herself an even more difficult task, one she could not go about openly. That task began after they'd moved into Drigo's house. As soon as she finished her morning duties, Trella spent two or three hours walking through the village. Accompanied always by a guard and dressed in the old shift she'd worn in Nicar's house, she talked to the women at the market, helped with their laundry at the river, even visited with the women working in the fields or on the wall.

She did more than visit. Her own labors at the wall were as strenuous as any man's, though she seldom worked more than a few hours. She carried stones and bricks, or dug in the trenches along with the other women. The first time Corio noticed her working, he tried to get her to stop. She refused, saying what she did was little enough compared to the other women.

Even that first day, groups of curious women gathered wherever she went, eager to speak to her and as eager to offer advice. After the first week, Bantor's wife, Annok-sur, began to accompany her.

A plain, practical woman a few seasons younger than Eskkar, Annok-sur showed she had the skills and experience needed to manage a large household. The two soon transformed the former house of Drigo not only into a home for Eskkar and his men but into a planning center for Orak's defense.

Between them, they organized the servants, assigned the day's tasks, and established a routine that began to run itself. Despite their age difference, they became friends.

Trella sat at a small table in her bedroom, while Annok-sur combed Trella's hair. Neither of them thought it the least bit strange for a free woman to comb the hair of a slave.

"Mistress Trella," Annok-sur said, keeping her voice low out of habit, though they were alone on the second floor, "your walks among the villagers have become the high point of the day for many of them. They stop whatever they're doing and wait for you to pass by, disappointed if you choose another street."

"I like to meet with people, Annok-sur. There is much to learn from them about Orak."

"Perhaps you're teaching them more than they realize. So many of them ask for your advice or help. And you give many of them copper coins. Why are you so generous to everyone?"

Trella countered with a question of her own. "You've been married to Bantor for a long time. It's a hard life, isn't it, being the wife of a soldier?"

"Very hard, mistress. My first two children died, one in childbirth and one a few months later. Only Ningal, our daughter, has survived." She sighed. "Bantor is a good man who works hard, but sometimes he is a little slow of thought. Until Eskkar promoted him, we had very little and no hope of improvement. There were many bitter things I had to do to help Bantor and Ningal survive."

Things better left unspoken, Trella thought. "But now life is better, is it not?"

"Yes, for now. But after the barbarians are defeated, then I fear the hard times will come again."

"You are certain that we'll defeat them?"

"No, of course not. I know how strong they are. But if our

men fail, then it won't matter. If we're not killed out of hand, you and I will become slaves in some warrior's tent, taken and beaten at his pleasure. No, what I fear most is growing old with only a soldier's pay, with no dowry to find Ningal a good husband. Since Eskkar became captain, my husband's future seems blessed by the gods. Bantor is very loyal. We both know what Eskkar has done for him."

Trella reached up and touched Annok-sur's hand, taking the comb from her and turning to face her. "I, too, am the woman of a soldier. And I have the same fear as you, Annok-sur, that when the barbarians are driven off, things will return to the old ways. Eskkar is powerful now, but when Orak is no longer threatened, then perhaps the nobles will not need so strong a captain of the guard. Perhaps they will not need so many soldiers, either, especially those they did not raise up themselves."

"So this is why you walk through the village, mistress, to gain the friendship of the people? Their friendship won't be enough to protect your master."

"There's much more I want from the villagers. And there's much you can do to help me, if you choose. Such help would not be forgotten in the future, Annok-sur."

"I will help you gladly, Trella. You won't be a slave for long. Everyone knows that. No, you will be a great lady in Orak, and Eskkar will found a great House. And as he rises, so may Bantor."

"Then there is much to be done to ensure that future. We must use the people to help secure Orak after the barbarians are defeated. The villagers must bind themselves to Eskkar and his future so that one cannot be without the other. There must be no return to the old ways."

"You see a way to make this happen? The nobles would not like to hear of such things."

"No, they wouldn't. There would be much danger, in fact." Trella said nothing further, just waited while Annok-sur considered.

"I don't wish to return to the old ways. Tell me what I can do to help you."

Trella spoke of her plans. When she finished, the older woman took her hand once again and squeezed it. "It can be done, Trella. We can make these things happen. I'll do whatever is needed."

"Help me, Annok-sur, and you will have a great House of your own someday. I promise it."

11

More weeks passed, with Eskkar too busy to notice Trella's quiet maneuverings or to care about them if he did. Instead he worried about Jalen. Almost three weeks overdue, Eskkar feared not only had he lost a capable commander, but that he lacked any information about the barbarians' progress or location.

An even gloomier thought troubled him—if they'd captured and tortured Jalen, the Alur Meriki would know all about Eskkar's plans. He didn't want them sending a raiding party early, before they finished the wall.

Whatever Jalen's fate, Eskkar needed to send out another patrol, one he'd lead himself. The barbarians must be located, and he didn't trust anyone else to do it. Men continued to arrive with stories of barbarian hordes only a few paces behind them, but almost all their sightings had no value. As each day passed, Eskkar worked harder to appear confident.

More than two months had elapsed since Eskkar became captain of the guard. Each day he met with Corio and Sisuthros to talk about the wall's progress. Their work proceeded smoothly, and Eskkar had no doubt the wall would be completed in time. Nevertheless he needed Jalen's information. He decided to wait three more days for Jalen. Then he'd lead the second scouting party himself.

This morning's training had gone poorly. Eskkar's worries distracted him, and a sword swung by an eager recruit had struck Eskkar's head and knocked him to the ground. If the blade had been bronze instead of wood, he'd be dead.

A few hours after the sun reached its zenith, one of Bantor's messengers found Eskkar at Corio's side, inspecting the day's progress. "Captain, Bantor asks you to come to the gate. There are travelers there who wish to speak with you."

"Tell Bantor I'm on my way." Eskkar smiled at the grinning youth, who dashed off at a run to return with this new message. Eskkar bade goodbye to Corio, then followed the path to the main gate, where he found Bantor and two guards speaking to three strangers.

As Eskkar approached he understood why the travelers stood out from those who wandered into Orak. These strangers must come from a land far to the north, where men had darker beards and hair that contrasted with their lighter skin. All were unusually tall and well muscled. Even their clothing looked odd, a mix of leather and somber colors rather than the raw linen or flax shades preferred by those in the surrounding countryside.

Each stranger carried a heavy bow and a fat quiver full of arrows, but no sword or axe, only a long dagger at each hip. A small ass, tethered a few steps away, rested wearily under its load of packs, blankets, and cooking utensils, no doubt holding all the travelers' worldly possessions.

"Greetings, Bantor." Eskkar nodded to the accompanying guards as well. He tried to remember as many of his men's names as he could. When he couldn't recall a name, he still gave each man some kind of greeting. It pleased him to see a simple gesture of recognition made them stand a little straighter.

"Greetings, Captain," Bantor replied. "These travelers asked to speak to the leader of the village, and I thought it would be better for you to meet them here."

Bantor had learned much in the last few months. In the beginning he would probably have directed them to Eskkar's house and forgotten about them. Now he kept them under guard until his captain could determine what to do with them.

Eskkar turned to the newcomers, easily selecting the old-est and guessing by his age and resemblance that he was the father of the other two. "Greetings. I'm Eskkar, captain of the guard."

Eskkar was one of the tallest men in Orak, but he found himself looking straight into the eyes of all three strangers, an unusual sensation for him. "What business brings you here?" He knew they weren't merchants or farmers. Even the boys, the youngest probably no more than fifteen sea-sons, looked hard and capable.

The elder man bowed slightly to show he considered him-self an equal. "My name is Totomes, and these are my sons, Narquil and Mitrac. We've come south to fight against the Alur Meriki. We may consider fighting with your village if, indeed, you plan to fight." The man's voice had a strong ac-cent and his words came slowly, as if he had to translate each thought into words.

Eskkar's eyes narrowed. Not one villager in twenty knew the name of the advancing steppes people. Most villagers thought all barbarians the same, and the fact that a particu-lar clan actually might have a leader with his own name never seemed to occur to them. The Alur Meriki took their name from one of their early leaders, though Eskkar knew the original Alur Meriki had been dead for at least a hun-dred years.

That these strangers would know such a name seemed unlikely, unless they had some encounters with them. "Why do you wish to fight them?"

Instead of replying, Totomes leaned closer to Eskkar's face, staring hard into his eyes before drawing back. "You're from the steppes yourself, Captain, are you not? From what clan do you come?"

Eskkar felt his mouth harden at the unexpected question, one that few dared ask, and he felt tempted to order them out of the village. Instead he remembered Trella's warnings about losing his temper. "I've been gone from the steppes people for nearly twenty years, Totomes, and here in Orak it's rude for strangers to ask too many questions. Now, what's your business here?"

"Our business is to kill as many Alur Meriki as we can. That's why I ask you—from what clan do you come?"

"If you wish to fight, go back through the gate and head north. I promise you'll find all the Alur Meriki you desire." He turned to the men standing behind the strangers, keeping his voice calm but firm. "Escort these visitors outside the village and see them on their way."

The youngest put a hand to his bow though it remained strung across his chest. "If you touch that bow again, boy, you'll leave here without it." As Eskkar spoke, the guards behind the strangers drew their swords with a rasp and moved apart, while Bantor stepped to the side and put a hand on his sword.

Totomes spoke sharply to his son in a language strange to Eskkar's ears, and the youth immediately took his hand from the bow shaft. "My son Mitrac still has much to learn about the ways of strangers. But I warn you that should anyone try to take one of our bows, they will die."

Eskkar kept his voice calm. "I think you should be on your way before my guards put their swords in your backs or I regret my generosity. You'll do no killing in Orak."

"Are you the ruler of Orak," Totomes said, his temper flaring, "that you can threaten those who want to enter your village even though they wish to fight against the barbarians?" Eskkar stared for a moment at Totomes. These men were hard of head, no doubt of that, but they looked ready to fight barbarians, or anyone else for that matter. They'd journeyed through a countryside filled with warriors, bandits, and thieves, and had somehow managed to survive.

The fact that they were foreign to these lands made that journey more remarkable. Travelers from distant lands took more risks in their journeys, always the first choice of robbers, since the victims would have no kin to demand revenge. One more reason why most men seldom traveled more than a few miles from where they were born.

Eskkar glanced at the bow the man was carrying. It was hard to judge its size, stretched diagonally across the man's back, but it looked to be a foot longer than the ones Eskkar's men trained with, which might make it a formidable weapon.

Eskkar glanced at the weapons of the two boys. Their bows were every bit as long as their father's.

Someone behind him coughed. Eskkar realize a crowd had formed, everyone frozen in place, ignoring the hot sun and staring at the men, caught up in the sudden tension and expecting to see blood spilled at any moment. He decided that such men as these could be useful, but harsh words had been spoken and now needed to be undone. He wondered what Trella would do. Probably offer them a cup of water. Or wine. Well, why not? He turned to Bantor.

"See that care is given to their animal." He turned back to Totomes. "Follow me."

Without waiting for a reply Eskkar turned on his heel and began retracing his steps, walking purposefully and moving at a good pace. His guard struggled to keep up with him, and Eskkar resisted the urge to turn around to see whether Totomes and his sons were following. Traveling down the main street of Orak, he turned left on a smaller lane and almost immediately entered a small tavern, one that catered to travelers.

He paused for a moment, letting his eyes accustom themselves to the dim light, and he felt his bodyguard bump into him. Not many customers patronized the alehouse at that hour, and the innkeeper's largest table stood empty. Eskkar headed there, calling out to the serving girl as he went. "Ale for myself and my companions."

He sat down facing the door and saw the strangers standing just inside the doorway, squinting into the darkness. Eskkar motioned to his bodyguard. "Sit down and keep your hand off your sword."

The guard grinned with admiration. "Captain, I thought they was going to stick us both in the back."

Eskkar smiled grimly. "We could use men like these. Now sit down and keep your mouth shut." He kept his voice low as Totomes approached the table and stood hesitantly before it, looking around the shadowy room. "Are you going to stand there or sit down and drink some ale? Or aren't you thirsty after your travels?"

Totomes looked as confused as he'd been angry, and

before he could reply or even sit, the serving girl approached carrying five wooden beakers and a large bucket of ale. As the men stood there, she expertly poured the dark brown brew into the cups.

"I hope, girl, that this is decent ale," Eskkar remarked as she finished. "I wouldn't want my friends to be offended."

She giggled, then looked at him with a provocative smile. "Our finest ale, Captain, in our best cups. Anything you want, anything, just ask." She smiled at him, then gave a quick bow and walked off.

Totomes slipped his bow over his head and placed it lengthwise across the table between himself and Eskkar. His sons followed his example and sat down on either side of their father. The table was scarcely longer than the bows.

Eskkar raised his cup. "Welcome to Orak, Totomes." He searched his memory for a moment, then added, "Narquil, Mitrac," glad that he had repeated the boys' names in his mind when he heard them, another trick he'd learned from Trella. "My name is Eskkar, and this is my lazy bodyguard for the day, Hykros."

Totomes picked up his cup and matched Eskkar's gesture. "To Orak." The five men all drank deeply, though Eskkar put his cup down first, still half-full. "I'm glad that we left the gate, Captain. I don't like weapons at my back."

"If we're going to talk, Totomes, we might as well do it in the shade and with a drink in our hands. But if you think you're any better off here than at the gate, you're mistaken. I can have you driven from Orak at any time. You've no place to go inside the village where you couldn't be found."

Totomes considered that for a while, then nodded. "I suppose you're right." He drank more ale, then wiped his mouth with the back of his hand. "We came here looking for a chance to kill barbarians. In the countryside, men say Orak is planning to resist them, though I don't see how that's possible. But we decided to come and see for ourselves."

"Oh, it's true enough." Eskkar leaned back against the rough wall. "Though we may all die in the trying. As you saw when you passed through the gate, we're building a wall around the village. When it's completed, we intend to fight the barbarians from it and kill them with arrows."

"You'll need many bowmen for that, Captain," Totomes remarked. "And skillful ones. Barbarians aren't easy to kill, even with arrows. We should know. My sons and I have killed many in the last two years."

Eskkar considered those words. If these three had been fighting the steppes people for the last few years and managed to survive, they must indeed be capable. He picked his words carefully. "I don't wish to offend, Totomes, but how have you been able to survive so long? Unless there are more of you somewhere."

An expression of sadness passed over Totomes's face. "Our people live far to the north, high on the steppe, near the great northern sea, where the clime is much colder than here. An earthquake forced my clan to move south, and we'd started to build a new home when our camp was attacked by an Alur Meriki raiding party. They killed almost all of us. My brother, my wife, and several children, all dead." He looked down into his ale cup.

"My sons and I, and some others, were away, exploring in the mountains, looking for ores and timber. When we returned, we saw the barbarians riding away. Not all of our clan were dead when we arrived. Many had been tortured and mutilated, then left to die. My sons watched their mother's slow death."

Totomes glanced at his sons. "Those of us who remained swore a blood oath to take revenge, and fourteen of us began to trail the barbarians. Some of us died fighting them, and others have turned back. But my sons and I have not yet killed enough to satisfy our oath."

Eskkar nodded in sympathy, though it was an old story to him, one repeated a hundred times. "Well, Totomes, if you wish to kill barbarians, you've come to the right place, providing that you can take orders. I need as many expert archers as I can find, and more than that, I need men who can teach others. Even now, we're training men to use the bow."

Eskkar glanced down at the bows resting on the table. In the dim light they appeared different from any he'd ever seen. "May I examine your bow? I don't think I've seen one quite like it."

That brought smiles to their faces. "Nor are you likely to, Captain." Totomes handed him one of the bows. "They're a new design that my grandfather created, made from the heartwood of a special tree that grows only in certain parts of the steppe. The wood closest to the heart of the tree is thicker and stronger than the outer wood, so it acts as if two pieces were glued together."

Eskkar examined the bow carefully, aware from his experiences with Rufus the bowyer that he had just learned a great secret. The bow had considerable heft but was not so weighty as he had expected. Lifting the bow toward the light, he saw that it was indeed made from a single piece of wood.

Eskkar knew a bow made from only one piece of wood could not take much stress and certainly could not fire a heavy arrow any great distance. The wood on the outer side of the bow had to bend so much farther than the wood on the inner side and so tended to break. To solve that problem, the bowyers fashioned their war bows from several pieces of wood bent at differing angles, joined into a center socket and held together with glue.

On Totomes's bow the wood on the inside looked as if it had been dyed, but closer inspection revealed only the wood grain's normal coloring. The bow's center had been wrapped with thin cords and leather strips to add strength as well as to provide a better grip. Putting the bow down, he looked at Totomes. The man took an arrow from his quiver and handed it to Eskkar.

Eskkar noted that it was almost three inches longer than the arrows his own men used and so slightly heavier, but otherwise seemed no different. "How far can such a bow fling an arrow like this?"

"We can hit whatever we aim at up to two hundred paces with the full weight of the arrow. The bow can shoot such a shaft well over five hundred paces. We've hit targets at even longer distances." A hint of pride sounded in his voice.

That sounded like boasting to Eskkar, but he let it pass.

Hitting anything at two hundred paces was fine shooting. Handing the arrow back to its owner, he picked up his ale cup. "So what are your plans, Totomes? If you wish to stay and fight, then you'll fight under my command and follow my orders. Otherwise, you may stay a few days in Orak to rest and buy what you need before you move on. I cannot have fighting men loose in the village. All men carrying arms in Orak are under my command."

"I'm the leader of my clan. I cannot take orders from . . . others."

"Well enough," Eskkar answered, sipping at the last of his ale. "Then in three days, you must leave. If you're still here, I'll take your bows and whatever else of value you have and have you driven from the village."

He stood up. Hykros did the same. "You can sleep here in safety, and they'll not charge you too much now they've seen you drinking with me. Good day, Totomes." Eskkar nodded to the two boys and started to walk out.

Totomes rose also. "Captain, please stay. There's still much I would discuss with you."

Eskkar turned and stared at the man until Totomes let his eyes drop. "You say you're the leader of a clan, Totomes, but your clan is dead or far from here, and now you have only these boys following you. You say you wish to fight, but here in Orak we fight the barbarians my way or not at all."

Eskkar let that sink in, but continued before Totomes could reply. "If you wish to stay, then you pledge yourself to me until the barbarians are defeated and gone, or until we are all dead. You'll obey me in all things, as does every other man who fights in my command, and you'll draw the same pay. If you can use those bows as well as you claim, you'll help train my archers, and that will keep you from carrying rocks or digging ditches, though you'll do that, too, if need be. I've said all that needs to be said. Choose now."

Totomes stood there, pride struggling with his desire for vengeance. Narquil, who looked to be the older of the boys, spoke to Totomes in his own language. They exchanged words, and even the younger boy had his say. Totomes turned back to him.

"I accept your offer, Captain. Will you please sit down," he asked. "There's much we would like to know."

Eskkar bowed formally, sealing the bargain, and returned to his seat. The serving girl, who had stood there listening to every word, rushed back with more ale, and poured another round. "Then I'm glad to have you join our forces, Totomes, and there is much . . ."

The door flew open with a crash that startled patrons and customers alike. Everyone's hand reached for knife or sword, the bright sun illuminating the same messenger who'd summoned Eskkar earlier. "Captain! . . . Bantor says come to the gate at once!" He gasped a moment to catch his breath. "Riders are coming. He thinks it may be Jalen!"

Eskkar bolted upright, bumping his head on the low ceiling, and started toward the door before he remembered his new recruits. "Hykros, take Totomes and his sons to Gatus. Tell him we have new instructors for the archers, then bring them to my house."

Eskkar ducked under the doorway and began to run, the messenger leading the way back to the gate. As Eskkar reached the gate, Bantor descended the last steps of the wooden ladder that provided access to the top of the wall, a big smile on his face that grew even larger when he saw his captain.

"Is it Jalen?" Eskkar couldn't keep the excitement out of his voice.

"I think so. It looks like his horse, at least."

Walking with Bantor to the gate, he looked down the road and saw a small group of horsemen riding slowly toward them. He counted four men, only two less than had departed, and when they drew closer, he noted that the youthful servant had survived, though two fighting men obviously had not. Eskkar stood at the side of the old wooden gate as a group of villagers rushed through. A hand took his, and he looked down to see Trella had joined him.

"How did you hear so quickly?" he asked, putting his arm around her, enjoying her touch. He looked behind him to make sure her guard was present, since his own had been left with the visitors. A few of Drigo's men remained, though most had left weeks ago. While the danger from Drigo's followers had lessened, the number of villagers who had no kind thoughts for Orak's war leader and his hard discipline had increased.

"Bantor wasn't sure where you'd gone, so he sent a messenger back to the house. The boy told us about the three archers that you turned your back on and invited to go drinking after they threatened to kill you."

Eskkar laughed. "It wasn't like that, Trella. They're interesting folk, though."

"No, I'm sure it wasn't," she answered, tightening her grip on his hand. "But I'd like to meet them."

"You will, tonight. We've just enough room in the small house for three more, I think."

Conversation ceased as Jalen trotted through the gate in a swirl of dust to the cheers and shouts of the crowd. He swung down from his horse, stiff from his long ride. Eskkar found himself hugging his lieutenant, pounding him on the back, while the villagers called out Jalen's name.

"Gods below, Jalen, I'd given you up for dead days ago! Now you ride in as easy as can be. Come back to my house. We can talk there."

"By the gods, it's good to be back." Jalen glanced up at the wall, his mouth agape at the sight. "And much has changed since I left." He stepped back to his horse and untied a leather pouch from his blanket, then followed Eskkar and Trella as they headed home. Halfway there they found Nicar waiting for them in the street. He invited them all to his house, saying the other nobles would be coming there as well.

Moments later Nicar's guests filled his meeting room to capacity, with every seat and stool occupied. A dozen others stood wherever they could find space. All waited for Jalen.

He'd stopped to wash up, though Eskkar knew it would take more than a few moments at the well to remove the smell of horseflesh from body and clothes. The room already felt warm from the presence of so many bodies.

Once again Eskkar sat at the foot of the table with Trella near his side. Gatus, Sisuthros, and Bantor stood behind their captain. When Jalen entered, damp from his washing, he wore one of Nicar's old tunics, a garment too large for his frame. Jalen sat down in the last open seat, next to his captain, and drank from the wine cup already poured in front of him.

"Noble Nicar, I thank you for your wine and the loan of your tunic. Mine is not worth saving, I'm afraid."

"Whatever you want, you have only to ask," Nicar answered. "But come, we're eager for news. Did you find the barbarians?"

The smile disappeared from Jalen's face. "Yes, I found them, and there's much to tell." He reached for the leather pouch he'd entrusted to his captain. Jalen removed the cloth map and spread it out on the table. Torn at the edges and dirty from much handling, it had obviously served its purpose well. Eskkar saw many new threads sewn onto it.

All heads craned toward the cloth as if its secrets would be clearly visible. Looks of concern replaced the smiles as they wondered what news they would hear. Jalen put down his wine and began his tale.

"Before we'd gone five days, we began to hear word about the Alur Meriki. As we went farther north, we met people moving west, and we learned of raiding parties that ranged far to the northeast. To avoid those, we traveled closer to the river, and there was little activity for another week until we began to encounter many folk moving south trying to stay ahead of the main party. Many of these people knew of Orak and were heading here. Have any arrived?"

"Yes, more and more are on the roads, all coming here," Eskkar replied. "Some stay, if they're willing to fight or work. Others camp outside and move on in a few days."

Jalen nodded. "More will come. We continued to ride north for another week and began to see small scouting parties, five or ten barbarians. We ran south each time they saw us. Once they chased us for a full day before we lost them. Thank the gods for our strong horses. Each time, we circled back north again and moved farther away from the river."

Eskkar leaned forward, his eyes hard. "You saw no big

raiding parties, only scouts?" They should have encountered at least one large band of warriors.

"Yes, only scouts. We couldn't continue north, so we moved east. We talked to many travelers and even some bandits. The farther east we went, the clearer things became."

Jalen drank again from his cup. Every eye rested upon him. "The barbarians have a plan. The main body of the tribe, with at least seven or eight hundred warriors, is coming slowly toward us, more or less following the river. Two large raiding bands are ranging far to the south and east of the main body, killing everyone in their path or forcing them to head west." He put his finger on the map, and everyone stood or left his seat to get a closer look, the nobles jostling each other, dignity forgotten.

Jalen pointed at some red threads. "Here is where the main camp is, or was about two weeks ago. They travel slowly and stay close to the river. The raiding parties range eastward, sweeping everyone toward the river."

Again Jalen pointed to the map, indicating two curved seams of black threads that hooked far to the southeast. "They ride great distances, but always to the east and south, though sometimes they send captives and loot back to the main camp. They do that every week or so, and perhaps they exchange men as well, so all can share in the looting."

Eskkar stared at the map, as did the others, but already he could understand the strategy. He sat there, lost in thought, until Nicar's words interrupted him.

"Well, Eskkar, what do you make of it? It seems they may pass us by if they are raiding so far to the east. When the river bends, the main party may continue eastward. That's the path they traveled the last time they passed through these parts."

Eskkar glanced at Jalen and saw that his subcommander understood all too clearly what the barbarians had in mind. Eskkar leaned over the map, tracing on it with his finger.

"The main body follows the river Tigris, and right now that group is traveling almost due east. When the river bends, they'll continue to follow it and will be moving southeast. When the river straightens, they'll be heading almost due south, and we'll be right in their path. By then these raiding parties will be ranging far to the southeast of Orak, and they'll start to move toward us as well, first driving west, then north. They'll approach Orak from the south, following the river and driving anyone seeking to escape from Orak back toward us." He looked up at the men and saw them all listening intently to him, mouths open, as they tried to grasp his meaning.

"This time the barbarians are not just passing nearby, and we're not just another village near their path. This time they make straight for Orak. We're their main destination. They herd everyone toward us, knowing that the crowds of escaping farmers and villagers will overwhelm us with their numbers even as they concentrate all their goods and livestock here. They expect to pluck a rich prize before they move on."

Eskkar's words silenced everyone for a moment before Nicar spoke. "How sure can you be of this, Eskkar? They could still turn east and not head directly here."

Nicar's question rang of desperation. They heard the words, but not what they meant. "Tell them, Jalen. Tell them what you think."

"I think it's as Eskkar says," Jalen said. "They're coming here. Otherwise the main band would have turned east weeks ago. That's why they're moving so slowly. They want people to get word of their approach and to come here, thinking themselves safe, until they have nowhere to go. The village will be overwhelmed with people from the countryside. The barbarians know there's no easy ford of the Tigris for forty miles on either side of Orak."

That put another thought into Eskkar's head. Pulling the map toward him for a moment, Eskkar glanced at it and grunted, then shoved it back toward the center of the table. "Yes, and eventually they'll send a band of warriors across the river to make sure nobody crosses over, even from the ford here. That will keep us penned up. They won't care whether Orak resists or not. We'll have nowhere to run."

For a long moment no one uttered a sound, each man deep in his own dark thoughts of the future.

Caldor, the younger son of Nicar, broke the silence. "You speak of ignorant barbarians having a strategy just because they wander along the river! They may just as soon head back the way they came as come here."

Nicar whirled toward his son, his voice hot with anger. "You are not to speak at this table unless asked to. If you're unable to obey, leave." The words chilled the room. Everyone remembered the brash words of another youth killed in this very room. Caldor flushed red at the rebuke and sat back in his chair, looking away from the group. Everyone turned to Eskkar, expecting an outburst of some kind.

Eskkar heard Trella's stool scrape softly on the floor behind him, a reminder she was close by. He didn't answer Caldor directly, responding as if Nicar himself had asked it.

"If any here think the Alur Meriki leaders, who've led their clan through hundreds of battles and thousands of camps, are not capable of planning their route with care and forethought, you are mistaken. If you think that it takes no wits to rule three or four thousand people, organize hunting and food gathering, repair your own wagons, smelt your own ores, forge your own bronze, make your own tools, and raise your own livestock, all while moving hundreds of miles, then you're even more mistaken. If we make mistakes of that kind, we're as good as dead or captured."

No one said anything in answer, and they avoided looking at Caldor.

"Jalen," Eskkar said, breaking the silence. "Did you get any idea of how big the tribe is? How many men, wagons, horses?"

Jalen clutched the empty cup, no doubt wishing for more wine but too nervous to ask for any. "The great clan has grown. There must have been a joining in the last few years. They say the tribe numbers more than five thousand, not counting slaves."

Eskkar thought that over as gasps of amazement went around the table. Five thousand was an incredible number of people, more than twice the number of people in Orak. But

Eskkar knew it wasn't the number of clansmen that counted, only the number of warriors they could hurl against the wall. Everyone started talking at once, but Eskkar rapped his cup on the table.

"Five thousand is a great number of people, but only about one in five will be a warrior. The rest are old men, women, and children. At most, there will be fifteen hundred warriors, probably less, maybe only around twelve hundred. It's a great number of warriors, but we'll have over three hundred defenders. It will be more difficult, but still possible."

"When we agreed to defend Orak," Nestor said, his voice tense with anxiety as he leaned across the table, "we spoke of possibly six or seven hundred barbarians. Now we speak of twice that number, and you say it's still possible? Are we mad to think we can stop that many barbarians?"

"The wall can stop them." Corio's words made everyone turn toward him. "It will be high enough and strong enough. I've seen Eskkar's men in their training, firing arrows into targets at a hundred paces, seven and eight shafts each minute. I've watched, and I believe what I've seen."

"You're committed to building the wall," Rebba countered. "You're being swayed by your own work. No matter how strong the wall, there won't be enough men to defend it."

"It's true I believe in the wall," Corio admitted. "But if we can get additional men, then it can be done, I'm sure of it."

"And where are you to get these additional men?" Nestor shouted, putting his fist hard on the table. He turned to Eskkar. "Your plans to recruit and train are already stretched thin. There are fewer men willing to fight each day. Isn't that so, Captain?"

Another silence fell over the table as all eyes turned back toward Eskkar. He saw the fear in their faces, and found he had no words. If the barbarians hurled everyone at the wall in one rush, he didn't know for certain they could be stopped. Everyone waited for his answer.

The sound of Trella's stool being scraped along the plank floor made every eye turn toward her, including Eskkar's. "Pardon me, Nobles, for speaking out, but are not the barbarians sending you all the men you desire?" She kept her head bowed as she spoke, properly submissive, her words just reaching their ears.

"By the gods, Trella, you're right. The more fool I for not seeing it," Eskkar's confidence returned, and he looked first at Trella, then at Jalen, who nodded his head in agreement. "We'll have more men than we know what to do with. And many of them will be fighting men at that, driven here from all the smaller villages to the south and the east, looking for a chance to strike back. We'll easily add another hundred or more men, and many will know how to swing a sword."

He grasped Trella's arm in excitement. "We can do it! We don't have to match the barbarians in numbers. One man behind the wall will be worth four or five below it. We'll have to plan on more people inside the village, but it can still be done."

"Then you think Orak can be held? Enough men will be found?" The excitement in Nicar's voice betrayed his emotions.

Eskkar turned back toward the table, the smile that Trella's words had brought still on his face. "Yes, Nobles, I'm sure we can. With another hundred fighting men, we should . . ." He stopped and turned back toward his slave. "Is there anything else we should be wary of, Trella?"

She lifted her eyes for a moment. "I should not speak at your gathering."

"Speak up, Trella," Corio snapped, "and forget those customs. If you have anything to say, just say it and let us decide if it's worthy."

Nevertheless Trella kept her voice humble. "Nobles, it seems to me that you will soon be facing the problem of what to do with so many people. If hundreds more farmers and villagers flock to Orak from the south and east, they'll overwhelm the village, even as you work to defend it. Already there are many strangers in the streets. I fear they interrupt the work or cause other problems. Perhaps you should consider closing the gates to all except those who will fight and their families, and send the rest across the river."

That sounded wise to Eskkar, and he was about to agree before he managed to get hold of his tongue. Let others speak first, Trella kept telling him. Listen to what they say before you speak, and you'll know better what to say yourself.

Corio's voice rose once again. "Yes, by the gods, I've already been slowed down by interruptions and people wandering in and out of the work areas, asking stupid questions. Each day it grows worse. It's hard to keep men working when newcomers stand there gawking."

Murmurs of agreement sounded around the table. "We're risking all that we have," Nicar said, "to save Orak. These strangers owe nothing to us or to the village. Let us take those who we want and send the others away."

"Fight, work, or move on," Eskkar said quietly. "That's what we've been saying, and it's the choice we'll offer those who can help us. We can establish a camp for the newcomers at the old village site to the south. They can stay there until they decide to move on. That will keep them out of Orak."

The first people to settle in Orak had dug a well about two miles to the south and lived there for many years before moving the village to its current site.

"More guards will be needed at the gates and at the old site," Jalen suggested. "And you'll need more patrols in the countryside."

Eskkar smiled at that. "We already have over a hundred and eighty men under arms, and well-trained men, too. Another sixty are in training and will be ready in a few weeks. Now that we've enough men available, we can increase the number under training."

"Are you certain you'll have enough men?" Nicar voiced everyone's concern.

"Yes, Nicar, I'm sure of it now. I want to have three hundred and fifty men ready to defend Orak, with another five hundred villagers behind them to help fight and carry loads. With that many men, I can hold Orak as long as the wall stands and the food holds out. But I think we'll need another fifty fighters to send across the river."

Nestor looked puzzled. "Why send men across the river when they're needed here?"

"To guard your livestock, Noble. All the spare cattle, sheep, and horses must be moved out of the village and the countryside. We won't have food or space to keep them here anyway, and the stink and filth would be unbearable. Besides, the barbarians will learn that we have no livestock here. It will make them less eager to fight. Remember, gold is not so important to them. Horses first, then animals, then women, that's how they think. So we send all our beasts away, across the river and to the west, with fifty men to guard them."

Eskkar reached out and pulled the map toward him, putting his finger on the spot indicating the main barbarian camp. "Jalen, when do you think the barbarians will arrive? Do we have enough time?"

"Based on what I saw and heard, I think they will arrive here in two months or so at the earliest. Raiding parties could be here sooner, of course, but I don't think that's their plan. They're moving slowly, taking their time, enjoying their conquests. They see no need to rush."

"What if they learn we're building a wall to stop them?" Nicar asked. "Won't that make them change their plans?"

Jalen shrugged. "It's likely they've already heard about our wall. We found plenty of peasants up north who knew we were planning to resist."

Eskkar pushed the map back to the center of the table. "They won't change their plans," he answered firmly. "They won't believe a wall can stop them. Still, we must take no chances in case a big raiding party arrives early." He looked at Corio. "How long before the first section is completed?"

Corio must have expected that question. "In a few days, we can seal the main entrance to Orak. The new gate will be ready in a week or so, but until then we can use wagons and men to close it." He turned toward his eldest son, seated beside him. "Alcinor, you will make the gate functional, even if it's not fully reinforced, as soon as possible."

When his son nodded agreement, Corio turned back to Eskkar and the others. "We've already speeded up our pace on the wall's construction. Materials are arriving in sufficient quantity, and we've enough laborers, though we can always use more." He glanced around the table as he made his commitment. "I will give you your wall at least a month early."

"What about the ditch?" Nestor inquired. "No one speaks about starting on the ditch."

"The ditch is the last thing we will do," Corio said. "Eskkar and I have discussed this. With three or four hundred men, we can dig the ditch completely around Orak in a week or ten days. We'll do that at the very last moment, so that even if the barbarians learn of the wall, they will not think it very formidable."

Nicar looked around the table. "Is there anything else we should consider?" Everyone glanced around, but nobody had anything to add. Then Nicar saw Trella's eyes come up to meet his. "Trella, do you wish to say something?"

She bowed humbly again. "Noble Nicar, I know you've discussed flooding the land alongside the village, but no work has started on that. Perhaps now we should prepare to do so in case the barbarians come early. I don't know how long it will take or how much water will be needed."

Apparently no one else did either, because no one spoke up. Nicar turned to Rebba, who sat there stroking his beard in thought. Rebba owned two large farms north of the village, and he'd been the original force behind draining the swamps many years ago. In matters of agriculture, he decided what crops would be grown for Orak, how much, and by whom. His family built the largest irrigation ditches and knew more about moving water than anyone. Rebba took his time thinking, and Eskkar felt his patience about to snap before the man spoke.

"My family will work with Corio's men to build some wooden breakwaters. If we place them properly, we can divert thirty or forty feet of river into the surrounding farms. That should flood the land in less than a day and be more than enough to stop the barbarians from trying to drain the water. After a few days, the water will sink deep into the earth, and the land will return to a muddy swamp that will take months to dry out. We'll build additional ditches to allow the water to flow where we wish it."

"I'm sorry that your lands must be covered with water, Rebba," Nicar answered, "but you know it must be done."

"Don't be sorry, old friend." Rebba smiled resignedly. "The crops would've been ruined by the barbarians anyway. Instead the waters will refresh the land and afterward it will be even more fertile than before."

Nicar's eyes went around the table and stopped again at Trella. "Anything else, Trella?" His tone was calmer now, and his look encouraged her to speak.

"Noble Nicar, there's one thing more that you might consider." She paused, then went on. "When the livestock is sent across the river, you may want to include men from the village, perhaps from your own families. If anything should happen to the animals, Orak would be without food and herds for the coming season. The soldiers may be loyal, but there will be great temptation. Perhaps an equal number of villagers, under your direction, should accompany them, and rewards promised for everyone's safe return."

Nicar sat quietly for a moment. "Yes, that's worth considering. There will be a rich value of livestock and grain, and if it's not returned safely, Orak will face starvation. We will speak further about it." He glanced around the table, but no one seemed to have any more words. "Then we're finished with our meeting. Again, let's give thanks to the gods for Jalen's safe return."

And for his information, Eskkar added to himself. He left the house, his commanders following, and he invited them to dine with him.

Bantor, Jalen, and Sisuthros headed off on their separate ways, but Gatus walked with Eskkar and Trella, though they went in the opposite direction to Gatus's house. When they were alone in the street, Gatus jerked his head toward Eskkar's bodyguard to move him out of earshot. Then he grabbed Eskkar by the arm.

"Captain," he began, moving close to Eskkar, then turning to include Trella. "I'm not sure whether you saw the look on young Caldor's face when Trella spoke out. I could just catch a glimpse of him seated behind his father. The puppy was hot with anger when his father put him down."

Gatus scratched his beard. "Well, if looks could kill, young Trella here would already be in the ground." He looked worried. "You'd better watch him, Eskkar. I wouldn't put it past him to do some hurt to you or Trella."

"Gatus, thank you for your concern," Trella answered kindly. "And for your warning. We'll be watchful."

"Good. And if needs be, I can have one of my rogues put a blade in his back. I'll even do it myself. Just let me know." He nodded to Eskkar. "Till dinner, then," and went on his way, striding down the street.

Eskkar looked thoughtfully at Trella, then put his arm around her. They started walking back to their house, his guard moving in a few steps behind. "Mistress Trella," he said, echoing the title of honor given to the senior woman of a household. "I see we have much to talk about this evening. Much, it seems, goes on that I know little about."

"When you have much to say at night, then I know I will be sore the next morning. Though you've been too busy and too tired for me lately."

"Then I'll have to make time for you. Perhaps you should make sure tonight's dinner is short and our guests depart early. Afterward, we'll have plenty of time to . . . talk."

"Yes, master." But she took his hand and held it until they entered the courtyard of the former House of Drigo.

12

~~~~~~~~~~~~~~~~~~~~~~~~~~~~~~

I t took little effort to keep dinner brief that evening. Jalen, weary from his journey and eager to return to the girl he'd started bedding just before his mission north, left the table first. Gatus and the others took the hint from Annok-sur. Jalen's news interested everyone, but once he left, nobody really wanted to linger.

Eskkar found Trella in the kitchen, helping the cook and Annok-sur clean up. He took her by the hand and led her up the flight of stairs that hugged the wall and gave access to the second floor. At the top, covered by a linen curtain, was a small privy containing a large chamber pot. This allowed the servants to empty the container without disturbing the master at his work.

A marvel of construction, the upper level of Drigo's home boasted many wonderful features not even Nicar's house possessed. A stout door led into a good-sized room Drigo used for his private workroom. It now contained a large table, an impressive cupboard, six chairs, and a smaller table.

From the workroom another heavy door provided the only entry to the bedroom. The bed chamber's size, nearly twenty-five feet long by twenty wide, had astonished Eskkar. Four small openings, spaced evenly and high up on the two outer walls, provided light and air. Not even a child could crawl through them. A narrow window, covered by a thick shutter and fastened with two beams, provided the only means of escape in case of fire. The shutter would take more effort to force than the door.

A coil of stout rope waited in a decorative clay pot beneath the window for use in an emergency, and the opening could be observed and guarded from the interior courtyard below. Drigo had taken care in building his private rooms, to ensure no one could enter or eavesdrop on his private bedroom activities or conversations.

All this effort now benefited Eskkar, as they passed through the workroom into the bedroom making sure to fasten each door. For the first time in his life, he had something more valuable than gold—privacy. He could speak and be assured that no one could hear.

He took her in his arms and held her, looking down at her face and breathing in the scent of her hair. "Trella . . . all day I've wanted to hold you, to thank you for your words at Nicar's table. You make everything possible, and now even the Families listen when you speak."

Her hands went around his neck, and her face pressed itself to his breast. "You said you wanted to talk, master," teasing him with the slave's salutation. "Or did you bring me here for other reasons?"

Once again she'd roused him with a few words and the press of her body. "I think . . . we will talk later." He took off her dress, pulling it slowly up over her head, enjoying the sight and feel of her body against his. She spoke the truth earlier. Three days had passed since he'd taken her, a length of time that suddenly seemed far too long.

"Then . . . we should make haste," she whispered, loosening his belt and letting it drop to the floor. She helped remove his tunic, her desire no less than his.

Eskkar guided her gently down into the bed and ran his hands over her, taking his time, forcing himself to hold back while he aroused her, wanting her pleasure as much as his own.

He'd never done such things before. Until Trella he'd cared little whether any of his women felt much of anything. He'd heard such things described, and men told stories of women who enjoyed lovemaking as much as their men, stories he had previously dismissed as lies or soldier's tales. Whatever magic Trella possessed, she brought to him something special, something that increased the love act and made it better than simple coupling. He resolved to keep it that way.

Later he lay there, relaxed, resting on clean pillows and a soft linen mattress filled with cotton and feathers. A small lamp provided just enough light to see. Trella left the bedroom and when she returned, she carried a tray holding a water pitcher and two glass goblets.

The expensive glass cups, rare and hard to fashion, came as a gift from one of many merchants seeking favors. Eskkar drank gratefully, but Trella drank only half of hers, then poured what remained onto a cloth. She used that to wipe Eskkar's brow, then rubbed down his chest and wiped clean his genitals. Turning the cloth over, she rubbed down her own breasts and loins as well. When she finished, she snuggled against him, pulling the blanket up over them.

He loved the way she looked after him, almost as if he were a child. "You know, Trella, this life is very good. We've a fine house, servants, and gold to pay for everything. For me it's like a dream." His arm went around her shoulder. "And most of all, I have you."

"And if you did not have me, you'd have some other girl in your bed. Men are much the same. My father, Nicar, the rulers of my village . . . ouch!"

He pinched her to stop her words. "Yes, I'd have some other girl, but it would not be this bed. I'd be in the barracks with a dozen men grinning as they watched."

Eskkar turned on his side to face her, serious now. "I know to whom I owe this soft bed. All this is because of you, and I'll not forget that." He moved the hair away from her face, then kissed her cheek. "So say what you wish even if you know it's untrue."

"Then you still want me," she whispered, her voice suddenly that of a timid young girl. "Even if I'm not as pretty as the women who now cast their eyes on you?"

"Yes, more than ever." He slapped her thigh playfully.

"But you must tell me how such a young girl knows so much about lovemaking? If all the girls from Carnax are like you, then I must visit this place." He pulled her on top of him. "Where did you learn to make a man so happy?"

She hid her face and he knew she was blushing, though the lamp barely revealed her face.

"One day my father caught me watching him take his pleasure with one of the servants. He decided that since I was so curious, I should learn how to please a man, to make sure I would be well treated by my future husband. So he had one of his slave women instruct me in the mysteries, and . . . I . . . was allowed to watch her with her husband."

He wondered what else she'd done, not that he cared. "Your father was a wise man. He gave you a great gift, one that I will always keep close to me." That reminded him of something unpleasant. "Now, tell me about Caldor. What about this look?"

She sat up, pulling the blanket close around her and turned toward him. "I saw the same look Gatus did, just for an instant. He was embarrassed by his father before everyone. The foolish boy should have kept silent. Then when I spoke and the nobles listened, he was even more angered, that I could speak when he was forbidden. He . . ." her voice trailed off.

Eskkar took her hand, pressed it to his lips, then squeezed it. "Yes, what else did he do?"

"When I was at Nicar's house, Caldor wanted . . . he wanted me. He told me he was just waiting for his father to take me first, and then I'd be given to him. But he didn't even want to wait for that, he wanted me to . . . to . . . get down on my knees for him."

She stopped, the words coming hard. "I pushed him away and ran off. I would have run from the house, but Creta grabbed me and made me tell her what happened. She must have spoken to Caldor because, after that, he only looked at me and smiled. I . . . I was afraid of him."

I'll kill him for that, Eskkar decided, but he kept his hand steady on Trella's, so she wouldn't know what he was feeling. He cursed himself for a fool, not to have asked her anything about her life at Nicar's house, as if nothing that had gone on before mattered once he'd taken possession of her.

Still, he couldn't go around killing everyone who wanted to bed Trella, since that now included most of the men in Orak. "Then what happened?"

"Nothing. A few days after that, Nicar returned from his travels. Two weeks passed, and Caldor and Lesu went off on their trip. Then you came to dinner and I was given to you."

"And you didn't know who was worse, the barbarian or the spoiled child," he said lightly, glad to coax a small laugh from her. "You seemed reluctant enough to come with me. Why didn't you tell me of this before?"

"Because I didn't think it mattered. I'd decided anything was better than being a slave, so I planned to run away. But you were gentle and treated me with respect. After I heard you speak to the crowd that night, I decided to help you, to do as Nicar asked, but for my own reasons."

She touched his cheek. "And then, after we made love together, I felt . . . different, and now I want only to be your woman. I will have no life but with you, Eskkar. If we fail, then we'll both die here and nothing will matter. If we win, then Caldor is of no importance."

Eskkar's hand tightened at Caldor's name.

"You cannot kill him, Eskkar, much as I would wish you to. If you kill another one of the Families' sons, they'll never forgive you." She twisted in his arms so that her cheek pressed against his. "You must listen to me. More is at stake here than just the barbarians. If we win, the victory may be as deadly for you as the barbarians. You'll have to survive the Families, who will remember you were born a barbarian, remember Drigo's death, remember those of their own families killed in battle, and remember how much of their gold you've spent."

He started to speak, but she put her finger to his lips.

"Even the soldiers may try to take power from you, with the help of the merchants and the Families. When this is over, many people will be dead, many of them your friends, and you'll have made new enemies. To hold power over them, there is much you must do, starting now."

Her breath was against his cheek, and he wanted to hold her in his arms and forget about everything but her. Damn the gods, wasn't it enough to fight the barbarians? Now he had to worry about a knife in the back and plan for the future at the same time—when he didn't even know if he'd survive the coming battle.

Demons take them all to the fire! Better a hard fight than all this cursed planning and plotting. He could take Trella and leave Orak behind, trusting to his sword and the gold he'd already earned. Part of him still longed to live from day to day, without having to worry about the schemes of men.

He reached out to touch her hair. "Trella, we don't have to stay here. We can still leave anytime. There are other villages, other lands, and we've enough gold." When she said nothing, he went on. "Isn't that better than staying here and risking all, fighting the barbarians and whatever will come afterward?"

"You must choose for both of us. My choice is already made, and I will follow you as long as you want me."

Esskar had a flash of insight. Trella would accept a lesser existence as his woman, traveling the roads in search of a new life, if that were all he could offer.

He sighed. "We'll stay, and we'll fight. Now, tell me what I must do."

"I've watched you closely, Esskar, and I've learned much from you. But now it's time to make new plans. The men are training well. The wall grows every day, and your commanders have settled into their roles. Watching you train, I see you've improved your strength and skills. Now we should show Orak a different captain of the guard."

"And how will we do that, wife?"

"I think you should leave Orak for a while. I have thought much about this." She sat up and poured more water into his glass.

"Which of your commanders is the most important to you right now?" she asked.

"Sisuthros is the most important. He has the quickest wits, and I've given him the most responsibility."

"No, I think not. I say Bantor is the most important because he deals every day with a multitude of people, and he can speak for you to them. Also, he's slower of thought, and he knows that you've been patient with him, so he is the most loyal. But you'll lose that loyalty if you don't spend more time with him and make sure he gets the respect he deserves."

"You may be right about his loyalty, although I would have chosen Gatus as the most loyal."

"Gatus is a good man, and like an uncle to me, but now he merely trains the men, and there are many here who could do that. Think of Jalen, who wants only to fight and will be loyal to you if you let him gain his victories."

Eskkar considered her words, seeing his men in a different light. "And Sisuthros? What of him?"

"Sisuthros is the most dangerous to you because he's the one the Families will turn to when they want you removed. Already Corio and some of the others are more comfortable with him than you. And that is something we must change. Remember, he hasn't killed any of them, nor does he travel about Orak with armed guards. And remember, too, that thoughts of Drigo's fate are never far from their minds. Sisuthros has spoken to Caldor at least once that I know of. So when you leave, you should take Sisuthros with you."

"How do you know so much about Sisuthros and Corio and their affairs?"

"For the last month, I've met each day with dozens of women, slaves as well as wives and daughters. I've given copper coins to those in need and befriended others. Because of you, there is respect for me, and now they come to me for advice or assistance or just to talk. Women are everywhere, and men like Caldor don't even notice them. For those who bring me information, there's a copper coin or whatever they need. Many of our servants have given me good information or have access to those who talk too much. These and others are helping me gather all the secrets men think their women don't hear or are too stupid to understand. Between all of them, I hear many things, and soon there will be little that goes on in Orak that doesn't come to my ears."

Trella had been spending his gold, but he had more than enough for his needs. And she spoke the truth. Men did talk in front of women as if they were deaf and dumb. He'd done so himself numerous times. Well, he would talk carelessly no more, lest his own words come back to haunt him. "And these . . . women . . . report all they hear to you?"

"Yes, they spy on their husbands and lovers. Most men talk too freely in their lovemaking, as well you know."

Spy. A new word to deal with, and Eskkar thought about what it meant. A gatherer of information, of secrets others did not wish you to know. Such knowledge could certainly be useful. "And you'll continue to get this information?"

"Yes, and more. But I'll need much more of your gold, Eskkar."

His twenty gold coins per month was about to vanish. He stroked her neck, thinking that his attitude toward gold had certainly changed in the last few months. Now it was just a means to an end. "Take what you need, Trella. What else must I hear before I can sleep?"

They spoke long into the night. When he disagreed or questioned her, he listened carefully to her reasons until there was agreement or at least understanding between them.

And so they whispered, watching the moon rise and fall, watching the lamp burn itself out, well into the morning hours, Trella challenging not only his thoughts but his very way of thinking. One thought, however, he kept to himself. When the time was right, young Caldor would die. That put a smile on his lips before they both drifted off into a deep and sound sleep.

The next morning Eskkar trained as usual with the latest batch of recruits. His natural fighting ability, enhanced by months of exercise and good food, now allowed him to teach as well as to train with the recruits.

Nevertheless he often received as good as he gave. For some of the new men, "recruit" meant only that they hadn't been trained as Gatus wanted, not that they weren't experienced fighters. So Eskkar observed different styles of sword-play and had already picked up several new techniques.

Today luck favored him. No new bruises pained his body. Tired and dirty, he joined the men as they washed up, before moving on to the next part of the training. Eskkar guided the recruits through the lanes, out the river gate, and to the archery range on the north side. The bow remained the most important part of the training in Eskkar's mind—the only weapon that could give villagers a chance against the barbarians.

Eskkar and Gatus discussed this training often, and both were determined that by the time the barbarians arrived, every man would be an exceptional marksman. The soldiers needed not only to become proficient with the bow, but to master the shooting techniques Gatus developed specifically for use from the wall.

As Eskkar and his troop arrived they found a large crowd at the range. Soldiers made up most of the throng, but enough idle villagers, men and women alike, joined them, bringing a frown to Eskkar's face. Villagers and soldiers should be at their assigned duties, not wasting time watching archery practice.

His anger grew as he pushed through the crowd, the recruits following him. The crowd roared as he reached the firing line, and Eskkar saw Totomes pointing downrange with his bow. Another roar went up. He watched Totomes's son Mitrac draw his bow and launch a shaft at the farthest target. The spectators voiced their approval with another cheer, even before the boy tending the targets signaled a hit to the center of the mark.

Eskkar stood there, as impressed as any, while Narquil loosed his arrow at the same mark. When the boy had finished shooting, Totomes and his sons moved back twenty paces and began again. The master bowman and his sons already stood well past the maximum range at which the most experienced archers practiced. Gatus, standing on the edge of the crowd, noticed Eskkar and joined him.

"Morning, Captain. You should've gotten here sooner. This Totomes and his boys have been putting on quite a show. They've hardly missed the mark at any range. Forno says he's never seen anything like it."

Forno, the senior archer among Eskkar's men, had slain Naxos's man. Forno led the archery training for the recruits. "So they're marksmen. But can they teach their skill to others?"

Gatus rubbed his beard as the crowd shouted approval at another hit. "Forno thinks so. He's already been given some tips by Totomes, who even let him draw his own bow, though only at close range."

No archer ever wanted to break another man's bow by trying to hit a distant mark. It said much for Forno that Totomes had allowed him to try his weapon. Another round of shafts were delivered, and again the crowd backed up another twenty paces. Totomes caught sight of Eskkar standing there and nodded.

By now the distance stretched over three hundred paces, and even the butts behind the targets looked small indeed. Despite the distance, Totomes's arrows reached them easily enough, with only a slight arc. Forno walked over to join his captain and Gatus, shaking his head in disbelief.

"Marduk's blood, but that man can use a bow better than anyone I've seen." Forno turned and squinted at the marks. "And his boys are almost as good. Narquil shoots slower but is the most accurate, though Mitrac hits his marks nearly as often."

"Can they help you train the men?" Eskkar asked.

"Captain, I think I'll be helping them train in a few days," Forno replied. "I'd like to see them shoot with our bows, but I'm sure Totomes has been training archers for twenty years."

Totomes and his sons, as far away from the butts as possible, still arched arrows into the sky that almost always struck the targets. Eskkar made up his mind and turned to Gatus. "Let Totomes start by training this group of recruits. And Gatus, I'll train with them."

Gatus raised an eyebrow.

Up to now Eskkar had postponed any intensive training with the bow, concentrating mainly on his swordplay. This might be as good a time as any to begin.

Before long, Eskkar stood at the head of the recruits, bow

in hand, quiver of arrows strapped to his waist, the targets a mere thirty paces away.

Totomes began his instructions. He put aside his weapon and demonstrated with one of the soldier's bows. If anyone thought it strange that the captain of the guard should be standing rigid with the latest batch of recruits, no one said anything, as Totomes stood next to Eskkar and watched him notch an arrow, aim, and let fly.

"Again," Totomes ordered, his eyes fixed on his pupil. Eskkar launched another, though the first shaft had hit the mark almost dead center. Totomes shook his head. "You'll not hit a target of any distance like that, Captain." He turned to his sons. "Show him."

The two boys moved on opposite sides of Eskkar, grasping his elbows, adjusting his stance and shifting his weight more to his rear foot.

"You shoot too much on your front foot, Captain," Totomes continued, "so, as you draw the bow, you become unbalanced, and make unnecessary movements. And you bring the arrow up from the ground as you bend into the bow. Always raise the arrow skyward and bring it down as you put your shoulder into it. That way a shaft released too soon may strike a target in the rear rather than the ground in front of you."

The two boys held Eskkar firmly, making him draw the bow slowly, keeping more weight on his rear foot and adjusting his right elbow. Eskkar held the drawn bow while they checked his stance and grip, taking plenty of time until they were satisfied. Eskkar's left arm began to tremble before Totomes gave the order to loose. The shaft flew into the straw butt but missed the wooden target hanging in its center.

"It feels awkward at first, Captain, but you'll get used to it. It's different from the way the . . . the way you learned. Try again." Totomes moved on to the next man, leaving Narquil to keep an eye on Eskkar.

And again and again, until Eskkar's left arm felt weak as water and the fingers on his right hand swelled and burned from the friction of the bowstring. But his pride drove him, and he refused to show weakness in front of his men. Up and down the line, Totomes, Mitrac, Narquil, Forno, and even Gatus kept close watch on the recruits' every movement, making sure they followed Totomes's instructions exactly. By the time they finished, Eskkar felt as exhausted as any of the men and wasn't even shooting as well as some.

"You'll do better in a few days, Captain," Totomes said with a friendly laugh as he walked with Eskkar back toward the barracks. "If you want accuracy, you'll have to unlearn some of your bad habits, but you'll do fine. You have the eye for it. If you like, Mitrac can work with you privately if you feel uncomfortable with the others watching."

A little late for that. He offered to train with this batch of bowmen, and now his honor had been challenged. He determined to do as well as any of them. "No, Totomes, though I thank you for the offer. I'll stay with these men for a while."

That meant an extra four hours per day with the bow for at least a week, in addition to his usual hours each morning training with the sword, spear, and battle-axe. But he couldn't avoid it, not if he wanted to experience exactly how Totomes and Forno trained the men. Orak's fate would rest in the arms of these bowmen.

It took ten days before he felt comfortable with the changes in his shooting style and before he could again plant his shaft within the mark with confidence. He'd long since admitted Totomes knew his craft. Eskkar led the recruits with the best scores until he realized some of the men would occasionally let a shaft or two fly wide to make sure their captain always scored higher. But by then he could hit a target at seventy paces three times out of four, and he felt more than satisfied with that.

A few days later they practiced from the main wall, looking out toward the low hills where their real enemy would appear. Now the soldiers fired as a group, aiming not at individual targets, but at a particular range. The targets had changed from the straw butts to stick figures planted in the earth at various distances. The men drew, aimed, and loosed their arrows together on command, learning how to gauge the distance and walk their shafts in from the farthest mark to the closest.

The first day on the wall Eskkar noticed something unusual. The men were always laughing, raising coarse jests, or doing all of the usual things soldiers and recruits did to take their minds off their own discomfort and to pass the time during training. But the first time they stood on the wall, the laughter stopped of its own accord. Taking their places, exposed from the waist up, they realized that a deadly business would soon be at hand. So they listened to the instructor's words a little more attentively, and took a little extra care in their work.

At the end of the first session, Totomes took Eskkar aside. "You're finished with your training, Captain," he said. "You're as good as you'll ever be. But you'll never make a master archer. You're too old for that. Leave the training now before too many of the others pass you by. You've proven your skill to your men. There are other, more important tasks for you."

13

Eskkar rode out of Orak six days later, taking Sisuth-ros, nine riders, two boys, and one pack horse with him. They traveled south at a steady pace. Jalen had explored north to get information about the barbarians' main camp. Eskkar wanted to observe the far-ranging Alur Meriki war parties reported to the south.

The men were fit, hard, and ready to fight. Six were hard-bitten veterans. Recent recruits made up the remainder, men who'd proven both their fighting ability and horsemanship. When you went to war against the barbarians, skill with a horse was as important as fighting.

Mitrac excepted. Totomes's youngest son had only limited experience with horses. Nevertheless Mitrac practiced hard for the last week under Jalen's tutelage. Once Eskkar saw Totomes's expertise, Eskkar wanted someone with him who could draw one of the great weapons.

Even so it had occasioned a four-sided argument between Eskkar, Totomes, and his sons before the father consented, worried he might lose Mitrac on some minor raid. Totomes gave in only when Eskkar promised to look after the boy personally.

Each day they rode south, resting the horses often. Esk-kar spent time with Sisuthros, Mitrac, and the rest, talking to them, asking their advice, or just joining them in rough song. *Get close to your men, from the lowest recruit to your commanders,* Trella advised. *First make them respect you, then let them know you. That's how you build loyalty.*

Her words matched what he'd seen in Corio and Nicar. Eskkar didn't know where Trella had learned so much about leading men, but her ideas made sense. He'd only to recall all the mistakes of his previous commanders or even his own to see the wisdom in what she said. So he began in earnest to build respect, then loyalty, in his men.

Only with loyalty can you have true power. The words echoed in his thoughts. *If enough of the soldiers and people believe in you, you will be safe, because your enemies will fear the anger of those who trust in you.* And so Eskkar made sure he got closer to his men.

In this Eskkar had changed greatly in the last months. Gold, women, horses, weapons, all the things he'd previously considered desirable, meant nothing to him. He wanted power now, power to place himself above the reach of the nobles, power to found his own House, power to build a clan that would last forever. Most of all, he wanted to safeguard Trella, to make sure their future remained secure.

But now Eskkar needed to concentrate on the present, so he put thoughts of Trella and Orak out of his mind and focused on his mission. By the fifth day they'd traveled over a hundred miles south of Orak, and soon he began hearing stories of an Alur Meriki raiding party.

Wayfarers, refugees, and travelers turned pale with fear when Eskkar and his riders approached. Their faces turned to smiles when they learned Eskkar came from Orak. From these wanderers he pieced enough stories together. The barbarians had finally reached the banks of the Tigris almost two hundred miles south of Orak. As yet they hadn't started north.

They would do that soon enough. No one had any real idea of the size of the war parties. Wild estimates of hundreds of warriors stripping the lands meant nothing. Eskkar divided every count by four, knowing fear and inexperience would inflate the numbers. He felt certain that two separate raiding parties existed.

Eskkar warned those they encountered not to go to Orak unless they wanted to fight. Otherwise they should cross the river as soon as possible.

That night, after caring for the horses, they sat around the small fire, enjoying fresh meat for only the second time since leaving Orak. They'd found a dying calf, separated from its mother, and the young animal had barely enough flesh on its bones for a hearty meal. The warm meat provided a respite from grain cakes and stale bread.

When the meal ended, Eskkar sent one of the boys to a nearby hill to keep watch and gathered the rest of the men. Each night he spoke about the coming day, so everyone knew what they were likely to confront.

"We've gone south long enough. Any day the Alur Meriki may turn north. So tomorrow, we head eastward. The barbarians have already passed through those lands."

"Why not go farther south," Sisuthros asked, "to see how many men they have?"

"We'll learn nothing more by going south. The barbarians have reached the river with at least one large raiding party. If we encounter them after they have turned north, they'll pursue us, and in a few days ride us down, even with our fine horses."

"What will we find to the east, Captain?" Sisuthros still sounded unconvinced.

"We should find groups of men and slaves moving north and south between the main body and these southern raiders. They won't be expecting men to come at them from this direction, now that their warriors have swept this land. I'd like to capture one or two, to learn how many they are and what they plan. Remember, we're not out looking for a fight, just information. I want to get you back to Orak alive."

Most commanders gave little thought to the lives of their men, so he knew his words had touched them.

"So if we encounter any barbarians," Sisuthros said, "we run?"

The men itched for a fight. Young and brave, they trained hard for weeks, and that training had given them confidence and the urge to test themselves against the enemy. "Yes, we run unless we meet a small party, one closer to our size. Then maybe we'll have a chance to test our blades."

The next morning they traveled at a moderate pace, with two men ranging ahead, and another to their rear. They rode that way for three days, stopping often to rest the horses, traveling only ten or fifteen miles each day, seeing fewer farms or people, and instead more empty land as the cautious riders moved deeper into rough country to the east.

They reached the beginnings of hill and canyon country, with the great mountains looming ever closer. By now Orak lay far to the northwest.

The ninth day since leaving Orak, the morning showed a sky gray and heavy with clouds, hinting at rain. They kept to their usual pace, keeping away from the hilltops and stopping often to rest the animals.

An hour past noon, after they dismounted to rest the horses, the man keeping watch raised a shout and pointed toward the mountains. In an instant Eskkar leaped on his horse, looking eastward. He saw the southernmost of his scouts galloping back toward them. Turning to his left, he saw the other scout also returning, but at a more reasonable pace.

The first scout, a veteran named Maldar, pulled up in front of Eskkar. All the men had mounted their horses, readied their weapons, and let their eyes scan the horizon in every direction.

"Captain, there's a large band of barbarians about three miles ahead." Maldar's voice betrayed his excitement. "Or maybe two bands. I couldn't be sure, but it looks as if they're fighting, lots of dust and noise."

Fighting among the barbarians! That didn't sound right to Eskkar. The Alur Meriki had serious penalties for fighting amongst themselves when on the clan's missions. At home in the main camp, individuals often fought, but conflicts between groups of warriors seldom occurred. Even if two clans opposed each other, everyone preferred to let the leaders fight it out. But who else could they be fighting?

"Maldar, switch horses with one of the boys." He wanted Maldar on a fresh mount. "Sisuthros, get the other scout in and follow us, but keep at least half a mile behind."

Eskkar waited until Maldar had moved his gear to the new animal. The fright Eskkar saw on the boy's face would have made him laugh once, but now Eskkar smiled encouragement. "Stay steady, boy, we'll not leave you behind." Then Eskkar and Maldar rode off at a canter. A small cloud of dust rose and soon settled in their trail.

Before long the two men reached the base of the outlying hills. From there successive ridges of earth rose ever higher, until the base of the great peaks blocked the path. Eskkar imagined he could hear the distant clash of bronze weapons and the cries of men fighting, but when he stopped and listened, he heard nothing.

"Here, Captain, from this hilltop I saw them." A winding trail, marked by the hoof prints of Maldar's horse, led to the top. Eskkar could ride up, as Maldar had done, or he could climb the steep hill on foot. Eskkar decided not to risk the horses.

"Come," he ordered, "we'll climb on foot." They rode the last few paces to the base of the hill, dismounted, and tied the horses fast to a small tree. Eskkar made sure he tied his knot tight and that Maldar did the same. If they had to run, Eskkar didn't want to be fighting his own man over a horse should one of the animals get loose.

They began the long climb, scrambling much of the way and slipping back occasionally until they reached the top. None of his recent training had prepared him for climbing steep hills, and he was breathing hard by the time they gained the summit. Low boulders covered the narrow crest, with patches of grass sprouting between them. He dropped down between two rocks.

Looking out over the spreading foothills, Eskkar found himself on a hilltop somewhat higher than those in front of him. It provided a good vantage point to observe the grayish-red slabs of rock that protruded down from the higher mountains and formed a labyrinth of canyons and gullies that twisted and turned back on themselves.

Maldar pointed to the northeast. "See, there they are. No, wait, they've moved toward us."

Another ridge crest separated Eskkar from the swirling cloud, but he could make out the dust of many riders, a constantly churning cloud that moved and shifted as he watched. It did look as if two groups battled each other in a running fight. As he watched, one band broke through the ranks of the other and headed toward Eskkar's position, following the line of hills that ran roughly parallel to the ridge Eskkar occupied, but more than a mile away.

In moments the other riders regrouped and took up the chase. "Count the first group, Maldar," he ordered while he tried to estimate the second and larger body. The strange riders were still far off and the horses moved and merged, making counting difficult. Sixty-five or seventy men, he guessed.

"Forty, maybe a few more. Why do they fight each other, Captain?"

Eskkar turned his attention to the first troop, close enough to distinguish some detail. They either had no standard or had lost it in battle. Yet even the dust couldn't hide the yellow streamers that decorated many lances and bow tips. Yellow meant another clan, for red marked the predominant hue of the Alur Meriki. So a different tribe of steppes people had somehow gotten involved in a fight with the Alur Meriki.

Eskkar watched the leading band turn toward them, seeking a path out of the hills and canyons that threatened to pen them in. The pursuing band began to gain on their quarry, their horses obviously fresher, though all the animals would be tired by the fighting and the chase. He'd seen enough. "Let's go, Maldar. We don't want to be here when . . ."

His voice trailed off as he watched the yellow riders gallop into a canyon. From his vantage point, Eskkar could see their path led nowhere. In a few moments the yellow riders whirled their horses about and rode back out, the gap between pursued and pursuers shortened by the time wasted on the false trail. A short ride would bring them to another fork. One branch led to a narrow, twisting trail that would lead to the open plain where Eskkar's men now waited.

The other branch, twice as wide, led into another, larger canyon, one that twisted and turned alongside the cliffs, but one he could see ended in a second cul-de-sac. But it wouldn't look that way to the harried riders. A flash of insight possessed him, almost as if he could see what would happen. At the same time, an idea, a foolish one perhaps, took hold of him. His eyes marked the landmarks beneath him.

"Come," he ordered, his mind made up, and he began scrambling down the steep hillside, grasping at roots and the hard rock edges that jutted through the thin grasses.

At the bottom Eskkar waited for Maldar to come rattling down, then grabbed his arm to halt him. "Walk slowly toward the horses, Maldar. Don't spook them."

They reached the horses that watched nervously, nostrils flaring and eyes wide at the unusual sight of men and stones sliding down the hillside. Eskkar made sure he had a firm grip on the halter before he undid the knot, looking at Maldar to make sure he followed his example. Once mounted, Eskkar led the way back to Sisuthros and the rest of his men, hidden from view by yet another tiny rolling swell sprinkled with skimpy grass.

"Captain, we should hurry." Maldar's voice betrayed his excitement. "They'll be here any moment. We're right in their path."

Eskkar reached the top of the grassy mound that opened up to the plain and spotted the rest of his men. He waved to them, summoning them forward. The faint sounds of the barbarian horses could be heard now, echoing off the rocks. The warring parties were less than half a mile away.

Maldar began again, but Eskkar cut him off. "No, they'll take the wrong turn into the canyon, and be caught in a trap.

They don't know this ground or they'd never have gone up the first blind canyon. We're safe for now."

Sisuthros rode up at the head of the men and looked toward the hills. Eskkar saw fear on each man's face, especially the new men and the boys. Everyone could hear the pounding hooves, amplified by the cliff walls, and they all knew danger lay just over the ridge. He waited until they'd bunched up around him.

"Listen carefully." Eskkar kept his voice calm and assured. "There are two tribes of barbarians engaged in a battle inside the canyon over there," he pointed to his left. "The larger band is Alur Meriki, and there are about fifty or sixty of them." No sense frightening them even more by telling them the exact truth. "They fight against another, smaller band of about forty barbarians, one that I don't recognize but clearly from a different clan. By now the Alur Meriki have trapped the first band in a box canyon and will soon be attacking them."

"Then we've time to get away." Sisuthros's voice showed his relief. The men nodded agreement.

"No, we're not riding away." Eskkar watched their faces go blank at his words, their mouths opening in surprise. "We're going to attack the Alur Meriki from the rear. We've enough men on fresh horses to tip the scale of battle."

"Why fight to save barbarians?" Maldar asked. "Why not let them kill each other, while we get away?"

Eskkar shook his head. "Barbarians have a saying—the enemy of my enemy is my friend. If we help this other tribe, we gain allies against the Alur Meriki, and Orak needs all the help it can find. With our help, these Alur Meriki can be defeated." He saw the doubt and disbelief on their faces. "You said you wanted to fight, didn't you? Well, here's your chance! Or would you rather run away?"

He gave them no time to answer, as he turned his horse's head back toward the canyons. "Mitrac, come with me and ready that great bow of yours. Sisuthros, prepare the men and walk the horses two hundred paces behind us."

Eskkar rode off without a backward glance. In a few moments Mitrac reached his side, pale but determined, his eyes wide. Eskkar looked at the young man. "Trust me, lad, we can do this. I promise that you'll kill at least five Alur Meriki today."

Eskkar rode through the creases in the hills, the sounds of shouting and excited horses growing louder. The first party realized they'd ridden into a trap, and now both sides took their time readying their men for further battle. No doubt the first band had ridden to the end of the box canyon and would regroup from there. But the battle hadn't started yet, so Eskkar knew he had some time.

Checking the landmarks he'd noted from the hilltop, Eskkar took his position and dismounted. He tied his horse to a gnarled tree limb, then retied Mitrac's mount.

"That was a poor knot," Eskkar said. "Your horse would have bolted loose at the first sound of trouble. Always make sure of your horse." He slapped the lad lightly on the shoulder. "Now, string your weapon and follow me."

Without waiting or looking behind, Eskkar moved silently the last hundred paces up the narrow trail. Boulders rose up on either side, twice his height, until he came to the final bend in the path. He slipped through the rocks and took a quick look up the trail.

The barbarians had left two riders to guard the opening against the chance of any opponents breaking through their ranks and escaping. Their gazes were fixed down the canyon. Mitrac's rapid breathing announced his arrival, and Eskkar stepped back behind the rocks.

"Mitrac," Eskkar said, noting the youth's bow was strung and an arrow fitted to the string. "There are two warriors, both with bows across their mounts, just around the bend, about forty paces away. Neither has an arrow to his string yet. Shoot the one farthest away first because he's closest to the canyon entrance, and I don't want him getting away. Then shoot the other one. If you miss, keep shooting. If he charges, I'll take him with my sword."

Eskkar looked at the lad, who seemed steady enough though his lip trembled and the bow shook a little in his hand. "Are you ready?"

Mitrac swallowed hard but managed to nod.

Eskkar had seen the signs of fear before. "It's an easy shot, and they won't be expecting it. Just do it, and think about it later. Now, let's go. Take three good paces and let fly. I'll be right behind you."

Eskkar pulled his sword from the scabbard, more to give Mitrac a sense of security than out of actual need. At that moment, a great war cry sounded from the Alur Meriki inside the canyon, mixed with the pounding of horses put to the gallop as they launched their attack.

Mitrac's hands shook a little, just enough to betray his nervousness. He bit his lip, took a deep breath, exhaled half of it, and stepped forward. Three long paces, then he turned and braced his left foot.

The boy's long training under the stern tutelage of his father paid off. The bow bent smoothly and, with scarcely a moment to aim, he launched the shaft on its flight. The first warrior cried out when the arrow struck him behind the right shoulder. The second man looked the wrong way. As he turned back to his rear, Mitrac's second arrow, which had leapt from quiver to string, struck its target full in the chest. The Alur Meriki pitched slowly off his horse.

Eskkar darted back toward his men and, waving his sword, urged them forward. He raced back to Mitrac, clasping him on the shoulder to give him confidence. "Take a stance up in those rocks. Shoot anything that comes your way wearing red."

Pushing him on his way, Eskkar ran ahead and gathered up the two riderless horses, leading them away from the canyon's opening. Up close, he saw that the gap between the canyon's walls was about forty feet wide at the entrance. He handed the horses off to Sisuthros, who rode up, sword in one hand, leading Eskkar's horse with the other.

Eskkar nodded at his subcommander, partly from relief that his men had followed him. He handed the ropes of the captured beasts to one of the boys, then took the halter of his own mount and swung back astride.

"Hold these animals fast. We may need extra mounts."

Eskkar turned to Sisuthros and the men. "Follow me, and once in the canyon, form a line. They won't be expecting an attack from behind. When we charge, ride as hard as you can and kill everything in your path wearing red. Red, remember that!" Eskkar spoke rapidly, giving the men no time to think or doubt.

In a moment Eskkar was at the center of a line of ten mounted men that stretched across the canyon's mouth. The noise of the battle sounded loud in his ears, just out of sight. "Mitrac," he called out to the lad standing in the rocks with his bow, an arrow to the string. "Follow us in, but stay in the rocks. Kill as many as you can. Don't let any get away."

Eskkar glanced at the men on either side. "Remember, kill only red, or we'll be fighting the whole lot."

He gave them no more time to worry. "Think about all the gold they're carrying! Use your horses and scream your heads off. I want them more scared of us than the other barbarians. Now, follow me, and do as I do!"

He kicked the horse forward and hoped his men followed. If they didn't, he'd be dead very soon. His own fear rose up bitter in the back of his throat, as it always did at the start of a battle. Death might wait a few paces ahead, but he refused to think about the danger or his decision to fight. Eskkar took a deep breath, glad that the time for thinking had passed.

Rounding the small bend just inside the canyon's mouth, the full sound of men and beasts fighting and dying hit them in all its fury. Huge clouds of dust swirled madly but Eskkar paid no mind, urging Nicar's best horse forward with savage kicks even as he gripped the beast tightly with both knees. He reached the rear of the fight as the first Alur Meriki heard the horses behind him and turned his head.

Eskkar's sword swept down, and he sliced through the man's shoulder as the warrior tried to wheel his horse around. Without slowing, Eskkar urged his horse directly at the next man, letting his beast's shoulder crash into the warrior's horse, knocking loose the man's grip as Eskkar followed up with another savage stroke. The fighting madness enveloped him, possessed him completely. Only killing mattered now.

His own men rode close beside him, yelling at the tops of their lungs and hacking away like madmen. An Alur Meriki warrior whirled his horse around and launched himself at Eskkar, swinging his sword high in the air. Before he could strike, one of Mitrac's arrows thudded into the barbarian's breast and he pitched backward off his mount.

The fight turned into a melee. Horses bumped each other, screaming and biting. Warriors clung to their mounts and tried to fight at the same time. But the fresh horses of Eskkar's men pushed the tired animals of the Alur Meriki back, and Eskkar's long sword rose and fell again and again, spattering blood from both man and beast.

Attacked from behind by an unknown force, they had no idea how few assailed them. The shouts of Orak's men rose up and mixed with the cries of the dying and wounded, the din resounding louder in the confined canyon, echoing off the walls and adding to the confusion.

Eskkar tried to keep track of the battle even as he struggled to master his horse and fight, but the chaos of the combat overwhelmed him as desperate men fought one on one. One moment Eskkar found himself practically surrounded by attackers. In the next, the clashing waves of men left him almost alone.

A dismounted barbarian flung himself upon Sisuthros and pulled him from his horse. The two men rolled together at Eskkar's feet. He reached down and pushed his sword's point into the barbarian's back as the warrior raised his knife for the killing blow.

Then Sisuthros was forgotten as another warrior rode at Eskkar, leaning forward over his lance and screaming his war cry. Eskkar had faced lances before and knew he only had to turn the point a few inches to survive. He kicked his horse forward, hugging the animal's neck and keeping his arm rigid and his sword low until the lance point passed over the tip of the blade. Then Eskkar pushed his sword out and up, catching the wood just behind the bronze tip and feeling it burn its way across his arm. His arm stayed locked and his blade straight as the horses crashed together. The hilt of his weapon smashed against the man's chest before the impact wrenched the sword from his grasp.

The collision sent Eskkar's horse to its haunches. Eskkar pitched backward and fell, going heels over head as he hit the earth. From the ground, everything looked different and more frightening. A barbarian spotted the easy victim and twisted his horse around to head for him. But a dozen steps from Eskkar, the horse suddenly reared up, an arrow protruding under its neck, its rider suddenly fighting for control of the dying animal.

Eskkar scrambled over to the warrior he'd just killed and retrieved his sword. Grabbing the hilt with both hands, Eskkar braced one foot on the body and heaved with all his might, pulling the sword free of both earth and carcass. An arrow hissed by his head, but he didn't know who shot it or where it went.

His horse, back on its feet, spun and twisted in panic, too confused to get free of the melee. Three quick steps and Eskkar launched himself across the back of the beast, nearly going over the other side. Struggling to regain control of the terrified mount, he called out to it so that it would recognize his voice. It took a moment to shift his weight and lock his knees on the horse as he reached forward for the halter. Another arrow hissed just beyond the horse's neck, and this time Eskkar looked up to see another red-clad barbarian pitching off his horse a few paces away.

The moment Eskkar had the halter, the animal steadied. Looking around, he saw the Alur Meriki being pressed back, Orak's men hacking away like fiends. He stretched his body upward in an effort to see more of the battle. Eskkar spotted six or seven warriors still pressing forward against the yellow riders. The red standard moved closer to a small knot of the unknown tribesmen.

"Follow me, Orak, follow me," Eskkar bellowed as he urged the horse forward, aiming the beast straight at the red standard. "Orak, Orak," he screamed as he crashed the horse against a rider, knocking the other man's beast back and slashing down with his sword. Then Eskkar burst into their midst, hacking left and right, screaming to his men to follow. The fighting madness came over him again. No thoughts, no fear, just strike and strike again.

He'd pushed through the line of barbarians who had turned to face the men from Orak. Now he reached the backs of those Alur Meriki fighting the weakening group of yellow riders. He stabbed his sword into the haunches of one horse, then slashed at the head of another wild-eyed mount. The stricken and terrified beasts reared up, lashing out with their hooves, their screams joining the battle din.

Eskkar drove his horse between the two wounded horses, killing one man outright as he struggled to regain control of his mount. Eskkar then turned toward the other and struck downward at the man's arm. A burst of blood and a scream erupted as the man's hand disappeared, severed at the wrist. Eskkar whirled forward once again.

He'd nearly broken through the Alur Meriki ranks, but one of the red warriors wheeled to face him, the two horses standing shoulder to shoulder as the swords clashed. A thick-bodied warrior in the full strength of manhood, he struck down at Eskkar's head. Eskkar blocked the blow, but the man struck again and again. The strokes pushed Eskkar's blade back, giving him no time for a counterstroke. Eskkar fought harder, trying to overcome with sheer strength what he couldn't do with skill. But the Alur Meriki proved as strong and determined.

Eskkar jerked at the halter, trying to disengage, but his horse was trapped from behind. He felt his sword arm growing weaker, and saw the gleam of victory in his enemy's eyes.

That light suddenly flickered out when a heavy feathered shaft appeared as if by magic at the base of the man's throat. The dying man's horse felt his master's knees relax and yielded to the pressure of Eskkar's mount. He rode past the man, whose dying eyes turned toward him as he pushed by. Esskar's right arm shook with weakness, but he kicked his horse forward and struck down another man from behind.

An Alur Meriki rider appeared and crashed his horse into Esskar's. Esskar tumbled yet again to the ground, but an Orak rider arrived and cut the barbarian down almost in the same instant. Esskar gained his feet and lurched toward the last few Alur Meriki still fighting to reach the leader of the yellow riders. Esskar saw that the clan chief of the yellow riders had been wounded and unhorsed, with a single warrior standing in front of him for protection.

Again Esskar's sword stabbed into the rear quarters of a horse that turned in pain and bucked its rider off, hindquarters lashing out and nearly catching Esskar in the face. An arrow hissed by and struck down another red-marked warrior as Esskar raised his sword to slash at the legs of the last rider.

The Alur Meriki saw the danger, turned and swung his sword at Esskar. He tried to parry the heavy blow, but his sword arm trembled with exhaustion. The impact pushed Esskar's blade back and nearly tore the weapon from his grasp. The force of the blow knocked Esskar to his knees, and he struggled to meet the warrior's killing stroke.

But the final stroke never came. The last of the yellow warriors struck the horse a savage blow on the fetlock, crippling the animal and sending it into a frenzy, before it sank to its knees in pain and terror. The Alur Meriki rider, fighting to keep his seat, raised his sword toward Esskar, then turned his eyes toward the last of the yellow warriors. His instant of indecision cost him not only his life, but also any chance to strike a blow.

Esskar, still on his knees, thrust out with his sword at his assailant now just within reach, lunging forward with his whole body, determined to strike one more blow, to thrust his blade into his enemy's body even if he took a death blow in return. The blades of Esskar and the yellow-clad warrior struck at the last Alur Meriki warrior from either side, and the man grunted in agony before he died, with Esskar's sword low in his stomach and the barbarian's blade thrust under his armpit.

The struggling horse fell on its side, tearing the sword from Eskkar's grasp. He struggled to get back on his knees and finally managed it. Eskkar reached out and tried to pull his sword free but couldn't, the fatigued muscles in his trembling arm refusing to obey, and he found himself unable to get to his feet.

Letting go of the hilt in disgust, Eskkar fumbled for his knife, but there was no need. Looking around, he saw the fight was over. No warrior wearing red survived. Only the men from Orak and the yellow barbarians remained alive, and they immediately began eying each other.

Eskkar forced himself to his feet, knowing the moment of danger had come. He struggled to catch his breath, and his legs shook with exertion and excitement. He raised his voice and shouted to his men to dismount and put away their weapons.

The warrior who had shared the final kill with Eskkar turned to help pull his fallen chief to his feet. The younger man, holding the bloody sword he'd pulled from the dead Alur Meriki, looked suspiciously at Eskkar. His chief called to his men who moved quickly toward him, lowering their weapons as they came. Apparently the chief shared Eskkar's concern about more fighting. The younger warrior repeated the chief's words in a louder voice, and this time they made some sense to Eskkar, who hadn't heard his native tongue spoken for some time.

At least they weren't going to start killing each other, if Eskkar understood the chief's words. As Eskkar's men gathered around him, swords still in their hands, but pointing at the ground, Mitrac joined the group, his face flushed with excitement.

Eskkar wanted to get his men aside, to make sure nothing unexpected happened. He tried to speak, but couldn't get the words out. He took a deep breath and tried again. "Get the horses . . . stand over there . . ."

He stopped as Maldar stepped up to him and took

Eskkar's left arm and placed it over his shoulder. Sisuthros moved to his other side and grasped him around the waist.

"You're wounded," Sisuthros said, looking down at Eskkar's right arm covered in blood.

"Aye, and you can't stand for shaking," Maldar added. "We need to bandage that arm, before you bleed to death, and take a look at that leg."

The two half-carried him to a spot near the canyon wall where the carnage had left some empty space, then set him down. No wonder his right arm had betrayed him, Eskkar realized, as he glanced down at the blood that ran from shoulder to wrist. It must have happened when he turned the lance thrust. The weapon's tip had sliced open half the length of his arm.

Eskkar felt his left leg trembling uncontrollably and saw a huge bruise already arisen in the center of his thigh. Getting knocked off his horse must have done that. Suddenly waves of pain shot through his leg, making him gasp. His eyes didn't want to focus.

He cursed as he realized that if his thigh bone had snapped, he was as good as dead, unable to ride and so far from Orak. His men propped him against an outcropping of rock, and Maldar ripped a garment off one of the dead and tore it into strips. Sisuthros held a water skin to Eskkar's lips until he could swallow no more, then poured more over the cut in his arm to rinse most of the blood off and clean the wound before Maldar quickly and efficiently bound it up.

"How many dead?" Eskkar sat there stoically as they worked on him. Sisuthros and Maldar looked at each other, everyone mentally counting.

"Four are missing." Sisuthros's grim voice removed the smiles of victory from their faces.

"And the horses?" Eskkar had to force the words out. "What of the boys?"

Sisuthros turned and ordered one man to go back to the canyon entrance and bring back the boys and horses.

"One boy is dead." Mitrac squatted on the ground near Eskkar's feet. "I saw him fall."

"They were told to stay back," Eskkar said angrily. A village boy wouldn't have lasted a moment in that fight. "And the other?"

"I'm not sure," Mitrac answered. "They both joined the fight, but I didn't see him fall. He's probably dead, too."

"I owe you my life, Mitrac, at least twice that I remember." He turned to Maldar sitting on the ground a few steps away. "And to you, too, Maldar."

Eskkar turned back to Mitrac and saw his quiver of arrows held only two shafts. "Better go and collect your arrows, before the strangers use them for firewood." He looked to Sisuthros, who seemed to have no major wounds. A wave of dizziness swept over Eskkar, and he had to fight to keep his thoughts from wandering. His leg began to tremble again and he gripped his knee to stop it.

"Look after the men's wounds. And see to the horses." They went off to do his bidding, and Eskkar leaned back against the rock as another wave of dizziness blurred his vision. He closed his eyes for a moment.

It must have been a long moment, for he suddenly sat upright, looking around in confusion. Ishtar's blood, he must have fallen asleep. A leader should never show such weakness in front of his men. Eskkar tried to get up, but Maldar pushed him back down and held on to his good arm.

"Rest easy, Captain. You passed out for a while. You've lost a lot of blood."

Eskkar recognized honest affection in his voice.

"And we got some good news as well, Captain. Zantar's alive. They found him under a pile of bodies, knocked senseless. The barbarians were stripping his body when he awoke. Scared the piss out of him, they did."

Maldar laughed at the thought. "And one boy is still alive, that rat of a pickpocket," he added, referring to the petty thief who'd begged and pleaded his way on the mission. "His arm's smashed up pretty bad, but he may live. He won't cut any more purses, though."

Eskkar tried to think. They'd lost only three men if Zantar survived—two veterans and one of the newer recruits. Not a bad trade, to finish off a war party of this size. He wondered what the other tribe's losses had been. Glancing around, they looked to have scarcely more men standing than those surrounding Eskkar.

Sisuthros returned, slumping on the ground next to Eskkar. "Four dead, counting the boy, and we lost three horses, not counting yours, which one of the barbarians seems intent on keeping for himself. The rest of us are in pretty fair shape, only minor cuts and bruises. We should go back to the stream and get cleaned up. Or at least send for more water."

No one knew why wounds washed with clean water healed faster than unwashed ones. "Yes. If they can ride, send them back to the stream. Bring water back for the others."

"I'll take care of it, Sisuthros." Maldar pushed himself to his feet. "You stay and keep an eye on these barbarians." In a few moments Maldar had collected all the intact water bags he could find, and he and two others rode off.

Sisuthros leaned close to his captain and kept his voice low. "I told the men to keep their weapons close, in case they try anything."

"Just make sure we don't start any trouble." Eskkar wanted their help, not another fight.

"Captain, the barbarians are stripping all the dead of their valuables. Some of our men tried to do the same but the barbarians put their hands on their swords, so they backed off."

"Don't worry about the loot," Eskkar said with a tired laugh. "After a battle, all the captured weapons and trophies belong to the chief. He divides it up according to how well each man fought or who's in most need. Tell the men they'll get their share."

A voice called out from the direction of the barbarians, and Eskkar twisted his head toward the battlefield. The chief of the strange band moved toward him, assisted by the same warrior who'd stood over him during the last of the fight.

"Here comes their leader." Eskkar tried to get up, but his leg failed him and he couldn't seem to manage with his one arm. "Help me up, Sisuthros."

Sisuthros put his arm under Eskkar's shoulder and started to lift, but the younger warrior, now only a few steps away, called out in the trade language, telling him to leave Eskkar on the ground. A few moments later, the commander of the barbarians sat down gingerly opposite Eskkar. The young warrior stood directly behind his chief, a grim look on his face.

"Greetings, Chief of the Strangers. I am Mesilim, leader of the Ur Nammu. This is my son, Subutai." He twisted his head slowly, as if in pain, to nod toward the warrior behind him. Mesilim had a great bruise on his forehead and cuts on both his arms, bound up with rags already soaked in blood. He spoke the language of the steppes people. He paused, then glanced at Eskkar's men sitting nearby.

Eskkar realized his mistake. When clan leaders spoke, only the chief's family or his subcommanders could be present. All others must be out of earshot, lest they heard words not fit for their ears.

"Sisuthros, move the men away." Sisuthros looked apprehensive, but led the men about twenty paces away, barely out of earshot.

Eskkar waited until Sisuthros returned. Sisuthros followed the example of the warrior, and stood behind him. "My name is Eskkar, war leader of the village of Orak, and I give honor to the great clan leader Mesilim who has killed many warriors this day."

Eskkar looked up at the son. "And to his strong son who slew all Alur Meriki who dared to face him." Better too much praise than risk offending anyone's honor.

"Your men fought bravely, Chief Eskkar," Mesilim said, "but I would know why you joined the fight. You ride and dress as people of the farms, and they've little love for any steppes people."

A delicate way to put it. "People of the farms" was about the politest way a tribesman could say "dirt digger." Still, Mesilim had made an effort. "My people fight the Alur

Meriki. Is not the enemy of my enemy my friend? We were on a scouting party when we saw your warriors attacked. Who would not join such brave fighters?"

The hint of a smile crossed Mesilim's face. Eskkar wondered whether he'd overdone the praise. Nevertheless, Mesilim and his men would have all been dead by now without Eskkar's help, though of course the chief couldn't ever admit that. Out of respect and politeness, Eskkar couldn't mention it either.

"It's as you say, Chief Eskkar. The enemy of my enemy is my friend. You saved many lives today, including my own. But can you tell me why you fight the Alur Meriki? They are a clan of many, many warriors, and the people of the farms cannot stand against them."

"It is not our wish to go to war against any of the steppes people, Chief Mesilim. But the Alur Meriki march toward our village with all their strength, and we've chosen to fight rather than run."

Eskkar saw disbelief cross Mesilim's face and guessed what Mesilim was thinking—that no farmers stood a chance against such a great force of warriors. "My village has many people, almost as many as in the Alur Meriki tribe. We've built a great stone wall around our village, and we will fight the Alur Meriki from the wall, not from horseback."

Mesilim looked down at the ground, too polite to show either his doubts or disgust with such an un-warrior-like strategy. Instead he explained his own clan. "My people first fought the Alur Meriki more than two years ago. We fought bravely and killed many of them, but they overwhelmed us with their greater numbers. Now the Ur Nammu are almost gone. Most of our warriors have been killed. Only we are left to carry on the fight. Almost all our women and children . . . dead or taken by the Alur Meriki." His voice couldn't conceal the sadness of his heart. "We fight on because I've sworn the Shan Kar against them, though it might have been better if I'd fallen in battle today."

Eskkar glanced up at Subutai with even more respect.

Many a son would put a knife in a father's back some dark night rather than continue a death fight. For that's what the Shan Kar proclaimed, a fight to the death, and Mesilim had condemned his followers to that fate since they had no chance of victory. The son must have great loyalty as well as great strength to protect such a father.

"Great Chief, there's much I would ask you regarding the Alur Meriki. You have knowledge of my enemy and it would aid my people to learn these things from you. If you'd be willing to share your knowledge with me."

Mesilim nodded. "Yes, we've much to talk about. But first, let us take care of the wounded, bury the dead, and divide the spoils. It'll be dark soon." He offered up his hand to his son, who reached down and helped him to his feet, then escorted him back to the Ur Nammu.

His men rushed back as Mesilim moved away, their questions coming fast. When they gathered around, Eskkar explained their position. "For now, we're considered to be friends to the Ur Nammu, since we fought beside them. They'll collect all the valuables from the dead, and it will be divided later amongst all who fought. By custom, Chief Mesilim will make the division since he has the most warriors on the field. We must bury our dead and tend to the wounded." He saw doubt in some eyes, and decided to explain further.

"Don't worry. They could kill us easily if they chose to." The Ur Nammu had about twenty-five warriors still fit to fight. "These people have much knowledge about our enemy. More than that, they could help in our own fight. So make sure you give no offense to any of them. They're all that's left of a proud people, fighting a war to the death against our own foes. Now, help me up."

Sisuthros and Maldar pulled him to his feet and watched as he tested his leg. The swelling on his thigh looked enormous now, but he took a few steps with their help and realized gratefully the bone hadn't broken, or the leg would not have stood his weight. Nevertheless, whenever he tried to put weight on it, sharp pain lanced through him. Eskkar asked for a crutch of some kind. Maldar picked up a broken lance and gave it to him.

Despite his injuries, Eskkar insisted on examining each of his men. Most of the wounds didn't appear too severe, mainly cuts and slashes. Zantar, knocked unconscious during the fight, remained stretched out on the ground, his eyes unfocused, still woozy and barely coherent. Only Mitrac had escaped without a scratch.

The surviving horse boy, Tammuz by name, had the worst wound. Standing over him, Eskkar saw the boy's left arm was badly broken, probably in more than one place. The slightest touch or movement brought a moan of agony to Tammuz's lips.

"Well, Tammuz, I see you disobeyed my orders. Next time, maybe you'll know better." Aside from the arm, the rest of his cuts and bruises seemed minor enough.

"I wanted to fight, Captain," Tammuz answered, his voice thin as he fought back the tears. Even the effort to speak made him wince. "I killed one of them, I did, with the . . . bow. Mitrac saw it, I'm sure . . . he did."

Eskkar had brought two riding bows with the expedition, but they'd been left behind with the other horses. The foolish boys had strung them and followed behind the men when they could. "I'm sure you did, Tammuz. Rest now."

The broken arm was beyond Eskkar's ability to bandage and the boy would likely be dead in a day or two. He turned to Maldar. "Give Tammuz water, then wine, lots of it, to ease his pain." Using his crutch, Eskkar turned and looked toward the Ur Nammu.

Mesilim and his son, nearly finished caring for their wounded, had begun the burial process. As Eskkar watched, several riders dashed off on some unknown errands, while others started clearing a burial space against one of the canyon walls. He hobbled toward Mesilim, leaning heavily on the crutch, until he reached a knot of warriors around Mesilim. They eyed him curiously but parted to let him through. Mesilim looked up.

"Honorable Chief," Eskkar began, "I have a wounded

boy. His arm is badly broken and is beyond our skills to set. Perhaps you have someone who can tend to him?"

Mesilim considered the request. "A boy must be tended last, after the warriors. We have a healer, though he has his own wounds. I'll send him to you after our warriors are tended."

Mesilim looked toward those men clearing the burial site. "We'll bury our dead there as soon as possible. Do you wish to put your dead with them?"

"Yes, we would gladly bury our men with yours. Thank you for the honor. Would it be allowed for my men to help digging the burial mound?"

A mass grave would have to be dug out of the hilly earth, deep enough to keep wild animals out. It would take many men's efforts to get it done. "We have one digging tool with us that might make the work easier," Eskkar added.

"I must consult my men about that," Mesilim replied.

Any handling of the dead must be done with great care and the proper rituals, to make sure their spirits rested in peace for all time.

Mesilim began speaking to his son and two warriors. Each had something to say, but they all seemed to agree. He turned back to Eskkar. "Your men may help us and we are grateful. Your dead will honor our own."

Eskkar bowed in thanks and walked to his men, leaning heavily on the stick and clenching his teeth against the pain. "Mesilim will send a healer to help with the . . . Tammuz." You didn't call anyone who'd killed an enemy in battle a boy. "Gather our dead and prepare them for burial. Then all who can dig will help Mesilim's men prepare the grave. We bury our dead with theirs, and they honor our own by the offer."

"What are they doing now?" Sisuthros asked. A dozen or so warriors had mounted horses and ridden off, half of them leading spare animals.

"They'll gather the bodies from the other battleground. After everyone is buried, the corpses of the Alur Meriki will be left to rot on top of the grave and to feed the carrion, so all will know how many died here. Then, I think, we'll all get out of this damned canyon."

Leaving all this behind sounded better and better every moment. Flies buzzed everywhere, and vultures and crows circled above, waiting their chance, attracted by the blood and death. Eskkar tried to ignore the coppery-blood smell that wanted to make him retch. He saw Mitrac swat at a fly. "Mitrac, have you recovered your arrows yet?"

The guilty look on the boy's face answered the question. "Go find your shafts. We may need them again and while you're doing that, count the number of your kills." It would give the young man something to do. "Sisuthros, leave one man to watch Zantar and the . . . Tammuz. The rest of you, get the shovel and start digging."

Digging turned out to be too much for Eskkar, who found he couldn't put any extra strain on his leg. But five of his men began digging alongside the Ur Nammu, and the small bronze shovel they'd brought with them proved a big help. In all, twenty men were soon digging as hard as they could, though Eskkar knew darkness would fall long before they finished.

Mesilim planned for that as well. Two men returned carrying firewood. They started a fire, then rigged up some branches to serve as torches. Strips of fat torn from the dead horses would keep them burning.

Eskkar's men dug as hard as the tribesmen, to prove themselves as strong and tough as their newfound friends. Despite their help, it took twenty-five men nearly four hours to dig a pit long and deep enough to hold almost fifty bodies. That included the Ur Nammu killed in the earlier fighting.

Those bodies were brought to the gravesite, tied two to a mount. Almost two thirds of Mesilim's people had died today. They'd fought bravely and if their numbers had been more evenly matched, they might have defeated the Alur Meriki by themselves. Now only about twenty-five Ur Nammu warriors, many of them wounded, remained to carry on their leader's sworn vengeance.

Darkness fell and men built up the fire and lit more torches. An hour later the moon rose and helped illuminate their work. Nevertheless the effort exhausted every man who finally staggered from the pit.

"By the gods, Captain." Sisuthros appeared ready to fall down. So much dirt covered him that his eyes gleamed white in the torchlight. "I don't think I've ever worked as hard." He looked around at the other equally tired Orak men and grinned. "But we showed them that we could keep up."

"Get yourself some water, then bring our dead here."

One of the Ur Nammu began chanting a death song to consecrate the ground and prepare it to receive the bodies. Eskkar and his men stood and watched silently in the firelight until the brief ceremony ended.

Mesilim walked stiffly but on his own over to Eskkar. "You may put your men at this end of the pit to signify the direction from which you came. We'll cover your dead with ours to protect them in the afterlife."

"We thank you for honoring our dead," Eskkar replied formally, then nodded to Sisuthros, who began moving the bodies into the ground. The Ur Nammu bodies followed, each corpse handled as gently as possible, legs straightened out and arms crossed over their chest. At last all the dead rested at the bottom of the pit.

Eskkar approached the end of the grave where his men lay, completely covered by the other bodies. In a loud voice he spoke the words that gave honor to the dead, calling out each man's name and his deeds, so that the goddess Ishtar and great god Marduk would know to receive and honor true warriors.

When Eskkar stepped back, Mesilim strode to the other end and did the same, though his words lasted longer and included more details of the bravest. At last all the gods, demons, and shades were appeased. The men began refilling the hole, a process that took almost as long as the digging, because of the need to tamp down the earth as tightly as possible.

When they'd filled in the grave, the warriors walked their horses back and forth across the dirt to pack it even harder. By the time they finished, midnight approached, making it much too dangerous to try to leave the canyon. Eskkar's men found a clear space as far away from the killing ground as possible. Everyone fell to the earth, wrapped in their horse blankets, and slept the sleep of the completely exhausted, all of them too tired to eat or worry about anyone slitting their throats in the middle of the night.

14

The morning sun woke Eskkar. He sat up with a start, then flinched in pain. Lifting his hand, he shaded his eyes and looked around the camp. His men were moving about, except Zantar and Tammuz, who remained in their blankets. Mesilim's healer had done his best for the boy's arm, but his screams had echoed through the camp despite the wine poured into him. He'd fainted twice during the ordeal. Now the boy slept, but feverishly. Nothing more could be done. Tammuz would recover or die, assuming riding a horse didn't finish him off.

Someone left a water skin at hand and Eskkar emptied it before he got to his feet, fighting the pain in his leg. He hobbled back and forth a few times, his teeth gritted, until the stiffness in his limbs lessened and he felt confident the leg wouldn't give out. At least he didn't need the crutch.

Eskkar checked the bandage on his arm. No fresh blood stained the crude dressing, though pain accompanied any sudden movement. In daylight he saw blood, dirt, and even worse covered his body. The rank smell turned his stomach.

"Morning, Captain." Maldar walked over. "The barbarians brought in some more firewood. We'll have fresh horsemeat soon."

Bile rose in Eskkar's throat at the thought of food and he

had to swallow before he could speak. "I want to wash in the river. Bring me my horse."

"Good idea, Captain. The rest of us have already cleaned up."

The men had gone to the river and returned while he slept. Eskkar swore at his weakness.

Maldar returned leading the horse, then held it while Eskkar mounted cautiously. He rode slowly out of the valley, ignoring the throbbing in his thigh and the dizzy feeling in his head.

At the bank of the stream he dismounted, wincing as his leg took the sudden weight. He let himself fall into the slow-moving water, where he washed his body and his clothes at the same time. The effort exhausted him, so he lay back in the cold water until the last of the stink and dried blood faded away.

When Eskkar could stand the cold no longer, he pulled himself out and rested next to the stream, letting the sun's rays warm him as they dried his garments. He thought about what the day would bring.

When he returned to the canyon, he found his men standing about, waiting. The horses had been fed and watered, weapons cleaned, and the wounded tended. The Ur Nammu had completed the burial pit. A single lance buried in the earth, blade thrusting skyward, marked the site. A long yellow streamer bearing the sign of the Ur Nammu fluttered from the tip.

More prayers had been chanted to appease the gods and sanctify the ground. The bodies of the Alur Meriki lay in a tangled heap around the lance. They'd be left to the carrion eaters, so all would know they'd been conquered in death as well as in life. When the Alur Meriki discovered this place, they would leave the bodies untouched and unburied. The dead would suffer in the afterlife for their defeat.

One of Mesilim's warriors greeted him with a slice of well-roasted horseflesh, the meat burned almost black and nearly too hot to hold. Eskkar wolfed it down, surprised at his hunger. It took a second strip to satisfy him.

Mesilim walked over. "Chief Eskkar, we're ready to leave

this place. We'll camp on the other side of the stream. I'll
send scouts out in case another war party arrives."

If one does, we'll all be dead. It took time to load the men
and animals with the captured weapons, food, and loot. At
last they walked their horses from the canyon, their pace
dictated by the wounded men and animals. As Eskkar left
the canyon, he glanced back at the place where so many had
died. Already a flock of vultures and other birds fought over
the dead flesh. The steppes people had lived and died this
way for generations. It might be as good a way to die as any
other, though he hoped his bones would find peace under a
patch of earth someday, instead of above.

They camped at the small stream where Eskkar had bathed
earlier. Everyone felt glad to be out of the maze of canyons
and back on the sparse grasses where the air didn't smell of
blood. A dead tree provided firewood and more horsemeat
soon sizzled on the flames.

Eskkar talked with Zantar. He'd recovered his senses and
could speak coherently. Zantar had an enormous bruise on
his forehead. Strangely, the man remembered nothing of the
fight or even the hours leading up to it, and had to be told in
detail what happened.

As for Tammuz, he remained fretful. They had no more
wine to give him. They'd supported the boy on his horse
during the brief ride to the stream, but he fainted again
when they lifted him down. Mesilim's healer examined his
patient and rebound the injured arm tightly to the boy's side
to prevent further damage. Now Tammuz slept on the soft
grass, his head pillowed by a horse blanket. He tossed and
murmured in his sleep.

Three Ur Nammu scouts rode off, while other lookouts
took up posts on the surrounding hills. Finally all the animals had been fed and watered, the men had eaten a second
time, and the time for talk had arrived.

Mesilim and his son came to Eskkar. He kept Sisuthros
with him, even though Sisuthros did not understand the
language. The four men found a quiet place on a grassy
knoll a hundred paces from the stream, where they could
speak privately.

Eskkar shared what information he had about the Alur Meriki, then listened to what Mesilim had to say. Eskkar asked many questions about the numbers and movements of the Alur Meriki. As they spoke, the leaders sketched a map in the dirt between them, using twigs, stones, and knives to represent various landmarks.

"Now I understand why they march as they did," Mesilim remarked. "We wondered what they searched for in their movements and why they didn't ride to the west. It will not bode well for you and your village when they do."

"Mesilim, I truly believe we can resist them," Eskkar said. "I'll have many bowmen to man the wall or swing a sword."

Eskkar didn't wait for their polite concurrence. "But I'd like to have your clan's assistance in my fight. If you help us, I believe you can satisfy your Shan Kar without sacrificing the rest of your men."

"The Shan Kar is to the death," Subutai answered firmly. "We've all sworn the oath and there's no turning aside."

Eskkar nodded gravely. "Of course. I'm a stranger to your clan, Subutai, and ignorant of your ways. But cannot a Shan Kar be satisfied by a great defeat of the enemy in battle? At least that's what I've heard."

They knew Eskkar came from the steppes, probably from the Alur Meriki clan they'd just fought. But diplomacy prevailed. Neither Mesilim nor his son wanted to ask any questions whose answers might offend them.

"That's true," Mesilim responded, "but we're not numerous enough to create a great battle. The days of our clan are numbered, and we will not recover our strength before we're overwhelmed. In a few days another ten or twelve warriors and a handful of women will join us, and that is all of the Ur Nammu."

Eskkar hadn't known any more of them survived, but took that as good news. "Orak is strong enough to create a great battle. We have almost as many people as in the tribe, and more come every day. It will take all of the might of the Alur Meriki to capture our village. If you join with us, then you could share in the great battle. If we win, your Shan Kar would be satisfied. And if you fight with us, I can help your people with weapons, horses, and supplies."

Mesilim and Subutai exchanged glances. A Shan Kar sworn in the heat of defeat two years ago condemned them all to death.

"We must satisfy our honor, Eskkar," Mesilim said, his head held high. "But if there be such a way . . ."

Eskkar breathed a silent sigh of relief, then reached to the ground and rearranged the twigs and stones. "Here's the Tigris to the north," three small twigs bent at angles to show the big curve of the river. "And here's Orak," a small stone set next to the twig. "The main body of the Alur Meriki are here." He placed a larger stone near the river. "The two raiding parties," he put two pebbles at the lower end of the Tigris, "will sweep everything in their path toward Orak, and in six or seven weeks the entire clan will be camped before Orak's walls."

Mesilim nodded.

"Except for one other war party." Eskkar picked up a stone and set it across the Tigris, opposite Orak. "This party will cut off those who try to flee, and then round up the cattle and horses we've sent across the river.

"This will be a smaller party, probably seventy or eighty warriors, just enough to hold the river and scour the countryside. With your help, I will ambush this party and kill all of them."

Eskkar's knife traced a groove northward along the Tigris. "After they are slain, your people can ride north, cross the river well upstream, then turn south and strike their main camp from behind at the height of the battle. There should be few watching their rear, because they know they've killed everyone in their path. The camp should be lightly defended. You can ride in and capture as many women and horses as you need to rebuild your tribe."

His knife traced another line going northeast. "Then you can return to these mountains far to the north and rebuild your clan. If you remain north of the Isogi river, you can help guard Orak's borders. We'll establish trade with your people, and even give you protection should you need it." Eskkar planted the blade firmly in the earth.

"How will this satisfy Shan Kar?" Subutai's curiosity got the better of him. "Even if we're victorious, the Alur Meriki will still be undefeated."

Careful, this has to be said properly. Eskkar took a deep breath. "The Alur Meriki have planned this attack on Orak for many months. All their marches and raids have been done only to put their full might against our village. They know we're fortifying Orak and building a wall, but they think we cannot stop them. If they fail to capture Orak, if they are forced to move south without taking the village, then they will have failed in their plan. By fighting alongside us, you'll help defeat the Alur Meriki in a great battle. That should satisfy the Shan Kar."

Whether it did might be open to debate, but it offered a way to save face and would look a lot better than fighting to the death without any hope of survival. And another battle would satisfy honor. Eskkar put his hands on his knees and leaned back. He'd made the offer as best he could. Now Mesilim would have to decide.

The Ur Nammu leader pondered Eskkar's words for a long time. "The Alur Meriki will return in another ten or fifteen years," he said finally. "Even if you drive them away now, you may be defeated later."

Eskkar and Trella had talked about that possibility often enough. "Times are changing, Mesilim. I believe that when the Alur Meriki return, all of the countryside around Orak will be defended, and the walls of Orak will be higher and stronger than they are now, with many more trained defenders. I've seen what can be done to prepare for the onslaught, and we've learned much. The future is always shrouded in mystery, but I believe Orak will survive, and it will be the Alur Meriki who are again driven off."

"How would we get across the river?" Subutai's subtle question left no doubt as to where the younger man stood. His words would send the same message to his father.

"When you're ready," Eskkar went on, "in a few weeks, cross the lines again and come to Orak. We have a ferry to move your men and horses across the river. We'll watch for your coming and escort you in, lest anyone attack you by mistake."

"Why do you do all this, Eskkar?" Mesilim countered. "And why are you so concerned about warriors across the great river?"

"If I cannot destroy all the barb . . . Alur Meriki on the west bank, those who escape will warn the main camp. If even a few survive, it could be disastrous for Orak. A dozen men could set the land ablaze. We've no provision for war parties on that side of the Tigris, and we don't have enough men to guard our livestock. The villagers would lose heart to find their herds destroyed or scattered. We need that livestock to rebuild the herds once the Alur Meriki have gone."

Eskkar stared into the eyes of the chief. "I need to tell my people I can destroy those Alur Meriki on the west bank and get back to Orak in time to man the walls. I must destroy them completely, and I cannot do so on open ground. I don't have enough horses or men who know how to ride them. So I need your help to make sure they're driven into some trap where I can kill them with my archers, and use your warriors to make sure none escape."

"I will speak of this with Subutai and the other leaders," Mesilim said. "We'll give you an answer by nightfall." He stood up, then extended his hand to help Eskkar to his feet. "You are . . . you were born on the steppes. Now you've cast your lot with farmers and herders of goats and sheep, and they will never accept you fully. Do you not wish sometimes to return to the life of a warrior?"

It was not a casual question. Mesilim offered him a choice—Eskkar could ride with them, if he chose.

The offer tempted him, but the thought of Trella banished the idea. "Many times, Mesilim. Many times I've wished to return to the warrior's life on the plains and steppes. But I've lived too long with the villagers, and I'm more used to their ways than those of our fathers. And I have a woman, a gifted one, who calls me back to her side. But if fate is not kind to me, then I will remember your words."

"Even if you win, can you be sure of how you'll be treated afterward?" Mesilim's concern showed he understood much about villager ways.

"It's true there is much treachery among the village leaders. But I've learned much in the last few months, and my power grows each day. Also my woman gives me good advice in these matters."

Barbarians thought one woman much like another. They also believed any warrior who listened too carefully to his woman showed weakness. Nevertheless, Eskkar had referred to Trella as a "gifted one" and perhaps Mesilim understood the power and strength of a woman who occasionally showed such wisdom and strength of character as to be accepted at the council fires.

Mesilim nodded in understanding. "We've fought together and we can never break the bond of thanks the Ur Nammu owe you. Now we must decide our own future." He turned, and his son followed.

Eskkar's men waited, curiosity whetted by watching the four men speak for almost two hours. He stopped in front of them. "Mesilim has told us everything he knows about the barbarians. I've asked him to join us in our fight. If he accepts, I think he can help us. If he chooses another path, then ours will be much harder."

Eskkar turned toward the sudden activity that had broken out in the camp. In a moment Eskkar understood the commotion. "Enough for now. It's time to divide the spoils."

That task took the rest of the morning and lasted into the afternoon at a maddeningly slow pace. Eskkar forced himself to smile and remain patient. The spoils were divided equitably, with Eskkar's men getting a little more than what he would have considered their due, so no one complained. Eskkar's share filled a sack. Trella would find good use for the gold and jewels.

The kills had to be counted as well, another involved task that required much sifting of evidence as to who killed whom, how it was done, and who witnessed it. Eskkar received credit for eight kills, though he doubted the number was that high. He certainly hadn't killed the last warrior

himself, though both he and Subutai received equal credit
for that body. The highest number of kills went to Mitrac,
whose arrows were found in fourteen bodies, plus more than
a half dozen horses. Eskkar thanked whatever gods protected archers that no arrow had struck any Ur Nammu.
Mesilim personally presented Mitrac with a gold and copper
ring of great value, in addition to the double handful of jewels and gold nuggets the boy had earned as his share.

Afterward many Ur Nammu touched Mitrac and his bow
for luck, and all wanted to know whether the rest of the villagers had weapons such as his.

Everyone spent the rest of the day eating and resting. Eskkar agreed that his men could use the time to heal their
wounds. Subutai persuaded Mitrac to demonstrate his archery skills and some warriors matched him shot for shot
until the distance grew too great for their smaller bows. The
force of his weapon impressed all the warriors. Even a hit
that might not be fatal would send a man to the ground, unable to fight any further.

The feasting extended into the evening with still no decision from Mesilim. Eskkar found himself a little withdrawn
from the circle of his men. Finally he got up and walked
over to the stream to relieve himself. Sisuthros came over to
join him.

When they finished Eskkar started back, but Sisuthros
held his arm, keeping him out of earshot of the men sitting
around the fire. "Captain, I would speak with you. There's
something I have to say."

Turning to face his commander, Eskkar heard the strain in
his voice. "What is it, Sisuthros? Unhappy with the spoils?"
Even in the moonlight, Eskkar saw confusion on the man's
face.

"Captain, I . . . there is . . ." He stopped and fumbled for a
moment with his belt, then brought out a small pouch he
handed to Eskkar. "This is gold, twenty pieces, that I was
given before we left Orak. It was understood that another
ten would be mine if you didn't return."

Eskkar felt his face flush with anger. For a moment he
wanted to strike Sisuthros down, kill him for what he'd been

planning. But the rage passed. If it hadn't been Sisuthros, it would have been someone else. A man always had enemies, and as Eskkar grew more powerful, the number of enemies would increase. Besides, he needed a fighter like Sisuthros, both now and probably even more in the future.

Eskkar hefted the pouch in his hand. "Thirty gold pieces. That's a great amount of gold." He handed the pouch back. There wasn't much light, but he detected surprise on the man's face.

"Don't you want to know who gave this gold to me? Or why?"

"I already know, Sisuthros, even before we left Orak. That's why I selected you to come with me. Caldor isn't very careful with his words. Nicar's whelp should keep his mouth shut."

Sisuthros's eyes widened in astonishment. Eskkar remembered Trella's words—always act as if you know more than you're saying. "Who else of the nobles approached you?"

"Nestor. I was in the tavern one night, and they bought wine, then we went for a walk. They said you were no longer needed, that others could take over now that the preparation was well begun. They worry you will have too much power and will turn on them once the barbarians are gone. That is, Nestor fears that. Caldor hates you for some other reason. His anger is strong, Eskkar."

"It's because of Trella. He's insulted that she's quicker in her wits than he, and that she's listened to by the Families. He wanted her when she was in Nicar's house. Now he wants me dead to have her for himself. He cares nothing about the future of Orak, and he's too stupid to see he might be destroying someone who could save his life."

"Trella befriended my wife and watched over my child." Sisuthros's voice hardened as he caught the drift of Eskkar's words. "I didn't know he lusted after her. You're right, he is a fool."

The young man stood there for a moment. "And I'm a fool as well. You saved my life in the battle, Eskkar. If you knew of this, why did you do so? You could have let the barbarian kill me."

"I saved your life because you're a good man with sharp wits, and because I need you to help defend Orak. But you've much to learn. They would never let you live even if I were killed. No matter what they promised, you're too young to command so many men, and I doubt you would have seen any more gold. The nobles want no strong captain of the guard who might have opinions of his own. Why do you think they put up with Ariamus all these years? Because he was greedy, and they knew they could control him through his greed. Nestor's just an old fool who doesn't realize the barbarians will return, even stronger than they are now."

Esskar laughed. "Or maybe I saved your life because I didn't have time to think about it. I would've done the same for any of my men, as would you."

"I'm not sure what I would have done in your place. I . . . took the gold."

"And what were you going to do?" Esskar's voice hardened. "Kill me in front of the men? Challenge me to a fight? Or murder me in my sleep? You had plenty of chances, and it's still a long way to Orak."

"I don't know what I wanted! I didn't want to do anything. I wish I'd never taken the gold. But I did. Perhaps I am not the man you think I am."

He heard the anguish in Sisuthros's words. "Then become the man you should be." Esskar gripped Sisuthros's shoulder. "Forget the gold. Look at these barbarians. They'll slit each other's throats over a woman or an insult. But in battle, they die for their comrades because that's the code of the warrior. You are a warrior, Sisuthros, but if you deal with merchants and shopkeepers on their terms, then that is what you will become."

Sisuthros stared at the ground. "I'm not worthy to be under your command." His voice choked with emotion. "You've treated me fairly, promoted me, and I nearly betrayed you. Even these strange barbarians respect you."

"And what do you want now? Do you want me to hate you? No, I think I'll give you more responsibility because you've earned it, earned it by what you did yesterday when you followed me into the canyon, though I saw in your eyes you thought we rode to our death. But you will earn more honors by what you do from now on. And when this is over, there's even more that will be asked of you, and greater rewards to be had."

"You would reward me after what I've done?"

"Done? You haven't done anything except listen to a young fool and an old fool in a tavern. You're not a murderer, Sisuthros." He moved closer. "Listen to me. When this is over, we'll have to rebuild the countryside. You'll be a ruler in a village of your own, and we'll fight the next wave of barbarians together. Forget about Caldor and Nestor. They don't understand what's at stake here."

"I'll kill Caldor and Nestor then." Sisuthros's voice was hard again. "I'll throw the gold in their faces and kill them."

"Nestor is nothing. But killing Caldor would give me great pleasure. But not yet, because we . . ." A call from the campfire interrupted him, and Eskkar turned toward the firelight to see Mesilim coming toward them.

"We'll talk more of this later, Sisuthros. But remember, you showed great courage yesterday, and we fought together against great odds. That's more important than gold." Eskkar stepped back to his men's fire circle to receive the Ur Nammu chieftain.

"Chief Eskkar," Mesilim began formally, his voice loud and clear in the night. "I've met with the elders of the clan. We've agreed to join you in your fight and help you defeat the Alur Meriki. Tomorrow we will begin our preparations."

Mesilim extended his arm, and Eskkar clasped his hand around the chieftain's forearm. They had sealed the bargain publicly and according to custom. Now their fates intertwined, at least for the next battle.

"I must go and tell the rest of my warriors." Mesilim turned away and returned to his own campfire.

Shouts of joy mixed with battle cries greeted the news, as Mesilim's men learned they had both a chance to live and an opportunity to regain some of what they'd lost.

The Shan Kar will be satisfied, Eskkar thought later, as he settled in for sleep, wishing he had some wine to numb the pain that throbbed in his thigh. I've gained an ally not only for the battle across the river, but perhaps for the future, should I need to keep the villagers in check. And Sisuthros will be loyal, at least for now. Trella will be pleased, he thought, and he drifted off to sleep with her face in his dreams.

Ten days later just before sunset, Eskkar and his weary band of riders topped the last hill and saw the village of Orak. After spending three days resting with the Ur Nammu, they had all ridden hard in a northerly circle to throw any pursuers off their trail. Then the two groups had split up, with the Ur Nammu turning toward the mountains.

The well-rested Ur Nammu clan would travel quickly and leave a plain trail, like men who had enough of hard fighting and only wanted to escape. They would ride far to the east, wait a week or ten days, then return to monitor the progress of the Alur Meriki. With luck, they'd slip back through the lines before the barbarians closed them tight around Orak.

Meanwhile Eskkar and his band headed back to the west, riding as hard as they dared but always favoring the horses. During the journey Eskkar spoke often with Sisuthros. They would ride side by side, letting the others stay ahead. After a few such conversations, Eskkar felt his subcommander had acquired a new respect for his captain and the difficulties they all faced.

Even from afar Eskkar saw the wall had grown. The eastern side, the one that would bear the brunt of the attack, had been completed, as had the great wooden gate, already blackened by fire to harden it and make it resistant to flames. On each side of the gate, towers rose up even higher to protect the entrance.

As Eskkar and his men drew closer, someone recognized them. Even at that distance, Eskkar could hear the roar of welcome that steadily increased in volume. Men and women began pouring out of the gate, some running toward them, a few claiming vantage spots on the roadway, while others stood shoulder to shoulder atop the new wall.

At the outskirts of the village, he turned to his men.

"Mitrac, you go first, then I'll follow. And try to look like fighting men instead of tired old women for a change."

The men laughed as he knew they would. He could call them anything now. During their time with the Ur Nammu, Eskkar had thought about what else he could do to strengthen their bond to him, and an idea had occurred to him. He would form a new clan. Not a clan of men related by blood, but a clan of arms.

He had spoken of it while they rested with the Ur Nammu, and all the men had eagerly accepted the idea. Most had no kin or close friends, and this new clan would give them a brotherhood to make up for what they lacked. They'd have something greater than themselves to belong to, and they'd share a bond of allegiance to their new brothers.

So they had sworn a great oath of loyalty, first to each other and then to Eskkar. Afterward Zantar took needle and black thread and stitched a crude outline of a hawk on each of their tunics. The hawk represented both strength and fierceness. Eskkar's Hawk Clan was born, resurrecting the symbol of his father's clan in the Alur Meriki.

Now they returned as true warriors, proven in battle and united in a clan of honor. Each man sat a little straighter on his mount, ignoring his wounds and aches. Mitrac carried his bow upright, a thin strip of leather with fourteen thumb bones hanging from its tip. Eskkar had eight bones dangling from his sword belt, and the rest carried their bones in a similar fashion.

They walked the horses the last hundred paces, unable to move any faster because of the crowd. Riding at the rear was Tammuz. The boy had surprised them all by surviving his wounds. Though he still grimaced in pain from his arm, he sat proudly on his mount, though Maldar held the halter. Tammuz carried the small bow in his good hand, displaying his single trophy.

Eskkar's eyes searched the crowd until he spotted Trella waiting just outside the gate, a smile on her normally reserved features. Her guard stood behind her, and nobody in the crowd dared to push in front of her.

Seeing her brought a grin to his face, and as he rode through the gate, he reached down and pulled her up to sit sideways in front of him. The crowd laughed and cheered even louder as her arm went around his neck.

"Well, girl, I've returned, and I've much to tell." She could scarcely hear him over the noise. The villagers continued to call his name, and the skittish horses began to flatten their ears at the growing crowd.

The men dismounted and walked the horses to Eskkar's house. The crowd followed behind, still shouting with as much enthusiasm as if the barbarians had already been defeated. Arriving home, Eskkar ordered that Tammuz be carried inside. Annok-sur sent one of the women to fetch a healer.

Eskkar went to the well and took advantage of his first opportunity to clean himself properly in over three weeks. A servant brought clean clothes, but Eskkar only donned them after he'd scrubbed as much of the horse scent from his body as he could.

Maldar remained at Eskkar's house. The men chose Maldar as custodian for their loot, to be stored in Eskkar's chambers until they called for it. None of them ever had so much of value before, and they didn't know what to do with it. No one felt comfortable carrying all that gold on their persons. They approached Eskkar and asked him to guard it for them.

The idea of holding gold for others made him uncomfortable, but he agreed his house was a safer place for their money than leaving it in the barracks. They decided Maldar and one other of the Hawk Clan would inspect the valuables once a week to make sure they remained safe. Each man took only what he needed for a few days of wine, women, and gambling.

Alone in their rooms Eskkar took Trella in his arms and squeezed her tightly. He stroked her hair and felt happy just to hold her. The feel of her body aroused him, and he would have taken her, but the summons had already come from Nicar. Reluctantly he let her go.

Later Eskkar, Trella, and Sisuthros sat down at Nicar's

crowded table with all the Families and their important followers present. A feast had been declared for all. Villagers shouted and sang in the streets, gladdened by Eskkar's return and a chance to celebrate.

Nicar served his finest wine, but Eskkar took only a single cup. When he'd drunk half of it, he refilled it with water. Wine no longer tempted him. Eskkar didn't want his wits dulled by wine. He did eat, enjoying the fresh bread and chicken Nicar's servants provided.

When he described the battle, not a sound could be heard, and he had to repeat the story, adding more details. Sisuthros told part of the tale, filling in the fight as he'd seen it, and telling of Eskkar's exploits.

Their faces registered shock at what he'd done. That Eskkar would risk his life to help another tribe of barbarians seemed incredible. Nevertheless they rejoiced to hear that, together, they'd wiped out seventy Alur Meriki.

"The Ur Nammu will be of great use to us," Eskkar said, ignoring the skeptical looks. "We'll meet them again, and they'll keep track of the main force for us."

More questions kept coming, and Eskkar encouraged Sisuthros to answer several, while he studied the faces of Caldor and Nestor. The old man just smiled, revealing no emotion.

But young Caldor did not repress an occasional flash of anger, though he kept silent. No doubt he wondered what his gold had purchased. *You will be dead soon, Caldor, like Drigo's whelp, and this time it will give me much more pleasure.* Finally Eskkar had a question of his own.

"Corio, I see the east wall is complete. How goes the rest of the work?" The new walls were not laid out strictly according to the compass. The east side, where the wall stood highest and where the main attack would come, actually faced southeast, toward the crossroad where the two main roads met to form a single track that led to the gate.

"You've been gone three weeks," Corio said. "In that time, we've made good progress, and are ahead of schedule, mostly due to the numbers of new men willing to bend their backs to avoid the barbarians. The entire wall will be finished in less than three weeks, and the river sluices and canals have been widened and are ready for release. We can let loose the water and begin to flood the plains in less than one hour."

Eskkar turned toward Gatus and Jalen. "And the men? How goes their training?"

"Sixty men finish training this week, and another seventy will start." Gatus had a big grin on his face. "The training goes faster, now that we have so many veterans. By the time the barbarians arrive, we'll have over four hundred and twenty well-drilled men ready to defend the walls."

"Then there's much to give thanks for," Eskkar said. "And you are satisfied with our progress, Nicar?"

"Eskkar, I'm more than satisfied. Up to now, I've been hopeful we could fend off the barbarians. When we first spoke, you promised me no better than an even chance. Now I'm sure that we have at least that, especially now that you have returned. The whole village worried while you were gone." Heads around the table nodded in agreement.

"But now that you are back, the people will have confidence again. Permit us to give thanks to the gods and to honor your return with a celebration tomorrow."

Eskkar felt surprised by the warmth in Nicar's words, but the sight of Caldor clenching his jaw reminded him of what was to come. "I'm grateful to return, Nicar . . . honored Nobles. But now I would like to return home and get some rest."

That ended the dinner. Everyone seemed excited by the prospect of a celebration. The village hadn't relaxed for months, and the people could do with a reason to cheer. In the street outside Nicar's, a few idlers lingered to shout greetings to Eskkar and, to his surprise, Trella as well.

They walked back to the house, Trella's hand in his. He closed the door to their private chambers, slid the wooden bolt into the hole with a sigh of satisfaction.

"Don't you want to eat more supper, Eskkar? You hardly ate anything at Nicar's, and we have much to talk about."

Her smile looked the same as he remembered it. "Yes, Trella, I'm still hungry." He took her into his arms and ran his hands over her body.

Eskkar kissed her hungrily, and she returned his passion, rising up on her toes as she put her arms around his neck. When they finally paused for breath, she lifted up her arms and he drew her garment up over her head, then let it drop. He took her hands in his and stepped back to look at her, letting his eyes feast on the sight of her naked body in the lamp's flickering light before picking her up and carrying her to the bed.

Two hours later Trella arose and called down to the servants for food. Sitting at Eskkar's work table, they ate another meal of bread and cold lamb, washed down with watered wine. For dessert, Trella peeled an apple while Eskkar savored a handful of fresh dates. She listened attentively as he described the trip and what he'd learned. When he finished, she shook her head.

"You leave too much out." She put her hand on his. "I want to know everything about the battle: what you thought, what you saw, why you did what you did, even how your men reacted. I know nothing about such things, and if I'm to help you, I need to know what and how men think in such situations."

Unlike most fighting men, Eskkar found it difficult to talk about battle. It was too personal, too intense. He knew he'd dodged death too often to boast about his own skill, all too aware that luck or chance was as important as one's prowess. The terror of it all, the horses screaming, the stink of fear in the air and on men's bodies, the knots in your chest when a sword slashed at you, the trembling in your bowels, the weakness of limb and mind afterward.

Eskkar began again, this time taking her as best he could through the entire episode, starting from the hilltop when he first saw that the Ur Nammu would be trapped. He tried to explain to her what thoughts rushed into his head and why he decided to help them. He recalled the fear he saw in Mitrac's face as Eskkar pushed him into the battle, the tenseness and doubts of Sisuthros, who had never been involved in such a close-fought battle, and even the struggles of those Eskkar fought and killed.

Words and emotions he didn't know he possessed helped him describe something almost beyond description. When he finished, she took his hand and led him back to their bed, and this time she made love to him with such tenderness that she left him weak and trembling.

Afterward she bathed him again. They relaxed in each other's arms, the light from the lamp almost gone, the wick already smoldering. But Trella had more questions. "Tell me more about Mesilim and his son."

That led to the conversation with Sisuthros, the division of the spoils, the formation of the Hawk Clan, and eventually their return to Orak. Eskkar even repeated conversations with Tammuz and Maldar, surprised he could recall so many details. By the time he finished, the moon had risen high in the night.

"You have done well, husband, better than well. My father said that few men have the ability to command large numbers of fighting men. You're such a man, Eskkar. You saw your opportunity and you took your chance. Luck is the favor of the gods, and it's sometimes better to be lucky than skillful. All your decisions were sound, and you've prepared for the future by turning Sisuthros back to your side and by establishing the Hawk Clan. That will bind many fighting men to you. You've established a family clan overnight."

"Seven men and a boy are not a large number," he pointed out, though pleased at her words. "But you're right, we were lucky."

"Yes, you were lucky you weren't killed, that you didn't lose all your men, that the Ur Nammu didn't turn on you after the battle and kill you. But tell me, who else in Orak would those men have followed into battle against seventy barbarians? I can think of no man. And you've proven yourself and your men in combat, and now a thousand will follow wherever you lead as easily as did ten."

He thought about that for a few moments. The men wouldn't have followed any one else into that canyon, certainly no one in Orak. The more he thought about it, it seemed unbelievable they had followed him at all. But perhaps what she said might be possible, perhaps he could command five hundred men, or maybe even a thousand.

She interrupted his thoughts. "But you must not risk your life again. Never take such a chance. You've proven your bravery. You say you plan to take the soldiers against the barbarians on the other side of the river? Go if you must, but do not fight in the front lines. You cannot risk your life so carelessly. You'll be needed to defend Orak and for what will come afterward."

"A fighting man needs to fight, Trella, or the men lose respect for him. The battle across the river will be easier, but I must be there to make sure it's successful. After that, I will stay in the rear." He let his fingers drift across her breasts, his hands still delighted by her body. "And now, perhaps you will reward me one more time."

She leaned down in the darkness and kissed him, then dug her elbow sharply into his side, making him gasp with surprise. "Just like a man, to think only of himself. Don't you want to hear what I've been doing while you were gone, or do you think nothing happens without you?"

He felt glad the darkness hid the guilty look that crossed his face. Indeed, he hadn't thought much about her or her plans. "Couldn't we talk of that tomorrow?" he ventured, unable to keep the plaintive tone out of his voice.

"No, we cannot wait until tomorrow. There is much that you need to know, and you've had enough lovemaking for one night! Now, would it not please you to know that the villagers panicked completely when they thought you were dead?"

"Dead? What made them think I was dead?"

"I spread the rumor you'd been killed. That is, Annok-sur and I spread it. The whole of Orak had it in less than an hour, and there was panic in the marketplace. The villagers were afraid and people were getting ready to flee the village. People shouted that we were lost without you to protect us."

"And those people . . ."

"More friends of Annok-sur." Trella's voice held a satisfied tone. "Nicar had to speak to the crowd and tell them it was merely a rumor, that no news had as yet returned. He spoke just in time and even I was brought to the marketplace to agree with him. In a few more hours, half the village would have been on the move. Many had already begun to pack their belongings."

"And you did this to . . . ?"

"To make sure that Nicar and the other Families know how much they need you, and to make sure the villagers understand that as well. Remember, when the battle is over, we'll need many friends to make sure you're accepted into the Families. Now everyone knows you're favored by the gods."

So she had been busy. He didn't bother to ask what she would have done if he'd gotten himself killed. She would have considered that possibility as well. "What else did you do while I was gone?"

Another hour passed as he listened to all she had to say, the weariness gone from his eyes. At last the talking ended, and she curled up in his arms and held his hands against her body until they fell asleep.

15

Eskkar was up before dawn the next morning. The day's activities started at the breakfast table with his subcommanders. Afterward he and Sisuthros spent several hours with Corio inspecting the wall.

By now both the soldiers and the laborers understood their roles, and the work proceeded steadily. Corio needed only thirty soldiers to keep everyone at their tasks.

Eskkar spent more hours inspecting the soldiers still in training. That necessitated one more retelling of the battle in the hills. He didn't mind. These men needed to know as much about the enemy as possible, and the more confidence they had in their leaders the better. Eskkar answered many questions regarding Alur Meriki fighting techniques.

The sun had passed its high point when Trella rejoined him, wearing a scarf to shield her head from the sun. They walked through the village, greeting the people and talking to them, reassuring the villagers by their presence. But Eskkar had to grit his teeth and force a smile to his face when they visited the temple of Ishtar and knelt in the shadows before the gloomy image of the goddess, Trella at his side.

Eskkar gave thanks in a loud voice to Ishtar for his victory, repeating the words Trella had suggested that morning. He had never been in Ishtar's temple, or any temple in

Orak for that matter. Since his family's death, Eskkar had no use for priests and their outstretched palms. He stood there stoically, hiding his impatience, while the priest offered his interminable prayers to the deity for Eskkar's safe return.

At last the ceremonies ended. When Eskkar returned to the sunlight he felt as if he had escaped the demon's dark underworld. His smile returned as he took Trella's hand, and turned toward their home.

"Master, have you forgotten our visit with Rebba this afternoon?" she asked. "We're already late, and there may be much to see before the sun goes down."

Eskkar's feeling of contentment vanished. He had forgotten about the meeting with Rebba. That was natural enough, because he really didn't want to spend three or four hours with the noble responsible for the farms surrounding Orak, listening to him explain how to grow wheat or herd goats. Eskkar thought about postponing the meeting, but he'd done that several times before he departed on his scouting mission. He knew Trella considered it important, important enough to arrange the visit as soon as possible on his return.

With no convenient excuse, he forced another smile and changed his direction. Together they walked to the river gate, then turned north, two guards accompanying them.

Once outside the village, they increased their pace, and Eskkar's muscles soon found the walk a good challenge after the weeks of hard riding. The sun shone brightly and the air off the river smelled clean and fresh. Within Orak a background smell of people and animals living too close together permeated the air. After a few days you didn't notice it as much, but Eskkar had been breathing fresh air for several weeks.

Finally they crossed the last of the innumerable irrigation ditches and entered the grounds of Rebba's farm. Eskkar had never gone there before, and unlike most of the farms he'd seen, this one had nearly a dozen huts scattered about. Rebba's dwelling didn't look much larger than any of the others. Grain storage places, built higher than the average hut and recognizable by their high entrances reached only by ladders, accounted for several of the structures.

Attached to almost every building were corrals that held goats, sheep, or cattle. Eskkar and Trella passed a few pigs that wandered by, picking at anything on the ground and fighting with dozens of chickens for anything that crawled beneath them. Close to the main house several willow trees provided shade. Eskkar noted four good-sized dogs taking their naps under the trees. Tame enough by day, at night the dogs would guard the property from petty thieves.

The smell of animals hung in the air, and Trella wrinkled her nose as they passed the corrals, though to Eskkar the odor seemed more pleasant than the village air.

Rebba greeted them at the door. At home he didn't bother with the fine clothes he wore when business called him into Orak. Today he wore a tunic as well worn as that of any field hand. "Welcome to my home, Eskkar." Rebba offered his hand to Eskkar as they arrived. "A spring day like this is too pleasant to spend indoors."

They sat on benches beneath a willow tree, at a table whose surface was gouged and pitted, no doubt from numberless days of chopping and cutting vegetables. A young girl of nine or ten seasons, one of Rebba's grandchildren, brought cool water for them to drink.

Rebba waited until they drank before speaking. "I offer my congratulations again on your victory, Captain. Trella tells me that you wish to learn more about farming. Where would you begin?"

Eskkar knew nothing about farming and wished to know even less. Farmers were the least important people in Orak. In fact those that actually farmed the land rarely visited the village, except for those few, mostly wives, that came each morning to sell their goods in the market, or the men who visited the smith's to have some tool repaired. Nevertheless Trella had insisted he learn something about farming, so he put another smile on his face.

"Noble Rebba, I know little about farming. I know that farmers provide much of the food for Orak, but I grew up among the barbarians and they don't think highly of farming."

"They consider us dirt diggers, do they not?" Rebba answered with a laugh. "I suppose that's true enough. But they do enough farming on their own, despite what they think of us." He saw the look of puzzlement on Eskkar's face. "Ah, I see that you are not aware of how important farming is even to the Alur Meriki." He stroked his beard. "Perhaps that's as good a place to begin as any." He turned to Trella, sitting at Eskkar's side. "I understand you grew up in a village to the south. Did you learn the ways of the farmers there?"

"No, Noble Rebba," Trella answered. "I know very little about the mysteries of the farmer and the herder."

"Then I'll try to explain a little to you both. A farm is not only a place to grow the wheat and barley, but a place to hold herds of goats, sheep, and other food animals. The barbarians herd their own flocks, even as we do, only they take them with them as they wander."

"But they don't plant crops," Eskkar countered. "They're never in one place long enough for crops to grow."

"Ah, but they do harvest, Eskkar. But they do it in a different way." Rebba smiled. "The Alur Meriki harvest crops as they travel, looking for stands of barley, emmer wheat, even peas and other vegetables. These crops they encounter along the way are as important to them as they are to us. And there are many wild crops throughout the land, such as wheat, beans, and flax. They gather those as well."

Eskkar accepted the correction. "Well, yes, I know the women gather anything they find on the march."

"Exactly. Even warriors cannot live on meat alone. They need milk and cheese from the goats and cows, wool from the sheep, as well as vegetables and fruits from the lands they pass through. And of course, they seize much grain and other crops from the farmers of the lands they occupy. I'm sure you know a horse grows stronger and more powerful if fed a mixture of grains besides what it gathers grazing. So farming is as important to them as it is to us."

"Yes, horses need grain," Eskkar replied. "Whenever possible horses are fed a mixture of grains before being ridden hard." He began to think along the lines Rebba had suggested. "And extra grain is carried to feed the horses when they raid, while the women bake bread for the warriors to carry with them."

Bread was light enough to carry on horseback as well as nourishing, and would last longer without spoiling than meat. Eskkar's men had done exactly the same when they rode out on their own scouting party. He'd forgotten these little details of steppes life, and now he realized they might be more important than he'd thought.

"Yes, bread is very important to us all," Rebba agreed. "It is bread that feeds your soldiers. More than that, bread pays the wages of your soldiers. Without bread, there would be no builders, smiths, taverns, or weavers. Bread makes possible the trade on the river that brings you the lumber and ores from the north for your wall. Without bread, there would be no gold, no silver, no horses, no weapons. Without the farmer, there would be no great village of Orak."

Despite himself, Eskkar had become interested. "I'm ashamed to admit I do not understand these things, Rebba. But I'm willing to learn."

"You learn very quickly, Eskkar, as all of us have noticed." Rebba smiled at that, and his eyes took in Trella as well. "But that's all to the good. If you're to defend the village, you should understand these things. And don't be embarrassed by your lack of knowledge; few even in Orak understand these things. It's like the mystery of counting. That is a mystery I see you understand."

Eskkar had never considered counting to be mysterious. Difficult, to be sure, and many men never grasped anything beyond the basic concept of ten fingers. But as a soldier, Eskkar had been forced to learn to count many things.

Like everyone he started with his fingers and some pebbles. You used your fingers to count to ten, then you moved a pebble from one hand to the other, and started over again. When you were finished, you counted your pebbles, knowing that each represented ten of whatever it was you were counting. In this way you counted how many men you had, exactly as you counted how many were with your adversary. You counted your arrows, your horses, your weapons, and even how many handfuls of grain you could feed to your horse.

"I didn't know counting was a mystery, Rebba," he said, "though I admit that I have difficulty when the sum is much over a hundred."

"It is a very great mystery, and one I believe was discovered as men learned to farm. We learned to store grain in bushels, baskets, and sacks, and then count the sacks for storage or trade. Farmers had to learn how to divide grain among themselves, and they had to learn how many loaves of bread come from each bushel. A special part of that counting was learning how to divide up the land, so that each farmer could have the same amount of earth to sow. Now farmers know how to count into the thousands, and we've learned to mark these numbers in clay as a permanent record."

Rebba sipped from his cup before he went on. "Did you know, it was something you said months ago that made me support you and your plan to fight off the barbarians? It was when you said that the barbarians would be back in another five or ten years. You're right about their migrations. It's that cycle of migration we must break, and that's why I decided to stay and resist. We may fail, but it must be tried. We can no longer rebuild everything we create every ten years at the whim of every passing band of marauders. The crops are too precious to lose, even for a single growing season."

"What's so valuable about the crops?" Eskkar asked, his curiosity aroused. "Crops have been burned many times in the past. They can always be replanted."

"Ah, now we're back to the mysteries!" Rebba answered, smiling again. He stood up. "Come. Let's take a walk down to the fields."

They walked to the rear of the house, then went down a narrow dirt track that curved between the canals. Here rough planks that could be easily moved bridged the water channels, each barely wide enough to get a small cart across. In moments they were surrounded by crops—large fields of waist-high wheat and barley, smaller fields containing peas, lentils, beets, and even some melons. Another field grew flax, which even Eskkar knew was grown not for food but for its stem fibers that could be spun into linen. There were other plants that Eskkar didn't recognize.

The smell of animals had vanished and now the air held strangely pleasant odors given off by the growing plants, all of them at various stages of growth. The occasional fruit tree and jasmine added their scents to the air, and the mix of all these growing things combined to create a kind of perfume, hard to describe but somehow satisfying.

Rebba led them down a narrow path and soon they were surrounded by wheat, most of it still growing, but already above the farmer's knees. "This is emmer wheat," he said, indicating the field on his left. "And this is einkorn wheat. These two are the most important crops on this farm. From them we harvest the seeds that we grind into flour to make bread. It's the wheat that gives us the most food for each hectare."

Rebba moved in among the growing plants, looking closely at some, glancing quickly at others. Finally he selected a handful of wheat from one plant, then a few moments later, another handful from a different plant. Then he rejoined his two students.

"Here, Eskkar, look at these clusters of wheat." Rebba held one in each hand, extending them to Eskkar. "Now, tell me which of these you would plant next year, and which you would make into flour."

Eskkar stared down at the clusters, looking from one to the other. "I see no difference between them, Rebba," he answered. "They look the same."

Rebba offered his hands to Trella. "And you. Which would you choose?"

Trella examined them more closely than Eskkar. She took first one, than the other, into her own hands, and brought them within inches of her eyes, looking at them from all sides. "They seem the same to me also, Noble Rebba. Though, perhaps, the grains in one are slightly larger than the other."

"You have good eyes, Mistress Trella," Rebba said. "Yes, this plant is producing slightly larger seeds than the other." He let the smaller cluster drop to the ground and held up the other. "This plant, and others like it, will be used as seed for the next crop. When we are ready to harvest the field, my farmers will look at every plant, selecting first those that produce the largest clusters and the biggest seeds, until they've gathered enough for the next year's planting."

Rebba lifted the cluster up to his nose, then took one of the seeds into his mouth for a moment. "Of course, we must taste each one, to make sure the flour we grind is not too harsh or bitter. It wouldn't do to harvest a crop next season that made poor or bitter bread. If we did, no one would eat it, and we'd get less for what we sell on the river."

Eskkar shook his head. The seeds had seemed the same size to him. "So, the largest seeds will go back into the earth, to start the next crop? Why does that matter?"

"Do you know how much wheat a hectare of land produces, Eskkar?"

Eskkar shook his head. "I am not even sure what a hectare is."

"Ah, I've rushed ahead," Rebba apologized. "A hectare is a square plot of earth exactly one hundred long paces on each side." He waited until Eskkar nodded in understanding. "Each hectare of wheat yields about thirty-three bushels of seeds. Each bushel, after it is ground into flour, will make over seventy loaves of bread. On this farm, there are thirty hectares planted with wheat, so we will harvest almost a thousand bushels. Some will be saved for the next planting, a few go to feed the farmers and their families, and some are lost to rodents or rot during storage or transport. Say, three hundred bushels in all. The remaining seven hundred bushels are available to be stored or sold. With what we sell, we can pay the smiths for our tools, the carpenters for our plows, the builders for our houses, and the traders for what few luxuries we need. And do not forget the herders—whose animals we use or sell for their meat."

Rebba smiled at Eskkar. "With all the excess food produced on this farm, and others like it, those of us who own the land around Orak can even afford the most expensive luxury of all—supporting soldiers and their insatiable demands for weapons and horses."

A thousand bushels of wheat! Eskkar was astonished. And that was just from this farm. There were dozens of farms around Orak, though not many larger than Rebba's. "I didn't know so much could be harvested, Rebba."

"Orak is very fortunate in that the soil is very rich and water plentiful. A few miles away from the river, the farms produce much less. The farther you go from the Tigris, the smaller the harvest; eventually a farm will produce only enough to feed those who labor on it. Go beyond that and the lands are too dry to support even the poorest and most desperate farmer. That is why we choose to risk our lives staying here and fighting the barbarians."

Rebba shook his head at the follies of men before continuing. "So you see, each cycle of growth and harvest is important, and that's the answer to your question, Eskkar. The largest seeds go into the earth, and from the next harvest we will select once again the largest seeds. In this manner, over tens of years, we increase slightly the amount of wheat grown from each hectare. So each season there is a tiny bit more food produced, because we select and plant with care." He turned back to Trella. "That is the mystery. The cycle goes on each season—sow, grow, harvest, select, and sow. And with each cycle we can feed more people. Or buy more weapons.

"And that's why, Eskkar," Rebba continued, "we don't want to lose even a single crop to the barbarians. Once the crops are destroyed or the land damaged, the work of ten or twenty years is undone, and the next harvest will yield less food. Instead of a rich harvest, we may not have enough to feed our own people. We've planted early this season, because of the news of the barbarians. We will harvest earlier, so this season's crop will already be smaller. And this season's seed crop will be stored in Orak, hidden in underground chambers so that even if the village falls, our families across the river may yet find them for the next planting."

"Eskkar will not let the village fall, Noble Rebba," Trella said.

Rebba looked from one to the other. "When Nicar declared his intent to stay and fight, I had grave doubts about our chances. Nevertheless, I remained here, even though I know my fields will be burned or flooded." He shook his head sadly at the thought. "Let's return to the house. There's still much to show you." Rebba looked up at the sun and saw that nearly an hour had passed. "You will never be a farmer, Eskkar, but by sundown, you will at least know the value of a farm."

For the rest of the afternoon Rebba talked about each crop, explaining the differences between the various types of wheat, how linen was made from flax, and how the animals were bred and raised. The last hour they studied the irrigation ditches, the channels that carried water not only to all parts of the farm, but continued on to the next farm, one owned by another wealthy villager.

Rebba and his family knew all about moving water, explaining how the ditches grew narrower and narrower as they carried precisely the right amount of water to the fields. "The water must move with the right amount of force. If there is too much force, we cannot control the water flow. The amount of water used to irrigate the plants is important also—too much water and the plants drown, or are sickly. Too little, and they die from the heat. Too much force, and the channels themselves collapse. Too little, and the water dries up before it reaches its destination."

Eskkar had known that fact, though in a casual way, and without really understanding how critical the transport of water through the irrigation ditches was. Water was another one of the mysteries—a key to another part of the puzzle. Between the wells and the river, there was plenty of water for everyone, including the farms and all the herds of animals.

And it was good water. No one got ill from drinking the water in and around Orak, though Eskkar had gotten sick enough times in other lands drinking bad water, and he'd seen men die from drinking tainted water. He knew that in the dry lands away from the river, wells often produced a bitter-tasting water that could make even a strong man sick to his stomach.

Now Eskkar understood that the water in the river by itself didn't help the farmers. What made the farms successful were the irrigation ditches that delivered the water
where it was needed. The river merely provided the force to
move the water, while Rebba and his people channeled it.
He hadn't realized how critical the hundreds of ditches that
criss-crossed the land were, or how complicated their design and construction.

By the time Eskkar and Trella left Rebba's house it was
quite dark and one of the guards carried a torch to light the
way. The cook had saved their dinner, and Eskkar and Trella
decided to eat alone in the upper room. Eskkar said little
during the meal; he kept thinking about Rebba's words.
When he finished eating, he found himself staring at the
crust of bread that remained uneaten on his plate.

"You're quiet tonight, Eskkar," Trella commented as she
finished her bread and vegetables. "Did Rebba tell you more
than you wanted to know about farming?"

Eskkar looked at Trella across the table. "Until today, I
had always thought farming was for those too weak to fight,
or too unskilled to learn a trade. Now I learn that farming is
the most difficult of trades, and the one most important to
the village."

"What is important is that you now understand how the
village works. You know how the farmers grow their crops
and deal with the traders, how the artisans make tools, and
the builders create homes. You know how the smiths make
bronze and how the boatmen ply their trade. From now on,
when the nobles speak, you'll understand not only what
they say, but how they think."

Eskkar didn't answer. After a moment Trella arose and
gathered up the empty plates and carried them out of the
room. He scarcely noticed her going. He sat there, thinking
not only about Rebba's words, but Trella's as well.

Eskkar had lived in and about villages for half his life and
had never given them a second thought. A village was only
an opportunity to get food or wine, buy or repair weapons,
trade horses, or even spend the night in relative safety. They

provided places to visit, pass through, or stay for a while. Some were large, others small, but always they were surrounded by farms and herds, so commonplace as to be unremarkable. But now he understood that everything started with the farms. The farms held the real wealth.

For all of his life Eskkar had sought gold. With gold, one could buy food, weapons, horses, even men. Since he'd left the Alur Meriki, gold, or the lack of it, had always been the most important element in his life, driving him from place to place, from fight to fight. Now he learned gold was less than nothing. The farmers on their land created the gold. By producing grain and other food stocks, they started the chain of events that lifted gold from the earth. The farms were the foundation for all of Orak's activities. Without the farms, there could be no village. Without the village, there could be no artisans or smiths, no nobles or soldiers. Without the farms, there would be no need for a wall to defend the village.

Suddenly he had an insight about the Alur Meriki. Their leaders must understand these same mysteries. Why else were they always burning and destroying the farms as they passed through the land? It wasn't enough to simply take the crops, but the farmers must be killed, and the land made barren as often as possible. The steppes people, too, understood the need to keep the crop production down, lest there be too many farmers producing too much food. That might lead to too many men opposing them someday. Exactly what had happened here in Orak.

If the farm production in Orak could be increased further, then even more men would be available to fight. That led Eskkar to another insight. The other villages up and down the river had their own ways, their own petty nobles. But if those villages could be brought under Orak's control, then their surplus would add to the wealth and strength of Orak.

By explaining how the crops were sown and harvested Rebba had indeed revealed one of the mysteries of life. Now Eskkar had learned another, one that Trella, Nicar, and the nobles already knew. The villagers might all rely on each other's skills to survive, but they all depended on the farms to create the wealth that allowed Orak to grow and prosper, and that allowed the gold to flow throughout the land.

The thought of gold made him smile. Eskkar remembered his feelings when Nicar had sent his first month's pay. His delight at the twenty gold coins now seemed childish. The real wealth grew in the fields. The golden coins that passed from hand to hand were only another way of storing grain. In the last few months he'd come to value gold less and less. He now understood that it was just a means to an end, something he needed right now to pay for the wall and the soldiers, but just a tool nevertheless. Trella had understood that from the start.

A sound made him look up from the table. He saw Trella leaning against the door. "Have you been there long?" He shifted in the chair and held out his hand to her.

"You seemed lost in thought and I didn't want to disturb you. Are you still thinking about Rebba and his farm?" She crossed the room and took his hand.

He put his arms around her waist and held her for a moment, his face against the softness of her breasts, then pulled her down onto his lap. "No, I was thinking about you. Do you know that you are very wise for someone so young?"

She put her arms around his neck and let herself lean against him. "I'm not so young anymore, Eskkar. Some girls my age have birthed two children. Now I'm just a woman . . . your woman."

"Yes, woman," he answered, looking into her eyes. "How much gold do you think you are worth to me?"

The odd question surprised her, and for a moment doubt appeared in her eyes. "Do you wish to sell me, then?"

He ran his fingers through her hair, enjoying the feel of it. "Today Rebba explained many things to me. But today, Trella, I learned what the true value of gold is." He kissed her gently. "Now I know why you're worth more than all the gold in the land." Again he kissed her, harder this time, and let his hand trace the outline of her body. "I think it is time to go to bed."

"Yes, master," she answered, as she put her arms around him. But her smile and her eyes promised much, much more.

PART II

Sargon's Wall

16

Thutmose-sin led the way along the winding trail, his horse avoiding the loose stones and debris. The hooves of many horses marked their passage in the rocky soil. His men trailed behind him. None of them spoke. No one laughed; not since they reached the place where the first clash occurred.

A mile behind them, a dozen Alur Meriki bodies, flesh already picked from their scattered bones, showed where they had engaged the Ur Nammu. The absence of Ur Nammu bodies confirmed what Thutmose-sin already knew: a force of warriors had defeated his men so completely that their conquerors had time to gather and bury their dead.

The trail led deeper into the foothills, winding its way between cliff walls and alluvial flows. Thutmose-sin knew immediately when he reached the canyon where the slaughter had taken place. Even eight days had not settled the signs of earth churned to clods by a hundred horses.

Urgo waited for him there, just outside the canyon's entrance, with a handful of men.

Thutmose-sin stopped beside him, trying to visualize what had happened. The Alur Meriki had pursued the Ur Nammu to this place. Either that, or they had been lured there. Whatever the reason, his men had ridden in, and none had survived.

"Issogu . . . Markad . . ." Thutmose-sin called out to his subcommanders riding just behind. "Send trackers along the canyon walls. Look for tracks, anything left behind." He turned to his remaining subcommander. "Behzad, bring ten men on foot, and follow me. Search the ground as you go. The rest of you stay here."

He touched his heels to the horse. The animal lifted its head and stepped forward. Urgo guided his horse alongside. The trail twisted along the rock wall almost immediately, and as soon as Thutmose-sin entered the curve, the smells and sight of the dead reached him.

At the far end of the canyon carrion eaters, birds, animals, and insects, thronged about the Alur Meriki carcasses. Even animals that normally fought each other for food feasted together, so plentiful was the human flesh. As Thutmose-sin drew closer, they moved grudgingly away, annoyed at the interruption of their repast, scurrying up the slopes or flapping wings until they lurched noisily into the sky.

A single lance protruded from the pile of broken bones and rotting flesh, a dirty yellow streamer spotted with bird droppings hanging limply in the still air.

Twisting about, he studied the death scene, examining the steep ramparts surrounding him. The nearly sheer walls held no easy place to position men, let alone hide them. Thutmose-sin saw only a few places where a man might cling to his footing long enough to work a bow.

Beneath him, battle debris littered the ground. Shattered swords, broken lances, and bloodstained rags lay amidst the animal and human bones. Arrows, most of them snapped off, still protruded from some of the bodies. Thutmose-sin's eyes searched the ground, but he stayed on his horse; the animal had to be firmly urged to guide it close to the pile of the dead.

"Sarrum, look at this." A warrior, holding an arrow in his hand, ran up to Thutmose-sin.

A glance told Thutmose-sin why the man had noticed it. The arrow's barb was missing and the shaft broken off just behind the binding. Even so, the shaft stretched longer than any arrows his men used, and when he took the arrow in his hand, he felt the extra thickness.

He handed the unusual shaft to Urgo, who studied it for a moment.

"Ah, I've seen these before, a few years ago, when we raided to the far north. There was a clan that used such long shafts. Good bowmen." He scratched his beard for a moment. "But they were not horse people. They lived high on the steppes, in thick forests."

"Look for more of these," Thutmose-sin ordered, taking the shaft from Urgo and handing it back to the warrior. "Show it to the others as well."

His men found three more such shafts, all broken or damaged. Their presence convinced him that others beside Ur Nammu had fought his men. Thutmose-sin turned to the old clan leader. "Bring twenty men in. Have them clear the bodies from the burial place. Then have them dig up the grave."

Urgo's mouth hung open for a moment. "But Thutmose-sin, the dead . . ." His voice trailed off at the look on his leader's face. "Yes, Sarrum. I'll get the men." He wheeled his horse about and rode back, shouting orders.

Issogu returned, jogging to his leader's side. "No tracks or any stones disturbed on the canyon walls, Sarrum," he said, pointing to the eastern side. "Nothing."

Thutmose-sin turned to the western side, where Markad had paused to kneel on a rock outcropping, studying the earth. "Help him," he ordered.

Urgo returned, leading twenty gloomy men behind him. One look at their leader convinced them not to complain. They began clearing away the bones, using their lances and knives as much as possible, to avoid touching the decaying flesh. They muttered incantations to ward off the spirits. Soon the rotting bodies were being dragged and pushed away, the flesh sometimes falling from the skeletons of Thutmose-sin's former warriors. Clouds of flies rose up in the air as the men sweated at their tasks.

Markad walked over, his face wrinkling in disgust at the stench. "Sarrum, there was little to see. But a few men might have followed the rocks on that side. I found one of our arrows up there, the tip broken against the wall where a man might stand. Archers might have been there, firing arrows down into our men."

"How many?"

"At most a handful, Sarrum, even less," Markad said, shaking his head. "More would have left tracks, scratches on the rocks. There was nothing, just the one arrow."

Then it wasn't an ambush, despite the strange arrows. "Good, Markad. Keep searching for any other sign."

He sat there, enduring the grave stink and the flies in silence, until his men finally cleared the dead and began digging into the rocky soil. He knew they cursed and swore at him beneath their breath, but no one dared refuse. The earth had been tamped down, to keep the carrion-eaters at bay, and at first the ground resisted his men's efforts. At last one of the diggers gave a shout. A few moments later, his warriors dragged the first Ur Nammu body from the grave.

Thutmose-sin ordered another twenty men to join the work, using them to clear the ground and lift the bodies from the grave. The heat added to the miasma of death that now flowed around them like a mist. Body after body came forth, more than forty of them, and still they kept lifting Ur Nammu from the earth.

One of his men cried out in surprise, and Thutmose-sin moved toward the man. They'd dragged out another body, but this man looked different. The body's clothing remnants showed the tunic of a dirt-eater. The man's face had the broad, flat look often found in those who worked the earth.

Two more bodies came up, with the same look about them. One looked to be a boy, barely old enough to ride. After that, nothing. They'd exposed the entire grave.

The sweating men stood about, covered in filth and dirt, waiting, while Thutmose-sin considered what he'd seen.

The Ur Nammu had buried dirt-eaters with their own warriors. He'd never heard of such a thing before, to dishonor fighting men by burying them alongside farmers. The Ur Nammu, like the Alur Meriki, had no use for dirt-eaters. They were to be hunted and killed. But not these men. These men . . . their bodies buried properly . . . he thought about the strange arrows, looking down at the one still in his hand.

His warriors weren't fools. They hadn't been ambushed, and they'd killed plenty of Ur Nammu and wounded many more, as the bloody rags scattered about attested. But then the tide of battle turned, and they all died, killed by . . . not enough arrows, not enough to account for so many dead. So riders had joined in the fight, helped by a few archers along the cliff wall. These strangers had turned the battle, probably striking the Alur Meriki from behind. A sudden attack from the rear, even by a handful of determined men, must have changed the battle's outcome. Instead of wiping out the last of the Ur-Nammu, his men had found themselves trapped between two forces—trapped and annihilated.

The shaft of the arrow snapped between his hands. His warriors had died—vengeance cried out for the blood of those responsible. The Ur Nammu must be destroyed, along with those who helped them.

Thutmose-sin looked up. His men stared at him, waiting for his orders, the silence broken only by the flies buzzing about the dead. What all this meant, he wasn't sure. But he knew a way to find out.

"Urgo, rebury the dead Ur Nammu." He ignored the shock on his men's faces. "Bury them properly, then walk the horses over the ground. Have the prayer-givers offer up sacrifices to the spirits, to atone for disturbing the dead."

Without looking back he rode out of the canyon. At the entrance, he called out to Markad and Issogu. "Follow the trail, wherever it leads. Find out where they went. And look to see if a band breaks off and rides to the west. Take as many men as you need."

Two hours later, he gave the order to camp for the night, at the same place where the Ur Nammu had halted and rested from their wounds. The camp's fire rings showed that men had used it for several days. Urgo found another of the large arrows from the north, broken off in a tree obviously used for target practice. So the northern archers and the Ur

Nammu had become friendly enough to shoot together, no doubt after celebrating the destruction of his men. A broad trail led north, made by perhaps thirty or forty riders.

In the next few days, Markad and Issogu would track the Ur Nammu. But Thutmose-sin could guess what they would find. The surviving Ur Nammu would flee to the east, and another trail would head west, back toward Orak.

A band of riders from Orak had either tracked the Ur Nammu, or, more likely, his own Alur Meriki raiders. The dirt-eaters then joined with the Ur Nammu or just attacked the Alur Meriki from the rear. Whatever their method, Orak's riders turned the battle, losing only a few men in the process. Then the two bands of hereditary enemies had camped together for several days, recovering from their wounds and taking time to sharpen their archery skills.

That much time together . . . that meant whatever the Ur Nammu had learned, Orak's dirt-eaters now knew also.

Even worse, it told Thutmose-sin that Orak had a leader, someone who knew the ways of war. That meant that the dirt-eaters would fight this time, not run. They'd beaten his men, and such a victory would give them strength. His own losses mattered little. At least the Alur Meriki had effectively finished off the Ur Nammu, ending that conflict at last.

The loss of his own men didn't trouble him. He had too many warriors as it was. But his men would look at each other and wonder. An Alur Meriki force had suffered defeat, annihilation, something that hadn't happened in nearly a generation. And that would make his men begin to doubt. They would look at their clan leaders differently. If warriors could be defeated once, then why not again?

Thutmose-sin went over this with Urgo, who sat across from him in silence, unable to challenge his sarrum's conclusions.

"Your plan, Urgo. Are you still certain we can trap the dirt-eaters?"

Urgo chewed on a blade of grass, taking his time. The loss concerned him, too, since any reduction in warrior numbers limited the number of fighting men available.

"We're driving everyone toward the village. Unless there are so many that they can resist us, we'll take the village."

Thutmose-sin stared at his kinsman. "And the wall you say they are building?"

"A wall without fighting men is useless, Sarrum." He met his leader's eyes. "Are their fighters now equal to our warriors, after one small skirmish? An ambush, on favorable ground, and with archers on the walls?"

"They have a leader now, someone who knows how to fight, when to fight, someone who can defeat our men."

"Perhaps, Sarrum. But even a few such men, however strong, cannot defeat all the Alur Meriki."

"Nevertheless, I want to know more about the war chief who led this force. Find out who he is. If this Orak has a new leader, someone skilled in the ways of war, then we should learn what we can about him."

17

For the next ten days, Eskkar spent the mornings with his commanders, preparing for the different kinds of battles they might face. Then he trained with the soldiers, primarily to encourage the men. The Hawk Clan helped build morale by retelling the story of how Eskkar destroyed the Alur Meriki raiders. The embellishments grew with each repetition, and the soldiers' trust in their leader soared. With the wall nearly finished, their self-assurance increased even more. Eskkar wanted the men to feel confident in their skills and commanders. They'd need that certainty when the fighting started.

The soldiers practiced with sword, spear, and axe. The proud Hawk Clan took the lead, playing the role of attackers, making spirited assaults on the wall. The master archers paced off distances from the wall and half-buried stones in the earth. Painted different colors to mark the distance, the markers allowed the bowmen to gauge the range to their enemy. The old targets were torn down. Bowmen practiced shooting only from the wall, to make sure they had the feel for every shot. Under Totomes's guidance they learned to fire volleys at specific distances.

Weapons and food continued to pour into Orak. The refugee traffic on the roads had diminished as the Alur Meriki drew closer, but men continued to arrive, many eager to work or fight, asking only that Orak protect their families. River trade increased, and the ferry plied its path back and forth countless times each day. Every vessel brought some much needed cargo. Stockpiles grew, and everyone complained they had no space to sit or stand.

When Eskkar walked about, the villagers cheered him, calling out his name or wishing him luck in the coming fight. Trella was just as popular, especially with the women, the poor, the children, and the elderly. She visited many of these people daily, assisting and organizing them, and making sure the women knew their roles in the coming fight.

Gatus finally had enough soldiers to train the women and old men. His men showed them how to fight fires and to use short, stabbing sticks from the wall. Men and women alike practiced using forked sticks to push ladders back.

Hundreds of rocks and stones were carried to the parapet and thrown down by villagers. When one group finished, they recovered the stones for the next group, a labor that went on all day, until everyone's muscles ached with pain and the rough stones had rubbed their hands raw. Thousands more stones stood in great piles beneath the parapet.

The training for soldier and villager continued until they mastered each technique, tool, and weapon. Women coated every exposed wooden surface inside Orak with a layer of mud, leaving no combustible targets for fire arrows or torches hurled over the wall. The village prepared for the siege, but Eskkar saw as much optimism as fear on everyone's face.

Eskkar shook his head in amazement at it all. He clapped Gatus on the back and praised him publicly for his labors.

At the end of a long but satisfying day, Eskkar returned home just before sunset. He went first to the well at the back of the house. The luxury of the private well still pleased him. He enjoyed the chance to wash the sweat and dust from his body.

As he finished he heard the gate to the courtyard bang open. A ragged youth slipped under the surprised guard's arm, though the man was stationed there to prevent just such an intrusion.

The boy rushed toward the house, his voice a high-pitched shrill. "Captain, Captain, come quick . . . Lady Trella's been stabbed!"

The boy dodged past a servant coming from the house. Bantor appeared in the doorway and grabbed the lad, holding him fast. Eskkar ran up, went down on a knee, and faced the boy.

"Here, lad, here I am. What happened to Trella? Where is she?" Eskkar felt dread growing in his stomach.

"Lady Trella was returning here, when a man came up behind her and drew a knife." The boy's high-pitched voice rushed the words together. "I called out to warn her, but I was too late and he stabbed her. Then he turned to run, but I grabbed his leg and held him until her guard reached him. The guard sent me here to find you."

"Where, boy? Where is she?"

"In the Street of the Butchers, near the carpenter's shop."

"Keep him here!" Eskkar pushed the boy into Annok-sur's hands as she approached.

Eskkar ran back through the courtyard and out the gate, headed for the Street of the Butchers. Before he'd gone more than a dozen steps a crowd approached, led by a burly soldier carrying Trella in his arms. One arm dangled limply. Her dress, covered in blood and cut open down the side, dragged on the ground. Trella's eyes rolled in her head and Eskkar couldn't tell if she was still alive. He recognized the guard, Klexor, assigned to guard Trella that day.

Klexor pushed right by Eskkar as if he didn't recognize him. Three soldiers of the watch, all white-faced and with drawn swords, followed close behind.

"Is she alive?" Eskkar forced the words out of his throat, his voice hoarse.

The guard carried Trella through the courtyard and into the house. Someone had cleared the big table and he placed her down gently. Annok-sur pushed him away and pulled open Trella's dress. Someone had cut a strip of cloth from the garment and used it to bandage her wound, the fabric wrapped completely around her body, just under her breast.

Eskkar reached the foot of the table. He saw Trella's

breast rise and fall, so she still lived. But her face was pale and blood oozed from her left side.

"Send for a healer." Annok-sur shouted the words over her shoulder as she placed a folded blanket under Trella's head.

Klexor stood dumbly where Annok-sur had pushed him. Eskkar strode to his side and grabbed his arm. "What happened? Who did this?"

The man turned and stared at Eskkar for a moment. "Yes, Captain, she's still alive," the bodyguard replied, as if recalling Eskkar's earlier question. "A man stabbed her in the lane. But a healer was passing by and came when he heard the shouts. He bound her wound, then said I should bring her here." The guard glanced around. "He said he'd follow . . . ah, there he is."

An elderly man, his bald pate ringed with wisps of white hair, came puffing through the door. He carried a large leather pouch slung over his shoulder that contained his instruments. Eskkar recognized Ventor, a healer often used by the soldiers. Too common for the upper classes, Ventor was better at binding war wounds than treating headaches or queasy stomachs.

"Don't just stand there," Ventor ordered as he headed directly to the table, "bring fresh water and clean cloths. And lamps and candles, as many as you can."

Annok-sur moved aside for the healer. Ventor opened his bag and used a knife to cut off the crude bandage.

Eskkar stood there in shock, pushed aside by the women. He watched helplessly as Bantor's wife and another servant wiped the blood from Trella's body while the healer poured water over the wound.

At first Eskkar thought she'd been stabbed in the chest, but as the blood washed away, he saw the blow had taken her from the left side, starting a little below the armpit and slicing down towards the hip. The long, jagged cut still bled, but Ventor ignored the blood as he washed the wound, pouring water from the pitcher up and down the length of the opening. The bloody water spilled to the floor.

"Bring another pitcher," Ventor demanded. He took a

candle and slowly scanned the length of the wound, holding the flame close to her body. The examination went on for a long time, before he straightened up and put down the candle. "Nothing in the wound."

Taking a needle and thread from his pouch, he threaded the needle carefully, then quickly bound the end of the thread with a large knot. Ventor rinsed the wound one more time, then, assisted by the women who held the flesh together, he began sewing the wound closed.

It was nothing Eskkar hadn't seen before. He'd suffered the same treatment, even watched while it was done, but this time he had to turn away. His hands shook and he forced himself to stop, clenching both hands into fists. Bantor's wife joined Eskkar and her husband.

"I think she'll live, Eskkar," Annok-sur whispered. "The wound is long but not deep, and the blade glanced along her ribs. Though I've no doubt she would've bled to death if the healer wasn't close by to staunch the bleeding."

"My thanks to you, Annok-sur. Please stay with her." Eskkar stared at Ventor, bent low across the table as he finished closing the wound. At last the healer began to bandage his patient, using clean linen brought by the servants. "When the healer is finished, keep him here to watch over her."

Eskkar faced Bantor. "Now let's find out who dies tonight."

He stepped out into the courtyard. He found it full of armed men. A few torches provided light against the deepening darkness. When they saw the grimness on Eskkar's face, a groan went up.

Bantor called out quickly, "No, no, she lives. The healer is with her."

A ragged cheer went up, echoed from beyond the wall, and Eskkar realized the street outside must be crowded with people, all concerned about Trella. Two members of the watch pushed their way through the soldiers, dragging a ragged man already covered with bruises, his hands tied tightly behind him and a gag in his mouth. The prisoner shook so hard he would have fallen if the men hadn't held him upright.

"This is the one who attacked her, Captain." The guard gave the prisoner a jab in the ribs. "Klexor caught him before he could escape."

Cries of "kill him . . . kill him now" went up from the soldiers, but Eskkar raised his hand for silence. He turned to Bantor. "Watch him, and keep him alive."

Eskkar fought the urge to strike the man, but that could wait. Think first, then act, Trella always told him. He started thinking coherently for the first time since they'd brought her in. He looked around the garden and spotted Klexor, sitting alone on the ground, disconsolate, his head in his hands.

"Klexor, come here," Eskkar called out, then said to Bantor, "Clear out the courtyard, but keep twenty men here. Close the gates and send the rest of the men to the walls. I don't want anyone to escape by slipping over in the darkness. Kill anyone that tries. Then come back here. Gatus, Sisuthros, come with me."

Klexor stood up, shaking, and nearly fell. Eskkar took the man's arm and guided him into the house. Ignoring the crowd around Trella, he led the man upstairs and sat the bodyguard on a chair in front of the table. Eskkar poured two cups of wine, a small one for himself and a large one for Klexor.

"Here, take this." Eskkar waited until the soldier had drained half the cup, then pulled it away from his lips. "Easy, now. Tell me what happened. Take your time and tell me everything."

Eskkar went to the other side of the table and sat. He looked carefully at the guard. A seasoned veteran and a bull of a man, Klexor stood a few inches shorter than Eskkar, but broader and wider, with hands like hammers. He wasn't one of the original soldiers, but Eskkar knew him well enough, and the man had guarded Trella before.

Klexor wiped the back of his hand across his mouth. "Captain, it wasn't my fault, I . . ."

"I just want to hear what happened, Klexor. It wasn't you that struck her. Tell me exactly what happened. Leave out nothing."

Klexor took another sip of wine, then glanced at Sisuthros and Gatus, who leaned against the wall.

"I was assigned to guard Lady Trella today, and we walked all over the village, back and forth, visiting people, training with the women. Finally we started back here, but some women wanted to talk to her, so she stopped and spent time with them."

His voice cracked and he took another mouthful of wine. "By then dusk was approaching. We were in the Street of the Butchers. The lane's narrow there, and I walked in front, making a way through the crowd." He stopped and ran his fingers shakily through his hair.

Get on with it, man, Eskkar wanted to shout.

"We were only a few steps from the carpenter's shop, you know, the big one where they make wheels and . . ."

Eskkar nodded his head.

"That's where we were, when there was a shout . . . some street boy screamed out '. . . knife, he's got a knife.' I turned and there was this man, his blade striking down. Trella screamed, and fell."

Klexor emptied the cup and set it clumsily on the table. "I stood there, Captain, for a moment, I couldn't move. But the boy, the one who shouted, he grabbed the assassin by the leg as he tried to run off and tripped him. Good thing he did, or he would've been killed himself. I saw the knife flash by the boy's head. By then I'd recovered my wits and ran at the man just as he got up. I hit him, he went down . . . I hit him a few more times."

The man stopped, thinking. "I heard Lady Trella say, 'Alive . . . keep him alive' before she fainted. That man, Ventor, I think his name is, came up and pushed me away. He bound up the wound and told me to send the boy ahead to you, then ordered me to carry Trella here."

"And the one who stabbed her, do you know him?" Eskkar asked.

"No, I never saw him before," Klexor answered, "though . . . wait, I did see him earlier in the afternoon. He could've been with the crowd at the wall when the women went there to practice. I'm sure I saw him there. The women may remember him."

Klexor started to shake again, aware he could be put to death for failing in his duty.

"You said he tried to stab the boy? Did he still have the knife when you struck him?"

The guard concentrated on what had taken place, then answered. "Yes, Captain, he still had the knife. But he was trying to get away, not use the knife."

"So you hit him. Why didn't you use your sword?"

"Lady Trella said to keep him alive . . . no, that was later. I don't know, I just wanted to get to him. I don't remember what I was thinking. I forgot to draw my sword."

Eskkar tried to visualize what the man had seen and done. "My thanks to you, Klexor. I'm sure no man could have done better. You did well to keep the assassin alive. Now go to the kitchen and get some more wine, but only one cup. You need to stay sober. Others will want to hear your words later."

The man got up, his relief evident. "Captain . . . I'm sorry about what . . . she's . . . she's a good woman . . ." His voice choked, and he couldn't get the words out.

"I know. Go now, and send up the boy who brought us the news." He turned to Gatus and Sisuthros, then paused as Bantor returned, squeezing past Klexor on the landing. "It sounds as if the man was following Trella, and that Klexor did his duty."

"The men have complained that it's impossible for one man to guard either of you," Gatus said. "You know that, with all these crowds. But Lady Trella didn't want another guard assigned. Klexor performed as well as any man."

"Nobody takes good advice, Gatus. She said the same thing to me. I should have . . ."

The door opened again and Annok-sur escorted the boy into the room, a crust of buttered bread in his hand, with crumbs and grease on his chin. He looked frightened.

Eskkar stood and guided the boy to the seat just vacated by Klexor, but this time Eskkar pulled a stool around and sat down next to him. He judged the lad had about nine or ten seasons. "Don't be afraid, boy. What's your name?"

The urchin's eyes went wide as he looked around. No doubt he'd never seen a room this big in his life, nor one as finely furnished. Eskkar prompted him.

"Enki, Noble One, I'm called Enki."

The name of the water god who dwelt in the river. "A fine name, Enki. You've done a great deed today, and I'm in your debt. Without you, Lady Trella's attacker would have escaped. Now I want you to tell me everything you did today, where you went, when you first saw Trella, everything. Do you think you can do that? Start from where you first saw Trella today."

"It was at the training ground, Noble. I went there to watch the women train. Sometimes they slip and fall, or their dresses come loose. When Lady Trella came, many of us ran over to her. Last week I carried a message for her, and she gave me a copper coin." He looked crestfallen as he remembered. "But then some older boys took it away."

"I can fix that." Eskkar stood up and went back to his table, opened the drawer and extracted two copper coins. He presented them to Enki who took them with his free hand, the other still firmly clutching his bread. Eskkar sat down again. "Then what happened?"

"Lady Trella watched the women practice, then she began to train, too. She's very strong for a girl, you know, and she can handle the short spear by herself, or the forked stick. Many were cheering and laughing. When they finished for the day, the women washed themselves at the well. I like to watch that."

Many of the women would take off their shifts and pour water over themselves. Eskkar smiled briefly. He'd watched such things himself. "Yes, that's always fun to watch. Now, Enki, while you were there, did you remember seeing the man who attacked Trella? Was he there?"

Enki frowned as he tried to remember. "No, not there. I didn't see him there. But later, when we began walking, he walked by me and Trella. I was following along, hoping she might need another message delivered or something.

The man pushed past her and moved ahead. Then he came back and walked behind us again. He kept looking around, I remember that."

"Good, Enki. What happened next?"

"Lady Trella stopped to talk to someone. Some of the boys crowded around her and the guard pushed them back. She and the women talked for a long time, whispering to each other, then Lady Trella smiled and gave one of them a coin before she started walking again. The guard had to push people out of the way so they could get through."

The boy looked around the room and saw everyone watching him. Probably no one had ever paid any attention to him before, and now four grown men listened carefully to his every word.

"Don't be afraid," Eskkar reassured the boy. "Go on."

"I got left behind, and was trying to catch up when the man pushed past me again. I almost fell, and I cursed at him. Then I saw him pull the knife from under his tunic. He walked very fast, and headed for Lady Trella. I yelled, and she started to turn around. Then she saw the knife and she raised her arm, but he stabbed her anyway. I kept yelling. He turned and ran away, ran right past me, so I grabbed his leg and held on until we both fell down. He got up, but the guard caught him and started hitting him."

"Do you remember what you yelled, Enki? The exact words?" Eskkar wanted all the details.

"I remember. I yelled, 'Lady Trella, he's got a knife. Lady Trella . . .' Then I saw the blood on the knife as the man ran past me."

"How loud did you yell, Enki? Can you show me?"

Without hesitating, the boy screamed out the words, showering Eskkar's face with bread crumbs, the high-pitched voice piercing in the closed room. It was loud, all right, loud enough to make anyone stop and turn around. If Trella hadn't turned, she would have taken the blade in her back.

Eskkar made the boy go over the story again. When nothing new emerged, Eskkar glanced up at the three subcommanders, standing quietly against the wall. "Anything you want to ask?"

Gatus and Bantor shook their heads, but Sisuthros stepped over and bent down to examine the back of the boy's head, pushing the unruly hair back and forth until Enki jumped in pain.

Sisuthros withdrew his fingers, some dried blood stuck on them. "I thought I saw blood. The blade didn't miss by much, though I doubt it would've killed him."

Enki's eyes grew wide at the sight of his own blood. Sisuthros rubbed the boy's head. "Just a scratch. Nothing for a brave man to worry about."

"Thank you again, Enki," Eskkar said as he stood. "Who is your family?"

"I have none, Noble. I had an older brother, but he disappeared. I sleep in the stables, or near the river."

The brother had probably been picked up off the streets and sold to a slaver. "Then you'll stay here from now on." Eskkar turned to his men. "Now it's time to talk to the assassin."

Taking the boy's hand, Eskkar led the way downstairs, where he turned Enki over to Bantor's wife before checking on Trella. The healer sat quietly beside her, his work for the moment finished. Ventor stood as Eskkar approached.

Eskkar stared at her pale face, her body covered with a soft blanket and another folded under her head. They'd combed her hair. Her eyes were closed but she was breathing regularly.

"How is she, Ventor? Will she live?" Eskkar couldn't stop his voice from breaking.

"Yes, Captain, I believe she will recover," Ventor said. "Unless the wound fills with pus. The blow struck her ribs and glanced downward. Her attacker should have directed his blade upward toward the heart. The ribs open to a thrust from below, but a downward stroke glances from rib to rib. Not a very expert assassin."

Ventor lifted the blanket and looked at Trella's wound. "She's young and strong and should heal quickly. I gave her some wine and ordered that she be fed soup as soon as she's able to take some."

Eskkar breathed a sigh of relief. "Thank you, Ventor. I'd

like you to stay the night. Then come at least twice a day to look in on her. You'll be well paid for your good work tonight."

"The nobles use their own healers, Captain."

"Yes, but I'm just a soldier, and you're more familiar with battle wounds. Besides, I'll not have a dozen healers standing around arguing about what potions to give her or gods to pray to. Tend to her wound, as you would for any soldier."

Eskkar walked out into the courtyard. A cheer went up from the men. Despite his order, more than twenty soldiers still crammed themselves into the courtyard, which now blazed with torchlight.

He held up one hand. "Trella is being cared for by the healer. Now we've work to do here, and you'll be needed later. So clear the courtyard. The Hawk Clan and the house guards remain."

"Get the rest of them out of here, Gatus. Bantor, bring the assassin to the back of the house."

Eskkar followed the guards as they dragged the man into the cul-de-sac behind the house.

The small garden contained only one bench and two small trees scarcely taller than a man. He stepped in front of the attacker. Two men held the prisoner by his arms. The man knelt in the dirt, arms bent up backward behind him, the gag still stuffed in his mouth.

Eskkar went down on one knee, his face close to the prisoner's. His eyes bulged wide with terror, and the stink of urine hung over him. Eskkar pulled the gag from the man's mouth, heard the quick gasp of air as the man filled his lungs. He started to speak.

"Silence!" Eskkar ordered savagely. "If he speaks or cries out, give him some pain."

Both men tightened their grips on the man's wrists, twisted high behind him, until he yelped with pain and saliva ran from his open mouth. Eskkar studied the man carefully but didn't recognize him. That didn't mean anything. He could have been in Orak for months or days, though he was more likely to be a newcomer. "Anyone know this man?"

No one said anything. "What is your name?" The man said nothing, and Eskkar nodded at the men holding him. They jerked the man's arms up a little, and the fresh pain loosened his tongue.

"Natram-zar . . . my name is Natram-zar, Noble." He spoke in a hoarse voice with a trace of an accent. Eskkar guessed the man came from the south, probably Sumeria.

"Why did you attack my woman, Natram-zar?"

"I meant to rob her, Noble One. I'm just a thief. I only wanted to steal her purse." He was pleading now, fear showing in his eyes as they darted back and forth.

"Then you're a very poor thief, Natram-zar. Her purse was still around her neck." Eskkar stood up. "Did he have anything on him?"

Bantor stepped forward, holding a small leather pouch, much worn and repaired, that contained five copper coins as well as other odds and ends, and the man's knife as well.

Eskkar took it, tightening his lips at the sight of Trella's blood. A good weapon, the copper blade fit perfectly into a carved and curved wooden handle. Small and well made, it wasn't a soldier's weapon, but perfect to hide under a tunic for a quiet murder. Much too good a weapon for a common thief. Of course, he could have stolen it from some wealthy victim. "Nothing else?"

"Nothing, Captain. Only this purse and the knife."

"Stand him up, then cut off his clothes." The man started to complain, but the guards lifted him up, ignoring his protests that quickly turned into moans of pain. In moments, they'd stripped him bare, and his clothes lay in a heap around him, including the dirty and reeking undergarment where the man had pissed himself in fear.

Using the man's knife Eskkar poked through the clothes. He almost missed a small pocket, sewn closed, that ran lengthwise along the bottom hem of the tunic. Eskkar sliced open the threads and heard the faint clink of coins. Each coin had been wrapped in a bit of cloth to muffle the sound.

Eskkar counted ten gold coins, all flickering bright in the torchlight. He looked at each disc, but they were all well handled and worn, with the different marks of various merchants and nobles. He checked the rest of the clothes, but found nothing. The gold told its own story—a murder for hire.

Standing, he faced Natram-zar. "You've lied to me once. Don't make that mistake again. If you want to avoid the fire, you'll speak the truth." Eskkar heard Gatus call his name. "What is it?"

"Many of the nobles are in the street. Nicar and the others wish to enter, but I've kept everyone out as you ordered. Also, the men guarding the walls heard something in the darkness. When they went to search, they found a horse tethered to a rock three hundred paces from the wall. Whoever was with the animal disappeared in the darkness. It's a fine beast, loaded with food and a water skin."

I should have anticipated that. The murderer would need to escape quickly after his deed.

Now the nobles waited outside. Eskkar wasn't sure whether he wanted them here or not, especially when it could have been Nestor who paid the man. Nevertheless, if he didn't have them present when the man confessed, they might not believe Eskkar's witnesses. Damn the gods.

"Bantor, find out who knows the horse, who owns it, where it came from. I doubt if this filth kept a good horse stabled in the village for days, but if so, somebody will know him."

Eskkar looked toward Gatus, still waiting. "Allow in only the heads of the Families, no one else. If they don't want to come in, don't make them."

Eskkar turned back to the prisoner. "Ready to speak, Natram-zar? The time for lies is past."

"Noble One, I'm just a thief." His voice sounded hoarse from dryness and pain.

"Tie him between the trees and spread his legs well apart. Bring fire from the house. And plenty of wood."

Natram-zar cried out as the men holding his arms started to drag him away. One of the guards dropped his arm for a moment, stepped in front of the prisoner, and punched him savagely in the stomach, the force of the blow doubling the prisoner over. "Keep silent, dog, or you get another."

They secured the prisoner between the two small trees, spreading his arms wide apart and tying them to the largest branches. Then they tied the man's ankles, spread-eagling his legs and fastening them to the base of each tree. They pulled each rope tight. When they finished, Natram-zar hung there helplessly, unable to do more than twitch.

While this went on, the heads of the Families came in, looking unnerved, the sight of the naked man reinforcing their apprehension.

"Just in time, Nobles," Eskkar began. "This man tried to kill Trella, and only a boy with quick wits and a loud tongue saved her life. The dog was captured in the act. His name is Natram-zar. He had those ten gold coins lying at his feet sewn in his tunic and a horse waiting for him outside the walls. Any of you know this man?"

The sight of the coins gleaming in the torchlight changed everything. No thief could have such an amount, and only the nobles and a few of the wealthier merchants could afford such a sum for a hired killing. And no thief carrying that much gold would risk his life for a slave girl's meager purse, not even if the slave were Trella.

Eskkar watched Nestor, but the old man seemed as shocked as the rest. Nicar, Decca, Rebba, and Corio all looked blankly at Eskkar. Nicar found his voice first. "Who paid him to do this? Why would anyone want to hurt Trella?"

"You will all wait over there and say nothing," Eskkar ordered, his voice hard. "Not a word."

He glanced at Gatus, who had little love for any of the nobles. "Gatus, escort the nobles to the side of the house where they can see and hear everything. Make sure they say nothing." From there, the prisoner could not see them.

By now Natram-zar had gotten his breath back and he lifted his head. A wide clay bowl, packed full of wood and a few chunks of coal, was placed on the ground before him. Another man came from the house, carrying three burning coals on a clay shard. He dumped them into the bowl and began building the fire, moving chunks of wood atop the coals. In moments, a small fire burned steadily.

Eskkar reached down and held his hand over the low flames. The heat rose to his hand, and he withdrew it.

"Warm him up a little." Maldar knelt down and pushed the fire between Natram-zar's legs. With his legs spread apart, the top of the flames reached within a foot of his testicles.

Natram-zar screamed as soon as the first warmth reached his genitals, long before the heat could have affected him. He struggled to move his body aside, but the men on either side of him used their knees to push his body back, keeping him centered over the flames. Maldar tossed more wood chips on the fire. The flames reached even higher.

Eskkar waited patiently, watching the fire's glow, watching the man as he jerked his body back and forth in a frenzy, trying to move his groin out of the path of the heat building up beneath him, trying to pull his genitals up into his body. .

But Natram-zar's frantic exertions quickly tired him. He had to slump against the ropes, which once again positioned him directly over the low flames. In a moment, the pain made him stretch upright, twitching and jerking once again, until exhaustion brought him back to the flames and the process repeated itself.

Eskkar let it go on for a while, while Maldar made sure the flames didn't lessen. The screams came without ceasing now and Eskkar knew the sound would be heard many streets away. From out in the lane came the sound of cheers as the crowd guessed what was happening.

When the smell of burning flesh started to rise, Eskkar nodded to Maldar, who pulled the bowl forward, removing most of the heat. The prisoner slumped limply from the ropes, the hair scorched away from his thighs, his genitals a deep red from the heat.

Eskkar stepped forward. "Who hired you to kill Trella? Talk now, or go back into the flames."

The man moaned as pain continued to shoot through his body. Blood flowed from his mouth where he had bitten his lip. "Mercy, Noble . . . mercy! I'm just a thief!"

"Back into the fire." Eskkar stepped away, and Maldar returned the bowl underneath the prisoner, bringing the flames back into position, before tossing more wood chunks on the fire. The top of the flames rose up to nearly touch the man's body.

The assassin's screams split the night air, loud enough to be heard throughout Orak. Jerking about, his cries for mercy echoed off the walls that surrounded him. Natram-zar must have known he was going to die, but that didn't matter anymore, only that the pain stop.

Eskkar gave the signal to stop. "Give him water, then we'll hear what he says." A soldier brought a ladle of water from the well and held it to the man's lips.

"Now, talk, and if you lie, you go back into the flames. And speak up, so all can hear your words."

Natram-zar sucked in gulps of air before he could speak, then his voice croaked with pain and fear. "It was Caldor. Caldor paid me. Caldor, son of Nicar. I was only doing what the nobles wanted." His voice trailed off and tears streamed down his cheeks.

A murmur of disbelief ran through the men in the courtyard, while Nicar cried from the wall, "No! It can't be true."

Even Eskkar felt surprise. He expected the man to name Nestor as the one who hired him. That was foolish. Of course Nestor wouldn't want Trella killed. He might want Eskkar out of the way, but he had no grudge against Trella. He'd been more than kind to her at all their meetings. But Caldor? Could he be that stupid? A wave of anger went through Eskkar. This was his fault. He should have taken care of Caldor sooner.

"Who else, Natram-zar, who else?" Eskkar grabbed the man by the shoulder and shook him. "Speak, or I'll put you back in the fire!"

The words poured from Natram-zar. Now he would do anything to avoid the flames. "Nobody else . . . only Caldor . . . and his servant, Loki. They approached me in the tavern . . . asked what I would do for gold, a lot of gold. He offered me . . . ten gold coins to kill her. I told him I'd need a horse . . . to escape, so he gave me twelve silver coins for that as well."

"Where did you buy the horse? Who sold it to you?"

The wretched man mumbled the name of Zanar, a livery-man. "Send someone for him, Gatus. Hold him in the street outside and have him describe the man who bought the horse, when he bought it, and how much he paid."

Eskkar turned back to the would-be assassin, who trembled uncontrollably. The smell of Natram-zar's burning flesh hung in the air. "If the liveryman's story differs from yours I'll put every part of your body in the flames, piece by piece. Now tell me! Why did Caldor want Trella killed?"

"He said it was for the good of Orak. I don't know why." Natram-zar saw the black look on Eskkar's face and screamed again. "I don't know! I asked, but that's all he would tell me. I swear it." The man began to sob.

Eskkar had no doubt that he spoke the truth. "When did all this happen?" He had to shake the man hard to stop the sobbing. "Tell me the day and the hour!"

"Three days ago, Noble . . . in the tavern of Dadaius. I swear it. He gave me the gold and told me never speak to him again. Only Loki, when he brought the silver for the horse."

Eskkar asked a few more questions. The man had lived in Orak for less than two months, avoiding the work gangs and living off his wits and his knife.

Leaving Natram-zar hanging there, Eskkar walked over to the nobles. They looked ashen-faced after watching the torture, their fear plainly visible. Their guards remained in the street outside. The nobles were at Eskkar's mercy. He could kill all of them, and no man would protest.

"Not pleasant to watch, is it, Nobles? A man tortured for information. It's easy to sit in a tavern and pay someone to murder, but not to watch death take a man. And it takes a special coward to pay for the murder of a woman."

They flinched at his words, but he no longer cared what they thought of him. He stepped in front of Nicar. "Where is Caldor, Nicar?"

Nicar appeared incapable of speech, just shaking his head.

Eskkar turned to Sisuthros. "Find Caldor. If he's not in

the street outside, he's probably at home. And the servant, Loki. Make sure you search Nicar's house thoroughly. There may be hiding places within the walls or floors. Tear it down if you have to, but find him."

Nicar tried to protest, stepping toward Eskkar, but Gatus shoved him back so hard that he bounced off the side of the house. "Stay where you are, Noble. Unless you wish to join your friend over there."

Eskkar knew how fond Gatus was of Trella. The old soldier would be more than willing to kill anyone who'd tried to hurt her.

"Bantor, make sure nobody leaves the village, and keep the extra guards on the walls all night. I want a horse patrol to ride out first thing in the morning to run down whoever held the horse. We'll get his name from Natramzar. I want him caught. Have the trackers ride out at first light."

"Well, Nobles," Eskkar faced them again, "is there anyone else who knows anything about this among you?" He stood directly in front of Corio. "Answer me!"

"Captain, I swear I know nothing about this. I like Trella, you know that. I would never try to hurt her."

Eskkar repeated the question before the others, getting the same answer, until he came to Nestor. "Well, Noble Nestor, what of you? Do you know anything about this?"

Nestor shook his head. "Captain, I know nothing about this. Nothing, I swear it by all the gods. I would never harm Trella."

Staring into Nestor's eyes and trying to read his thoughts, Eskkar felt tempted to believe him. The man hadn't said anything to deny that he might bribe a man to kill the captain of the guard, but Trella was a different story.

Disgusted with them all, Eskkar stepped away. He wanted to think, and it would take a while before they found Caldor. He turned to his men. "Keep them here. Gatus, come with me."

Eskkar left the nobles standing there while he went into the house, Gatus following. Inside, he stopped and gripped the old soldier's arm. "Watch them, Gatus. I don't want any of them speaking to each other or sending messages to anyone. Have your men with them at all times."

Gatus nodded and returned to watch over the nobles.

Inside the house, Eskkar found the big dining table cleared. The servants had finished washing it down, and now they scrubbed the blood from the floor. They looked up as Eskkar entered but his grim face turned their eyes quickly back to their work.

Eskkar ran up the stairs to the bedroom. Ventor and Annok-sur sat perched on stools on either side of the bed. To his surprise, Trella had regained consciousness. Her eyes turned to him.

Her guardians rose and left the room, leaving him alone with Trella.

Eskkar took Ventor's place on the stool and picked up Trella's hand, trying to keep his from shaking. "Are you in much pain?" He leaned down and kissed her cheek.

She smiled. Her voice sounded weak but steady. "It's not so bad, husband. Now I know what a warrior feels from his wounds. Your hand shakes, Eskkar. Is something else wrong?"

"Nothing is wrong, Trella. We caught the man who did this. Just a common thief hired to do murder. Caldor paid him ten gold coins, plus a fine horse, to kill you. I should have killed both him and Nestor as soon as I returned to Orak."

He shook his head in disgust at his failure. "We're searching for Caldor, and we'll find him soon. No man will risk hiding him, and the village is sealed."

Her eyes closed for a moment, and her next words surprised him. "Poor Nicar, to endure this. He knew nothing of this, I'm sure. Don't hurt Nicar, Eskkar. You need him."

Eskkar shook his head. "This will cause a blood feud between us. Caldor dies tonight and Nicar will never forgive his death. Better that he and his family go the way of Drigo. No one in Orak cares. None will deny me my revenge."

"We need men like Nicar and his son, Lesu. They're good men and must not die over Caldor's foolishness. Find some way to avoid killing Caldor."

Her eyes closed before he could protest, but Eskkar knew she was thinking, so he waited, holding her hand.

She opened her eyes and began to speak. He had to lean closer to hear her words. When she finished, he looked at her. "It may not work, but I'll try."

A knock on the door made him look up. Ventor stood in the doorway. "Let her sleep, Captain. She needs to rest now."

Trella tried to speak, but Eskkar leaned down and kissed her lips gently. "Rest, as the healer commands. You're safe now, and I'll be with you soon."

He left the chamber and went downstairs, turning into the kitchen and asking the cook for wine and something to eat. Eskkar sat on a stool at the small cutting table for a long time, ignoring the wine and the cheese placed before him. Everyone in the house feared to speak to him.

He remained there unmoving until cries from the courtyard announced Sisuthros had returned. Rising, he found Maldar and Bantor waiting outside the kitchen, standing silently in the main room.

"Did they find him?" was all Eskkar asked as they went out. In the torchlight, he saw Nicar on a stool someone had given him, his head slumped forward in his hands. Corio looked up, saw Eskkar in the doorway, and shook his head in disbelief.

The soldiers dragged two men toward him, their hands bound—Caldor and Loki.

Nicar's younger son had blood on his face and a cut above his eye. Loki's face showed fear. A mere servant, he had no powerful father to protect him. The crowd's hate would frighten anyone.

One of the soldiers grabbed Caldor and threw him to the ground, while another kicked the legs out from under Loki. Both twisted about in the dirt, trying to get back to their knees.

Sisuthros stepped forward, a grin on his face. "Here they are, Captain. Caldor was hiding in a secret room in the cellar. Loki tried to get away over the back wall. Nicar's guards tried to stop us from entering and I had to kill one." Fresh blood stained Sisuthros's arm and tunic.

Eskkar moved closer and looked down at the two men, his face expressionless.

Caldor saw his father held back by guards. "Father, help me! Don't let them do this!"

"Bantor, take Caldor into the house," said Eskkar. "Keep him quiet. If he makes a sound, break something."

Bantor's men grinned as they scooped Caldor up and dragged him into the house, one of them clapping a hand over his mouth to keep him silent.

Eskkar turned his attention to Loki, a man of thirty seasons who'd probably been Caldor's servant from his youth. "Bring him around back."

Soldiers dragged the terrified servant to the back of the house where Natram-zar still dangled from the tree, unconscious, blood oozing from his mouth. One of the soldiers had probably knocked the man out to stop the screaming.

Loki saw the man's genitals burnt black and caught the smell of burning flesh that lingered in the air.

"Bring the nobles closer." Eskkar waited until the five men approached, each escorted by one of Gatus's men. Eskkar grabbed Loki by his hair and twisted it savagely so the servant stared directly at Natram-zar.

"Look closely, Loki. This is what awaits you, if you don't speak the truth. We know what happened. Natram-zar told us everything. Now you'll tell us everything you know about the attack on Trella. One hesitation, one lie, and we'll put you in Natram-zar's place, and you'll suffer an even worse fate." He pushed the man hard, and Loki fell to the ground.

"Look at me, Loki, and remember. One lie . . . one hesitation. Now, start at the beginning and tell me everything."

Loki's breath came fast, the shallow breathing of a man in great fear who can no longer control his emotions. He looked beseechingly at Nicar. "Noble Nicar, please help me. I didn't do anything. I just . . ."

"Strip him and tie him to the tree. Bring more wood for the fire." Eskkar wasn't going to waste time with the servant, not with Caldor waiting inside. But Loki twisted free as the men tried to lift him and threw himself at Eskkar's feet. "No,

please, Noble! I'll tell you everything, everything! . . . I'm
sorry! . . . I'm sorry!"

Eskkar ignored his cries as the men cut Loki's clothes off.
Others untied Natram-zar, then fastened Loki in his place.
Loki screamed when a soldier brought more fuel, dumping
fresh coals on the fire.

The soldier fanned the embers with the shard until the
flames rose up again. Then he picked up the bowl and moved
it under Loki's legs. Another man tossed more wood chips
into the fire, as guards took position on either side of the
helpless prisoner.

Loki cried out, then began to urinate uncontrollably as
his body twitched from side to side. The flames hissed from
the man's piss, but kept burning. Loki's eyes were wide with
terror and his voice shrill with panic as he begged for
mercy.

"Add more wood," Eskkar ordered. "Make it burn hotter."

"Caldor made me do it, Noble." Loki's voice sounded
frantic. "It was Caldor. He paid Natram-zar ten gold pieces
to kill her. He wanted her dead . . . he wanted her dead."

The soldier looked up at Eskkar.

"Wait."

In a broken voice, Loki's story came out with scarcely
any prompting. The amount of gold, the silver for the horse,
the meetings with Natram-zar in the tavern, Loki knew it
all. The details matched the assassin's story. None could
doubt it now. Caldor was guilty, and every man in the courtyard knew it. When Loki finished, he sagged against the
ropes, tears running down his cheeks.

"Gag him, then bring out Caldor," Eskkar ordered. "It's
time we heard his story." When Bantor dragged Caldor from
the house the soldiers let out a roar of curses as they demanded his death. The sound echoed against the walls,
carrying to those crowding the street.

They dragged Caldor before Eskkar and again shoved
him to his knees, his hands still tied behind him.

"Silence!" Eskkar roared, then waited until everyone
quieted down. It became as quiet as death and his words carried throughout the courtyard. "Caldor, we've spoken with

Natram-zar and with Loki. They told us everything. About the gold, the horse, the plan. It's all out in the open. Now it's your turn to speak, or you'll replace Loki on the tree. Tell me why you wanted to kill Trella."

Caldor looked at his father, held upright by two guards, more to keep him from falling than to restrain him. "Father, this . . . it's all lies! I did nothing, nothing. Tell them, father." Caldor's voice sounded high and shrill, like a child's, as he realized for the first time in his life that even his father might not save him.

Eskkar turned toward Nicar, who stood ashen-faced at the horror facing him. The mob and soldiers would demand his son's death, and now Nicar must fear the same fate for himself and his House.

"Tell them, my son." Nicar forced each word from his lips. "Tell them the truth and save yourself from the torture."

"I didn't do anything, Father, it must have been Loki who did it! He wanted Trella from when she was in our house. Loki . . . it was Loki!"

Strangled sounds came from the gagged Loki as he heard his young master blame him. Loki twisted and struggled, but the men and ropes held him fast.

Eskkar's anger flared and he grasped Caldor by the hair. "Where did Loki get ten gold coins, Caldor? And twelve for the horse? Did Loki have that much gold, and would he spend it simply to see a woman die? Do you pay your servant that much?"

A sound of satisfaction went through the courtyard as the soldiers saw how easily their commander had caught Caldor in his lies.

"Please, Eskkar, please spare my son." Nicar begged as his son knelt in the dirt, trying to find words to answer. "We'll give you gold . . . leave Orak . . . do anything you want. Please spare his life, Noble Eskkar."

Nicar had never used the honorific toward him before, but Eskkar ignored the words. "Should I spare his life so he can try again to kill Trella, or give more money to Sisuthros to betray me?"

A gasp went through the soldiers, all eyes turning to Sisuthros. "Yes, it's true," Eskkar went on. "Caldor gave another bag of gold to Sisuthros and promised more for my death. But Sisuthros came to me and told me about it. I should have killed Caldor, but I thought the young fool would learn his lesson and behave himself."

While Eskkar spoke, Sisuthros reached into his belt and drew out the small pouch that contained Caldor's gold. Opening it, he flung the coins in the dirt at Caldor's feet.

Caldor's terror was complete now. "Father, please! She's only a slave! Give him silver, no, gold to satisfy him!"

Nicar's son knew the customs of the village. If a man injured another man's slave, or even killed him, the usual penalty was ten silver coins. "He can buy ten women better than her! I can't die over a slave! Please, Father! Please! . . ." His voice trailed off.

"You fool, Caldor!" Nicar, his face red with anger as he twisted helplessly in the guard's arms, shouted the words at his son. "She's not a slave! Eskkar freed her before he left the village, witnessed in secret before myself and Corio. They were married by the priest in Ishtar's temple. She's his wife!"

Everyone looked at Eskkar in astonishment.

"Let him go," Eskkar said to the guards holding Nicar's arms.

Nicar stood there, swaying on his feet. Then he stepped forward and struck his son across the face, a hard blow that knocked him backward off his knees. "You foolish child! You've tried to kill a free woman, not a slave." Nicar struggled to catch his breath. He looked ready to collapse.

"Nicar." Eskkar stepped toward him. The soldiers waited for the order that would slay Caldor and his father. "Nicar, you've shown nothing but respect for me and Trella. I gave you my word to defend Orak because I saw how much the village means to you. So I'll spare your life, even the life of your foolish son."

Eskkar glanced around at the soldiers, who listened in shock to his words. "Instead, I'll leave Orak. If the Families want to get rid of me so badly, I'll save them the trouble. As soon as Trella can ride, we're leaving Orak. You can defeat the barbarians yourself, or not. It will mean nothing to me. If any wish to follow me, they are welcome."

He turned toward Bantor. "Release Nicar's child," he said scornfully, then turned again to face Nicar. "Now go. Take your gold and hope by all the gods that I never see your son again."

Bantor didn't move. No one moved. No one said anything as the moments passed by. Even Nicar stood frozen, until Caldor's voice broke the spell.

"Yes, Father, yes! Take me home. Let the barbarian go! Let him go!"

Gatus slapped his hand on his sword. "By Marduk, I'll go with you! I'll not fight for cowards who would stab a woman in the back. But first I'll take care of this little shit." He pulled the weapon from its sheath and stepped toward Caldor.

Eskkar blocked Gatus. "No. Put your sword away."

Bantor spoke. "I, too, will go with you." He stepped past Eskkar and used his foot to push Caldor back down. "And any of the men who want to fight."

Sisuthros joined in, and his voice rose up over all the others. "We'll all go! We don't need Orak. We can build our own village to the west with Eskkar as our leader. Better to build and battle for our own than to fight for cowards and murderers."

A roar of assent went up, echoing off the courtyard walls into the night sky. Swords flashed in the torchlight. The men called out Eskkar or Trella's name, others shouted "death to Caldor."

Outside the courtyard, men took up the cry. Dozens had listened from the edge of the garden, hanging over the top of the wall to see and hear what went on. But others joined in, repeating the shouts from the courtyard, without fully understanding what had happened.

Eskkar stood there. He could scarcely believe what he heard. Never had he seen such emotion, such loyalty. No leader, no war chief, no village noble had ever been cheered like this. Right now, these men would follow him anywhere, do anything he said. He could lead a migration of his own. With nearly four hundred fighting men, they could go where they pleased and take what they wanted. This was power—suddenly he understood—real power, not the kind that one buys with gold. And he realized something else—that he ruled in Orak now. The soldiers and the villagers had given him the power.

Another voice had risen up, trying to be heard over the din. Corio pushed away from his guard and the master builder raised his arms high, asking to speak. Eskkar bellowed over the shouting, demanding silence.

It took time before it was quiet enough for Corio's words to be heard. "Soldiers! Villagers! Listen, I beg you! Eskkar must not go. You must not go! You need not go! The customs of Orak condemn Caldor, not the hand of Eskkar. His evil deed sentences him to death for attempting to kill a free woman. Is that not so, Nobles?"

Corio turned sharply toward the heads of the other Families still clustered together, dread visible on their faces. "Is that not so?" Corio shouted the question at the top of his lungs, his anger and fear putting force into his words. "Answer me!"

Rebba stepped forward, his eyes darting nervously around the courtyard: "Death to Caldor!" The phrase was repeated by Decca, then Nestor—"Death to Caldor."

Only Nicar remained, staring down at his son, until Corio's hand gripped Nicar's shoulder and shook him hard, forcing him to lift his eyes. He stared dully at Corio, as if he didn't even recognize him.

"Death to Caldor." Nicar's words could barely be heard.

The courtyard erupted. Swords flashed in the torchlight and everyone screamed the words, "Death to Caldor!" over and over.

Again Corio held up his hands for silence. "All have agreed. Take him to the market and stone him to death. Take all of them. Walk them through the streets and proclaim their guilt to everyone. Let Lady Trella be avenged. Let the women stone them."

A deafening roar burst from the crowd.

"Wait. Let me speak." Eskkar's words stopped the soldiers

before they rushed off. "Do you want me to stay and fight the barbarians?"

Another roar went up, repeated from the street, "Stay! . . . Stay . . . Stay!" They repeated the words without ceasing.

The soldiers went wild now. Their bloodlust had spread to the crowd in the street. Nothing would stop them.

Eskkar turned and jerked Caldor to his feet. He had to shout to make himself heard, his face close to the boy's blanching face. "You'll die slowly, Caldor, as you deserve, and when you're dead, I'll place your head at Trella's feet, right here in this garden. You should have listened to your father."

Two Hawk Clan soldiers pulled Caldor out of Eskkar's hands. Other soldiers cut Natram-zar down from the tree and dragged a screaming Loki toward the gate.

"Gatus! Make sure it's done right. Then bring me his head. I promised it to Trella."

"No! Mercy! Father, help me!"

Gatus shoved Caldor into the hands of his men, the action unleashing another roar to the heavens. Half pushed, half dragged, they led Caldor through the courtyard. Many took the opportunity to strike at his head or shoulders. Another roar went up as they reached the street. The crowd screamed for his death.

In moments the courtyard had emptied itself. Eskkar heard the crowd's progress as it began the journey down the streets of Orak. The victims would be shown to all. Looking around, Eskkar found himself alone. No one had stayed behind. All wanted to see the men die.

Eskkar trod back into the house and found that empty, too. Even the servants had joined the mob, screaming for blood and wanting to see the execution. He thought about going up to see how Trella was doing but decided to wait awhile. Emotionally drained, he went into the kitchen and sank tiredly back onto the stool. He felt weak. The wine and cheese remained on the table, untouched.

Draining the wine, Eskkar refilled the cup. He forced himself to take a bite of the goat cheese, which he could hardly taste and barely swallow.

He managed as best he could. Caldor would die, though not as slowly or painfully as Eskkar wanted. There might be a chance to make peace with Nicar.

Eskkar had learned a hard lesson, one he would never forget. From now on, anyone who plotted against him would die quickly. He'd never give any man such an opportunity again. Like a fool, he'd thought the danger to himself gone when he returned to Orak, with the barbarians only weeks away. Instead, Caldor had struck at Trella.

Eskkar thought of his woman lying upstairs. Now everyone knew she'd been freed, that he'd taken her for his wife. Despite her objections, he'd insisted on freeing her and marrying her before he left. She would act the slave no longer. He was glad of that.

18

Eskkar found Trella dressed, sitting on her stool and combing her hair. Only seven days since the stabbing, she was ignoring the advice of Ventor and everyone else in the household. He stood in their bedroom doorway. Her face lacked color, either from the injury or confinement indoors, and she had to move slowly so as not to disturb the bandages, but other than that, she looked remarkably well. The young heal quickly. She had just passed into her fifteenth season.

He enjoyed watching her comb her hair. Perhaps because the long tresses were her most beautiful feature, or because she obviously enjoyed the task. She saw his reflection in her tiny silver mirror and smiled, but the determined look stayed in her eyes. She would not return to bed.

When she tried to change hands, Eskkar saw a moment of pain on her face. He moved to her side and took the comb. "Let me help you. You don't want to open up your wound." It gave him pleasure to run the comb awkwardly through her hair, using his other hand to guide and straighten the wavy strands. He'd never combed another woman's hair, thinking it unfit for a man. Now he no longer cared what anyone else might think.

"You don't make a good handmaiden, Eskkar," she said, smiling to show her appreciation. "I'll have Annok-sur finish it."

"My hands are clumsy," he agreed, putting down the comb. "You should not be out of bed yet. The healer said . . ."

"I know what Ventor said. I was here when he said it. But the wound has closed, and there's no need for me to stay in bed like an old woman. Besides, I have a gift for you."

"A gift?" Presents were rare among the villagers, but even rarer among barbarians. "What kind of gift?" He couldn't keep the interest out of his voice.

"One you'll like. I was going to have it on the table when you came home this evening, but now you'll have to get it yourself. It's under the bed."

Puzzled, he stooped beside the bed. At first he didn't see it, the shadows blending with the dark material. As soon as he touched it, he knew what it was, and he brought it out from under the bed, then unwrapped it. A magnificent bronze sword glinted against the black cloth.

He held it up to the light, turning it this way and that, amazed by its feel and how it seemed to merge with his hand. Esskar had never seen such a blade, forged so fine that it seemed a single edge from tip to pommel. The bronze metal looked darker than usual, except at the edge, where the sharpener's wheel gave it a brighter glint that reflected the sunlight.

The hilt, encased in hardwood and criss-crossed by tough leather strips to improve the grip, was longer and wider than usual, to better balance the long blade's weight. The pommel, a simple large ball of bronze, looked hard enough to crush a skull. His eyes returned to the blade. Though wider and thicker than his old sword, the weight was less, with a shallow groove down the center for a blood channel. The guard differed, too, with a strip of slightly angled metal designed to protect the hand, but flat enough to allow the weapon to be carried comfortably across the back.

"By the gods, Trella, what a weapon! I've never seen such workmanship before. Where did it come from? What did it cost?" Esskar swung the blade through the air. A true horseman's weapon, meant more for slashing than thrusting.

She smiled at him, like a mother watching a child play

with a new toy. "Master Asmar made it right here in Orak. Do you remember our meeting with him?"

Eskkar remembered it all too well. They'd called on Master Swordmaker Asmar to inquire about weapons for Orak. To his embarrassment, Eskkar discovered he knew even less about metal smithing than he did about bows. He hadn't known bronze weapons were a new improvement, a method of working with metals less than a hundred years old.

Asmar had sighed, then explained that with the discovery of bronze, the sword became the warrior's preferred weapon, replacing club or axe. Before that, swords had been made of copper. But copper weapons were soft, didn't hold an edge, and tended to shatter, so fighting men continued to rely on more dependable weapons. Bronze changed all that. A far harder metal, bronze kept its sharp edge, and a bronze blade could cut right through a copper one.

Daggers and knives, weapons not intended for use against metal, were still made of copper. But copper swords were rare now.

How the ores were discovered, mined, and turned into metal, how that metal was forged, beaten, and shaped, the entire swordmaking art proved a mystery to Eskkar. He hadn't known bronze could only be made by combining specific amounts of copper and tin, and that these elements required the work of many slaves to dig the veins of metal from the earth. The two ores, each soft and flexible alone, could then be heated and combined. The resulting molten metal was poured into a mold where it cooled into the desired shape, hardening in the process into a metal far stronger than either of its original parts.

"Yes, I remember Asmar. I remember I had to spend the whole day listening to him and watching him work his magic so the next time someone spoke of swordmaking, I'd understand what they were saying." After that, Eskkar promised himself to never again take any craftsman's trade for granted. He'd learned more than just the Mystery of Bronze.

"This sword seems cast for my own hand. When did Asmar find time to make such a master blade?"

Asmar and his family labored all day and long into the

night, often working by the light of their forges, to produce all the swords, lance tips, arrowheads, and battle-axes Orak needed. Every day smoke from Asmar's fires rose into the sky, as he and his helpers created weapons.

His battle-axes, easier and cheaper to make, remained a favorite of many. With its simple bronze blade attached to a wooden handle, it would be very useful in defending the wall. While a sword took months to master, a villager could be trained to swing an axe in a few days.

"I told him to make you a new sword," Trella answered, "one befitting the man who would save Orak. Asmar said he'd already begun working on a master weapon, but it would take many months and be very expensive. We haggled over the price, but he finally lowered his demands."

Leave it to Trella to bargain down the cost. Eskkar hefted the sword again, and itched to test it against the training posts. He remembered his manners in time.

"This gift, it's the most valuable thing I've ever owned, and I have no words to express my thanks."

Her smile vanished. "The cost is nothing if it saves your life. Take it with you when you ride across the river. That's why I gave it to you today, so you can test its strength.

"But, remember, the sword is nothing and another can always be made. Don't do anything foolish because you have it. It's only a lump of metal. If the sword helps you return safely, it will have achieved its only purpose."

He nodded, remembering those he'd seen die because they'd grown too attached to one weapon or another. "I'll use it well, Trella."

Eskkar tossed the weapon on the bed and took her in his arms. "Now, how can I thank you? Perhaps you could return to your bed, as the healer ordered, and I could show you how much I appreciate your gift."

"I don't think I would get much rest, and there is much to do. Besides, I thought you would be glad to see me up and around." She turned back to her table and sat down.

"I like you better in bed," he said, moving his hand to the back of her neck and rubbing the muscles there with both hands. "You give me much less talk and much more pleasure though you moan and cry out loud enough to wake the dead."

She leaned back against him, her head resting on his hip. "If you like, I will return to bed, husband. And try to be quiet."

Standing over her, he saw her left breast inside the loose dress, uplifted by the bandage that passed under it, and the sight still excited him. It was the hour of noon, and everyone was taking their meal. But he didn't want to do anything that might slow her healing. "Perhaps later, after you've changed the dressing." He kissed the top of her head. "And you need not worry about being quiet."

"I will try to wait until tonight." She straightened up and turned back to her mirror. "Now, what took you away from your training?"

"Jalen has returned from across the river." Esskar had sent the man out to find a suitable place to ambush the barbarians. "He was surprised to hear what happened. Jalen offers prayers for your speedy recovery. He joins us tonight for dinner."

"Did he find a suitable place?" Jalen's mission interested Trella far more than his prayers.

"He thinks so. We'll talk about that tonight." Esskar sat down on the edge of the bed.

"Do you think the barbarians will come soon?" She might have been asking about the weather.

"The main host is moving faster. They'll be here in less than a month."

"Must you go across the river?" Now she sounded like a soldier's wife, fretting about her husband, worrying that he must risk his life in some minor skirmish when he'd be needed for the great battle before the walls.

They'd had this discussion before. "Yes, from what Jalen tells me." He hesitated. "I'll wait a few more days, in case Mesilim can get through."

He worried more about that than he admitted. Mesilim should have sent word by now if he were coming. The noose had started closing around Orak, and fewer people came asking for shelter or transport across the river.

In another week, it would be too late for Mesilim to come at all. Eskkar's men had begun burning the fields and crops, riding as close to the barbarians as they dared, then falling back, torching everything behind them. The Alur Meriki would find little to sustain man or beast when they arrived. And the villagers' lives would depend on the grain and livestock sent across the river, at least until the next harvest.

"What else troubles you, husband?"

She could tell when something bothered him. "Nicar wishes to speak to me . . . to us. He sent a messenger asking if he could meet with us today. I haven't yet sent a reply."

Eskkar hadn't seen or spoken to Nicar since Caldor's death. The father had stood there, hands over his eyes, as they stoned his son to death. Gatus had to protect Nicar from the wrath of the crowd that cried out for his blood.

"It must be a terrible thing to watch your child die." For a moment Trella seemed lost in thought. "What should we say to him?"

He'd come to ask her that very question. But he sat there and thought about what would be best for Orak, for himself, and for Nicar. After Trella's attack, he'd considered banishing Nicar and his family, despite Trella's advice, but now he knew that would be a mistake. Orak needed men like Nicar, open-minded, fair men who could deal honestly with people.

"We must find a way to make peace between us, Trella. But how we can accomplish that, with blood shed on both sides? A blood feud can only be settled with blood."

"There must be no more blood shed, especially from the noble families. Besides, we owe so much to Nicar. He raised you up to captain of the guard, stood by you when Drigo was killed, and convinced the other Families to give you the gold you needed and to submit to your orders. He gave me to you so that I could help you. I think he was protecting me even then from Caldor."

"Perhaps he was afraid you would slip a knife in Caldor's ribs while he slept." Eskkar made a face. He couldn't contemplate the thought of Trella in Nicar's or anyone else's bed. "You're right. There's much we owe him. But how do we make peace?"

"What thoughts must be in Nicar's mind now? What will concern him the most?"

"Lesu! He will be worrying about his son," Eskkar said. Weeks before they'd put Lesu in charge of all the cattle, grain, and livestock taken across the river, along with thirty-five soldiers and forty armed villagers to herd and care for the animals. They'd established a camp in the hill country at least a hundred miles away. "Nicar dispatched a rider across the river six days ago, no doubt to carry the news about his brother. Perhaps Nicar comes to plead for his son's life."

"Yes, that's likely. But you mustn't let him plead or beg for anything. That would destroy his dignity. You must treat him with respect and we must assure him that he and his son will come to no harm." She reached over and took his hand. "Let's talk about what we will say."

The long summer sun still blazed in the afternoon sky when Nicar arrived. Eskkar had spoken to the household, and everyone greeted Nicar respectfully before escorting him upstairs. Eskkar and Trella were standing when Nicar entered. Eskkar bowed formally and offered Nicar one of three chairs arranged around the small table. Platters of fruits and dates rested on the table, along with a pitcher of wine.

Eskkar studied Nicar and saw a man who had aged greatly. Until now, Eskkar's hatred of Caldor had overshadowed any sympathy toward Nicar. But seeing him like this, Eskkar felt a pang of sorrow for the man.

The man who'd been the most powerful in Orak now knew that all his wealth couldn't bring back his influence. Caldor's deed had weakened his father's authority, and the barbarian invasion would change the foundations of village life. The new Orak would be very different from the old. Nicar sat awkwardly for a moment until Trella spoke.

"Noble Nicar, the loss of your son must pain you greatly. If there's anything we can do, please tell us. We need your help in the coming days."

Nicar stared at her for a moment, then looked at Eskkar. "Trella . . . Lady Trella, you seem much recovered. I am glad. I came to beg your forgiveness for what my son did." His head went down for a moment. "It was a weak and shameful act, the deed of a foolish child spoiled by his father. The fault was mine. I did not restrain him . . . didn't teach him to respect others . . ."

Trella reached out and touched his arm. "Nicar, there's no need to say such things. We understand. Without you, Eskkar and I wouldn't be here today. We owe you more than we can ever repay. But now we must think of the future. If we survive the battle, there are years of work ahead of us and we need your help."

"That night, the crowd wanted to kill me." Nicar turned to Eskkar. "Why did you have your men protect me? It would have been easier for you with me dead, my House broken. Each day since, I've waited for your revenge."

"Let there be no talk of revenge, Nicar," Eskkar answered, seeing things clearly now. "You've been nothing but honest with me. I put no blood feud between us. I know you had nothing to do with it. Caldor paid the price for his deed and that can be the end of it."

True enough, and Nicar hadn't known anything about it. If he had, the attempt would never have been made—or it would have been better planned and executed.

Nevertheless Eskkar couldn't stop from saying what he felt. "If Trella had been killed, it might have been different." If she'd died, he would have taken every drop of blood from Nicar and his family, then left their bodies to rot in the sun.

Nicar looked at both of them, almost as if seeing them for the first time. "You've changed much, Eskkar, since we first met. You've become a great leader. And Trella has become a noble woman, wise beyond her seasons. I failed to see what the rest of the villagers saw months ago when they first called her a great lady. And now I find mercy from you both." He shook his head as if all this were beyond his understanding.

"Do not talk of mercy, Nicar, only of friendship," Trella replied. "We need your wisdom. The village has changed greatly in the last few months. If the barbarians are driven off, we can never return to the old ways. Orak will become a great city, larger than any of us can imagine, and every man's hand will stretch out to take it as a prize. All will hear of Orak and come here for protection. Such a city must be governed by a strong ruler, and this ruler will need a wise council to advise him."

Nicar smiled wanly. "I'm sure as long as Eskkar has you at his side, Lady Trella, he'll need few others to advise him."

"There are many people in Orak, Nicar," Eskkar said, "and more will come in the years ahead. You told me once that you built Orak and you wanted it to last. Because of your will, I stayed to fight. But many hands will be needed in the future to make your dream come true, and the customs and laws of the village must be more than the whims of the Five Families."

Eskkar took a breath. "I ask for your help, Nicar, help to make Orak into a great city for all the people who will dwell here, including your own family."

"I give my help gladly and that of my son, Lesu. He's a good man and grows in wisdom each day. There will be no blood feud between our families, I swear it." Nicar paused for a moment. "What is my future?"

Trella had prepared Eskkar for this question. "Tomorrow the three of us will walk the streets of Orak together. That way all can see that there is no anger between us, and that you remain an important voice in Orak's defense. Once the barbarians are upon us, the people will have other things to think about."

"And afterward," Trella added, "they'll remember only your good works in their behalf."

Nicar seemed much moved by their words. He stood up and bowed. "You're right, Eskkar. I'd forgotten about Orak and its future. That is more important than anything else. And now, Captain . . . Lady Trella . . . I thank all the gods that you're both here in Orak."

After Nicar had gone, Eskkar left word that they were not to be disturbed, then bolted the door to the outer room.

"So I am to be the strong ruler of Orak. When did you

decide that, wife?" As he said the words, he picked her up in his arms and carried her into the bedroom.

"I did not want your head to swell too greatly," she answered with a smile as he helped her remove her dress. "Nicar had to be told what his place will be. He'll be grateful now and give you his support." She breathed a sigh of pleasure as Eskkar began to run his hands over her body, carefully avoiding the bandaged areas. "And with Nestor terrified of his own plots, he, too, will support you. Along with Corio, who rises in importance every day and owes everything he has to you, there should be no problems from the Families. For a while, at least."

"Then be quiet, girl, and let's begin working on the Sixth Family."

19

Under the noonday sun, sweat covered Eskkar's half-naked body. Calluses had formed on his hand to match the grip of his new sword, and in five days he'd shattered half a dozen posts. The fine blade kept a sharp edge, and its weight now felt natural to him. His muscles rippled under his tanned skin. Nothing remained of the soft village life. He'd never been as strong and fit in his life.

Jalen stood breathing hard on the other side of the training post. Each man countered the other's moves. But instead of striking at each other, the thick wooden beam took the brunt of the parries, thrusts and hacks. Any barbarian who made the mistake of thinking them easy victims would not live long enough to regret his error.

A horse galloping toward them made them look up. No one ran a horse in the crowded streets, unless on urgent matters. As the rider dismounted in a swirl of dust, Eskkar saw the Hawk Clan emblem on his chest.

"Captain, I've word from Sisuthros. He's met the Ur Nammu and asks that you come at once."

Eskkar muttered thanks to the gods. Time was running out and he had to take a force across the river in a few days, with or without the Ur Nammu. But if they could help . . .

"Well done, Ugarde. Find yourself another horse. We'll leave at once." He turned to Jalen. "Get ten men ready to ride." They needed the extra men. Barbarian patrols might be encountered anywhere.

Eskkar checked his new sword, making sure the edge was still keen, then wiped it down with a rag. So far no tarnish spots had developed. Eventually tarnish would cover the blade completely, though Asmar claimed the metal would only become stronger as a result.

At the well Eskkar washed himself down before drinking deeply. He dressed in his leather vest and cap despite the heat. Then he dispatched a messenger to inform Gatus and Trella where he was going.

They rode out of Orak at a gallop, riding the last horses remaining in the village. Four hours of steady riding across the countryside found them many miles from Orak. Riding slower now to conserve the horses, their eyes constantly searched hilltops and horizons looking for dust clouds that might indicate either a friendly patrol or a hostile war party.

Instead they found another Hawk Clan rider coming toward them at an easy canter. He told them that Sisuthros followed only a dozen miles behind. They kept riding, and soon saw four riders approaching them.

They met near a stand of rock that rose above the tall grass. One rider proved to be an Ur Nammu warrior. The man appeared near exhaustion and every rib showed on his chest. He rode a thin pony that looked more spent than its master.

Eskkar dismounted and extended his hand in greeting. He remembered the tribesman from the camp, but hadn't spoken with him and didn't recall his name.

"Greetings, Eskkar, war leader of Orak," the man began formally. "I'm Fashod, sent by Mesilim, to learn if you still seek our aid."

"I welcome a warrior brother, as I welcome the Ur Nammu. We've food and drink for you, but first, tell me of Mesilim. He's well?"

"Yes, but all are weary and the horses grow weaker each day. As soon as it grows dark, the Ur Nammu will slip past the last of the Alur Meriki patrols," he paused to spit on the ground at the mention of the name, "to join you in your fight. I've shown war leader Sisuthros where they will cross. Now I must inform Mesilim that you await his arrival."

"Your news is good, Fashod, but first you must rest. We've food and water."

Sisuthros, Esskar, and Fashod sat together on the sand, apart from the rest of the men, most of whom had never seen a barbarian this close. Jalen stayed with the soldiers and kept reminding them not to stare. Fashod drank thirstily from one of the water skins, then devoured two days' worth of the bread Esskar's men carried.

"That horse doesn't look strong enough to make it back," Sisuthros commented. "It's been pushed for a long time."

Esskar nodded. A few weeks of hard riding could finish most horses. He'd noticed the animal, too, and it started him thinking. "Fashod, take one of our horses in exchange. You may need a strong beast tonight."

Fashod looked at each man in turn. Until now he'd been polite but aloof, doing his duty as his clan leader ordered it and nothing more. The offer of a horse, even for a temporary exchange, was a significant gesture. He put down his food and wiped his mouth with the back of his arm. "Chief Esskar, I thank you. My mount is a good one and needs only a few days' rest and grass to recover."

"Finish your food and drink," Esskar said, as he climbed to his feet, thinking the animal would need at least a week to recover. "I'll go and see to the horse."

Returning to where Jalen waited, he told him about the horse swap. "Pick someone small who can walk and ride Fashod's horse back to Orak. Get him started at once. Otherwise he'll get left behind if we have to run."

Esskar glanced back at Fashod. "Jalen, I want you to return at once to Orak. If all the Ur Nammu are as bad off as this man, they're going to need weapons, food, and fresh horses if they're to fight at all. Tell Trella and Gatus what they need."

Jalen nodded, and went off to choose a horse for the exchange.

Eskkar returned to Fashod. "A horse will be ready soon, along with extra food. Tell Mesilim we await him here, to escort him to Orak."

."Mesilim will be pleased," Fashod said.

Jalen came over, leading a horse stripped down to the halter. Fashod gathered his weapons and the food, and galloped off to the east. A few moments later, Jalen cantered in the opposite direction, quickly passing one of his men who'd started walking Fashod's horse on the same path.

"Mesilim and his men may be finished," Sisuthros remarked. "He would've sent one of his best men to find us. They may not be of much use to us after all."

Eskkar had the same grim thought. "Maybe. We'll see what Mesilim has learned. Besides, it can only help to have thirty or so horsemen protecting our rear. And tired or not, they'll kill at least that many before they're finished."

The Ur Nammu didn't arrive until long after midnight and even in the moonlight they looked played out. Eskkar bade Mesilim rest while Orak's riders kept guard. At dawn they started moving west, though at a slow pace. Some Ur Nammu horses were going lame, and their riders spent as much time leading them as riding. Everyone kept looking behind, wondering when a horde of Alur Meriki would appear.

Eskkar took stock of Mesilim's band. Eskkar counted thirty-eight men, five women, and seven children of various ages riding forty-four horses. There were no infants or small children. Those would have been left behind to die or killed by their parents. Both men and beasts looked ready to drop. The exhausted children, eyes wide with hunger, looked as pitiful as the warriors. All would reach Orak none too soon.

Eskkar walked his horse between Mesilim and Subutai. From a captured Alur Meriki scout, Mesilim had learned much, and they'd watched the Alur Meriki raiding parties traveling south. For men trapped within an ever-shrinking circle around Orak, any information was welcome.

By nightfall they'd journeyed far enough away from danger and close enough to Orak that Eskkar began to relax. They made camp, and the Ur Nammu fell asleep as soon as they finished eating the last of the soldiers' food.

In the morning Eskkar gave half his men to Sisuthros and told him to return to his patrols. The extra men would help the subcommander begin the final burning. The Alur Meriki would reach Orak soon. Eskkar was determined that they find nothing of value in their path. Crops burned in every field. Houses, corrals, anything that would burn would be put to the torch. Only the wells remained untouched. With so many small streams and irrigation canals nearby, it would have done little good to contaminate wells by dumping dead animals into them. He hoped the Alur Meriki would leave them as clean when they moved on.

They topped the last hill ringing the plains around Orak at midafternoon. Everyone breathed a sigh of relief at the sight of the village's walls. During the day Eskkar had twice been challenged by patrols from the village. Bantor's men would take no chances on a barbarian band slipping through their midst.

The men and women riding behind Eskkar began to talk at the sight of Orak, its wall rising out of the earth. Even at this distance, they saw the gangs of men laboring before the wall, digging out the final stretch of the ditch.

None of the Ur Nammu had ever seen a village so large, nor a wall so strong and tall. To the north the flooding of the fields had begun. The south side would be flooded as soon as the Ur Nammu departed.

"Rest tonight, Mesilim. Tomorrow you can give me your advice as to how you would attack Orak."

Mesilim and his son stared at the village, impressed as much by its size as its wall.

"With all the people driven here by the Alur Meriki," Eskkar commented, "there are nearly three thousand people in Orak. More have crossed the river."

"Until now," Mesilim began, "I didn't believe you could resist the Alur Meriki. Now I see that you may have a chance."

"More than just a chance." Eskkar smiled with satisfaction. "There's much to show you."

They rode slowly toward the gate and as they neared the walls, the laborers paused to stare at the unusual group. Soon curious villagers crowded the walls. A few began cheering when they recognized Eskkar riding at the head of the small band of allies. Eskkar led them away from the main gate and guided Mesilim's people along the ditch that ran parallel to the south wall, then on until they reached the river.

As they paced their horses along, people kept shouting from the wall and waving their hands in greeting. The Ur Nammu seemed astonished at the sight and Eskkar realized that they hadn't given any thought about how they might be received by the villagers. When the little band reached the river, they turned once again. They'd camp alongside the wall at the river's edge, out of sight of anyone on the hilltops to the east.

An open space awaited them, with two water barrels, hay and grain for the horses, a great stack of firewood, and two bullocks on spits, already butchered and ready for roasting. A pile of blankets lay stacked beside the water barrels. A small rope corral would hold their horses, with fodder placed inside. The animals had sorely lacked grain in recent months.

Eskkar signaled their journey's end by dismounting. "Camp here, Mesilim. If there's anything you need, it will be provided. If you bathe in the river, be careful. The current is strong except along the water's edge. It can pull down a horse and rider even at this time of year. I'll return in a few hours."

He led his horse through the river gate and found Trella waiting for him. Two soldiers now guarded her at all times. He took her hand and they walked back to the house. Inside the courtyard, Trella went to fetch him clean clothes while he headed to the well to wash the dirt and horse smell from his body. By the time he'd finished, Trella rejoined him, a clean tunic and undergarment in her hands.

"I watched from the wall," she said. "As soon as you left, they rushed for the food and water. They must be nearly starving."

"They're in bad shape. They were lucky to get past the Alur Meriki's lines. But they've already paid their way with information. They captured an Alur Meriki messenger and tortured him until he told them all he knew. The messenger revealed that they plan to send a force across the river in four or five days' time. That means we'll have to meet them across the river soon. By then, warriors will be on the hills surrounding Orak. A few days later, they'll be ready to attack."

"You'll be back before then, I hope."

Her tone implied that he would be in more trouble with her than with the barbarian raiding party if he weren't.

"Yes, even if the ambush fails, I'll come straight back. I'll leave in three days. It will be a slow march north to the ambush site and we may need time to prepare. Did you make the preparations I requested?"

"We met with the craftsmen, and everything should be ready by noon tomorrow. But you didn't tell me they had women and children."

"There were so few of them, I didn't think it was important."

She looked at him, but Eskkar held up his hand. "I know, everything is important. But truly, they didn't mention them except in passing. Do they really matter?"

"Perhaps. But now there are more things I must do. Come inside. Supper is on the table."

"Yes, wife," he answered dutifully. Village women could prove a trial for their men. There were advantages to being a barbarian after all, especially when it came to dealing with women.

Two hours later Eskkar returned to the Ur Nammu camp dressed in his best tunic, but wearing his short sword, and accompanied by Jalen and Gatus, whom he introduced to Mesilim and Subutai.

Much had happened in the last hours. The horses had been fed, then led to the river to be washed and groomed. The men and women had taken their own baths, probably the first in many weeks. Their clothing had been soaked and scrubbed, and now was drying on their bodies.

The children had been fed, then wrapped in blankets. The littlest ones slept, their stomachs full for the first time in weeks. For the adults, food was now the main order of business. They gathered around the fires, eagerly slicing off chunks of roasting meat. Four wineskins had been provided, enough to give everyone a good drink, but not enough to get anyone drunk.

"I have some gifts, Mesilim," Eskkar began, as he and his men sat down a little away from the fires, facing Mesilim and Subutai. Eskkar motioned to Gatus, who placed a blanket on the ground between them and unwrapped it. Inside was a slim lance tipped with bronze, an arrow, a bowstring, and a sword.

Eskkar saw the confusion on Mesilim's face. "Your men have lost much equipment, so tomorrow you will have sixty lances such as this. Also, for each man, fifty arrows and five extra bowstrings, and as many swords and knives as you need."

Bowstrings always seemed to be breaking. As important as the bow itself, they proved even harder to come by in the field.

Subutai leaned over and picked up the arrow, eyeing it to make sure it was the proper size for their curved bows. "Your arrows are longer and heavier. Where did you get so many shafts this size?"

"We made them, Subutai. That is, they'll be finished by tomorrow evening. The fletchers started as soon as I sent word. The same with the lance. These are weapons for those who fight from horseback, and though we don't use such weapons ourselves, we can make them quickly now." That impressed them. It would have taken them weeks to make so many arrows.

"Whatever else you . . ." Eskkar's voice died away as Mesilim's eyes shifted from him. Turning, Eskkar saw a group of seven women approach the camp, two of them carrying torches now that dusk had fallen. Each woman carried a bundle or basket of various size and shape. Trella walked in their midst, wearing her finest dress and escorted by her guards, Annok-sur beside her, carrying one of the torches.

The torchlight procession had a strange effect on the tribesmen. They could see that a woman of importance was coming. Trella's fine dress and the guards conveyed that fact, as much as the obvious respect shown by the accompanying women. Conversation and eating ceased throughout the camp. Everyone rose to their feet in respect, an unusual gesture for such men.

The leading women stopped when they reached Eskkar's group and Trella passed through them to move to Eskkar's side. Once there, she bowed to the visitors, then turned to Eskkar.

He felt her effect as much as did the others. In the flickering torchlight she looked like one touched by the gods. Only the hissing and snapping of the torches broke the silence.

Eskkar found his voice and made the introductions.

She bowed low again, then straightened, erect and proud. "I welcome you to Orak, Clan Leader Mesilim, and your brave son, Subutai."

Eskkar translated her words, then nodded to her to continue.

"We honor your fight against our common enemy. My husband did not tell me you had women and children, so we had not prepared for them. Now we bring them gifts and clothing."

Trella's voice sounded serene and regal. Mesilim might not understand her words, but he clearly recognized her presence. He looked at her, as much at a loss for words as Eskkar had been a moment ago. Subutai stared at her with his mouth open.

"Honored wife, Trella," Mesilim began, "you honor us by your presence and your gifts. We welcome you to our campfire. Eskkar told us you were a 'gifted one,' but we did not expect you to visit us."

Trella glanced at Eskkar as he translated, and he read the question in her glance. "Gifted One?" she would say tonight, followed no doubt by the "everything is important" speech.

She bowed again to Mesilim. "Your visit honors us, as does your offer to help in our fight. How could I do less? Now, I must leave you to your talk while we tend to your women, if I have your leave?"

When she left, they sat back down. No one spoke for a moment. Eskkar saw Gatus struggling to keep a grin off his face. Trella did look and act as if she had the power to command both men and spirits. Perhaps it wasn't just superstition. Maybe she did have the gift, and maybe a group of barbarians could see it more clearly than Eskkar could.

They watched as she went to the women, but found herself surrounded by Mesilim's men. The Ur Nammu women had to push the men aside. Fashod stood at Trella's side, translating for her, then helped with the distribution of clothing and other gifts. The commotion went on for some time until the women led Trella and her companions away from the men. They sat a short distance from the fire, to talk about things that concerned women only.

Even Fashod stayed away, leaving one of the women to do the translating. Trella asked her guards to move back as well. After watching for a while, the tribesmen returned to the fire and their food, but their eyes often returned to Trella and the women, lighted now only by the flickering torches that began to burn low.

Mesilim shook his head and turned back to Eskkar and his men. "Never have I seen the women act like that, to take a stranger into their midst and pay honor to her. She truly has the gift, to move my people so easily."

"She's wise beyond her seasons," Eskkar added. "Her wisdom guides me and gives me strength."

Gatus spoke unexpectedly. "Her wisdom guides all of us, Mesilim. My wife, who has more than twice her seasons, stands at her side and heeds her every word."

Eskkar translated Gatus's words with another smile.

"Chief Eskkar, why do those men guard her?" Subutai inquired. "Surely no one would harm one with the gift."

Eskkar shook his head in disgust. "I have not been war

leader in Orak for long, Subutai. Two weeks ago, one of my enemies tried to kill her. He was angered at her wisdom and thought to attack me by killing her. She was wounded but survived, and now I make sure that it doesn't happen again."

"The clan responsible was killed?" Mesilim made it more of a statement than a question.

"All those involved died, slain by the people," Eskkar said carefully. "I don't think it will happen again." No sense trying to explain local politics to tribesmen who tended to see everything as white or black. Depending on the offense, barbarians might hold an entire clan responsible for the misdeed of one of its members.

"Nor will it," Gatus added firmly, after Eskkar explained Subutai's question. "Everyone has been warned."

"Guard her well, Eskkar," Subutai suggested. "If the Alur Meriki knew you had one such as her, they'd tear the walls down to take her."

Eskkar looked at him, reading beneath the man's words echoes of what Subutai himself might like to do. Eskkar felt surprised at his intuition. But where Trella was concerned, his eyes had become quick to see and his wits and words just as swift. "Subutai, such a gift cannot be taken by force. It must be given freely. An enemy cannot capture it, and a friend would never try."

"May her wisdom guide you, Eskkar," Mesilim said, bringing the conversation back to the matter at hand. "You'll need her help in the coming fight. Now let's talk about weapons."

They discussed the weapons and reviewed the plans for the next few days. They were almost finished when laughter coming from the women made all heads turn toward them again.

Trella stood now, holding hands with some of the tribeswomen, as all of them sought to touch her. Finally they released their clasp. Trella bowed to them and walked toward the leaders, passing through most of the warriors, who seemed to pay more attention to her than to their leaders.

Mesilim and Subutai again rose to their feet, as did Eskkar and his men a moment later.

Trella stepped between Mesilim and his son and stopped with them close on either side. "Eskkar, some of the children are too weak to travel. I've offered to care for them here until the battle is over." She looked at Mesilim. "That is, if Clan Leader Mesilim will allow it?"

"My women suggested this?" Mesilim questioned in surprise, as soon as Eskkar finished translating.

Eskkar felt as astonished as Mesilim. He'd never heard of such a thing, to leave children with not only strangers but hereditary enemies. "Trella, there's danger here as well. They may not understand what they are asking."

Before Trella could reply, one of the women approached the group, calling out as she did so and slowing down until Subutai waved her forward. The woman spoke softly but rapidly to Subutai, and Eskkar couldn't keep up with her words, so fast did she speak. Whatever she said, it took a long time and when she finished, she didn't move away, though custom decreed it.

Subutai turned toward Eskkar. "It is as Honored Trella says. My woman wants to leave the five youngest here, saying they will surely die if we have to travel hard once again. My daughter is among those." Subutai looked at his father. "We'll have to speak of this."

Mesilim nodded thoughtfully, then turned to Trella. "We'll consider your offer with great care. But our thanks are yours already."

"Then I will leave you men to your work." She touched Eskkar on the arm and wished him goodnight. As she started to leave, one of the tribesmen called something out to Mesilim, then added several sentences, and Trella, hearing her name, stopped and waited.

Eskkar heard what the man said but it made no sense. Something about "touching the gifted one."

Mesilim turned toward Eskkar. "My men request a great favor, though you've already done so much for us . . . but, if it is permitted, they would like to touch Trella to give them strength and a blessing from the gods." Mesilim sounded a little uncomfortable with the request, but did not withdraw it.

Trella came back to Eskkar's side and looked inquiringly at him. "They want to touch you, for luck or something," he said. "It may be a custom I don't remember or something I've never seen before. Mesilim seems embarrassed by it but probably thinks it's a good idea."

"What should I do? How should I touch them?"

Eskkar thought for a moment. "Touch each man on his upper right arm to give him strength in battle."

Trella handed her empty basket to Annok-sur, at her side as always, and approached Mesilim. She put out her hand, but not to his arm. Instead, she placed the palm of her hand on his forehead. "May you have the wisdom to lead your people through the coming fight," she said, then touched his right arm as Eskkar suggested. Turning to Subutai and placing her hand on his forehead, "May you have the wisdom to guide your people in the days ahead when many things will change and all will be sorely tested."

By the time she finished, a line had formed behind Subutai, some of the men pushing each other to gain a higher place. She went down the line, touching each man on his battle arm, offering them strength for the coming battle. Fashod followed alongside her, translating her words.

The women had gone to the end of the line, and with each of them she clasped hands. When she finished, she retrieved her basket and left without a word, her guards and the women falling in behind her.

They stood there, watching in silence until she passed through the gate and out of sight. Then Eskkar turned to Mesilim. "Rest tonight, Mesilim. My men will close the gate to keep the curious away, and they'll keep watch from the walls. I don't think any will approach you here, but you may want to post your own guard. No man from the village will be outside the walls tonight. Tomorrow, I'll return and we'll talk further."

When they had walked out of earshot, Jalen made a comment. "That was the strangest thing I've ever seen. They looked and acted as if Trella were a goddess."

"Nothing strange about that," Gatus answered. "Is there, Eskkar?"

"Nothing at all, Gatus," Eskkar said with a laugh. "Nothing at all."

20

Two nights later and three hours after sunset, Eskkar led a hundred men through the river gate. It took half the night to ferry them and their equipment across the river. By dawn the soldiers had marched well inland, out of sight of any watchers.

They traveled slowly. Each man carried seventy pounds of equipment: a wooden shield, a bow, two quivers of arrows, plus a sword, food, and water. Gatus informed Eskkar that men on foot could carry no more than sixty pounds at a steady pace. So the first day's march would be the hardest. The weight would decrease each day.

Eskkar walked with the men. He'd brought only four horses for the scouts, plus two donkeys to carry food and water. They didn't expect to be gone more than a week; if they were, they'd have to live off the land. On this side of the Tigris, nothing had been put to the torch, and herds of goats and sheep still grazed in the hills.

Gatus insisted on coming. He'd trained the soldiers to fight together and wanted to see his work put into practice. Sisuthros stayed behind to oversee Orak's defenses. The following night, Jalen would cross with Mesilim and the Ur Nammu, then guide them to Eskkar's soldiers at the appointed place.

During the march Eskkar thought about his talks with

Mesilim and Subutai. The day after the Ur Nammu's arrival, Eskkar and his commanders had taken Mesilim and his son around the walls. Eskkar went over his battle plan, putting Mesilim in the role of the Alur Meriki war chief. Back and forth they'd ridden, looking at the wall from every angle, searching for weaknesses.

Afterward he took Mesilim inside and showed him the great stores of arms and the preparations for defense. Mesilim's eyes widened in surprise at the vast quantity of arrows and stones. In the end, he found no flaw in Eskkar's defenses. "But you must not let them over the wall. Once inside, they will overwhelm your men."

Eskkar and Gatus had looked at each other in satisfaction. They'd drilled that same message into the men since the first day. The barbarians must be stopped beneath the wall.

Time was running out, for both Eskkar and the Alur Meriki. The great battle would be fought soon enough, and he needed to protect his back by destroying the barbarians sent against them from the west. The men, cattle, and supplies sent across the river must not be lost, or Orak would starve even if its people drove off the attackers.

Eskkar wanted to take more men with him, confident that he could return before the Alur Meriki arrived. But the looks of panic among the families convinced him not to take too many soldiers away from Orak at this late stage.

Mesilim and his men would depart the following night, to give them an extra day's rest. In the four days since they arrived at Orak, they'd had plenty of food and sleep, and restored much of their strength. Mounted on refreshed horses, they'd easily catch up with Eskkar and his slow-moving soldiers.

Counting Mesilim, thirty-seven warriors and two boys remained. One warrior had been judged too weak to ride and left behind. He'd been told to guard the women and children staying in Orak.

Eskkar pushed the pace as hard as he could for two days, walking beside the men and carrying his own equipment.

He could have ridden, but the horses were better used by the scouts, and this let him stay close to the men.

They'd just made camp at the end of the second day when Mesilim and his men rode up. Eskkar studied them as they arrived. Four days' rest showed in their faces. The new clothing each man wore replaced their old garments. Many of their weapons were gifts from Orak.

Every lance carried a yellow strip of cloth, another gift from Trella, and each bow dangled a smaller yellow ribbon. Each warrior wore a yellow sash around his waist. The colors were more than simple decoration—in a close-up battle they helped identify friend from foe, something needed even more by his soldiers.

The Ur Nammu's mounts looked stronger as well, and those that hadn't fully recovered were replaced by the last of Orak's horses. Mesilim's warriors looked confident and strong, a far cry from what they had been only days before.

Mesilim swung down from his horse and saluted Eskkar, while Subutai led the riders to their campsite, a few hundred paces away from Eskkar's. His men had little enough experience with barbarians, without getting into some argument or fight with the Ur Nammu over an unexpected or careless insult. Better to keep them apart until the time for battle, when no man would turn down an ally. Neither leader wanted any incidents.

"Your men look fit, Mesilim," Eskkar extended his hand in the sign of friendship. On the war trail, formality disappeared. "Any trouble following our path?"

"No. We rested the horses often, else we would have caught up with you hours ago."

After everyone had eaten, the two leaders stayed by the fire and discussed what the next few days would bring. Much would depend on the ambush site itself, and they wouldn't know about that until tomorrow. After Mesilim left, Eskkar spread his blanket on the hard ground and fell asleep in moments.

In the morning, Eskkar mounted a horse for the first time.

With Jalen and Gatus, he joined Mesilim and Subutai, riding ahead of the men until they reached the site chosen for the ambush, a few miles away from the river and well into the rough hill country. Clumps of pale-green grass still showed on the land, though the hills would turn brown soon enough from the merciless sun.

The small valley chosen for the ambush ran roughly north-south and was surrounded by steeper hills. At the southern entrance some farmers had built a half-dozen mud houses, penned some sheep, goats, and chickens, and tried to farm the land. But as Jalen reported, they were too few for such a task, less than a dozen men, and none used to living by their swords. They'd have made easy victims for the first band of rogues who came by.

They should have welcomed Eskkar and his men, but they acted sullen and angry at having their land taken over, even temporarily. They calmed down when Eskkar told them a large barbarian force was heading their way, and would undoubtedly slit their throats.

The settlers included several women. Eskkar wanted no women hanging around his men. Women led to rape and fights. He gave the settlers a dozen silver coins to pay for the loss of their houses and corrals and ordered them to head south immediately. When they complained, he offered to take back the coins and turn them into slaves if they preferred. That got them moving, loading their possessions onto three carts and shepherding their flocks before them.

The narrow valley ran fairly straight, rising slightly from south to north. At the south end, where the settlers established their homes, the opening was ninety paces wide. Once past the entrance, the vale widened quickly to more than twice that. The far end lay more than a mile distant, and that entrance spread about two hundred and twenty paces across. About five hundred paces before the north opening, however, the cliff walls closed in, narrowing the valley at that point to approximately one hundred and twenty paces.

Eskkar approved of the valley walls. Steep and rocky, they offered few places where a horse and rider might, with great care, scramble to the top. Inside the basin the land was open and flat with no places for concealment or defense. Nevertheless, neither Eskkar nor Mesilim looked satisfied with the location.

Jalen saw the frowns. "Captain, this was the best location I could find. You wanted something close to the river where they could be closed in. And it's nearly on the line of march to Orak."

"I'm sure it's the best we could find," Eskkar said. "But it's going to be difficult to spring a trap here. We'll have to split the men, and that means the Alur Meriki will outnumber each half. And the length of the valley means a long run for the men to close up."

"The canyon is wide here," Mesilim added. "Our lines will be thin and our enemy can concentrate their forces at any point." He turned to Eskkar. "Remember, you say we need to kill them all, not just defeat them. If they see the size of our force, they'll simply turn away and ride south by another route."

Jalen looked doubtful. "Without a fight?"

"They won't fight unless they expect to win. They see no dishonor in running away, or shooting arrows at us from a distance for hours or even days." Eskkar shook his head. "We'll have to think of something, first to lure them in and then to stop their escaping."

The group of commanders rode slowly to the north end and inspected the ground there. The entrance proved as wide as Eskkar had feared, though the walls did pinch in before the opening. Eskkar decided he had no choice. This place would have to do. The Alur Meriki might be here any day and he didn't have time to search for someplace better.

Eskkar, Gatus, Jalen, Mesilim, and Subutai rode back to the center of the valley, close to the east side, dismounted and sat on the ground in a circle. For two hours the five of them went over their options, taking into consideration the

capabilities of the bowmen, the Ur Nammu warriors, the
ground, and what they thought the enemy would do. Once
they had made their decisions, they spent even longer im-
proving the plan, until each knew where and how they would
fight.

While this went on, soldiers and tribesmen rested and
watched while their leaders scratched lines in the dirt and
argued over their fates.

When the leaders finished planning, no one felt completely satisfied, but nobody could offer any further im-
provements. Esskar and his men returned to the south end,
where the soldiers waited, tense, waiting to learn their future.

Esskar looked at them, then raised his voice. "You men
wanted to fight, didn't you? Well, you'll get a fight to remember, I promise you that. This will be a fight like no other.
You'll obey orders or wish you were never born. And work
like slaves if you want to live through this one. Remember
that if you want to live!"

With that, the camp burst into activity. Subutai gathered
what supplies he needed and took fifteen of the fittest and
best mounted warriors. He had the most dangerous
assignment—the bait for the trap. They rode south, back the
way they came, planning to swing completely around the
entire valley so as not to leave a trail. They would eventually
ride north and find the Alur Meriki, let themselves be seen,
and lure the enemy into the valley.

Gatus took a work crew of thirty and some digging tools
from the farmhouse. They walked along the steep east side,
to avoid making tracks down the center of the vale. Meanwhile, Mesilim posted men as lookouts on the valley's
heights to make sure no one surprised them. Another work
party took the donkeys and marched out through the south
entrance, to gather as much wood as they could find.

For the rest of that day and the next, Esskar's men labored
and practiced their movements, their archery, and their signals. The lead bowmen marked distances up and down the
valley, so the archers would always know the range. The

steep sides would negate any wind. Finally everything was ready.

Now all depended on Subutai. Not only did he have to find the Alur Meriki but he had to entice them into the valley, close enough behind him for the plan to work, but not too close for them to discover the trap.

So much could go wrong that Eskkar refused to think about it. Instead he complained about everything the men did, cursing them even as he urged them to work harder. As they sweated, everyone kept an eye on the horizons and hilltops, keeping their weapons close at hand. When all the preparations had been made, they finally rested and tended to their weapons.

The waiting began. Mesilim looked tense as well, shouting at his men over every little annoyance. The Ur Nammu leader worried about his son. Jalen kept pacing back and forth, certain his choice of the valley would be blamed if anything went wrong. Only Gatus seemed above it all, calmly making sure the men did their tasks properly, saw to their arms, and trained in every spare minute.

At midmorning the next day, one of the sentries on the north rim gave a shout. Moments later a rider came into view, galloping an obviously weary mount into the valley. Every eye followed the lone horseman. Sweat covered his mount's sides as he rode straight down the center of the valley until he reached the huts at the south end where Eskkar and Mesilim waited. It was Fashod, sent by Subutai with the news.

Dismounting, Fashod spoke so quickly to Mesilim that Eskkar had trouble understanding. Finally Mesilim turned to the waiting commanders.

"Subutai found a small scouting party of the Alur Meriki yesterday and ambushed them, letting a few escape. Then he rode west, pretending to hide his trail, before turning south. The main force of the Alur Meriki is following him, and he's riding slowly as if his horses are tiring. Fashod thinks there are about seventy men in the war party. Subutai will be here in an hour with the Alur Meriki right behind him, if all goes well."

Eskkar felt the sweat start on his hands but didn't wipe them on his tunic, a gesture every man would see and understand. Anything could go wrong. The barbarians could catch up with Subutai earlier than expected; they could stop for some unknown reason; or simply turn away and head back toward the river. But now was not the moment to show fear or doubt.

"Then it's time. Gatus, take command here." Eskkar looked at Mesilim. "May the gods smile on us today."

"I'll be at your side when the battle begins," Mesilim answered. He turned to Fashod. "Stay here with Gatus, and make sure when Subutai arrives, he knows where we are and what we do." With that Mesilim went to his men and, in a few moments, all twenty-two remaining Ur Nammu rode south out of the valley, leaving only Fashod with Gatus and fifty soldiers at the south end. Mesilim had an hour's ride through the hills to circle the valley and appear at the north end.

Eskkar turned to Jalen. "Start the men moving, and by the gods, they'd better not leave anything behind or forget what they've been told."

Eskkar, Jalen, and fifty bowmen moved north, in single file, hugging the east side of the valley and treading carefully so as not to leave any trace of their passing. For the last two days, everyone avoided trampling the grass in the center of the valley. When the Alur Meriki rode in, they must not see any sign of Eskkar's men.

Near the north end of the valley, where the walls pinched sharply, Eskkar and each of his men paused long enough to leave their weapons in the deep pit they had carefully created and cunningly concealed.

Then they continued moving, still in single file, exiting the valley's north entrance and turning to the northeast. The last two men used pieces of brush and took care to remove any trace or scent of their passage. Three hundred paces from the valley entrance, Eskkar, Jalen, and fifty men packed themselves into a tiny cul-de-sac, sat on the ground shoulder to shoulder, and waited.

One man with good eyes and who could count was

assigned as lookout, crouching in some rocks a few paces from their hiding place. Esskar squatted down in the dirt with his men. The battle smell, that familiar combination of sweat, urine, and feces, soon filled the tiny space, as fifty unarmed men were wedged together in a space little bigger than Esskar's workroom.

Weaponless except for a few knives, a child with a sword could probably kill all of them. Esskar knew this would be the most dangerous part of the trap. He'd decided to stay with the men most exposed to danger, to keep them steady by sharing the risk.

"Riders coming!" The sentry called out softly.

Esskar pictured Subutai's men riding into the valley from the north. They'd be moving slowly, letting the Alur Meriki catch up. He strained to hear them, but there was too much hillside in the way, and Esskar felt no vibration in the earth.

The men looked edgy, their breathing rapid, waiting the release of energy. Esskar fought the urge to join the sentry, but there wasn't much cover, and one man could see as well as ten. The waiting played tricks with his senses. One moment Esskar could hear nothing, then he fancied he could hear the roar of flames and Subutai's war cries.

"The barbarians are in sight. They're moving . . . they've stopped! Keep silent!" the sentry hissed the last words.

The man would be hugging the ground. The men jammed behind Esskar ceased all movement. No one spoke or made a sound, no stone kicked loose, and each man watched his neighbor closely for a cough or a sneeze that could ruin everything.

The barbarian riders would be little more than three hundred paces from Esskar's hiding place. Would the Alur Meriki sense a trap, would they see the men's hiding place, or spy the sentry? Perhaps their horses would catch their rank smell. He tried to put himself in the mind of their war chief.

The Alur Meriki would see the Ur Nammu had ridden into a tiny valley, one with a small settlement at the far end, a settlement already sending fire and smoke into the sky.

The war chief would hear men screaming, others sounding war cries, and would think the Ur Nammu too busy looting and killing to notice that riders had gradually overtaken them from behind.

Take the bait, Eskkar pleaded. *You can have your enemy and the loot, too. Just ride in and take it.* He heard the sound of horses. The much larger band of Alur Meriki warriors made more noise than Subutai's smaller party. Then the sounds began to fade, and Eskkar knew the enemy had entered the valley. He saw the excitement in Jalen's eyes.

The last hoofbeat disappeared. Eskkar remained immobile until the sound of scraping earth announced the sentry at the opening.

"They entered the valley, Captain, like you said they would!" The man's grin looked like it would split his face in two.

"All of them?" Eskkar asked. "How many were there?"

"I counted seventy-three," the man whispered, "and they all entered!"

Eskkar leapt to his feet. "Let's go, men! Keep silent, and run as you've never run before!" With that he began racing toward the entrance of the valley, the sentry passing him in a flash and leading the way. Eskkar ran hard, and reached the opening of the gorge just in time to see the Alur Meriki, already more than halfway down the valley, burst into their charge as they launched themselves at what they thought were the unsuspecting Ur Nammu.

At the far end flames and black smoke rose high into the sky as the buildings and corrals burned, stoked by heaps of wood and dried grasses carefully placed under or inside them. In a moment, Gatus and his men would rise from their hiding places and launch the first flight of arrows, though they would wait until the last moment to give Eskkar as much time as possible.

He ran as hard as he could, head down, feet pounding. They had to cover more than a quarter of a mile to reach the weapons cache and arm themselves, and all this must be done before the Alur Meriki spotted them. In practice, their best runners had covered the distance in the time a man could count to seventy-eight.

This time they ran for their lives and their weapons, and Eskkar's men kept passing him, Jalen already far ahead, as the younger and faster men easily outpaced their leader. Eskkar cursed himself for being so old and slow. Though for his men, he'd chosen those who could run the fastest. They had to reach the weapons, arm themselves, and form a battle line across the narrowest part of the valley before the barbarians recognized the snare and escaped back the way they came.

If the plan worked the trap would be considerably smaller than the valley's full length, maybe small enough to allow Eskkar's men to support each other when the barbarians hurled all their force at one contingent or the other in an effort to escape.

Eskkar reached the weapons pit at last and found his great sword out and leaning against a rock. Even with his head start, all the men had passed him. The line had already started to form, the men struggling with their equipment as they extended toward the middle of the valley. A gold coin had been promised to the first man to reach that station. The men moved slower now. Each had to carry a sword, bow and quivers, the wooden shield, and a thick staff to support it.

Snatching up his sword, he didn't bother to buckle it on. He ran toward the valley's center. He saw the first soldier reach the midpoint of the valley, plant his shield, and notch an arrow. The trap was nearly complete.

A few moments later Eskkar reached the center as Mesilim and his band rode slowly in to complete the line of battle. The Ur Nammu formed into two ranks. The riders, a few feet apart, bows in hand, lances slung across their backs, had determined looks on their faces, prepared to pay back their hated enemy for the killing they'd endured.

Eskkar's fifty men stretched across two-thirds of the gap. Mesilim and his twenty-two warriors filled the remaining portion.

Gasping for breath, Eskkar stopped a few steps from Mesilim's horse as the Ur Nammu chief took his place. Eskkar took his first good look down the valley.

The Alur Meriki milled around, trying to understand what happened. One moment they'd been charging toward a dozen dismounted Ur Nammu raiders. Then a line of men had risen as if by magic from the earth and launched a flight of arrows toward them. In the same instant the looting and burning Ur Nammu had leaped to their horses and launched their own arrows.

The Alur Meriki, taken by surprise, had wheeled their horses and galloped back out of range. Eskkar knew they'd already lost their best chance to escape. If they'd continued with their charge, they would have taken heavy losses but at least some would have broken through Gatus and Subutai's men.

Eskkar picked out their leader, surrounded by his men as he tried to figure out why the strangers didn't pursue the attack, why they stood there shouting and cursing and waving their bows, while the Ur Nammu rode back and forth. Eskkar counted thirteen riderless horses scattered among them, attesting to the damage done by the arrows from Gatus's men.

Those arrows had flown at the Alur Meriki until they stopped and turned, then ceased abruptly. The Subutai's warriors remained behind Gatus's bowmen. Those archers, protected from foot to midchest by the heavy shields, propped upright by a stake, waited for the next charge.

As Eskkar watched, one Alur Meriki warrior, shouting and waving his bow, finally reached the side of his chief and pointed toward the north. The chief looked back the way they had entered and saw a line of men stretching across the narrowest part of the gorge, more Ur Nammu at their side.

The Alur Meriki had ridden into a trap, and now their leader knew it.

Eskkar glanced back down the line and saw that it had fully formed up. Each man stood two paces from his neighbor, behind the shield that gave him partial shelter from Alur Meriki arrows. Each man had one quiver on his waist, the other resting on the shield, arrows splayed out for easy grasping. Every man's sword was thrust into the earth, ready for instant use should the Alur Meriki survive the arrow storm.

Jalen commanded the men closest to the walls, standing behind the line, sword in hand, while Hamati, one of Gatus's subcommanders, took his position at the center of the bowmen. Hamati would direct the archers' fire.

Everyone was in place. Everything had gone as planned. Now Eskkar and his men waited. Only one more piece of the plan was needed to make the trap complete.

Hamati, calmly chewing on a blade of grass and with a big smile on his face, walked up to Eskkar. Three water skins had been stored in the hole, and Hamati had just handed off the last of them to the soldiers. Every man would have his fill of water before the fight.

"Well, Captain, they've got their water. Now they can piss all they like." He squinted down the valley. "I think they're still in arrow range of Gatus's men and don't know it."

"They're confused, all right," Eskkar agreed. "This isn't how they're used to fighting, but they'll make a new plan soon enough. Are the men ready?" A stupid question, and Eskkar regretted the words as soon as he uttered them.

The veteran Hamati had heard a hundred such questions from senior leaders. "They're ready. And I've told them again to aim at the horses." He smiled at his captain's worries. "They've got confidence now, too, knowing that Gatus stopped them. Don't worry, we'll hold them."

There was movement in the Alur Meriki ranks and their horses began to turn toward Eskkar, a ragged line forming. Their leader had evidently decided to take no more chances with what might lie before him. He'd try to escape the way he came.

Gatus saw the same movement and knew what it meant. Eskkar couldn't hear the order, but suddenly arrows winged their way toward the barbarians, just within range of the

soldiers' long bows. Mitrac, with his longer and more powerful bow, would be able to reach them easily. Eskkar had
left Mitrac with Gatus, thinking the youth would be safer
there.

The deadly rain fell on the Alur Meriki again, wounding
man and beast, throwing the unformed mass into more confusion. One horse went wild with pain, kicking and biting
until someone killed it.

The Alur Meriki trotted out of range, but Gatus reacted
almost as promptly, moving his men forward fifty paces before they stopped to reform the line of shields. The Ur
Nammu warriors paced their horses right behind.

"Time to get to work, Hamati," Eskkar said grimly.
"They've figured it out now." He walked back to Mesilim.
"What will they do next? Your side or mine?"

"Your side," Mesilim answered without turning his eyes
away from the enemy, sitting tall on his saddle blanket, trying to see as much as possible. "They'll try to ride right
through the center of your men, as far from ours as possible.
Now they only seek to break out, and they don't think your
bowmen can stop them. If your men can hold, we'll break
them."

Something in Mesilim's voice gave Eskkar a chill. He'd
heard that tone before, the battle fury that made men berserk
with rage at their enemies. But he had no time for such
thoughts. The Alur Meriki began to move toward the east
side of the valley, driving their horses to a gallop as they
rode up the slight incline.

"Bows up, full range," Hamati shouted, using the same
words as he had done in a thousand training sessions as he
gauged the distance for the first shot. "Aim for the horses. If
any get through, use your swords on the horses' legs."

The bows were drawn and the shafts held, angled up for
long-range shooting.

"Ready!" Hamati's voice carried up and down the line.
"Loose! At will!"

Fifty arrows leapt from the bowstrings, their fall timed to
arrive at a distant spot of earth at the same moment the bar-

barians reached it. The shafts whistled as they burst into the air. The second wave launched less than three seconds later, then another, the volley becoming more jagged as the faster men got off shots a bit quicker than the others.

Men and horses went down, but not many, and the barbarians kept coming. Eskkar saw the soldiers' bows were at level now, the men firing as fast as they could. The Alur Meriki war cries mixed with the thunder of the horses' hooves and the earth shook from their impact.

The Alur Meriki had to cover more than half a mile to reach Eskkar's men, which should take them about the time a man might count to seventy, and they'd be in bowshot for almost half that distance. Automatically, Eskkar counted the volleys. One . . . two . . . three. Each volley equaled fifty arrows, all aimed at about sixty warriors. Four . . . five . . . six.

Arrows flew both ways. A bowman went down, then another, even as an arrow whistled by Eskkar's ear. Seven . . . eight . . . nine. But the soldiers' heavy shafts kept finding their marks as the range decreased. Ten . . . eleven. Horses and riders spilled to the earth, slowing the riders behind them. Orak's archers had turned the rapid-fire tactics of the steppes people against them, with even greater efficiency and accuracy.

Eskkar heard Mesilim shout an order and saw the first rank of Ur Nammu riders begin to move. Twelve . . .

With a shout, Mesilim led ten men in a sweep, curving his line to the left and aiming to strike the Alur Meriki from the flank just before they closed with the bowmen. Mesilim's men launched arrows as they rode. At the same time, the second line of Ur Nammu wheeled their horses behind Eskkar's men to back up the line should any of the Alur Meriki break through.

When the Alur Meriki leader saw the Ur Nammu moving up behind the archers, he knew the line wouldn't break. Thirteen . . . fourteen. Then, less than seventy paces from the soldiers, the Alur Meriki warriors started pulling their mounts up, unable to continue in the face of the withering fire.

Eskkar saw their leader shouting, trying to swing his men to his left, to crash through the open space where the Ur Nammu had been. Instead he found Mesilim and his ten riders smashing into them in a fighting melee.

The remaining Ur Nammu were supposed to wait behind, to cut off any that tried to escape. But seeing their brethren in action before them, they ignored their orders and spurred through the bowmen, knocking soldiers down in their eagerness to reach their enemy.

Their actions forced Orak's archers to stop shooting, as friend and foe mixed together.

Mesilim's men and horses were rested and prepared. Their first wave of arrows cut down their foes before they could bring their superior numbers to bear. Then lances and swords were swept up. Eskkar saw Mesilim bring down a horse with his first arrow, then kill a warrior with the second, before the Ur Nammu leader crashed his horse into the Alur Meriki leader's beast. Eskkar saw Mesilim drop his bow and swing up his lance before he disappeared from sight in the swarm of horses, men, and dust.

Cursing at every god he could think of, Eskkar broke into a run, determined to stop as many as possible from escaping into the now-open gap to his right. Three Alur Meriki did get through, but Hamati had seen the danger and pulled men off the line, turning them to stop this new threat. They launched their arrows and brought down the men, multiple shafts protruding from horse and rider, before the Alur Meriki could get away.

The surviving attackers had broken off in defeat, turning their horses and heading back to the center of the valley. Eskkar saw Mesilim again. The Ur Nammu chief clung to his horse's neck, unable to recall his men. Blood covered both horse and rider when Eskkar arrived at a run to grasp the halter just as Mesilim started to fall.

Eskkar caught the wounded man and lowered him to the ground. Mesilim's horse had taken a slash across the neck as well, its eyes wide and stumbling in its gait. Many riderless animals milled about and some of Eskkar's men began wasting time trying to catch them.

The Ur Nammu jumped down from their horses, surrounding their leader and pushing Eskkar aside in their haste, but in moments they returned to their horses. One of them turned to Eskkar. "Mesilim is dying. But he orders us to obey you until Subutai says otherwise."

"Check every horse. No one must escape clinging to a horse's belly. Send five men to guard the north entrance and tell them to stay there no matter what. And make sure every Alur Meriki is dead. Thrust a lance into every body."

Turning his attention back toward the center of the valley, Eskkar saw the retreating barbarians had gotten another surprise. Gatus had moved his men forward at a dead run as soon as the charge began, and now his men formed up two hundred paces closer in. The barbarians found themselves under long range fire from both sides, as Hamati ordered his men fifty paces forward.

They could go no farther. Any greater advance would put them into the widest part of the valley and spread the line too thin. Nevertheless, arrows began to fly from both ends of the valley. The shafts flashed high into the sky before arcing down upon the enemy.

Eskkar caught a glimpse of the Alur Meriki chief. He'd survived Mesilim's attack but looked wounded. Eskkar took a quick count; only about twenty barbarians remained alive. Gatus moved again, advancing another fifty paces before setting up the new line.

Alur Meriki men and horses, hit at long range by lethal, bronze-tipped arrows, continued to fall. Their chief didn't have enough men left to break through either side now. He gave another command and his men began racing toward the west wall.

They began to climb, scrambling up the steep sides. The Alur Meriki had to dismount to lead and drive the horses up the slope. The moment they'd started toward the cliff, Ur Nammu from both sides charged, ignoring the soldiers' arrows still arcing over their heads and striking at the fleeing men.

Eskkar saw horses slip and fall, screaming in pain, men and beasts dying as shafts found their marks, but the Alur

Meriki kept climbing, fighting up the rocky slope as they strove to escape the valley. But as the first man reached the top, four Ur Nammu strode to the edge of the cliff and began firing arrows down into the struggling mass.

These were Subutai's men, plus the two boys who had ridden with their elders. He'd sent three men and a boy to the west side, and two men and the other boy to the east side in case any Alur Meriki tried to climb out. It had taken these men this long to get into position, but they'd arrived just in time to partake in the killing.

The few surviving Alur Meriki left alive were helpless. If they let go of the horses, the animals would immediately turn and try to descend. And they couldn't shoot a bow with one hand. In moments they were all dead or dying, either from the carefully aimed arrows fired at close range by the men above, or the storm of missiles from Subutai and his men below. The Ur Nammu had joined together at the base of the hillside to finish the slaughter, some of them jeering at their victims as they handled their bows.

One of Eskkar's men captured a horse and brought it to his captain. Eskkar swung onto the back of the wild-eyed animal. Once he had control of the excited brute, he rode deeper into the valley and reached the Ur Nammu as the last body came crashing down the hillside, pushed down by the men descending from the top.

Subutai, blood on his lip and a look of triumph on his face, looked otherwise unharmed. His jubilant men shouted their war cries. He saw Eskkar. Then his eyes went wide as he realized his father was not with him.

"Your father is dying, Subutai." Eskkar knew no way to soften the news.

Subutai gave a gasp of anger and frustration but said nothing.

Eskkar couldn't wait. "Subutai, we must check all the bodies, make sure that none are playing dead or hiding in the rocks. We have to count the dead, you understand?"

Subutai took a long time before replying, his face betraying the anger he tried to hold in check. "Take me to him."

Nevertheless, he shouted orders at his men before turning his horse away from the hillside.

The two rode back to where Ur Nammu warriors attended their chief. Mesilim lay still, either dead or unconscious, so Eskkar left the tribesmen to their grieving and rode off, to make sure Jalen and Hamati sealed the valley and counted the dead. Then he turned and galloped back to Gatus, who followed orders and retreated back to the south end of the valley.

"Gatus, guard the entrance, and keep men at watch along the walls of the canyon."

Gatus would take care of the details, so Eskkar wheeled the horse around and headed back to the warriors, now bunched around Mesilim's body. Dismounting, Eskkar found he was still carrying his sword, never having thought to belt the scabbard to his waist, and he'd done nothing with the heavy blade but carry it from place to place.

This time he saw Mesilim had died. Eskkar stood beside the body and offered the warrior prayer to the gods. When he finished, he nodded to Subutai, then withdrew to leave the Ur Nammu to their death rituals. Eskkar had work enough to do.

He started with the Alur Meriki dead, and it took some time before Eskkar felt satisfied, and then only after he'd counted the bodies personally. He ignored the numbers of Jalen and Gatus and demanded all the bodies be gathered at one site to make sure seventy-three dead Alur Meriki lay on the earth. Darkness began to fall, coming earlier in the hill-shaded valley, and the men built a fire. When Eskkar sat down near the flames he felt exhausted, as if he'd been fighting all day, though he hadn't raised his sword once.

Someone brought him a wineskin stolen from the farmhouse, and Eskkar drank it gratefully, for once not caring there was only enough for himself, and the men would have to do without.

Gatus had lost only three men, with two more wounded. The men with Eskkar had taken more losses, five dead and four wounded, but with only one or two likely to die. The heavy shields the men had complained about carrying for days had undoubtedly saved lives and prevented wounds.

The Ur Nammu had lost four men and two wounded, all occurring when Mesilim led his men at the barbarians. It was an amazing victory, seventy-three enemy killed, while losing only twelve of their own. Eskkar had never heard of such a battle before, in which a large and powerful force could be defeated so easily and with so few losses.

Normally when men fought, the side with the greater number won unless the other side proved tougher, better armed, or more rested. Here the battle had first been considered weeks before. Then the details of the trap carefully plotted. Eskkar decided more such victories could be achieved with the same forethought, like the way they planned the defense of Orak. He'd think more about it later.

When Eskkar dropped the empty wineskin to the ground, the soldiers had gathered around the fire. Those closest to the blaze sat, while the rest stood behind. Almost ninety men waited patiently, wanting to hear what he would say.

A few whispered to one another, but most remained silent. Everyone stared at him and Eskkar saw admiration in their eyes. It took a moment before he understood. Trella's words came back to him. *The men first, Eskkar, build on their loyalty. Remember how much you need them.* He must say something to them.

He stood up. Instantly all conversation ceased, and every eye rested on him. Taking a deep breath, Eskkar raised his voice.

"Today we defeated the barbarians in battle. But this was no common clash in the hills. We had to kill all of them. Well, today you men killed seventy-three barbarians and we lost only twelve men. To win, you had to follow your orders exactly and fight bravely. You needed to work together to save each other's lives. You did that well, and at the same time you proved that the enemy could be beaten with the bow. Now they'll have no force behind us when they come to Orak, and we'll beat them there just as we did here. Today, the glory was yours. Today I did nothing but run so slowly that all of my men passed me by."

They laughed at that, a few calling out comments about Eskkar getting old.

He raised his arm and pointed toward the other fire fifty paces away, where the Ur Nammu sat silently, watching Eskkar speak to his men. "But never forget that we would not have been so lucky without their help. Some of them died today, including their leader, to help us. For that we must honor them and join them as brothers."

Eskkar glanced around the ring of men. He could see some eyes glistening with moisture. "Tonight we'll take many new men into the Hawk Clan. Gatus, Hamati, Jalen . . . we all observed many men who fought bravely. But each of you stood at your companion's side, and each of you can speak up about his courage. First, I call out the name of Phrandar, the fleetest runner and the first to reach the battle line, earning a gold coin for his speed. He held the end of the battle line. I ask you, is he Hawk Clan?"

A roar of approval answered his choice. Men shouted out other names. Then someone began to chant the name "Eskkar! . . . Eskkar! . . . Eskkar!" Others took up the cry, until the walls of the valley echoed from the din. It went on for so long he thought their lungs would burst. When they quieted down, the men sat there, looking at him.

Eskkar had never seen such honor given before. Though he'd done little, the soldiers gave him credit for their victory. The men believed in him. More than that, they trusted him to keep them alive. Trella had been right. He no longer needed to fight himself, to prove his valor, to keep their respect. They accepted his leadership, as they trusted him to lead them to future victories. He'd won their loyalty. Now he needed to build on it.

"Soldiers of Orak," he began, "the Hawk Clan awaits the bravest of the brave. Give me their names!"

Another roar went up into the night. Again they shouted out names, until Gatus stood up and restored order. When they finished, eighteen more men would be entitled to wear the Hawk symbol. And they all swore they'd follow Eskkar into the demon's pits if he led them.

Eskkar finally slipped away and walked over to Subutai and his men. They silently mourned their leader, as they watched the soldiers celebrate. "Subutai," Eskkar began,

"I've come to offer my thanks to you and your men. Without your help, we would not have achieved this victory. I also offer my sorrow for Mesilim. He was a great fighter, a brave man who led his people well."

"You honor my father, and that is good. He died as he wanted—in battle." Subutai kept his voice strong and clear for all to hear, the voice of a chief. "But you, too, are a great leader, and you've led us to a great victory. Because of this I have declared the Shan Kar of my father satisfied. He gave us the Shan Kar and this victory, but now both are finished. We'll return to the north from whence we came."

The moment Subutai had declared the Shan Kar over, Eskkar knew the Ur Nammu would fight no more. Mesilim had made the arrangement to fight with Eskkar, not Subutai, and his son wasn't bound by oath or duty to abide it. In his heart, Eskkar could not argue with the decision. Too few now to do much damage, the Ur Nammu would be lucky to stay alive.

"I'm glad your Shan Kar is ended. But the friendship between our people will not end. We owe you much, and we'll remember our debt."

Eskkar described his plan to begin the march back to Orak in the morning. They'd both bury their dead at first light. Subutai would return with Eskkar to gather the women and children left behind.

Hours passed before everyone finally settled down to sleep. Eskkar felt dog-tired, more from worrying than fighting. At last the sentries were posted and the watch established. He was about to wrap himself in his blanket when he heard his name. Turning, he saw Subutai walking through the crowd of soldiers toward him. He started to get up, but Subutai sat down close beside him, their faces close together.

"Eskkar, I would speak with you a moment." Subutai kept his voice low, and he spoke in his native tongue though the nearest man was ten paces away. "I know what my father promised you, and I'd help you if I can. My men are weary, and need time to rest, and we must regain our lands before another takes them. But I don't want to leave you as a friend in the morning and find ourselves enemies by night."

Eskkar understood Subutai's problem. "There's no dishonor in your course. You must do what's best for your people. When you cross the river to the north, the land there is yours. None from Orak have ever claimed it, and few have even seen it. It doesn't grow wheat or vegetables, so it is of little use to us. As long as you do not war across the river, we won't be enemies."

"It will be long before we're strong enough to ride across the river."

"Even then, there will be no need. When all this fighting ends, we'll need help to watch our borders and warn us of new attacks and new enemies. We could establish trade for what you need, set up a trading camp. Your people would benefit."

"Perhaps it can be as you say," Subutai said, "trade instead of war. But first I must gather my people and return to the mountains. Still some of my warriors favor the idea of raiding the Alur Meriki, as you and my father discussed. We'll see what the next few weeks will bring." He reached out and grasped Eskkar's shoulder. "We part as friends, as my father would have done."

Eskkar returned the grip. "As friends we will part. But there may yet be some things I can do for you before you go. I'll think about it and send word to Trella."

When the Ur Nammu chief departed, Eskkar sank back down on the grass, thinking about Subutai's words "the next few weeks." The new Ur Nammu leader had just said Eskkar and the village would have to withstand the Alur Meriki's attacks for at least that long, no matter what. Eskkar grimaced as he rolled up in his blanket.

Trella had seen how these people could help Orak now and in the future. More important, she'd looked at them with kindness, seeing past the warrior trappings, even as she'd overlooked the barbarian in the man to whom she'd been given.

Bar'rack crawled to the top of the ridge, ignoring the insects that welcomed his presence as they nibbled on his flesh. Peering through a clump of tall grass, he watched the approach to the valley. He couldn't see much. The entrance lay more than three hundred paces away, but what he saw kept him hugging the ground.

Two riders sat their horses near the valley's mouth. Both carried lances tipped with yellow streamers and bows slung across their backs. Their relaxed posture made Bar'rack grit his teeth in anger. His clan brothers had ridden into that valley only hours ago; he could still see the broad trail of hoof prints that stretched from just below him all the way to the passageway that led into what must be a good-sized valley.

Another rider appeared along the crest of the valley wall. This one waved his bow toward the riders below him. They waved back, but didn't move. After a long moment studying the land beneath him, the third rider turned away, vanishing from sight.

Bar'rack swore at the flies and fleas biting at him, then cursed his clan brothers for leaving him behind, though now he began to think the gods had saved his life. His horse had stepped into a hole, breaking its leg and throwing its rider to the earth. Too dazed even to cling behind another rider, they'd left him behind in their eagerness to close with the Ur Nammu. He'd slipped into unconsciousness and when he awoke, he found himself alone.

Angry at being left behind, Bar'rack started walking, an activity that normally consisted of moving from his tent to his horse. It had taken him the better part of two hours, following the twisting trail left by his clansmen, to reach this place. Fortunately the riders hadn't spotted him when he approached.

Another hour passed as he watched, but nothing happened. The crest rider had reappeared twice in that time, his movements telling Bar'rack that the Ur Nammu patrolled the valley's heights as well as its access. His Alur Meriki brothers hadn't returned the way they entered, so either they'd ridden out the far end of the valley, assuming that it had one, or they'd all been killed. How that might be possible he had no idea, but he'd heard the story of the warriors trapped and killed by the Ur Nammu a few weeks ago. In his worst dreams, Bar'rack couldn't believe such a thing could happen to his clansmen.

A handful of riders appeared at the valley's mouth, and for a moment Bar'rack thought his clansmen had returned. But these new riders showed no colors, didn't even carry lances or bows. Dirt-eaters, he decided, from the way they handled their horses, except for their leader. A tall warrior with the look of a horseman, he spoke as an equal to the two Ur Nammu guarding the exit. The way they answered, showing respect and deference, surprised Bar'rack. He watched as the tall rider acknowledged their response. Then he wheeled his horse and rode back into the valley, his men following behind.

Bar'rack had seen enough. He put his face on the ground and tried to think. Dirt-eaters had banded together with the filth Ur Nammu. They'd either wiped out all the Alur Meriki warriors, or driven them to the south. In either case, Bar'rack would be on his own. His duty to his clan was clear—he had to get back across the Tigris and warn the Alur Meriki clan leaders.

A moment of fear swept through him. If the Ur Nammu rode back this way, they might see his footprints overlaying the horse trail. They'd hunt him down, track him wherever he went, until they caught him. Bar'rack looked up at the sun. Only a few hours of daylight remained. He didn't dare start moving until dark. He'd have to travel all night, put as much distance as possible between him and the Ur Nammu, who would surely send out patrols at dawn.

Getting away, finding and stealing a horse somewhere, then getting back to Thutmose-sin: that's what he needed to do. Bar'rack rolled over on his back and covered his eyes with his arm. He still had his water skin and his bow. He'd rest until dusk, then start moving. With luck, he could travel far enough to escape the Ur Nammu patrols.

Beneath his arm, Bar'rack found his eyes watering. His younger brother had ridden into that valley. Now Bar'rack would have to tell their mother of his death. He let the tears come, something he couldn't do in the presence of warriors. But when the tears dried, he swore vengeance to the gods, in the name of his brother, against both the Ur Nammu and the miserable dirt-eaters. The gods heard his oath, and he knew they would honor it. The dirt-eaters and Ur Nammu would pay for his brother's death.

21

At first light Eskkar dispatched a rider to Orak to deliver word of the victory. He also wanted Trella aware of Mesilim's death and its effect on Subutai.

The men spent the morning burying the dead and caring for the wounded. The sun had climbed high before they began their journey back to Orak, but the long summer days promised them extra hours of daylight.

The injured who could cling to a horse had been given mounts, while parties of men took turns carrying the three wounded men unable to ride. Thirty-two horses had been captured. Eskkar gave thirty of them to the Ur Nammu. The rest of the Alur Meriki mounts had been killed in the fighting. Every man had their fill of horsemeat, while what was left of the farmhouse had provided fuel for the cooking fires.

They camped as soon as darkness fell, and the next morning Eskkar had them on the march almost as soon as the sun rose. By early afternoon they'd covered nearly three-quarters of the distance home and Eskkar expected to reach Orak just after dark. He didn't push the pace and the men walked lighter now that they didn't have to carry the awkward and heavy shields.

They carried no food, either. The last of it had gone with this morning's breakfast. It wouldn't hurt the men to miss one dinner.

The sun had started to set when a rider appeared over the hilltop and lashed an obviously tired beast toward the column of soldiers.

Subutai rode alongside Eskkar, though only ten of his warriors accompanied him. The others had stayed behind in the valley, guarding the horses and resting. Eskkar watched the rider as he approached, the horse covered with sweat and finished for the day. Halting the column, Eskkar dismounted and sat on the ground, motioning to the rider to join him. The rest of his men, eager to hear the latest news, crowded around them, all discipline lost in a moment.

"Captain, I come from Lady Trella. She says to tell you the barbarians have been sighted." The man paused to catch his breath. "A large column rode up from the south two days ago. We saw more than a hundred riders. Now they keep a watch on the village."

"Did any of them attempt to cross the river?" The water ran a bit lower now, and a strong swimmer might make it across.

"No, Captain. There's plenty of water at the farms, so they don't need the river."

Nor did they want to call anyone's attention to it just yet, Eskkar thought. "Is there anything else?"

"Yes, Captain. Lady Trella will join you in a few hours. She crossed the river with me along with the barbar . . . the women and children that the warriors left behind. She said she wanted to get them out of Orak before the enemy prevented them from leaving."

Trella on her way here! Well, a small group of men and women crossing the river should arouse no suspicions. It didn't matter. He wouldn't take any chances on this side of the river.

"Gatus! Start the men moving and pick up the pace. I'll not have Trella walking through the countryside with a group of women. We keep moving until we find her."

"Captain, she has four soldiers with her," the messenger said hastily. "Sisuthros wanted to send more, but she said it would attract too much attention."

Four or forty made no difference. Eskkar wouldn't rest until he saw her safely back in Orak. Climbing back on his horse, he led the way, moving at a quick trot that drew grumbling from the men as they struggled to get moving and keep up.

Once again Subutai rode beside him. "Perhaps I should ride ahead, Eskkar, to see to Trella's safety."

Eskkar appeared to think it over for a moment. "No, it's better that you stay at my side. The men guarding Trella might be surprised if they saw warriors riding toward them."

"I would be willing to take such a chance. We could call out to them, tell them who we are. Our women would recognize us."

"No, I will not risk it. Stay here with me. We'll meet up with them in another hour or two at most."

"And if my horse suddenly broke into a run, what would you do?"

For the first time Eskkar turned to look carefully at the man at his side. He regarded the new chief of the Ur Nammu closely for a few moments and chose his words before replying.

"In the village, Subutai, many men now cast their eyes at Trella, and I'm sure some of them would slit my throat if they thought that would help them get her. But that could never happen in Orak. The entire village would rise up and punish anyone who tried to take her by force."

His voice hardened. "But out here, any man with a horse can take a captive, and I remember the saying of my clan: 'Trust no man with your woman, especially your brother or your friend.' Now the warrior in me sees danger everywhere, and I'll take no chances with her safety."

Subutai digested Eskkar's words. "Put your fears at rest. I'll ride with you until we meet up with them." After a moment he added, "Though I think you have learned much wisdom from your woman."

"She has many sayings, so many that sometimes my head turns. One of them is to always try to put yourself in another man's place, to understand him from within. Sometimes it's not an easy thing to do, but often it helps to understand a man."

He turned toward the Ur Nammu chief again. "You're now the leader of your people. But whether you'll be a great ruler, only time will tell. But it might be a wise saying for you as well."

They rode in silence for a hundred paces before Subutai spoke. "I did think about it, Eskkar. For a moment it was a great temptation. But I knew I would have to kill you first. After all you've done for my people, I'm content to seek her wisdom. But remember your instincts. Always keep a close watch on her."

"That's one lesson I've already learned. Now, let us talk about the future."

The moon had not yet risen when they crested a small hill and saw two torches twinkling in the distance. A few moments later Trella's party spotted them and waved their torches.

The men groaned in relief when they saw Trella's group. They hadn't stopped moving for the last three hours. Orak was close now, little more than another two or three hours at an easy pace. Trella had not traveled very far, burdened with the Ur Nammu women and children in addition to a great amount of supplies.

Eskkar galloped ahead as soon as he saw the torches. He jumped down from his horse and took her in his arms until she gasped for breath.

"You should not have left Orak. This was dangerous. You could've been attacked on the road. You haven't even recovered from your wound."

She looked at him in the flickering torchlight. "Orak is only a few miles behind us. But the ford may be blocked at any moment. I didn't want to be alone on the other side of the river, away from you."

"We will talk of this later. Now we must deal with Subutai. I hope you've more influence with him and his women than I."

He told her about the battle in the valley, of Mesilim's death, and Subutai's plans. While they talked, Gatus and the men arrived. The soldiers built a small fire and a ring of soldiers formed around Eskkar and Trella. The men drank the last of their water and rested. Eskkar told Trella what he thought about the new situation, then listened carefully to her replies.

They sent for Subutai. He'd been with his wife and daughter, listening to what the clan's women had to say, examining the supplies and gifts Trella had given them. The supplies would make a great difference in how the Ur Nammu lived in the months ahead.

Eskkar moved back his guards so his men formed a wide circle, leaving himself and Trella in the center. Now Subutai and his men entered the circlet, bringing with them their women, though Eskkar knew this was not their custom. But these were highly unusual circumstances. With only five women for thirty men, these wives would command a greater say in their fates.

Eskkar watched Subutai as he regarded Trella, who sat on part of a fallen tree one of the soldiers had dragged up for her. How she managed it, Eskkar didn't know, but she appeared both regal and desirable even in her rough travel dress. Maybe it was the combination of the firelight on her face, while two torches burned behind her. She had an indisputable presence, one she'd become well aware of and worked hard to enhance.

When the Ur Nammu were seated, the women behind the men, Eskkar began. "Our two peoples have fought together against their common enemy not once, but twice, and we've defeated them both times. Now Subutai will take his people back to their homelands, north of the river Enratus. When the Alur Meriki are defeated and driven from Orak, our people will stay to the south. In that way, our two peoples can live in peace."

Eskkar gestured toward Trella. "Trella and I have offered to help Chief Subutai in any way we can." He turned to Subutai, who had to speak next.

"Lady Trella," Subutai began, adopting the phrase Eskkar used, "we thank you for your help with our women and children. You've given us many gifts of food and clothing, as well as tools and healing medicines. We're embarrassed we have nothing to give you in return. Now we are too few to fight against the Alur Meriki. Yet we know you are wise, and so my people ask you for your wisdom."

Eskkar guessed that Subutai doubted she had any wisdom for him. But Trella had planted the seeds with the women-folk even before they left the village, and no doubt that had been part of the quiet discussions between Subutai and his people moments ago.

"It is we who are in your debt, Chief Subutai." Trella's soft voice floated on the night air like music from a lute, and not a sound was heard around the circle except for the crack-ling of the fires and the whispers of the translators as every-one strained to catch her words.

"Without your help, there would have been no victory two days ago, and the Alur Meriki would now have a strong force behind Orak. But a great challenge stands before you—the need to return to your homelands and re-build your people. It is something that you must do quickly, else you fall victim to some larger clan. You'll need more wives for your men to give you many children, and you'll need tools and food before you can stand on your own again. It may be that Eskkar and I can help you with these things."

Eskkar smiled inwardly at the box Trella had placed Sub-utai in. She offered him a way to rebuild his people, but he'd have to ask for it, and that would place him in her debt. If he turned it down, some of his men would begin to doubt his leadership, especially if her ideas had merit.

Subutai worked it out quickly enough. He had to ask, then examine her suggestions seriously. "Lady Trella, if you have any thoughts that can help my people, we ask for them."

"Nothing is certain, Chief Subutai," Trella answered. "We face a great battle against your own enemy, and it may be that we will not survive. But if we do, and if the Alur

Meriki are driven off, then the lands that they have passed through will be filled with chaos and confusion. There will be many masterless and landless men who'll kill and destroy whatever little has survived the Alur Meriki. Even among your kind, there will be many steppes clans wandering these lands. They'll fight each other as well as the soldiers Orak will send out into the countryside to protect our farmers and herders. Even now, several small bands of steppes people are on the west bank of the Tigris, moving north, avoiding the Alur Meriki while they take whatever they can."

Eskkar watched Subutai as he listened to Trella's words. So far she'd said nothing unexpected.

"If you wish," Trella continued, "we can speak to these small bands, or you can ride south and seek them yourself. Gather them together into a new clan within your own land, with a truce between your people and the men of the villages and farms. With supplies and trade goods from Orak, life in the northern lands could be easier. Orak would give you gold, and you would need only to watch the mountains and send us word of any dangers. You could trade for anything else you needed. All we would ask is that you raid no lands south of the Enratus."

Eskkar saw Subutai thinking it over, the same way Eskkar had when Trella proposed it. The havoc caused by the Alur Meriki had created many bands of homeless men. By absorbing them, one band at a time, perhaps a new tribe could be built in months rather than in years.

"We would still need women as wives for our men, Lady Trella. These will not be so easy to find, and without them the true Ur Nammu will diminish."

"My husband has told you of a way to obtain many women by taking them from the Alur Meriki at the height of their attack on us. They'll be distracted and you can capture as many as you like."

"Even if the Alur Meriki are defeated before your walls, they'll give chase to anyone who raids their women." Subutai spoke confidently. Doubtless he'd given much thought to such a raid. His father might have been willing to chance it, to bring death and shame to the Alur Meriki, but not Subutai. "If we were burdened with captives, Lady Trella, they would quickly catch up with us, and we would be destroyed."

Eskkar spoke up. "Subutai, much can be accomplished if the plan is good. We've seen how easily the Alur Meriki can be beaten when everything is thought out in advance. Now you have many horses, more than you will need, maybe even more than you can easily drive back to the mountains. The raiding party could capture the women and throw them on horses. If the raid were planned carefully, you would have thongs ready to bind the women to the horses, and torches prepared to burn as much of their camp as possible. If your men did not waste any time or strength in fighting, you could be gone in a few moments. Then the horses could be run until they were exhausted. Change to a relay of new mounts, kill or scatter the old ones, and the Alur Meriki would be chasing you on tired animals. Kill a second string of horses and they'd be left far behind, in danger of being cut off from the main body of the tribe. They would have to turn back. Any few that went on could be easily trapped and killed."

Some men would never give up the chase, those whose wives or daughters were important to them. But most would turn back when they saw no quick opportunity of either revenge or loot. There would be plenty of widows in the main camp after the battle at Orak. Those would be easier to obtain than chasing a small band of determined Ur Nammu far into the distant north.

"A raid planned so carefully would have little risk and much chance of success," Trella offered. "And a wise leader would treat these new women as wives, not slaves. If they were treated better than they were with the Alur Meriki, they'd soon dry their tears and look with admiration on their new husbands."

She turned to the women. "For your clan to survive, you would have to accept these new captives as equals, not captured concubines, and treat them with friendship, not the whip. In this way, their children and your own would grow up to be brothers."

The fire had burned down. No one bothered to add more fuel, so Eskkar gathered some wood himself, dumping it on the flames, then arranging the new sticks. Others joined in, and for a few moments everyone focused on rebuilding the fire, giving Subutai time to think. When Eskkar sat down, the circle went silent again.

"Both of you have given me much to think about," Subutai said cautiously. "And in return for your help, you only ask us to raid the Alur Meriki at the height of the battle?"

"Yes," Eskkar answered, a little too quickly, so he checked his pace. "It may be that your help isn't needed to defeat them, or it may be that we are fallen. But at the height of the main attack, your diversion might turn the battle."

Subutai took a deep breath, and his lips came together for a moment. "I'd hoped we were finished with fighting for a time. Now we must decide if there is yet one more battle to risk."

"Chief Subutai, we, too, have one more battle to fight," Eskkar answered. "But there is always one more battle to wage. Each season brings some new threat. What's important to remember is to fight only those fights that make your people grow, not those that gain nothing except lasting hatred."

Eskkar spoke the words, but the idea and thoughts were Trella's. They'd spoken many times about the future, after the Alur Meriki were defeated.

Subutai stood up and bowed, his people rising to their feet with him. "You would have me change the ways of my people, and that is not an easy thing to do. But we'll consider your words."

He left the circle and moved back to where his people had gathered before, his warriors and their women following. In a few moments, they had started a small fire and sat down around it.

"Do you think he'll do it?" Eskkar asked Trella in a whisper as he slipped his arm around her.

"Oh, yes. He will have no choice. The women will see to it. They know that if the tribe does not grow, they'll all be dead or captured soon enough. And they want the goods Orak can provide to make life easier for them." Trella rested her head on his shoulder.

"I was angry when I heard you had left Orak," Eskkar murmured. "But now I'm glad that you came. I tried to convince Subutai myself but I couldn't think of a way. But I did manage to change his mind about riding ahead and making you his captive."

He smiled at the look of confusion that crossed her face. "Never mind. I'll tell you all about it when we return to Orak. Now rest. We march for Orak and our own great battle in an hour."

Two hours after midnight, Eskkar and Trella stepped off the ferry and onto the east bank of the Tigris. They'd scarcely left the flat-bottomed craft before the gang of ferrymen and soldiers began heaving on the ropes, sending the unwieldy craft slowly back across the river, their grunts of effort seeming to boom across the river, which amplified the slightest sound.

They couldn't do anything about the noise, and it would take another four trips to move everyone, including the horses, back to Orak, so the men would be at risk for another few hours.

Sisuthros waited anxiously for them at dockside, his face filled with relief at their safe return. Once inside the village, Eskkar, Trella, and Sisuthros walked quickly back to their house. They went directly to Eskkar's workroom, where Corio and Nicar awaited them. Cold food, water, and wine were on the table, while two lamps provided light.

"By Ishtar, we're glad to see you back," Sisuthros began excitedly. "The villagers were nearly in a panic with you both gone. Another day, and half of them would be trying to get across the river to join up with you."

"The barbarians are here?" Eskkar asked as he picked up a cold chicken leg and took a bite.

"Yes, the big band that's been pillaging to the south arrived two days ago. Our scouts had to run for the gate. Now they're camped about two miles away at the farm belonging to old Gudea and his sons. He and his family are as mad as hornets that their house was chosen by the barbarians. We could see about a hundred men from the walls, but there are probably at least twice that number."

"And the main party? Any news?"

"Nothing in the last few days, but they can't be too far away now. We're locked in here now, and there have been no patrols to the north since you left. It's likely the main force will be making camp a few miles away from here in two or three days." The tension sounded in his voice. "Your own battle went well?"

"Very well. We lost only eight men during the battle, though one of the wounded died on the return trip. But all seventy-three barbarians were killed, and their horses, those that survived, were given to the Ur Nammu. It will be at least a week, probably longer, before the Alur Meriki begin to wonder what happened to those they sent across the Tigris."

Eskkar smiled grimly at that thought. "At any rate, we now have ninety more veterans to put on the wall, men who know the barbarians can be beaten."

"And the Ur Nammu?" Corio asked. "Will they help us in our fight?"

Eskkar shrugged. "I'm not sure. Their chief was killed in the battle, and his son now decides for the tribe. But Trella did her best to persuade him. They may yet give us some small help."

"We didn't want Lady Trella to go," Nicar said, looking at Trella as he spoke. "We knew you would be angry. But she insisted, and there was nothing we could say to prevent her."

"It matters little, now that you're both safely back," Corio remarked. "It is time to get ready for the first attack. When do you think they will attack?"

"Just as soon as their ruler arrives," Eskkar answered.

"He'll want to see the first attack, and he will probably bring his own warriors ahead of the main party. But he may not want to leave the main camp unguarded and too far to the rear. So tomorrow or the next day should bring the first assault."

Nicar stood. "We should let them get some sleep. They're tired and need their rest."

The others nodded, said their goodnights, and departed for their own beds and a few hours' sleep. Eskkar escorted them downstairs. When they were gone, he returned to the workroom to find Trella seated at the table. She had extinguished one of the lamps to save oil.

"You're not tired, Trella?" He sat down next to her. "Is there something you want to talk about?"

"Everything is starting now." Her voice was low and her eyes stared at the table. "I mean, all the planning and building and training . . . everything is finished. Now the battle begins."

It took him a moment to understand her words. "Yes, this is the way of war. All the preliminaries are over, and luck or the gods decide your fate. We've prepared as best we could. Now swords and arrows will determine if we live or die. All our decisions and choices will be held up to the light for all to see."

She turned toward him. "You don't fear tomorrow! Why am I suddenly filled with fear? I wasn't afraid until now."

"All men are afraid of their first battle, Trella. When we waited for the Alur Meriki up in the valley, the men's fear was so thick I was sure the Alur Meriki could smell it three hundred paces away. Men's teeth were chattering, their bowels loosening, and their hands shaking. But once the battle starts, there's no time for fear. This is your first battle. Don't be concerned about these thoughts."

The night before battle, every man had to face his fear, some men of sword thrusts, others of arrows or lances, and most worried about their own bravery. He realized a woman could be as afraid. "Anyway, we have nowhere to run."

"And death? We could both be dead by tomorrow night!"

That was more likely than she realized. He pulled her from her chair onto his lap, holding her close as her arms went around his neck and she squeezed him with all her strength.

"All men fear death, but I've been fighting all my life, and should have been dead many times. Now I only fear losing you." He kissed her hair and neck, then turned her head toward him.

"When you sat at the fire across from Subutai, you looked and spoke like a goddess come down from the heavens. Every man in camp envied me when you lay down beside me to rest, and I'm sure many wished themselves in my place, with their hands upon you."

He kissed her again and this time she kissed him back, though the tears were starting now and her body shook with the effort to hold them back.

"I'm just a frightened girl, pretending to be all-wise, because that's what the people need. Now all I want is for you to take me away, someplace where five thousand barbarians won't be trying to kill us."

He smiled. "No, it's too late now. Once, perhaps, I could have done that. But that's not enough for me any longer. You are wise and you care about many people, and you deserve something better than a hard life as a soldier's wife. Here you are . . . will be . . . a queen in Orak, and all men will know your wisdom and beauty."

She wriggled on his lap as she tried to hold him closer, and suddenly he felt excited by her touch, or the heat from her body, or maybe by the threat of dying on the morrow.

Lifting her in his arms, he carried her into the dark bedroom. "Now I need you to love me, to give me strength for the days ahead."

He sat her down on the bed and helped her remove her dress, as she seemed too weak to do it by herself, then pushed her back gently. When he slid under the blanket, she moved into his arms and buried her face in his neck and he barely heard her words.

"Give me your strength, Eskkar, and I'll be strong for you forever."

22

Eskkar awoke with a start, alone in bed, with the morning sun making bright patterns of light on the blanket and the floor. Sitting up, he realized the soft bed had let him sleep at least an hour past sunrise. He'd told Trella to waken him an hour before dawn. Two hours wasted.

The house seemed strangely quiet as he hurriedly dressed. The outer workroom was empty and the door that led downstairs closed. When he opened it, subdued voices and the smell of crisping meat floated up from the kitchen. He went down the stairs two at a time. At the bottom, he found Gatus emerging from the kitchen, dressed for battle, a piece of chicken in his hand.

"Good morning, Captain. I was about to wake you." Before Eskkar could reply, he continued. "We decided to let you sleep a little longer. All the men are posted at the wall and there are only a few barbarians watching us from the hilltops." He wrinkled his nose. "You might want to wash up before you eat. You still smell like a horse."

"Where's Trella?" Why hadn't she awakened him? The barbarians might have attacked at dawn.

"Where she's supposed to be, out with the women." Gatus took another bite from his chicken leg. "This is good. I think it was supposed to be your breakfast."

Eskkar swore at the grinning soldier, then strode past him into the kitchen. Bantor's wife stood there, tending the kitchen fire, ready with his breakfast. Halfway to the table, he decided Gatus was right.

"Hold the food, Annok-sur." He went outside to the well, stripping off his tunic and using it to scrub himself down. A servant came and drew bucket after bucket of water for him until Eskkar felt as clean as he could be without a swim in the river. Wrapping his wet tunic around his waist, he returned to the bedroom and dressed again, this time for battle.

He took his time, binding his undergarment tightly around his loins, then donning a clean linen tunic. He strapped on the sandals that Trella had purchased for him that first day, making sure the wide leather straps were tightly knotted around his calves.

The servant entered the bedroom with a knock, holding a thick leather vest. He laced a leather protector onto Eskkar's lower right arm, then a smaller one onto his upper arm. Eskkar belted the great sword around his waist and thrust his knife, almost as long as the men's short fighting sword, into his belt. Last the servant offered the bronze casque, the helmet that would protect his head, but Eskkar shook his head. "Leave it. It's too hot."

He nodded his thanks to the servant and returned to the kitchen. He wolfed down the remains of the chicken, ripping it apart with his fingers and washing it down with water and handfuls of bread.

"Salt, Annok-sur." She handed him a bowl containing the rough crystals.

Men fighting or working in the heat did better with extra salt, though no one knew why. Eskkar swallowed a bitter mouthful of the gritty stuff, then washed it down with the last of the water.

"Good fortune to you today, Captain," Annok-sur offered when he finished, wiping her hands clean on a rag and following him to the door.

She would have duties of her own today. "Good fortune to you and Bantor."

Eskkar turned and stopped so suddenly that she bumped into him. "And thank you both for what you've done for Trella. Bantor is a lucky man to have such a good wife, but don't tell him I said that."

She laughed and touched his shoulder. "There are many things I don't tell Bantor, Captain."

Eskkar wondered about what things Trella didn't choose to tell him as he stepped outside into the bright sunlight. His men had converted the courtyard into a command post. Gatus sat at the main table, along with Jalen and a handful of soldiers. A dozen messenger boys were packed into a corner of the yard, all wearing distinctive red bindings around their arms so the soldiers would recognize them and let them through.

Clerks mixed with subcommanders who would coordinate the defenses. Nicar and the other members of the Families sat at a second table, each with his own duties and his respective attendants. The spacious courtyard barely accommodated those responsible for Orak's defense.

Eskkar walked over to the main table, reminding himself to take his rest wherever and whenever possible today.

"All the men are in position, Captain." Gatus spoke formally. "Bantor and Sisuthros are at the gate, along with Corio and his eldest. Jalen has inspected the rear gate. Maldar will command the men on the riverside, and I'll command the north wall. Hamati and Alexar direct the east and west walls. All the men have been fed and the water buckets are full. Each man has been given his instructions for the hundredth time, though I'm sure they'll forget them as soon as the first barbarian starts for the wall."

In a few words Gatus had given Eskkar all the information he needed and at the same time had communicated that all was as it should be.

"So, I should have stayed in bed longer. Maybe you would've called me after the fighting was over."

"They're not going to attack for hours, even days," Gatus offered reasonably. "First they'll try to frighten us with their presence." He looked squarely at his leader. "Now it's time to inspect the men and give them some words."

Meaning I'd better get to work. "Then let's begin." With Jalen and Maldar in tow, they walked out to the street where more messengers leaned against the wall. They cheered at the sight of Eskkar and he smiled at them. Yet another surprise waited for him. Four of the Hawk Clan, including two of its newest members, stood waiting.

"This is your personal bodyguard from now on," Gatus explained. "These four rogues are the least valuable of the Hawk Clan, so they've been assigned as your guard. If they stay sober, they may be of some use."

Each stood taller than average, two of them with less than twenty seasons, but all with hard muscles stretched tight across their chests. They looked as if they could chew stones for breakfast, though they all smiled at Gatus's backhanded words of praise. Each wore as much leather armor as he could carry, and every one bore the Hawk Clan emblem on his chest. Eskkar started to protest, but Gatus cut him off.

"Save your breath. They have their orders, which are to keep you alive. So don't bother trying to order them away, and don't try to take any foolish risks. They won't allow it." He started walking, not waiting for an argument.

Eskkar shook his head and strode after him. Eskkar saw few people in the normally crowded lanes, most of whom called out nervous greetings. At the main gate, the last of the dwellings behind the structure had been torn down, leaving a clear space roughly fifty paces in length. That opening narrowed as it followed the wall in each direction, but there were always at least twenty paces from the wall to the nearest building, so men and equipment could move easily from point to point.

He stared up at the gate. Four great timbers braced it, two to each side, resting in holes dug deep into the earth and reinforced with rock. Across the top, small wooden troughs ran the length of the opening, already filled with water. A catwalk extended underneath the troughs, so men could tip the contents over the top of the gate to put out fires.

This top platform could also hold a dozen archers who'd be able to shoot through slits carved into the gate. Another platform, wider and stouter, hung just below it, with more slits for the defenders. The structure's outer surface, hardened by fire, would be slow to reignite, but Eskkar knew there was nothing wooden that couldn't be made to burn. A gang of women waited nearby, ready to replenish the troughs with buckets of water as needed throughout the day.

On each side rose a square tower, ugly in its unfinished rock and mud bricks, but rising above both wall and gate, allowing the archers to fire down at anyone directly below.

Corio's oldest son, Alcinor, saw Eskkar's party approach and waved. That triggered a massive shout as the villagers and soldiers recognized him. Eskkar decided his venture across the river must have worried Orak's inhabitants. His return, added to the reports of another victory, gave the crowd something to rejoice about.

It felt strange to be cheered simply because he was seen. He still didn't know what to do about it.

"Captain, it's good to see you back in Orak," Alcinor said with a smile and a bow, "and congratulations. We hear you killed all the barbarians with great ease."

Eskkar grimaced at the soldiers who couldn't keep from bragging of their victory. Now everyone would expect an easy defeat of the barbarians. "Greetings, Alcinor." He kept his voice cold and hard. "And don't speak of easy conquests. There will be none from the Alur Meriki."

Alcinor's smile vanished at Eskkar's tone and the young man's eyes widened in fear. "I'm sorry . . . I meant no disrespect . . . I . . ."

"Enough, Alcinor. I know what you meant. Is everything here as you planned?" Curse the gods, he hadn't meant to frighten the man out of his wits.

Alcinor tried to recover from his embarrassment. "Umm . . . yes, of course. We've prepared everything as Sisuthros ordered. We have . . ."

"You've done well, then," Eskkar interrupted, trying to undo the effect of his harsh words. "Your gate will be one of the main points of attack, so you must help the soldiers keep the gate secure. If you need anything . . ."

Sisuthros called to them from atop the left tower. "Captain, there's movement on the hillside."

Eskkar and his guards filed quickly into the tower, treading carefully on the dark, narrow steps that followed the walls as they ascended to the top. Bantor came over from the other tower to join them. The soldiers stationed there stepped back so their leaders could see better.

The sight made Eskkar grunt in annoyance. The barbarians surveyed the village and its defenses from the same hilltop where, months before, he'd first considered defending Orak. From there they could see much of the village and the surrounding lands, now flooded, except for the main approach.

"There were only ten or twelve horsemen there until a few moments ago," Sisuthros informed him. "Now I see standards there."

Eskkar counted as quickly as he could, using his fingers to keep track, his lips moving slightly. "At least forty now, and with three clan chiefs." The extra-long lances that bore the Alur Meriki symbols also carried each clan leader's emblem. The distance was too great to distinguish details, but the standards stood out clear enough. "Another raiding party has joined with the two war parties from the south," he commented, then cursed himself for stating the obvious.

"From the main camp," Gatus asked, "or just another raiding party?"

"Probably the main camp," Eskkar guessed. "But the Great Chief's standard isn't here, not yet. You'll recognize that when you see it."

The third chief and his men probably formed an advance party from the main force, sent ahead to meet with the others and begin planning the attack. It might mean the War Chief had arrived. Or it might mean something else.

"Curse my eyes," Eskkar swore, "I can't make out any detail. Can you see anything on the banners, Sisuthros?" He was younger and presumably had better eyes.

"No, nothing," Sisuthros said. "They'll move closer soon enough."

"Where's Mitrac?" Eskkar asked. "That boy has better eyes than anyone in Orak. Send for him."

Gatus dispatched a messenger to find the archer. It took some time before Mitrac arrived, carrying his bow and breathing hard.

"Ah, Mitrac." Eskkar grasped the boy by the shoulders and led him to the tower's edge. "See those three banners out there? Those are the standards of a war chief. I want you to remember those three banners, because one of them is probably the fighting chief who'll be responsible for the attack. That's the one I want you keep looking for. If you get a shot at him, take it, but only if you think you've got a good chance to hit him."

The boy nodded, his hand over his eyes as he stared at the hillside.

Eskkar tried to think about what the enemy might be thinking. Put yourself in the other man's place. What would I see? . . . what would I do? Ignoring the chatter of the men, he set himself to the task. After a moment he turned to his men.

"From where they are, they can't see the open areas directly behind the wall. They may think the northeast section is the farthest from the center of the village, and that it will be the most difficult for our men to reach in an attack. If I were them, I'd strike at the gate, where we expect them, but push the real thrust at that corner."

Eskkar looked at his men and waited, but no one offered any argument against it.

He shrugged. "We'll plan for it. Sisuthros, Bantor, stay here with Mitrac and keep watch. They'll come closer soon enough and Mitrac should be able to figure out who's in charge. Gatus, let's check on the rest of the wall."

Eskkar descended from the tower and began walking quickly toward the northeast corner. Halfway there, a large group of villagers began to block his way, asking frightened questions that had no answer.

"Gatus, keep this area clear of villagers," Eskkar ordered loudly. "Send those who don't have duties here packing."

He stopped about fifty paces short of the northeast corner

and climbed the steps to the parapet. A cheer went up, this time from the soldiers as well as villagers. Damn the gods. He'd have to say something. He turned and faced the crowd beneath him. Fear and doubt showed plainly on every up-lifted face.

"Soldiers! Villagers! In a few hours, the barbarians may launch their first attack. They will try to rush the gate, but I think they'll attack this part of the wall as well. So ready yourselves." He turned to Gatus. "I think Sisuthros and Ban-tor can handle the gate. You and I will command here."

Eskkar looked up and down the parapet. He was about sixty paces from the corner. "This is the spot where they will hurl their attack, here and at the corner. I think everything else will be a ruse. Get the men ready. Make sure the men with the least experience are up front."

Gatus looked surprised, and he showed no inclination to move.

"I want as many as possible to get experience, Gatus. This first attack should be the easiest to beat off. Keep some vet-erans in reserve at the base of the wall, ready to come up if needed. I don't want them to know how good we are yet. I want them to keep thinking they can take the wall, if they just send enough men. Bring Maldar and half of his reserve up here as well."

That would take men from the rear gate, but Eskkar didn't think it likely the Alur Meriki would attack there.

Gatus nodded and hurried off, dispatching messengers as he did so. Eskkar turned to his bodyguards. "You heard the plan. If I fall, you continue it. Now, help me pick the men."

Everyone began moving and the activity lasted for some time. When Eskkar thought everything was in place, he stopped for a drink of water from one of the water barrels, as Totomes and Narquil, his older son, arrived with Mitrac. Jalen accompanied them and they moved to the wall's edge to assess the situation.

Eskkar smiled at the three archers. "Good to see you again, Totomes . . . Narquil. Did you learn anything at the tower?"

"Yes, another standard has joined the first three," Totomes answered. "They're starting to move toward us."

Eskkar looked out toward the east. Four Alur Meriki chieftains and about thirty warriors were riding slowly toward the village at an angle. In a few minutes they would be in front of the gate, about half a mile distant, still out of bowshot.

A mutter of excitement raced along the wall. "Keep quiet, men," he snapped. "Remember, they've never seen a wall like this before, and they're only looking. Keep your heads down and don't show yourselves."

The Alur Meriki probably lacked information about the number of people in Orak. Eskkar wanted them to think he had fewer fighting men than were actually available.

Jalen pointed toward the hills to the north. Eskkar saw men and horses, the hilltops dotted with curious warriors. No doubt they disobeyed their own orders to stay below the hill crests.

Meanwhile, the chieftains halted a little past the gate and resumed their discussions. Behind him Eskkar could hear the leaders of each file of ten cursing their men, who kept peeking over the wall. Eskkar didn't even bother swearing at them. The instant you gave an order, some fool would disobey it. Soldiers never changed.

The Alur Meriki resumed their inspection, riding leisurely until they passed opposite Eskkar's position on the wall and continuing until they reached the flooded lands. Villagers crowded against each other, despite orders to keep the wall clear. Everyone wanted to see what the barbarians looked like.

Eskkar watched some warriors splash their horses into the newly formed swamp. The animals kicked up spray as they struggled to move through the thick mud covered with at least a foot of water. He smiled when the horses slowed to a crawl. The barbarians tested the wetlands in several places, but always with the same result. Finally they gave up and returned to dry ground, where they sat on their horses, staring down the length of the wall toward the river.

The dry land between the ditch and the flooded basin was only about thirty paces wide, about the same as the width of the ditch. Those two distances, taken together, would give them more than enough room to operate. Eskkar knew that they were thinking it shouldn't be too difficult to surround the village and attack from many points at the same time.

Gatus strolled up to where Eskkar stared at the Alur Meriki. "Well, Captain, what do you think? Should we have flooded the ditch or not?" He said it seriously, without any hint of second-guessing his leader.

"It's too late, now, Gatus. If I'm wrong, you'll probably not get a chance to tell me so." If the enemy came in full strength against many parts of the wall, the village might fall. Eskkar swore again, worried that he had guessed wrong about the first attack.

"Looks like a little disagreement out there," Gatus commented, shading his eyes. "Maybe they're already arguing over the spoils."

One chief did look a little angry, his horse moving restlessly as its master gesticulated, at one point slapping his breast to emphasize some point.

Eskkar wondered what they could be quarrelling about, even before the first attack? *Put yourself in their place.* His mind went over the possibilities. One situation seemed likely—that the fourth standard belonged to the war chief, and that he wanted to wait before attacking. The more excited warrior probably wanted to attack at once. Eskkar couldn't be sure, but . . . *if you decide something, be firm about it. Mistakes can be overcome, but never moments of indecision.*

"Where's Mitrac? Mitrac! Come here," Eskkar shouted. In a moment the young man approached, having followed his captain's travels along the wall. Eskkar pointed to the chiefs. "You see that chief that's arguing out there? Can you see who he's arguing with? That's the war leader, and he's the chief you'll go after when the time is right. Always look for him, but not in the first fight. Don't try to kill him yet."

Mitrac studied the distant horsemen. "Yes, Captain, I think you're right. From the tower, we saw each of the three speak to him in turn. He says little, just seems to listen. It's the others who talk the most. His horse is that bay, the one with the white spot on the shoulder."

Eskkar cursed his eyesight again. He couldn't distinguish any markings on the horse, but the chief appeared to be wearing something white around his neck. "Good, good. Now, you see the one doing all the arguing? I don't want him killed either."

Mitrac turned to stare into Eskkar's eyes. "But, why . . . I mean . . . why not shoot at either of them?"

"Because the loud one is probably the war chief who'll lead the first attack, and he wants all the glory for taking the village by himself. I think the other chief is the one in charge. He's probably the smartest one they have, while the other is the most reckless and ambitious. For the first attack we want the reckless one in charge, not dead by some lucky arrow fired at long range. After the attack fails, then you can kill him. And after today, you try and kill the other man every chance you get. Understand?"

"Why, yes . . . yes, I understand. I think I understand." Mitrac's eyes had gone wide in awe of Eskkar's reasoning. "I'll go tell my father," he added, anticipating Eskkar's next command.

"Good, and make sure he understands why. Off you go."

When the boy trotted off, Gatus came over, shaking his head but smiling at the same time.

"Well, old man, what are you laughing at?"

"By sundown the story will be all over Orak. How Eskkar picked out the war chiefs and figured out their plans." He smiled again and lowered his voice. "If I didn't know you better, I'd almost believe you know what you're doing."

"If I knew what I was doing, I wouldn't be standing here with you behind this puny wall. But it's better to be lucky than smart, so let's hope our luck holds out."

Voices rippled along the wall and Eskkar turned back to watch the riders. They'd started to move, not returning the way they came, but moving toward the north. He watched them ride, graceful on their wiry horses, so much at home as they rode across the burnt-out stubble of what had been, until a few days ago, a grassy plain. He glanced up at the sun and saw noon approached. They'd watched the horsemen for almost two hours.

"Gatus, do whatever else you need to strengthen this corner of the wall. Make sure that the whole length from here down to the river is ready. No matter what that eager war chief decides, there will be some attacks down this side."

"We'll be ready. Now you go and talk to Trella. She's waiting down there for you."

Eskkar looked down into the village. He picked her out at once, surrounded by half a dozen women and her two bodyguards. Eskkar recognized the burly Klexor standing behind her.

Walking along the wall until he could descend, Eskkar strode across the open space toward the house that shaded Trella and her party. He greeted everyone as they moved aside.

"Good morning, husband. I've some food and water for you." Trella carried a small basket under her arm.

She looked serene and confident, not a trace of last night's frightened girl. She wore her poorest shift, the one she had on that first night. Today she carried the dagger Eskkar had taken from Drigo's dead hand. He felt glad that she'd been trained in its use.

They sat on the ground, their backs against the wall, while the others moved away to give them some privacy. "You seem much better today, wife. Did you sleep well?" Eskkar ignored the smiles that appeared on some of the nearby faces. He wondered whether they knew everything that went on in his bedchamber, including how often and how well he made love to his woman.

"Yes, I slept very well. Now eat and drink. You may not get a chance later." She handed him a piece of bread. "Will they attack today?"

"In a few hours. They're waiting for the great chief and more men, just in case the first attack is successful." He told her what he'd seen from the wall and his thoughts on what the barbarians would do.

"You know how they think, Eskkar. More important, the rest of the villagers feel secure when you act confidently." She put the basket between them. "Finish your food while you can."

Her agreement made him feel surer of himself and he took pleasure in that. He fell to work on the slices of bread and chicken, the meat still warm. Though he'd eaten breakfast only a few hours ago, he found himself hungry again, and the heat of the day had already given him a thirst. Eskkar almost drained the water skin before he remembered to offer her some.

She finished the water. "Give the rest of the chicken to Gatus. I must return to my duties. The old men grow nervous and quarrelsome if I'm not there to reassure them."

"Be careful," he warned her. "Don't stand where a stray arrow can find you. And don't . . ."

She stood and smiled at him. "Yes, master, I will obey, and you don't need to repeat yourself a dozen times." He must have looked crestfallen, for she leaned down and kissed his cheek. "Good fortune to you today, husband." And she walked off, her followers trailing behind, some of the women looking back at him and giggling.

He hadn't adjusted yet to that new experience, the constant stares and giggles from the women, who acted as if they knew all the intimate details of his personal life. Before Trella, no woman had dared to laugh at him. Barbarian customs had much to recommend them, he decided once again.

He walked back to the wall, carrying the basket. He found Gatus underneath the parapet, swearing at two of his men for some infraction.

"Trella sends you some chicken for lunch, so I suppose you'll have to eat it." He pushed the basket into his hands. "Get some rest." When the man started to protest, Eskkar held up his hand. "You won't have time later." He turned to one of the ever-present Hawk Clan bodyguard. "Bring water for Gatus, and make sure you men get something to eat and drink as well."

Eskkar spent the next hour pacing the wall, making sure everyone stayed alert and that the archers knew their roles, places, and orders. He had to be careful where he stepped— the top of the parapet creaked under the weight of stones piled upon it. Any more and there would be no room for his archers.

Satisfied with the preparations, he reviewed the signals that would allow him and his men to communicate through the chaos of battle. He even found time to talk with some of the villagers, those who stood ready to use short spears, axes, and forked sticks.

Three hours past midday shouts went up from those manning the wall. Eskkar ran lightly up the steps to the position he had selected to defend, about fifty paces from the northeast corner. He looked to his left and saw Gatus standing at the corner. Eskkar had to push men aside to get to the wall, but one look told him the attack had begun.

The hills were covered with mounted men, riding slowly toward Orak, most of them still more than two miles away. Their numbers seemed endless, and he felt the doubt rise up inside him.

"Mitrac," he shouted, and this time the young man reached his side in a moment. "Get a count of their warriors." Some of the barbarians carried ladders or climbing poles, sticks with crosspieces tied or nailed to the upright. They didn't seem to have very many of those, he noted.

While Mitrac counted, Eskkar scanned the riders, looking for standards as the men walked their horses slowly toward the village. Three . . . four . . . five . . . six . . . seven. That's all he could see, and nowhere in sight was the giant standard of the sarrum. Riders continued to come over the crest of the distant hills, but fewer now, though he did see one new standard. They rode slowly or walked their horses, coming toward the village, mostly silent, strong men on fine horses, ready to do battle, all of them eager for glory and loot.

Gatus walked over to his side, as Jalen came up the steps

behind him. "By all the demons, is there any end to them?" Jalen asked. "Ishtar, they're still coming!"

"I think we'll see about two-thirds of them today," Eskkar said. "They'll wait for the clan chief before they attack, so he can witness their bravery." The leading riders had stopped now, waiting, as their leaders held up lances or bows horizontally to mark out a rough line less than half a mile from the wall.

"How long before the big chief shows up?" Gatus inquired. "He won't keep them waiting long, will he?"

"Less than an hour," Eskkar answered, staring at the warriors. "Enough time for us to become weak with fear."

"Then he can come right now, as far as I'm concerned," Gatus said. "Maybe we should have stayed across the river."

Jalen looked shocked, but Eskkar laughed. "You should've thought of that yesterday." He turned back to Mitrac. "Well, how many, lad?"

The boy's lips moved wordlessly as he checked his fingers. "Captain, I count about eleven hundred, maybe a few more."

Eskkar had done his calculation the easy way, figuring a hundred men to each standard, with extra men for the chief who would lead the first attack. The answer made him feel a little better. If the first attack were a full assault, with every warrior participating, there'd be even more men facing him.

War cries rose up from the barbarians, shouts that quickly swelled into a thunderous roar that went on and on, as the warriors lifted their swords and lances and shook them against the sky.

Over the crest of the hill appeared the grand standard of the Alur Meriki clan chief. The tall banner, carried by a giant of a man on a massive horse, swayed in the breeze. The cross-shaped emblem, draped with many ox-tails and streamers, signified all the battles won and clans absorbed into the tribe. The leader rode in front of the standard bearer, undistinguished by any trappings visible at this distance, looking quite ordinary. He carried neither lance nor bow.

Around him raced twenty or thirty warriors, galloping

their horses back and forth while raising war cries. Another thirty or forty rode more sedately behind him.

Everyone, villager and barbarian alike, followed his progress and Eskkar could see the great chief turn his head from side to side as he surveyed the burnt grasses and empty landscape.

"By the gods, I've never seen so many horses." Gatus shook his head. "How many do they have?"

"More than you see, Gatus. Every warrior has at least two mounts. Many will have four or five. When a warrior dies, his horses are given to the rest of his clan."

"Let's hope there are many horses to divide up tonight," Gatus responded.

Eskkar put thoughts of horses out of his head and turned to Jalen. "Tell the men to get ready, then go to your position. I think they'll be coming soon." Jalen would defend the section between Eskkar and the gate.

Jalen nodded, then clasped Eskkar's arm in salute. "Good fortune to all of us, Captain."

"Well, he said he wanted to fight barbarians," Gatus commented as Jalen raced off. The old soldier placed his leather cap on his head and fastened the strap. "And I've brought this for you. Make sure you wear it." He handed Eskkar a copper helmet, the metal glinting in the bright sunlight. "Trella had it made for you. For some reason, she doesn't want your head taken off."

Eskkar looked at the helmet as he hefted it in his hand. It weighed much less than the bronze one he refused to wear, complaining that it was too hot and heavy. He hated having anything on his head. This helmet had·a simpler design, hardly more than a cap. It came down low across the forehead yet covered the back almost to the base of the neck, with two short strips of copper extending down to cover the temples. Inside, a thin layer of leather acted as a lining.

He tried it on. It fit almost perfectly, only a little too tight over his temples. Pulling it off, he bent the soft metal flanges slightly, then replaced it on his head.

"Trella said to give it to you right before the battle, so that you wouldn't have any excuse to lose it." Gatus turned to the bodyguards. "If he takes it off, carry him off the wall, no matter what he says. Understand?" They muttered their agreement, and Gatus turned back to Eskkar. "Wear it for her sake, Eskkar. You'll need it with all these arrows flying around. Good luck to you."

One of the bodyguards helped Eskkar with the straps as he fastened the helmet under his chin. Copper wasn't as good as bronze at stopping a sword stroke, but it would probably turn aside a barbarian arrow, even at close range. Moving his head tentatively from side to side, he tested the helmet's feel. It rested lightly enough on his head, so he had no cause to complain. He turned back to the wall.

The leader of all the Alur Meriki had nearly reached the front of his men, riding up a slight incline that permitted a better view. The other chiefs already waited there. Eskkar watch them exchange greetings before they began to speak. The discussion went on for a long time. Everyone appeared calm, no angry words or gestures that he could see, as the chiefs presented their plans for battle.

The talk ended abruptly. The war chief rode back to his men on the front lines, while two other chiefs returned to their own clans. Probably three hundred in the attack, with an equal number ready to join in if the attack succeeded or looked close to success. The other chiefs remained with their sarrum, to watch the battle with him and point out any mistakes made by their counterparts.

"Those chiefs seem pretty calm," Gatus said. "Is that good?"

"I think so. If the attack chief hadn't gotten approval, he would have argued with the clan chief, so we'll have our attack. Which is good, because they don't have enough ladders to climb the wall. They're expecting us to collapse in fear and abandon the wall and gate."

Eskkar watched as the Alur Meriki gathered themselves, every tenth man raising lance or bow to show his readiness.

"Then I'd better get moving." Gatus left, walking slowly to his own position, as unconcerned as if this were just another training exercise.

Eskkar took a deep breath and raised his voice. "Archers! Don't fire until they cross the second mark. Not the first! The second. I'll flog any man who launches an arrow before I give the word." His voice carried down the wall, and he heard his words repeated by others even farther down by the gate and beyond.

"Are you ready, men?" This time his voice thundered and a roar of approval went up. Everyone had grown tired of waiting, and even those who felt fearful were past that now, just wanting to get it over with.

On the plain the barbarian chief in charge of the attack rode slowly down the line of warriors, speaking to men as he moved, his standard bearer and guards following him. He reached the end, then rode back toward the center. He stopped almost directly opposite Eskkar's position. The fool had pinpointed the focus of the attack. They'd start any moment now. Eskkar swallowed to moisten his suddenly dry mouth.

"Remember, the second mark," he shouted again, and this time he heard laughter from his men at his need to repeat his order.

The first marker indicated the maximum range of their arrows. Eskkar wanted the barbarians to reach the second marker, one hundred paces closer, before they began firing. The third marker stood one hundred and twenty paces from the wall, and the bows would need almost no arc at that range.

The time for orders and questions had passed and every soldier on the wall kept silent, while the war cries and challenges from the warriors mixed with the neighing of the excited horses. Eskkar saw the war chief's standard rise up as its bearer raised it aloft. Then it dipped and the line of men and horses burst into a gallop, the riders' shouts suddenly muted by the thudding hooves.

Totomes, in charge of the bowmen, took command. His orders echoed along the wall. "Draw your bows . . ." the same words and cadence used in a thousand practice sessions.

"Aim . . ." the riders were past the first mark. No one had

loosed an arrow that Eskkar could see. Hours of relentless practice ruled out any time for thoughts or worries.

"Fly!" and two hundred and fifty arrows were launched at the rapidly approaching horsemen. "Draw . . . aim . . . fly." The chant repeated, again and again.

Eskkar watched the oncoming riders, saw some go down as the first flight arrived, but not as many as he had expected. The next flight did better. The third flight looked a bit ragged, as the more proficient men worked their bows a little quicker, but it was fired with the bows almost level and its effect was devastating. Horses and men went down all along the line, though the Alur Meriki ranks had opened up somewhat.

The fourth wave of arrows struck fifty paces before the riders reached the ditch. Now arrows flew both ways. Eskkar saw an archer go down, struck in the forehead, even as he heard something hiss over his own head. But most of the Alur Meriki's shafts struck the wall, making a dull snapping sound as they struck the hard surface. The barbarians had only a small target to aim at, the upper bodies of the men on the wall, and they had to find that target while aiming and loosing their shafts from horseback at a dead run.

Then the enemy reached the ditch. Some riders showed their skill by jumping their horses off the ten-foot drop. Most of the horses, however, balked at the descent, stiffening their legs as they stopped at the very edge in a spray of sand and dirt.

Eskkar saw three riders tossed forward, one going headfirst into the ditch, the others clinging to their horses' necks. Arrows rained down on the warriors, as every soldier worked his bow as fast as he could. They didn't need a cadence now.

The Alur Meriki plied their own bows, some from horseback, others dismounted by force or choice, kneeling on the ground and loosing their shafts at the defenders. At least a hundred warriors jumped from their horses, leaped into the ditch, and raced to the wall.

Eskkar heard the thud of the first ladder as it slammed against the wall, saw the tip of it a few steps from where he stood and walked over to it, drawing his sword as he did so.

He had already started to swing the blade with all his strength when a head appeared. The heavy weapon cut through the man's arm and into his head with ease. Twisting the blade loose, Eskkar dug the tip into the wooden ladder and pushed with all his strength, sending the ladder as well as the next warrior sailing backward into the ditch.

Looking out over the plain Eskkar saw another Alur Meriki standard on the move toward him, the men moving quickly to support the first wave.

Totomes's voice rose up over the din, taking control again. The archers stepped back from the wall and notched their shafts to the string. "Draw . . . aim . . . fly!" The chant began again, as the bowmen's shafts sought out those across the ditch. Volley followed volley and the Alur Meriki reinforcements erupted into a confused tangle of men and horses crowding against one another. The Alur Meriki bowmen got caught by the confusion, and for a moment, few arrows flew toward the wall.

Villagers did their work, using the forked sticks to push away the ladders and swinging axes at any head that appeared. Totomes's commands kept sounding. Flight followed flight, fired together and on command, the shafts sent into the crowded mass of men and horses, with practically every arrow hitting something, man or beast.

The men began to cheer. Eskkar saw the barbarian bowmen were finished, broken by that deadly fire, their reinforcements driven back in confusion. His archers kept up the pace as the Alur Meriki wheeled their horses and rode back to safety. Arrows whistled overhead, but fewer now, as the barbarians continued their retreat, leaving those in the ditch the difficult task of climbing back out.

None had made it over the wall. Those mounted barbarians in the ditch found it much more difficult to get a horse to climb up a ten-foot embankment than to jump into it, and all who tried soon had arrows in their backs. Those on foot found themselves trapped. They were targeted and shot, as archers returned to the wall's edge and risked exposure by leaning over, selecting a target and loosing their arrows.

In less than a minute, all movement in the ditch had stopped, except for the riderless horses that trotted back and forth, eyes wide and whinnying in fear, searching for a way out of the ditch and away from the scent of blood.

"Captain, should I take a shot at the chief? He's still within range."

He turned to find Mitrac at his side. Eskkar's eyes followed where the boy was pointing. The two chiefs who had been involved in the attack were talking, no, shouting at each other, no doubt each accusing the other of some failing. Eskkar's eyes hunted for the marker stones and he saw that the two chiefs had halted between the first and second marker. Arrows kept landing near them, and they would move out of range in a moment.

"Yes, take the shot." Before he'd finished speaking, the lad's feet were braced and he drew back the shaft, taking one last check of the wind. A fraction of a second to aim and then the great bow twanged. Mitrac immediately drew another shaft, aimed it and let it fly. A third was in the air before the first one landed.

The chief who'd led the attack pitched forward as the long shaft slammed into his back. Three seconds later, the next arrow arrived, aimed at the other chief, but the man's horse moved and the arrow took the beast in the neck. Mitrac's next three arrows missed, as the wounded beast reared and lashed out in pain, tossing its rider onto the earth.

Eskkar swore at the bad luck that caused the horse to move. He saw the dismounted chief, stunned for a moment, scrambling to his feet, then falling back, an arrow in his leg. Mitrac kept shooting, but by this time warriors had surrounded the two chiefs and carried them off, though Mitrac did get one more rider before the warriors galloped out of range.

"Fine shooting!" Eskkar shouted, clapping the grinning lad on his shoulder. Eskkar turned back to the wall, leaning over the edge to see what had happened below, then turned his eyes south toward the gate. The barbarians there had already retreated, the hundred or so warriors far too few to force the gate. Eskkar and Gatus had faced more than three hundred men, plus part of another group, and they had still routed their foes.

Every voice on the wall erupted into cheers, shouting and waving fists or bows at the retreating barbarians. Gatus appeared, walking carefully along the wall, alertly dodging the excited soldiers, not wanting to get knocked off the back of the parapet. It had happened often enough in training.

"Well, Gatus, you survived another fight."

Gatus smiled. "Yes, Captain. And you can put away your sword. Better clean it first, though. How did it strike?"

Eskkar still held his bloodied sword in his hand. "Smoothly. Any problems at your end?"

"None to speak of. Most of the attack was here. Shall we go check at the gate?"

That was good advice. But first Eskkar raised his voice. "Silence!" It took three times before the men realized who'd given the order and the celebrations died down.

"You men did well." That brought another cheer and this time Eskkar raised his hand for quiet. "But this was only a little test, just a push to see what we're made of. The next attack will be worse, much worse, so stop all this noise and get to work. Where are the ditch men?"

Everyone looked around, but no one answered. "Get them moving. You know what to do."

The ditch men, mostly young men and older boys, would climb down ropes into the ditch, to recover arrows and weapons, and loot the dead. In a few moments thirty men and boys began sliding into the ditch, armed only with long knives to finish off the wounded. Each carried an empty quiver or sack to recover anything usable.

Each shaft was precious. Most arrows would be broken, damaged beyond use, or simply lost. As every person who'd ever drawn a bow knew, nothing could disappear right before your eyes as completely as an arrow falling to earth. You could mark its fall and yet the shaft would burrow itself under the grass or earth, never to be found. But every arrow point was forged of precious bronze and mustn't be wasted.

Eskkar and Gatus strode quickly to the gate, where they

found a smiling Bantor and Sisuthros waiting for them. Sisuthros had a small cut on his cheek that still trailed blood.

"It's only a scratch, Captain. But we held them off here easily enough. Most of the attack was at your end."

"You both did well, Bantor . . . Sisuthros. How many did you kill? How many did you lose?"

The two men exchanged glances before Bantor said sheepishly, "Uhm . . . I don't know, Captain. We haven't counted them yet."

Eskkar's orders had been plain enough. Immediately after the attack, send the ditch men out to retrieve weapons and count the enemy dead. "Get to it, then," he said quietly, managing to get more emphasis in his tone than his words. "Use the shaduf to get the dead horses inside. We can use the fresh meat."

The shaduf was a long pole mounted to a beam buried in the earth, used to lift heavy objects or water from the river. One end of the pole was weighted with stones, so that the laborers could add their weight to the stones and use the pole as a lever to raise heavy objects. Builders used the shaduf when building houses, as did traders at the wharf to lift heavy cargoes onto or off the ships.

He turned to Gatus. "Let's climb the tower and see what's happening."

The tower had become the tallest structure in Orak. From its top Eskkar could clearly see the Alur Meriki leaders about three-quarters of a mile away, talking things over. They'd dismounted, as they argued their cases. "I'll bet some of them are for trying again."

"They'd better change their tactics, then," Gatus answered.

"Let's hope they don't." Eskkar shaded his eyes with his hand as he looked out over the plain. The Alur Meriki had attacked Orak as though the wall wasn't there, using their usual tactics of launching a hailstorm of arrows followed up by lance and sword. They must have expected the villagers to break and run. But the wall deflected their arrows, and the defenders had stood the first test of fire. Meanwhile the barbarians had no cover at all.

"They have no more ladders," his second in command offered. "They'd be fools to try without more ladders."

Eskkar leaned out over the tower wall, where men had already begun the gathering. "You men down there! First pick up all the ladders and climbing poles, and throw them up over the wall. Pass the word!" He turned to Gatus. "You're right. They never had enough ladders and now they'll have to make more, many more. So we're probably through for the day, maybe tomorrow as well."

"There isn't much wood in the countryside, either," Gatus noted. "They'll have to ride quite a few miles to gather new supplies."

Every stick of wood the barbarians could use had been taken down. No houses, no carts, no corrals, nothing. Even the barbarians' horses would need to travel for fodder. The Alur Meriki knew how to live off the land, but the countryside around Orak was going to give them very little.

"Well, Gatus, when they come again, they'll have plenty of ladders, ropes, ramps, and anything else they can think of."

Gatus scratched his chin, rasping his beard in the process. "They'll not try to match arrows with us from horseback, either."

"No, they won't try that again," Eskkar agreed. "They'll look for an easy way and they'll wait a few days, expecting the war party to arrive from across the river. If I were them, I would try to burn the gate next time—really go at it with fire and axes."

"Or maybe they'll try at night."

It was the old soldier's primary worry, though Eskkar didn't think it very likely. Night fighting didn't stand high on the list of warrior skills. You couldn't use your bow very well, the horses would have to be left behind, and even more important, no one could see your bravery, which meant quite a bit to their way of thinking.

"That's why you're in charge at night," Eskkar said cheerfully, "because I know you'll keep the men alert and watchful. But I think they'll try the gate first. They know how to use fire, so I expect we'll see plenty of fire arrows next time they come."

Shouts made them look north, where a small party of Alur Meriki had ridden back, angered by the sight of village men scampering around their dead. But a few flights of arrows from the nearest defenders drove them off, leaving another body lying on the blackened grass.

Eskkar and Gatus left the tower and descended to the ground, where they found Bantor coming to meet them.

"Captain, there are sixty-nine bodies that we can see, plus at least that many horses. We had eight killed and seventeen wounded, but only two badly hurt."

The barbarians probably had another fifty or sixty wounded men, a third of whom could be expected to die, as well as many injured horses. So it had been a good exchange, eight for more than seventy. As for the wounded soldiers, if you took an arrow in the face or neck, you were either dead or dying. Wounds to the arms would be much less dangerous and the leather vests and caps worn by the men might stop an arrow, except one striking head-on or at close range. But now wasn't the time for the men to be patting themselves on the back.

"Only seventy barbarians! Gatus! Did you see how many arrows missed in the first few flights? Hardly any warriors were brought down at all. Tell the men that they'd better start aiming better, or I'll toss them over the wall."

Bantor and Gatus looked at each other but said nothing.

"We just killed off their weakest and most foolish warriors," Eskkar explained, raising his voice so that as many as possible could hear his words. "The next lot will be tougher and stronger and will know what to expect. So tell the men to stop bragging and get ready. And Gatus, as soon as the ditch men are back inside the walls, tell Corio to start pumping. Make sure the wells and water wheels are fully manned until the ditch is turned into mud."

Corio estimated that it would take at least two days to soften the earth properly in the entire ditch, longer for the area in front of the gate where the trench was twice its normal width.

"I want that ditch turned into a swamp by tomorrow." That would give the men something to do besides cheer and pound their own chests, Eskkar decided. He walked off, well satisfied with the day's results in spite of his harsh words to his men.

Two hours later Eskkar met with his commanders at the courtyard table. The late afternoon shadows had lengthened, providing a little relief to the partly shaded table.

"The wells are being worked to bring water up for the ditch, as are the water wheels," Gatus reported when they were all seated. "We've brought in thirteen dead horses and they're roasting on fires made from barbarian ladders." He laughed at the irony.

"Let's hope we have more wood and meat after the next attack," Eskkar said with a smile. "We'll have plenty of fire next time. They'll bring branches and grasses soaked in oil. They'll charge the walls at the same time and every section will be under attack. Many of them will be dismounted to provide cover for those who rush the walls and gate. And this time they'll send all of their warriors, not just a part of them."

He turned to Corio. "Now is your time, Master Builder. They'll heap firewood at the gate, try to burn it, or pull it down, while they try to shoot our men off the walls and towers."

Corio shifted uneasily on the bench. "The gate will stand, Captain, and it will not burn easily. If the men stand at the walls, the gate will hold."

Eyes turned toward Sisuthros, then to Bantor. The two men had worked closely in the last two months, building and guarding the walls and gate, training their men. "Captain, we'll hold the gate," Bantor said. "Many will die, but we can hold it."

Eskkar considered that for a moment. "We'll add half of the Hawk Clan to the towers and the gate, except for a few to scatter along the rest of the wall. Keep the experienced men in reserve for reinforcements." He turned toward Nicar. "We'll need the best villagers as well. And we'll need water, stones, weapons, arrows, and the men to help repel any who scale the wall."

"This is what we've trained for, Captain," Nicar answered calmly. "We understand the risks."

Looking around the table, there didn't seem to be anything else to say. Months of preparation resolved many decisions. "Now, what else do we need to talk about?"

Darkness had fallen hours ago before a weary Eskkar decided to get some sleep. He'd taken one last turn around the walls, making sure the men were fed. Food would be in short supply for the next few months and had to be carefully guarded and rationed. Now he slipped past the soldiers and villagers who continued to labor under torchlight in the courtyard. Stopping by the well, he washed the dirt of the day from his face and chest.

From today until the barbarians departed, the walls would be heavily manned day and night, with extra vigilance after dark. Fires would burn each night, with torches nearby ready to be raised over the walls, while men with bows in their hands watched ceaselessly. Gatus would sleep little this night, as he planned to inspect the men throughout the darkness. Ten lashes awaited any man found not fully awake.

Upstairs he found Trella waiting, sitting at the big table in the outer room. When she looked up, she seemed different. It took him a moment to realize that she looked tired, almost exhausted, a look he hadn't seen on her before. A wan smile crossed her face as she saw him. He went over to her and bent down to give her a kiss. "Have you eaten?"

"No, not since this morning. I was going to, but then the attack started and everyone was rushing around." She looked up at him. "I saw you on the wall, and suddenly I was afraid that you would die."

He sat beside her. Annok-sur called out from the door, though it stood open, then entered without waiting for acknowledgment. She carried a tray holding strips of roasted horsemeat, bread, and warm oil. She put the tray on the big table, then went to the smaller side table and filled two cups with wine.

"You should be tending to your husband, Annok-sur," Eskkar commented as he gratefully took one of the cups from her hand. The smell of the roasted meat reminded him that he hadn't eaten since before the attack.

"I already have," Annok-sur answered. "He returned an hour ago and is already asleep." She looked at him sternly. "You should be more concerned with your wife. She worked twice as hard today as anyone. Make sure she eats and drinks some wine. She'll need her strength." Her hand rested on Trella's shoulder for a moment before she left the room.

Trella smiled again, a little brighter this time. "Annok-sur is like the older sister I never had. She worries about me all the time. But I'll eat a little."

"No, you'll eat your share and drink some wine as well," Esskkar said as he reached for a strip of meat. "As I will, before Annok-sur returns and takes a stick to us both." They ate in silence. Esskkar finished his portion and took a deep draft of the wine. Sitting back in the chair, he watched Trella until she finished. "Now, what's troubling you?"

Trella drank more of her wine, though she usually limited herself to only a few sips. "When the attack started, I was watching from the roofs across the street. I saw you standing there, saw arrows flying past your head. So many flew over the wall." She looked away. "I thought I might see you die, right before my eyes. If not today, then tomorrow, or the day after." Her eyes met his. "What would happen to me if you die, Esskkar. What would become of me?"

The question took him by surprise. "If the village falls, Trella . . ."

"No, that's not what I mean. What happens to me if you die and the barbarians are driven off?"

His mouth opened in dismay. So now this frightened her. Not the thought that she might die, but that she might live. He hadn't bothered to think about the consequences of his death. He'd risked his life too many times to be much concerned about it. In battle you either lived or died, and those who spent too much time worrying about their fate often ended up dead.

If the village fell Trella would become a slave in some barbarian's tent, beaten at will, traded regularly among the male warriors who enjoyed new slaves, the property of anyone her new master might offer her to, and abused by her master's regular wives and children. Many women killed themselves rather than endure such a hard, brutal existence.

Tonight that fate didn't hold her thoughts. She would probably be one of those who killed themselves rather than endure captivity. For Trella, no torture could be worse than not being able to think, to use her mind, and to have no control over her fate.

He raised the wine cup and drained it. The wine jug tempted him, but he refilled his cup with water instead, using the time to think.

Trella waited patiently, as she always did, never prodding or rushing him, knowing that he needed more time to work things out than she did.

"If I die, you have the house and the gold. Gatus and Bantor would protect you, until . . ." His voice ran down. The soldiers could be killed as easily as he, and they had their own wives to consider. Trella had no relatives to turn to. With some property would come the pressure to remarry, and the Families might select a new husband for her, their duty for any widow with no family.

"A new husband would be found for you, or you might be able to select one for yourself, since so many know you and respect you. You're young and there are many sons from the Families . . ."

"So I would be sold once again," she answered harshly, "this time for my gold and my reputation, to be put on display until my new husband gets tired of me or grows angry with my words."

Eskkar tried to think about what he could say, suddenly wanting more wine and wishing that she'd brought this up some other time. "I can't say what the future brings. Let's talk about this tomorrow, when we're both rested."

She said nothing, just sat there, eyes downcast. When the silence dragged on, he stood and went into the bedroom. He stripped off his tunic and threw himself down on the bed, longing for sleep, but his mind thinking about Trella. What made it worse was knowing that she couldn't find any good solution to her problem. Otherwise she would have suggested it already.

He tried to think but his body, weary as only those who have fought in a battle could be, betrayed him and he fell into a deep sleep. Nor did he awaken when Trella, after a long wait, put out the lamps and slipped under the blanket with him, put her arm across his shoulder and silently cried herself to sleep.

23

Four days passed with little sleep or time to talk, as all attention turned to the spectacle beyond Orak's walls. The main body of Alur Meriki arrived late in the afternoon on the second day after the attack. They spent the rest of that day and the next establishing a semipermanent camp. Hundreds of women and children soon filled the hilltops, staring at Orak and its wall. The villagers, equally curious, stared back at their counterparts, and Eskkar had to set aside a section of wall so gawkers could see the barbarian encampment without disturbing the soldiers.

Even Eskkar felt impressed as he watched the traveling village re-create itself, as it did almost every day. Most of the encampment remained hidden behind the low hills, about two miles from Orak, but he knew a broad, open expanse would divide the camp into two parts. The warriors would pitch their tents, forges, corrals, and anything else needed for the battle on the side closest to Orak, while the families, their carts, herds, and animals settled in on the other side. At the extreme limits of his vision, Eskkar saw herders tending the flocks of cattle and goats that provided milk, cheese, meat, and hides. The horses grazed close by the river, more than two thousand of them, in three separate herds.

Nicar had scribes try to estimate the numbers of Alur

Meriki. It took most of the day, accompanied by much squabbling and arguing, before they agreed upon an estimate of more than fifty-seven hundred. Nicar shook his head in despair at the total, while Eskkar swore under his breath.

On the fourth day Eskkar invited Trella to the tower. They sat there for most of the day, while he explained Alur Meriki ways and how everything functioned for the good of the clan. Smoke from hundreds of fires trailed up into the sky and they caught the smell of burning dung mixed with wood chips whenever the wind changed direction. They watched as slave crews working under the whip built ladders and climbing poles. Another group constructed a battering ram, using a tree trunk dragged up by a team of horses. Carts arrived and departed, carrying lumber that would be used to form shields for their archers.

"They're a great number of people, Eskkar, but most are women, children, and slaves," Trella said. "And the horses. There must be more than a thousand of them. What will they eat? How long can they stay before the grass is all gone?"

"More than two thousand horses," he corrected. "And the warriors, they can eat the cattle and, if need be, the horses as well. A warrior can go for many days without food."

"If they eat too many animals," Trella said, "they'll have none left to breed. Any they expected to find here are across the river, out of reach, and they have no easy way to cross over. They've already stripped the land behind them. They must attack the village quickly, overcome it, and move on. Even the land in front of them is burned to the earth."

That matched Eskkar's assessment of the situation. The farther away the food source, whether grain or animal, the more difficult to bring it back to camp. Riders would use up as much food as they could carry back in a few days' ride, so there was little benefit in trying to move supplies on horseback. The cumbersome wagons traveled slowly and broke down often. A team of oxen could generally cover two miles an hour, and no amount of beating would make them move faster. Even herd animals couldn't be driven too hard, lest they die. So the main camp remained on the move, and always moving in the direction of fresh food and grazing.

"The Alur Meriki lost about sixty men in the first battle with the Ur Nammu, then another seventy across the river, and another seventy here, plus their wounded," he mused out loud. "That is . . ."

"About two hundred men," Trella finished the sum. "They seem to be waiting for the band across the river."

The day after the battle, the Alur Meriki built a signal fire on the highest ground next to the river, and green wood smoke rose into the air each day since. By now they'd be wondering what delayed their raiders, but Eskkar doubted they'd think the entire party wiped out, at least not yet. In a few more days, when no word came, they'd suspect the truth. That would make them wonder how strong a force opposed them across the river, and whether they dared risk another sizable force in a second crossing.

"When do you think they will come?"

Everyone asked the same question. "Tomorrow, I think," Eskkar said. "They are almost ready."

"Can you hold them off?"

Eskkar gazed into her serious brown eyes. "I don't know, Trella," he answered, his voice low so nobody else could overhear his words. "I just don't know. I do know they'll pay a heavy price, more than they ever imagined. We'll have to see." He kissed the top of her head. "Don't be afraid for either of us."

She straightened up, in control of her emotions and her expression. "Make sure you come home early tonight. We'll have much to talk about."

But when they found themselves alone in bed that night, there wasn't much to say, though he held her close and felt a tear on her cheek.

"Enough of my tears." She sat up in the bed, her voice firm once more. "You will hold the village, Eskkar. I believe in you and I will not be afraid of the future. You don't need to worry about me. Just take no unnecessary risks."

He couldn't see her in the darkness, but he ran his fingers up her arm, then touched the softness of her breast. "I'll take care, Trella." Eskkar ignored the whisper in his mind that suggested that tomorrow might be the day of his death. Holding each other, they drifted off into an uneasy sleep.

The next morning Eskkar stood on the wall and watched the sun rise over the hills to the east, the barbarian camp already alive with activity. One look confirmed his fears. The attack would be today, probably between midmorning and noon.

His men looked ready and every face showed determination. They'd be fighting for their families as well as their lives. Some sought revenge for blood spilled. Whatever the reason, each would put strength in a man's arm.

"By noon today," Gatus commented, lifting his leather cap and wiping the sweat from his brow.

"Yes, or sooner," Eskkar answered, shading his eyes as he tried to estimate what forces would be placed where. "But we have a surprise for them, I think."

After the first attack, the water wheels had fed water into wooden troughs that led through the wall. The troughs could be pushed out to varying lengths into the ditch. Two such devices had been built on each side of the main gate. In addition villagers lifted water from Orak's wells and fed a constant stream into the ditch, backbreaking labor that exhausted the laborers after just a few hours.

Even now, leaning over the edge, Eskkar could see water trickling out into the ditch and turning the earth into mud three or four inches deep. He'd tested it himself last night, lowered from a rope to the base of the wall, where he'd tried to walk around. Instead he had slipped and fallen flat on his face, to the muffled laughter of those above. After more sinking and stumbling, they pulled him back up, his feet encased in mud.

Now he sat on a tall stool halfway between the gate and the northeast tower that had borne the brunt of the last attack. Once again Eskkar expected this site to receive the main thrust. He felt self-conscious about sitting and resting while everyone else stood. But Gatus, who used one himself, urged him to take his rest whenever possible.

Out on the plain, the barbarians began their maneuvers. The war leaders shouted and waved their bows as they moved huge numbers of men and horses into position.

Ordinarily the Alur Meriki found it a simple task to position a warrior at a certain place. But today the war chiefs had much more to do. They had to assign men to attack certain parts of the village, this group of fifty to the rear gate, that group to follow them to the north wall, and so on. And this time each group had to carry ladders, ropes, and fire arrows, items not usually handled by warriors. Many would be complaining or resisting the assignment. Eskkar smiled when he saw ladders passed from one warrior to another, accompanied by much shouting and shoving.

"Warriors want to fight, not carry ladders," he said to Gatus. "The strongest hand the ladders to the weakest. But there are a great many men. And today they have plenty of ladders."

Gatus stepped away to ask one of the clerks assigned to counting the enemy whether he had finished his task, grunted, then returned to Eskkar's side. "It looks like about fourteen hundred men out there. At this rate, it will be noon before they're ready," Gatus said. "Look, they're bringing a battering ram."

Eskkar squinted into the sun and saw that a huge tree trunk rested atop a cart, pushed along by a group of slaves, a task that wouldn't please those assigned to it. About twenty horsemen escorted them to make sure they kept to their work. The slaves carrying firepots wouldn't be any happier. The pots needed to be replenished with fresh fuel, which apparently no one had remembered to bring. Resolving these issues took time and more hours passed before all the men and their burdens reached their assigned places. Other carts lumbered up behind the warriors, and the horsemen moved forward a hundred paces to allow the carts to come closer.

At the first stirrings of the horsemen a ripple of sound had run up and down the wall. The soldiers thought the attack had begun. When the horsemen halted, waiting for the carts to close up, Eskkar and Gatus turned to each other with smiles on their faces. The leading edge of the riders stood just within long range of the bowmen. The leading warriors sat on their animals while they waited for the final arrangements, believing themselves out of range, when in truth they stood about thirty paces past the first mark.

Eskkar turned to Totomes, who'd taken his station behind the commanders. His face showed that he looked forward to sending arrows into the unsuspecting riders. "Master Bowman, I think it's time to show these invaders what they're in for."

A villager readied his drum and waited for the order. He'd relay Totomes's commands. Totomes leaned back and waved his bow to signal the other lead archers. He took but a few moments to assure himself that everyone stood ready, and then he gave the order. Three quick beats sounded, repeated a few seconds later as another drummer relayed the signal down the length of the wall.

Two hundred and sixty archers in two ranks on the wall readied their weapons, drawing their bows to the fullest and aiming up into the sky. Totomes gave the command, and a single drumbeat echoed along the wall.

A storm of arrows burst upward into the sky, followed by another and another. Leaders of ten called the cadence out, exactly as they had during the months of training. Eskkar's eyes stayed fixed on the distant horsemen even as he heard the rasp of wood on wood, followed by the grunts of the men as they let the shafts fly.

The first flight landed, many falling short, but enough striking the leading ranks as they sat there, many looking up at the wave of arrows that approached, more surprised than worried about any danger at that range. That didn't last long. As the second cloud descended, animals reared up in pain and wounded men cried out or slipped from their horses. Though nearly spent at such long range, the heavy bronze-tipped shafts could still kill.

The leading warriors tried to move back, but the riders behind blocked their path, and no chief gave any orders to retreat or move forward. The carts continued their journey and added to the confusion, as sweating slaves under the lash and their masters kept directing men and animals forward.

The Alur Meriki milled about in confusion while eight hailstorms of arrows fell upon them. A few rode forward, trying to move under the cloud of missiles, while others forced their animals to the rear. Those who rode forward became targets for the lead archers, allowed to pick their own shots, and soon shafts flew at those who had moved toward Orak.

Eskkar saw one such rider knocked clean off his horse. Another warrior clutched his stomach and hunched over his mount. Suddenly the whole mass of men surged rearward, any semblance of order gone. Warriors might charge fearlessly through arrows in a wild dash for glory, but none wanted to stand in one place and be a target.

Laughter and jeers rang from the walls as the horsemen galloped back out of range, leaving their dead and wounded behind. That would delay them for at least another hour, Eskkar decided, sitting back down on the stool. Totomes walked over, smiling.

"Well, Captain, that was a good lesson for them. They'll not stand that close again."

"Good shooting, Totomes," Eskkar said approvingly. "How many did we strike?"

That required some closer observation. Totomes stepped to the wall, his lips moving as he watched the activity on the hillside. Others were counting as well, but Totomes apparently had faith in his own eyes. "I'd say that we killed another twenty or twenty-five men and horses, and wounded as many more. Better than I thought these men could do, with such small bows."

Eskkar felt quite pleased. Half a hundred barbarians would be out of today's attack, at no cost to his men. "I still say it's good shooting, Totomes. Not everyone can have your eye and your arm."

Totomes snorted. "Good shooting, indeed. To hit only half a hundred? Two hundred and fifty archers shot at least eight arrows each at a standing target. That's . . ." he paused a moment, eyes closed and lips moving as he did the sum, a feat far beyond Eskkar's ability. "That's . . . over two thousand arrows, or about one hit in forty. Not very good results at all."

"At five hundred paces, Totomes, I'll take any kills they can make. We've plenty of arrows and we've delayed their attack for at least another hour. Meanwhile they've been standing in the hot sun for most of the morning."

"Standing without water," Gatus added, coming over and joining in on the last part of the conversation. "Both the horses and men will be thirsty."

Eskkar glanced up at the sky, for once grateful of the heat that burned down from the heavens. The defenders had plenty of food, salt, and water, as evidenced by a steady stream of men using the latrines.

The Alur Meriki took more than an hour to regroup. Eskkar could see the frustration as they readied themselves. One clan leader struck a man with a sword, knocking him from his horse, and farther down the line a fight broke out in the ranks with a dozen men involved.

Finally everything was in place and an Alur Meriki drum began to pound. With shouts of relief the horde began to move, walking their horses up to the line of arrows that protruded from the earth and marked plainly the true range of the villagers' shafts. As they neared it, Eskkar heard Totomes ready the men. They nocked their arrows and drew their bows. The waiting is over, Eskkar decided. One way or another, five months of work would be decided in the next hour.

Along the wall, Totomes, Forno, and the other lead archers calculated the range perfectly. At the same moment the Alur Meriki began to gallop their horses, the first flight of arrows flew free, rushing to meet the approaching horsemen. Eskkar stood up, gathered the stool and slipped to the back edge of the rampart. He dropped the stool down to one of the villagers below. Then Eskkar stood beside Totomes and watched as the northerner directed the archers.

The barbarians rode quickly through the hail of arrows. Eskkar watched the bows, lowered slightly for each shot, until the archers held them level and fired directly, the height of the wall giving them another small advantage in range. The first arrows from the Alur Meriki arrived with a clatter, most of them hitting the wall, some flying overhead, and only a few striking the men.

At that extreme range, many of the spent shafts bounced off leather jerkins. Nevertheless cries of pain sounded, as arrows pierced bare arms and shoulders. Eskkar saw one man struck in the eye and killed instantly. But the creak of wood followed by the twang of the released bowstring went on steadily. Enemy horsemen were dropping even as they reached the ditch. This time the horsemen pulled up, not wanting to be caught in the ditch. But a few jumped their beasts in, while others split to each side of the eastern wall, turning along the narrow path to ride down the north and south sides.

Those who jumped into the ditch found more than they bargained for. The horses sank into the mud and despite the din Eskkar heard leg bones snapping as they pitched, man and beast, to the ground. The high-pitched screams of horses in pain rose above the cries of wounded warriors.

But many of the warriors remained on their horses, trading arrows with their foes on the wall, while others dismounted and leaped down into the ditch. The soldiers kept firing their shafts into the mass of men and animals, with barbarians so crowded together that almost every arrow struck something. If this keeps up, Eskkar thought, we'll break them right here.

Totomes's voice boomed over the men, shouting orders that echoed along the wall. The first rank of archers leaned over the wall and began killing those on foot below. A few volleys and the attackers below began trying to scramble back out. Meanwhile the second rank of archers continued to fire into the enemy across the ditch.

Even with only a single row firing, they devastated the riders. The bowmen could scarcely miss such a massed target at close range. Soon the far side of the ditch was littered with men and animals, some writhing in pain, many with multiple shafts protruding from their bodies. A drum began to sound at the rear of the barbarian ranks and the riders broke off, riding north and south to get away from the deadly arrow storm. Others dismounted to attack the walls on foot as carts finally reached the edge of the ditch, pushed into position by slaves and warriors.

With the carts providing some shelter the barbarians began to shoot back at the men on the walls. Totomes directed all the archers to aim at the bowmen behind the carts. Arrows struck home there, instantly turning the carts into a forest of arrows as dozens of shafts hit.

But the carts made a difference. A mass of Alur Meriki moved forward and into the ditch, while the defenders continued to exchange shafts with the warriors protected behind the carts. At least three hundred fighters plied their bows, so they more than matched the defenders. However, the Alur Meriki shot at longer range, about ninety paces, an easy distance for the practiced archers behind the wall. Under their fire the men standing next to the carts went down first. And as more and more men crowded behind the wagons to fire their weapons, even the smaller targets offered were being hit.

The men needed little guidance, each man firing as quickly as possible. Eskkar turned away from the wall to look back down into the village. The villagers, men and women, kept on doing their jobs. Fresh quivers of arrows continued to reach the bowmen, and enough dead men lay behind the wall to provide replacement bows.

Totomes bellowed orders that brought villagers, armed with axes and forked sticks, up the parapet. The archers continued to ply their bows, moving back just enough to allow these new defenders to take their positions directly behind the wall. The rampart was only four long paces wide, and three ranks of men could barely fit on it at one time.

Ladders slapped against the wall, some pushed away instantly by the villagers, but others remaining as the attackers below used their weight to hold them in place. Eskkar looked out across the ditch. The defenders' deadly archery continued to take its toll. The barbarian bowmen, carts notwithstanding, seemed to show little stomach to go toe to toe with Orak's bowmen. Less than half of their original number remained standing. Many of these now huddled behind the carts, themselves barely visible beneath the hundreds of arrows protruding from them.

Eskkar's archers kept firing, grunting steadily with the effort to bend the stiff bows and launch the heavy shafts. Weeks of practice had toughened those muscles and he saw no one fail to pull the shaft to his ear before releasing. A thrill of pride went through him that they could take such punishment and continue to fight so effectively.

In front of him Eskkar saw a man and a woman struggling to push back a ladder. He added his weight to the forked stick and the ladder moved slowly vertical, then toppled backward. As Eskkar moved closer to the edge an arrow rattled off his copper helmet. Barbarian archers stood below, waiting to shoot at any target that appeared on the walls. He looked at the man and woman, their eyes wide with fright, and grinned at them. "Rocks! Rocks!"

All along the parapet, the same command rang out. The villagers dropped their axes and sticks and began tossing the hoard of stones over the wall. The rounded river rocks, about the size of a melon, made a deadly missile. They were heavy enough, and with fifteen feet to fall, dealt a blow that could snap an arm or crack a skull. For those at the bottom of the ditch, which gave the stones an extra ten feet, the rocks would crush a skull even inside a helmet.

The rain of stones provided yet one more shock to the attackers, struggling in the mud that hampered their movements and now trying to dodge the deadly rain from above.

Of all the practice drills the villagers had conducted, stone-tossing had been the most physically demanding. The men had trained to throw the stones in a random pattern, but always to try and drop them close to the base of the wall. It had been exhausting, backbreaking work, first to place the stones on the wall, toss them down, then retrieve them and repeat the process. Now that effort proved its worth. In the time a man could count to sixty, more than a thousand stones rained down on the Alur Meriki.

This new tactic stopped any attempt to climb the wall.

Meanwhile, a cheer went up from Totomes and the archers, as the barbarians' bowmen behind the carts began to move back, unaccustomed to this kind of exchange and surprised at their losses.

Totomes's voice rang out, ordering the villagers away from the wall. He ordered the rear rank to continue firing at the departing archers and moved the first rank up to the wall's edge, so they could lean over and shoot at anything below. A few archers were struck by arrows from the men below but the rocks had disrupted the attackers and forced the men carrying ladders away from the wall, pushing them into the kneeling archers behind them. Now Eskkar's men delivered a volley of arrows, ducked, then fired another. After the third volley, they didn't bother to duck back down, as the barbarians began to flee. Eskkar moved forward and took a quick look, then immediately ducked his head as two arrows flew over him.

The copper helmet made him too conspicuous. He'd have it painted brown tonight. But the quick glance had told him what he wanted to know. The fight would continue, but the attack against this part of the wall had failed.

He decided to check the gate. Slipping away from the wall he swung down from the back of the rampart and let himself drop to the earth, his bodyguards following him. His horse stood ready under the rampart. A scared youth held the halter, the rope wrapped so tightly around his wrist that it took a moment to loosen it.

Eskkar thanked the lad as he mounted and cantered toward the gate. The short distance made it hardly worth the trouble to mount and ride. But it looked better to arrive by horseback rather than appear out of breath by running from one place to another. At the gate he found confusion everywhere. Fire arrows still struck the mud-covered houses behind the gate, some shafts still burning harmlessly. Eskkar needed only a glance to see the fighting there had been brutal, with bodies of the dead lying beneath the rampart, most with arrows in their faces or throats.

Smoke and the smell of burning wood floated in the air. A few men, far less than he expected, struggled with buckets of water or bundles of arrows, carrying their loads to those in the towers or standing on the gate itself.

A boy ran up and took the halter from Eskkar as he dismounted. Moments later, the twenty men of the reserve arrived, breathing hard from the quick run. He divided the reserve force and sent half to each tower, but he climbed the steps that led to the top of the gate. Only a few men stood atop the upper rampart and these were busy pouring water over the top of the gate, trying to keep the wood wet.

The lower rampart, only ten feet off the ground, held fewer than ten men firing arrows through tiny slits carved at the intersections of the vertical logs. The supply of rocks on both ramparts had been exhausted and no one carried replacements. He saw the other reserve force of soldiers had already been committed. He turned to find Nicar and Bantor at his shoulder, his subcommander's arm covered with blood.

"Where are the men bringing the stones?" he shouted before they could speak.

"They've run away." Nicar had to raise his voice to be heard over the din. "I sent for more men but they haven't arrived yet."

"Get men from anywhere and have them bring stones as they come. Hurry!" He turned to Bantor. "Are you holding?"

"Yes, but barely . . . the fires are beginning to grow. We need more water as well." As he spoke, they heard a huge crash as something hammered against the gate.

"If we drive them away from the base of the gate, the fires will go out by themselves." The gate shuddered again. Eskkar sprinted up the ladder, swinging himself onto the top rampart, shouting down for his bodyguards to find bows and follow him.

"Archers! Get to the upper rampart." Eskkar and his guards, plus the men still fighting, now numbered a dozen. He spaced them out along the rampart. When they were ready, Eskkar commanded, "Start from the back of the ditch. Don't try for the ones directly beneath. We'll take them from back to front . . . Ready . . . loose."

The archers rose over the wall. Instead of one or two bowmen being the targets of many warriors, it was a line of archers who fired their arrows and ducked immediately back below the crest of the gate. The effect of the volley fire might not be impressive, but at least the archers, firing together, knew they would not be singled out. That gave them courage and at Eskkar's command they launched another volley. "Again!" The rain of arrows at such close range proved deadly to the attackers.

Eskkar glanced at the walls on each side of him. The men from the towers and the adjacent areas of the wall still exchanged shafts with the remaining barbarian archers across the ditch. If the barbarian bowmen directly below the gate could be stopped, then the men working the ram could quickly be killed. So far, it was working, four volleys fired and not a man lost.

Breathless men began arriving below, scooping stones from the piles, forming a human chain, and handing them up the wall. The gate shuddered regularly now, the ram's blows starting to take effect. Soon cracks would appear. The archers continued their deadly work, but already two had been struck by enemy shafts, one pitching off the rampart. Meanwhile from across the ditch, the barbarians targeted the men atop the gate, making exposure dangerous.

Eskkar grabbed two stones as they began to arrive. "Wait," he shouted at the fresh men who now filled the rampart. He moved to the center of the rampart and put down one stone. He waited until a row of men was crouching beside him, all on their knees beneath the line of archers. The rampart creaked and groaned under its weight of stones and men.

When the archers fired their volley, Eskkar stood, one stone held in both hands. "Now!" Glancing quickly over the top of the gate, he saw at least thirty sweating barbarians handling the ram, using ropes slung underneath the giant log to swing it back and forth. He hurled the stone down and saw it strike the ram, then bounce onto the shoulder of a man, who screamed as his bones snapped. In a flash, Eskkar gathered the second stone, and sent it down as hard as he could, this time not bothering to see what effect it had. Meanwhile his archers fired another volley. A shaft from the attackers buzzed right past his ear.

"Archers! The next volley is for the ram. Aim at those carrying the ram! Ready . . . now!" They went over the top, firing their arrows. The archer next on Eskkar's right dropped his bow with a cry, an arrow through his upper arm. Eskkar seized the weapon and took an arrow from the man's quiver. He'd spotted the warrior in charge of the ram, a shield raised over his head to protect him. This time Eskkar aimed carefully before he fired, ignoring the arrows that whizzed by his face, hoping his helmet would protect him as he targeted the man directing the battering. His arrow flashed low into the man's stomach, just below the shield.

Arrows and stones rained down on the men carrying the ram and the heavy log slipped sideways and fell. Too many bearers on one side had been killed or wounded. That stopped the ramming. The barbarians would need a sizable effort to upright the ram and get it into action again. Eskkar was amazed they'd managed to wield it even that long on such uncertain footing.

Stones kept crashing down from the gate and now villagers dropped them carefully, aiming them to fall directly at the base of the gate. In a few moments the barbarians realized their cover had disappeared and they turned and ran, staggering through the mud, easy targets for the men in the tower and the nearby walls. Moments later the ditch held only the dead and dying.

Eskkar saw a body of horsemen arrive across the ditch and realized that they'd been coming to reinforce the attackers. If he and his men hadn't managed to stop the ram, there would have been a hundred fresh men at the gate, more than enough to drive its archers below the wall. The warriors hesitated as they saw their comrades fleeing, and soon arrows began to strike among them. Some went bravely forward to help the men on foot, and a few paid the price for their courage.

The barbarians had started giving ground across the entire length of the wall as Totomes's archers finally swept the carts clear of enemy bowmen. Once again the Alur Meriki had to run the same gauntlet of arrows as they retreated.

Cheers sounded everywhere across the wall, even as leaders of ten cursed their men for using their mouths not their bows. But the defenders had tired, too, so they watched gleefully as the barbarians ran back to their original position of that morning. Eskkar glanced up at the sun and saw that less than an hour had passed since the attack began. Looking out again at the ditch, he found he could scarcely see the earth, packed as it was with bodies of men and animals.

The barbarians began to regroup under individual standards. Even half a mile away defeat and disbelief showed in their postures. The first attack a few days ago had been a probe, nothing more. But this had been a full-scale effort, and they weren't used to being beaten in battle. Even worse, they'd had to leave many of their clan brothers lying on the earth. Eskkar could see a group of chiefs, their anger and frustration visible even at nearly half a mile. They argued for some time, surrounded by hundreds of dejected and weary men. Finally the standards were raised. Men turned their horses around and headed back toward the main camp. The battle had ended for today.

Eskkar leaned heavily against the gate, breathing hard, then looked down behind him into Orak. Men and women from the village filled the space, all eyes turned upward, waiting in silence. They'd come because the fighting had ceased and they knew the enemy was moving off. Now they waited to hear the outcome.

Wiping the sweat from his eyes, Eskkar straightened up. He knew he had to speak, that this was one of those times when words were more important than swords. Taking a deep breath he raised his voice, inwardly reviling himself as a hypocrite.

"Men of Orak! The barbarians have been driven off for today." His last words were drowned out in an uproar that reached all the way to the barbarian camp. Eskkar shouted out the words again, but the jubilant shouting went on, until he raised his hands to silence them.

"We have won a battle, but the struggle is not over. They're driven off, but they will be back! And now they're filled with anger and hate, and they'll want revenge for those we've slain. As long as they're outside our walls, the danger grows each day. Return to your duties. There is still much to do."

That would have to satisfy them. He scrambled down from the gate, to find Gatus and Bantor waiting for him. Bantor had blood running down his arm and his eyes looked vacant as he swayed upon his feet. "Where is Maldar?" shouted Eskkar. "We almost lost the gate because the villagers ran off in fear!"

Furious, Eskkar's pent-up energy and frustration of the last few days rushed to the surface. The gate could have been stormed and the village captured for lack of a few stones and men to carry them.

Neither Gatus nor Bantor spoke, so Eskkar continued shouting orders, his anger apparent to all. "Send men over the walls to gather up their ladders and weapons. And wood-cutters to break up that ram and bring it inside."

He saw Corio pushing through the crowd. "Corio, get your men over the wall and check the gate. I saw men trying to dig underneath it, and the ram made cracks in the timbers. Make what repairs you can before dark. And don't forget to recover the stones!"

Gatus nodded and moved away, shouting orders to his men. But Bantor leaned heavily on one of the villagers and Eskkar realized his subcommander was seriously wounded. Blood dripped steadily from his neck, as well as from the ragged bandage wrapped around his upper left arm.

Eskkar turned to his bodyguards. "Carry Bantor back to the house and find a healer for him."

A horseman pushed his way through the thinning crowd. Eskkar saw that it was Jalen, come from the rear gate.

"Captain, do you need help here?" Jalen's voice showed his concern.

"No, not any longer. Any problems at the river?"

"A small party of barbarians rushed the gate, but we drove them back without much trouble. Everything is secure there."

Eskkar nodded, still hot with emotion. "Where's Sisuthros? And Maldar?"

Soldiers approached him nervously and the story came out in bits, as each contributed what he knew. Sisuthros had been wounded early, an arrow striking him in the mouth. The missile had passed right through and come out in front of his ear, taking out two of his teeth. He'd been bleeding badly when they took him away.

Maldar had taken an arrow under his right arm and passed out from loss of blood, just as his second in command had been slain. With their commanders wounded, the men had done the best they could. In the tumult, no one noticed when the villagers abandoned their duties and ran off.

Eskkar stepped toward the last of his bodyguards, so enraged that the man instinctively took a step backward. "Find the men who left their posts. Get them and bring them to me. Every one of them! I want them all."

The cowards had jeopardized everything, though they'd faced little danger themselves. They had seen men die and had run off to hide in their houses or under their beds. As if that would save them. He swore they'd pay for their cowardice. He took a deep breath and tried to control himself.

"Jalen! Take command here. Make sure the defenses are ready for another attack. Clear out the bodies from in front of the gate as well. Get the men water and food, then exchange some of them for fresh men from the other walls. Have the men change their bowstrings, get more arrows and stones . . . curse all the gods below, you know what to do!"

Everyone burst into activity, any thoughts of celebrating vanished by their captain's rage and all glad of any opportunity to move away from him. Eskkar took the time to inspect the men in both towers, keeping his anger suppressed and making sure they knew what to do and that help was on the way. When he felt the gate secure, he called out to Jalen. "Send word to Gatus that I'm going back to the house."

His horse still waited, the reins held by a boy of about twelve seasons. Esskar swung onto the animal's back, took the reins, then reached down and caught the boy's arm, pulling him up in front of him. "Come with me, lad. You've earned a coin for doing your duty today, and I have none with me." He kicked the horse and they cantered through the narrow streets, people scattering before him, his grim face frightening most of them into silence.

At the house he swung down from the horse, holding the boy in his arm as if he were a child. "Stay with the horse, lad, but get him some water. I may need him again."

Pushing his way into the courtyard he saw much of the space taken up with wounded. Nicar stood there, directing men and dispatching messengers. Esskar walked into the house where he found Trella and a dozen women working with the healers. She gave him a brief smile, but went on with her work. Four wounded members of the Hawk Clan lay there, including an unconscious Maldar. Bloody bandages covered his upper body and under his arm.

Esskar found Sisuthros sitting on the floor, his back against the wall and his chest covered with dried blood. His mouth, jaw, and neck had all been wrapped tightly. These bandages oozed only a trace of blood, though, and the man's eyes seemed alert enough. Sisuthros couldn't speak, but he lifted his left hand a little when Esskar saw him.

Walking over to him, Esskar took Sisuthros's good arm gently in his hand. "You look like you've been wrapped for burial." The man tried to shake his head, but the movement brought pain to his eyes. "Rest. We drove them away and the battle's finished for today and probably the next few days." Esskar looked around. "Have you seen Bantor?"

Sisuthros raised his hand again, pointing upstairs. Esskar ran up the stairs to the workroom. He found Ventor there, finishing his work, assisted by Annok-sur, her lips trembling even as she helped bandage her husband, unconscious on the big table.

Esskar stood there a few moments until the healer stepped back and began putting his instruments into his pouch. "How is he?"

"They pulled an arrow out of his arm," the healer replied slowly. "That must have been early in the battle. Then another arrow went through the side of his neck." He looked at Annok-sur. "Your husband is a lucky man. The arrow missed the big blood carrier." He turned back to Eskkar. "I've washed the wound and bandaged it, but he's lost much blood and his life now rests with the gods."

Ventor started to walk away, but Eskkar put out his arm. "Do everything you can for him. He fought bravely today."

"So did many others, as I can see by their wounds," he answered tiredly. "But I will come back when I can. Annok-sur will call me if something happens." Ventor pushed past Eskkar on his way down the stairs.

"I should be helping the others." Annok-sur's voice trembled and her shoulders shook with the effort to hold back the tears. "There are wounded all over the village."

"Stay here," Eskkar ordered, "and watch him carefully. Send word if you need anything." She stood there, twisting a bandage in her hands. "He's strong, Annok-sur. The gods will surely help him to recover."

There was nothing more Eskkar could do, so he returned downstairs, pausing halfway down to survey the aftermath, trying to shut out the moans of the injured. On the battlefield, far from water or healers, with any kind of a serious injury, most men died. Here, with many to care for them, maybe half might live. The women had prepared as best they could, making bandages from clean rags, setting up benches and tables for the injured, and ensuring that water and wine were plentiful, both for those wounded and those helping them.

Eskkar went out into the courtyard, striding over to the table where he found Gatus, Corio, Nicar, Rebba, and the other leaders. Gatus had emerged without a scratch, though he had been exposed often enough. As Eskkar heard their reports he ground his teeth in anger.

The problem was the towers. They drew arrows from every warrior. He swore silently that next time the Alur Meriki came to Orak, they would find more and bigger towers, so that the men defending them were not singled out. And future towers would project out over the wall, so that the defenders would not have to lean out over them to shoot at anyone at the base of the gate or the wall itself. He swore at himself for not thinking of that in advance, though nobody else had thought of it either.

Gatus took one look at his captain, poured some wine into a cup, and handed it to Eskkar. "How are they?" His head turned toward the wounded.

"Sisuthros is good . . . just can't talk. Maldar is bad, but may live, if the rot does not set in. Bantor is . . . has lost a lot of blood and the healer doesn't know. Or won't say if he does."

He held the wine cup to his lips and had to concentrate to keep his hand from shaking—though he wondered why he bothered. Plenty of brave men shook after a fight, grateful to be alive and away from the stress of battle.

"Get the Captain a bench," Gatus ordered, and one of the Hawk Clan pushed a stool over to Eskkar. "The scribes have finally finished counting our dead and wounded." Gatus squinted over the clay tablet. "Fifty-one archers dead, sixty-two wounded. If they come again, we'll have to strip the men from the rear and side walls."

Eskkar struggled with the numbers for a moment. A quarter of his fighting men were dead or out of action, and most of the casualties came from the towers and the gate. More than a hundred precious archers it had taken months to train. Now the defenses would be stretched thin.

"They won't be back today, I'm sure of that. How many did we kill? Do you have the count?"

"No, not yet. The ditch men are still doing their work. Jalen will send word when they've finished the counting."

"The ladders have already been picked up and the ram will soon be chopped into firewood, Captain," Corio added. "It will take them time to find wood and make new ladders. The gate is in good condition. The fires didn't burn long enough to damage anything, and the ram made only a few cracks. We're nailing new wood over the damaged places. It should be completed before nightfall."

Eskkar nodded in satisfaction. "Good, Corio, your gate

did well." A horse galloped up and a grinning clerk from Nicar's staff flung himself from the horse's back outside the gate and then rushed over to the table.

"Captain, I bring word from Jalen. We've counted the barbarian dead." The messenger paused dramatically before imparting his news. "Three hundred and thirty-two dead, Captain. That includes those killed in the morning," he added, then remembered the rest of his report. "Jalen is collecting the weapons and arrows, and he went over the wall to fire the carts they left behind."

"Ishtar!" Gatus smacked his fist on the table. "The fool will get himself killed over a few wagons."

The clerk looked around nervously. "The archers are protecting them and . . ."

"That's enough, boy," Eskkar said. Too late now to order Jalen back inside. By the time someone reached the gate, he'd either be finished with his burning or dead. "Anything else?" When nothing new was offered, Eskkar thanked the clerk and sent him back to his duties.

"Well, Gatus, the barbarians were fools to leave those carts behind. It will be good to burn them. Nevertheless, if we can count three hundred dead, then there are probably another hundred wounded. This is a terrible defeat for them. They've lost many men, including some of their best archers."

"What will come next?" Nicar asked. "Will they come again?"

"Oh, yes, but not until they have a new plan. They've learned their lesson today and they won't try to match bows with us again. Not like that at any rate. And today they learned we won't collapse in fear at the sight of them."

Eskkar took a deep breath. "If they come at the gate again, they'll be better prepared. They might have taken the gate today if they'd been more organized. They were slow bringing up their reinforcements."

Even the mighty Alur Meriki could blunder in the heat of battle, Eskkar realized. But they wouldn't make that mistake again. His eyes met Nicar's again. "Or maybe they'll come at night." Nicar looked uncomfortable, and that reminded him.

"Did we find those men who left their posts?" Eskkar looked at Gatus. "Where are they?"

Gatus and Nicar exchanged a look before the old soldier replied. "There are thirty men outside in the street," Gatus said calmly. "Four men were in charge of them. Three have been found and they're outside as well. We're still searching for the fourth man." Gatus leaned back and looked at Nicar.

"Captain, they just did as their leaders did," Nicar said defensively. "Most are good men and shouldn't be punished for their leaders' failures."

A silence fell over the table, though the moans of the injured and the voices of those tending them continued. Eskkar paused for a moment, trying to get his temper under control.

"Those men were supposed to bring stones to the gate. The reserve force was called up. Bantor, Maldar, and Sisuthros were wounded." He looked around the table. "If the fight on the north wall had lasted any longer, the gate would have been taken and the village lost. And now one of those who ran is hiding from us!"

Eskkar closed his fist and tapped it gently on the table. "I should kill them all, all thirty of them. Perhaps Bantor and the others would not be lying wounded if these villagers had stayed at their posts." No one met his gaze. "I'd kill every one of them, if I might not need them tomorrow." He let his fist open.

"The four leaders are to die and their goods confiscated, to be distributed with any other loot taken. The others will be assigned duties of greater danger. If they falter, the soldiers are to kill them instantly. What they did and why they're being punished is to be explained to every man in Orak, so that everyone understands what will happen if they run again."

Nicar swallowed nervously but kept silent. The look on Eskkar's face was plain to all. No entreaty would change his mind.

Gatus turned to Nicar. "It's better than they deserve. The villagers must see that their leaders are willing to fight for them." He looked back at Eskkar. "We'll find the fourth man soon enough. How do you want them to die?"

Eskkar wanted them tortured over the fire, but knew he couldn't order that.

"Just kill them, Gatus, as soon as you find the last one, just kill them and make sure everyone knows why. Do it in the marketplace, with a sword thrust. It's a better fate than the barbarians would have given them. Nicar and Rebba can handle the details."

He put all thoughts of those men out of his mind. "Now let's get ready for the next attack."

Two miles away, a disgusted Thutmose-sin sat inside his tent, still thinking about the failed attack he witnessed earlier. The dirt-eaters had not quailed at the sight of his warriors. Instead they fought bravely, their cursed arrows wreaking havoc among his men. Their outcast leader had prepared his men well, training the cowards to fight with the bow while hiding behind their wall. And each time the Alur Meriki pressed the attack, this Eskkar had rallied his men.

Now Thutmose-sin had to deliver even more bad news to the council. Bar'rack had ridden into the camp an hour earlier, near exhaustion. Bar'rack's clan leader, Insak, heard the story first. Insak then gathered Altanar, the other clan leader who'd provided warriors for the raid across the river, and the three of them carried the evil tidings to Thutmose-sin.

Bar'rack again related what had happened on the other side of the Tigris. Thutmose-sin sat stone-faced as the tale unfolded. The news didn't surprise him. He'd already assumed the riders were dead or scattered, otherwise they would have signaled days ago. It was one thing to be a day or two late in arriving, but it would be a foolish leader who disobeyed his sarrum's orders for more than a week. When Bar'rack finished, Thutmose-sin told him to keep silent about the loss and dismissed him.

"It must have been this Eskkar," Thutmose-sin said when they were alone. "He moves quickly. Across the river only a few days ago, then back to Orak to meet our attack."

"How did he know about the warriors," Insak asked. "It would take time to gather men, to prepare this ambush. Is there a spy within our camp, someone who . . ."

"No, I don't think so," Thutmose-sin replied. "From the Ur Nammu he learned about our plans to encircle the village. With that knowledge, he guessed we would send a force across the river. So he recruited the Ur Nammu to provide riders, made his preparations, and moved northward."

"He's a demon, then," Altanar said, "one of our own turned against us. He must be killed, flayed alive, and burned over the fire."

"On that we agree, Altanar," Thutmose-sin said. "But first we have to capture him. Summon the rest of the council. I'll tell them the news."

The two clan leaders left, and Thutmose-sin resumed his thoughts. Orak had turned into a disaster. Today's failure, coupled with this latest news, would turn the council into an angry mob. Outside his tent, he could hear the clan leaders gathering, some still quarreling about today's attack, blaming each other for the failure to capture the village. Their voices rose in anger, and the accusations and recriminations flowed freely.

"All the clan leaders are waiting, Sarrum."

Thutmose-sin cleared his thoughts, buckled the sword around his waist, then stepped outside. The full council of the Alur Meriki, with every clan leader present, turned toward him. His presence stopped the bickering, and they took their seats on the open ground before his tent. Only then did Thutmose-sin join them, taking the last empty spot that completed the circle. Markad and Issogu took their places behind him. No other guards were permitted when the full council met. Thutmose-sin nodded to Insak.

"One of my warriors has returned from across the river," Insak began. He repeated Bar'rack's story, taking his time and leaving nothing out. The council sat there, mouths open, stunned into silence at hearing that another force of Alur Meriki warriors had ceased to exist.

"These dirt-eaters," Insak concluded, "must be swept

from the earth. My clan demands vengeance on these filth. They are even worse than the Ur Nammu who shame their clan by joining forces with them."

They all started talking, asking more questions at first, then beginning the argument that Thutmose-sin expected. Some wanted to hunt down the Ur Nammu, some to raid the lands across the river. Others wanted to attack the village again, as soon as possible. A few, Thutmose-sin noted, wanted to move on. He counted these, relieved that only four clan leaders spoke openly of leaving Orak.

At last Thutmose-sin raised his hand, and the conversations trailed off. "My clan brothers," he began, "we must destroy this village. For us, there is no other way."

He gazed at every clan leader as his eyes went around the circle. "We are committed. We've driven the dirt-eaters to this place, and destroyed their farms and fields. Our men across the river were to prevent them from escaping, but they are not trying to escape. The few boats they might have are inside the walls, unused. This Orak offers a challenge to us each day that it resists. Its people are prepared to die here, and die they must. We planned for this battle. We traveled out of our path. Now we must finish it. If we had food enough, I'd stay here and starve them out. But the lands are empty, and we cannot remain here much longer."

"But the loss of the raiding party. Do we not need them . . ."

"The raiding party was to keep the dirt-eaters from crossing the river." Thutmose-sin stood. "Our men have watched the crossing and none of the villagers have tried to flee. Our warriors across the river would not be of any help to us even if they were alive. And I'm sure Insak and Altanar's men killed many dirt-eaters before they died. Now it falls to us to avenge our kin."

No one spoke. He'd shamed them all into silence, and now no one met his gaze.

"So nothing has changed. The dirt-eaters held us off today only by luck. Next time will be different."

He let his voice grow hard. "The Alur Meriki have never

been defeated. Remind your warriors of that. Tell them to prepare to attack the village again. Tell them that no matter what the cost, the next attack will succeed, or every Alur Meriki warrior will die in the attempt. And this time, my clan brothers, we will hold nothing back, and we will not fail."

24

Eskkar returned to his bedroom well after midnight and closed the door. Bantor remained on the table outside, resting under his wife's eye on a layer of linen blankets. Ventor didn't want to chance reopening Bantor's wounds by carrying him down to his bed. Instead the healer, along with his apprentice, took what sleep they could in Bantor's room downstairs.

He found Trella waiting for him, sitting cross-legged on the bed, a single, small lamp shedding smoky light throughout the chamber. He knew he'd kept her from sleeping, that she stayed up because he might need her.

"You should have slept," he chided her gently, though grateful she'd stayed awake.

Trella stood and came into his arms. "It's been a long day for you, Eskkar. I thought you might need to talk." She spoke softly, reminding him that others slept in the outer room. She held him close for a moment, then stepped back and helped him remove the great sword from his waist. "I saw what you did with the men at the gate. I was in the marketplace when they were killed."

Most of the wounded received treatment at the marketplace, and she'd gone there after doing what she could at the house.

He held her for a moment, then sat tiredly on the edge of

the bed. "I was angry. The gate could've been taken and all of us killed. They deserved to die. I wanted to kill them myself, put them to the torture."

Trella filled a cup with a mixture of water and wine and handed it to him. "They said that Nicar asked for mercy on their behalf."

He smiled at her, then drained the cup. "So you were at the table after all."

She took the empty cup from his hand and put it on the floor, then got on the bed behind him and began to rub his shoulders, her fingers strong on the muscles of his neck. "You did the right thing, killing only the leaders, and doing it quickly before anyone could feel sorry for them. But Nicar also was right to ask you for mercy for the others. You should thank him for it, you know." She kissed his neck. "He gave you good advice, though you did not ask him for it."

Eskkar started to relax. The massage stopped for a moment and he heard the rustle of her dress as she removed it. Then her hands were reaching around to hold him and he could feel her breasts soft against his back, her nipples hard.

"You need to get some sleep, Eskkar, before the morning is upon us. Let me help you sleep." She blew out the lamp and pushed him down on the bed. Her mouth found his and she kissed him tenderly, her hands moving over him, her body twining against his.

Suddenly Eskkar wanted her. His fatigue vanished and he felt the urgings rise up inside him. He'd survived another battle and now he wanted her, as much to prove that he still lived as for any other reason. He pulled her down beside him on the bed and moved atop her, heard her moan softly as he entered her and felt her arms encircle him. Then he thought of nothing else.

The sun had climbed well over the horizon before he awoke, the street sounds finally rousing him. Again Trella had let him sleep but had risen early for her own work. Eskkar felt annoyed at himself. The village lay surrounded by thousands of savage enemies and Orak's leader slept in his soft bed until well past the dawn.

He shook the sleep from his eyes and dressed, then went into the outer room, stopping abruptly when he found others there. To his further surprise, Bantor was awake, propped up by blankets and being fed soup by his wife. He looked pale and weak but his eyes seemed alert.

"Bantor! I'm glad to see you awake." Eskkar looked at Annok-sur. "Did the healer . . . I mean . . . is he . . ."

"Ventor said he is doing better." Annok-sur couldn't disguise the happiness in her voice. "He isn't allowed to speak. And he's very weak and must not move or exert himself for several days. The healer has already changed the bandages and says the blood flow has stopped."

"Well, that is good news," Eskkar replied, a smile lighting his face. "I must go, before the whole village thinks I sleep the day away." Bantor's eyes were full of questions but Eskkar waved them away. "Everything is taken care of, so don't try to speak. Annok-sur will tell you everything." Eskkar looked at her. "The women around here seem to know everything that goes on."

He checked in at the command table, where he learned the barbarians were keeping out of sight and that nothing had happened during the night. He went to the well, washing and drinking deeply of the cool water before he poured it over himself. Returning to the house, he entered the kitchen where he got bread, figs, and some fresh-cooked strips of horseflesh. Placing everything on a wooden trencher, along with a cup of water, he carried it all outside to the command table.

By then a tired Gatus had arrived, his watch just finished. Eskkar remembered that his second in command was getting on in seasons.

"I walked the walls at dawn," Gatus reported. "Everything is as it should be. Work continues on the gate and there's a huge stockpile of stones there now. Jalen is on watch and Hamati is making another circuit of the wall. Corio wants to know what he should do about all the bodies in the ditch. The smell will be rank soon enough."

Eskkar took a bite of the horsemeat and washed it down with a gulp of water, then chewed on a piece of bread, using the time to think. Trella had spoken several times about the need to keep the village as clean as possible during the siege. When he hadn't shown much interest, she took the responsibility on herself. He didn't understand her reasons for wanting to take charge of the sanitation but it seemed harmless enough.

She'd organized work gangs to cleanse the streets and make sure the villagers cleaned up after themselves. Carts now collected the human and animal waste each day and took it to the stables, where a huge pit had been dug.

Before the attack closed the gates, the carts had simply dumped their contents into the river, letting those downstream worry about the occasional floating gifts in their water. But the dead bodies in the ditch would soon be stinking. Not that he cared about that, but they might block the flow of water needed to keep the ditch muddy. In a few days there might be dry patches that the barbarians could use for their attacks.

"Gatus, I want the bodies dragged to the river and dumped in. We can't let anything interfere with the water flow. So let's use all the men who ran yesterday. I'll tell them they can redeem their honor by this task, if they do it well. We'll let them do the dirty work but we'll need soldiers and others to help, maybe even horses and some carts. If we prepare everything in advance, we can probably clear the bodies in a few hours, and maybe the barbarians won't try to interfere."

"It's a filthy job, not even fit for slaves," Gatus replied with a laugh. "They'll think twice before they shirk their duties again. I'll get everything ready and go out with them."

Eskkar thought it more likely that the sight of their leaders being executed yesterday might keep them better focused on their duties. "You prepare everything, but I'll watch them," Eskkar ordered. "You get some rest."

Gatus opened his mouth to protest but Eskkar held up his hand. "If I do it everyone will see how important it is, and I can get a chance to stretch my legs. I'll promise a few coins for those who work the hardest."

He stood up and went to the well for more water, carrying his empty water cup. A servant was there bringing up water and a fresh bucket soon appeared, cold from the depths.

Men always forgot to drink enough water when they had the
chance, and then a long day in the heat would leave them
weak from thirst.

A little after midmorning they opened the rear gate. Soldiers stood ready, just in case a horde of barbarians had hidden at the river's edge. But nothing greeted them except the
swirling sounds of the river. In a steady stream nearly two
hundred men and women slipped out, leading a few horses
and carrying ropes and planks. Everyone went quickly to
their assigned locations and duties.

They didn't have far to go before they found the first
corpses. The hot sun and slippery mud made it hard work,
and the bodies of men and horses were already covered with
flies that rose up in a cloud as they were disturbed. Many of
the dead had loosed their bowels as they died, adding the
stink of human waste to the smells of blood and open flesh.
They saw marks on the bodies indicating that during the
night, many small animals had feasted well.

The men slogged through the mud, dragging the bodies
toward the far side of the ditch, where other men tied ropes
to the corpses' feet, then coaxed nervous and excitable
horses to their dreary task. As they shifted the bodies, the
smell of death rose fresh in the heated air.

The worst jobs went to those men who'd fled their duty.
They had to wrestle the bodies from the mud to the edge of
the embankment. But yesterday's offenders weren't enough
to move all those dead by themselves. Soon almost everyone
was in the mud, all of them more fearful of being caught out
in the open than worrying about the dirt and stench.

They started from the river gate, working both sides of
the walls. It didn't take long to clear the rear, and soon they
began working on the sides. But most of the dead lay in the
front of the east wall, and before long the barbarians saw the
activity and sent horsemen to investigate.

They were a small party, fewer then ten riders, and they
held their distance, showing a newfound respect for the archers standing ready on the walls. Eskkar kept pace with the
laborers, shouting encouragement and laughing each time a
man fell on his face, or slipped backward on his ass. He had

led his horse down into the ditch, walked it carefully across the muck, then helped it scramble up at the other side.

Now he could ride back and forth as needed, keeping an eye on things and giving directions. His four bodyguards followed on foot behind him, no doubt cursing the heat and their captain's idea of exercise. Mostly, though, he sat and watched, letting the men know that he was there, while Nicar and others from the Families directed the actual work.

Eskkar heard his name called and looked up toward the wall. Trella waved at him, surprised to find him on the far side of the ditch. He waved back at her, feeling like an apprentice on holiday, before he rode slowly toward the front of the village.

At the southeast corner of the wall he stopped and watched his men's progress. Not that they looked much like men any longer. Rather they seemed to be made of mud themselves, having fallen so many times.

Eskkar looked east toward the barbarian party now less than a half-mile away, just out of long bowshot. As he stared another twenty or so riders joined the first party. They pointed their bows at him. Three of them rode toward him, staying out of range and shouting challenges at him, offering him a chance to fight them in single combat.

Ignoring them Eskkar turned his horse past the corner of the wall and rode toward the front gate, his animal picking its way carefully around the bodies and the remains of the burnt carts. The horse shied repeatedly at the corpses, snorting and jerking its head, as disturbed by the stink as any of the men. Eskkar kept his knees locked tight on the beast's ribs. Reaching the area in front of the main gate, he surveyed the damage.

Even though the gate was blackened by fire before the attack, he could see where the flames of the Alur Meriki had done their mischief. The cracks caused by the ram seemed large to him, but if Corio professed himself happy with the repairs, then it must be satisfactory. He had a big crew of men at work, making sure that the ground beneath the gate stayed firm and cleared of obstacles. A dozen ropes dangled from above, should the men need to be pulled quickly back

into the village. The gate would not open until the Alur
Meriki departed.

A shout from the wall made him turn, and Eskkar saw the
barbarian party had swelled to more than sixty or seventy
riders. By now they realized he must be someone of importance, probably by the way the villagers cheered and shouted
as he passed them. Eskkar moved on, walking the horse
slowly toward the northeast corner, inspecting the ditch and
the wall, trying to put himself in the mind of his enemies,
trying to guess their next point of attack. When he reached
the corner, he saw that a dozen warriors had paralleled his
course, staying out of range, but watching his movements.

His guards looked nervous, fingering their swords and
constantly watching the barbarians, but the line of archers
on the wall kept the enemy at bay. Eskkar knew the Alur
Meriki must be sorely tempted to ride in close enough to
launch a wave of arrows, but they seemed unwilling to risk
the danger, especially since Eskkar could easily ride away
from them.

The villagers continued to clear the bodies and by noon
they had worked their way around from both sides to reach the
front. By his order bodies not in the ditch would be left alone,
so plenty of stinking corpses would remain. But Eskkar wasn't
willing to risk villagers or soldiers' lives any further than the
ditch. Turning the horse he came slowly down the north side,
splashing a little into the swamp, letting himself feel the mud's
stickiness as the animal sank to its fetlocks in the man-made
marsh and had to struggle to free itself.

At the rear of the village the activity continued at full
speed. Bodies arrived steadily and were untied from the
animals. Men dragged the corpses down to the river's edge
where other laborers pushed them over the embankment.
Then they used long poles to shove the dead out into the current. In a few more moments the work would be done. The
river looked cool and inviting. Impulsively Eskkar swung
down from the horse and handed the halter to his guards.

"I'm going to take a swim," he announced as he unbuck-
led his sword and stripped off his tunic, grinning at the nervousness in their eyes. "If anyone wants to join me, come on

in." None of them moved and in a moment, he dove in, about fifty paces above where they were dumping the bodies. Here the water flowed fresh and clean and he soon felt refreshed and cooled. He refused to think about those who would be drinking the water downstream for the next few days.

Eskkar swam for only a minute or two, just enough to feel clean, before he climbed out. After drying his body with his tunic, he took the horse by the halter and guided the animal slowly down into the ditch and then through the mud until he and his guards had reached safety back across the ditch.

He stopped outside the gate and watched as the villagers shoved the last of the bodies into the river. With the filthy job finished, villagers and soldiers followed Eskkar's example, jumping into the river, laughing as they washed off the dirt and blood, and splashing water on each other. They looked cheerful, their task done.

The last work crew continued, their task almost completed as well. More than eighty villagers, mostly women and old men, wielded rakes, planks, and shovels, to rake the mud as level as possible. Wielding their implements, they smoothed the mud and filled in any holes. Another backbreaking task, but one that needed to be done properly to insure the even flow of water.

A boy came over to take his horse back to the stable, but Eskkar waited at the rear gate, watching until everyone finished their work and the last man and woman passed back inside. The guards pushed the gate closed, then barred it.

As the men passed by, Eskkar spoke to them, thanking them for their work. That had been Trella's idea, to make sure the villagers knew they'd been forgiven and to let everyone know he appreciated their efforts. Those disgraced by their cowardice now felt absolved, and he no longer saw any sullen or dejected looks on their faces, though he'd seen plenty of both this morning when he ordered them into the ditch. He felt surprised, though, at the looks they gave him in return. They had pride again and seemed glad he had noticed their work and thought it important enough to join them outside the wall.

Walking back home he found Trella upstairs, helping

Annok-sur change Bantor's bandages. Bantor looked even better than he had this morning, though Eskkar knew there was an even chance the man would die. Sometimes wounded men, no matter how strong physically, would suddenly take a turn for the worse and die, even after they seemed to be recovering. Bantor's eyes held many questions, so Eskkar sat down and described what had happened, though his subcommander had probably already heard most of it from Annok-sur.

They dined that night outside in the courtyard, at the same table where the morning's meetings occurred. Gatus, Jalen, Totomes, Corio, Nicar, and Trella sat at the big table, joined by two of the Hawk Clan. Alexar would take over the duties of Maldar, and Grond, who had been recommended for promotion by Gatus. Alexar, a small man, with a thin wiry body, claimed to have been a thief before he joined the soldiers. Grond was his opposite, tall, just a shade under Eskkar's height but broader in the shoulders. Grond's back showed marks from the lash. According to Gatus, Grond had been a slave in the distant lands to the west, but had escaped and found his way to Orak. Both men served under Gatus in the fight across the river.

After dinner, everyone sipped their wine, relaxing a little. Eskkar brought up the ideas he'd considered during the day.

"Though we hurt them badly yesterday, the barbarians will be back," he began, "and this time they'll be better prepared. They've lost many men and cannot afford to do so again. They've attacked the wall twice now with no success. So I think they'll hurl the next assault at the gate. They'll use more fire and find ways to protect their men while they attack." He paused to give anyone a chance to speak up, but no one did.

"That kind of attack will take them many days to prepare, so they may try something else first, maybe a night attack."

He paused, but nobody spoke. That silence had become more frequent. After each victory his words were received with more and more importance. Now anything he said was taken almost as if coming from the gods, and lately he had to prompt them for their ideas and opinions.

"Gatus, keep the wall manned each night, with men every twenty paces. I want them awake and alert. Keep the watches short so they don't get sleepy, and make sure they know the punishment for not being alert. During the day ensure they get plenty of sleep and that they are not awake gambling or wasting time with their women."

At least he didn't have to worry much about them getting drunk. Wine and ale were in short supply and the price of what little remained had gone up sharply.

The meeting ended and everyone went their way. In bed Eskkar took Trella in his arms and held her close. "The next few days will be hard ones, Trella. I worry more now than I did before the first attacks. Then, I felt certain we could surprise them. But after two attacks, they know how strong we are, and they'll be wary and cunning. And they're angry, filled with revenge for those we have killed."

"Perhaps they'll give up. Even if they could take the village, they know that they will lose many more men."

"That's what everyone would like to believe, but warriors don't like to be beaten. They'll fight harder, if anything. They'd be shamed in front of their women if they just slunk away."

"Then there is nothing we can do but defeat them when they come."

25

Ten days slipped by. Each morning as dawn broke, the men on the wall searched the plain before them, saw nothing, and breathed a sigh of relief. Today would not be the day. Bands of warriors occasionally rode about, but little could be seen, with most of the encampment behind the hills. The less activity they showed, the more Eskkar worried.

Almost every night brought some new threat. For the barbarians, the night gave them an easy opportunity to keep the villagers off guard. Using the cover of darkness, men would slip up to the wall, fire a few arrows at the sentries, then disappear. Sentries covered themselves with leather, but men still fell dead or wounded. By the time soldiers hoisted torches over the wall, the attackers were gone, and seldom did the soldiers have a target. Besides the cost in men, the antics kept everyone on edge and losing sleep.

Tonight Eskkar had little to say to Trella. He'd held her until she fell asleep, then rolled onto his back, wide awake, thinking about the besiegers. If he had enough men at their rear, even a hundred would do, he could attack the enemy and disrupt the camp, burn their wagons, scatter the horses. But he was not in their rear, he was trapped inside Orak with no way to get out.

Meanwhile, the barbarians continued with their preparations. The thought made him uneasy, so he got out of bed, pulling a tunic over his body and slipping out of the bedroom. Moving silently, he descended to the main floor, then out into the courtyard. A torch burned there at all times and the guards walked by, alert even at the end of a long day.

Eskkar nodded at those manning the command table, but walked toward the rear of the house. He sat on the bench, facing the trees where Natram-zar had been tortured. Already that time seemed long in the past, a mere trifle hardly worth considering.

One pleasant memory remained, however. A few feet from the base of the tree, where it came closest to the wall, Caldor's head had been buried deep in the earth. Both young Drigo and Caldor had insulted Trella, and both were dead, a fact all in Orak knew well. Caldor had even put his hands on Trella's body, but that would never happen again. No man would ever touch her and live.

Eskkar returned his thoughts to the Alur Meriki. He stared into the darkness, wondering what they would do next. He needed a spy, he decided, someone who knew their councils. If only he had a way to visit their camp, spend a day or two there, observing and listening. But no one could get out of Orak. The attackers had sealed up the village too well.

A shadow moved on the ground. He looked up and found Trella in front of him, a cloak wrapped around her body, though the night air held little chill.

"I thought you found it pleasant in our bed," she said quietly. "Or do you plan to sleep in the garden?" She sat down and leaned against him.

Eskkar put his arm around her and inhaled the scent of her hair. "I couldn't sleep. I started thinking about the barbarians, wondering what they're planning, where they'll attack next."

"You always seem to know what they think. Are their plans a mystery now?"

"Yes. They've many clan leaders, and right now they're all thinking about the same thing. They wonder about the best way to crack the nut Orak has become. How can they get past the ditch and the wall, or through the gate, so they can kill all of us? And now they have a new problem—how to do it without losing too many more warriors. So they prepare themselves and when they're ready, they'll attack."

He sighed. "Perhaps the gods will smile on us."

"The gods have already smiled on us. Nobody can doubt that, not even the priests. Why do you think they've been so quiet these last few months? They know you're touched by the gods."

The thought of the priests always brought a frown to his face. In the past the quarreling priests and their demanding gods had caused trouble enough in Orak, though the danger from the Alur Meriki had quieted them down. The less he had to do with them the better.

She rested her head on his shoulder, the cloak coming loose. She wore nothing beneath it.

He slipped his hand inside the garment and felt the heat from her body. Her breast felt soft and heavy in his hand. Eskkar settled back, letting himself enjoy a moment of pleasure.

She relaxed under his touch, closing her eyes, then lifting her face to his. "It's time for bed, and this time I'll make sure you go to sleep."

He smiled, then pulled the cloak off her shoulders, so he could gaze at her body in the faint light from the stars and the torches. The longer he looked at her, the stronger the urge became to take her right there in the garden. The guards would hear the noise and come to investigate, not that he cared about what they saw or thought.

"Then we should return to our chamber, wife." He pulled the cloak back around her and took her hand, then walked her back into the house, nodding at the guards whose smiles were tinged with envy at their fortunate commander.

Wide awake now, they returned to their bed. Eskkar forgot his worries and made love to his wife, a task that took considerable time as each seemed to hunger for the other. Trella seemed on fire, her own urges demanding satisfaction. Even after the passion overcame her, it only whetted her appetite for him, and it was a long time before they lay exhausted in each other's arms, sweat-soaked, the bedding a mess of twisted blankets.

Neither of them knew or cared that the shaking and half-muffled cries had awakened half the household and brought smiles to the guards who paced the courtyard below. When they'd finished, Eskkar held her close, before he fell into a deep sleep.

The alarm drum roused him instantly, the rapid beating telling him an attack was in progress, even before the soldiers' shouts penetrated his consciousness. Eskkar jumped to his feet, pulling on his undergarment and grabbing his sword before Trella was fully awake. He raced barefoot down the stairs, following the reserve soldiers as they ran down the street to the north wall.

As he ran his fear increased, since they headed toward the site that he had deemed most suitable for a night attack. Eskkar heard the clash of swords, but by the time he reached the wall the fighting had ended.

"Down, Captain!" someone shouted, even as an arrow hissed by his head. Cursing under his breath and bent double, Eskkar scuttled swiftly along the wall until he found Jalen. His subcommander had everything under control. Villagers shoved torches attached to poles out over the ditch, giving the crouched archers some targets. As usual, the nighttime attack initially favored the enemy, who could put their archers in place in the darkness while the defenders would be outlined against the wall and lighted from behind. Barbarian arrows had killed at least two men, as Eskkar saw by the bodies lying below the parapet.

But by this time the parapet held at least forty archers, and volleys of arrows flew into the darkness. Gradually the shafts from the attackers came less frequently. More torches added their light but little now remained to be seen.

Jalen finally had time to report. "A guard heard them splashing in the ditch and gave the alarm. Their arrows drove us down and they tried to climb the wall. Stones soon put a stop to that, and three who reached the top were killed." He looked around for a moment. "This was a real assault, not just a raid. I saw at least a hundred men out there. Did they attack anywhere else?"

"I don't know. Gatus was at the command table, and I heard only one alarm. Can you hold here?"

"Yes, we've plenty of stones, and the men are wide awake now."

"I'll go check with Gatus." Eskkar gripped his subcommander's shoulder for a moment, then swung down from the parapet. He dropped lightly to the ground below and raced back to the command house, now lit more brightly than when he had left it. He found Gatus speaking to several soldiers, all looking tense but displaying no signs of panic.

Gatus answered his question before he could even ask it. "No other attacks, Captain. Only on the north wall. Does Jalen have everything he needs?"

So the reports had come in smoothly to the command table. Eskkar could have stayed here and learned just as much without his mad dash. Well, next time he'd know better and keep his head. "Yes, but keep the messengers busy."

Gatus stared at him, and Eskkar realized he'd given another unnecessary order. Maybe I should have stayed in bed, he decided, since Gatus had everything under control. "I'll take a horse and check the walls myself, Gatus." At least that would give him something to do.

He found a horse and swung onto its back. In his rush to the attack site, Eskkar had forgotten that, by his own order, a horse was always kept ready for his use. Instead he had followed the running men. Curses flowed steadily under his breath as he jerked the horse's head harder than necessary and began to canter toward the rear gate.

Someday, he swore, if he lived long enough, he would learn to think before acting. He made the circuit of the walls not once but twice, taking his time and speaking to the men, urging them to keep silent and to listen for the sounds of men on the move. Three hours later he returned home, to try and get some sleep before dawn.

In their bedroom Eskkar hung up his sword, then sank onto the bed, as reaction to the long night began to set in. Trella lay down next to him and took his hand.

At that moment a hard knocking came from the outer door. "Lady Trella . . . Captain . . . please open the door." They heard Annok-sur's voice.

Eskkar pushed himself up off the bed, knowing something important had occurred or they wouldn't have troubled him. Trella reached the door first and unbolted it, to find Annok-sur standing there.

"Jalen sends word for you to come. A slave boy escaped from the enemy camp."

Seated at the big table in his workroom, Eskkar waited for the strange boy to finish his meal. Simcar claimed to have twelve seasons, but his stick-thin body looked younger. Trella and Annok-sur had insisted on cleaning the boy up first. When Trella escorted him to the workroom, Eskkar, Gatus, and Sisuthros waited, eager to learn what the boy could tell them.

But then Trella had insisted the boy first eat his fill. So the three tired soldiers, who had no sleep that night, watched Simcar eat and drink. Eskkar had to admit the boy looked as if he hadn't enjoyed a real meal in months. Finally the eating slowed and at last stopped.

"Now, Simcar, tell us who you are and what you've seen," Trella began encouragingly, reaching over and wiping the boy's mouth with a bit of rag, then taking his hand and holding it. "Take your time and tell us everything."

Simcar's eyes widened, nervous under the gaze of the men. At first he had trouble speaking, his voice high and uncertain, but under Trella's smiles he gradually gained confidence.

"Three months ago, the Alur Meriki raided my father's farm. We lived in the lands to the north. They killed my older brother, but they wanted us for slaves. They beat all of us, and we had to work very hard just to get something to eat."

"Did you learn their language, Simcar?" Trella smiled at the boy.

"Oh, yes, we had to learn fast. They beat us every time we didn't understand. My mother helped me, as long as she could."

"What happened to your family?"

"They killed my father a few weeks ago. He did something bad . . . I'm not sure what. My mother is a slave to one of their clan leaders. I don't know what happened to my sister."

Eskkar saw moisture in the boy's eyes, but pretended not to notice.

"I'm sorry for your family." Trella patted his shoulder. "What made you run away from them?"

"My mother told me. She said I had to try to escape to Orak. She'd heard the stories about the fighting, and said this was my best chance. I didn't want to leave her, but . . ." Simcar's voice choked, and he stopped for a moment. "She told me to sneak across the plain if the night attack failed, that they wouldn't be looking for anyone trying to get into Orak."

"You're safe now, Simcar," Trella said reassuringly. "Your mother was right to send you here. But we need to ask you some questions. We're trying to find out what attacks the Alur Meriki have planned. Can you help us?"

Eskkar and the others leaned closer, each of them with a dozen questions but they'd agreed to let Trella guide the boy through his story. Eskkar forced himself to smile to conceal his impatience. "You were very brave to slip through their lines, Simcar. Go on."

The boy brightened at the compliment, and Trella began her questions. What were the other boys like? Were there many women in the camp? Was there enough food for all the boys? How did the animals look? Well fed or lean? Was water in plentiful supply? How about firewood? What did you eat each day? What did the other boys say about Orak? How did the warriors look? Were they angry or patient? Did you see any clan chiefs? What were they like? Did you hear anyone speak about them in anger? Where were the horses? How many were there? Were there many guards? Did the warriors quarrel among themselves. Over what?

With each question Simcar's replies grew longer and more detailed, as if he were proud of the fact he'd noticed all the things Trella inquired about. Eskkar kept the smile fixed on his face and by now Gatus and Sisuthros had taken the hint and nodded encouragement to the boy as well, masking their eagerness as best they could. Esskar saw Gatus biting his lip and Sisuthros's hand gripping the edge of the table. But Trella chatted away, keeping her tone light and her questions short, stopping once to ask if Simcar wanted more food or water.

Gradually the picture unfolded and Esskar realized he was seeing the Alur Meriki encampment through the boy's eyes. The large central camp, flanked by two smaller ones. The herds of horses pastured up against the river. Another, smaller herd kept to the south, though the grass was poorer there—the lands closest to the river had already started to see some regrowth after the burning. The wagons and carts moving to and fro, changing owners as men died in the fighting and their wives and possessions were taken or traded to the remaining warriors. The path the women and girls took to get water from the river.

From the boy's story Esskar visualized the line of sentries hidden beyond the low hills that overlooked the approaches to and from the village. A band of forty or fifty warriors waited behind the sentries, in constant readiness to prevent anyone from trying to enter or leave the village, or to repel any sorties from the gate. Esskar could almost hear the women weeping late into the night and the sullen looks of the boys whose fathers had been killed.

As Simcar went on Esskar pictured the warriors' angry faces as they strode about the camp, unable to attack the village, yet with no other target for their rage within fifty miles. Fighting men forced to remain in idleness, with too much time on their hands, and not even the usual activity of the day's march to occupy them. Naturally they would take to drinking and quarreling when the sun went down.

Simcar had been talking for some time and Trella's questions became more direct as she and the boy grew comfortable with each other. ". . . so, Simcar, did you hear of any plans the Alur Meriki have to attack Orak?" The question seemed casual, but Esskar found himself leaning forward a little more.

"Yes, Lady Trella. Six nights ago their leader, Thutmose-sin, met with the council, and I decided to go listen to them talk about the battle." By now the words flowed easily from his lips. "I crept up to the campfires and found a place where I and some other boys could watch and listen. We heard them plan how they would attack Orak at night."

Under the table, Eskkar's hand knotted into a fist again and he had to force himself to relax it. If the boy had heard their plans . . .

"And no one chased you away?" Trella poured more water into Simcar's cup.

Simcar took several large swallows before replying. "No, the guards didn't care, and there were many others even closer. So I went again last night, after the battle. The chiefs met again, along with many of the warriors. There was much shouting and pushing, and Thutmose-sin raised his voice many times. The guards didn't even notice us this time, there were so many warriors there. They wanted to listen, too. I could only hear them when they raised their voices, but they did that a lot."

Trella patted his shoulder. "Tell us what you heard. Start from the beginning."

"Well, Thutmose-sin began talking about why the night attack did not succeed. He blamed one of the other chiefs for the . . . failure." Simcar had to stop to think of the right word. "Said it was something he'd told them wouldn't work. He was very angry that they had been defeated. There was more shouting and cursing. Some raised their fists against Thutmose-sin. Others said the Alur Meriki should move on, that there was little to gain here even if the fire attack is successful."

"What's the 'fire attack,' Simcar," Trella asked unconcernedly, picking at some threads on her dress, merely another in the long list of questions. "Is that something special that they have planned?"

"Oh, yes! They have loaded a great number of carts, all piled high with wood and logs and anything that will burn, enough to burn the whole village down, my master says. They'll place the carts against the gate and set fire to it until the gate is burned away. They've been collecting wood from the countryside for more than a week, soaking it in the black oil or drying it in the sun."

"What else did they say about the fire attack?" Trella's voice remained soothing, as if this topic were no more important than questions about the camp's food.

"Well, nothing more. Thutmose-sin said the fire attack would succeed, that the other attacks had just wasted time and men. They argued about it for a long time, and then everyone just left and went back to their tents."

So Thutmose-sin remained the great chief, Eskkar thought. All these months and they hadn't even been sure who led the Alur Meriki. But now Thutmose-sin's time was running out. The sarrum argued openly with his chiefs and nothing less than a quick victory would save him. He'd failed to capture Orak, so he would be doubly dangerous as desperation forced his hand.

"Do you know when they will come with the fire wagons, or how?" Trella went on. Once again she held Simcar's hand and smiled at him.

"Oh, yes, Lady Trella, it will be soon. I heard all about it from my friend. All the camp knew of the plans. They'll use great wooden shields to protect them from the archers. Then they'll heap the dry timber against the gate. They'll fire the wood and keep adding more until the gate is destroyed. Then they will cross the ditch and attack through the gate."

Trella questioned the boy for another few moments, but eventually she sat back and looked at Eskkar. "Well, Simcar, you were very brave. Now I think Eskkar would like to ask you a few things. Do you need to rest first?"

The boy shook his head.

By now Eskkar had only two questions. "Simcar," he began, keeping his voice calm, "where is this great pile of wood and carts, and do you know if they keep a guard on it?"

"Yes, lord. The wood is stored behind the rise to the south. My mother and I tried to get close once, but the guards there threw stones and chased us off. They knew we wanted to steal firewood. There's always a guard there, otherwise women would take all the wood and use it for the campfires. I think," he paused to remember, "I think there were three or four men guarding it."

Gatus and Sisuthros had other questions but they learned little more. After a while, Trella suggested they let Simcar get some rest. She escorted the boy to the door and turned him over to Annok-sur before returning to the table.

"Best to let him sleep for a few hours, then we can go over his story again. He may remember something else of importance." Trella leaned back in her chair and looked at the three men.

"Well, we knew they were coming soon," Gatus said, shifting in his seat and twisting his shoulders. They'd scarcely moved for nearly an hour, not wanting to disturb the boy's tale. Sisuthros poured water for all of them.

"And we know how and where," Eskkar finished. "This time there will be nothing held back. Thutmose-sin must win or lose control. Too many men have died. The other chiefs will try to kill him the moment the attack fails. Even his own clan won't be able to protect him."

"We can strengthen the gate," Sisuthros suggested in a whisper, his words still coming with difficulty.

"Aye, we can do that well enough," Gatus agreed. "We'll need a lot more water at the gate, for one thing." But he didn't sound confident, and all three men knew water alone wasn't going to stop the burning.

"I thought if we knew their plans," Eskkar said, "we might do something, raid the camp, stampede the horses, anything . . . but all that isn't important now and wouldn't even delay their attack. And we can't get to the store of wood. It's too far from the walls and we'd have to get past both their sentries and the armed party. By the time we fought our way through, the whole camp would be roused."

"It would take too long to start fires and burn the wood anyway," Gatus agreed. "And if you took enough men to do the task, they'd hear you coming, just as we heard them."

No one said anything. Trella stood and went to the cabinet. She withdrew a map of Orak and its surroundings, a copy of the one Corio had shown them months ago. She unrolled it across the table and smoothed the surface with care.

"Can you show me where the wood is stored?" she asked, as the men instinctively moved closer. Sisuthros sat on the table's edge and leaned over Gatus's shoulder.

Gatus picked up the wooden pointing stick rolled up inside the papyrus. "Here. If the boy is right, this must be where the wood is being collected. These hills are high enough to keep us from seeing what's behind them. They could've been moving anything there for days without our noticing."

Eskkar stared at the map. The site was too far from Orak's walls, a mile at least and well to the south. Even if a raiding party got there, none would ever return alive, even at night.

"And where do they keep the horses?" Trella continued. "I couldn't follow what Simcar said about the river."

Gatus moved the pointer. "Here. We can even see one herd from the walls."

Eskkar took the pointer from Gatus's hand. "If I were in charge, with that many horses, there would be at least three herds, each a few hundred paces apart, with rope corrals to keep them separate and hold them in against the river."

"That makes sense," Gatus said. "The curve of the river and the rise of the ground would make that the easiest way to control big herds like that." He looked at Eskkar. "How many in each herd? Three or four hundred?"

Eskkar closed his eyes and tried to visualize the land. He'd seen it often enough, even ridden along it once or twice during the last preparations for the siege. Opening his eyes and pointing to the land closest to Orak, "I'd put the largest herd here, probably close to four hundred horses. Then about three hundred each in the other two places." He looked up at Trella and saw that she continued to stare at the map.

"It would be good to set fire to the wood they've prepared, isn't that right?" Trella asked, her eyes directly on Eskkar. "If we could destroy it, then they might not be able to attack."

"Yes, that would set them back considerably, maybe even stop the fire attack or at least weaken it. They've stripped the land bare for lumber and there can't be much more left out there, even if they could find and bring it here."

"But you can't raid the wood store, because it's too far." She pointed to the place where they guessed the main herd was kept. "But you could raid the horses, could you not? I mean, in the place closest to us. What would you do there?"

Eskkar didn't answer because he caught the glimmer of her idea and began to think it through. Shifting in his chair, he began to think aloud. "We could move a small party out at night, either slip them by the sentries or kill them silently. Then we could stampede the horses and drive as many of them as we could into the river. The current is swift there and many would drown, while others would be swept downstream. The whole camp would be in an uproar, and every warrior would rush to the river to see to his horses. Then . . ." he moved the pointer back to the location of the wood, "during the confusion, we could slip another party through the lines to this place and we could burn the wagons."

Sisuthros let out a sound that could have been a laugh if his wound weren't so painful, and Gatus swore softly before answering. "Attacking their horses would draw every man to the river, I'd bet my life on it. We could slip in, burn the carts, and race back to the walls. But it would take time to fire the wagons."

"What about the men who attack the horses?" Trella asked. "Could they get back to Orak?"

"No, they'd be trapped there," Gatus answered soberly. "Once the horses began to stampede, the riders who guard the approaches to Orak would cut them off." Silence followed his words. "Still, it would be worth it, even if we lost the men. As Eskkar says, if we burn the wood, then we can weaken the attack, even if we can't prevent it." His eyes turned to Eskkar, as did Trella's and Sisuthros's.

Their captain remained lost in thought, his eyes focused on the map. Nobody wanted to interrupt him. He tapped on the location of the horses with his finger, forgetting Corio's admonishment about touching the papyrus. "Perhaps there's a way to get the men back after all." He looked up and found them all staring at him.

"The carts and wood must be destroyed," Eskkar said softly, "even if we have to chance losing men. But I think it can be managed." He turned to Gatus. "Get the other leaders here, even Bantor. We have much to plan if we're to attack tonight."

"Tonight! By the gods, we've hardly finished one battle and you're planning another?"

"Tonight. It must be tonight. If we let another day go by, they may launch their own attack." He smiled at Trella and took her hand. "As always, you give us good ideas, wife. And I think we'll add Simcar to our household from now on. Just in case the gods are slow in their duty to send us a son."

26

Eskkar awoke to the smell and feel of Trella's hair on his cheek and the brush of her lips against his. For a moment he just lay there, soothed by her touch as he awoke. Then he glanced at the window. The full darkness of evening covered the sky. He sat up in the bed, words of anger coming to his lips.

"Be easy, husband, there's plenty of time. Gatus told me to make sure you got some rest before you go." Trella lowered her voice. "If you still insist you must go."

They'd argued about that most of the morning. Gatus and Trella remonstrated against Eskkar's going. No one wanted him dead out there in the countryside, putting the village into panic.

Eskkar insisted, determined to lead the raid. In truth, he didn't trust anyone else. Sisuthros and Bantor were wounded, and Gatus couldn't move fast enough at his age. That left only Jalen, and his blood flowed too hot for such a mission. Eskkar spoke the language, which might be critical. In the end everyone had finally given way.

That decided, he and his commanders spent the rest of the day planning the details. They selected men to raid the horses, choosing eight men for the task, all experienced liverymen who knew how to handle horses and, more important, how to stampede them. Jalen would lead them, a simple raid well suited to his abilities. Eskkar reviewed the preparations, then turned the details over to Jalen.

Finding volunteers for the fire carts took less time. When the soldiers learned Eskkar would lead that party, dozens offered to go, despite the risk. For this he needed only level-headed men who could follow orders and strong enough to carry what they'd need. He and Gatus selected six men, talking with them individually and making sure each had the right temperament and would follow orders.

Eskkar finally took some rest just before sundown, at Trella's and Gatus's insistence. By then even Eskkar felt tired enough that he agreed to rest for an hour.

Instead Trella let him sleep more than three hours. By the time he'd dressed and eaten, only two hours remained before midnight, the time set for both parties to depart. Actually there would be three parties. The third consisted of a small team of archers, all good hunters and trackers, men who could move quietly through the darkness. They'd slip out first and eliminate any enemy sentries in their path.

Before Eskkar left the house Trella pressed herself against him with such force that he nearly lost his balance. Her words breathed against his cheek. "Don't take any foolish chances. Come back to me, Eskkar."

At the river gate Eskkar assembled his men, wondering what the next few hours would bring. The guards had removed most of the braces that secured the gate and now they eased open the heavy frame, its hinges moistened earlier with oil and water to muffle any sound.

Twenty-six men slipped out in single file and moved as silently as possible across the ditch. As soon as the last man passed the gate, the sentries closed it behind them.

Across the ditch, the two raiding parties stopped and knelt in the darkness, while they waited for the archers to remove the enemy sentries. Led by a hunter named Myandro, they disappeared into darkness, their bows wrapped in cloth to lessen any noise. All had hunted wild game in the hills and knew how to move with care.

Nearly an hour passed before Myandro returned, slipping up to Eskkar's side so quietly that he jumped in surprise.

"Captain, the sentries are dead," Myandro whispered. "There were only three as far as the first line of hills. You'll have a few hours before any come to relieve them. But go quickly. I'll send Jalen out as soon as you are gone."

Eskkar grasped the man's shoulder. "Good work, Myandro." Jalen and his men had a much shorter distance to travel and would move faster, since they carried no heavy loads. Eskkar turned to Grond, his second in command for this mission and kept his voice low. "The way is clear. Come."

Eskkar waited while Grond passed the word down the line, making sure every man understood the order. Then Eskkar stood up slowly, letting any stiffness in his muscles stretch their way loose. He carefully picked up the two clay pots, bound in thick cloth for protection and linked by a rope that he slung around his neck, allowing him to carry a pot under each arm. His sword already hung down his back, leaving nothing that might bang against a pot and make a sound, or worse, break the container.

The burden was heavy and he heard the muffled breathing of the men as they shouldered their loads. Only Grond seemed unaffected by the weight.

Myandro took the lead. In single file Eskkar and his men followed, traversing the north side of the village, stepping with care to make sure they didn't trip over some obstacle, fall into the ditch, or splash into a pool of swamp water. That caution slowed them down, and it took some time before they passed the point where the wall turned to face the east.

Grateful to be away from the ditch and the flooded lands, they traveled now in the open, exposed to any close scrutiny. Gradually they turned south and began the long walk across the face of the main wall, moving farther away from Orak with each step. At first Myandro stayed with them, leading them at a steady pace. Then he vanished into the darkness ahead, to make sure the way remained clear.

At last they reached the first of the low hills, nearly opposite the main gate but more than a mile away.

Myandro reappeared at Eskkar's side, placing his hand on his captain's chest to stop the column. Eskkar sank to his knees, grateful for the chance to remove the millstone from his neck, even for a moment. Between the weight of the pots and the coarse rope, the flesh already felt raw.

His men welcomed the respite. The need for complete silence and the effort to ensure that no misstep caused a stumble had stretched every muscle, and Eskkar felt the strain in his body. They waited as Myandro and two of his men slipped ahead through the darkness.

Looking up at the stars Eskkar guessed that not quite two hours had passed since they left Orak. It would've been shorter to leave by the main gate, but that meant more sentries to get past, as the Alur Meriki watched the main gate more closely.

Myandro reappeared, ghostlike, putting his face directly to Eskkar's ear. "The barbarian troop is just over this hill and about a hundred paces away. Most are sleeping and they only posted a few guards. A sentry is there, supposedly watching the village, though he spends more time looking at the campfires. They suspect nothing. But they're between us and the wagons, so we must wait here."

Eskkar repeated the message to Grond, who would whisper it to each man. Eskkar turned back to Myandro. "Jalen should have attacked by now. It grows late."

Myandro checked the progress of the moon before answering. "We'd have heard something if he were seen or captured. I'll go back on watch. More can be seen and heard from the hilltop. Keep close against the side of the hill, and make sure nobody makes a sound."

Again he vanished, leaving Eskkar envious of his ability to move so quietly. But the idea of the sentry made him nervous, and Eskkar moved down the line of men, whispering to each and making sure every man hugged the hillside as much as possible.

More time passed as the moon seemed to race across the sky. When the moment came they felt it in the ground before they heard the noise, the rumble of hundreds of pounding hooves. The horses over the hilltop heard it as well, and a few began to whinny nervously, the first sounds they'd made.

Eskkar pictured the raid in his mind. Jalen would have gotten his men into position and built a tiny fire. Each man would light the thick, oil-soaked bundle of rags already fastened to the ends of the ropes. Whirling the ropes overhead would create a big flaming circle that would frighten any horse, let alone a herd suddenly awakened to see eight circles of fire rushing toward them. The horses would bolt from the sight, and with luck, directly into the river if Jalen positioned his men properly.

Other noises came to Eskkar, horses screaming, the distant alarms of men, and above everything the thunder of hooves in the night. Behind the hill, men shouted and cursed, warriors suddenly jerked awake, fumbling for their swords, scrambling for their horses, damning the darkness and whatever unknown disaster had struck the herd. Each warrior probably had a mount or two in that band, and all would be keen to learn what had happened.

Myandro loomed up out of the darkness above them. "Down! And don't look up!"

Eskkar and his men froze into the earth, hardly breathing, all of them pressing against the hill. He heard horses climbing the other side. At first Eskkar thought they'd been discovered, but realized that someone, likely the leader and a few others, had ascended the hill to see whether Orak showed any activity.

When the horses stopped moving, Eskkar glimpsed three or four horsemen, not forty paces above their heads and as many to their left, looking over the empty plain to the village walls. If any of them looked down toward the base of the hill . . .

But the riders searched toward the village, where nothing moved. At the base of the hill deep shadows covered the motionless men. Eskkar heard the horses snort and one of them neighed. The animals had probably picked up the scent of men beneath them. The warriors, however, ignored those small signs, certain the animals were spooked by the stampede.

At last the Alur Meriki leader shouted an order and the horses turned about and started back down the hillside. As they did so, the whole band burst into a gallop, riding off toward the north.

Eskkar remained rooted in place, waiting while Myandro climbed up the hill, looking for any guards left behind. If any remained, they'd have to be killed. Time again dragged by before Myandro called to them from above.

Instantly Eskkar and his men grabbed their pots and began climbing up the face of the hill, cursing silently the clumsy weights around their necks that unbalanced them and made them slip and stumble. At the crest they found Myandro and one of his men. Hugging the ground so no silhouette would show against the faint moonlight, Eskkar could see the main encampment about half a mile away. Only a few scattered fires glowed in the darkness, but more were lit each moment as the camp roused itself to learn what had stampeded their horses.

"There, Captain," Myandro gestured with his bow to the east. "See that small fire there? That's where the carts are." He pointed to a tiny fire about six hundred paces from where they stood. "Shall we go with you?"

Eskkar hesitated a moment, but realized a few more men wouldn't help. "No, stay with the plan. Remain here and cover our retreat if you can. If not, save yourself."

The man nodded, not bothering to tell Eskkar that Gatus had ordered him specifically not to return without the captain of the guard. "Then hurry, before they return and block the way. And there may be guards."

Of course there would be guards, wide-awake ones at that, based on the sounds coming from the north. Moving as quietly as possible, Eskkar's men descended the back side of the hill, still moving south, so they could approach the outpost from the rear, hoping to find the guards focused on the confusion in the north. They hadn't far to travel now and they moved at a faster pace, helped by their brief rest.

When he reached his position, Eskkar gave the order to halt. He dropped to one knee to let his burden slip carefully to the ground, then pulled the rope over his head. Another movement freed the sword strapped to his back and he buckled it around his waist. He carried no other weapon.

Eskkar chose two men to come with him. One carried a short bow and six arrows, the standard weapon of the barbarians, an item now in plentiful supply, taken from dead warriors. The other man carried two knives.

The three men walked openly toward the campfire. The first cart loomed in his path and Eskkar stumbled over the tongue hidden in the darkness at his feet. Up ahead, just past the small fire, he spotted two men facing north, away from him. Eskkar turned to the man with the bow. "Stay here in case there are more guards," he whispered. "We'll take care of those two. Come, Tellar," he ordered the other man, "and give me one of those knives."

Tellar could handle a knife better than most, one of the reasons for bringing him. He handed Eskkar one of his daggers and Eskkar held it concealed against his arm.

He walked straight toward the guards, making no effort to keep quiet. Nevertheless they closed within thirty paces and hadn't been noticed, so Eskkar pretended to slip and swore loudly. The guards turned at the sound, hands on their swords as they saw two men weaving toward them.

"Who are you?" the smaller of the two snapped out.

"Rest easy, friend," Eskkar replied in the barbarian language, slurring his words as if intoxicated. He kept walking slowly forward, grateful to the Ur Nammu for all the recent language practice. "We were drinking out in the plain when we heard the noise. What's going on?" He let his words tail off and moved sideways a little, as if he were finding it difficult to walk a straight line.

The taller guard spoke up, apparently eager to talk. "Something must have stampeded the horses. Maybe the dirt-eaters."

"No! How could they do that?" Eskkar stopped a few steps from the men and turned to his companion. "Did you hear that? Someone's after our horses."

When he turned back, the knife flashed in his hand and he leapt at the smaller, more alert guard, shoving his dagger into the man's stomach before he could clear his sword. At the same instant, Tellar flung himself on the other and dragged him down to the ground, where they wrestled a moment before Tellar arose, bloody knife in one hand and the man's sword in the other.

Eskkar wasted no time with the bodies. He climbed up the nearest cart to look around but saw nothing, no more guards, not even horses, just more torches and fires being lit in the main encampment. "Tellar, get Grond and the men. We don't have much time."

Grond appeared out of the darkness almost instantly, carrying Eskkar's burden as well as his own without apparent effort. Eskkar found time to grin at the man's strength.

"Push as many carts together as you can. Tellar, unseal the jars." The wrapped pots contained the heavy black oil that burned for hours. The contents of one jar should be enough to turn any two carts into a pyre of flame within moments. Tellar's sharp knives easily cut through the ropes and leather sealing the pots.

Eskkar left his men to their task as he walked over to inspect a different pile of wood. Long planks had been nailed together, perhaps to form shields for five or ten men at a time. The barbarians had planned for their fire attack well. They could use these great shields to protect them from arrows and stones as they piled the wood and carts against Orak's gate.

Eskkar didn't know whether he could do anything about them, as it would take at least four men to lift one and they had no tools to break them apart. Perhaps they could drag some of them against the burning carts.

Two carts squealed loudly when the men pushed them together. Within moments six carts were practically touching. Already two men had climbed atop them and started pouring oil over the contents.

The men moved fast, carrying the oil, pouring it, then moving to the next cart. In moments they'd emptied the pots. The guards' campfire came in handy now, as they tossed burning brands onto the carts. The oil-soaked wood caught fire at once and the flames began to grow.

"Grond! Help me with these shields." Men rushed over and four of them picked up the first shield and leaned it up against the nearest cart, before running back for another. By now at least twenty-eight fires had been set, emptying the fourteen jars they'd carried with such care. The dark of night erupted into a wall of flames.

Eskkar and Grond ignored the waves of heat against their flesh. They carried the huge shields to their destruction, placing them against whatever burning cart was closest. Ten . . . twenty . . . Esskar lost count of how many they'd dragged to the fires, though his arms ached from the effort.

"Captain! They've seen the fires. They're coming," Tellar shouted to be heard over the crackling flames. "We have to go now!"

The fire roar grew deafening, as more dry wood burst into hot flames that shot up into the night sky. Eskkar glanced at Grond, who nodded. "Help me with this last shield, Grond." The other men joined them to heave one of the most massive shields into position.

"Get moving," Eskkar ordered, gasping for breath against the heat of the fire, his men already melting into the darkness, eager to return to safety.

Warriors near the main camp had spotted the flames. Men came on the run but so far none on horseback. Any warrior with a horse nearby would have headed straight for the river, anxious to recover his mounts. Esskar started back toward the village when three warriors burst into the firelight and charged at him. He started to run, saw they'd quickly overtake him, and turned, pulling his sword from its sheath as they flung themselves at him.

Thutmose-sin woke with a start, feeling the ground trembling beneath him. For a moment he thought it might be an earthshaker, but he recognized the sound of many horses on the move. The two wives he'd chosen for that night called out in fear, but he ignored their questions. Men shouted outside his tent, and by the time the first guard pushed open the tent flap, Thutmose-sin had arisen and buckled his sword around him.

"Sarrum," the breathless warrior gasped out, "the horses have stampeded. They all . . ."

"What caused it? Do you know?" Anything might set horses moving, a strange scent, a strong breeze, even a clumsy nightrider.

"No, Sarrum. Not yet . . ."

"Find out," he ordered. Stepping outside his tent, Thutmose-sin looked up at the stars. Still a few hours before sunrise. All the fires had burned out, except for a few scattered watch fires that still glowed on the outskirts of the camp.

Around him, warriors milled about in confusion. Everyone had horses in the herd. Those who'd kept mounts nearby soon galloped off toward the river. A young warrior approached, leading Thutmose-sin's horse. He swung up onto the animal, then rode off toward a nearby hilltop, his guards scrambling along on foot behind him. When he reached the small rise, he looked first toward the village. Everything there seemed quiet, so he turned his attention to the river. He couldn't see the horses, but a few torches danced about, all moving toward the water's edge.

A rider galloped up, calling out Thutmose-sin's name. In a moment, the horseman had raced his horse up the hilltop.

"Sarrum, the dirt-eaters stampeded the horses." The man had to pause for a moment. "They waved fire at them, drove many into the Tigris."

"Did you capture them?"

"No, not yet, Sarrum. The horses blocked the way, but the patrol moved to cut them off, so they're trapped along the riverbank."

Thutmose-sin again looked toward the village. Still no sign of activity. He shifted his gaze toward the south, but saw nothing, just the watch fires. Reassured, he decided to ride toward the commotion. Then he noticed the fires farthest away, where the carts and wood for the assault had been gathered. The watch fires there burned brighter . . . too bright for a campfire, he realized. And there should only be one campfire, not . . . even as he stared, he saw new fires come into existence, their flickering flames rising ever higher.

"Get men back from the river. Send them to where we're holding the carts. The dirt-eaters are raiding the carts. Bring men. Cut them off."

He looked about him. Only a dozen or so of his guards remained; the rest had gone to the river to see to their horses. "Follow me. Hurry, before they burn everything."

They broke into a run down the hillside. He followed more slowly, letting the horse pick its way down the slope. By the time he reached the bottom, his men had outdistanced him, stringing out in a ragged line and shouting for more men to join them. Thutmose-sin put the horse to a canter, as fast a pace as he could coax from the animal in the darkness. He soon began to pass his men. Fire from the burning wagons now illuminated the night, and he saw that more than a dozen wagons were covered in flames.

He urged the horse faster. For a moment the animal responded. Then it shied away from the approaching flames, stiffened its legs, slid to a halt, and refused to move. Swearing at the frightened beast, Thutmose-sin leapt down and ran after his men. Darker shadows moved before the flames, and he could see men shoving wood against the burning wagons.

"Stop them," he shouted, drawing his sword. The sound of swords clashing told him men fought just ahead of him. By now the fires had gown so bright he could see the dirt-eaters working frantically, trying to burn the carts and wood his warriors had so laboriously collected.

One of his men cried out, then stumbled and fell, clutching at the arrow in his arm. Damn these accursed village archers. Just ahead of him he saw another of his men cut down, this time by a tall warrior with a long sword. Ignoring an arrow that hissed by his head, Thutmose-sin raised his sword and rushed at the warrior.

Eskkar met the first warrior with a savage sweep of his arm, knocking the man's blade aside and thrusting into his attacker's chest before he could recover. The second warrior, little more than a boy, swung his blade at Eskkar's head, expecting to catch him before he could free his sword from the first man's body. But Eskkar ducked and shoved his shoulder into the youth, his sword coming free at the movement. Before the warrior could strike again, Eskkar swung the sword around with all the force he could muster. The parry, weak and off balance, did little more than slow Eskkar's blade as it slashed into the base of the young man's neck.

The third warrior reached Eskkar with a vicious overhand stroke, and Eskkar knew from the first contact he faced no gangling youth, but a warrior in his prime, with a powerful arm of his own. Eskkar parried a second blow, and a third, then a fourth, but he had to give ground with each stroke. The warrior kept pressing forward and Eskkar couldn't mount a counterstroke as the vicious blows clanged against his weapon, pushing him back into the firelight, toward the heat of the flames.

Eskkar saw an opening and thrust at the man, the stroke stopping his adversary's advance and giving Eskkar a chance to set his feet. Wielding the great sword, he lunged and slashed at his opponent with half a dozen strokes, before cutting deep into the man's sword arm. The wounded man staggered back with a curse, his sword slipping from his grasp. Eskkar swung his sword up for the killing blow, but another half-dozen Alur Meriki arrived, shouting their war cries, and he turned to face them. Before they could overwhelm Eskkar, Tellar, Grond, and two others reached their captain's side, forming a rough line to Eskkar's left.

Eskkar barely had time to catch his breath before the first of these new warriors rushed in, using his momentum to take a powerful cut at Eskkar's head. He deflected the blow, but felt the shock up his arm. The impact slowed him down as the warrior's momentum carried him into Eskkar's chest, the two of them falling to the earth. Eskkar got his arm under the man's neck and heaved him away, then scrambled to his feet. Fighting raged all around, but for the moment, no new Alur Meriki appeared. The warrior Eskkar had flung aside rolled twice and somehow regained his feet, faster than Eskkar thought possible, and again the sword came at Eskkar's head, shifted at the last moment and aimed at his shoulder. Eskkar blocked the blow and countered with a thrust that forced his opponent to twist his body to the side.

The movement swung the necklace the man wore, and the firelight glowed against the polished copper medallion, the medallion that proclaimed its bearer the Alur Meriki's sarrum.

"Thutmose-sin!" Eskkar spat the words at the ruler of the clans.

Then he had no time or breath for anything else. The two leaders stood toe to toe, neither man willing to back off, too close to effectively use the long swords, but each man making up for the lack of room by cutting and thrusting. Eskkar's anger flared up. This man's father had killed his family. Bloodlust overcame him, and the sword slashed viciously at Thutmose-sin's neck.

But the Alur Meriki ruler had honed his expertise since his youth, with muscles hardened by hours on horseback, and he blocked every stroke with skill that bespoke of years of practice. Stroke fell upon stroke, and Eskkar's opponent moved effortlessly. Eskkar's rage began to fade as he felt his arm growing weaker. Forcing himself to ignore the tiredness in his arm, he lunged at his opponent.

The sarrum of the Alur Meriki pivoted as he brushed the point aside, and countered with a stroke so fierce it drove Eskkar back two steps. The blows kept hammering at him, giving him no time to counter. Eskkar's arm began to tremble and he knew his opponent sensed it as well. The man increased his efforts, his mix of thrusts and cuts coming faster and faster, never allowing Eskkar time to recover.

Eskkar felt fear rising up. Any moment now and a stroke would catch him off guard. The heat raged at his back, all-enveloping now. He retreated another step, but a wagon wheel burned hot against his shoulder and he knew he'd run out of room. Already Eskkar had to use both hands to parry the endless blows that arrived with the force of a woodsman plying his axe.

Grunting with confidence now, Thutmose-sin swung his blade at Eskkar's head but at the last moment aimed at Eskkar's shoulder. Eskkar's counter nearly came too late. He barely managed to get his sword in front of his chest, its tip bumping against the burning wagon. The two blades met with a clang and a shower of sparks, and then the unthinkable happened.

Thutmose-sin's sword shattered against Eskkar's new blade. The weapon's failure caught the warrior by surprise for a single instant. Eskkar pushed forward, ramming his hilt into Thutmose-sin's head, knocking him backward and off balance. Thutmose-sin's heel caught on a wood scrap, and he fell flat on his back, stunned, his sword dropping from his hand. Gasping, and with the last of his strength, Eskkar lowered his sword's point and lurched toward his blood enemy, ready to thrust the blade savagely into the fallen man's chest.

Before he could avenge his family, an explosion blew Eskkar to the ground, a wave of searing heat passing over him. The wagon behind him, pushed into the flames only moments earlier by Eskkar and Grond, had contained more than just wood for shields. Unnoticed, half a dozen jars of oil rested beneath the wood, and the fire set by Eskkar's men had finally reached them. The clay containing the oil had cracked from the heat, adding a flood of fresh oil to the roaring inferno that turned the cart into something beyond his comprehension.

A blast of fire shot up into the night, as burning pieces of the cart flew in every direction. All fighting stopped in an instant, the men knocked to their knees or flat on the ground, forgetting their enemy to look in awe at the writhing flames climbing into the dark night sky. No one had ever seen or heard anything like it before.

Stunned by the blast, Eskkar felt Grond helping him to his feet. Eskkar, mouth sagging, still clutched his sword. A dozen paces away, he saw Thutmose-sin being dragged to safety in the opposite direction.

The flames from the oil cart had collapsed from their height, but the other fires raged on, merging and growing ever hotter, with the roar of the combustion increasing until Eskkar thought his ears would burst. Tellar, his sword gone and blood dripping from one arm, flung his good arm around Eskkar's waist. With Grond carrying most of the burden, they stumbled away from the firestorm.

Another Alur Meriki appeared out of the darkness and raced at him, his sword high. Eskkar, still dazed and unable to react, saw Grond raise his weapon, but suddenly the man tripped and fell, nearly at Eskkar's feet. An arrow protruded from the man's chest. Eskkar caught a glimpse of Myandro notching another arrow at the far edge of the fire. Eskkar heard without comprehending the clash of other swords at the edge of the blaze. His back felt scorched. Grond shouted something, his blade reflecting fire and blood from the flames, as the bodyguard pulled Eskkar into a run.

At the same time two more of Myandro's archers arrived, loosed their shafts, then fell back with the rest of Orak's men, rushing into the darkness and leaving behind the angry shouts of the warriors.

Eskkar's head began to clear as he lurched along. The cooler air away from the conflagration helped restore his strength. He shoved Tellar away as the weakness in his legs lessened, but Grond's grip stayed firm on his left arm. Eskkar staggered along, trying to lengthen his steps.

They ran for their lives, Grond pulling Eskkar along until his captain hit his stride. Moving as fast as they could over the uneven ground, they had no breath for words. As they reached the top of the hill, Eskkar pulled himself loose and stopped. He took a quick glance behind him.

A fiery mass lit up the sky. Shouts from angry warriors mixed with the roar of flames that illuminated dozens of Alur Meriki who had reached the burning carts. Some tried to pull wagons and wood away from the inferno, while others searched for the raiding party.

Grond jerked hard on his captain's arm and Eskkar turned back to the darkness. Orak remained more than a mile away. They'd covered barely half the distance when the fearful sound of hoofbeats gave their legs a fresh burst of energy. The terrifying vision of what happened to men on foot, caught from behind by mounted riders, flashed into Eskkar's mind.

They raced on, Grond and Eskkar slipping farther behind the others. Eskkar's heart pounded in his chest and his legs trembled with exhaustion. His breathing came raggedly.

Two nights with little sleep and the hard fight took their toll. Grond moved behind him now, his hand on his captain's back, urging him along.

Orak's walls, outlined against the moonlight, were growing in size and the ditch couldn't be more than two hundred paces ahead when Eskkar saw a line of men rising up in the darkness. He slowed, thinking the barbarians had gotten in front of them. Then he heard the welcome voice of Gatus calling to them. Eskkar lowered his head and kept running, ignoring the piercing pain in his chest at every breath.

They reached the line of soldiers, passing between men who stood with bows drawn to the ear. The moment they passed out of the line of fire, Gatus shouted. "Loose!"

Twenty arrows whistled into the night.

Eskkar stumbled and nearly fell, but Grond, still at his side, caught his arm. The big man had remained behind him the whole time, protecting his back, when Grond could easily have outrun him. Now he resumed his grip on Eskkar's arm and pulled his captain along. Behind them, the archers sent two more flights of arrows into the approaching horsemen before they, too, turned and fled for the safety of Orak's walls. The rescuers soon caught up with Eskkar's weary party. All reached the ditch together, jumping down into the mud, the loud slap of feet revealing their position.

A loud voice from the tower reminded the archers to shoot only at men on horseback. The ditch became a horror in the dark, and Eskkar heard arrows whistling overhead. Men fell facedown in the muck, cursing, scrambling up only to pitch forward again as the treacherous footing and darkness slowed them down to little more than a crawl.

Finally reaching the base of the wall, Eskkar leaned for a moment against it, unable to see anything as the structure blocked out the feeble moonlight.

Next to him Grond swept his hands along the rough surface, found a rope, and wrapped it twice around his captain. Another instant to knot it, and Grond shouted to those on the rampart above.

Eskkar ascended as if by magic, his sword shoved tightly under his arm, until hands seized his shoulders and pulled him into the safety of Orak. Moments later Grond arrived, pulling himself up as soon as he saw his captain reach the top. Eskkar lay on the parapet, trying to catch his breath.

Arrows whistled overhead or plinked against the wall. At least some of the barbarians had pursued them to the ditch. Orak's archers soon drove them back. The flames from the burning carts rose over the low hill and provided enough light, even at that distance, to outline anyone on horseback. By the time Eskkar pulled himself to his feet and looked over the wall, the last horsemen were riding back out of range, heading toward the pyre of flaming carts.

The sight of the fire rising over the hill amazed Eskkar. In his whole life, he'd never seen such a burning. Flames thrust their way high into the night as if to set the heavens afire. The enormous store of wood, dried by the fierce sun and fired by the black oil, produced a blaze impossible to put out or even approach. The barbarians would probably save some carts and shields, but at least half, maybe more, of their precious wood supply was being consumed.

The raid was worth it, Eskkar decided, then caught himself. Better to see how many men had died before he started gloating.

"A pretty sight, isn't it, Captain?" Gatus's words sounded calm enough.

Gatus stood at his side, mud-covered from head to foot. The comical sight made Eskkar grin—before he remembered to look at his own body. Gatus had been the last man pulled back up the wall. Grond stood there, too, as muddy as the others, his teeth gleaming white in the moonlight. All the men from the raid crowded around Eskkar.

"It's a sight I owe to Grond here. He practically dragged me back to Orak."

"Captain was tired from fighting three warriors by himself." Grond raised his voice so that all could hear. "He turned to attack them, so the men could get away. Killed them all, too."

The terror of the fight flashed into Eskkar's mind. He couldn't stop a shudder from passing over him as he remembered Thutmose-sin, who'd driven him against the wagon wheel. Eskkar had faced danger often enough but never had the certainty of his death felt so close.

Shaking off the chilling thought, he heard the men telling of his deeds, bragging about how strong their captain was. If they only knew how fear had almost overpowered him. "How many men did we lose, Gatus? And what about those who went for the horses?"

Gatus looked sheepish for a moment. "By the gods, I'd forgotten about them." He shouted for a body count, but no one knew anything. "I'll go and find out, Captain."

"No, stay here and keep watch until morning. I'll go see what's happened to Jalen."

Eskkar pushed men out of the way until he could descend the steps. Trella was waiting for him. She clutched him fiercely for a moment, but then he took her hand and they ran toward the rear of the village. Grond and the others followed. All wanted to know what happened to the men who had provided the diversion.

Anxious villagers crammed the streets, wandering about, wanting to know what had happened. Grond formed a wedge with a couple of men and simply pushed the crowd out of Eskkar's way. It seemed to take forever before they reached the river gate.

The gate stood open. Archers stood ready, bows in hand, facing the opening, now brightly lit from a line of torches that stretched to the river's edge and even into the dark waters. Men lined the walls on each side of the gate. Eskkar heard shouting, even a few cheers, coming through the gate's opening.

They pushed their way through the men and crossed the ditch, Grond seizing a torch to light their way. As they reached the riverbank, a soaking-wet man staggered up to them and slipped to his knees, exhausted from his battle with the river. Another appeared, this one falling flat on the earth as he gasped for breath.

Eskkar pushed past both of them and stopped at the jetty. The flickering torches showed a line of men extending out into the Tigris, each clinging to the thick tow rope used to pull the ferry back and forth.

As Eskkar watched, they hauled more men from the river, gasping and spitting, until seven had been pulled in. He saw no sign of Jalen. Eskkar waited a few more moments, watching the men standing against the current to make sure they stayed alert and looked with care for anything coming down the river.

The diversion had worked exactly as Eskkar planned. Jalen's men had driven the horses into the river, then waited until the last possible moment before they jumped in themselves, letting the current take them quickly around the curve of the bank and downstream to Orak. They should all have been carried to this spot. But they should have gotten here long ago, well before Eskkar and his men returned to safety. Something must have gone wrong.

Abruptly he turned his attention back to the first two men who'd reached shore. "Where's Jalen? Why did you wait so long before returning?"

One man looked up blankly but the other shook his head, then took a deep breath before speaking. "Captain, the horses blocked our path to the river. They just raced back and forth along the river's edge. We couldn't get past . . . had to hide until the way was clear."

The man struggled to his feet, and Eskkar extended his hand to lift him upright. "When the way was finally clear, the barbarians spotted us. They rushed us, and Jalen got wounded in the fighting. He slew one man, but he was bleeding badly when I saw him go into the water."

A shout went up from the men in the river, and the words "Jalen's dead" echoed over the water. The men began wading back to the shore, carrying a body.

Cursing under his breath, Eskkar went back and arrived as the men set the body onto the earth. In the wavering torchlight, Eskkar had to stare for a moment before he recognized Jalen, a broken root clutched tightly in his hand and a gash in his side where he'd been wounded.

"He must have been too hurt to fight the current, or maybe just got tangled in some vines." Eskkar could guess what had happened. By the time Jalen pushed free of the vines, he didn't have the strength to keep his head above water. Either that, or the loss of blood from the wound had finished him. Eskkar shook his head in frustration, a brave man they could ill afford to lose.

By now Jalen's second in command had steadied enough to tell the story. Following orders, he'd made certain all of the men went into the water, including Jalen, who was last to jump. He assured Eskkar that he'd counted them as they went into the river. Nevertheless, one other hadn't made it and must have been swept unnoticed downstream, likely drowned by the currents, his unnoticed corpse mixed in with dead horses that had floated by.

By the time the man finished, everyone had climbed out of the river. In a few moments they began moving back across the ditch. Last came the men carrying Jalen's body.

Eskkar took Trella's hand. Together they returned to the safety behind Orak's walls. Sisuthros stood inside the gate, his face reflecting the pain he felt.

Eskkar put a hand on Sisuthros's shoulder for a moment. "Get the whole story, then tell Gatus." Eskkar felt Trella's hand pushing at his arm, and realized he was gripping her hand so tightly that he'd hurt her. He loosened his grip, and they walked back home in silence.

At the well Trella helped him strip and she washed the mud from his body herself. Servants lifted water from the well and brought drying cloths and fresh clothing. Under the torchlight she bound up a nasty gash on his left arm, after making sure it had been washed clean. The hair had burned off his right arm, when the wagon exploded. On his back she found two burn marks and she washed those as well, but left them uncovered.

The servants withdrew, leaving only a single torch burning in the tiny garden. Trella and Eskkar sat together on the bench at the rear of the house. He drank his fill of fresh water, followed by a cup of heated wine that he drained almost as easily.

Trella examined his arm, checking his bandage to see if he still bled. She waited until he was ready to speak.

"Jalen was unlucky," he began, "unlucky to be wounded, unlucky in the river. He should be alive and I should be dead." He pointed at the great sword leaning up against the tree, already wiped clean and oiled by the servants. "Your sword saved my life, Trella. I fought against Thutmose-sin. He is a true swordsman and he had me beaten. I knew I was about to die. I felt helpless before him, until his sword shattered on your blade and I knocked him down with the last of my strength. One more stroke and I'd have died out there. Even then, I'd have been killed or captured if Grond hadn't practically carried me back to the village."

He looked at her. "I've never been so certain of my death, not in all the fights, in all the years. I felt fear, the same fear I've seen in others' eyes . . . other men I have fought . . . killed." He shook his head as if disbelieving his words, ashamed to admit his fear and weakness, even to her.

When she spoke, her voice was calm and matter-of-fact. "Then the sword has served both of us well. Since I can't fight at your side, the sword must take my place, and so it must defend you. You know, husband, it's true the gods favor and watch over you. They protected you even from the Alur Meriki leader. No man can fight so many men without tiring, especially after a long walk carrying a heavy burden. But it's even better that you admit your fear."

Eskkar looked at her, puzzled. He'd never confessed fear to a woman in his life, nor had he ever heard of any warrior doing so. He wouldn't have done it now, except he felt exhausted, and perhaps the hot wine had loosened his tongue.

"The gods grow angry when men become too presumptuous, too sure of their own strength and power," she went on, her hand stroking his arm. "Remember this time and this feeling when you're tempted to think you are all-powerful. Then remember Jalen and his sacrifice."

He sat in silence. Eskkar knew what she hadn't said. She hadn't reminded him who placed the sword in his hand, who guided him all these many months, whose strength supported him when he worried in the night.

"Tomorrow, we'll give honor to Jalen. His funeral will be attended by all. We'll give him praise for the success of the raid." He put his arm around Trella and held her close, feeling her strength as she gripped him in return. "And you . . .

you will remind me if I grow too proud, or if I ever forget the lesson of tonight."

"You will not need to be reminded. You're too wise to forget what you learn."

He'd never considered himself wise, and wondered if she might be saying that simply to ease his mind.

She looked up at him, reading his thoughts. "You are a wise man, Eskkar, wise enough to know your own strengths, wise enough to learn from your mistakes, and even wiser to learn from the mistakes of others." She pulled free and stood up. "Now come to bed, husband. You need to rest, and there will be much to talk about in the morning."

Eskkar glanced up at the sky. Morning would soon be upon them.

"I wonder what happened to Thutmose-sin," he said. "I struck him with the sword hilt, and he went down." He told her about how the cart had burst into a mountain of flame and heat, about the strange noise that knocked them all off their feet. "His men dragged him away, away from the fires and away from us. He might even be dead. I wanted to kill him, to avenge my family. That would have been worth dying for. But he fought . . . he was too strong."

"No more talk about dying, husband. And we'll know soon enough about Thutmose-sin," she answered. "But whether he lives or dies won't change what the next few days will bring."

"I suppose not." He looked at her, recalling how he'd felt during their first days together, when he'd started to learn just how special she was. Now she spoke just a few words, and the unimportant disappeared. She was right. The battle would go on, with or without Thutmose-sin.

He took her in his arms and held her tight for a moment, forgetting the pain in his arm and back, letting her strength wash over him. They walked together back into the house, ignoring the servants and soldiers who stared at them with respect and admiration. Falling across his bed, he had time for one more thought before sleep claimed him. Wisdom, he decided, was becoming less a matter of what you knew and more a matter of admitting how much you did not know.

* * *

Thutmose-sin regained consciousness in his tent, surrounded by his women. The first rays of dawn shone
through the opening, telling him the night had passed. At
first his eyes wouldn't focus, but his wives helped him up to
a sitting position. Touching his head, he flinched at the tenderness when his fingers, still clumsy, bumped against the
swollen bruise just above his temple. His head hurt when he
moved it, but he sat still for a moment, and the waves of pain
began to lessen.

The fight came back to him. He remembered his sword
breaking. In battle, anything could happen, and he'd seen
enough swords shatter before, though never one of his, and
never just as he'd readied the killing blow. One more
stroke . . . the weapon's failure had unbalanced him, and the
tall warrior managed to strike him with his weapon's pommel. Thutmose-sin had twisted his head trying to avoid the
blow, and the bronze ball had glanced along his skull, instead of hitting directly.

If it had, I might be dead.

His first wife, Chioti, lifted a water skin to his lips, and he
drank and drank, letting the water spill down his chest. When
he finally pushed it away, he looked at her. "What happened?"

"Your guards carried you back here a few hours ago. You
were unconscious. They said the dirt-eaters burned the wagons. We saw a great burning."

He shook his head, then regretted the movement. "Help
me up, Chioti."

Some of the wives murmured that he should rest, but
Chioti knew his ways. She placed his arm over her shoulder
and helped get him to his feet.

"Fetch Urgo," she ordered, keeping an arm around her
husband's waist. "Urgo wanted to know when you awoke."
Chioti moved in front of him and looked into his eyes. "Stay
inside the tent until you're sure you're all right. You don't
want to stumble and fall."

Or look weak in front of my men. Thutmose-sin smiled at
her. "I will take care, Chioti."

By the time Urgo arrived, Thutmose-sin felt strong enough to leave the tent. His guards looked at him. The relief on their faces mixed with fear; they'd failed in their duty to remain at his side, to protect him last night.

He looked at them coldly as they gathered around him; he would deal with their dereliction later. The morning sun had lifted well above the horizon. His strength grew with each breath of fresh air, though his head would likely hurt for days.

Urgo arrived first, carrying a bow in his hand. Rethnar, Altanar, and two other clan leaders were on his heels. They sat on the ground in a half-circle, facing Thutmose-sin.

"The dirt-eaters burned the fire wagons, Sarrum," Urgo said without any preamble. "We lost about half the wood, and one wagonload of oil. Fortunately, the other two carts carrying oil were spared."

Thutmose-sin restrained himself from shaking his head in disgust. "And the horses? The dirt-eaters that raided them?"

"The men got away, jumping into the river." Urgo shrugged. "They may have drowned. We lost about thirty horses. The rest scattered all over the plain. The men are still rounding them up."

"And those that burned the wagons?"

"We found two bodies, Sarrum." He saw the question on his leader's face. "We lost ten men. That included the two guards. The rest were killed in the fighting." Urgo handed the bow to Thutmose-sin. "One of the dead carried this. The dirt-eaters sent their archers to raid us."

"That was no bowman I fought," Thutmose-sin said, examining the weapon with interest. They hadn't recovered one before, and it took but a glance to recognize a well-made, powerful bow. "He recognized me, called out my name. He might have been from our clan."

Urgo shrugged. "A renegade warrior . . . what does it matter? You may have wounded him. His men had to help him away."

"And the wood? Do we have enough left?"

"I've already sent men out for more. We have plenty of oil, and we'll have enough wood in a day or so."

"He knew how to fight, Urgo."

"The gods may be saving him for us to capture later, Thutmose-sin."

"Or the gods may be sending us another message, Sarrum." Altanar spoke for the first time. One of the older clan leaders, he'd said little up to now about the campaign. "Perhaps the gods are saying we should move on, that there is little here worth the death of so many warriors."

"You would run from dirt-eaters!" Rethnar spat the words across the circle. "Are you afraid to fight cowards who hide behind a wall?"

"No, Rethnar, I'm no more afraid of them than I am of you." Altanar's hand went to his sword hilt. "But many more warriors are sure to die before we take this place. Will slaves make up for warriors lost? The dirt-eaters have no horses. Where will we find new horses even to replace those mounts lost last night?" He shrugged. "If Rethnar wants to stay behind and capture the village, so be it. But I say there is nothing here for us."

"You are a coward," Rethnar said, leaping to his feet and drawing his sword.

Altanar rose with him, his own blade flashing from its sheath.

"Sit down!" Thutmose-sin shouted the words, but the two clan chieftains, if they even heard his command, had gone too far to stop.

Pandemonium broke out in the camp. Clansmen of Rethnar and Altanar rushed up. Thutmose-sin's guards, extra alert after last night's failure, scooped their leader up and pulled him away from the circle. They formed a barrier between him and the melee that had exploded before their eyes. A dozen men were fighting in a moment, and more would be rushing to join them. Thutmose-sin knew it needed to be stopped now.

"Guards," he shouted in a voice loud enough to be heard over the fighting, "kill anyone who doesn't stop fighting *now*! Kill them!" His men surged forward. They easily outnumbered the handful of fighters, who saw the menace in their advance. The two clan leaders broke off their duel, and their clansmen followed reluctantly.

"Stand between them," Thutmose-sin ordered, his voice carrying to everyone now that the clash of weapons had ended. "Kill anyone who doesn't put down his sword! I'll not have you killing each other because of the dirt-eaters."

With an oath, Rethnar lowered his sword. A moment later Altanar did the same. The two men glowered at each other. Thutmose-sin stepped forward, moving into the center of the space. "Or would you rather fight me?" He looked around the circle. "Chioti, bring me my sword."

Thutmose-sin waited, surrounded by angry men still clasping bronze in their hands, until Chioti pushed the guards aside and handed him a sword. Taking the blade, he hefted it, then swung it hard over his head, the weapon hissing through the air. "Do you want to challenge me, Altanar?" When the clan leader didn't respond, Thutmose-sin turned to Rethnar. "Do you, Rethnar?"

Rethnar took his time answering, and Thutmose-sin knew the clan chief was wondering how much the fight last night might slow Thutmose-sin down. He walked over to Rethnar, the sword pointed at the ground. "Are you challenging me?" Thutmose-sin spoke softly, but everyone heard the menace in his words.

"No, Sarrum. It's just that . . ."

"Then you, both of you, sheath your swords, send your men away, and sit down. I've something to say."

He waited until Rethnar and Altanar settled onto the ground. "Altanar is right," he began. "We will lose many more warriors in taking this village. And it's true there will be little of value inside Orak to make up for those who die." Thutmose-sin turned to Rethnar. "But Rethnar is right also. If we don't defeat these miserable villagers, every dirt-digger in the land will begin moving to the nearest village. They will band together and resist us. Once they know we can be driven off, we'll be fighting over every farm and mud hut we encounter."

He moved in front of Altanar. "Would you change the

path of our migration, Altanar? If we fail to take this place, we can never come back to these lands again. If we do, Orak will be twice as strong, with twice as many fighters within. Is that what you want your sons, your clan to face?"

Thutmose-sin walked around the circle, his eyes challenging each clan chief and his subcommanders. "No, my clansmen, we are no longer fighting here for horses or loot, not even for honor. This Orak must be destroyed, or these lands will be forbidden to us. We're fighting to live the way our fathers before us lived."

He moved back to his place and sat down, keeping his sword across his knees. When he spoke, he lowered his voice, so that only those within the circle could hear. "This village must learn the price of war. We must kill many more of them, just as we've destroyed their crops and burned their houses. This battle must be fought, not because of what we might gain, but because of what we will lose if we just ride away."

No one said anything. "Then it is settled," Thutmose-sin said. "We attack as soon as the wagons and wood have been replaced. For this next attack, nothing will be held back. Every man and boy that can fight will march on the village." Again he looked around the circle. "And when it is taken, we'll put any survivors to the sword and tear down every wall and house until there's nothing left but the mud from the river."

Eskkar got less than two hours' sleep, the pain in his back wakening him. The window showed only the faintest light in the dark sky to indicate the approaching dawn. Despite the lack of sleep his thoughts seemed as alert as if he'd slept the whole night. But every muscle in his body protested as he began moving about. The bandage on his arm had slipped a little. He ran his fingers over it, but felt no traces of fresh blood.

Slipping quietly from the bed so as not to waken Trella, he dressed quickly. He gathered his sword and entered the workroom, where he unfastened the outer door as a yawning Annok-sur was about to knock and awaken her mistress.

Eskkar held his finger to his lips. "Good morning, Annok-sur," he whispered, "I'll wake her. Can you bring breakfast up, and send Bantor and Gatus to me when they arrive?"

"Captain, Gatus just sent word. He asks that you come to the gate."

He stared at her but she had nothing more to add. "Bring breakfast for Trella, then. Make sure she eats before she goes out." Eskkar returned to the bedroom and sat down on the bed. The movement made Trella turn over but she remained asleep. A bit more light came through the windows, just enough to illuminate her. She lay with a hand flung up over her head, her dark tresses scattered across the pillow.

When she slept, she seemed so young, too young for the burden she carried. Her life and future hung on the same thread as his, the thread he'd created in his pride when he told Nicar the barbarians could be beaten. Nothing must harm her, Eskkar decided. The barbarians, the nobles, nothing and no one must hurt her again. First he would defeat the barbarians, then he would increase his power over the nobles. He swore it by all the gods he didn't believe in. Eskkar wanted to kiss her but worried that his touch might awaken her. Better to let her have a few more moments of peace.

By the time he was downstairs he'd put all thoughts of Trella behind him. He stopped in the kitchen where he drained a cup of water and picked up a round loaf of bread that he chewed as he went outside in the early morning sun. Eskkar nodded to his guards, checked briefly with those at the command table, then mounted the ever-present horse. He rode slowly out of the courtyard, his guards jogging after him, the loaf of bread held firmly in his hand.

Few villagers had risen early this morning. Many had stayed up late last night celebrating the victory over the Alur Meriki. Another victory. Like thieves in the night, he and his men had crawled on their bellies into the barbarian camp, stampeded some horses, and burned a few wagons. Then they'd run for their lives. Today the whole village might pay the price for our "victory." Eskkar kept these black thoughts to himself. When he reached the gate, he swung down from the horse, tossing the halter to a half-awake boy.

Climbing to the top of the tower he found Gatus sitting on a stool so tall that he could see more than if he were standing. His second in command had traces of mud over his body, and Eskkar realized that Gatus had remained on the wall all night.

The rising sun shone in Eskkar's eyes as he peered into the east. "Well, Gatus, I see you've missed another night's sleep. What is it now?" He tore the remaining bread in half and handed it to Gatus, who took the still-warm bread gratefully.

"Last night, a few hours after you left, we saw something." Gatus took a bite of the bread, then chewed it thoughtfully before continuing. "Another fire broke out in their camp. Not near where you burned the wagons, but close to the center of the plain. We watched it for a while and, just as it disappeared, we heard sounds of fighting. That went on for a few moments, then stopped. Then just before dawn, we thought we heard fighting again."

Putting the last of the bread into his mouth, Eskkar shaded his eyes as he scanned the horizon. Thin trails of smoke still rose from behind the low hill where he'd burned the wagons but he saw no other sign of fire. Many men on horseback moved about on the low hills, and he could see dust trails from those out of sight. As he watched, a line of riders appeared on the top of the slope where Eskkar had crouched last night, about twenty in all. Clan leaders come to inspect the damage in daylight and plan their next move.

"We've made them very angry, I think." Eskkar kept his eyes on the riders as they moved slowly across the hilltop. "They lost horses and wagons last night, as well as much of the wood they've gathered in the last few weeks. Most of all, they've been humiliated, raided by dirt-eaters. The warriors and chiefs are very angry at their leader or whoever they decided to blame for our attack. They may have tried to kill Thutmose-sin. If they succeeded, we'll be facing a new chief, one who may have entirely different ideas. Or Thutmose-sin may have blamed some of the other chiefs and attacked them."

Gatus finished off his portion of the bread. "Well, the more they fight each other, the better I like it. Or maybe they've had enough and will move on? I don't suppose anything will happen today, do you think?"

Eskkar wasn't about to take any chances. "Not today. But I'll stay here for a while. Send Sisuthros to me. Then you get some sleep."

Gatus opened his mouth to argue, then thought better of it. "Very well. I'll go to your house to sleep. Bantor is well enough to manage the command post for a few hours." He waited a few moments, but Eskkar didn't say anything, just stared across the plain. Shrugging, Gatus left the wall, after first telling his men where he would be and when he should be called.

Eskkar scarcely noticed his departure. There seemed to be an unusual amount of activity in the barbarian camp. Without thinking, he sat down upon the now-vacant stool. Small clouds of dust hung everywhere, signifying riders moving from place to place, most of them out of eyesight. He tried to put himself in Thutmose-sin's place.

If I survived a challenge to my authority, I'd have to attack the village. For Thutmose-sin to abandon the siege now would be to admit failure, and too many had died in too many clans to allow that. Tempers and hatreds would have exploded in fury last night, and blood would have to spill to settle the score. So if Thutmose-sin remained in control, Eskkar decided, then we can expect an all-out assault today, or more probably, tomorrow. The Alur Meriki would first try to replace some of the lost wood, and they might need more time to round up their horses.

Eskkar felt certain about one thing. If . . . when the attack came, it would be unrestrained. The barbarians had more than enough men for one final assault. Every man would be flung at the walls, and it would be victory or disaster for the Alur Meriki. For if they failed, their ranks would be so diminished that other large villages or clans would seize the opportunity to oppose them.

But if Thutmose-sin had been removed, then maybe . . .

there might be a chance that the new leader would move on. The new ruler, whoever he might be, could blame all the failures on his predecessor, could say it was too late in the season to keep fighting, could claim they'd be back in a few years to take their revenge, anything. The Alur Meriki had enough reasons to satisfy those ready to abandon the fight. The clan would move on, and the new leader would be busy for the next few years consolidating his power. And there would be plenty of wives, concubines, and horses to distribute to his new supporters—the former property of those killed.

So Orak's best hope was that Thutmose-sin was dead. Eskkar thought about that, wishing for some way to kill the leader of the Alur Meriki, hoping that some clansman had solved his problem with a knife in Thutmose-sin's back.

Eskkar stayed on the wall the rest of the day. No attack came, a fact he attributed completely to the raid. At least, no attack on the village. Late in the afternoon, for a few moments, some of those watching the plain claimed to hear more sounds of fighting in the enemy's camp. But nothing could be seen, and Eskkar heard nothing.

Nevertheless, even if there were no actual fighting, plenty of sharp words and accusations would be exchanged by clan leaders unhappy with Thutmose-sin's performance. And warriors don't fight well when their leaders quarrel, he knew, both from his own experience and the old days under the command of Ariamus.

The sun finally set. The soldiers maintained their vigilance throughout the night, taking no chances. Gatus again walked the walls much of the night. Still the pause gave Eskkar time to catch up on his sleep, though dawn found him on the wall again, anxiously watching the hilltops. But the morning sun brought nothing new, and that day passed as well, with no noticeable activity.

With the arrival of darkness, however, the men on the walls saw the lights from campfires reflecting up into the darkness, and these seemed to burn brighter and longer into the night than usual. The men watched and waited through-out the early evening.

Finally Eskkar turned to Sisuthros and Gatus. "I think our waiting is over. Tomorrow . . . I think it will be tomorrow. They'll come with the dawn."

"Then we'll be ready," Sisuthros answered grimly.

27

A small lamp in the workroom gave more smoke than light, its oil nearly gone. Trella paused to add more, enough to see by. She opened the door to their bedroom and listened to Eskkar's breathing. At least he'd gotten a few hours of restless sleep. She slipped into bed and put her arms around her husband, letting her body wake him.

Enough light reached the bed to see Eskkar's eyes open. For a moment he sighed contentedly. Then he tried to sit up, as he remembered what today would bring.

She kept her arms around him. "Stay a moment. It's more than two hours before dawn." She buried her face against his chest and held him with all her strength.

He kissed her gently, then turned on his side, keeping one arm around her. "I have to go."

Trella heard men talking and moving about downstairs, as they prepared for the battle. She knew the sounds called to him and that she must let him go.

"How long have I slept? You said you . . ."

"Almost three hours. You've scarcely slept in three days. Gatus told me to let you sleep." Her arms couldn't prevent him from sitting up.

"I must go, Trella. The men need to see me before the battle."

"I know, husband. Just remember to take care. There's

no need for you to take chances. Let others earn the glory today."

She stood and watched as he laced up his sandals.

Eskkar took his time, knotting them securely, then stood and buckled on his sword. He hadn't undressed before lying down. "This is the last battle. For five months we've prepared, and now it's upon us. Today we either win or fall."

Trella shook her head. "There is never a last battle. Remember that and you won't act rashly." She came into his arms and pressed against him, then lifted her arms around his neck. He tried to kiss her, but she clung so tightly all he could do was brush his lips against her forehead.

"Trella, I . . . you have to let me go."

She said nothing, but loosened her hold on him and stepped aside, her head downcast.

"Take care for your own self, and remember what I've told you if we fail."

He spoke the words calmly, but their meaning brought pain to her heart. She stood there as he turned and left the room. Trella heard his steps down the stairs. "May the gods go with you, husband, in all the places of danger that you will find today." She spoke the prayer aloud, but more to herself than to the gods. The tears came, but briefly. She had her own duties to attend to.

Eskkar went first to the well, quenching his thirst and washing his face in the flickering torchlight before returning to the kitchen. A single lamp showed Bantor, Alexar, Grond, and a few others seated at the table. Eskkar joined them, and they picked at the cold fowl and drank the weak ale the women set out. No one spoke, each in his thoughts, occasionally glancing at the tiny window to see if the stars had begun to dim. Each, as he finished eating, took chunks of bread and stuffed them in his pouch before leaving. There might not be another chance to eat the whole long day.

In the courtyard Eskkar found Sisuthros making sure each man knew his duty and station. Sisuthros hadn't slept during the night, offering to let the others sleep while he patrolled the walls and prepared its defenders. In the flickering light,

Eskkar thanked him for the long night's work, then clasped his arm in farewell.

Orak slept little during the night, as word spread the barbarians were mustering their forces and would attack at dawn. The commanders and village leaders inspected their men and ordered everyone to be at their station before first light. The cooking fires started early. Villagers and soldiers ate tasteless meals in silence and near-darkness, then drank again from the water jars in preparation for a long, hard day.

Parents, husbands, and lovers said their goodbyes, their voices low, faces grim, their futures uncertain. The whole village felt fear and tension. By sundown their fate would be decided.

The water wheels had run steadily since yesterday, filling the ditch with as much water as possible. Corio no longer worried about weakening the base of the wall. Senior men inspected weapons, checked water stores, and made sure each man knew his place. Archers strung fresh bowstrings on their bows, then tested them by torchlight. The rasp of sharpening stones grated endlessly, as men honed swords and axes to fighting edges.

Followed by his bodyguards, Eskkar strode to the main gate. Gatus and the other commanders had begun one last circuit of the village. They'd make sure all the men stood ready and at their posts, their weapons, equipment, and tools at hand.

Eskkar found Corio checking the ropes on the parapets that stretched across the gate, Alcinor at his side. The upper, smaller one sagged in the middle under its load of stones. The lower, wider and better supported, held an even greater weight of men and stones. Corio looked ready to collapse from the strain. Fear showed on the faces of both father and son in the torchlight. Today the master builder's wall and gate would face their greatest challenge.

As Eskkar watched, a line of villagers passed buckets of water up to the top of the gate, where others gently upended them in a slow stream designed to soak its outer face. That process would continue all day, to keep the wood as wet as possible.

"The night before a battle is always a long one, Corio," Eskkar said reassuringly.

"We're nearly ready, Captain," Corio answered, his voice pitched higher than normal. "Only a few more tasks . . ."

"You've plenty of time." These men needed calming more than anything else. "Try and rest, or you'll be useless when you are most needed. Once the battle begins, you'll be too busy to worry about anything."

Before they could reply he walked past them to enter the north tower. As he climbed the still-dark steps, he called out greetings, letting the men know he'd arrived, sensing rather than seeing the relief on their faces. When he reached the top, the sentries cleared a place for him at the wall.

Eskkar had spent much of yesterday at this same spot, watching for any hint of the barbarians' plans. He'd stared at the enemy camp until midnight, when Gatus demanded he get some rest. Eskkar left the wall, but only when they promised to awaken him three hours before sunrise. He didn't expect to sleep, but his body surprised him and he fell asleep moments after lying down, an arm thrown over his eyes as if to keep the dawn away as long as possible.

Now the time for sleep had passed. Eskkar looked toward the eastern sky. He thought he could detect a lighter shade of blackness. Lowering his eyes, he saw the line of the hills etched sharply against the glow of Alur Meriki fires. Nothing moved atop those hills. In front of the hills, darkness still covered the plain.

Leaning against the wall, Eskkar waited for the first glimmer of dawn. He closed his eyes and concentrated on his hearing. Though the hills lay more than a mile away, he could hear faint sounds of activity and knew preparations would have continued throughout the night. He recognized the rumble of wagons mixed with the occasional neighing of a skittish horse, frightened as it moved through the darkness, uncertain of its step or startled by torches that snapped and hissed. There would be plenty of fire to light their preparations, but only behind the hills, giving the defenders no glimpse of what lay hidden.

Behind him he heard the tread of feet on the steps. Men

moved beside and behind him as the soldiers filled their positions on the wall. The archers said little, as if they feared words would hasten the dawn or disturb the enemy.

"Well, Captain of the Guard, it sounds like barbarians are on the move out there." Gatus had returned, his loud voice breaking the spell. "They'll come early today, I think. We've been hearing movement from behind the hills all night."

Eskkar turned to face his second in command. In the torchlight, he saw most of his subcommanders. Sisuthros, Maldar, Grond, Totomes, even Myandro and a few others. Bantor remained at the courtyard, too weak to do much more than sit at a table and help coordinate the reserves.

Along the wall everyone watched and waited. Each wanted to be first to learn what the day had in store for them. The soldiers remained silent as the false dawn ebbed in the east, but they pressed forward as the stars began to disappear.

The noise coming from the plain increased, more horses moving about, the faint clink of sword and lance, the deeper groaning of cart wheels. The hilltops seemed to move and waver in the dim glow. The sky began to lighten, with tiny fingers of red and gold reaching up into the darkness, then a broad stream of sunlight flowed into the heavens as the first rays of true dawn swept into the sky.

The edge of the sun appeared over the hills and bathed the plain with soft, reddish light that revealed the enemy's movements at last. Eskkar saw wagons everywhere along the top of the hills, all moving slowly but purposefully down toward the plain, finding their positions and gathering themselves for the long journey toward Orak's walls. Hundreds of men pulled and pushed at the carts, assigned to make sure each wagon reached its destination. Warriors walked alongside the wagons.

Many in the front ranks carried no weapons and Eskkar realized that slaves and captives would be human shields to protect the warriors. Huge shields appeared everywhere, each large enough to protect three or four men, carried at each end by warriors or slaves. Not many rode their horses today, and those on horseback moved toward the flanks of the village, away from the main gate.

Eskkar stared in wonder at the number of men coming toward them. They'd killed hundreds of warriors and yet the enemy still had so many to send into battle. "And so it begins," he said, more to himself than to those standing beside him.

Only Gatus heard the odd remark and the old soldier turned toward him. "I care not how it begins, only how it ends. And we'll know that soon enough."

"They fight on foot today," Sisuthros commented. "No more wild charges. They'll be easy targets and our archers will cut them to shreds."

"It looks like every wagon in their camp is coming our way," Gatus said. "They intend to bring them to the very edge of the ditch and fight from behind them."

"And the sun will be in our eyes the whole time." Totomes's accent still sounded strange after all these weeks. "A long morning for our archers."

"They're coming right toward the gate." Sisuthros shaded his eyes with his hands. "And smoke is coming from the wagons. They carry fire."

Eskkar watched the Alur Meriki as they deployed their men in a slow but orderly fashion. No signs of confusion today, no aimless galloping back and forth, no loud boasting from the riders, only a few warriors on horseback directing men who pulled or pushed their loads. Thutmose-sin had prepared well. They'd had enough weeks to get ready.

Eskkar worried about the number of wagons and their wooden burdens. He'd burned an enormous amount of wood two nights ago, yet it all appeared to have been replaced.

"Look at the size of those shields," Gatus marveled. "I've never seen anything like that before."

Just crossing the distant hilltops, ten or twelve men appeared carrying a huge wooden shield, maybe six paces wide and twice as long. They looked like those he and Grond had burned.

Eskkar studied them for a long moment. "I think they're platforms to lay across the mud. They plan to cross the ditch on those. There's more of them on the wagons."

Nobody spoke for a moment, as each commander

contemplated what these unusual implements would mean. It seemed that today the attackers would be the ones with new tactics.

"Totomes," Eskkar said, "do your archers have any fire arrows?"

"No, Captain, we didn't think they'd be necessary."

"Better start making them. A lot of them."

"Yes, Captain." Totomes started down the tower's steps.

"Good hunting today, Totomes." If the man heard him, he didn't bother to reply. Eskkar turned back to his men.

"Sisuthros, get Nicar and anyone else you can find. Have them gather torches and as much of the oil that burns, if we've any left. Bring everything to the gate. We may have to burn these wagons and platforms ourselves."

He looked intently at each man for any sign of panic or fear, but saw only determination. "Everyone get to your positions and tell your men what's coming. The more they know what to expect, the less likely they'll be to panic."

As Gatus started down the steps, he grabbed one of Eskkar's bodyguards. "Make sure he puts on his helmet and wears as much leather as you can find, or I'll personally have your head."

Eskkar smiled at the old man's worries. It was a waste of time to argue with him. Turning back to the wall, he studied the advancement before him, shading his eyes. Horses, men, and wagons now covered the plain, all moving slowly, the leading edge already halfway to Orak. Before long the foremost barbarians would be in range and today the arrows would start as soon as possible.

Behind him men began shouting and moving about. He heard Totomes giving orders to his archers, including those who would target only clan leaders. His two sons would target little else. *Well, Totomes, this is your day for taking your revenge on the Alur Meriki.* By sunset, no matter how it ended, the master archer and his sons would slay more than enough of their foes to satisfy their blood feud.

Eskkar scanned the plains. Two streams of riders, backed by archers and men carrying ladders, moved toward the north and south walls. They'd try and draw soldiers away from the gate and towers. The bulk of the Alur Meriki came straight at the gate. They meant to bridge the ditch by pushing wagons and wooden platforms into place until they could attack the gate itself. Wagons and shields would provide protection for their archers.

Looking at the hills, he saw men still coming from the camp, but fewer of them. Almost all those in the front ranks were weaponless slaves, many of them women. They pushed wagons, or carried wood or pots of fire.

The Alur Meriki considered the slaves expendable, since a new supply could be obtained once they captured the village. So nothing would be held back today—every slave that could walk and every man that could hold a weapon. Eskkar signaled to one of the messengers kneeling against the wall. "Find one of the scribes and try to get a count of their fighting men."

How many men did Thutmose-sin have left? At least a thousand, Eskkar guessed. The horde in front of the village slowed, stopping just out of bowshot as they found their stations and took up their shields, preparing to face the arrows they knew awaited them.

Only silence came from the enemy. There would be little shouting or taunting, no eager war cries. They'd learned their lessons and knew they faced hardened soldiers who would not easily yield. They'd miss the joy of battle, Eskkar decided, no quick slaughter of men on foot, no feats of horsemanship, just moving forward into the rain of arrows.

Eskkar understood why they didn't use the horses. They'd lose too many, more than they could replace. He smiled at that thought. Thutmose-sin must be worried about how big a price he'd pay today, even in victory. The Alur Meriki leader must have a victory, and it must be cheap enough to satisfy those who hoped for his failure.

We just have to give them a reason to turn back, and some will take it.

Calls for silence moved up and down the walls as Totomes and his men finished testing their bows. The master archer had no more instructions for his men and needed no

orders from Eskkar to tell him when and what to shoot.
Huge stocks of arrows stood ready and the archers would
begin loosing shafts as soon as they could, for as long as
they could bend a bow, until every last arrow was gone.

Eskkar nodded in approval. He'd done all he could, and
now the arms of his archers would determine whether Orak
stood or fell.

He felt a gentle tap on his arm and turned, surprised to
find one of the women standing there. At first he didn't comprehend her words, then he saw the water jug in her hand.
An elderly matron, she had long gray hair that blew around
her shoulders in the light breeze. The jug's weight made her
hands tremble. She'd carried her burden first to him, bypassing others on her way.

Eskkar took the jug and lifted it to his lips. He didn't feel
particularly thirsty yet, but the sun already warmed the wall
and the full heat of the day would be on them soon enough.
So he took a long drink and returned a much lighter vessel
to the woman.

"Thank you, elder," he said, not knowing her name, as he
wiped his mouth with his hand.

"Good fortune," she answered soberly. "My sons fight
with you this day. So bring us victory." She didn't wait to
hear his reply, moving down the wall with her water, a task
she would perform throughout the long day or until an arrow took her down.

Behind her stepped Grond, newly promoted leader of the
captain's personal guard, carrying Eskkar's copper helmet,
now painted brown to look similar to the leather ones. He
handed it to his captain, as well as a leather vest and gaunt-
lets for his arms. Eskkar fastened them on his body, taking
care to lace them properly, letting Grond help him. The
other bodyguard handed Grond a thick leather collar.

"I'll not wear that." Eskkar shook his head. "It itches, and
I feel like I'm in a noose."

"I'm sorry, Captain, but Gatus and Lady Trella insisted."
Grond stared at him. "Or we'll have to carry you from the
wall. The enemy will be targeting you and we don't want
you to take an arrow in the throat."

Eskkar could have browbeaten the bodyguards, who looked nervous. But so long as Grond stood firm, they'd obey orders to carry off their captain. For a moment Eskkar's annoyance flashed, but Grond waited patiently, meeting his eyes, still offering up the collar. Eskkar felt tempted to take it and pitch it over the wall, but that would be childish. Besides, Grond would probably climb down into the ditch to retrieve it.

Eskkar ground his teeth and jerked the collar out of Grond's hand, then wrapped it around his neck. Immediately it began to chafe. Grond stepped around him to fasten the laces. "Make it loose, damn you. I don't want to choke to death."

Grond knew his business and the nearly three inches of stiff leather sat on the base of Eskkar's neck, loose but capable of deflecting, with luck, an arrow. That duty done, Grond nodded to the two bodyguards and they moved in front of Eskkar, bringing their wooden shields up to rest on the wall.

Eskkar would be able to peer between and over them, but the thick wood would shield most of his body. More men moved into position, including two special marksmen assigned by Totomes. These archers looked grim as they glanced at their captain. Their job was to kill anyone targeting Eskkar.

A messenger arrived, breathing hard, eyes wide as he reported to Eskkar. "Captain, Corio says there are at least eleven hundred armed men coming toward us, with about five hundred slaves."

"Send word to the command post." Eskkar spoke calmly, though he swore to himself at the number. He hadn't thought they had that many warriors left. They must have recalled every outrider and pressed into service all the old men and young boys. Or perhaps another raiding party had joined them. Wherever they came from, it would be a lot of men to stop.

"Already done, Captain," the boy answered.

Eskkar thanked the boy who moved aside, wedging himself out of the way in an empty space near the back of the tower. Out on the plain, a drum began to beat. Everyone turned toward the sound. The Orak bowmen looked nervous, almost anxious to get on with the battle. Their day had come and they'd be put to the test in the next few hours.

The barbarian horsemen moved to the flanks, staying just out of range. They'd try to keep as much pressure on the other walls as possible. They'd probe for any weak points, and they had enough men to mount a rush. But their primary task was to draw off as many defenders from the main gate as possible.

Meanwhile the main force of Alur Meriki paused, crowded together, carts ready, and wooden shields lifted on high. Suddenly the drum changed its rhythm. With a few shouts the mass of slaves, warriors, horsemen, and carts began to move. Eskkar glanced up at the sun, well above the horizon. An hour had passed since dawn.

The men on the wall fell silent. All eyes focused ahead as they took their stances and put arrows to the string, waiting for Totomes's order. The tall archer took his time. He waited until the thick block of men reached the range of even the weakest of his archers before giving the command. That order echoed along the rest of the wall, as the first flight of arrows told everyone the battle for Orak had begun.

The main wall held just two hundred and twenty archers, with the rest spread thinly along the other three walls. They faced at least seven hundred warriors heading straight for the gate, plus the mass of slaves used as shields and beasts of burden, well over a thousand men.

Arrows rattled up into the sky, flight after flight. His men were loosing between fifteen and eighteen arrows a minute. Out on the plain barbarians fell to the earth but the wagons kept coming, slowed for a moment as one or two men went down, but moving steadily forward.

So far no one fired back, but that would soon change. The enemy advanced, stoically absorbing the losses. War cries sounded on all sides now, as warriors raced their animals along the north and south walls.

The drumbeat quickened. The barbarians broke into a run, driving their slaves in front of them by the flat of their swords. Before long the leading edge of Alur Meriki knelt in the dirt and planted their shields about fifty paces from the ditch, as archers moved up behind the protection and began to return fire.

For their shorter bows it was still long range, and the advantage lay with the defenders, aided by their stronger bows and the height of the wall. But already more than three hundred enemy warriors plied their bows and began to score hits, even at that distance. The wagons still advanced.

An arrow whistled past Eskkar's head. Totomes directed his men to target the men advancing the wagons. Men went down again and again, but others took their places.

Eskkar grimaced. Most of these were slaves, not even warriors, forced to labor until an arrow took them. To turn away meant facing the swords and lances of warriors behind them. At last the first of the wagons, one piled high with planks nailed together and showing scorch marks on its high sides, reached the edge of the ditch. The attack would begin in earnest now.

An arrow glanced off Eskkar's copper helmet and a moment later another brushed his right arm, gouging the stiff leather. Grond pulled him down behind the shield, then ordered the archers to kill those who aimed at their captain. Eskkar saw a sudden flurry of activity behind the first wagon, already sprouting a thicket of arrows as defenders shot at every barbarian around-it.

About twenty leather-clad warriors ran alongside the wagon and grasped the topmost planks. They lifted a section and carried it forward into the ditch. Many went down with arrows, but enough stayed on their feet and managed to get the bridging section to the ditch and fling it down, before running back behind the wagons for shelter.

Another group of men tried to repeat the effort but this time Totomes's archers stopped the second attempt with a wave of arrows that brought warriors, screaming in pain, to their knees before they reached the edge of the ditch. It proved only a momentary setback. More men rushed up to aid them, and they managed to grasp and lift the heavy platform once again and rush it forward, some leaping down into the mud, others dropping onto the first piece of bridge.

In their haste they failed to place the second section properly. For a moment no warrior would venture out to correct it. Instead they brought up more archers from the rear and a hailstorm of arrows drove the defenders beneath the wall for a few moments. Esskar could only watch through the narrow gap between the two shields as two gangs of men rushed forward, one to straighten the second section and another to lift and carry the third section.

By now all the barbarian archers were shooting from behind some sort of cover, making it harder for Orak's archers to hit them. Their enemies needed only to aim for the top of the wall to keep the defenders pinned down.

With the third bridging section in place, the barbarians had reached more than halfway across the ditch, even though the trench here stretched twice as wide. Esskar turned to Gatus. "Get every archer you can find up on the wall. I'm going to the gate."

Without waiting for a reply Esskar dashed away, Grond and the bodyguards following him. Esskar ran down the tower steps, pushing past a constant stream of men climbing up to reinforce or resupply those already there. Emerging into the sunlight he took only a few steps before he found Corio directing a handful of villagers carrying three heavy clay pots.

"Good work, Corio," Esskar shouted. "Is this the oil?"

"All that's left. The storehouse is empty."

The lands around Orak held numerous pools of the oil-that-burns, but no such pool existed inside Orak. The countless torches needed every night had drained the stores of oil faster than expected. Esskar's fire raid had taken the rest.

Esskar grimaced but there was nothing he could do about it. "We'll need more than that. Find more. And send one jar up to the top of the gate."

"Captain, be careful, we might set fire . . ."

Esskar left Corio and climbed up the narrow wooden steps leading to the upper parapet. Several archers manning the slits had taken wounds, but a few cheered at the sight of their captain. He moved to the gate's center, then pushed an archer aside to glance through the firing slit. The barbarians had placed another section into the ditch and looked ready to move up another. That one would completely bridge the ditch.

A burly villager bumped into Eskkar's back, breathing hard and carrying the largest of the pots of oil. Eskkar took the vessel and almost dropped it, surprised by the weight.

"Fetch as many torches as you can," he ordered. The man nodded, then swung over the edge of the platform and just dropped to the parapet directly below, before jumping to the ground.

The last bridging section had the farthest to go and again Totomes's archers waited for the Alur Meriki effort. A wave of arrows from the defenders cut the first attempt short, hitting a half-dozen warriors before they could even take up the burden. Another attempt failed as well, until a horde of nearly fifty men rushed up and by sheer numbers carried the section down into the ditch and heaved it into position. Despite the heavy losses, a shout of triumph accompanied their success.

Eskkar turned to Grond, who'd stayed right behind him. "We'll hurl this as far from the gate as we can. Understand? At the count of three!"

Together they lifted the clay jar, each holding it with one hand on the bottom and using the other hand to steady it. Eskkar took a deep breath and braced himself, nodded at Grond, then gave the count. "One . . . two . . . three!"

With a mighty heave they hurled the pot of oil over the top. The jar landed at least twenty feet away from the gate, bursting into a hundred pieces as it emptied its contents between the fourth and fifth sections. Without bothering to look Eskkar seized the flaming torch that the laborer had brought and hurled it over the top. By the time he reached a slit, the torch had ignited the oil and a sheet of flames burned hotly wherever the oil had spread. Even the mud in the ditch caught fire.

Two arrows hissed through the slit and Eskkar felt his heart jump. If he'd stared an instant longer . . . Alur Meriki archers below now waited for any target. "Get another pot of oil, Grond. That should slow them down."

Men crowded the gate now, its parapets sagging danger-ously as ten more archers added their weight to the plat-forms. Another jar of oil arrived, this one smaller, and again Eskkar and Grond heaved it over the gate. It landed closer to the mud this time but shattered well enough to cover the burning wood again. A strange whooshing noise and a wave of heat accompanied flames that rushed into the air. The few warriors who had ventured out onto the platform quickly retreated. For a moment the conflagration rose even higher than the gate.

The last two sections of the bridge burned steadily, and nothing would put them out until the fire reached the muddy underside of the wood. The barbarians halted, surprised to find their own tactic used against them. The vicious ex-change of arrows continued taking its toll on both sides. Grond readied the last pot but a quick glimpse told Eskkar it wasn't needed yet. He leaned over the edge of the platform and shouted down at Corio. "Corio, we need more oil. Send women to gather every drop from every house."

"Yes, Captain. We'll find some."

Eskkar turned back to the parapet. Alcinor had his work-ers pouring water over the top, nervous about the fire their leaders had ignited. A fire behind the gate might be disas-trous. Then a cry from the tower made Eskkar take another quick glance through the slit. The barbarians had lifted an-other bridging section from a wagon and were gathering for a new rush.

Eskkar understood immediately what they planned. Placed on top of the burning ones, the new section would smother the fires and be even firmer underfoot. The warriors gave a shout as they braved the archers' volleys to take up the plat-form on both sides and begin moving it toward the ditch. Eskkar picked up a bow from a wounded archer and strung a shaft himself. "Find yourself a bow, Grond."

The big man returned in a moment, as archers crowded around the slits. Eskkar looked at him. "They're watching the slits. We'll shoot from over the top. Try to bring down the first man on your side." This was dangerous. They'd have to expose more of their bodies. But Eskkar needed to stop the attackers now.

Warriors, stumbling under the weight of the new section but moving rapidly, had reached the halfway point of the ditch.

"Now!" Eskkar shouted. In that instant, both he and Grond leaned over the top of the gate, Eskkar firing as the rest of the defenders did likewise, ducking back not an instant too soon as a flock of arrows whistled into the space their heads had just occupied. A peek through the slit told Eskkar his shaft had hit the mark. The stricken warrior had fallen onto the man behind him. The whole section had crashed into the ditch. The warriors tried to pick it up, but arrows from each tower and the gate struck among them and drove the Alur Meriki back behind the wagons. By now even the bridging sections were riddled with arrows.

The section the Alur Meriki had tried to bring forward sat half in the mud and half on the bridge. It looked too far for Eskkar to reach with another pot of oil. Or was it?

"Wait here, Grond," he ordered. He swung down to the lower parapet then dropped to the ground. He shouted for messengers even as Corio and Alcinor raced to Eskkar's side. "Find some small jars, about this big," he held his hands about six inches apart. "I want to throw oil further out on their bridge. And get me more oil!"

Corio nodded to his son and Alcinor raced away. "Can we hold them, Captain?" The master artisan looked frightened.

A meaningless question. "Only the gods know, but they're not inside yet. Just keep the gate wet and our own torches away from the oil." Only a few paces from where they stood, villagers frantically pumped at the water wheel, sending a steady stream out into the ditch.

Eskkar mounted the steps, ignoring the tiredness in his legs, and returned to the top. He knelt beside Grond, picked up a shield, and used it to cover himself as he looked through the slit. He saw warriors trading shafts with the defenders while others prepared for another rush.

Alcinor arrived, breathing hard and carrying two small

clay jugs, the kind used to hold wine in the alehouses. He also carried several long pieces of cotton. Alcinor dipped the wine jug into the last remaining pot of oil and held it until it was almost filled. He stuffed one of the rags in the mouth of the jar. Finally, he took another rag and wiped the outside of the jug clean, rubbing hard to remove every trace of oil.

Alcinor saw the puzzled look on Eskkar's face. "The rag will act as a stopper, like a wick in a lamp," Alcinor explained. "We light the rag before you throw it." To demonstrate, he called for a torch, then touched the rag to its flame.

Eskkar watched in fascination as fire blossomed from the rag. It did burn like a wick in a candle, without being instantly consumed. Eskkar took the flaming wine jug, braced his feet, and hurled it over the wall. The pot almost went too far but landed on the new section of bridge, shattered, and burst into flames. The fire didn't burn as intensely as before, but would certainly slow the attackers.

For a few moments it did. Then a large group of warriors rushed down into the ditch, where they used their hands to scoop up the damp mud and toss it on the burning planks. That smothered the oil and flames at the same time. Arrows struck down many, but others replaced those killed or wounded, throwing more wet earth onto the platform. Wherever the mud landed, the fire hissed and smoked, then died out immediately.

"Damn them," Eskkar swore. The archers' fire from the walls wasn't enough to impede them. "We need more archers," he shouted to Grond. "Stay here and throw as many jugs as you can." Eskkar dropped down from the parapet, running back to the north side where he found Gatus directing men and shouting orders. "Gatus, we need more archers. They'll be at the gate in a few moments."

"I've sent you every man I could find. Totomes says they're driving the barbarian archers back."

"It's taking too long. They're almost ready to assail the gate. Strip every archer from the other walls. Send villagers to take their place. Just get more men to the towers."

Leaving Gatus, Eskkar raced back up the steps to Grond's side, who'd prepared another oil-filled wine jug.

An arrow whistled through the slit just as Eskkar was about to look, the shaft passing between the two men's faces. They looked grimly at each other. But he needed to see, so he took a quick look. He saw plenty of activity across the ditch, but so far the Alur Meriki hadn't tried to push another section out. They would at any moment.

"Captain, this is the last of the oil," Grond said. "But I think I can throw this close to their wagon, if you can cover me."

Eskkar looked at Grond's huge arms and shoulders. This jug appeared smaller than the others. If anyone could do it, Grond could. Nevertheless, he'd have to stand up, brace himself, and make the throw. But if he could reach the wagon. . . .

"Archers," Eskkar shouted, "ready yourself for a volley." He picked up his shield. The soldiers readied themselves. Grond held out the jar and Alcinor touched the torch to the rag, which flamed up for a moment before it began to burn steadily with a smoky haze.

Eskkar glanced up and down the parapet. The archers looked grim but ready with their bows. "Now!" They rose up and released a hasty volley, enough to distract the closest barbarian archers for a moment.

In that instant Eskkar arose, holding the shield to protect Grond, who grasped the top edge with his left hand and hurled the wine jug.

Eskkar pulled Grond back down with his free hand as arrows hissed above them. Eskkar's shield had four arrows protruding from it. Glancing through the slit he saw that Grond's throw had been true. The jug landed just in front of the wagon and burst into flames. Splashes of oil reached and immediately began to burn the dry wood of the cart. The warriors tried to quench the flames, but Orak's archers drove them back.

Covering most of the slit with his shield, Eskkar watched as the warriors reacted. At first they did little. Then an Alur Meriki war leader gathered warriors with shields and ordered them in front of the cart, to protect those who would extinguish the flames.

This time the attackers not only extinguished the fire, but draped two hides over the wagon's front. Meanwhile warriors loosed arrows at a rapid pace as they prepared once again to place the final bridge section. Eskkar and his men had slowed their advance but not stopped it.

With a shout the barbarians swarmed around the wagon and took up another section of bridge. They ignored the flickering flames that lingered in places underfoot as well as the arrows that flew into their ranks. Eskkar heard the heavy section drop into place beneath the gate. This time a few of the attackers paused long enough to scoop mud and dirt from the ditch onto the new platform, trying to wet the wood before the villagers could throw more burning oil.

Fresh reserves of enemy fighters, most with bows but many with axes, rushed out from behind the wagons, shouting war cries as they came. They raced across the muddy and smoking bridge, stepping on the bodies of their fallen, whose dead and dying bodies littered the ditch. Now twice as many barbarians stood under the gate, arrows nocked and ready to shoot at anything that moved.

Eskkar felt the first axe thud into the gate. "Stones!" he bellowed. Men dropped their bows and began heaving the river rocks over the gate.

A second and third axe began plying on the gate, the sound ringing throughout the village. Their shields protected the Alur Meriki somewhat from falling stones.

"Stones! Arrows! Now," Eskkar yelled. Stones flew over the top, until the melon-sized rocks fell like rain.

Alcinor, his voice cracking, shouted at the men, reminding them to drop the stones straight down, for the men below surely pressed themselves as close as possible to the wall, to avoid the bone-breaking missiles.

In a few moments of frenzied activity the defenders exhausted all the stones on the parapet. Alcinor screamed for more rocks, and Eskkar risked an arrow to take another look through the slit. The first wagon side had been pushed into the ditch. The Alur Meriki wanted to move the wagon as close to the gate as possible. They'd tried to guide it directly onto the bridge, but one side must have gone over faster than the other and now one of the wheels had caught in the mud. Still, three of the wagon's wheels rested on the bridge, and another cart carrying a fresh supply of wood and oil had taken its place.

Warriors crawled and stumbled in the ditch now, ignoring the arrows that flew at them, to free and move the first wagon forward. Eskkar heard them cursing the clumsy vehicle that clung to the mud and resisted their efforts, until nearly twenty men lifted and pushed it free and completely onto the bridge. Meanwhile other barbarians seized tools and axes and rushed back to the gate, ignoring the flames that still burned in places.

A fresh group of warriors, weaponless but carrying large wooden shields, came forward to protect the axe men hammering at the gate from the stones. Damn the gods, there seemed to be no end to these barbarians.

Eskkar turned back to Grond. "I'll try and find more fire jugs. The first wagon is within reach now, and they're bringing up another." The big man nodded, and Eskkar swung from the edge of the parapet to the ground for the third time. There he nearly knocked over Narquil.

Totomes's son had just descended from the right tower. He staggered toward Eskkar, blood pouring down his right arm, two arrows protruding from it. Eskkar grabbed the man and shouted for a messenger. A boy, eyes wide, appeared from under the wall.

"Bring Narquil to the women and have them stop the bleeding."

Narquil, his eyes wide with shock from pain and loss of blood, grasped Eskkar's arm with his left hand. "Captain . . . look at the arrow."

He slurred the words, and at first Eskkar thought Narquil wanted him to look at the wound.

"The arrow, Captain . . . it's one of ours. They're running out of arrows."

"Yes, I see. Go with the boy now." Turning to the messenger, Eskkar ordered him to get moving, then raced up the tower where he'd started the morning. Emerging into the sunlight, he found blood and bodies everywhere. Death had thinned their ranks, but archers still worked their bows. He found Totomes. The grim archer had held his place, calmly aiming and firing shafts at his hated enemy, using the tower's vantage to kill as many clan leaders as possible.

"Totomes, can your archers sweep the ditch of warriors?" he shouted, almost in the man's ear. "They're at the gate with axes."

Totomes loosed the arrow on his bowstring before ducking below the wall, pulling Eskkar down with him. "Not yet, Captain. We'd have to lean too far over the wall to get a shot at them. We're killing the bowmen behind the barricade. Their fire is slowing and they're running out of arrows. The men in the ditch will have to wait."

"We may not have that much time left. They're weakening the gate and fire will be upon us soon."

"I'll do what I can, Captain, but you must hold them off a little longer. Are my sons still alive?"

"Narquil was wounded in the arm and I sent him to the women. He'll fight no more today. I haven't seen Mitrac." Eskkar started to move away, then turned back to the master archer. "Narquil said the same thing, that they were running out of arrows. One of the arrows that wounded him was one of ours. Does that mean anything?"

Totomes grimaced at the news of his son's wounding. "Our arrows are heavier than theirs, and longer. If they shoot them at us, they risk breaking their bows, or not shooting them full strength. That means they'll fire more slowly as well. Now let me get back to my work. I've killed two clan leaders already and there are more out there." He strung another shaft to his bowstring while they spoke. Now he rose up, aimed, and loosed in one easy motion.

Cursing the gods in frustration, Eskkar started back down the steps, pushing past a woman carrying a sack of arrows up to the men. At least his soldiers would have no shortage of missiles today. Out of the tower and back at the gate, he heard axes ringing against the structure. Looking up, he saw Grond hurling stones over the top of the gate.

Men scrambled up the steps, carrying baskets of stones, but the defenders dropped them over the top faster than they could be resupplied. Men passed baskets from hand to hand to make sure they covered the entire section of the gate. Eskkar started up the steps, then stopped when he heard his name called. He turned back to find Gatus running toward him, blood on his hand and a cut across his cheek.

"Eskkar! The barbarians crossed the ditch on the south wall and nearly carried the wall. Bantor went there with the last of the villagers, when there were no other soldiers to move up in support."

Eskkar could do nothing about the other walls. The villagers would have to keep the attackers at bay. "I need more men here, Gatus, and now." Pointing up at the gate, Eskkar saw only a few men hurling rocks and firing arrows. "Otherwise they'll be coming through soon enough." The gate's big timbers had begun to shake under the axe blows.

Gatus coolly appraised the gate. Alcinor's workers swarmed everywhere, carrying heavy planks to reinforce its base. "The gate will last a little longer. I'll find you more men."

Eskkar swore again and ran toward the steps, pausing only to take a basket of stones away from a woman who could scarcely manage the load. He grunted under the weight and ducked beneath the slits until he reached Grond's side. The big man picked up two stones, one in each hand, then positioned himself directly over the pounding before he flung the missiles over the edge. Eskkar stayed on his knees, handing Grond the three remaining stones, one at a time. When they were gone, Eskkar tossed the empty basket to the ground and shouted for more.

A bowman at the slit beside him gave a strangled gasp as an arrow pierced his throat. Eskkar grabbed the bow from the man's hands, then pushed the dying man off the parapet. Notching a shaft, he went to the slit, as another arrow flew through it. The attackers had grown bolder. They had discovered that the safest place was directly under the wall, and many had positioned themselves there, shafts ready to fire at any target that showed.

Peering through the slit at the sharpest angle he could

manage, Eskkar saw an Alur Meriki archer in the ditch and let fly. The arrow feathered itself in the man's chest.

Eskkar's action drew a flurry of arrows and another hissed through the slit, narrowly missing him. Still, he had the helmet and collar for protection, and he needed to stop the barbarians now. Eskkar shoved the bow into the slit for a moment then ducked back, letting another flight of arrows come at him. Then he moved up while they were notching their shafts and again sent an arrow into an Alur Meriki archer.

Ducking again he took a quick glance toward the ditch and saw that a third wagon had been pushed to the edge. Warriors now carried burning fagots and torches onto the platform. They had their own jars of oil. They'd stuff the burning wood into the holes the axe men had created, douse everything with oil, and try to fire the gate. And the defenders had no more oil to oppose them.

Grond reappeared with another basket of rocks. Two bodyguards came behind him, carrying more. The gate shuddered continually under the axes, the sounds of splintering wood carrying over the frantic shouts of the defenders. "There's a group of bowmen right below us. Let's feed them some stones."

Grond nodded and pulled the bodyguards into position on each side of him. Then the three men began tossing the rocks in unison over the edge. As soon as they started, Eskkar moved to a slit and shot another arrow, cursing as his intended target moved back, the shaft disappearing harmlessly in the mud. In the same instant he saw another warrior struck in the shoulder by a stone. The man screamed in pain and dropped the shield he'd held over his head. Nevertheless, more barbarians moved into the ditch, carrying bundles of wood and straw, as well as pots that surely contained oil.

Eskkar, Grond, and the others fought like demons, while the brutal fighting raged all around them. Stones provided the main weapon for the defenders now, the gate's archers almost useless now, afraid to lean out or even use the arrow slits. Too many enemy archers, bows drawn, waited for any movement, most of them protected by shields. The barbarians still hacked away at the gate, taking losses but maintaining their stubborn attack. The continuous pounding shook the structure.

A shout behind him made Eskkar turn around. Corio and Alcinor had returned with a crowd of villagers carrying the last of the stones. Forming lines, villagers passed the rocks to the top of the gate as fast as they could. Under the parapet, carpenters continued to reinforce the base of the structure. Suddenly the ringing of the axes ceased. Eskkar risked a peek through the slit.

The axe men were racing away, back to the safety of the wagons, their task done for the moment. Others ran forward to replace them. These warriors carried large bundles of dry grass they placed against the gate. The barbarians had chopped and shattered much of the gate's bottom and now stuffed bundles of oil-soaked straw and wood into the openings. Eskkar saw a dozen men with torches race across the platform before hurling their torches. The gate ignited in a whoosh of flames.

The defenders kept hurling rocks and water over the gate. Eskkar leaned back and looked across the ditch. Arrows coated all the carts, and new shafts kept striking at the mass of men huddled behind them, aimed at any warrior who exposed himself. Orak's archers were slowly stopping the bowmen behind the ditch. Totomes had been right. They were winning the archery battle. If only they had enough time.

Eskkar looked down behind him. At the base of the gate, a thick plume of smoke already curled underneath, carrying the stink of burning oil with it.

Everyone screamed for water. Men and women alike passed buckets to the top of the gate. Every available villager, even children, had come there, drawing water from the wells, then passing the buckets hand to hand to the men on the walls. Others continued to carry stones and arrows to the wall's defenders.

It had become a race between the fire at the gate's base and the water that poured over its top. Others hurled water at the gate's bottom, at any place that looked likely to burn through. Eskkar glimpsed Trella among them, keeping the villagers in order and directing them where they would do the most good.

Eskkar gazed along the parapet. "Grond, these men are exhausted. I'll send fresh men up and you move these men down, or they'll be too tired to fight." He swung down again to the ground.

Someone shouted his name. Eskkar saw Alexar running toward him with archers taken from the other walls, ten men in all. "Replace the men on the top of the gate. They'll be needed soon to use the stones as well."

Alexar nodded and moved off, shouting orders, and Eskkar moved to the base of the gate. Eskkar laid his hand on the structure, but felt nothing. The fire roared louder now, and he saw thick, greasy smoke flowing over the top. The shimmering flames leapt higher than the gate.

Grond remained on the top, making sure the men kept tossing stones, while on the lower parapet men risked arrows to hurl water through the arrow slits. Nevertheless the oil-soaked wood continued to burn, and the Alur Meriki kept bringing up more and more bundles of dry grass to feed the burning gate.

Eskkar watched as the flames steadily ate away at the gate's beams. But no villagers left their labors and more men and women kept coming, carrying anything that could be used as a weapon. Despite the confusion, everyone was doing their duty.

He saw a break in the line of men carrying water up to the parapet. Grasping a bucket, Eskkar carried it to the upper parapet, then poured it over the side where Grond pointed. Another voice shouted for Eskkar's attention. He looked over to see Sisuthros standing at the back of the south tower.

"Captain, they're massing their warriors," Sisuthros shouted, cupping his hands to make sure his voice carried. "They're bringing up a ram, getting ready to attack."

Eskkar wiped sweat from his brow and took a look, keeping his head back far enough so that the bowmen below couldn't see him. He studied the men moving into position. Something looked different. Eskkar moved his head a little higher, then dropped down as an arrow snapped through the slit and glanced off his helmet.

"Grond, I need to see this." Eskkar snatched up a shield and raised it over the gate, holding it an inch or two above the top, ignoring the arrows that thudded into it. Behind the shield, he rose almost to his full height.

The barbarians were massing across the ditch, forming a V-shaped line of shields and wagons that curved slightly away from the ditch. The Alur Meriki had concentrated their fighters here, drawing most of their warriors away from the other walls and focusing their attention on the gate. The attackers were betting all on breaking through here.

Sisuthros joined him. "I've ordered every man I could from the rest of the walls," he gasped, "and told Maldar and the others to do the same."

Eskkar noticed fresh soldiers arriving on the parapet, each one carrying a basket of stones in addition to his bow.

"Keep the towers at full strength. Have them start killing the warriors at the base of the gate, even if they have to lean out to do it. We've got to drive them away from the gate!"

Raising his voice, Eskkar shouted to the defenders. "Hold fast! More soldiers are coming. And the barbarians are weakening!"

A few cheered but most just looked at him, exhaustion and despair in their faces. But no one stopped working and then, as bowmen began arriving, they appeared to take heart.

Eskkar climbed down to the first parapet, creaking and swaying even more ominously as the ropes continued to stretch. A great shout came from outside the gate. After a quick look, Eskkar ducked his head back. For once, no arrows flew in through the slit, though he heard at least one strike the gate nearby. Orak's archers were taking their toll. But a mass of barbarians, at least sixty or seventy warriors, had moved forward into the ditch, carrying with them a great ram made from a huge tree trunk. The ram swayed beneath a wooden frame, suspended by a mass of ropes. Warriors carrying shields held high protected those who bore the burden, and the ram reached the base of the gate without falling to the earth. Soon it would begin hammering the structure where the fire had done the most damage.

The fire-weakened wood couldn't take too many blows from something that size. A renewed storm of Alur Meriki arrows flew at any target that exposed itself, as the attackers tried to protect the warriors carrying the ram.

The sound of hammering made him look down. At least twenty villagers labored there. Men with mauls nailed a notched plank into position. Others, struggling under the weight of a beam, moved forward to angle the log into the notch. Carpenters immediately began hammering it home, fastening the beam to the plank. Everyone ignored the thick black smoke curling around their feet, though many began coughing, choking on the stench of the burning oil.

Suddenly the gate shook as if a mighty fist had struck it. Two men cried out as they lost their balance and toppled backward from the upper parapet. Eskkar might have followed but for Grond's huge hand, covered in blood, that reached over and grasped him. Eskkar had barely recovered before another blow struck the gate.

Risking another glance through the slit, Eskkar saw a near-solid wall of shields protecting those manning the ram. The attackers might be taking terrible losses, but they fought on. He hadn't killed enough to make them lose hope, give up, before they broke through.

The gate reeled again, this time accompanied by the sound of splintering wood. Villagers screamed at each other to hurry.

"Do what you can here, Grond, but don't stay too long. Be off the parapet before it falls. The gate's going to be forced. I'm going down to get the men ready." Once again, Eskkar swung off the parapet, holding for a moment until he could drop all the way to the ground. He landed heavily enough to fall to his knees.

Getting to his feet he stared at the base of the gate. The ram was breaking through. The heavy beam, hammered in place on the left side of the gate only moments ago, had already been knocked out of position, and the ram's head had crashed through part of the planking that supported it. Maldar ran up, with another half-dozen men, bows in hand.

"Form a line here, Maldar," Eskkar ordered.

The gate shuddered again. A section of the lower parapet gave way, sending men scrambling to avoid its imminent collapse. Eskkar studied the gate, watching it vibrate every few moments as the ram struck again and again in a powerful rhythm. The leftmost portion looked weakest, but the right side stood mostly intact, its main brace firmly in position.

Corio, his eyes streaming from the smoke, tripped over the fallen beam. Eskkar seized his arm and pulled him to his feet. "Corio, brace the upper parapet before it collapses, too, or we'll have no men manning the slits. See if you can keep it in place, even if they break through underneath. Hurry!"

Eskkar gave the man no time to reply, just shoved him on his way. Another file of five soldiers arrived, and Eskkar called them to him, shouting for shields. Grond came scrambling down from the upper parapet with two of Eskkar's original bodyguards.

Wiping the sweat out of his eyes, Eskkar turned to his men. "Give your bows to the villagers and find shields. We'll need swords and spears for this work."

Grond pointed the two guards toward weapons stored against the nearest house. They returned in moments, carrying four shields.

Eskkar looked back at the gate. The left side of the once-solid gate had splintered badly. The giant logs, weakened by axe and fire, trembled and shook from the ram's mighty blows. A glance at the towers and walls on each side showed them crowded with archers desperately trying to stop the rammers.

They would be too late. The Alur Meriki were going to open a breach. But it might not be a large opening, and maybe it could be held. As he watched, the leftmost side of the lower parapet swung down with a screech of nails and snapping of ropes, accompanied by the shouts of men who jumped or tumbled to the ground. It collapsed slowly and dropped directly in front of the opening. The same blow pitched two men off the upper platform as it swayed precariously from its ropes. That platform still held, though it shook and rattled under each blow of the ram.

The ram crashed against the gate once again and this time its fire-hardened tip penetrated the wooden structure. As the ram's head withdrew, some of the archers fired at the opening, and Eskkar heard a scream from the other side.

"Keep shooting," he ordered, moving well away from the gap as the archers loosed a volley, a few shafts going through the narrow, jagged opening. Then the ram, repositioned slightly, smashed into the next set of vertical logs. Four more times the ram struck before another log snapped in two.

The ramming stopped for a moment, as warriors with axes pried at the weakened logs. Then the ram began its hammering again. It took less than a dozen strokes before another pair of logs gave way. The din increased, as more axes hammered at the loosened logs, widening the aperture. A warrior tried to climb through the breach and was riddled with arrows that knocked him backward from sheer force of impact.

Eskkar gripped his shield and drew his sword, then turned to Grond and the bodyguards. "We have to stop them here. They can't be allowed past the gate!" He grabbed the nearest bodyguard and shouted in his ear. "Make sure the archers hold their fire when we move to the breach. Go!"

The man nodded and raced back to the line of archers, who stayed in their rough line, still loosening their arrows at the opening. Alur Meriki shields appeared, pushed through the breach, protecting the attackers massing behind them. Eskkar and Grond gave out mighty shouts and rushed toward the gap.

The attackers shoved their way through the narrow opening, crouching low and using their shields to avoid the defenders' arrows. Rushing forward, Eskkar had no time to worry about an arrow in his back from his own men. Raising his shield to his eyes, he took four quick steps and crashed against the shield of the first Alur Meriki warrior. Caught off balance, the man reacted slowly, stumbling in the jumble of beams and splinters, and Eskkar took a half-step back and swung the great sword down on the warrior's head. Again Eskkar lowered his shoulder behind his shield and shoved with all his might, pushing the dead body into the man behind him.

Battle fury took all of them, as Eskkar, Grond, and four soldiers formed a half-circle around the breach and defended it with a ferocity that surprised the attackers. The defenders were fresher, while the attackers had been working the ram or ducking arrows in the hot sun without water for nearly two hours.

The first wave of Alur Meriki fell back, driven by the vicious blows of Eskkar and his companions. But as the defenders exulted, a second horde of screaming attackers, seeing victory within their grasp, fought their way through the opening, a gap that grew wider as the enemy outside kept hammering away with their axes.

These attackers wielded lances as well as swords. They quickly widened the half-circle of warriors who had pushed through the opening. Eskkar struck again and again, using his shield to turn their swords and spears and striking at anything within reach of his great sword.

Suddenly a loud voice behind them commanded, "Down!"

Eskkar and his men responded by habit, so well trained were they, dropping to one knee and ducking their heads under their shields. A wave of arrows flashed over their heads. Instantly Eskkar and the others arose. They'd practiced this tactic so often that now they did it without thinking. The volley had stopped the invaders for a moment. Eskkar and his men, behind their shields and thrusting with their swords, attacked the wavering men before they could recover, forcing the warriors back. The besiegers gave ground for a moment, but once again fresh warriors pushed their way through the ever-widening breach into Orak.

Eskkar and his swordsmen anticipated the next command, and when the shout of "Down" came again, they dropped, letting another flight of arrows cross over them before they rose and again rushed the barbarians.

The Alur Meriki hesitated, taken aback by this strange

tactic, not used to fighting swordsmen and archers at the same time. Before they could recover, Grond pushed his way nearly back to the breach, carrying a dead man pinned to his shield and hurling the body into the opening.

Swinging his sword over his head, Eskkar brought it crashing down with all his strength on a warrior's shield, slicing through it and into the man's arm.

More defenders surrounded him. A spearman pushed in front of Eskkar, even as fresh swordsmen arrived. Twenty swords now blocked the opening. But surprisingly, no new attackers tried to force the breach, so Eskkar stepped back and looked up at the gate. The upper parapet hung crookedly from its supports, but men continued to hurl stones down on their attackers. Only now they shouted with glee and worked with renewed energy. Something strange was happening, but he had no idea what.

Eskkar turned to Grond. "Hold them here." He needed to see what had happened in the ditch. Racing to the right side of the gate, he dashed up the steps, nearly knocking over two men carrying baskets of rocks up to the defenders, and continued all the way to the parapet. He felt it sway precariously under his weight and hoped it would hold a while longer.

This time Eskkar didn't bother with a shield, just looked over the top of the gate, standing back to be out of sight of any archers beneath him. What he saw stunned him. Warriors were turning back, moving away from the ditch and running to the rear. Others backed away more slowly, firing their bows as they retreated. From the sides of the village, horsemen galloped back toward the plain, urging their horses hard and ignoring the fight at the gate. To his surprise they didn't slow their mounts, even when they passed out of range of Orak's arrows. They were racing back to their camp, but he didn't understand why.

He squinted into the sun as he looked toward the highest hilltop, ignoring the sweat that ran into his eyes. That looked different, too. More than a dozen smoke trails rose into the cloudless sky from the Alur Meriki camp. The fires themselves couldn't be seen, but they burned near the northern portion of the Alur Meriki main camp.

He saw movement all over the hilltop. More men came running down the hills toward Orak to join the battle. No, by the gods, they were women! Women running away from the camp. And dozens of riderless horses galloped toward Orak as well. Something had stampeded the animals. Another movement, something different, caught his eye and he strained to make out what it was.

On the crest of one of the highest hills a lone horseman stood, wheeling his horse and waving his lance high. Attached to the lance hung a long streamer. Even at this distance, Eskkar could make out its yellow color as it rippled in the breeze. The rider waved it for a few more moments, ignoring the rapidly approaching horsemen, before he leisurely turned away and galloped over the hilltop and out of sight.

"What is it?" Sisuthros stood at his side, breathing hard, his left arm covered in blood. "What's happening?"

Eskkar tried to laugh, but his dry throat wouldn't permit more than a cackle. A wheezing villager came behind him with a bucket of water destined for the fire below. Eskkar grabbed it and poured it over his face, filling his mouth at the same time.

"Can't you see, Sisuthros," he answered when he'd slacked his thirst. "That was Subutai, and by the gods, he's ridden clean through their camp!"

"They'll catch him for sure, won't they?" Sisuthros's voice showed concern.

Eskkar turned his gaze back to the vacant hilltop. He laughed now, his throat refreshed. "Subutai's not that foolish. I'm sure he put his horse to a full gallop the instant he left the hilltop. He'll have a hard run to escape them, but he'll make it. He must have raided the camp, burned some tents, stampeded the horses, and made sure the Alur Meriki knew he was there. That's what made them abandon the attack, knowing that their women and children were at risk. They don't know how few men attacked their camp."

They stood there in silence. Eskkar watched as the last of

the Alur Meriki scrambled out of the ditch and began to run as fast as they could to the rear. Many dropped swords and weapons in their haste, trying to outrace the angry arrows chasing them. Shafts struck down a few of them, as the defenders showed no mercy and lost no opportunity to take their targets.

A broad trail of bodies, arrows protruding from their backs, marked the flight of the barbarians. The sight saddened him and he felt strangely glad when the last escaped out of range. Many paused to shake their fists at Orak and its defenders, their anger and frustration all too evident. Others just knelt in the dust to catch their breath, too tired from fighting and running even to call curses upon their enemies.

Cheers echoed along the wall, ragged and hoarse, growing louder as those away from the gate grasped what happened. Esskar watched the retreat and counted the lines of smoke climbing into the hot sky. The smoke streams merged, making it difficult, but he guessed at least thirty fires had been set. Not a great number, but enough to send a lot of smoke into the sky. Subutai wouldn't have many men, but one horseman carrying a torch could do much in little time. Subutai must have prepared his men carefully. He'd learned well that lesson.

Esskar wondered how many more men Subutai had lost and hoped the number was small. Even if the Alur Meriki had no force of warriors guarding the camp, there would have been a few boys and old men who could draw a bow. Subutai's men faced a long and hard ride to the north, with at least a hundred warriors pursuing them.

"Could we have held them off? Without Subutai's attack?" Blood dripped from Sisuthros's cheek. The old wound had reopened, probably from all the shouting.

"Well, we'll never know for sure, but I think we might have held them. Their bowmen's fire was weakening. Still . . ." He realized the cheering had taken a different note. The shouts of joy remained, but now a new, simple cry began to rise up. "Esskar! . . . Esskar! . . . Esskar! . . ." the crowd roared, and in a moment it sounded as if the whole village had but one voice.

He turned and looked down into the village. It seemed like every man, woman, and child had come there, jammed into the open spaces and the lanes, with more coming and others appearing on the housetops or the wall. The shouts went on and on. He noticed movement in the mass of people crowded below. A half-dozen soldiers pushed their way through the throng, Trella in their midst. They had to force their way through the solid mass until the villagers saw who they escorted and let them pass. The chant changed and Trella's name, too, echoed from the walls.

Eskkar looked at Sisuthros and saw his subcommander had joined in the cheering. "I've never seen such a thing before." Eskkar's words went unheard, vanishing in the swell of sound. Then Trella reached the steps. Eager hands guided her up the parapet until she reached Eskkar. He took her in his arms and held her tightly, to another outburst of cheers. When he let her go, she clung to his side and shouted into his ear.

"Speak to them. Tell them what they want to hear."

He looked at her face, calm and serene, her head held high. She'd planned even for this. Eskkar raised both his arms and called for silence. At first they ignored him and shouts of "Eskkar" and "Trella" kept rising. Eventually they quieted down, helped by those who wanted to hear what Eskkar would say. He shouted before they could begin again. "Villagers . . . soldiers. We have driven off the barbarians!"

Another roar went up into the sky, everyone shouting with all their strength. Eskkar had to wait a long time before he could continue. "We've done what no village has ever done. Now they will have to move on. You fought bravely today. Now we must tend to our wounded and bury our dead, because many good men have fought and died today. We must rebuild Orak bigger and stronger than ever before."

Dozens of villagers cried out, "Lead us! . . . Protect us! . . . You must rule Orak!" In moments, every person in the village demanded the same thing. Soldiers waved their swords or bows as they shouted, while villagers uplifted their arms. Even Trella stepped aside and turned toward him, lifting up her arms and joining in the exhortation of the mob.

Eskkar raised his hand again, and after another long burst of cheering, the noise finally abated. When he spoke he used all the voice he could muster, his words carrying to all those below. "If you wish me to guide and protect you, I will do so. Do you choose me to rule in Orak?"

This time the noise sounded like thunder, Orak's inhabitants yelling themselves hoarse with excitement and joy, as well as relief at being delivered from the barbarians. Eskkar let it go on for a moment, then raised his hands and called for silence. "Then I will lead you. There's much work to do, but now we can begin."

The crowd cheered again. Eskkar stood there, keeping his right arm raised in acknowledgment. It took a long time before the voices began to die down. "Now, back to your tasks!" he shouted, and turned away from the crowd.

He led Trella down the parapet. At the base of the gate, Corio, Bantor, and Gatus waited. Eskkar gave instructions to secure the gate, tend to the wounded, and bury the dead. There would be no rest yet for the villagers. They had to rebuild the gate and secure it before nightfall. Eskkar told Gatus to send archers back to the walls, post sentries, and keep the soldiers alert.

When Eskkar finally finished giving these and a dozen other orders, Trella faced him.

"Now that everything is being done as you command, we must walk through the village and speak to as many of the people as you can."

He took her hand, smiling for the first time in days. "And what am I to say to the people?"

"Thank each of them for their work today and in the past months. Tell them how much our success today depended on their efforts. Say that in as many different ways as you can."

A group of women approached, carrying cloths soaked in water. They washed the blood and dirt from Eskkar's body, one of them kneeling to clean his feet and sandals. Then, surrounded by the Hawk Clan, he and Trella walked through Orak. They went down every lane and stopped at nearly every house. Esskar accepted thanks and praise while he repeated the same message—that Orak owed it all to them, that they were the real victors, and that he thanked the gods for their help. While they walked, messengers still came to him, with questions or requests for orders.

He answered these, but Trella refused to let him abandon the walk. "This is more important," she told him when he grew impatient. "Now, when the victory is fresh in their minds, you must win them to your side once again. They'll be your power in the coming months, until we're truly secure as Orak's rulers. They'll remember your words of praise and gratitude forever."

He sighed but kept smiling. Trella, who planned for everything, had foreseen and planned this moment as well, so he felt prepared for his task. As they moved through the lanes, several of the women, Bantor's wife among them, preceded their way, encouraging the people, suggesting to them what to say, and shouting blessings to them. Even at the moment of victory, Trella guided and directed the villagers, moving the common people to her will. He shook his head in wonderment, but kept the smile on his face as he gave thanks to the people, holding tight to Trella's hand.

28

By sunset Eskkar swore he'd spoken with every man and woman inside Orak's walls, a task that exhausted him almost as much as the morning's fighting. While he thanked the villagers, his men worked or cared for the wounded. Later Trella served a simple dinner with no thought of a celebration feast. Too many had died, and angry warriors remained camped beyond the hills.

Eskkar wanted to rest but despite the long and strenuous day, he felt restless. He decided to take one last look at the Alur Meriki camp. Taking Trella's hand and accompanied by four guards, they walked through the lanes, ignoring the revelry.

By the time they reached the tower the crowd had disappeared. They climbed the steps that still stank from all the blood shed. From the top they looked out over the empty fields that reeked of death.

Beneath them Corio's men worked on the gate in the fading light, though fires made from Alur Meriki shields had already been lit. Craftsmen hammered steadily, adding so much wood to the gate that it appeared twice as thick as before. They used lumber left behind by the barbarians. The thrifty master artisan had brought everything usable inside the village.

Sisuthros had cleared the ditch of the enemy dead, though

on the far side bodies still lay where they had fallen. That task had taken most of the afternoon. They stripped the bodies of their valuables, weapons, and clothes before dumping them in the river. The ditch had been swept smooth, the ruts and holes filled, and debris removed. They'd recovered the arrows and stones as well. The weapons had been inspected, cleaned, and readied for the next attack, and the stones again stacked in readiness.

Orak's dead lay in orderly rows near the river gate. Tomorrow the ferry would be dragged out of the village and its ropes reconnected. The initial cargo would be Orak's dead, to be buried in mass graves on the west bank. Earlier Eskkar had received the count of enemy dead—they'd killed more than three hundred and seventy warriors today. Many more Alur Meriki would be suffering from wounds.

The long summer sun dipped below the western horizon behind them but enough light remained to let them see across to the hills. Campfires outlined the hills against the coming darkness. Across those hilltops a line of mounted barbarians stood guard, watching the village.

"It seems strange, Trella," Eskkar said, after pointing them out, "now it's they who fear we may attack them."

"Not so strange, husband. In the last few months you killed nearly eight hundred of them and wounded many more."

"They've learned a bitter lesson. Half of their fighting men are dead. Even the Alur Meriki cannot ignore such losses."

"You're sure they won't attack again? Everyone just assumes the battle is over."

He stood behind her and wrapped his arms around her waist. "No, the siege is broken. They've lost too many men and too much equipment. Even their horses have been scattered again. It would take them weeks to get ready for another attack and they're already late in their journey south. Besides, the warriors have no stomach for another assault. Without a new plan, Thutmose-sin, or whoever leads them, dares not propose another assault unless he can guarantee victory."

"They almost captured the gate, didn't they? Might they

just try that again?" She leaned her head back against his chest.

He felt her relax against him, soft and warm in his arms, and enjoyed the sensation. "No. Because we held them, and they know in their hearts we could do it again. They fear us now. They won't underestimate us next time. When they return in ten or fifteen years, it will be different. By then they'll have new plans and new warriors ready for a fresh challenge."

He thought about that for a moment. "In a way we've changed them as much as they have changed us. They'll have to learn new ways of fighting. Knowledge of what we've done here will spread. Other villages will resist them."

Her hands clasped his and again her strength surprised him.

"Yes, other villages will try, but they will fail. They'll have no one with your strength and courage, Eskkar. You're a great leader of soldiers and you understand how and why men fight. The Alur Meriki came here not expecting any strong resistance. They made no real preparations to capture the village, even though they knew we were building a wall. You were always a step ahead of them. You anticipated their plans and they never caught up with yours. No other man in Orak could have accomplished what you did in the last few months. You have truly won a great victory."

Her hands caressed his. "But more important than that, is what you have become. More than anyone, you've changed into someone better, someone wiser."

"And without you, I'd have failed," Eskkar replied. "You made the villagers work, organized the craftsmen, got the people to support me, and kept the nobles at bay. Without you, there would be no victory. Every soldier that fought today knows that."

She stayed silent for a moment. "Today many may know that. But in a few months, only your name will be spoken as conqueror of the barbarians. Only the victors in battle are remembered, it seems. I suppose that is a good thing."

She turned in his arms and faced him. Placing her hands

on his shoulders, she looked into his eyes. "Do you truly wish to rule here in Orak, husband? Ruling the village will be different from planning for a siege. It will be even more difficult. A new wall, much higher and stronger, must be built, and it must encompass twice as much land as does this one. You will be building walls for many years, as well as training men to defend them. There will be more battles to fight, and not just against barbarians. Others from distant lands may come against us. To guard Orak and make sure we are safe, you will have to take control of all of the land surrounding us, every farm and village for great distances in every direction. It will be hard work, even for a great leader of men. But if you wish to rule, then we must begin tomorrow. It's a task that may last a lifetime."

"What you ask won't be easy. It's one thing to fight from behind a wall. It is another to carry war to distant places and defeat your enemies in their own lands."

"I have no doubt that you will find new ways of making war. But those battles are in the future. First you must decide whether you wish to rule here."

He gazed into her eyes in the gathering darkness. She was asking him to rule but he knew, without saying the words, they would rule together, that she would decide many of the rules and customs that would govern Orak's daily life. She would select who would have power and who would not, and he would need to listen to her advice. Many of his soldiers and the villagers would know the truth—that she ruled as much as he. Eskkar would see it in their eyes every day.

None of that mattered anymore. He'd accomplished enough. Even his father's death had been avenged. No one would ever forget his name now. Besides, all of Orak knew Trella was touched by the gods, that she was truly a "gifted one." There would be no shame in sharing power with her. They would rule together.

"Or," she offered, as his silence began to lengthen, "we can leave Orak in a few weeks." She lowered her voice and rested her head against his chest. "We can take gold and men, and go wherever you wish."

"You'd leave the village with me? To go wandering around the countryside, risking danger every day?"

She laughed, and the bright sound rang out across the tower. "I've risked my life every day for the last six months. I've been enslaved, sold, given away, stabbed, and nearly killed. Would there be any more danger out there than that?"

He squeezed her to him again. Much too late, he knew, for such a choice. Besides, he remained as much in her spell tonight as that first night when she came into his arms. His fate had been sealed then, and his life would revolve around her until the spell was broken or until one of them died, and perhaps not even then, if the gods' promise of an afterlife held true.

"We'll stay, Trella, and we . . . both of us, will rule in Orak." He reached out to touch the wall before him, the gritty feeling oddly satisfying. "Our blood is already in these walls. You're right. There must be a new wall, greater than this."

Trella laid her hand on top of his. "The wall will hold our voices for a hundred years, perhaps even two hundred. As long as the wall stands around Orak, we'll be remembered." She turned her head slightly to look up at him. "I can help you rule over a great village."

"You will guide me in all things, and I will protect you." He barely heard her next words, so softly did she speak them.

"Protect us, Eskkar. I carry your child. Now you must protect both of us."

He lifted her chin up and looked into her eyes as he'd done that first night. "You're with child? When were you planning on telling me?"

"If Orak fell, then there was no need. I didn't want to give you something else to worry about. It's still months away, but I'm certain I carry our child. Annok-sur agrees."

She turned again, still staying within his arms, but now she faced out toward the fields. Deep shadows hid the dead bodies scattered across the plain. Except for the faint glow from behind the hill, the darkness was nearly complete. Fewer campfires would burn tonight, Eskkar knew.

"There's so much to do, Eskkar. You must control the soldiers, establish outposts and villages up and down the river, overcome those who resist, and plan for the next barbarian migration."

She sighed. "The livestock and grain must be brought back from across the river. There will be more fighting, Eskkar, but in the future you'll be leading it, not fighting yourself, not ever again. In all the time we've been together, I've asked you for nothing for myself, but this you must promise me. The great sword must stay in your scabbard."

That might not be such a bad thing, Eskkar decided, his thoughts flashing back to that terrible fight in the Alur Meriki camp. He was getting old. Even among the steppes people, hard fighting was best left to the young. He brushed away such thoughts from his mind. "I'll leave the fighting to others," he said finally, unable to keep a hint of regret from his words, "but I'll keep your sword at my side, in case it's needed."

He took a breath. "And you will have to decide how to rule Orak, what customs and decrees will come to pass, what families to ennoble, how we will get enough gold to pay for the soldiers and for rebuilding Orak and everything else we will need. I see there's as much work in keeping power as winning it. Yes, there is much for you to do, Trella."

The sun had set completely now. The darkness before them stretched all the way to the hills. When she spoke, the question surprised him. "What would you name our child, should the babe be a son?"

He thought a moment, then shrugged. "I know only barbarian names, and they're not fit for our son, who will rule Orak after us. And villager names are as one to me. Do you have a name that you would choose?"

"I'd like to honor my father, since I owe so much to him. His name was 'Sargat.' If you allow, we could name our son after him."

Eskkar, still getting used to the idea of being a father, considered her request thoughtfully. Even among villagers naming a son was the husband's responsibility and not something to be passed off lightly. But her father's name did not convey the qualities of a leader. It was an ordinary name, used by many.

Eskkar knew some names had power of their own, as certain words had influence over men. He had no preference for any name himself, but still . . .

"Sargat . . . it's a good name, but a common one. Our son should have a name that shows strength and power." He thought again. The name "Sargat" had no equivalent in his native tongue, but if he had to translate it . . .

"Suppose we call him Sargon. That's a name that I haven't heard before and it seems to me to carry strength. Would that honor your father?"

"Sargon," she repeated, saying the strange name aloud, as if listening for the gods to approve. "Sargon. Yes, that is a fine, new name and it honors my father as well. He will be called Sargon, and he'll give honor both to his grandfather and his father."

"Sargon, who will rule the village of Orak," he repeated.

"No, Orak is no longer a village. It has grown into something greater. It is a city, with a wall and brave men to defend it, a city that will grow in strength and have greatness of its own. For the first time villagers and farmers joined together and resisted the barbarians. Who knows what we can do in the future?"

"It should have its own name, then, a new name, like the name of our son," Eskkar suggested. "Maybe we can think of a new name for Orak as well."

"Can you choose a new name for Orak, then? A name that will make them forget the old village, and instead remind them of you and your victories?"

Eskkar kept silent for a long time, thinking about names of places. Trella, as always, let him take his time. "When I was a boy, we spent part of a summer far to the north, by a tiny stream we called the Akkad. I saw my first lion there. It was the last happy time I had with my family." He smiled to himself at the distant memory. "How does 'Akkad' sound for the name of our city?"

"Akkad . . . Akkad. Eskkar of Akkad . . . Sargon of Akkad. Yes, it's a strong name, Eskkar, like your own. Perhaps the lion spirit will approve, and give his protection to both Sargon and the city of Akkad. But let's not tell the others yet what new name we plan for Orak. The new name can come in its own time, when everyone sees what we have accomplished."

So the City of Akkad would come to be in a few months, or whenever she thought it was ready. He understood her reasons. The village had endured so much change in the past months, with more to come. It would be wise to let them get used to some things gradually.

A cool breeze rustled through the stillness and for a moment the air smelled clean and fresh. He heard the bodyguards, waiting below to give them privacy, shifting their feet, probably impatient to join the revelry.

"Since there is to be so much work tomorrow, then perhaps you could find time tonight to please your husband." His hands moved up from her waist and he cupped her breasts and squeezed them, enjoying the feel of her body through her dress. That, too, hadn't changed from their first night. Her body, the scent of her hair, even her smile still excited him. "Or have you already forgotten your wifely duties?"

She leaned her head back and placed her hands atop his and pressed them to her. "No, master, I await your pleasure." Her voice was soft and her tone as seductive as that first night in his bed, only now she sounded happier than he'd ever heard her.

Eskkar shook his head at the mystery of women. "Sometimes I wonder, girl, who was the master and who was the slave."

Her answering laugh sounded low and enticing, and they turned away from the darkened battleground and its dead. They faced the village, brightly lit by many torches and fires as the villagers celebrated their deliverance. His village now . . . no . . . his city. And someday, if his luck stayed true and the gods approved, it would be his son's. But tonight—tonight there would be more magic, and tomorrow would take care of itself.

Epilogue

T he war drum sounded, faint at first, then growing in intensity and changing into a rolling thunder as a second and third merged in, the rapid strokes summoning every soldier and villager to his post.

Eskkar's feeling of contentment vanished in an instant as fear and doubt rushed through him. The bench flew backward as he rose from the table. He grabbed his sword from the wall as he ran down the stairs and out into the courtyard. A quick-thinking soldier brought out Eskkar's horse. He leapt astride the animal and galloped out of the courtyard, racing through the lanes, scattering stunned and fearful villagers as he burst past them.

At Orak's main gate soldiers milled about in confusion, cursing as they gathered weapons and climbed to their stations. Eskkar jumped down from the still-moving animal, dashed into the tower, and raced up the steps. Emerging into the sunlight he found Gatus waiting.

Gatus pointed to the east and Eskkar's eyes took in the still-barren plain. He saw the warriors lined up across one of the hilltops to the southeast. Automatically he began to count them, but Gatus saved him the trouble.

"About sixty of them, I'd say." The old soldier spat over the wall. "Not enough to attack us, not yet."

The distant warriors sat on their horses, staring in silence at Orak and its wall, or perhaps at the dead bodies of their kinsmen still littering the landscape. Moments passed, but the horsemen made no move, just waited patiently, as if expecting something to happen.

Eskkar felt just as confused as his men. Four days after the Alur Meriki failed to capture the gate, they broke camp and moved off to the south. Three days had passed since then, and he didn't understand why their horsemen would be back raiding around Orak. They had exhausted what little grass had grown back, and the barbarians lacked the strength to assault Orak again. Nevertheless, none of Orak's inhabitants dared leave the safety of its walls to return to their farms. So a raiding party didn't make sense.

The center of the line of horsemen parted. The grand standard of the chief of the Alur Meriki rose up from behind the hilltop, preceding another handful of riders. The warriors closed behind their leader as he passed through. Surveying the scene before him, the Great Chief sat on his horse in front of the standard. The only movement was the wheeling of crows and vultures circling over the bodies of his dead warriors. Finally he began to move forward, and the whole line of warriors followed, all riding slowly down the hill. At the bottom they set their horses to a canter and rode through the ruined fields toward the village. They stopped just out of bowshot.

As Eskkar watched, the clan's sarrum paced his horse a few steps forward. He drew his sword and raised it high over his head. The bronze blade flashed golden in the sun, as the sarrum, taking his time, moved the sword from side to side, from horizon to horizon, three times. Then he lifted it toward the sky once again. He held it there for a few seconds, before lowering his arm until the blade pointed straight toward the tower where Eskkar stood.

The words just carried across the gap between them. Eskkar cocked his head to hear, but understood them well enough.

Eskkar ignored the murmur that moved across the wall, as each man asked his companion what the words meant. Eskkar climbed onto the face of the tower, feet spread out and balanced precariously on the narrow ledge. The thickness of the tower's wall tapered near the top and he barely had enough room to place his feet. Gatus grasped his captain's belt from behind, keeping a firm grip on his leader.

Drawing his sword from its scabbard, Eskkar held it up to the sky for a long moment, whirled it three times around his head, then lowered the tip until it pointed directly at the Alur Meriki leader. Eskkar took a deep breath, and bellowed his response in the barbarian tongue, the harsh words echoing out over the empty plain between them.

The Great Chief thrust his sword once more up to the sky, sunlight again glinting off the blade, then drew it down, sheathed it, and turned his mount. Without a glance back, he put the horse to a gallop, his men wheeling their mounts around as they followed him, the grand standard waving in the breeze.

Eskkar watched as they rode back up the hill, crossed the top, and disappeared. Once vanished from sight, it was as if they had never existed. He sheathed his blade, and jumped lightly down from the wall.

"What did he say?" Gatus couldn't keep the curiosity out of his voice. "What did you say? I heard your name."

Men packed the top of the tower, his commanders, soldiers with their weapons, even a few villagers, fear showing on their faces. Everyone stared at him, mouths agape.

"He said, 'I am Thutmose-sin, leader of the Alur Meriki.'" Eskkar shook his head in disbelief. "Somehow Thutmose-sin survived. How he managed that . . . the gods must favor him."

Gatus stepped closer to his commander. "What else did he say?"

Eskkar took one last look at the empty hill before answering, raising his voice so that all could hear. "He said, 'You fought bravely, but it is not yet finished. We will return another day.'"

Nervous whispers ran through the crowd at the threat, and Gatus had to lift his voice to be heard. "And your answer?"

"I told him I am Eskkar, son of Hogarthak, that I had repaid the Alur Meriki for my family's blood, and never to come to these lands again." The soldiers nearby turned to repeat their captain's words, breaking into cheers and yelling their approval. A smile crossed Eskkar's face, though there was no warmth in his eyes. He lowered his voice, so that only Gatus could catch his words. "And I said I'll be waiting for him."

The End . . . Of the Beginning

Historical Footnote

And so began the era of walled cities. Others sprang up across the land, each fortified with its own great wall and surrounded by farms and herds, each a center of local trade and industry. These cities contended with one another for supremacy for many thousands of years, with power shifting from one to another and back again. But less than seven hundred years after the battle of Orak, in approximately 2500 B.C.E., armies united under the ruler of the City of Akkad swept over all the lands to the south, occupied by those who called themselves Sumerians. The Akkadians defeated the Sumerians and ruled over them for many years. The Akkadians had achieved their victories primarily through the skill and strength of well-organized infantry, equipped with powerful bows, and trained in siege warfare. It was history's first recorded use of an army of foot soldiers skilled in the use of the bow.

The land the Akkadians conquered and ruled became known to the western nations as Mesopotamia, the land between the rivers. Leading this first conquest was the first great king in recorded history. His name was Sargon and he built the world's first empire, uniting by conquest not only his own lands, but also the lands surrounding Mesopotamia. Eventually his son, also named Sargon, would extend the empire's reach as far as the shores of the Mediterranean Sea to the west and India to the east. From these places, the influence and power of walled cities would spread to many new lands, including one that would come to be called Greece. The Greeks would learn much from their eastern neighbors, and build many walled cities of their own, one of which would be called Athens.

In the east, the great walled city of Akkad would endure for many, many generations, even after the shifting of the Tigris gave rise to an even greater city called Babylon that would raise its walls higher than any other. But that is another story.

Acknowledgments

Sometimes, somehow, things do work out. This book, begun seven years ago, is an example of that. Thanks to the help and support of many, this book was drafted, written, critiqued, rewritten, revised, lengthened, shortened, revised, and shortened again. All this before my editor saw it. After that . . . well, you get the idea. I do thank all of you who contributed by reading and critiquing.

Foremost thanks go to my agent, Dominick Abel, who believed in the story and connected me with my editor at HarperCollins, Sarah Durand. Her suggestions added new material, and generally polished the entire manuscript.

A special debt is owed to those who helped in the beginning. Vijaya Schartz, an excellent author in her own right and past president of the Arizona Authors Association, who patiently red-penned the early drafts, along with others in her critique group, for nearly a year. Extra thanks to my own critique group members, who jumped in every time I needed help. Sharon Anderson, Martin Cox, Laura Groch (my niece, the newspaper editor), Jim Jasper, Deb Ledford, and Sally Mise all contributed to the final draft.

Extra thanks to Jim, for believing in the work enough to contact Dominick Abel on his own, relying on a twenty-year-old connection, to get the first few chapters into Dominick's capable hands.

And lest I forget, thanks to Gracie and Xena, my writing felines, whose paws and claws helped me get through many a writer's block.

Last, and not least, thanks to the spiritual father of this story, one of my favorite writers, J. Michael Straczynski, author and producer of the *Babylon 5* TV series. His encouraging email kept me going when I was about to quit. May the Great Maker forgive the occasional idea "borrowed" from *B5*.

SAM BARONE
Scottsdale, Arizona
August 2006

For more heroic battles, passion, and courage from the Bronze Age—

EMPIRE RISING

Available soon in hardcover from William Morrow

As the afternoon waned, Eskkar met with his commanders and the fifteen men chosen for the initial raid. They'd had to wait until all the farmers moved well away from the camp. The carefully selected soldiers received their instructions, and Eskkar used the few hours before darkness to make sure Sisuthros and the men knew exactly what to do. Only after Eskkar felt satisfied did they gather around the campfire for the evening meal.

Nevertheless, Eskkar kept reviewing the details of the attack during dinner, speaking to each man, making sure each knew his assignment. Finally even Eskkar could find nothing wrong. He went off by himself, to try and get some sleep, leaving word to wake him when the men were ready.

Sleep came slowly. Eskkar had never sent men out on a raid before, had never delegated such a command to another. Always he had led sorties like this himself. To send others out into danger while he remained safe in camp seemed unmanly. But he knew that he couldn't risk his own life on such a small raid, just as he knew Sisuthros could easily direct the men.

At midnight, Grond woke Eskkar from a restless sleep. Sisuthros and his men stood ready, each standing by his horse. Eskkar gripped Sisuthros by the shoulder, then stood

aside as his subcommander led the first two of his men out
of the camp. The rest of the soldiers left, two at a time, after
a slow count to one hundred, so that the horses wouldn't get
nervous in the darkness and begin whinnying, or making
sounds that might alert any keen ears in Bisitun. Eskkar
knew horses could do strange things at night, spooking at
some shadow, the moon, or even a breeze.

Each man would walk his horse a full half mile before
mounting and waiting for the rest of the men to join up.
When all the riders assembled, they would pace their horses
at a slow step for another mile before turning north.

The last of them disappeared from sight, and nothing remained for Eskkar to do except wait. He didn't expect Ninazu to launch an attack tonight, but Eskkar wanted his
remaining men alert and ready just in case.

The moon had risen late and progressed steadily across
the starry sky. The scouts stationed between the camp and
the village came in at regular intervals, all reporting no activity from Bisitun's defenders. Eskkar paced back and forth,
checking with the men as he went, urging them to stay vigi-
lant. Time seemed to slow the moon's journey across the
night, and he thought morning would never come.

A few moments before dawn, the sound of hoof beats came
from the south. Though expected, the sentries gave the challenge. Sisuthros called out his name in a loud voice, though
the approaching horses slowed to a walk a hundred paces
from the camp. Eskkar gave the word, and soldiers lit torches
that revealed a smiling Sisuthros leading his horse back into
the encampment.

As Sisuthros and the others passed in, Eskkar grasped
him by the arm and pulled him aside. "Did it go well? We
heard nothing from here."

Sisuthros's grin turned into a laugh. "Yes, Captain, it
went well. They never heard a thing. If we had more men,
we could have forced our way in by the river. I'll wager they
don't notice anything until well after sunup."

"You mean they saw nothing? And the men? All went according to plan?" By now, everyone pressed round Sisuthros

and his band, who came in laughing and swaggering, pleased with themselves and the ease of their mission. "Tell us what happened."

"We walked the horses, until we were out of earshot, then rode to the northern part of the river." Men jostled each other to hear Sisuthros's words, every one eager to learn about the first action against Bisitun. "I sent the rest of the riders, with all the horses, downstream of the village, telling them to swing wide of the encampment. My men and I boarded the boats with no problems."

The scouts had found a farm a few miles upriver that possessed two small boats, probably used mainly for fishing, but each large enough to carry a few men. No doubt by now the puzzled farmer wondered who had stolen his vessels.

"We let the boats drift downstream," Sisuthros went on. "Just before we reached Bisitun, four men from each boat slipped into the water and clung to the boat's sides."

Sisuthros had chosen only strong swimmers for this raid, men who stood ready to trust themselves to the river's current to carry them to safety, if need be.

"We drifted in among the vessels at the rear of the village," Sisuthros continued. "We untied or cut the ropes mooring all the boats there, and shoved them well out into the current. It didn't take long, and we stood by in the boats to carry the men off as soon as someone raised the alarm."

"We heard no outcry here, Sisuthros," Eskkar said.

"No one gave the alarm. We could see guards walking the palisade, but they noticed nothing, and no one raised a cry. The sound of the river must have muffled the noise."

"The guards were that lax in their duties?" Eskkar couldn't believe it. "They never saw you at all?"

"No. We made certain the current took all the boats downstream. Then, with our men again clinging to the sides of the boat, we followed, making sure none of the boats had grounded. A mile down river, we found our men and horses waiting, and rode back."

"Well done, Sisuthros! You're sure you cut all the boats loose?"

"Every one. We gave the river gods many offerings, for whatever gods and fortunate farmers live downstream!"

Everyone laughed. Sisuthros had to repeat his story in more detail, his men adding their own actions. By the time he finished, the torches had gone out, and the sun climbed above the horizon in the eastern sky. Eskkar, a smile on his face for the first time in many hours, ordered the men to get some food and rest, while he sat atop the rampart and watched the village.

So far, the plan that he had first sketched out in his mind back in Dilgarth continued to progress smoothly. When he'd learned the size of Ninazu's force, he had known that, even though he could probably take the village by direct assault, he would lose far too many men in the process. No, he knew he needed to capture Bisitun quickly, and with a minimum of casualties to his valuable men. Besides, he needed the village and its inhabitants as intact as possible. Now, in less than two days and thanks to Sisuthros's well-executed raid, Eskkar had bottled Ninazu's men in the village.

Now the next part of the plan would begin. Ninazu and his men would have plenty to worry about. They'd seen first hand that they faced a disciplined force, real soldiers who could throw up a fortified camp in less than a day. The threat of reinforcements coming soon would make some of them think about moving on.

With all the boats gone, Ninazu's quick escape across the river would be greatly reduced. At this time of the year, a strong horse, ridden by a good rider who could swim himself if necessary, might make it across. But that rider couldn't carry much loot, and Eskkar was willing to wager that if ten good men attempted it, three or four would likely drown.

So Ninazu would have to fight or run, before his own men began to slip away. Not that Eskkar wanted them to run. He didn't want them plundering up and down the river for the next few weeks, with his Akkadians wasting their days in pursuit. He wanted most of the bandits dead, and the rest as slave labor to rebuild Bisitun.

The village shone in the morning light, as the sun moved ever higher in the sky, and Eskkar fancied he saw fewer defenders than yesterday. Everyone inside Bisitun would know about the loss of the boats, and worry, if not fear or panic, would start taking its toll. Some would be thinking about escape. The more they thought about escaping, the less willing they would be to fight. Eskkar decided to apply more pressure.

He turned back to the encampment and found Grond waiting there, a few steps behind him. "Grond, get the men on their horses. Send ten riders and ten archers to each side of the encampment. If any in the village want to make a run for it, make sure they have to fight their way out. I don't want anyone going in or out of Bisitun."

Grond relayed the orders to Hamati and the other men. It took only a few minutes to get the forty men chosen something to eat, and send them on their way. When they reached their positions, each detachment would block any escape attempt by anyone, on foot or mounted, to pass through Bisitun's back gate, and follow the river to safety.

Of course if the defenders came out in strength on either side, then the situation would change. But they talked about even that possibility. While the full force of the bandits could certainly ride through twenty men, it might take some time, and with enough time, the rest of the Akkadians from the main camp might catch them with their backs against the river.

What Eskkar thought more likely was that a hundred men would burst out of the front gate, and attempt to ride right through, or around, the encampment. He now had only thirty-two fighting men, plus the scribes, boys, and liverymen remaining to defend the camp. Eskkar had stretched his forces very thin, but he needed to act as if he had the upper hand. As soon as the men in the camp finished their meal, he had them ready their weapons and stand to their posts. With his men in place, he returned to the embankment and watched the palisade.

Once again, the man with the silver bracelets stood there, studying the Akkadians, and undoubtedly making plans of his own. Nevertheless, the loss of Ninazu's boats changed the situation, and now the ground outside the palisade, with its tumbled-down houses worked to Eskkar's advantage. Men on horseback would only have a clear path directly down the main road, which would send them straight at the encampment, or along the river's edge, where they would encounter archers and mounted men. Ninazu would see all this, as could his men, and they would begin to worry.

For days Ninazu had assured his men that they could easily fight off Eskkar's small force from behind the palisade. Instead, the bandits could see a hard fight ahead of them if they tried to escape. Moreover, the worst worry of all would be knowing that, in two or three days, another strong force would reinforce the attackers.

Grond returned to join him. "All the men are in position, Captain. Sisuthros and Hamati are getting some sleep, but the rest of the men are resting at their posts."

"Watch the walls, Grond. If they all decide to run for it, the guards on the palisade will slowly be replaced by villagers. They'll be nervous and frightened. That might give us warning."

"Do you think they'll run?"

Eskkar thought about that. "His brother was brave enough. I don't think Ninazu will give up Bisitun without a fight. Besides, he sees us splitting our force, and that will make him wonder what we will do when night falls. If he thinks that we've weakened our force here, he may fall into our trap." Once again, Eskkar went through the thought process. "I still think he will come tonight, with a large force, right at our camp."

He faced his bodyguard, who still stood there, doubt still written on his face. "I know, Grond, I have my own doubts. But if he does nothing, and another hundred men appear, he'll be trapped. His men will run if he does nothing." Eskkar shrugged. "Well, that's what I would do. But I am not him, so we'll have to wait and see."

"Are you sure that we can withstand them, if he sends everyone against us?"

"These are bandits, Grond, not Alur Meriki warriors. They have no clan or family to fight for, no code of bravery to sustain them. They are held together only by their lust for gold. If thirty of us cannot break them . . ." He shook his head and headed back to the rear of the camp.

The daylight hours dragged by, one by one, with Eskkar pacing back and forth. The camp had to appear no different from the day before, so all the regular activities continued. Men stood to their watches, cooking fires sent smoke into the sky, and anyone not standing guard relaxed on the embankment, watching the village.

The detachments on either side of Bisitun reported in, but they saw no sign of anyone trying to cross the river or escape along its banks. Sisuthros, after he had taken his rest, declared that to be a good sign—if they weren't trying to run, then they would be ready to fight.

As the afternoon began to lengthen, Eskkar, Sisuthros, Hamati, and Grond met once again, and began to prepare for the night's work. They went over everything for almost two hours, thinking of what could go wrong, what evil chance could upset their plans, what they would do if the plan failed, and even what they would do if they were beaten.

The soldiers started the evening fires and prepared their meal before Eskkar and his subcommanders finished. At least the men continued eating well, thanks to his largess with the local farmers. With dinner finished, Eskkar and his commanders met with the other senior men. The thirty men in the camp would be at the greatest risk, and Eskkar wanted them to know exactly what he expected of them. Each of the subcommanders went over it yet again, this time with their men.

Eskkar watched, looking for signs of confusion, but saw nothing but confidence. No one showed any fear, or doubted their ability to beat off an attack. The men believed in him, believed in his luck if nothing else. At last, it was time to go. "Take care, Sisuthros. And good hunting to all of us."

Grond had made all the preparations, and he and Eskkar slipped out of the camp. They took their time moving across the dark landscape, swinging wide to their rear, lest some chance flash of moonlight revealed them to any sharp-eyed guards on the village palisade. Eskkar didn't want to trip and sprain an ankle in the darkness. Finally, they joined up with the men who guarded the southern edge of the river.

The small camp had only a single fire burning in front of it, lighting the darkness between it and the village. The men sat well back from the firelight, waiting for Eskkar to arrive. They'd spent the afternoon practicing their archery, the same as they had done every day before and during the siege of Akkad, and talking over what situations they would likely encounter and how they would respond. Every one of these bowmen could loose a properly aimed arrow every three seconds, and some even faster. Now they waited, confident in the skills and in their leaders.

Grond had briefed them earlier in the day, but as soon as Eskkar joined them, they checked their preparations again. These men were eager, anxious to go on the offensive, and ready to take their chances. Five of them were already Hawk Clan members and another seven, mostly experienced fighters, looked to prove themselves worthy of such an honor. Mitrac waited there, leaning on his bow, next to the two men he had considered his best archers, both men who had fought beside Hamati at Dilgarth. Even Eskkar felt satisfied that everyone knew what to do.

Midnight passed without event. Eskkar could do nothing to make the time pass faster, not even pace around. If Ninazu's attack came, it would likely be when the moon began to set, about two hours before dawn. Too excited and nervous to rest or sleep, Eskkar and his men just waited. Most of them lay on their backs and watched the silver orb slowly cross the night sky. At last the moon began to fade. The time had arrived.

Eskkar sat on the ground, drumming his fingers against his leg, a bad habit he had picked up during the siege of Akkad. He didn't like anyone knowing he felt nervous, and he stopped the motion the moment he became conscious of it. Except for the faint crackling of the fire, Eskkar could hear nothing. Another hour crept by, and still he heard no sign of any activity. He wanted to start moving, but he didn't dare take the chance. Any unusual sound might stop Ninazu's attack. If Ninazu even did plan to attack tonight. It should have come by now.

His doubts growing every moment, Eskkar had just decided that he had guessed wrong when a shout went up from the Akkadians' main encampment. A moment later someone hurled a torch into the sky, Sisuthros's signal an attack had begun. Shouts drifted across the black ground.

Without any commands, Eskkar and his men started to advance, trying to make as little noise as possible. They swung wide around their small fire. In single file, they moved rapidly toward the southern corner of the village, each man following the man ahead of him. Mitrac led the way. He'd studied the ground during the day, and now Eskkar and the others followed him. Behind Mitrac strode his two picked archers, trailed by Eskkar, Grond, and the rest of the men.

Time moved quickly, and they soon drew close to the village, where it came closest to the river. When Mitrac stopped, less than a hundred paces separated them from the palisade. They crouched among the rubble, and hoped no one watched this side of the village too closely. Mitrac and his chosen archers disappeared into the darkness.

Sound continued to drift in from the front of the village, though Eskkar couldn't tell what any of it meant. For all he knew, his men in the camp had been overrun and slaughtered, or they had already driven back Ninazu's men. Whatever the result, Eskkar was committed, and they hadn't much time. He hoped any sentries watching this side of the village would be lax, their attention focused on events happening in front of the main gate.

Precious moments dragged by with no movement or activity from Mitrac. Eskkar couldn't control his patience. He hated to restrain himself from action when all his instincts urged him to the attack. He started to move forward, when one of Mitrac's men slipped back to his side. "Come!" he whispered, "Mitrac killed the sentry."

Eskkar and the others began to move. Crouched over, they crept straight toward the base of the palisade, which they reached in moments. Unlike Akkad, Bisitun had no

ditch to give added height to the wooden fence. No alarm
had been given yet, but at any moment they could be discovered.

They reached the base of the palisade, hugging close to
the rough timbers. Grond and another man unslung the ropes
they carried coiled across their chests. One end of each rope
had been fitted with a short block of wood, wide enough to
secure the line against the top of the palisade. Mitrac had
already scaled the fence, boosted up by his companion, and
now stood guard atop the barrier.

Grond tossed the two ropes up, and Mitrac wedged the
wooden blocks between the strakes. The two archers started
climbing, the timbers creaking under their weight, though
they hoped not loud enough to attract any attention.

Eskkar could barely contain himself. The sounds of fighting had increased from the direction of the main gate. Or
perhaps the defenders cheered their own victory. Either way,
Eskkar could no longer tolerate doing nothing. If Sisuthros
had not held the camp, if he had not driven back Ninazu's
men . . . no, it was too late to worry about that.

The instant the two archers disappeared overhead, Eskkar
grabbed one of the ropes and began to climb. Grond pushed
him from below, and the rough wood of the stockade gave
Eskkar some purchase, the vertical beams creaking a little
louder under his heavier weight. He reached the top, and one
of the archers waiting there pulled him over.

Eskkar dropped down to his knee and looked about, until
he saw Mitrac kneeling on the rampart a few steps away.
The bodies of two men lay in front of him, but already the
arrows had been pulled or broken off from their bodies. The
silhouette of an arrow sticking out of a corpse was too easy
to identify, even at night. Eskkar crept over to the archer.

"What do you see?" Eskkar asked softly.

"Two more sentries up ahead, but they face the front of
the village," Mitrac whispered. He held his bow at an angle,
with an arrow fitted to the string. "They're staring at the
main gate."

Even as Eskkar glanced in that direction, he saw some
flames shoot up into the sky. Crouched down, he couldn't

see the front of the village. Suddenly a flaming arrow streaked up into the sky and fell over the wall. He grunted in satisfaction at the signal. Sisuthros and his forces had not only held the camp, they'd driven back the attackers and started counter-attacking the village with fire arrows.

Using the black oil that Drakis had brought up from Akkad, Sisuthros's men had made a hundred fire arrows, wrapping cotton thickly around the shaft, binding it with linen threads, and soaking the tufts in oil. When touched to fire, the cotton would burst into flame, a flame so hot that not even the arrow's flight through the air could extinguish it.

The palisade behind him creaked again, and Eskkar turned to see Grond come over the wall, the last man to make the ascent. Eskkar looked down at the village beneath him. The inner rampart stood only about ten feet off the ground, and even in the dim starlight, he could see a lane that seemed to lead toward the front of the village. The smell of a slaughterhouse reached him, and he could see animal pens below. A few houses backed against the enclosure.

The village remained indistinct in the darkness, lit here and there by torches or watch fires, but dawn approached and already the eastern sky seemed a bit less dark. As he watched, villagers emerged from the houses, roused from their sleep by the noise, talking excitedly and all looking in the direction of the main gate.

That might change any moment, and Eskkar had to get his soldiers off the rampart. He turned to Grond. "Get the men down now." Moving as he spoke, Eskkar grasped the edge of the rampart, and swung to the ground. His men joined him, all except Mitrac, who called softly to his two archers. Eskkar paused briefly, watching, as the three bowmen stood up, drew their bows, and launched their arrows at the sentries who guarded the next position on the palisade.

He heard a faint cry, followed by the sound of a body thudding to the earth, but nothing more, no outcry or alarm. Mitrac, followed by his two men, paced slowly along the rampart. Anyone giving them a casual glance would take

them for sentries. Ignoring the rampart for now, Eskkar
started off, striding with authority, followed by Grond and
eleven other men. It took only a few paces before they had to
push their way past the first confused villagers.

Nothing distinguished them from any of Ninazu's men.
In the darkness, they would seem merely another group of
Ninazu's followers, moving toward the main gate. Eskkar
saw one man's mouth open in surprise as he shrank back
from them, but the man said nothing, and in a moment
they'd moved well past. The lane forked and Eskkar didn't
know which way to go, so he grabbed the first villager he
encountered, an older man whose white hair shone in the
dim light.

As Eskkar's hand tightened on the old man's arm, the
man froze, helpless, as much from sudden fear at these men
as the hard muscles in Eskkar's grip. "Which way is the
quickest to the main gate?"

The man's mouth opened, but no words came, and Eskkar
repeated the question, shaking the man as he did. "Which
way!"

The man pointed to the left, and Eskkar kept his grip on
the man as they resumed walking, dragging his unwilling
guide with him. The lane twisted left and forked again, but
this time Eskkar had only to look at the man, and he gestured
the way. A few more steps and Eskkar could see his destination. He loosened his grip a little. "Return to your house and
keep silent, or I'll slit your throat!" He pushed the man aside
and increased his pace.

Fire blazed from the outer fence, and two watch fires had
been lit in fire pits on either side of the gate. Sisuthros's arrows would have started fires in several places, and now his
men, shooting from the darkness, would be targeting any
defenders who attempted to put out the flames.

Ninazu's men had recovered from their shock. Men raced
to the ramparts, and cries for water echoed all around them.
A dozen villagers, pressed into service, carried buckets of
water from the well to extinguish the arrows in the gate.

Eskkar paid no attention to all that, his eyes searching
until he saw what he wanted. A house with a low roof that

faced onto the open ground behind the gate. The passage to the house remained closed, but even as Eskkar approached, prepared to put his shoulder to it, the door opened. An elderly woman wearing nothing but a loose shift bumped into him, obviously intending to see what all the commotion was about. Instead, Eskkar pushed her back in, his hand over her mouth to keep her silent, though she seemed too frightened to cry out.

Inside, two more women and some children had roused themselves, fearful at the sounds of fighting that now rang through the village. Grond swept them together into a corner of the hut. "Keep your mouths shut if you want to live," he ordered.

Meanwhile Eskkar climbed the flimsy ladder that opened onto the roof. From the housetop, torches and the burning fence illuminated the scene before him. He knelt down, taking everything in as he studied the situation.

The outer palisade blazed in three places, and without immediate water, the fire would soon be unstoppable. Villagers with water buckets rushed about, pouring water down the palisade. On the ground just inside the main gate a dozen men stood, two of them with arrows still protruding from them. Ninazu's men struggled to fight the fire and the attackers at the same time, while others rounded up more villagers to bring water.

Eskkar noticed plenty of men carrying weapons and standing about, talking loudly and gesturing in frustration. Obviously Ninazu hadn't lost too many in his attack on the camp. Eskkar guessed that most of the bandits had turned and run back as soon as they realized their foes waited for them. He sought to pick out the leaders, those trying to restore order to the mass of confused and panicky men.

Grond tapped him on the shoulder. All the soldiers had climbed up on the roof and knelt behind him, including Mitrac and his two men. Every Akkadian had a bow, except Eskkar and Grond, who carried only their swords. Eskkar turned to Mitrac. "There, see them, to the right of the gate. And the one at the well, and those two on the rampart."

Mitrac nodded as Eskkar pointed out the first targets.

Mitrac took over, pushing in front of Eskkar and moving closer to the edge of the roof. Eskkar stepped further back and shoved the wooden frame that covered the access hole to the roof into place. He didn't want anyone coming up behind them. The dry rasp of arrows on wood sounded, as Eskkar's thirteen archers stood up, bows drawn, as Mitrac's low voice prepared the men for the first release. Then Mitrac drew his own arrow to his ear and released.

Even after all these months, Eskkar still found himself amazed at Mitrac's skill. He scarcely seemed to aim, and yet the shaft that vanished into the darkness would no doubt find its mark, while another arrow seemed to leap from his quiver to the bowstring. The other men fired as well and immediately the screams started. It would take the defenders a few moments to figure out that they'd been attacked, and many of their leaders would be down before they turned and located their attackers.

The men Mitrac had chosen for this raid had proven themselves among the best archers in the troop, and now, despite being crowded together, they poured arrows into their enemies at a rate that made them seem like twice their number.

The roof gave Eskkar's men clear shots, and the watch fires burning at the gate provided plenty of light for their shooting. For the defenders, the shafts seemed to come out of the darkness, and at such short range, little more than forty paces, the heavy shafts with their bronze, leaf-shaped points struck with lethal accuracy.

Before a man could count to fifty, the Akkadian archers swept the area beneath the gate clear of defenders, the defenders tripping and scrambling down from the walls, some of them tossing their bows and buckets aside. Out of the corner of his eye, Eskkar made note of every time the closest archer fired. The man had released his tenth arrow before anyone spotted them, and another four volleys were launched before anyone turned a bow against them.

Eskkar couldn't count that quickly, but he guessed nearly two hundred arrows had been launched, enough to break any small group of men, let alone those still recovering from being defeated by Sisuthros at the camp. The bandits broke and ran, determined to get out of the killing zone.

With the defenders fleeing, Esskar called out to Grond, who raised a small trumpet to his lips and blew a long blast that echoed out over the walls and into the darkness. Esskar heard an answering sound from the Akkadians outside the gate. Sisuthros and his men now pressed their attack in earnest, the trumpet announcing that most of the defenders had abandoned the walls. They screamed and howled like wild men as they charged, every man shouting at the top of his lungs, as ordered. They carried with them the rest of the ropes, and would soon be over the palisade and into the village, even if the gate remained fastened.

Esskar kept his eyes moving, and finally saw for what he searched. A flash of silver in the flames, and he saw the leader of the defenders on the move. Esskar cursed the bad luck that let the man survive the archers' arrows. Now Ninazu would need to be hunted down and killed before he could escape over the fence into the darkness. No, even now, the darkness had started to give way to dawn, and the first rays of the sun already climbed slowly into the heavens. "Grond! Mitrac! Come with me!"

Esskar ran to the side of the house and swung himself down, Grond, Mitrac and his two archers following him. Ninazu and a group of his men were moving down one of the village streets, already out of sight, and no doubt headed toward the river gate. The bandits' horses would be kept there, close to the rear gate and the river.

Ninazu had decided to run for it. The bandit leader would have no idea how many soldiers had slipped inside Bisitun, not that it made any difference. With all the causalities his men had taken, the Akkadians now outnumbered them. More important, Ninazu's men had lost the will to fight. Every bandit's thought would be on fleeing the village and saving his own skin. To stay meant death. Within hours, the villagers would turn in or denounce any of Ninazu's men still in Bisitun. Only escape could save them now.

Esskar didn't care if a few dozen leaderless bandits escaped, but a man like Ninazu, who could organize and lead others, would only cause more trouble if he remained on the loose. Ninazu must be stopped, before he escaped.

Heart-stopping action and suspense from
New York Times bestselling author

JAMES ROLLINS

DEEP FATHOM

978-0-380-81880-8/$7.99 US/$10.99 Can

Ex-Navy SEAL Jack Kirkland surfaces from an aborted
underwater salvage mission to find the Earth burning and
the U.S. on the narrow brink of a nuclear apocalypse—and
he is thrust into a race to change the tide.

EXCAVATION

978-0-380-81093-2/$7.99 US/$10.99 Can

For untold centuries, the secrets of life have been buried in
a sacred, forbidden chamber in the South American jungle.
Those who would disturb the chosen must now face the
ultimate challenge: survival.

SUBTERRANEAN

978-0-380-79264-1/$7.99 US/$10.99 Can

A hand-picked team of scientists makes its way toward the
center of the world, into a magnificent subterranean
labyrinth where breathtaking wonders await—as well as
terrors beyond imagining that should never be disturbed.

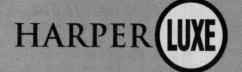